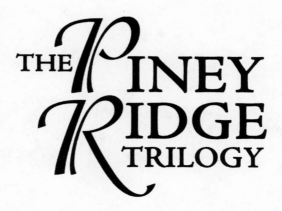

THE PINEY RIDGE TRILOGY

EXCLUSIVE 3-IN-1 VOLUME

The Enduring Hills

Miss Willie

Tara's Healing

The Enduring Hills

Janice Holt Giles

THE UNIVERSITY PRESS OF KENTUCKY

To Henry, of course,
and to
Libby and Nash —
my three!

This edition published by The University Press of Kentucky

Scholarly publisher for the Commonwealth,
serving Bellarmine College, Berea College, Centre
College of Kentucky, Eastern Kentucky University,
The Filson Club, Georgetown College, Kentucky
Historical Society, Kentucky State University,
Morehead State University, Murray State University,
Northern Kentucky University, Transylvania University,
University of Kentucky, University of Louisville,
and Western Kentucky University.

Editorial and Sales Offices: Lexington, Kentucky 40506-0336

3 in 1 ISBN: 0-7394-3237-0

Printed in the United States of America

FOREWORD
TO THE SECOND EDITION

The Enduring Hills is the first book of fiction I ever wrote. I had scribbled and written all my life, had always written long, vivid letters to my family and friends, told stories well. But I had had no lifelong dream of being a writer.

The summer of 1943, in the middle of World War II, I was going on my vacation. It was July. I was secretarial-assistant to the Dean of the Louisville Presbyterian Seminary, Louisville, Kentucky, and had the unbelievable good fortune to have a month of vacation each summer. Usually I visited my people in Fort Smith and Fayetteville, Arkansas.

That summer, however, I wanted to spend one week with a very dear aunt in El Paso, Texas, before going to Arkansas. I went by Greyhound bus, since "is this trip necessary" was the rule of the day during those war years and one traveled catch as catch can.

Henry Giles boarded the bus at Bowling Green, Kentucky. He had been visiting his family, near Knifley in Adair County, Kentucky, and was returning to Camp Swift, Texas. He sat by me and for almost forty-eight hours we were seatmates, talking much to each other, learning much about each other, and when we parted in Dallas it was with the promise to write often.

One thing led to another and before he went overseas we had decided to marry when he returned from the war. He did return, we were married, on October 11, 1945. We decided to live in Louisville where I would continue working at the Presbyterian Seminary. My salary there was fairly adequate and Henry's sub-

3

sistence on the G.I. Bill as he returned to school made us have a comfortable life.

It was soon evident, however, that he hated the city which I so loved. It was apparent that he *had* to return, eventually, to the country where he was born, where he was the seventh generation of his family to live. Any other way of life would make him ill, or it would wreck this marriage.

It was a real dilemma. I knew I could not live in the country without some work of my own to challenge my mind. But what could it be? Writing? What kind of writing? Fiction? I thought this would challenge me more than anything else. So during the winter of 1946–47 I decided to see if I could write — really write books, really write fiction. I had read all my life. Surely I had learned enough from all that reading to make a good stab at it. But I knew the books must be successful, they had to be published. I was not the kind of dedicated writer who could go on year after year trying, with no luck. I would have to succeed, to feel the books were worth writing.

I continued to work at the Seminary, an eight-hour day. We had a small apartment. After dinner Henry studied in the bedroom, and on a typewriter loaned me by the Seminary, on the kitchen table I wrote. I set myself a stint of three hours every night, five nights a week. Toothache, headache, flu, sinus trouble, no matter what, I wrote three hours, from 7:30 P.M to 10:30 P.M.

Henry actually gave me the idea for the plot. It was based very much on his own life, his own feelings, his ambitions, his hopes, his hurts. We knew the incidents in the book must be fictional, so we made them up. None of them really happened, nor were any of the people, except Hod Pierce and his mother and Mary Hogan, based on real people. There were certain similarities to many people, but I soon learned that it is impossible to work from real people. They are too inflexible. And real events are too inflexible. One must invent. Even Hod Pierce is not truly Henry Giles.

Nor is Mary Hogan really Janice Holt Giles, although we did use the way we met, some of the things we felt, said, saw in each other. But they became fictional people, too, as I worked with them.

The book was finished that winter and I sent it to the West-

4

minster Press. It was a small publishing house owned by the Presbyterian Church, U.S.A., and had just opened a fiction department. I believed the book would get a good reading there, since they needed authors. The book was sent in under both our names, Henry and Janice Giles, for Henry had helped me so much.

The book got a good reading and the editor, a young woman named Olga Edmonds, wrote me that if we would rewrite certain sections she believed it would be publishable. Right there, the difference in Henry Giles' inherent pessimism and my unquenchable optimism became evident. He did not believe the book had a chance, refused to have anything more to do with it, and told me not to use his name on it again.

I rewrote the book twice before I got it right. It was really very amateurish. It all had to be done at night, of course, but I kept plugging away. Finally, it came right, a contract was sent to me in 1949, I signed it and the book was published in April of 1950.

It caught the eye of Mr. John Beecroft, editor-in-chief of the Doubleday Book Clubs, who chose it for his Dollar Book Club, and it had a sale of 140,000.

On the strength of the contract, however, having already begun a second novel, we bought our first small farm, a little forty-acre place, and moved to it on May 30, 1949.

The Enduring Hills has been out of print for perhaps fifteen years. I am pleased to see Houghton Mifflin reissuing it because I believe it is timeless and as the hands of the clock have turned and turned, people are turning back to the earth, knowing now that saving this earth is the most important work in the world, that we must all become, as Hod and Mary Pierce did, a man and woman with faith in the earth.

JANICE HOLT GILES

Spout Springs
Knifley, Kentucky
June 18, 1970

FOREWORD

IT IS IMPOSSIBLE to reproduce the speech of the hill people exactly as it is spoken. There is no way to put it down in black and white. You have to hear it. I have therefore not attempted to use their forms with every word. I have, however, tried to do justice to the most common usages. But even so, a word of explanation seems necessary.

The people themselves are not consistent in the use of words. Much depends upon the emotions, the strength of feeling, the length of a sentence, or the vowel and consonant sounds immediately preceding or following a word. For example, the aspirate " hit " for " it " is practically always used at the beginning of a sentence. And it may be used any place in a sentence, but when it is, the speaker has paused for breath, as at the beginning of a phrase or clause. So it is not true that hill people say " hit " and " hain't " consistently. And the word " if." Where it is euphonious, and if the speaker is not hurried, it becomes " ifen." Otherwise it remains " if." The possessive " your " is expressed two ways. " Yer ma," or " yer pa." And again, " Ifen it's yore intentions." One is quick, the other is slow.

Some words are almost pure Elizabethan in origin. " Seed " for " seen," for instance. And " afeared " and " heared." The contractions " e'er " and " ne'er," come, of course, from " ever " and " never." They are slurred into " ary " and " nary " in some places.

Remember that it is a lazy speech, softly spoken, with no wasted motion. Remember that it is so euphonious that it is as

7

liquid as song. It falls from the lips with a honey sweetness. Take the phrase, for instance, "Hit's been a time an' a time." Is there a more lovely way of saying it's been a long time? Or, "forever and endurin'." Is there anything more eternal-sounding?

All the characters in this book are fictitious and all the events are imaginary.

CHAPTER ONE

THE EARLY MORNING SUN edged hesitantly up the first few inches of the sky. Each time Hod looked up it had risen a little nearer the tip of the trees that rimmed the far side of the cornfield. The long fingers of light meshed through the tops of the trees and shredded a pattern of lacy shadow halfway across the field. In a shy breeze the pattern rippled and broke, and wove a new pattern. It bent past the young corn and marked Hod's hoe with dark crossbars. It slanted off his blue work shirt and ran ahead of him in a thinned, pencil line.

The whole June morning was soft and easylike around him. The field was a rampart on the edge of the ridge, bold against the cresting sun. The corn was ankle-high, tender and green, and the faintly ribbed leaves rubbed a sigh down the long rows. It was caught and held for a moment here, then passed on there, only slightly diminished. It reached the farthest edge of the field and fiddled through the needles of a pine; it set a frenzied quaking among the leaves of a silver poplar, and then a wood thrush in an old hickory nut tree picked it up and let it tremble from his throat.

"Hod! H-o-o-d! O-o-o-h, Hod!" The round, high call split the air, curved high over the slope of the ridge, and dropped flutelike in the cornfield. Hod shifted the hoe to his left hand and straightened his back.

"Here," he yelled back. "I'm on yon side the field!" And he listened as his own voice was sent out of his chest full into the air, unseeing, but trumpeting out the sound. It was thick and hard and it sped, without partition, cleanly. Like as if I blew a silver note, he thought. Just like as if I blew on Grampa Dow's huntin' horn!

"Here," he called again, and he threw back his head and blew the sound high. "This here's Hod Pierce ablowin' his horn!"

"Horn — horn — horn — horn," came back the sound from the cliff across the holler, the echo making its own echo and sending it back into a cavern of space until at last it was only a piece of sound, flattened and spent.

"Horn," Hod whispered, and completed the cycle. Something went away from me and was gone and came back, and I am all together like I was before. Something was given and something was given back. It's a thing to think on. It's a thing to make a body wonder.

Hod let his arms go loose from the shoulder and let his fingers curl around emptiness, as he watched his sister step high and lightly through the green corn. She came hopping over the furrows with an uneven gait that brought her up to the place where he was standing, breathing fast and shallow. He noticed how red her hair looked in the sun, and how brown and smooth her face was. He wondered afresh at the clear green of her eyes and the queer slant at the outer corners of her mouth — like a smile was forever and endurin' tucked away there. He saw the faded dress molded tight and sharp across her thighs. He was surprised. "She's growin' up! Why, Irma's growin' right up!"

Hod let the hoe handle slide down his hand. "Breakfast ready?" he asked.

"Hit's ready an' waitin'! Did you fergit it's Saturday? Comin' on out to the field thisaway!"

Saturday was the day he took the corn to the mill at the Gap, and made the weekly purchases at the store for his mother.

"No, I didn't forget," he said, shouldering his hoe. "But breakfast wasn't ready, and I thought I'd have time to finish up that row I left last night."

"Never thought somebody'd have to come git you, I reckon," Irma grumbled.

Hod pulled a twig of her hair and grinned. "I don't reckon anybody minded very much," he teased.

Irma glanced cornerwise at him and stuck her chin up in the

10

air. Then she burst out laughing. "Race you to the house," she challenged, and was off like a flash. Hod followed, heels glinting in the morning sun.

Piney Ridge is the backbone of a group of knobby, stony, almost barren hills, lying in a remote and neglected section of South Central Kentucky. These hills ram each other so closely with their interlocking horns that the country around and between them is well-nigh inaccessible. A graveled pike winds through their jutting lower slopes, but the roads back into the hills are little more than trails.

Green River cuts a deep gash in the hills, but for a space after it leaves the hills it flows gently and placidly, and in the rich bottoms the land stretches black and loamy on either side. Piney Ridge rises like a hogback from the litter of the low, clustering hills, and broods timelessly over old Green.

Clinging to the rocky ledges, the thin level tops, and the deep-scarred hollows of Piney Ridge are the descendants of a resolute man who pushed past the great wall of the hills and settled himself and his wife behind it.

If Thomas Pierce was disappointed when he first looked on the six hundred acres granted to him in payment of his services in the Continental Army, no one knows about it. If he had hoped, when he and his wife Amelia packed their household plunder into one lumbering wagon and drove out of Virginia through the Cumberland Gap into the dark and bloody wilderness — if, then, he had hoped that the tract of land toward which he had turned his face would be fair and fertile, it is not recorded. That proviso which caused the dark hills and Wandering Creek to be peopled read only that " in payment of loyal service rendered the Continental Army from November, 1777, to January, 1779, by Thomas Johnson Pierce of Amelia County, the Congress of the United States deeds to him and his heirs 600 acres of land near and about Wandering Creek, in the territory of Kentucky." The grant was dated February 1, 1805.

Nothing was said about the hills and there was no way Thomas Pierce could know that practically the entire six hundred acres would be covered by their rambling, rocky ridges; because

11

Wandering Creek wanders, as lazy and easy as its name implies, all around and between the hills.

How often he must have thought of home and Virginia and the level fields beside the placid little river there! How bitterly he must have regretted leaving them! How like the drinking of the cup of hemlock must have been the tilling of these thorny acres! But he stayed. To him and his heirs had been deeded the land, and while Thomas Pierce has long since been forgotten, his heirs still till their thorny acres.

Along the saw-toothed lip of Piney Ridge runs a road. In the winter it is axle-deep in mud, and impassable except, perhaps, for a sure-footed mule. In the summer the hard-caked mud is churned to a thick dust which, when stirred, drifts lazily off into the holler like an acrid fog.

About halfway down the ridge the road is bisected by another narrow, rutted road, which, eastward, leads off over Blain's Ridge to Goose Creek and the little settlement of Pebbly. To the west lies Knobby Gap, where there is a post office, a blacksmith's shop, two general stores, a gristmill, and perhaps a dozen drab houses. A church raises its dingy, scaling spire between the two stores.

But all that lies between is Piney Ridge, and on the road running the length of the ridge live the numerous descendants of Thomas Pierce on what is left of his six hundred acres. A few have been ambitious enough to add to their holdings, but most have been content with their meager share.

None of the Pierces care how they came to be on the ridge. Piney Ridge has belonged to them as far back as they can remember, and beyond that they have little curiosity. Sometimes Grampa Dow, the oldest of the tribe, and getting long-winded in his old age, tells about his father, Jeems, who could remember when the deer, bear, and wild turkey would walk right up to a man's cabin. But for the most part the familiar pattern of today is all that matters on the ridge. The Pierces only know that this land is theirs, that Pierce feet have always walked it, and that Pierce feet will always continue to walk it.

Grampa Dow was Hod's grandfather. He had three sons — Gault, Lem, and Tom. As each married, he gave him a parcel of land, and when Tom, the youngest, married, he gave him the home place and moved himself and Annie down to the log cabin in the holler which Jeems had built. Lem took the piece down on the pike, and Gault settled on the middle eighty down the road from Tom. Tom was Hod's father.

And there were great-uncles and uncles and first and second and third cousins scattered the length and breadth of the ridge. Farther down the road, toward Wandering Creek, big Wells Pierce and Hardy Pierce divided Great-Uncle James's place, Wells taking the old house with fifty acres and Hardy building him a cabin on the far forty. Hardy's wife had died many years before and he had lived alone until he hurt his back; then his oldest girl, Matilda, who had married her own first cousin, Little Wells, had come to live with him and keep his house. Little Wells tended the forty acres for Hardy, along with his own, and they had a house full of young'uns which, some said, nearly drove Hardy out of his mind.

Still farther down the road was Great-Uncle Frank's place, and then Great-Uncle Tim's place was the last bit of level land before the ridge dropped off to Wandering Creek. Frank had seven sons to heir his hundred acres, and Tim had five.

Uncle James, Uncle Frank, Uncle Tim, and Grampa Dow had had sizable holdings in their time, but the land had been divided among their sons, and soon it would have to be divided among new sons. And so it went. There was no new land to buy without leaving the ridge, and few Pierces ever left the ridge. They could not seem to live away from their thorny acres.

Occasionally — only occasionally — was there born to one of the Pierces a son or a daughter with a trace of the vital spirit of Thomas Pierce who had cut a trail to this gaunt land. Grampa Dow was one. Once he had studied on being a preacher. He even got him some books and pored over them. Hod didn't know why Grampa hadn't finished his studying, but Gramma had always laughed about it and said, " The sperrit was willin' but the flesh was weak." Grampa Dow didn't rightly know what had happened to the books, either. " The young'uns must o' took 'em," he said. " I ain't seen e'er one in a coon's age."

And then there was Aunt Dorcas, Grampa Dow's sister, who somehow had got enough learning to teach the Big Springs school. Of course she didn't teach very long. She married one of

13

her pupils, a big, strapping hulk of a fellow, who was ten years younger than she, and went with him to live over in Bear Holler.

But the fact remains that occasionally there was a Pierce with a will to lift himself out of the general inertia that was characteristic of the clan. The will may not have been sufficient to lift very far, but it stirred a faint spark of hope and yearning which flamed for a brief moment before it sputtered out.

Such a will was part of the heritage of young Hod Pierce when he was born on a hot July day, to this land and to these people. He was seven generations removed from his pioneer ancestor, but in the strange, unfathomable way of nature Hod was endowed with qualities that made him the old soldier's spiritual son.

This may have been because both Grampa Dow and Hod's father, Tom, went off the ridge to find their brides. Grampa Dow married Annie Hobbs from Pebbly, and Tom had gone to Peachstone, near the Gap, for pretty Hattie Byron. Fresh blood may have offered a freer channel for the transmission of the stancher and nobler qualities of the line. However that may be, young Hod was destined from the start to chafe and pull at the pattern of his life, trying first to make his dreams fit the pattern, and then trying to make the pattern fit his dreams. The pattern of Pierce lives was the very warp and woof of his soul, but it couldn't stifle the spark of his dreams. From childhood he looked at his world with clear, judging eyes, and with a heart torn between what he loved and felt and what he saw and judged.

Hod was born in the home place and his childhood varied little from that of his father before him. His bare feet stepped out of the low kitchen door onto the same wood block that had been worn down by Tom's feet. He ate with the same bone-handled knives and forks, at the same oilcloth-covered table in the dark corner of the kitchen, from the same old ironstone plates. He took the milk down the steep, rocky hill to the same cold spring, and struggled back up with heavy buckets of water for his mother. He swung on the same sagging garden gate, and ate the spicy, short-core apples from the same gnarled old trees.

From July to February he went down the road past the church, turned off on a dim path through the woods and over the edge of the hill, and down the holler to the same school to which Tom

14

and Grampa Dow had gone. His father's initials were cut on one side of a giant beech tree in the edge of the clearing and Grampa Dow's initials were still plain on its other side. Hod cut his own there one day, fresh and bleeding, under his father's, and stood off to admire his handiwork.

It was at school that the Pierce pattern changed. His father and most of the others had suffered in the schoolroom as in a prison; had felt bewildered by the steady stream of facts and uninspired to open the door of knowledge. They were like birds released to fly again when each long day was over. But Hod's eager young mind soaked up knowledge and was ever thirsting for more. History and geography flamed with color and passion for him, and the precise accuracy of mathematics and science enthralled him. He loved every day of the short school term and raced through his books until the teacher was sore tried to keep him supplied.

"Why do you keep running ahead of the class, Hod?" she asked. "If you will study only the lesson assigned to you, you won't finish your books so fast."

"I don't aim to bother you," he answered, "but I can't seem to quit when I get to the end. I allus want to know what comes next."

"But you'll find out when we come to that part."

"Yessum, I know. But I can't seem to help it. I know it's there and I want to learn so bad I have to keep right on." And then he burst out: "Miss Bertha, I want to read all the books I can get a hold of. I can go faster'n the other kids, and if I can go faster without botherin' you none, why can't I? Seems like I can't go fast enough to learn all I want to, and I get afraid the books won't last me out."

After that Miss Bertha had let him move along as he could. She tried to find books for him, and even dug down in her trunk and brought him those of her college days. He seized joyfully on anything she brought him — history, fiction, poetry, even the dull stuff of theology, for her father had been a minister and she still had some of his seminary volumes. He read anything and everything she gave him. He seemed spurred by some frenzied need to keep forever reading.

"Hod," his mother said one night when he had forgotten to

15

chop the kindling for the morning fires the second time in a row, "I'm plumb wore out with you havin' yer nose stuck in a book all the time. Hit's the beatinest thing ever I seen how you go to school all day an' cain't git enough o' books. A body cain't git a lick o' work outen you if they's a book handy. I don't know what's come over you, an' you ain't even ahearin' me talkin' to you now!"

The strident voice brought Hod back from King Arthur's Court and he blinked in the dim light of the familiar room. "I'm sorry, Ma," he said, laying the book down. "I didn't aim to forget the kindlin' again, but I cain't seem to remember anything when I get to readin' a book like this."

"What's it about?"

"It's about knights and ladies that lived across the ocean. And about a girl called the lily maid of Astolat. The knights had to be very . . . very — " he groped for the word — "very gallant, and fight for the king and the ladies."

"Humph! Sounds plumb crazy to me! You better git out there an' fight that choppin' block or there'll be no more readin' to-night. Cain't burn the lamps much longer, noways. Hit's a pure waste of oil."

Hod, who had been making ready to go out, stopped at the door. "Can I have a candle in the loft room, then?"

"No, you cain't have you no candle in the loft room. Someday yer goin' to burn the house right down to the ground, an' us with it, aburnin' a candle up there with them straw ticks. You'll go to bed an' go to sleep like you'd orta, young man, an' now git goin' on that kindlin' 'fore I smack you."

Hod hadn't really expected to be allowed to read later. Seemed like Ma almost always said no. Like that time he had wanted to have a garden all his own. "Ma," he'd said, "kin I have me a little garden over here in the corner an' have me some radishes an' onions o' my own?"

"No," not interrupting her own hoeing.

"Why?"

Smack! The thin, calloused brown hand was likely to reach out surely and swiftly for his face. "Git to yer hoein' an' quit pesterin' me with yer why's! You ain't big enough to have you a garden, that's why! Besides, you'd fergit to take keer of it, an'

16

it'd jist be good seed wasted." And Hod never argued. Life was easier if you didn't argue with Ma. Things went smoother if you just did what you were told to do.

Hod set the lantern down by the chopping block and methodically went to work on the kindling. With sure, clean strokes the hatchet stripped the slivers from a pine log. Doggedly he worked in the winter cold, and doggedly his thoughts kept him company.

"I'm gonna" — he corrected himself — "I'm going to go away from Piney Ridge someday and see the whole world. I'm going to Louisville and California and Europe, and maybe to China too; and I'm going to see for myself what the rest of the world is like. I'm going to eat off of a white tablecloth with shiny knives and forks and I'm going to have good clothes and sleep in a real bed, and I'm going to *be* somebody. *Someday I'm going to be somebody!*"

This was Hod when he was twelve. By the time he was seventeen he had finished with the little country school. It went only through the eighth grade and Hod had gone as long as Miss Bertha was there, but when she left, there was nothing more for him in the schoolroom. He wanted to go on to high school, but that would have meant boarding in at the county seat, and Tom and Hattie could see no use in any further schooling. Money was too scarce, and his help was needed on the place.

Hattie said: "You've learned how to read an' write an' do a little figgerin'. Why would you need to know any more? 'Twon't he'p you none growin' tobaccer."

So now he was free of the schoolroom, for his father to shift most of the heavy work of the farm to his thin shoulders. Not unkindly. It was the way of the ridge. Sons took over the hardest work as soon as they were able.

Hod was up at first light in answer to his mother's call: "Hod! Git up!" Never was it softened. Never once did she climb the steep little stairs to the loft room to touch him and wake him gently.

He would tumble out of his straw tick and dress hurriedly, for the loft room was bitterly cold in the winter and stiflingly hot in the summer. In the summer, dressing consisted of pulling on his overalls and putting on his shoes, for he wore neither underwear nor socks, and he slept in his shirt. There was something faintly

17

repulsive to him in this, for his shirt always smelled of his own sweat and he shrank, fastidiously, from its contact. But he wouldn't have thought of asking his mother for a clean one. He put on the clothes she laid out for him, when she laid them out, understanding all too well that there wasn't enough money for him to have more than two pairs of overalls and three or four shirts. Since he carried the water from a spring on washday, he knew he couldn't have fresh clothes every day. At that he was cleaner than most boys he knew, for Hattie was a cleaner mother than most. But a bath once a week, with fresh shirt and overalls for him satisfied her standards.

Dressed, he stumbled down the steep, dark stairs to the kitchen, splashed warm water from the iron teakettle, which always sat on the back of the stove, into a tin washbasin, and washed the sleep from his eyes. Then he ran the snaggle-toothed comb, which the whole family used, through his hair two or three times, and his toilet was made. After that he was usually off to the barn, where his father had preceded him, and silently they fed the stock and milked the cows.

Breakfast was ready when they returned to the house. It was a meal that rarely varied: fried, home-cured bacon or ham; fried eggs; hot soda biscuits; milk gravy; scalding, black, boiled coffee; and homemade jam, jelly, preserves, or sorghum molasses.

Such a breakfast waited for Hod and Irma now. As they came through the door, Hattie speared brown pieces of meat and piled them high on the platter. Breaking eight eggs into the large iron skillet, she fitted the lid down and left them to simmer.

"Irma, you kin set the things down," she said sharply.

"Yessum," Irma said, flying to take up the hot biscuits, to pour the coffee, and to set a small pitcher of cream in the center of the table.

Hattie took the cover off the eggs and poured them into a warm, shallow bowl. She dropped a handful of flour into the hot grease in the skillet and stirred vigorously until it was blended. Then she filled the skillet with milk and gently moved the creamy mass back and forth until it thickened.

Hod sniffed. "Cream gravy, Ma?"

"I declare, Hod! You had cream gravy nigh onto ever' day o' yer life, an' you allus act like it was somethin' brand-new! Don't

18

you never git enough of it?"

"Never have yet! Just be sure you make enough. I'll need it to pass the day at the Gap."

Irma drew her mouth down at the corners. "I wisht I could go to the Gap with him today."

"Now, Irma," Hattie said, "we got a sight o' work cut out fer us today, hit bein' Saturday an' all. I cain't noways make out here by myself. Likely the meetin'll start tomorrer night too. Hit's powerful early to be startin' a meetin', but them White Caps, they allus have the first 'un. But White Caps or whoever else, I ain't aimin' to miss the startin', an' they's more work'n I kin make out to do. You'll have to he'p today."

Irma sighed and slid down the bench along the wall to her regular place, and Hod slid in next to her. When Hattie sat down, the family bowed their heads and waited for the blessing. She smoothed back her hair. She always smoothed her hair back before the blessing, as if she must be neat to approach the Lord. She then cleared her throat and murmured rapidly: "Lord, we thank thee for what we are about to receive. Keep us from sin and save us in heaven. For Jesus' sake. Amen."

The blessing over, each one filled his plate, sprawled his arms along the table, bent his head over his food, and shoveled it in as fast as he could swallow. It was an insult to a good cook to talk when a body could eat. As each finished eating, he shoved his plate back and left the table. Hod and Tom moved out into the yard.

"Reckon I better git on down to Grampa's," Tom said, moving the toothpick in his mouth from one corner to the other. "I give him my word I'd he'p in his corn today."

"You sure you wouldn't rather go to the Gap today yourself?"

"No. You go on. Ifen yer ma don't remember to put a plug o' tobaccer on the list, don't you fergit it."

"I'll not. And I'll be home in time to help with the evenin' work."

Tom's eyes twinkled. "Mebbe," he drawled, "ifen that Lily Mae gal ain't down at the Gap today too."

Hod flushed and kicked the toe of his shoe against the wood block. "I'm not aimin' to tarry with any Lily Mae girl," he muttered.

19

"I dunno, boy. Ifen I was yore age, I'm afeared I'd be bound to tarry some."

"Well, I'm not actually talkin' to her, yet."

"No? Well, don't be like them molasses in there agittin' started. Happen somebody else is agoin' to notice them blue eyes o' her'n first thing you know."

Hod grinned at his father and poked at him with his fist. "You better be gettin' on down to Grampa's, and I better be headin' for the Gap." He started toward the house.

Hattie had laid out clean denim pants for him, and a fresh-ironed shirt. As he pulled them on, Hod thought of Lily Mae. It would be something, now, wouldn't it, if she should happen to be at the Gap today too. He remembered her wheat-colored hair, and the bold, strong look of her eyes. The other night when he walked her home from the singing, was she mocking him when she said she liked bashful boys, or was she saying it for true? A thin silver stream ran through him and set his legs to quivering. He stared strangely at his reflection in the cracked mirror hanging over the chest of drawers. He looked closely at his own straw-colored hair, springing thickly from the scalp, pushing back in one high wave. He examined his eyes, blinking them rapidly and widening them to see exactly how they looked. They were hazel, there was no doubt about it. He pulled his lips away from his teeth and looked carefully at their strong, even whiteness. He looked at the deep dimple in the middle of his chin. He screwed his head from one side to another, looking at his jaw from first one angle and then another. It was lean and ruddy, but he wasn't much to look at, he thought. If a girl like Lily Mae took a fancy to him, it wouldn't be on account of his looks.

What, then? What drew a man and a woman together and lifted their eyes to each other shyly? What, across the face of the earth, pulled the male and female into pairs? This thin silver stream of loneliness? This emptiness inside of him in the night? This need to stand on high places and look beyond the hills? What, in all time, was the way of man on the face of the earth? And how was a man to know, and what was he to know? His thoughts ran vaguely, without definition. There was only a feeling of deep nostalgia . . . for something that eluded him.

"Hod?" his mother's voice recalled him. "I've done fixed out my list. You 'bout ready?"

He tucked in his shirttail and went into the kitchen. "I'm ready."

She handed him the list, written in pencil on the cheap, blue-lined tablet paper she always used. "Hit ain't so much today, an' they's no real heavy things to pack, so I reckon you better not take the wagon."

He folded the list and slipped it into his shirt pocket.

"Now, mind, Hod," Hattie went on, "an' don't fergit nothin'. Don't mislay that there thread, fer I'm plumb outen it, an' I've got to git Irma's dresses sewed next week fer shore. An' you watch the miller on the toll real keerful. Matildy was tellin' me he uses a awful heavy hand ameasurin', an' we ain't got no corn to spare to fatten up his hogs with!"

"Yessum," said Hod. "Anything else?"

"Ifen you see Brother Jim, you might tell him we're all well. An' ask him how Frony is. She ain't been very stout this winter, an' it wouldn't surprise me none to hear any day she's been took with another spell of her heart."

Hod moved toward the door. "Find out fer shore if the meetin's goin' to start tomorrer night, an' who's goin' to do the preachin'. But don't go givin' him no invite fer dinner tomorrer, though. I don't aim to kill e'er nother chicken till my little 'uns come on."

As he went through the barnyard gate, Hattie called once more. "Hod! Uh, Hod! Better git Tom a plug o' tobaccer."

He waved to let her know he had heard and went on. He led old Buck to the fence, slipped the bit between his teeth and threw the saddle over him. Then, turning back to the barn, he hefted the bag of corn onto his shoulder. Under the load he hunched over to Buck and threw the sack up back of the saddle. He took a double hitch around the bag of corn, making it fast to the saddle, and then he swung up and moved down the path toward the road.

As he turned into the road, Irma came running out the front door. "Here's the money, Hod! Hod! You done fergot the money!"

He reined up the horse and waited, laughing, while Irma

21

caught up with him. She handed it up to him and said: "That was about the foolishest thing I ever knowed of! What was you aimin' to use fer money?"

"Wasn't thinkin' about money one way or another. Just plumb forgot about it."

Irma stood, fingering the saddle strings. "Hod," she said, her voice low and her head down. "Reckon you'll see John Walton down at the Gap?"

Hod grinned at her. "It's possible."

"Well, ifen you do, an' don't go out o' yer way none, but jist ifen you do, an' ifen you find out fer shore the meetin's goin' to start tomorrer night, jist let it drop like that we'll all be goin'."

"How does a body go about just lettin' it drop like?" he teased.

Her face flamed. "You know what I'm meanin', Hod Pierce!"

"Now, just smooth down your red hair! I wasn't meanin' anything. I'll find a way to let it drop like if I see him." He slapped the reins against Buck's neck and the horse moved slowly away. "And if he's at the Gap I'll see him," he promised. The dust between them rose in a thick cloud and Irma went back into the house.

Buck stepped off the distance lightly and quickly, following the meanderings of the road. When they came to the crossroads, Hod took a path through a pasture, into the woods, and eventually came out at the road that went down off the ridge to the Gap. Hod loved that little place in the woods. It was always cool and quiet, except for the squirrels and birds.

This morning the sun sprinkled the ground with gold dust, and sprayed the leaves with shining lacquer. The birches stood whitely in their cleanness, and squirrels fretted childishly among them. An old mockingbird trilled high up next to the sun, and a jay scolded him from a sumac bush. Hod leaned out and stripped a sassafras twig from a young tree; and peeling it, stuck it in his mouth to chew on.

"You old jay," he teased the bird, "nobody's botherin' you! You go on about your business!"

He eased Buck on down the hill, smelling the clean June morning and the warm sun and the bright blue day. It was a fair day, for sure.

CHAPTER TWO

Horses, mules, and teams were hitched to the long rail in front of the mill, which on Saturday was the gathering place of farmers from the whole countryside. They came in from every direction, bringing their bushels of corn, whetting their gregarious appetites with anticipation of a full, unhurried day of male company. Here the wine of man's talk was distilled afresh each week, and mulled voluptuously over each tongue.

Hod pushed past the knot of men lounging in the doorway and eased his load of corn into the line of sacks on the floor.

"Howdy, Hod," said the miller.

"Howdy, Uncle Billy. Reckon I'll have time to do Ma's buyin' before you get to me?"

"Plenty o' time. Plenty o' time. Be another hour yit 'fore I kin git to you. Go 'long an' don't be in no rush. How's all yer folks?"

"Well as could be expected, I reckon. You seen Uncle Jim around today?"

The miller spat tobacco juice on one of the sacks near his feet and looked slowly around. "No," he said finally. "Come to think of it, I ain't. An' he don't hardly ever miss a Saturday, neither. Could be Frony's puny again, but I ain't heared no one name it if she is. Want me to tell him yer lookin' fer him ifen he comes in?"

"I'd be much obliged to you," Hod said, and moved out the door.

He crossed the road to the store, went up its three rickety steps and inside. When his eyes had become accustomed to its dimness, he walked diffidently back to where Miss Ettie, the storekeeper, sat crocheting. Hod always dreaded this moment, for the store was usually full of womenfolks and he felt out of place among them. But Ma's list burned his pocket until he had made her purchases.

As he threaded his way through the women, he nodded shyly to each, noticing who they were so that he could tell Hattie. His heart pumped suddenly when he saw Lily Mae Gibbs standing over by the counter. He could hear Hattie's tongue clucking

23

now. "So Lily Mae Gibbs was in town, was she? You'd think she'd stay home oncet in a while an' he'p her ma. She does a sight o' runnin' around fer a girl her age."

Maybe he wouldn't tell her Lily Mae was there after all. She'd been upset when she found out he walked Lily Mae home from the singing last time. Wasn't any need to tell her everything.

Among the women gathered at the counter Hod took note of Matildy, Little Wells's wife. She was a short, plump little woman, with crinkling brown eyes, and a good, hearty laugh. It rang out now and filled the store, and Hod smiled as he heard it. He had always liked Matildy. He would ask her about the meetin'.

Miss Ettie heaved her vast bulk up from the rocker and rolled her crocheting into a neat ball. The womenfolks always had to gossip awhile and look around until they made up their minds, but she knew Hod would have a list and wouldn't want to linger long.

"Howdy, Hod," she said, moving to meet him. "You got yer ma's list, I reckon. How's Hattie, an' all yer folks?"

"We're all tol'able, thank you. You all well?"

"Purty good. Ma's been ailin', but, as I tell her, when yer eighty-five year old you got to expect a few aches an' pains. She's right peart fer one her age. Lemme have Hattie's list."

Hod fished in his pocket for the list and handed it to her. "Ma said git Pa a plug of tobacco too. It's not on the list."

Miss Ettie nodded and went about filling the order. White thread, a bottle of Black Draught, a large can of baking powder, a box of pepper, a paper of pins, and Tom's cut plug. As she gathered together the articles, Hod listened to the women's talk.

Becky, Gault's wife, was telling Matildy and Lily Mae how she made her famous spiced peaches. "Hit's the way you make the sirup that counts," she was saying. "Ifen you bile it jist a mite too long, it hardens 'em. I never even let it spin a thread."

Matildy laughed. "I reckon yer right, Becky. But with that flock o' young'uns round my feet I'm lucky if I git e'er peach in a can, much less foolin' with sich fancies as spicin' 'em."

Becky, who had no children, looked wistfully at Matildy. "Air the young'uns all well?" she asked.

"Oh, tol'able. But with four you cain't never tell. I'm hopin' they won't come down with ever'thing till the meetin's over."

24

Lily Mae giggled and lowered her voice, but Hod could hear the clear whisper: " Ifen they ever' one had the whoopin' cough an' was coughin' their heads off, don't reckon you'd miss the meetin'."

Matildy's big, hearty laugh rang out again. " No, that wouldn't frash me none. I ain't aimin' to miss out on the meetin' fer nothin' like that! "

They bunched their heads together and Hod knew they meant to exclude him. This was hushed and intimate woman talk, meant only for a woman's ears. Self-consciously he kept his eyes away from them. He studied the canned goods on the shelves, whistled tunelessly under his breath, and stuffed his suddenly awkward hands in his pants pockets. When Lily Mae laughed too loudly and too meaningly, his glance was drawn to her like a magnet. He wanted desperately to talk to her. He thought of how it would be to walk boldly up to her and ask her whether she knew for certain the meeting was going to start tomorrow night and if she was going. He could feel how he would swing his shoulders back, uncaring, before all the women. How he would say for all to hear, " I'll be walkin' you home tomorrow night."

But he made no move except to shift from foot to foot uneasily. Miss Ettie handed him his purchases. He paid her and put the change in his pocket. As he walked past the women, Matildy spoke to him. " Hod, e'er one o' the folks come in with you? "

He stopped. " No," he answered. " Pa had to he'p Grampa today, and Ma and Irma cleaned house. So I came in by myself." He ran the rim of his straw hat around in his hands. " Say, Matildy, is the meetin' goin' to start tomorrow for sure? "

" I was aimin' to tell you," Matildy slapped her hand down on the counter, " and I plumb nigh fergot! The tent's all set up in the schoolyard at Big Springs, tell Hattie. An' Dan Wilson's goin' to do the preachin'. I ain't never heared him, but they say he's really got the sperrit, an' kin expound somethin' wonderful. Big Springs ain't as handy fer Hattie as 'twould be at Piney Chapel, but I reckon it's clost enough fer her to go real often."

" Well, much obliged, Matildy," and Hod turned to go.

" Tell her," Matildy added, " that he's goin' to take dinner with Lizzie tomorrer, an' if she figgers she kin take him e'er time durin' the meetin', she kin let me know."

"I'll tell her," he promised, and turned on his heel. He swung sharply into Lily Mae, who had moved back of him as he talked to Matildy. The girl gave no ground and lifted impudent, mocking eyes to him. Her face was only a few inches from his, and her bold, blue look held him brightly. His heart skipped a beat and then started pounding crazily. He felt paralyzed and rooted to the spot.

She tossed her yellow hair back and laughed. "I'm goin' to the meetin' tomorrer night," she said. "You aimin' to go?"

He swallowed hard and felt his voice cracking around the knot in his throat. "I reckon," was all he could manage to get out.

She leaned slightly forward so that for a brief moment her body brushed against him. Light as a moth's wing it was, but it sent an instant shock all over him. Even his finger tips tingled. She was so close her breath fanned his cheek when she said, "Ifen you do, bring yer gittar!"

He lifted his eyes to hers, and her shining, confident look darkened with promise. His tongue stuck to the roof of his mouth, and he thought wildly that his knees were going to give way. He could bear no more. He ducked his head and fled, hearing the women laugh as he stumbled down the steps. Lily Mae's laugh was loudest of all.

His nose burned with the depth of his indrawn breath, and he forced himself to walk away slowly. But his heart pumped loudly and there was a singing in his ears. Lily Mae liked him! She moved over on purpose so he would bump into her! He felt a joyful surge of exhilaration again, and he lifted his head high. She wanted him to come to the meetin'! Tomorrow! Tomorrow! Tomorrow was so fair a day!

"Ye-ay! Hod!" a voice hailed him. "Wait up!"

Coming around the corner of the store were two of his cousins, Wade and Sandy Pierce, Lem's boys, about his own age. They were handsome boys, taller than Hod, more solidly built, with brilliant curls and flashing, perfect teeth. Hod had envied them all his life, not only because they were so carelessly good-looking, but also because they were so wonderfully free. Lizzie was an easygoing mother, who showered love and affection on her young'uns and spoiled them out of all reason. She kept a slovenly house whose doors were open to everyone, and lived and let live as best she could. Her house was a scandal to as good a housekeeper as Hattie, and the way she was raisin' her kids was worse. But to Hod, Wade and Sandy seemed blessed by Providence' own kind hand.

He was proud of Hattie's smart ways and neat house, but he wished it didn't hedge him in so. Folks said Hattie Pierce had been as gay and purty as a bird when she was young. But ever since she was converted that summer, long before he could remember, she had been strict and, most times, joyless. Religion sometimes did that to a body. But folks all said that Hattie Pierce was a woman who really had the faith, now. And there was never a tongue set against her. She would die before she'd lift her skirts to a dance tune, and if a deck of cards had darkened her door, she would have burned them quicker than a flash, and her tongue would have taken the hide off him that brought them. Seemed like sometimes her religion was mostly don'ts, but one thing you had to say: she never talked one way and did another.

But Wade and Sandy, now. They could go swimming in the river whenever they liked; they could go hunting when they wanted to; they could have the horses to ride on Sunday; they could build martin boxes right in the house and Lizzie didn't say: " Git that stuff outen here! Yer jist makin' a mess fer me to clean up! "

They were even allowed to have a deck of cards at home, and Hod had seen Lizzie sit down with them, laughing just as hard as they did over the game. And they had a fiddle and a victrola in their house, and some mighty lively tunes they played on that victrola.

" We been wantin' to see you," said Wade, who was the older. " Pa said we could go over to the lumber camp this summer till the tobaccer's ready, an' hew ties an' make us some money. Reckon you could go? "

Hod's eyes brightened. What wouldn't he give to go with them! Why, he might make twenty-five or thirty dollars! It was a couple of months yet until tobacco would be ready to cut. He might even make fifty dollars! With fifty dollars he could go to Louisville. Maybe he could get a job there and work and go to school. He could hew ties! Why, hadn't he just last winter split enough hickory to fence the pasture along the road?

"When you goin'?" he asked.

"Monday mornin' bright an' early. Pa's goin' to take us over in the wagon, an' we kin stop by fer you easy as not," answered Wade.

"We're goin' to stay over at the camp too," spoke up Sandy. "Ain't no use to come home 'cept on Sundays."

An uneasy feeling crept over Hod. He didn't know what Hattie would say to that. She had always held that the lumber camp was a godless place. But surely she would want him to earn all that money. If he could make as much as fifty dollars, he could give her half of it and still have enough to go to Louisville.

"Well, you all stop by," he said, "and if I can go I'll be ready."

Wade nodded and turned away. Sandy followed him and Hod started toward the mill.

"You goin' to preachin' tomorrer night?" yelled Wade at his back. Hod swung around.

"I reckon Ma'll want to go."

"Betcha a dollar you go . . . fer the singin' anyhow," teased Wade. Hod flushed.

"What do *you* know about any singin'?"

"Oh . . ." Wade laughed, "news gits around. I hear you like the color of Lily Mae Gibbs's eyes."

Uncomfortably Hod pushed his old straw hat back on his head. "I couldn't even tell you the color of her eyes," he lied intensely.

"Well, what *was* you lookin' at when you was talkin' to her over at Smiths' the other Sunday?" howled Sandy, and the two cousins fled down the road, whooping and yelling.

Hod kicked angrily at a pebble in the road. This is the meanest place in the whole world for talking, he thought. Just because I looked off the same book at singin' with Lily Mae Gibbs, and then walked down the road a piece with her, the whole ridge has got me married to her!

Piney Ridge found nothing strange in a seventeen-year-old boy's thinking of marriage. Many boys on the ridge married at sixteen or seventeen and had families before they were twenty. But no such thought was in Hod's mind. The girl Lily Mae was exciting. He didn't ferret out his feelings beyond that. His skin

28

prickled when he thought of her. But he forgot her when he thought of the lumber camp Monday. And maybe the big city this fall.

At the mill he looked around for John Walton, but not seeing him, settled himself on a sack of meal on the fringe of the circle of men who were chewing and spitting and ruminating. Little Wells was there, a short, sawed-off little man with merry, winsome ways. He and Matildy were cut from the same piece of cloth, Hod thought, fitting together like the pattern from one bolt of goods.

Ferdy Jones was in the group. Ferdy was a tall, skinny fellow with a nervous Adam's apple and a sharp nose that was always smelling gossip and talk, most of it scandalous and obscene. Ferdy liked to drink too well, and the talk was that Corinna had a bad time with him.

Lem was there, tall and stooped, and Gault; and thin, wizened little Old Man Clark, who lived in the tenant house on Gault's place. Matt Jasper sat over in a corner to himself, tobacco juice making twin lines of dribble down his unshaved chin. None of the Jaspers was very bright, but Matt had fits, and while he could work a farm all right, his eyes had a staring, vacant look.

Other men drifted in and out the door from time to time, but these men were the hub of the wheel. Hod knew they would sit here several hours. He listened and watched as they talked. Funny, he thought. You can tell the strength of a man by the way the others listened to him. Lem is like a stout oak tree in a forest. When he talks, the others heed him. Little Wells will be a stout oak tree someday too. But the sap is still green in him. Gault is strong, but it's like his strength had frozen in him. He's brittle. Maybe if he and Becky had had children, he would have been warm and gentle. Having no children seemed to dry up a man.

Ferdy Jones was a windbag, and, like the wind, his words passed over and were hardly noticed. Old Man Clark they humored, knowing his strength was past. They pitied Matt Jasper, but their pity was mixed with something like shame. He had the form of a man and the manner of a man, but there was

29

something rotten and sick and unclean in him, and spiritually they isolated him and his disease fouled them. Are men like this the world over, thought Hod. Or is it the ridge makes them so?

The talk drifted lazily from one subject to another. Little Wells was speaking when Hod noticed. "That rain last week shore freshened up the tobaccer," he said. "Ifen we kin jist have a little spell o' rain along, we'd orta have a right good crop this year."

"How much you figger to have, Wells?" asked Gault.

"Oh, round seven, eight hunderd pounds, I reckon. What you figgerin' on?"

"'Bout the same. Mebbe a little less."

"I doubt the price'll hold this year, though," spoke up Ferdy. "What you think, Lem?"

Lem pulled at his chin and pondered. "Hit's untellin', but they's no real good reason to think it'll go down too fur. As a usual thing it builds up two, three year, an' then it'll start taperin' off. Ain't quite due to drap off much yit. But the tobaccer market's somethin' I ain't ever hopin' to figger out."

The miller came up behind Wells and laid a dusty hand on his shoulder. "Wells, how's that little Jersey I sold you awhile back doin'?"

"She's all right, Uncle Billy. A good little milker. 'Course she's dry right now, but she's due to come fresh in about a coupla months. I ain't got e'er thing to complain about in that cow. She's gentle an' she's easy to milk. You done me a favor when you sold her to me."

Ferdy Jones snickered. "That ain't the only thing that's due to come fresh over at yore place, is it Wells?"

Wells chuckled. "Well," he said, "I'm ahopin' Matildy an' the cow don't run too clost a race." The men laughed together, comfortably.

Hod saw John Walton come in and saunter over toward the hopper. He unfolded his long legs and drifted over toward him.

"Howdy, John."

"Howdy, Hod. Looks like nearly ever'body come in to the Gap today. All yore folks come?"

"No. Nobody but me."

The Waltons were one of the few outside families who had

30

settled in the ridge country. Old Man Walton had bought a little piece of land from Hardy Pierce and had brought his family from Tennessee. He had acquired more land from time to time from various other Pierces and now had one of the biggest farms on the ridge. Folks said he drove himself and his boys mighty hard, but they had to admit he made a showing for it.

John was an easygoing, quick-laughing young man. Hod knew him to be a diligent and dependable worker; and in that fraternity of quickening young men he knew him to be decent. He knew John would make Irma a good and faithful husband.

"You all aimin' to go to the meetin' tomorrow night?" he asked idly.

"They aimin' to start fer shore?"

"Matildy was just tellin' me they are. Tent's on the Big Springs school ground. She said Dan Wilson's goin' to do the preachin'."

"I've not heared of him."

"I've not either, but Matildy said he was a man with power."

John ran a thin stream of fresh-ground meal through his hands. "You all aimin' to go?"

"We'll be there."

"Well, I'll be seein' you then."

The word had been dropped like, and Hod could tell Irma that John would be looking for her. He turned back to the men, raising his hand to John.

CHAPTER THREE

HOME LOOKED GOOD to Hod as he came in sight of it. It was always thus when he had been away, even for so brief a spell as the trip to the Gap each Saturday.

The house Grampa Dow had given Tom Pierce when he brought Hattie home as a bride hunched low by the side of the road. There were four rooms now; two across the front and two in the lean-to across the back. A narrow porch with a railing around it hemmed in the two front doors, and at the back an old wood block served as kitchen stoop.

The house was built of rough lumber, battened vertically, and it had long since weathered to a soft, mellow gray, like the sky

31

on a rainy day; and the white-oak shingle boards of the roof were curled at the edges. Days the wind blew hard they slapped noisily against each other and occasionally one would wrench itself loose from its bindings and scurry end over end across the yard.

The yard was closed in with a paling fence, weathered like the house, and a tired gate swung between cedar posts. Honeysuckle matted the fence to the right of the gate, and a brilliant scarlet rose climbed thickly down the left side. A bronze bush stood at either end of the narrow porch, and cinnamon vines followed thin wires to the roof in between. Roses were dotted about the yard in tight little clumps, and just by the chimney at the end of the house was Gramma's little yellow rose. It was said the first Tom Pierce's wife had brought a slip from Virginny, and Pierce yards ever since had always had a yellow rose. It clambered valiantly up the old stone chimney, and each summer its green spikes were softened with pale, buttery buds which opened full into a brilliant, extravagant gold.

Hattie had not planted any of these pretties. She didn't have much of a hand with blossoms. But she did her best to keep the grass from choking them out, and she kept the yard as tidy as her house and garden patch would let her. Tom too was neat about the place. He kept his barns and sheds mended, his tools where they belonged, and his fences clean. Tom and Hattie Pierce had a pride in themselves and in all they owned. Gramma had planted the blooms, but Hattie tended them faithfully.

Hod stabled the horse and went toward the house, sorting over in his mind the doings of the day. He was elated over the encounter with Lily Mae, excited and flooded with eager hope. Bring yer gittar! Now, what did she mean? And he had good news for Irma. First off, he'd tell her he'd seen John Walton. He nodded his head approvingly when he thought of John for Irma. They'd make out fine together.

But it was when he thought of the lumber camp that something took him by the throat and shook him hard. He could hardly swallow past the knot of excitement that tightened there. But he must be sure to pick the right time to tell Ma. He'd promise to be careful, and with the work caught up she surely couldn't care for him going.

When he stepped through the door, the familiarity of home closed round him. Since he could remember, it had looked the same. The house was oblong, with a big and a little room across the front and another big room and little room across the back. The big front room was the heart of the house, with the great fireplace at one end, and Hattie's bed across from it in the corner. Her sewing machine stood against another wall, and a dresser with cracked and peeling varnish completed the furnishings. A steep stair wound up from the corner by the fireplace to the loft room, which was Hod's.

The kitchen was back of the big front room, so that Hattie had only to step from one part of her domain to the other. A huge, black wood stove took up one corner; and hanging all around it were the pots and pans, skillets and pails, and stretched on a line kitty-cornered the dish towels always hung drying. Across from the stove was the dough table, which Grampa Dow had made. No one else had a dough table whose tray slid so smoothly in its groove; and Grampa had thought of the clever little shelf in the corner of the flour bin to hold the soda and salt. It saved many a step to the shelves over by the window. Grampa Dow was always studying ways to fix things up.

In the far end of the room the long table stretched down the wall. It sagged in the middle and it had been scrubbed until it was splintery, but a heap of Pierces could sit around it for Sunday dinner, and it would hold a sight of victuals.

The little back room was a storeroom. Times when the house overflowed with company some folks had to sleep there, but mostly it was a store place for Hattie's jars of garden truck and dried apples, and old trunks and broken-down furniture, and all the other things a family had need to hide away.

In the little front room there was a neat iron bedstead spread with a patchwork quilt. Gramma had made the quilt for Irma on her fifth birthday, and when Irma was old enough to have her own room, she put it on her bed. It was called a crazy quilt, because its pieces were put together any size or color. But Irma loved its bright colors and its queerly shaped pieces. This piece was from a dress Gramma had had when she first came to Piney Ridge with Grampa. This piece, fitting so lovingly here alongside it, was from a little shirt of Pa's. This piece, now, was from the

33

dress Ma wore the day she was wedded, and this one was from one of her own baby aprons. It all went together, however the pieces were cut, and in the end it was square and true.

In Hod's attic room was an iron bedstead like Irma's. Gramma had given him his coverlet too, but she hadn't made it. She said Abigail Pierce had made it long years ago on her own loom. She had carded the wool herself, and then she had woven the coverlet. And now Hod had a coverlet for his bed, soft and white and worn.

An old chest with several drawers, and a table with two shelves nailed above it, completed the room. Hod's clothes hung on nails in one corner. He spent little time in his room, and gave it less thought. It was where he slept and changed his clothes. It was a part of home, without having any significance of its own. It bore no mark of ·him, boy or man. Hattie kept it as spotless as she did the rest of the house, and it had the immaculate austerity of a monk's cell, swept, aired, and virginal.

To this home Tom Pierce had brought young Hattie Byron twenty-two years ago. Gramma had already worn off its newness in her years of homekeeping there, so when Hattie took it for her own, it had the smell and the feel and the look of a place where folks lived.

Hattie was ironing when Hod reached home, but she pushed the irons to the back of the stove and set about fixing him something to eat. "I wasn't lookin' fer you till midafternoon," she said. "You nearly allus stay as long as you kin. But I kin fix you a snack that'll do you till supper, I reckon."

"Don't bother," said Hod, heaving the sack of meal to the floor. "Just give me a glass of milk and some corn bread and I'll make out."

She set the glass of milk and a plate with a chunk of cold corn bread on the table and placed a spoon by it. When he had finished washing, he sat down at a corner of the table and began crumbling the bread into the milk. Hattie drew up a chair and buttered a piece of bread for herself.

"Didja git my things?"

Hod nodded, and put his spoon down to unload his pockets.

34

Hattie laughed. "Ifen that ain't jist like a man! Man or boy, if they've got e'er thing to pack, they'll squeeze it into a pocket! Anything to keep from packin' a sack. I recollect one time when you was little an' I sent you down to borry some eggs offen Becky. You come home with a egg in ever' pocket!"

Hod grinned sheepishly as he laid the articles on the table before her. "How could I pack a sack ahorseback?" he asked

Hattie laughed again and settled back for him to finish eating. Sometimes when they were alone like this she seemed more relaxed and quiet. Her busy hands would lie still for a time in her lap and her voice would be gentle and soft. Hod loved such times with her.

"Didja see Jim?" she asked.

He shook his head. "He wasn't there. I asked the miller if he'd seen him and he said he'd not been in. Promised to keep an eye out for him, but he never did show up, I reckon."

A little worried frown appeared on Hattie's forehead. "I jist know Frony's been took with another spell. Ifen I didn't have that there sewin' on my hands this week, an' my garden to clean out, I'd git Tom to take me over there an' see."

Hod reached for the last of the corn bread. "If Frony's had a spell," he said, "Jim'll be over here after you. I wouldn't worry about it if I were you."

"Well, a body'd orta keep up with their own kin," she replied, "an' Jim's the last o' mine. I'd hate to think o' Frony down in bed over there with not e'er soul to take keer of her."

Hod was silent. Ma was always quick to go when someone needed her.

"Who all was in town?" Hattie went on.

He named the women he'd seen in the store, leaving out Lily Mae. As he'd expected she clucked her tongue over Matildy. He named the men who had been at the mill, and he told of seeing Wade and Sandy. But he didn't say anything about the lumber camp.

"What about the meetin'?" she prodded him.

"The tent's already set up on the school ground, and Dan Wilson's to do the preachin'."

Hattie sighed. "I was afeared they'd have it down there. Hit's jist too fur to go ever' night. An' I love to go so good too. But I

35

reckon they had to have it there this time. The last 'un was at Piney Chapel. Who tole you?"

"Matildy."

Hattie rocked her hickory chair back on its legs and smoothed her apron. "You aimin' to he'p out with the music any?"

"If I'm asked I might," he answered. "Where's Pa?"

Hattie was raking the crumbs off the table into the palm of her hand. She shook it out the door vigorously. "He's not come back from Grampa's yit."

Hod started toward the front room. "Where's Irma?"

"She went up to the mailbox. She'd orta be back here too."

As he went by the fireplace, Hod picked up his guitar and ran his fingers lightly over the strings, ear bent intently to catch the tone. Folks on the ridge said Hod Pierce could pick the heart right out of a guitar. He only knew that whatever he was feeling could find expression through his fingers on the strings, and that something wild and yearning inside of him was stilled when he played.

"Ma," he called, "you know where those strings are I got last week from the mail order?"

"On the clock shelf," she called back.

"Think I'll restring my guitar. Might need it tomorrow night."

"Bring yer gittar!" "Bring yer gittar!" The words sang in his mind while his hands worked lovingly with the instrument. When he had finished, he tested the strings, tuned first one and then the other. He plucked a few chords, and then settled his chair against the doorjamb.

> "'You git a line an' I'll git a pole,
>   Honey!
>   You git a line an' I'll git a pole,
>   Ba-a-abe!
>   You git a line an' I'll git a pole,
>   I'll meet you down at the crawdad hole,
>   Honey, Sugarbaby, mine!'"

Hattie came to the kitchen door. "Git it fixed?"

Hod nodded and let his fingers pick lightly at the strings.

"Sing me the one about the great speckled bird," Hattie said. Hod found the key, thrummed a rich chord, and his voice deepened to the opening words.

" 'What a beautiful thought I am thinking,
    Concerning a great speckled bird.
Remember her name is recorded,
    On the pages of God's Holy Word.

" 'With all other birds flocking 'round her,
    They watch every move that she makes.
They try to find fault with her teaching,
    But really they find no mistakes.

" 'I am glad I have learned of her meekness,
    I am proud that my name's on her book;
For I want to be one never fearing,
    On the face of my Saviour to look.

" 'When he cometh descending from heaven,
    On a cloud as he writes in his Word;
I'll be joyfully carried to meet him,
    On the wings of that great speckled bird.

" 'Now she's spreading her wings for her journey.
    That she's going to take by-and-by.
When the trumpet shall sound on that morning,
    She will meet her dear Lord in the sky.' "

Hattie sighed. " I've allus loved that song." Her eyes dreamed
beyond Hod into the past and her memories. The song made
her slender and bright and beautiful again. It went back down
the years to the tent meeting where she had first seen Tom, and
where she had sat on one of the back rows with him night after
night, letting her fingers lie warmly inside his. For the moment
she felt again the new and exciting tingle his big presence by
her side had brought her. At first he had said, "Miss Hattie,
could I walk you home tonight?" And after that he had simply
found his way to her side, and soon everyone knew big Tom
Pierce was talking to Hattie Byron.

There was a night when the moon was up, and her waist was
small to his arm and her mouth was soft to his kiss. And shortly
after, Hattie Byron was Hattie Pierce. Forever and enduring
Hattie Pierce. So brief the years. So long the time.

When Tom married Hattie, she had been as bright and beautiful as a dream. Her eyes were brown, speckled with green, like
the trout pool down in Wandering Creek. And her hair lay back

37

from its center part as smooth and black as a raven's wing. A man's hand reached for those smooth wings as naturally as it curved around a hoe handle. And a man could lose himself in her trout-pool eyes.

In twenty-two years Hattie Pierce had borne eight children. Six of them had died. Only Hod and Irma had lived. Hattie's beauty had been glossed over by grief and the hard passage of the years, and when Hod looked at his mother these days, he saw nothing of the brightness Tom's young eyes had beheld. The eyes were still fine and true, but the trout pool had long since dulled and dimmed. The hair was still parted severely down the center, but now it was streaked and gray. She had lost most of her teeth early, and her shrunken mouth had given her face a pointed, peaked look. Her shoulders were rounded and her stomach paunched.

She was worn and she was weary, but she was not defeated. A woman married her man and she bore him as many children as the Lord sent. That was a woman's life. There was no fretting in Hattie against the will of the Lord, nor any question of it. She tended her house, bore her children, buried them if they died, fed and clothed them and compelled their obedience if they lived, and lay by her husband's side at night. A woman's life was bound to be hard, but Hattie didn't feel her lot was any harder than the next, and she went through her days with determination.

She had not been " saved " until she was a grown and married woman. Hod was a baby that summer when she had been converted at the revival. She shuddered when she remembered how sinful she had been, but she felt certain the Lord had forgiven her. She had been like the heathen who didn't know any better until that night when the light had shone through on her. Since then there had been a zealous dedication of herself and her family to the Lord. She had purged herself of much of her gaiety and expunged all the innocent pleasures of vanity and worldliness. Her tongue had become more astringent since then and her judgments were sharper and more impatient. Tom and Hod and Irma tried to let her sharpness roll off their backs unanswered. She was Ma, and Ma's ways were her own. But Ma herself was the fixed and true pole of their existence.

For a moment after Hod stilled the quivering strings Hattie stood still. The stillness was all through her. Then she briskly came back to the present. "You better start bringin' some water up from the spring so's we kin all git a bath tonight."

Hod put his guitar down and followed her to the kitchen. He sniffed. "Something smells mighty good! What's for supper?"

"Squirrel an' dumplin's. Tom found two down in the holler this mornin'. But you don't git e'er bite till supper, so don't go sniffin' around! Git a move on, now."

He picked up the two buckets which sat on the narrow wash shelf by the door and swung off down the hill.

> "'You git a line an' I'll git a pole,
> I'll meet you down at the crawdad hole,
> Honey, Sugarbaby, mine!'"

"Bring yer gittar!" "Honey, Sugarbaby, mine!"

On the way back he saw Irma waiting for him in the road. He grinned at her, and hurried, sloshing water over the buckets in his haste.

"I saw him," he assured her at once. "He was at the mill, and I talked to him a minute. First I asked if they were goin'. And he wanted to know if we were goin'. I told him we were, so he said — and these were his very words — he said, 'I'll be seein' you then.'"

A flush started at the base of Irma's throat and slowly spread up her neck onto her face. She bit her lip. "You never said nothin' to Ma 'bout seein' him, didja?"

"Of course I didn't!"

"Well, don't."

"Doesn't Ma like him?"

"Ma likes him all right, but she'd change her tune ifen she thought I did!"

"You and John talkin'?"

"Not yit, we ain't. When would we have the chancet? That's why I was hopin' he'd be at the meetin'. I'll at least git to see him."

"Maybe something'll work out so's you can sit by him, or talk to him a little. But I sure don't know any way you could let him

39

walk you home! "

"Oh, they ain't a chancet o' that! I don't even hope fer sich. But ifen I kin see him an' jist feel him alookin' at me, it'll make me happy."

They walked slowly around the corner of the house, and Hod lowered his voice as he spoke. "I'm not much better off. Ma hasn't hardly quit sulkin' yet over me talkin' to Lily Mae the other Sunday. But I'm aimin' to walk her home tomorrow night, come hell or high water! "

"Oh, it's some different with you, anyhow! You're a boy! All she does is pout an' quote Scripture to you. But it's untellin' what she'd do ifen she thought I was even thinkin' about a boy. An' me nearly seventeen too. She's done fergot her'n Pa was married when she wasn't more'n my age! "

Hod shifted one bucket of water to open the kitchen door. As he stood with the screen thrown wide, the far cry of a whippoorwill came low and tender across the holler. It sifted through the screen and seemed to mourn a lost love. In a sudden, luminous moment Hod could see Irma bent and old like Ma. Married. Skirts dragged by the hands of kids. "Maybe," he said slowly, "maybe that's just what she's not forgotten."

CHAPTER FOUR

IT's ALWAYS COOL and damp down here, thought Hod as they walked through the holler going to the meeting Sunday night. The mist curled and drifted from the narrow creek, and he shivered as he felt its moist fingers on his throat. The high walls of the hills boxed in the ancient creek bed and he could hear the echo of their footsteps against the old cliff as they moved along the stony path. In the pools of the creek the frogs garrumphed, and from tree to tree the whippoorwills called that there was " cheap-butter-in-the-white-oak."

Hod lifted his head. There must be a million stars tonight, he thought. Like someone with an open hand had sowed a field of silver seeds. The Milky Way was a narrow, sifted band that arched the holler and rested on the hills. It's like being down in a deep, dark well, he thought, open only at the top. He stumbled.

"Mind the lantern, Hod," Tom warned. "You'll bust it agin a rock if you don't take keer." Hod shifted the lantern and set his eyes on the path.

The holler widened as the hills rounded off, and came out in a low, level valley. The creek, released from the imprisoning walls, slowed, paused to catch its breath, swelled in freedom, and threaded a more genteel way through the valley.

Hugging the last hill, in the wide mouth of the holler, was the Big Springs schoolhouse. A tent had been pitched on the grounds, its sides rolled up to permit the circulation of air. A platform had been built at one end of the sawdust-covered enclosure, and a pulpit stand of rough lumber stood about midway of the platform. The preacher's Bible and a stack of paper-backed songbooks rested on the pulpit. Seats, made of the same rough lumber, fanned out from the platform in three staggered sections. Strung inside the tent, and suspended at intervals outside, were dim, tired lights which flickered with the asthmatic breathing of a sputtering old engine.

The family joined the gathering crowd and said their howdies to all. There were no strangers here. At any gathering on the ridge or in the valley the people were the same closed group, kith and kin of Pierces or their in-laws, except for the little knot of White Caps who stayed to themselves usually.

Tom and Hattie seated themselves on one of the back rows. It would be cooler there. Hod propped his guitar against the end of the seat and went out to find the group of boys milling around the hitching post. John was in the crowd and Hod drifted over to stand by him. In case John missed seeing Irma in the bunch of girls he would know she was here when he saw Hod.

Irma joined the girls who were sitting, giggling, on the schoolhouse steps. Now was the time when the girls flirted their bright dresses and careful curls most enchantingly, parading their charms before the sidewise glances of the boys. After the meeting the two groups would merge and pair off, each boy seeking out his special girl to walk home. He might have to walk her whole family home at the same time, but over the rough trails and paths, in the dimness of lantern light, he would have a chance to slip a bold arm about her waist, or even to steal a kiss if they could drop far enough behind.

41

Out of the corner of his eye Hod saw Lily Mae in the circle of girls. He kept his eyes lowered, although he knew she was aware of his presence. His hands started sweating and he rolled a cigarette to occupy them. He dreaded the moment he would have to step up by her side and somehow find the voice to ask to walk her home, and yet, restlessly, he longed for it too. It would be an enduring shame if she turned him down. But she'd as good as promised! Well . . . he'd brought his gittar! Now let's see what she made of it.

He saw his mother looking around, seeking him and Irma. Other boys and girls might be allowed to sit on the ground outside the tent in the semidarkness, but not Hattie's. Hattie's children would sit by her side in decent respect to the Lord. He crushed his cigarette under his heel and walked over to take his place on the bench. Hattie nodded at him approvingly and leaned over to whisper, "Where's Irma?"

He caught a glimpse of Irma moving toward the tent and he motioned to her. "She's comin'," he answered. No, there wasn't a chance for Irma to have John by her side tonight.

Hod looked around the tent. It was comfortably full. The meeting was going to get off to a good start. Most of the ridge folks sat to the middle and back, the White Caps crowding the front. After all, it was their meeting.

Hod remembered the story Miss Bertha had told him about the White Caps — how, back in 1770 an old Mennonite preacher, one Jacob Engle, had grown desperate under the religious persecution of his people in his native Switzerland, and how he gathered together thirty Mennonite families and by might and main had secured ships to transport them to the new world. Miss Bertha had said one of the ships had not weathered the storms, and had gone down in an angry sea, taking all aboard with it.

The remainder of the small group settled in Lancaster County, Pennsylvania, and, because of their peculiar habit of baptizing in the river Susquehanna, had become known as the River Brethren. In time, Miss Bertha said, they had quarreled among themselves, mostly over small differences in their doctrinal beliefs — such a little thing, for instance, as whether in the washing of the saints' feet the one who washed should dry or whether another should stand by with the napkin and have the privilege.

42

They had split up into little bands, and some of them had migrated southward, into Ohio and Indiana and Kentucky.

Miss Bertha said their real name was Brethren in Christ, or "River Brethren," and their history went clean back to the Pietists of the Reformation days. But few, if any, of these people knew that. Here in the Kentucky hills they were called White Caps, because of the sheer little starched white caps the women wore at all times. The women also wore nunlike dresses, all made from the same pattern, ankle length, with long sleeves, high round neck, and a prayer bib. They wore neither jewelry nor make-up, and they were usually of quiet and modest manner.

Equally simple was the dress of the men. Their suits were dark, plain, and simply cut. In the old days they were homemade, but now the men were allowed to buy them in stores. Ties were prohibited, as were rings and other forms of worldly vanity.

The doctrine of the founding fathers had included several unique beliefs, such as that of trine immersion, and the efficacy of the prayer veil. On Piney Ridge folks watched the queer baptism, face forward three times, with curiosity; and occasionally a Pierce connection married a White Cap. He became less a Pierce when he did that, withdrawing from the clan solidarity and becoming one of a closer knitted band.

Hod's attention came back to the meeting. Little Wells was standing in front of the platform now, songbook open in his hand. Hod liked for Wells to lead the singing. He kept time with a firm, sure lead and never let the tunes lag. Books had been distributed, and while Wells held a last whispered conference with the preacher, an air of expectancy settled over the crowd. The meetin' was about to begin!

Little Wells walked back to his place and raised his hand. "Folks, we're goin' to start by singin' number sixteen . . . 'Joy Unspeakable.' An' I want ever'body to join in. Don't be bashful. You all know this song, so jist open yer mouths an' let 'er roll!" He spied Hod on the back row. "Hod! Hod Pierce! Bring that gittar o' your'n up here an' he'p us out. Hit ain't goin' to do you no good back there on the last row!"

Heads turned. Folks craned and laughed and whispered neighborly as Hod, flushed, made his way up front. Hattie modestly kept her eyes straight ahead. It would be unmannerly

43

to appear prideful, but even her rigid back bespoke her complacent satisfaction as Hod was singled out.

"All right now," said Wells as Hod tuned his instrument. "We'll take it in 'G,' Hod, so's the womenfolks won't have to reach fer that high note up there. Let's all stand up, an' don't nobody hold back! This song's a good 'un, so come on an' sing!"

It was a good song to start the meetin'. Five long stanzas and a chorus that was full of glory! Rapid, clean, four-four time, with powerful, exciting words. And the people lifted up their voices and the joy unspeakable coursed through their veins!

"Jist stay on yer feet, now," Wells commanded when the song was over, "an' let's sing number fifty-four . . . 'God Put a Rainbow in the Cloud'! The rainbow's a promise to all of us, so let's sing it like we was glad fer it."

This was still rapid, four-four time. The kind that made folks lift their faces to the hope and the promise. The kind that made them shout and rock on their toes! Yes, Lord! God put a rainbow in the cloud!

Wells kept the crowd on their feet for still another song — 'That Will Be Glory' — before he let them be seated, panting and hot. But the tempo had been set; the ice had been broken; and emotionally the people had been lifted joyously to a rainbow in the cloud and the glory road! Little Wells was an expert at opening a meetin'.

Ferdy Jones came forward now for his turn at leading. And Hod knew the tempo would change. Before the preacher took over, the mood must be shifted to sin and guilt. The probing finger of fear must dig into scared hearts, scavenge certain secret sins, and invoke judgment. Out of the clouds Ferdy's bellowing baritone would pluck them and remind them that the rainbow and the glory road were theirs only if their lives were pure and stainless. His right arm, pumping like a piston rod, would drive the pitiless rhythm before them. He would charge them with their sins.

"Amen," shouted Old Man Clark from the front row at the end of the first stanza. Amen . . . Amen . . . Amen, a chorus of voices fervently echoed. Have mercy, Lord, on me a sinner! Lord, hide me in the darkness! Let not the light shine! Lord, remember me, a sinner!

Ferdy led them into another warning hymn: "Hide Me, O My Saviour, Hide!" And the masochistic ecstasy of guilt and grief mounted. The flailing arm whipped accusingly, rising and falling relentlessly like the flagellant lash of a monk's rope on bare flesh. I went to the rock, but there's no hiding place there! Woe unto me! Ferdy's really got 'em goin', thought Hod. Now it's the preacher's time.

The preacher rose and lifted his chin to the sky. He spread his arms tenderly. "O God," he prayed, and his deep, full voice spread like a sheltering cloak over the people: "O God, we are as worms in the dust. Stained, spotted, and sinful. Our hearts are hard. We come to the throne of grace knowing we are not deserving of thy redeeming love. We have lived in sin and darkness in this weary world so long we have lost our way. We have hardened our hearts against you and followed the ways of the sinful world. We are doomed men and women. Yes, doomed, Lord, unless you remove the scales from our eyes and let us see the light again. Turn our feet from the paths of sin and lead us in the narrow way. Soften our hearts to see the error of our ways, Lord, and lift us up out of the mud and mire of the world. Lord, we are but poor pilgrims wandering in a world of woe! Take our hands and lead us home."

Amen . . . Amen . . . Amen. Take our hands and lead us home.

A general stirring and settling of the people followed. Songbooks were laid aside, fans began to flutter, small children were bedded down against the long sermon, heads in their mothers' laps; the flock made ready for the shepherd.

The preacher spread his hands on either side of the Bible and leaned forward. "Brethren," he began, "brethren, I have taken my text tonight from the book of Revelation. That's the book that tells us what awful things will be in the last days. And, brethren, I say unto you the last days are upon us, and we can't shut our eyes from those things. The bridegroom cometh, and no man knoweth the hour. Repent and be prepared!"

For an hour the lush, sonorous voice rose and fell majestically. He spoke of scorpions and seals and death and hell, and he charged the people with black sin and the lusts of the flesh. His face flamed and his voice roared as he pictured the fiery furnaces and the everlasting torment waiting down below. Fear, awe, and dread trembled visibly on the faces of the people, and the tension mounted until it seemed to Hod as if the very roof of the tent would rise to give them breath. An hour of the exhorting, threatening voice left him feeling limp and wilted.

At last the voice softened, rich and full, sweetly pleading. This was the signal for Little Wells to start a pleading hymn: " Softly and tenderly Jesus is calling, Calling for you and for me. . . . Calling, O sinner, come home! " Folks rose and stirred restlessly and began to shift and filter through the crowd, stopping to talk earnestly with man or woman, boy or girl, who had not yet been to the bench. The preacher's voice never ceased its entreating pleas, and Little Wells followed expertly with one petitioning song after another.

One by one persons were answering the call. They came forward to fall on their knees at the long bench in front of the platform. Some silently buried their faces in their hands; others moaned and sobbed and sang. The preacher's voice rose above the tumult as he went from one to the other, placing his hand upon them, encouraging them, and urging them to lay their hearts bare. The noise of the moaning voices and the hot odor of sweaty bodies fused into one purgatorial overtone and Hod felt himself sway unsteadily. His eyes focused again on the mourners' bench.

There was Becky, Gault's barren wife, at one end of the bench. Her thin, black-draped figure looked fragile and lonely as it kneeled apart from the others, and hunched over her hands. She surely doesn't need to get religion again, he thought. What drives her to the bench time after time? Does she think God has hidden his face from her? Does she think if she abases herself often enough, the Lord will give her life, like Sarah, in her old age?

Matt Jasper was there too, and beside him was Lutie, his wife. Hod closed his eyes, but couldn't keep out the sight of Lutie Jasper, forever hopelessly weary, forever bearing one thin, sickly baby after another; laying them in their graves within a few weeks, or a few months, or a few years. Or if they lived, tending their hopeless minds and bodies drearily. What were they praying for? Did they think the Lord would stop Matt's fits maybe? Or let the new baby live? Or not send any more? Even as Hod watched Matt, the shriveled, bony shoulders began to jerk convulsively. The big head on the thin neck swiveled grotesquely and stiffened, frozen at an angle. A high scream rent the air.

"He's got it," shouted the preacher, "he's seen the light! He's got the old-time religion in his heart! Praise the Lord! A soul is saved tonight!" And he raised his hands high over his head.

He's got a fit! thought Hod, and started toward him. Little Wells was quick before him. Together they carried him outside and laid him on the grass.

"He'll be all right, kid," said Little Wells. "These fits don't last long. They look a heap worse'n they are. Hit's a good thing it come right at the end of the goin's on, though. Preacher'll close up now."

"You reckon the preacher actually thought Matt had religion?"

"Why, shore. He wouldn't have no way o' knowin' 'bout pore old Matt's fits. An' what he don't know won't hurt him none. Hit'll mebbe encourage him some to have one take it so hard the very first night."

By the time Matt had revived, the meeting was breaking up, and Hod left him for Little Wells to handle. He had to get his guitar and hurry to find Lily Mae. Already some other fellow might be ahead of him.

In the tent Lem had crawled up on one of the benches and was shouting to make himself heard. "All them that lives up Piney way is welcome to a ride home in my wagon. I've got a bed o' straw in it, an' as many as kin pile in is more'n welcome to load on."

Hod saw Lily Mae talking to some girls at one end of the platform. He grabbed his guitar and started toward her. She saw him coming and laughed loudly and self-consciously. In the hurry and intensity of his purpose Hod forgot his shyness and blurted out, "Would you care to ride home in Lem's wagon?"

She tossed her curls back from her face. "Why, shore," she answered. "That'd be swell, ifen we kin find e'er place."

"I'll find us a place," promised Hod, and taking her arm

47

he steered her toward the wagon. It was already filling. Hattie and Tom and Irma were settling themselves; Lizzie and her children were finding places. Gault and Becky were waiting, and one or two others.

Hod placed his hands under Lily Mae's arms and swung her up into the wagon, letting them linger a moment and sliding them slowly and sentiently down her sides as he released her. How warm and soft girls are, he thought. "I'll be back in a minute," he whispered. "Don't let 'em go off without me." And he disappeared in the crowd.

He searched around the edges, and then he spied John standing disconsolately in a group of boys. He hailed him. "Hey! Hey, John! You wanna ride up the ridge in the wagon with us?"

John came to life. "I shore do!"

"C'mon then, Lem's about ready to pull out!"

When they came back to the wagon both boys vaulted up onto the end of the wagon bed and settled into the straw. Hod called to Irma, "C'mon back here and sit with us."

Irma scrambled over legs and bodies and Hod reached out to steady her. "Look who's here," he whispered.

John took her arm and pulled her down beside him. "I been awaitin' fer a chancet like this," he said. "I jist been hopin' an' prayin'."

Irma put her hand in his. "I been awaitin' too, John."

Hod settled himself by Lily Mae, and they pulled the straw up close around them and let their legs dangle out the back. By the time they were settled, Lem called from up front, "All set?" and clucked to the team. "All set," they called back and in a moment they were swallowed in the leafy tunnel of the road.

Lizzie spoke across the children to Hattie. "Well, whadja think o' the preacher?"

Hattie temporized. "Hit's too early to say yit. He seems like a powerful exhorter, though, if he kin jist hold out. We'll all have to uphold him an' he'p him ever' way we kin."

The talk flowed gently on, and Hod and Lily Mae were silent, feeling its edges curl about them. For the moment Hod was content, his fingers laced with Lily Mae's. It was good, and this was enough. Lily May swayed against him. "Where's yer gittar?"

"Right here."

"How 'bout a song?"

Hod hesitated. After the meetin' Hattie might not like a fancy tune. But he pulled the guitar around in front of him and thrummed the strings experimentally. Lizzie laughed and called to him: "That's a good idee, Hod. You play 'em an' we'll sing 'em."

"What'll it be?"

"'Buffalo Gal,'" called Lem from the spring seat. Hod's fingers trilled a run up the strings. "'Buffalo Gal' it is," he sang out.

> "'Buffalo gal, won't you come out tonight,
> Come out tonight,
> Come out tonight?
> Buffalo gal, won't you come out tonight,
> And play by the light of the moon?'"

"'Down in the Valley,' Hod," said Becky. Hod shifted the key, and the voices followed him. "Barbry Allen." "Lord Lovel." From one old song to another they went, melody lifted high in the night.

"'Crawdad Hole,'" whispered Lily Mae.

> "'You git a line an' I'll git a pole,
> I'll meet you down at the crawdad hole,
> Honey, Sugarbaby, mine!'"

"Are you my girl, Lily Mae?" Hod laid his forehead against her cheek.

"I'm yore girl tonight," she said.

Hod threw back his head and looked at a million stars. He laid his guitar aside and slipped his arm loosely around Lily Mae's curving waist. It was as soft and warm as a baby lamb's. He tightened his arm abruptly and pulled her close, turning her slightly against him. Lily Mae let her head rest against his shoulder and in the soft night breeze her hair blew across his face. It filled him with a gentle tenderness. His mouth, searching, found hers and clung for a long, still moment. Her lips were moist and slightly parted, and when he lifted his head he was breathing hard. This had been his first kiss. Lily Mae caught her breath and laughed, then, reaching back of his head, she pulled his

49

mouth down upon hers again. "Yer sweet," she whispered, "Hod Pierce, yer plumb sweet."

"Bring yer gittar!" So this is what she meant!

He felt warm and good. It was a fine thing to be ridin' in the back of an old jounce wagon with your girl. The wagon bumped and jogged along the rough road and the swaying motion threw them often together. The pliant, breathing softness next to him drooped and leaned against him. This was Tomorrow, his fair day!

Suddenly and impulsively, out of his warm feeling, he spoke. "Listen, Lily Mae," he said, "someday I'm goin' to leave Piney Ridge. I'm goin' to work and make enough money someway or another to get away. And I'm goin' to have a better life and see the world and get more learnin'. I don't aim to be a Piney Ridge farmer all my life!"

"What's wrong with bein' a Piney Ridge farmer? Ain't nothin' wrong with it as fur as I kin see. You eat an' sleep an' work anywheres, I reckon."

"There's nothin' really wrong with Piney," he said slowly, hunting for the right words. "There's nothin' wrong except it can't see any further than its nose, and it doesn't ever want to. If you get through the eighth grade you've got enough learnin'. If you raise enough corn to make do, there's no need to frash yourself raisin' more. Your grandpap raised tobacco and he cut it and stripped it a certain way, and what was good enough for Grandpap is good enough for me. If there's a drought and the tobacco's ruined, there's nothin' to do but tighten your belt and do without, because tobacco's the only way to get cash. If times get hard, you sit around and talk about it and hope something'll turn up so's you can make out. Lily Mae, there's a whole world out there where people don't wait for something to turn up. They make things happen. They don't stop goin' to school at the eighth grade. They go on and get a college degree."

"I don't see as a college degree would he'p you grow tobaccer here on Piney any better."

"Yes, it would. That's just the point. Maybe it wouldn't grow tobacco any better, but maybe tobacco oughtn't to be grown on

50

Piney. This land is poor and washed out. Maybe tobacco's one of the reasons. There's schools where they teach you about that. They teach you nearly everything in those schools."

Lily Mae laughed. "Tobaccer's been growed on Piney as fur back as I kin remember, Hod, an' I reckon hit allus will be. You've got too high an' mighty notions, I'm athinkin'."

He shook his head. "No. I've not. I'm goin' to amount to something someday."

"Well, jist be shore an' let me know when you do," she said pertly.

They were quiet for a time, rocking comfortably against each other. "Wade an' Sandy's goin' to the lumber camp tomorrow," he went on after a while. "They're goin' to hew ties until tobacco's ready to cut. They say the pay's real good. I'm thinkin' of goin' with 'em."

"Ifen you go to the lumber camp you cain't go to the meetin' no more," she protested immediately, straightening up.

"I know, and I hate to miss it too. But it's a chance to make some money, maybe forty or fifty dollars, and I could easy go to Louisville on that and see about a job."

"Well, of all things," she sniffed, "all the time you been aplannin' to go off an' jist now ast me to be yer girl! What do you expect me to do while you're gone? Set around an' hold my hands an' be yer girl till you git back? That's not my way o' doin', Hod Pierce! There's many another fish in the sea, an' don't think I won't ketch a few!" She jerked out of his arm and bounced angrily away from him.

"Now, Lily Mae, I wasn't thinkin' that at all," he protested. "I was just tryin' to tell you . . ." For goodness' sake, how had this ever got started? In a sudden burst of confidence, born of his feeling of closeness to her, he had only meant to try to tell her something of what he wanted out of life. How could she take it wrong and how did it ever get so mixed up!

"You don't understand . . ." He was miserably hunting for the words to explain.

But abruptly Lily Mae leaned across him and called to Becky, just as Lem pulled the team up in front of Gault and Becky's house. "Becky, kin I take the night with you?" She was scrambling down even as she asked. "I kin walk on home in the morn-

51

in'. I wouldn't want to disfurnish nobody to see me home to-night." Her words were dipped in acid.

Becky said she would be glad to have her, and Lily Mae walked toward the gate without another word. Hod could think of nothing to say or to do. The turn of events had been too rapid for him. What in the world had Lily Mae got her back up about! He sat motionless as Lem pulled back in the road and the wagon jounced into the ruts again. Let her go, he thought bitterly. Just let her go. There's many another fish in the sea. But his arm remembered the warm, firm flesh around which it had been pressed, and he felt empty and tired.

The next stop was home, and Hattie and Tom and Irma piled out. They called their thanks for the ride to Lem and Lizzie, and groped their way into the dark heat of the house. Hattie briskly lighted a lamp, and Hod could see that her lips were set in a thin, firm line. She's mad too, he thought. Probably saw me kissin' Lily Mae, and I'll either catch the devil or she'll sulk two or three days.

He set his guitar in the fireplace corner and went outside to smoke. Hattie wouldn't have it in the house. He drew deeply on his cigarette and settled his shoulder against the post. The moon rode high and there was a halo around it. He counted three stars within the circle. Three days of rain comin', he thought. And he hadn't told Hattie about the lumber camp yet. How was he goin' to bring it up with her lookin' like she could bite a nail in two! He flipped the cigarette into the grass, his eyes following its glowing arch. Maybe in the mornin' would do. Better be turnin' in now. The loft room would be like an oven tonight, and he dreaded going up there. He'd like to bring a pallet down and sleep right here on the porch. But he knew Hattie wouldn't hear of it. "Poor white trash," she'd say. The screen squeaked softly, and as he turned Hattie stood beside him.

"Out here moonin' agin, I reckon," she said.

"Just thinkin'," he said, leaning back lazily against the post.

"Yes! An' I know what yer athinkin'!" Her voice was vehement and tense. "I heared part o' what you was tellin' that Lily Mae . . . about the lumber camp an' makin' so much big money an' mebbe goin' off to Louisville!"

He started to speak, but she went on fiercely. " Yer not agoin'
to e'er lumber camp, not now nor never! You hear that! You
don't know e'er thing about hewin' ties, an' the first thing you'd
do would be to hew yer foot right off! Yer so clumsy! An',
besides, I'll not have you off over there away from home, up to
no tellin' what mischief. Lem an' Lizzie kin let their boys go if
they're a mind to, but I aim to see you stay as decent an' God-
fearin' as I've raised you. You jist fergit it right now! They's
plenty o' work right here where you belong, an' yer beholden
to stay an' he'p now that you kin do a man's work! "

He could see that her hands were tight knots, held stiffly in
front of her. " But, Ma," he argued, " I'd make forty or fifty
dollars and I'd give the most of it to you to help out."

She turned on him and scratched at him with her voice. " Do
you reckon forty or fifty dollars'd pay me ifen you happened to
a accident, like you shorely would? You think it would pay me
fer the nights I couldn't sleep aknowin' you was over there
roisterin' around amongst a bunch o' godless men? "

He sighed and closed his eyes wearily. This was Tomorrow!
Where had it gone wrong? How had he bungled it so badly?
First Lily Mae and now Ma. He felt hot and smothered, and as
if something were closing in on him. What is it they want me
to do, he thought. Nothing. Just plain nothing. Do nothing,
think nothing, be nothing but Piney Ridge. Plow and plant and
sucker and tend and strip and cut and dry and sell tobacco! Go
to mill on Saturday! Go to preachin' on Sunday! Marry and build
a two-room shack on the far side of the pasture! Have a bunch
of kids! Get up at daybreak and go to bed at dark! Sweat and
struggle and starve! No! That's not for me! That's not for me!
Life was meant to be sweeter. And I'll find a way! I'll find a way!

But tonight he was so tired. " All right, Ma," he said at last.
" Forget the whole thing."

She turned back to the house and opened the screen. Looking
back at him, she could see him silhouetted against the night
sky, and she paused with the door half open. " Hod," she said,
" Hod . . ."

" Yessum? "

But whatever tenderness she may have felt could not overcome the long years of stern repression. Whatever gentle thing she meant to say to this yearning son of hers remained unspoken. "You better git on to bed," and the screen slammed lightly behind her.

CHAPTER FIVE

TOM ROUSED HOD before daylight the next morning. "Git up, Hod," he called. "Git up. We've aplenty to do today. Git movin', boy!" He tugged at Hod's hair and shook him until he rolled sleepily to his feet. "C'mon now. Let's eat an' then you do the milkin' an' feedin' whilst I go down to Grampa's. Agin you've done with the chores you better light into that corn patch an' git it hoed out. I aim to start work in the tobaccer today. But we ain't got no time to be asleepin'."

Hod struggled with his clothes and followed his father into the kitchen. Irma was setting the table and she caught his eye as he went by to wash. A motion of her head toward Hattie at the stove warned him. He came awake all at once. So Ma was still sore!

The air was sultry with Hattie's displeasure, and they sat down to breakfast in a smoldering silence. Hattie's mouth was a tight line and her movements were quick and jerky. Irma and Hod kept their eyes on their plates and ate without comment. Tom alone seemed unaware of the brooding cloud.

"Ifen you git done in the corn this mornin', Hod," he said, "you better git on down to Grampa's an' start his'n this afternoon. You kin stay an' do up his night work then, an' eat yer supper down there."

"*Ifen* he gits done!" Hattie's voice shrilled across the table. "Ifen he kin hoe e'er row fer moonin' over that there Lily Mae Gibbs, hit'll surprise me!" Hod ducked his head and his face went scarlet.

Tom said soothingly, "Now, Ma."

"Don't you 'now, Ma' me, Tom Pierce! I reckon I seen what I seen! Him an' that shameless Lily Mae ahuggin' an' akissin' right under my eyes . . . an' Irma no better! Ifen she didn't do the same, 'twasn't because her own brother didn't set her no example! An' you, missy! You needn't to think I won't have my

54

eyes open the next time! You both think you was purty smart aputtin' somethin' over last night! Hit'll not happen agin, I'll promise you that! Settin' there all cuddled up in the straw, alookin' at the moon an' asingin' fancy tunes, when the fear o' the Lord orta been in yer hearts! I don't aim to have sich goin's on, an' you kin both remember that!"

"A little huggin' an' kissin' never hurt nobody, Ma," Tom said gently. "An' I should think you'd a ruther had 'em adoin' it right before yer eyes than asneakin' behind you."

Hattie's hands were shaking. "They ain't no use you takin' up fer 'em, Tom! You'd ortent to go encouragin' 'em in sinful ways! I'm tryin' to raise 'em up decentlike."

"I know," Tom said quietly, "I know."

Hattie jerked her chair back from the table and picked up her plate. She stalked stiffly to the stove and splashed it noisily into the dishpan. Tom poured his coffee into his saucer and blew on it. He sipped it cautiously and looked across at Hod and Irma. Shaking his head at them, he sighed.

"Hello!" called a voice from out front. "Hello! You all up yit?"

"Now who's that abellerin' at this time o' day?" Hattie snorted.

"Sounds like Lem," said Tom.

Hod slid out from behind the table. "Must be Lem's atakin' Wade an' Sandy over to the lumber camp. They said they aimed to go early this mornin'."

"So?" Tom followed Hod out on the porch, with Hattie and Irma close behind him. "Git down," he called. "C'mon in an' eat a bite."

"We've done et," Lem answered. "The boys is goin' over to the lumber camp an' they said Hod here might want to go too. Thought there'd be no harm stoppin' to see."

"Hod ain't goin'," Hattie said flatly. "He don't know the first thing about workin' in lumber. An', besides, I'll not have him off over there up to no tellin' what mischief. Are you an' Lizzie plumb outen yer minds to let them two o' your'n go aroisterin' around amongst that bunch o' godless men over there?"

Hod looked wistfully at Wade and Sandy, who could nearly always go where they pleased. Wade closed one eye mischievously and grinned. Nervously Hod grinned back.

Lem was talking. "Hit's all a matter of opinion, I reckon, Hattie." He turned to Tom. "I jist come by Gault's, an' Becky was tellin' me Grampa fell last night outen the hayloft an' sprung his ankle. She said Gault was doin' up the work this mornin', but she reckoned we'd all have to he'p out till he's on his feet agin. I don't see as how I kin make out to go today, though. Takin' the boys over to the lumber camp an' all. Reckon you an' Hod kin go?"

"Shore," Tom answered. "Well, I declare! I've told Pa more'n oncet he ortent to git up in that hayloft after dark. He's gittin' too old to go crawlin' around sich places." He rubbed his nose with his thumb. "I'll go on down this mornin', an' Hod kin go tonight. Hit works out jist the way I'd thought on anyhow. I been he'pin' him with his corn, an' I'd aimed fer Hod to finish it up."

"You better come go with us to the lumber camp, Hod," Wade prodded. "You git paid fer workin' over there."

"You shet up," said Irma fiercely.

"I reckon I better git ready an' go 'long, Tom," Hattie put in, "Gramma'll be needin' some he'p herself." And she turned back into the house.

Lem gathered up the reins and pulled the horses around. "Well, we better be gittin' on. I'll stop at Pa's this evenin' on my way back."

As the wagon wheeled into the road, Hod swallowed the hurting knot in his throat. There went his chances to make fifty dollars, or maybe more.

Irma gets the worst of these spells of Ma's, he thought, on his way to the barn. She has to stay in the house with her and hear it over and over again. Pa was always trying to stand between them and Ma. Like this mornin'. He was easygoing and hard to ruffle, but some days it looked like that just riled Ma more than ever. The best thing to do was to keep quiet and let the storm blow itself out.

He thought on the ways of Hattie. Nobody on the ridge kept a cleaner house, and nobody had the pride in washing and ironing and keeping her family clean that Hattie did. And her garden patch was always early and full. She took a pride in that too. Times she was in a good mood she was almost gaylike and

56

happy. And he remembered how soft and easy were her hands the time he had the fever. She hardly left his side, day or night, for weeks, and she tended him and made him broths and custards and egg dishes to tempt him. She was never too tired to do for those that needed it, either. Going out in all sorts of weather to bring a new baby, or to lay out someone who had died.

And then there was this other Hattie. This sharp and acid Hattie who clawed at them quickly and unexpectedly. This Hattie who pored over her Bible and strove to rid them of blemishes; who bound them so closely with tight wires of fear. This Hattie whose mouth was thin and whose hands were knotted and whose voice shrilled.

He sorted out all the ways of Hattie and tried to put them together smoothly. This one here. That one there. He set up the good ways and molded and rounded them, and he tucked the sharp and acid ways out of sight. Best to let them go. Let them prick and spear quickly, but let them hide darkly. Best not to mind. He was whistling when he reached the barn.

He worked in the corn all morning, his hoe making its steady way down the rows. His back soaked up the sun and he bent under it, taking the heat into himself. There was a content in bending his back to the sun, and in turning the earth beneath his hoe. It was porous and moist from the rain several days before. His feet were planted strongly, feeling the hot dirt and the looseness of the soil. He moved down the rows, feeling the earth give beneath his hoe; feeling it pull in his arms and back.

There was a way in which the warmth of the earth was like the warmth of the sun, all joined together and giving. The sun hot upon his back and the earth warm beneath his feet. The sun, day-giving, life-giving. The earth, absorbing and storing the warmth, and giving it back. This earth, strong and deep and loamy. This earth which sheltered the corn in seed, rooted it, bound and tied it, but gave it up to the sun. This corn, now, growing green and tender and ankle-high. He slid his hoe around a young green blade, and smiled at its brave upward thrust.

Irma came to the field at midmorning with a pail of cool water. He set his hoe against a tree and drank deeply. When he handed the pail back to her, Irma said, " I'm aimin' to take the night at Gramma's this night, Hod."

He made no answer. She went on. "I'm aimin' to see John Walton ever' chancet I git whilst this meetin's goin' on. I'm goin' up to the mailboxes now an' John'll be awaitin', an' I'll tell him he kin come by Gramma's an' walk with me to the meetin'. Ifen I kin work it out, I'm aimin' to stay at Gramma's ever' night. Long as Grampa's ankle is sore I'll have a good cause, an' this is my best chancet. But I ain't aimin' fer Ma to come between me an' John like she's done with ever' other boy I've looked at. I like him too good fer that."

Hod stripped a leaf from the tree and pulled it back and forth through his fingers. Irma waited quietly. Finally he threw the leaf down and picked up his hoe. "I'll help every way I can, Irma. You belong to know what's in your mind. I don't know why Ma's the way she is, but we aren't either one of us kids any longer to be kept under latch and cover."

"I don't look fer Gramma or Grampa to take no notice. But if they do, you reckon they'd feel called on to name it to Ma?"

"I don't reckon they would. Gramma's always been a sight easier on us than Ma. And I've never known Grampa not to be fair in his judgments. He'd likely give you a talkin' to himself. If I was you and they took notice, I'd just plumb out and tell 'em. My opinion is they'd likely think you were a big enough girl to know your own mind."

Irma picked up the empty pail. She ran her hand lightly across her hair which the wind had blown into loose strands. It curled redly in the sun. Hod watched her fasten it beneath a little silver clip. Now it was Irma and John Walton! She turned away, swinging the pail idly. "I know my mind, Hod," she said. And the sea of green corn parted and undulated in the wake of her passing.

Hod finished the corn by the middle of the afternoon and started down to the holler to work in Grampa's patch. He moved carefully through the thick grass, down the path to the road and down the road past the old church to the edge of the ridge where it dipped down into the holler. Here he forsook the road and took a thin trail which led off down the steep hill. Past the white birch, and around the big rock. Yonder was the last turn. Here was the creek, and he stooped for a drink before splashing

58

through its noisy chatter. Now he was in the meadow, with the grass to his hips, and it swayed and parted to let him through.

The house was on the far side of the meadow, but he angled off to the left and went on to the corn patch. Here the shade was already deep from the steep sides of the ridge, and the little creek rushed clear and bright over the white stones. The air was cool and damp, and Hod threw off his hat and pulled his shirt-tail out. He let the air wrap itself around him and lay chill fingers on his skin until he shivered in a transport of ecstasy. He felt the heat withdrawn from him and a fresh energy poured into him so that he worked rapidly and tirelessly until first dark. Then he left the field and set about doing up the nightwork.

When he had finished the feeding, he came up to the door and stepped onto the sagging old porch. Gramma swung around from the stove. " That you, Hod? "

" It's me."

" You fair frighted me! I've done got the milk pails ready, an' you better git on out to the barn an' git the milkin' done. I'm bound to git a snack o' supper here, but I'm behindst, what with tearin' 'round to Gault's, an' fetchin' fer Dow. Fortunate hit is it ain't winter time fer this to happen. There'd be a sight o' chores fer a body to do. The way it is, ifen you kin all take keer o' the milkin', an' feed the animals, an' bring me in a little mite o' kindlin' wood fer the breakfast fires, I kin make out."

Gramma's eyes were worried for all her tongue was wagging. She's talkin' to keep from lettin' on, Hod thought. Her little wiry body was as taut as a fiddlestring, and her hand kept straying to the knot of gray hair on top of her head. Her mouth was pinched in and a leader in her neck stood out hard and gaunt. She's worryin' a sight, Hod reflected. She's tuckerin' herself plumb out.

He picked up the milk pails, swung one from each hand, and made his way back to the barn. The pails clattered against the gate as he let himself through, and a cow threw back her head uneasily. Inside the barn he lifted the milking stool from its peg and settled himself beside the brindle cow in the near stall. He ran his hand down her side and talked gently to her. " So-O-o, Pet. Easy, Pet."

He drummed the first stream of milk into the waiting bucket. It made a thin, tinny sound, like a downpour of rain, but it

59

swished around the edges. Steadily he pulled the milk down into the bucket, and as it filled the sound was changed from emptiness into fullness, and there was no longer the tinny drumming against the bucket. Now it was rich and thick and heavy, and soon there was hardly any sound at all except a faint hissing as the hard stream of milk, forced by his hand, joined the solid heaviness of the milk waiting in the bucket. There was a rhythm in the squeeze and pull and release which pleased Hod. Pet stood easily and gave down her milk under his gentle hands.

From Pet he moved on to Star, and when he had finished milking both cows, he took the milk back to the house and gave it over to Gramma. Then he went back to the barn to feed the horse and to pull down some more hay for the cows.

The feeding done, he went to the house to light the lantern. It was too dark to cut the kindling wood without light. Gramma had it ready for him, and he touched the lighted match to the circle of wick and watched the flame run around the circle. Light chasing itself until it's joined together again. He lowered the glass and went out into the dark, not needing to feel for the step now that he had a light.

The wood block was solid and the ax was wedged into it deep, just like Grampa had driven it there this morning. The place for an ax is driven deep in the wood block. Hod jerked it loose and felt its heft in his hand. He chose a piece of pine and swung the ax down. He let the feel of the pine splitting run clean up his arm. It was a good feel, a finished and completed feel. Something done. Something final. He filled the basket and swung it up onto his shoulder.

"There, Gramma. That ought to start you a right good fire in the mornin'."

Hod filled the tin basin on the wash shelf and plunged his face in the water. He sputtered and splashed and groped for a towel.

"Hit's right in front o' you! Right there in front o' you! Ifen it'd been a snake, it'd a done bit you! I declare, men are the unseein'est things that ever was! Now you come on an' set down here an' eat you a bite. I know yer bound to be plumb wore out. They ain't much to eat, but they's aplenty of what they is."

Hod slipped back of the table onto the worn old bench and

filled his plate. Gramma might not call it much to eat, but when Gramma set a table there was always plenty. Tonight she had beans boiled with fat meat, tender green onions from her garden patch, a slice of red ham, and steaming hot corn bread.

Irma came in from the next room while he was eating. He looked up. "I see you made it all right."

She nodded and set about straining the milk into the big crocks already scalded and waiting for it. "John'll be by about good dark, in a few minutes, now. I'm aimin' jist to walk right out an' go on down the road with him. You goin' tonight?"

"I don't know. Lily Mae got riled up about something last night, and I don't know's she's expectin' me. If I'm goin', I'll catch up with you time you get to the meetin'. You can wait up a minute on the edge of the clearin'."

There was a shrill whistle from outside. "That's him awhistlin', now," Irma said. She untied the apron and hung it on a nail near the stove. She ran to the wash shelf and looked at herself briefly in the mirror and ran the comb through her hair. "Reckon I'll do," she said. "We'll wait a spell fer you." She laughed quickly. "But if you come, Hod, you kin take yer time!"

His mouth was full of bread and milk, but he grinned at her and motioned for her to be on her way. If Ma ever found out about this, there sure would be a stir! But maybe Ma wouldn't find it out.

Now Gramma was back in the kitchen hovering over him. "Hod, I saved you a piece of this here chess pie. I knowed you love it so good, so I says to myself, 'I'll jist save Hod a piece.' Hit come out real good, if I do say so myself. I allus say that chess pie is the best pie a body kin have. Ifen you got butter an' lots o' eggs an' cream, it's about the best eatin' they is."

Hod washed the pie down with the last of his milk. Let her talk. She's afraid to cease talkin'. If she stops her talkin', she'll have to think about Grampa. How is it when two people are one flesh? How does it come to be that a man and a woman can be so joined together that if anything happens to one the hurt spreads out over the other? Gramma's hands were picking at a rough spot in the oilcloth table cover. The hurt was already spread over her, and her hands were seeking a quiet place. A great pity ran all through him — a pity for Grampa in the hay-

61

loft and for Gramma dragging him to the house, and for the pain in Grampa's leg and the fear in Gramma's heart. The pity began in his throat and he swallowed it down into his stomach, and then it ebbed into his thighs and down into his legs. The hurt spread over him from Gramma and Grampa, and he felt it in his bones and muscles, and it was a hurt and a pity for all pain and suffering everywhere. A pity for all mankind who must hurt and die.

"Hod," Gramma's voice brought him back, "he's hurt bad."

"No, he's not, Gramma. He's just got a sprained ankle. Why, a sprained ankle doesn't amount to anything. He'll be up and around again before the week's out. You'll see. A sprained ankle doesn't amount to a hill of beans!"

"He's past seventy, Hod. An' mebbe it's broke. Who's to know? He won't have the doctor. An' its swole somethin' powerful. An' old folks' bones don't mend so good."

"Pa said if he could move it, it wasn't broken."

"He cain't move it none now. Hod, he was jist pitchin' down some hay, an' 'fore he knowed it, he was flat of his back. Said he never rightly knowed what happened. The pore thing laid there it's untellin' how long 'fore ·I heared him acallin'. Time I got there he'd crept to the edge o' the loft an' was lyin' there amoanin'. How I got him down the ladder an' into the house I've no idee. A body's give strength to do what has to be done, I reckon. Then I run for Gault, him bein' the clostest. An' Gault, he come an' looked at it an' wropped his leg up, an' said he didn't figger it was broke. But it's swole somethin' terrible. An' it's all black an' darklike."

"Well, sure, Gramma. A sprained ankle always swells up and turns blue. It'll go down soon, if he keeps off it."

"You go in an' talk to him whilst I do up the dishes. He's twitchylike with the hurtin' an' all. An' he'll want to know how you made out with the work."

Hod moved into the other room of the house. The square logs this room was built of closed round Grampa's bed like a brown frame, smooth and shiny in the lamplight. Grampa was propped up in the old wooden bed with the high headboard rising almost to the ceiling. His bad leg rested on top of the coverlet. His massive shoulders spanned the pillows stacked behind him, and his great gray head moved restlessly from side to side.

"Hurt pretty good, Grampa?"

"Now, that's a fool question! Certain it hurts! Man cain't pull his anklebone clean outen place 'thout it hurtin'. Fetch ye up a chair, boy. Fetch ye up a chair an' set down. Reckon you kin make out to do the work fer a spell till I git back on my feet?"

"I reckon."

"How'd you make out in that there corn today?"

"Got a good start. But your patch is so shady and the ground's so damp the weeds are rank. It'll take me a right smart spell to get it done."

"Yeah," Grampa agreed. "That allus was the most troublesome thing 'bout that there patch. But I've tried corn ever' other patch on the place, an' it jist natcherally grows best there. Same ground as makes rank weeds makes tall corn, I reckon. Ifen my leg gits better, though, 'twon't be long I'll be laid away. I'd orta be up from here agin another week passes."

"Well, I wasn't complainin', Grampa. You just rest yourself and we'll make out to get everything done." Hod dragged a chair over to the bed.

"I declare, Hod," Grampa said, "believe if you was to bring in my hickory strips an' them two frames in the shed I could be aworkin' on them bottoms. Mebbe you could sorta prop me up some higher here in the bed, an' lay one o' them frames acrost the bed, like. Ifen I could jist be aworkin' with my hands, seems like I'd be a heap easier."

Hod piled the pillows behind the old man's back and pulled him up higher in the bed. Then he went out to the shed and brought in two chair frames he found there, and the rings of hickory strips which had been soaking to make them pliable. He helped his grandfather get one of the chairs set before him at an angle that was comfortable for him to work, and then he loosened the circle of hickory. He watched the knotted, misshapen old hands test the texture of the hickory and then fasten it to the chair to begin his weaving. It went across, around, under, and back.

It was fascinating to watch how surely the old hands wove the strands together . . . how taut and firm the pattern was. Grampa was counted the best chairmaker in the whole of Adair

County. There were always three or four chairs out in the shed waiting to be bottomed, and folks came from all over to get him to make their chairs new from stout, dry hickory. Couldn't anybody hold him a candle. Folks said Dow Pierce's chairs never wore out. The bottoms maybe. You could sit out three or four bottoms of a chair during its lifetime. But if Dow Pierce made the frame, it would outlast a man. Hod ran his hand down the leg of his chair, and thought of how Grampa made it. With never a nail or spike. Just seasoned wood bored into green wood, careful-like and sure, and rounded and smoothed until it was shiny.

The lamplight wavered fitfully in a light breeze and made tall shadows across the logs. Outside, the burr of frogs was beginning and the whippoorwills were crying lonesomely. Hod reached out his hands. " Let me see if I can do it, Grampa."

Grampa gave over the chair frame and the strips and cautioned him, " Mind you keep the strips even, now, an' don't let no slack creep in."

The boy bent his head over the work. At first he felt clumsy handling the strip, and his movements were awkward. After a few laps, however, he found that the strips fitted into his hand naturally when he held them a certain way.

" Why, it's just all in gettin' the feel of it, isn't it? "

" Mostly," answered Grampa. " They's some couldn't never git the feel of it, though. They's some ain't the patience ever to mess with it. Hit's slow work, makin' chairs. An' ain't ever'body has got the turn fer it."

Hod ran his palm over the smooth, hand-rubbed legs of the chair frame before him. It was satiny to feel and the grain of the wood was finely etched. " I reckon I've got the turn, Grampa," he said. " I've always loved to whittle and make things out of wood, and I sorta love the feelin' of wood itself."

" Hit'd be natcheral to you. I reckon I got my turn fer it from Ma. Her that was Abigail Sawyer. She could make e'er thing you wanted outen wood. Right quare fer a woman too. But she was handy that way."

" How long you been makin' chairs, Grampa? "

" Why, I wouldn't rightly 'know, boy. Might' nigh all my life, I reckon. Hit jist come handy to me, an' the first thing I knowed ever'body was bringin' me chairs to bottom, an' then I commenced amakin' 'em new. Over fifty year I've been makin' 'em, that I know."

" There's something comfortable about makin' things out of wood, isn't there? "

" Ain't no feelin' like it. Put a good piece o' whittlin' wood in a man's hand, an' give him a good, sharp knife, an' ifen he ain't content he ain't my kind of a man."

The boy and the old man bent together over the chair. Hod finished the overlapping and Grampa fastened off the last strip for him. Hod swiped his hands down the side of his pants. " Some folks say the furniture places in Louisville make hundreds of chairs a day. Would you think that could be so? "

Grampa's head jerked. " Mebbe. I've heared tell. But they ain't turned by hand, an' they ain't framed of hickory. You cain't hurry hickory none."

" I've not hardly been out of Adair," Hod said, his eyes pinned to the dark square of the door. " Just over to Campbellsville, and Ma said she took me to Liberty once to an all-day singin'. But I don't remember about it. Campbellsville, now. There's a right smart of stores and things there, but I reckon Louisville must be a sight to see."

Grampa looked at Hod and there was a twinkle in his eyes. " Yer feet's itchin', huh? "

" Maybe," and Hod laughed.

The old man pulled the quilt close around his shoulders and settled his head against the pillows. " Well," he said, " most Pierces is content to stay by their land. But I reckon there'll allus be one or two yearnin' to git out an' see the world. Yer great-grampa — him that was called Jeems — he was one. Had him a good snug cabin here he built hisself, an' a good woman, but he was allus agoin' off somewheres. I mind how he used to tell about the Mexican War, an' all them fur places he seen. Texas an' Mexico an' the like. But I mind mostly how he'd tell how tired his feet got awanderin' over that strange land."

Hod stirred. He'd read about the Mexican War. He looked at his feet, and they were Jeems's feet. They walked silently across the ridge and they felt the stones and the sharp spine of the ridge. They stirred the pine needles in the woods and splashed

65

through the creek. They tramped down the earth for a cabin to be built, and they searched the hillsides for stout oak and pine logs. They marched off to war, and they wandered the red dirt of Texas. They crossed over onto foreign land and were sore and cracked from the long marches over scorching sand.

But they came back to Piney Ridge and walked again behind a plow in cool, fresh dirt. At last they stopped and lay still, shod and boxed, and were lowered into the dirt to become a part of the dirt. The boy shivered and pulled his identity back into himself. This here's Hod Pierce!

" I'd like to see them places."

Grampa eyed him quizzically and hitched his quilt higher. " They ain't no place so homey as Piney Ridge."

Hod picked up his hat from the floor. He turned it round and round in his hands, and picked at the frayed edge of the straw. " Grampa, you been content most of your life? "

Grampa raised his arms and stretched mightily. " Why? "

" Just wonderin'."

The old man held the boy's eyes with a clear, straight look. " Hod," he said finally, " I reckon they's a time in ever' man's life when he hurts all over with discontent. I've had mine. An' only the good Lord an' yer gramma kept me from makin' a plumb mess o' my life." He laughed gently. " An' the time was when I laid most of the mess to yer gramma." He paused, and his look strayed toward the kitchen where Gramma was redding up the dishes. Then it came back to Hod. " Content? I reckon we wasn't intended to be content for too long at a stretch. But mostly I've liked livin'. I've had me a little piece o' land o' my own . . . an' a roof over my head that belonged to me . . . an' I've raised what I put in my stummick an' it set light there on account of it. I've had me a good woman to go along with me, an' kids that's pleasured me. I've had work to lay my hand to . . . work o' my own choosin'. An' folks around to neighbor with. Don't know what more a man could want. Livin' jist about biles down to that, I'd say. Ifen you take e'er thing away from it, a man ain't got full measure. Ifen you try to add to it, hit won't hold no more. Yes, I been right content."

Gramma darkened the doorway, smoothing down her hair and wiping her hands on her apron front. " You goin' now, Hod? "

66

"I better."

"Tell Hattie to come."

"She'll come. Pa or me one'll be comin' every day. Don't worry."

Hod opened the screen door and stepped out on the small porch. The stars were sprayed across the night, thick and yellow and hot. The hills closed all around him, tight, pressed down, closed in. " Livin' jist about biles down to that, I'd say. . . . I been right content." But what if you want to push the hills back? What if you have a longing so fierce it pulls and tugs inside of you? To stay where the earth is sweet and dark and familiar. Or to go where the boundaries broaden into wide skies. What if a man seeks himself back beyond the place where the sun rises? What if he must find other suns and other hills and other streams flowing swiftly? Would he then be content? Would he then come into his own place?

He stepped out into the night and took the path with long strides, his feet finding the way unerringly. The path dipped by the meadow gate, and swung down to the creek. Across the shallow water it rose sharply, and a man had to get a long breath for the climb. A slow mist was rising all down the holler, trailing in thin wisps around the trees and settling softly over the land. It twined itself around his legs and he pushed through it ghost-like and walking easy on a cloud.

The climb was long and steep, and he walked out of the mist halfway up. By the time he reached the top of the ridge he was winded, and he stopped by the white birch to ease his breathing. Up here there was a moon, and all down the ridge he saw the spiny humps and saddles of the trees. Back down in the holler the mist lay, blotting out the light in the cabin; blotting out space and the edges of space.

Across the holler was the cliff, white and shining in the moonlight. It scarred the hillside in austere purity, towering above the trees and free of them. Hod cupped his hands around his mouth. " Hey! " he cried. " You over there! This here's Hod Pierce ablowin' his horn! "

Feebly the echo made its way back across the holler. It doesn't carry as well at night, he thought, and stepped on down the road. He had forgotten all about the meeting.

CHAPTER SIX

THE HOT, BRASSY DAYS slipped breathlessly by. Hattie's old wood range in the kitchen had a fire in it from morning until night as she started the canning season. It was a point of pride with her that she never left an empty jar in the house. So the pots and pans simmered constantly on the back of the stove, which made the big, low-roofed kitchen steam like a boiler room. Tom grumbled: "Looks like you've a notion to can ever' blessed thing on the place. Want me to pick you a mess o' them dog fennel weeds? I seen some tall 'uns over in the fence corner."

Hattie, whose temper was short with the heat and the hard work, snapped at him, "You won't be the one that'll pass up e'er thing fitten to eat come winter, Tom Pierce!"

The long, hot, dry spell made the menfolks uneasy. It wasn't good for tobacco. Tobacco must have heat, but it must have plenty of moisture too. And a ruined tobacco crop on Piney Ridge meant no cash for a long, bitter year. So, daily, Tom and Hod and all the other ridge farmers scanned the sky for signs of rain; and they hovered anxiously over their tobacco fields, feeling the texture of the leaves and shaking their heads ominously.

Grampa's ankle stayed swollen and sore, and the long, hot days held him housebound and fractious. Irma was still staying the nights with him and Gramma, and she and John were holding tight to their stolen hours together. The meeting was coming to an exhausted close after three burning, passion-charged weeks. The preacher was worn out by the heat and the violent outpouring of his energy; the people were sated of their emotional hunger. Hattie was too tired after a long day over the stove to go many of the nights now. But Hod continued to walk the long way regularly.

Mostly this was to keep Hattie satisfied about Irma. For his own joy in the meeting had been short-lived. Lily Mae continued to ignore him, punishing him by laying her bold glance on the other boys and never once favoring him. Evening after evening he miserably saw her gather a group around her, toss back her sunburned curls, and let her laugh ripple like wind in the trees, sweetly, lightly, over her shoulder in Hod's direction. He stayed away from her. Not for anything would he have risked a rebuff. With a measure of dignity available to him through his hurt he kept to himself, quiet and contained. But she stabbed him afresh each night. He felt a possession of her which he dared not think another shared. But Lily Mae was so prodigal with the gift of her eyes and her smile that he was tormented with doubt. The long, dry days drew him taut, and he felt stretched and thinned. He had an uneasy sense of impending trouble, and he knew he would be glad when the meeting closed.

The morning of the last day of the meeting dawned as still and stifling as the ones that had gone before. Even the sun had a limp, fried look, like an egg cooked too quickly. By noon, heat waves shimmered in the blinding glare, and the whole world lay quivering under them. Hod sought the shade at the side of the house and hacked away with a long knife at the overgrown grass. Nothing could be done in the fields till it rained, and the time had best be spent in small chores around the house.

He heard the swish and slide of a footstep in the grass and leaned sideways to catch a glimpse of Becky coming down the front path. "Hi, there, Becky," he yelled, waving the knife at her. "Aren't you afraid you'll get a sunstroke out in the sun this mornin'?"

"Reckon my skull's too thick," she laughed. "You aimin' to scythe the hull yard with that there knife?"

"No, I'm not that lively. I'm just aimin' to clear the paths. Ma's inside quiltin'. Go on in."

He went back to his chore, stopping occasionally to wipe the sweat out of his eyes. Inside, there was the buzz of Hattie's and Becky's voices, and at intervals he could hear Becky's explosive, raucous laugh. It always startled him. Becky was a little, thin, frail-looking woman whose voice should have been soft and gentle. Instead it was deep and nasal, and when she laughed it was like the clanking of tin pans.

He heard them come out on the porch and heard Hattie say something about its being cooler out there. Then he forgot them and was not conscious of them for nearly an hour. Hattie's voice recalled him. " Hod! C'mere! "

There was something like steel in it, and a harsh hand squeezed his throat dry. He laid the knife down carefully and moved slowly to the porch. Becky was sitting, white-faced and scared, her hand to her mouth. Her eyes met his. " Hod, I never aimed to tattle nothin'. I never thought but what she knowed."

" Knew what? "

Hattie's voice cut in cleanly. " Becky's jist been atellin' me that Irma an' John Walton's been ameetin' ever' night down at Grampa's. I'm askin' you what you know about it."

Hod looked at his mother, and he saw her hands knotting and twisting. His eyes met hers steadily. " I just know Irma's a grown girl, mindin' her own business."

" Hit ain't her business to go meetin' e'er boy on the sly! "

" It's your doin' it has to be on the sly. And it's for Irma to say when she meets him and where." His eyes held his mother's without wavering.

" You don't know what yer sayin'! An' she don't know what she's doin'! But I'll git the truth one way or another. Ifen the whole countryside knows but me, they's aplenty to tell."

She went in the house and reappeared with her sunbonnet on her head. She stood for a moment tying its strings firmly under her chin. " I'm goin' to git Irma now," she said, and walked past them without seeing them.

" You've sure done it," Hod said bitterly to Becky.

" Hod, I never knowed she'd mind. I was right proud that Irma was atalkin' to sich a good boy as John Walton, an' it come over me to name it to Hattie. I swear, Hod, I'd cut off both hands 'fore I'd a caused Irma e'er bit o' trouble." Becky was crying now, and the tears rolled down the lined cheeks and dripped forlornly off her pointed chin.

" Well, never mind now. What's done is done. Irma'll catch it, and we'll all pay for it for a week or two. Worst is, Irma and John really love each other, and this'll go hard with 'em."

Becky wailed and threw her apron over her head. " I wisht I could cut my tongue right out. I wisht I was deef an' dumb an' dead. Pore little Irma, an' it's me that's done brought this on her! I wouldn't a caused her no trouble fer nothin' in this world.

70

Oh, me! Oh, me!" And she rocked back and forth, moaning.

"Becky, you better go on home now. Ma's not goin' to be in any easy frame of mind when she gets back here with Irma. Everybody's goin' to be walkin' low. You best go on now."

"You tell Irma I never aimed to."

"Oh, if it hadn't been you, it would have been somebody else. Nothin' can be kept on this ridge. Don't go blamin' yourself too much. But you better get on out of the way."

"I'm agoin'. But you tell Irma I never aimed to."

"I'll tell her," Hod promised, and Becky shuffled down the road, stooped and weeping.

What Hattie said to Irma, Hod never knew. It had been said before they reached home, for when they came in they were both white and drawn and silent. Irma went directly to her room. The afternoon wore itself out and supper was a desolate meal. No one went to the meeting that night, and the first dark found them all in bed, weary with the tension of the day, and guarded against the spoken word which would bring on the storm.

At breakfast the next morning Irma appeared tight-lipped. She helped with the meal and ate silently, glancing at none of them. It was as if she had repudiated all of them. Hattie's face was a stone image, with lines frozen in place. She was remote and withdrawn, and her rounded shoulders sagged with a heavy burden.

Hod tried to find a moment alone with Irma, to proffer his help if she needed it. But she merely shrugged his words off and kept her face still and flat. Only once did she say anything. "This ain't the end. I promise you, Hod. This ain't the end of it."

This dreary day was Hod's birthday. This day he was nineteen years old. There was no mention made of it, nor any notice taken. But when Irma seemed to have no need of him, he thought he might give himself a present and go fishing. He put a cork, hook, and line in his pocket and set off down the road for the river. He felt an overpowering need to be alone. The house was dull with silence and thick with hidden quarrels. He wanted to be away from it. He wanted to be still . . . to be at peace.

At the river he cut a long reed and tied his fishing line to it, set the cork and hook, and threw it in. Then he settled himself in the shade on the bank. The river was low, but still the water swirled and eddied, as clear and green as an emerald. Green River. Rightly named, he thought. He stretched out and let his hands lie limp on the damp, spongy ground. One hand gathered a clump of the dark loam and crumbled it, letting it slip through his fingers. The earth is good, he thought. There's nothing wrong with the earth. Only people get mixed up. The earth is forever and enduring the same. It answers a man's need. If a man knows his need, that is. But supposing a man doesn't know his need. Supposing he only knows an emptiness. An emptiness that isn't always an emptiness, but is sometimes a fullness. How is he to know whether he is empty or full? Whether he's to go or stay? How is a man to know what makes him a man?

He sat up suddenly and shook himself. The cork floated placidly and undisturbed. I'm moonin' again, he thought. Believe I'll take a swim. He stripped and slipped into the cool water, thrashed and snorted and ducked himself, then swam rapidly across the river and back. This was the hole where he had learned to swim, he remembered. Right over there by the sand bar Little Wells had thrown him in that day and shouted, "Sink or swim!" And he had swum. This was the hole where he and Wade and Sandy used to try to touch the bottom. You had to bring up a handful of pebbles to prove it. You went down and down in the limpid depths until you could lay your hand against the cold white stones. In a second you scraped your hand full and shot back to the surface. "Touched bottom," you shouted, and held your hand aloft, the white stones sparkling in the sun.

He floated lazily on his back, squinting against the sun. He felt the inertia of time-space endlessness and was melted into the water which upheld him. He shifted his eyes to the gleam of his white body washed by the clean ripples. He thought of the words of a song he sometimes sang . . . lonely river . . . weary water. Old Green was a lonely river, but its waters were never weary. He lifted his hand and watched the drops flow in a thin, fine stream down his arm back into the mother water. These drops that touch my body, now, go on. They pass the Smith place and the Beaver hole, and the old covered bridge. They go

72

farther than I've ever been. They eat out the banks of the Ohio; they marry the waters of the Mississippi; they flow free into the receiving cradle of the ocean. O free and searching water!

The sun was tipping the trees when he crawled out, dressed, stripped his line from the reed pole, and set out for home. Supper was over when he arrived, but Irma set a plate for him and he ate cold beans and potatoes hungrily.

When she had served him, Irma said quietly, " Hod, me an' John is goin' to git married."

It struck him like a blow in the pit of his stomach, but he went on eating. " That's good," he said.

So this was what she meant when she said it wasn't the end. This was her answer to Hattie. He went on to think of her and John. Married, setting up housekeeping. She was so young and so little to be going away from home. Even Hattie's sharp tongue couldn't keep home from being a sweet place. Did she know what marriage was like? Did she know how it would be with her and John? He shrank from the thought of her shoulders bending so soon. He wanted her free of burdens yet awhile. But she was a woman grown, and if this was her choice, this was what he wanted for her. He said none of these things, however, and he kept his face impassive. " You sure? " he asked her.

" I'm certain," she answered steadily.

" What did Ma say? "

" I've not told Ma, an' I ain't aimin' to till it's all over."

" When you plannin' to do it? "

" Saturday. I seen John at the mailbox and we made it up fer me to go over to Frony's an' Jim's at the Gap tomorrer. John'll meet me over there, an' we'll go to the county seat an' git the license. Then ifen you'll come to the Gap Saturday like you allus do, we'll wait an' you kin stand up with us."

Hod nodded. They had it worked out and it ought to go off without any trouble. But Irma had always been a sturdy, independent little person. He didn't urge her to tell Hattie. In fact, he agreed that it would be best not to tell her.

Thus it was planned and thus it was consummated. On Saturday morning Hod took his half bushel of corn to the mill as usual. Later he stood by his sister's side in the spare, plain front room of the preacher's house and listened to the words that made

73

her John Walton's wife. "Forsaking all others, cleave only unto him."

Forsaking Ma and Pa and him; the clean-swept rooms and the slow-ticking old Seth Thomas clock on the shelf; the yellow rosebush by the chimney; the old dominecker hen that squawked when it rained; the sunset over the beech grove. Inexorably the words repeated themselves in his ears. "Forsaking all others." Now it was going to be Irma and John, forever and enduring. There was partition and creation. There was a dividing and a loss; and there was the making of a whole. No, he had the impulse to say. No. But he stood quietly and his face was calm, and he signed the certificate with a steady hand.

As soon as the brief ceremony was over, the young couple drove off in Old Man Walton's spring wagon. They would stay a week or two with John's folks, and then they were going to set up for themselves in the tiny, two-room tenant house on his father's farm. They would start with a bed, a stove, and maybe a couple of chairs. Friends, neighbors, and relatives would give them dishes, pots and pans, and bedding. Folks on the ridge always helped a young couple get a start.

Just before the wagon moved away, Irma slipped a note into Hod's hand. "Give this to Ma," she said.

She had written two short lines. "Dear Ma. Me an' John got married today. I will come when I can. Your loving daughter, Irma."

When he gave Irma's brief note to Hattie that Saturday afternoon, Hod expected her to grieve, to storm and rage, to weep and scold. But she did none of them. She read the note and folded it neatly twice over into a small square. She laid it carefully on the edge of the table, and walked past him to the door. Bracing a hand on each side of her she stood there, looking out over the fields to the hills beyond, with her shoulders straightened and her face lifted. Hod waited, feeling weak and a little sick. It was an interminable time before she moved again. But when she turned, her face was quiet. The deed was done. Irma was safe now. The God-fearing ridge mother's anxiety that her child might go wrong was laid. An' John Walton was a right good boy, folks said. A hard worker an' a decentlike man. Yes, she could rest easy.

There was a look of peace and even of happiness on her face, and an odd, strange, fleeting beauty. Her eyes were soft and her mouth was sweet. She smiled at Hod gently and reached out to pat his shoulder. " I'll have to git them quilts done now fer shore," she said. " Irma'll be needin' 'em, come cold weather."

CHAPTER SEVEN

I RMA WAS MARRIED and the house was empty of her walk and her talk and her bright laugh. To Hod the first week after she was gone was like a strange and bewildering dream. When he came in the kitchen to breakfast in the mornings, he expected her to be there helping Hattie. When he slid into his place on the long bench at meals, he was lonely, and the bench was now too long and empty. A dozen times a day he listened for her voice and waited to hear her call him. How can a family so quickly be less than a family? How can one who is part of home so suddenly become no part of home? What is there to prepare you for the cutting away of something dear, and how can you heal the gaping hole that such cutting away leaves? He had not thought he would miss her so.

They talked of her often. " Hit don't seem like I'll ever git used to her not bein' here," Hattie said fondly. The fact of the marriage had freed her love of the alloy of distrust, and it went out full and deep to this daughter who had now taken on a woman's greatest task.

John brought her home for supper one Saturday evening when they had been married about two weeks. The sun was easing its way down behind the hills when they drove up and John hitched his mare to the yard fence. Hattie pulled the curtain aside from the front window to see who it was. Her cry brought Hod and Tom from the kitchen. " Hit's Irma an' John! " she called. " I declare if it ain't! I knowed when that ole rooster stood on the back steps this mornin' an' crowed that somebody was acomin'. Hit's a good thing I set to right then an' cooked up some decent victuals. An' baked that there cake! " And then she was out the door running to the front gate.

" Git out," she called, " git out! Ifen I ain't the gladdest thing

75

to see you!" Irma crawled over the wheel and flew to her mother's arms.

Hod and Tom reached them, and Tom held out his hand, grinning at John. "Well," he said, "you takened on a man's-sized job, ain't you? Marryin' this girl right out from under her ma's nose?"

"I figger I'm a growed man, Tom," John chuckled.

"Well, you shore takened us by surprise, boy, but now yer in the family, yer shore welcome. As fur as I'm concerned, they's not e'er 'nother boy Irma could a picked would a suited me better."

Hod had gone around on the other side of the horse to unhitch the traces on that side. He stretched his head over the mare's back. "Reckon he must a suited Irma pretty well too. Leastways, she hooked him mighty fast!"

Irma wrinkled her nose at him. "You're jist awishin' somebody thought that much o' you! That's all's wrong with you!"

Hattie slipped her arm through Irma's. "You jist hesh, Hod. Hit allus takes two to make a weddin', I've noticed."

The men laughed. John handed Irma a bundle from the wagon, and she and Hattie went through the gate toward the house. "You jist come right on in now," Hattie was saying; "hit won't take me a minnit to git supper on the table. My, I'm shore glad you come!"

Inside, Irma laid her bundle on the bed and followed Hattie to the kitchen. "I brung you some quilt pieces, Ma. Miz Walton give me a heap, an' I knowed you was allus needin' some. They're real purty an' the colors is bright an' cheerful."

"Now, ain't that nice? I was jist tellin' Hod the other day I was aimin' to git yore quilt I started last winter done. Fer I know in reason yer bound to need it, come winter."

"Well, I was aimin' to take back some o' my things tonight. That coverlid Gramma made fer me, an' them summer quilts you give me, an' a few things like that."

"They're jist like you left 'em. Take e'er thing you need. Tom an' me, we was wonderin' ifen you wouldn't like to have yer little dresser. Hit's right purty, an' it would brighten up yer house."

"O Ma, could I? I'd shore love to have it. We've not got much yit. Jist a bed an' a table an' cookstove, an' some chairs. John, he said when the tobaccer's in, he'd git me e'er what I needed, but I've allus loved that dresser so good. I'd ruther have it than a new one. Don't disfurnish yerself none now."

"Hit won't disfurnish me a bit! Hit's your'n. Hit was bought fer you, an' yer welcome to it. You think you'll like over there?"

"In time, I think. Hit's a little ole house. Jist two rooms. But John an' me aim to fix it up. He's agoin' to whitewash the outside, an' I thought to paper the rooms, an' paint the floors. John's folks has been right nice. His ma's a sweet woman, an' she seems real proud fer him to be married an' settled. She give me some o' her dishes. An' they was her best ones too, mind you. I told her we was goin' to git ever'thing like that soon as we could git around to it. But she let on like she was jist pleased to do it. An' John said I'd hurt her feelin's was I not to take 'em."

Hattie was bustling back and forth, but she nodded her head as she listened to the stream of Irma's talk. "I allus heared Susie Walton was a good woman. That ole man now. He's a hard worker, but I reckon work never hurt nobody."

"John, he works hard too. Seems like they work different from Pa an' Hod. Or even Grampa. I don't rightly know how it is, but seems like our menfolks allus went at things sorta easylike. I know Pa's frashed you many's the time with his ways, but he's allus been so good-natured with it. John, he's good-natured like Pa, though. But he works hard an' don't never take no time off to go fishin' or huntin'."

"He'll be a good pervider, then. We ain't never went hungry here, but we been too clost to it fer comfort, times."

Hattie set the table and burdened it with the food she was dishing up. Green beans, tiny and tender, cooked with a piece of smoked side meat. Corn, heaped high on the platter, steaming and golden yellow. Small, round tomato preserves. Thin green slices of cucumber pickles. Jelly and jam and molasses. Proudly she opened a loaf of store bread and piled it high on the plate, with biscuits and great squares of flaky corn bread. She poured milk into a tall blue pitcher and set it at one end of the table, and then she set the bubbling coffeepot at the other end. Last of all, she brought out the chocolate cake, standing four layers tall on the old cut-glass cake stand.

When they sat down to the table, John and Irma slipped naturally onto the long bench at the back, and Hod took a strange place at the end.

Looking at Irma and John across the table, Hod had a strangely awed feeling. These two were now one. They looked the same, they talked the same, and yet there was a proud new assurance in their bearing. Irma laid a knowing hand on John's arm sometimes. And John bent an owning look on her bright head. Together they had explored a new land. Together they had come into the sweet knowledge that only those who are very deeply in love could know. And nevermore would they be without the touch of it. It would lie over their life, and give it glory. Irma took on a new growth to Hod. She was a little less Irma, a little more woman. And in her increased stature he relinquished his last hold upon her. The forsaking had taken place, and he, in turn, could at last forsake her, leaving her free to be wholly John's wife.

He thought of Lily Mae, and the familiar dull hurt went through him. She had looked the other way at the store last week. Pretended not to see him. How could she stay angry so long? Or did she mean to stay angry forever, never forgiving him? He could no longer say, "There's other fish in the sea." There weren't, for him. He hadn't thought a girl could hurt you so. He hadn't known how lost she could leave you feeling when she took her warmth away.

He didn't ask himself if he wanted with Lily Mae this belonging which Irma and John now had. He only knew that to look at them in their new belonging sent an ache down his arms and left them feeling empty and drained. And he came upon a truth then — that once a man has held a woman in his arms, they can no longer be satisfied to fold across the emptiness without her. Abruptly Hod pushed his chair back. No more would go down.

Hattie urged food on the others until they were stuffed, and then she made them go out on the porch while she washed the dishes.

"I'll he'p," Irma said.

"You'll do no sich! Yer company tonight! When you come agin, you kin he'p e'er way you kin, but you ain't goin' to turn yer hand tonight. You go set with the rest on the porch. Hit

78

won't take but a minnit, noways."

As she went through the front room, Irma picked up Hod's guitar from the corner by the fireplace. "Thought I might as well have it handy," she laughed. "I'm wantin' some music when yer supper's settled."

The night was beautiful with a still, languid beauty. A wash of silver stars was spread widely across the sky, and the trees across the road were massed in blurred and softened outlines. The katydids were fiddling, and down in the holler the old bullfrogs grumbled about a "jug-o-rum, jug-o-rum, jug-o-rum." Over in the pasture a cowbell sounded gently, mellow and golden and muted.

Hod sat on the porch step and leaned his back against the post. He soaked up the night sounds and let them thread quietly through his body. The grass around the steps was heavy with dew, and the cinnamon vines spiced the air with a pungent, heavy odor. He stripped the dew absently from a blade of grass. Dew was a funny thing, now. Some said it fell, like rain or mist. Some said they'd heard tell it rose. But all summer long, rise or fall, the dew was there . . . as wet as rain, but infinitely more personal than rain . . . more mysterious and more delicate.

Hod's eyelids grew heavy. The voices lifted and fell around him, as soft as a woman's waist. As slow as molasses. As sweet as the smell of the cinnamon vines. They faded to a hum, burred through with Tom's deep laugh occasionally. They made no sense at all, and he felt himself rising and falling on the gentle rhythmic waves that flowed around him.

Irma's foot prodded him awake. "How 'bout that music?"

Hod lurched and nearly fell off the step. Unkindly Irma poked at him again. "C'mon, wake up!"

"I'm awake!"

"Then let's have some music."

Hod laid the guitar across his knees and plucked lazily at the strings.

"What'll it be?" he asked.

"You know that there tune, 'Lord Lovel,' or somethin' like that?" John wanted to know.

"Yeah, but it's awfully sad and mournful," Hod said.

"I know, but hit's got sich a purty tune," John insisted.

79

"Well, all right," and Hod thumbed a chord and leaned his head against the post.

> " ' Lord Lovel stood at his castle gate,
>   A combin' his milk-white steed;
>   Then along come Lady Nancy Bell,
>   A wishin' her lover good speed,
>   A wishin' her lover good speed.

> " ' Where are you goin', Lord Lovel, she said,
>   O where are you goin', said she.
>   I'm goin', my dear Lady Nancy Bell,
>   Strange countries for to see,
>   Strange countries for to see.

> " ' When will you come back, Lord Lovel, she said;
>   When will you come back, said she.
>   In a year or two or three at most,
>   I'll come back to my Lady Nancy,
>   I'll come back to my Lady Nancy.

> " ' He'd not been gone but a year and a day,
>   Strange countries for to see,
>   When languishing thoughts came into his mind
>   And Lady Nancy he would see,
>   And Lady Nancy he would see.' "

The song went on and on through its long story. Lord Lovel rode and rode until he reached London town, where he heard the people all mourning. And when he asked who was dead, they told him it was Lady Nancy. He ordered her grave opened, and he kissed her grave-cold lips while the tears came trickling down.

> " ' Lady Nancy was laid in the old churchyard,
>   Lord Lovel was buried close by her;
>   And out of her bosom there grew a red rose,
>   And out of his, a brier,
>   And out of his, a brier.' "

"I declare!" said Irma, when Hod stilled the last lingering quiver of the strings, "that song makes me plumb sad. I kin allus see pore Lord Lovel acomin' home an' findin' Lady Nancy dead an' buried."

"Well, he hadn't orta left her, seems to me," Hattie put in.

"Guess he must o' had a itchin' foot," said John.

"Hit says ' strange countries fer to see,' " Tom added.

Strange countries for to see! Hod knew how it must be when a man had to go, strange countries for to see. Home was sweet, and love was sweeter. But strange countries were like a hand in front of you pulling. The wonder of them never ceased.

"Sing somethin' gay, now, Hod. Sing the 'Crawdad Hole'!"

Hod laughed and swung into the swift rhythm. Irma joined him, and then John took up the tune with a pleasing, full voice. They rollicked down the verses to a breathless finish. "Lily Mae likes that one too," Hod said when they had ended the song. Hattie cut her eyes at him cornerwise and lifted her chin obliquely.

Hod sucked in his cheeks and pulled a brash chord from the guitar. "'Oh, they call it that good ole mountain dew,'" he shouted. "'They call it that good ole mountain dew'!"

"Now, that'll do, Hod," Hattie's voice sliced through the music. "Man or boy, I ain't aimin' to have you singin' no sich a song as that! Jist put yer gittar up now!"

"O Ma, it's jist a song," Irma protested.

"You heared me." Hattie was immovable.

Hod laid the guitar aside and rolled a cigarette. Somewhere down the road a dog barked.

"That's Lem's old Spot dog," Tom said. "Reckon what he's doin' up on the ridge."

They were quiet on the porch, listening. Soon they heard the muffled sound of voices. A smothered laugh or two came down the road and the shuffling of many feet.

"What in the world you reckon's goin' on?" Hod asked, puzzled.

"Sh-h-h," warned Tom.

And when a shot broke the air, all bedlam turned loose. The noise of pans being banged against one another, of iron bars clanging together, of cowbells and whistles, of a dozen shotguns being fired at once, of people screaming and yelling, deafened those on the porch. They sat stunned by the first impact of the drowning sounds, unable to move or to think.

Hattie recovered first. "Hit's a shivaree," she said, shouting above the din to make herself heard. "They're ashivareein' Irma an' John!"

Hod grinned in the dark. But his heart was pounding hard.

Every young couple who got married on the ridge hoped for a shivaree. It was the ridge's way of voicing approval of the marriage. It was a token of esteem. And here the folks were shivareeing his own sister and her new husband. And by the sounds of it, it was a bang-up shivaree! He slipped off the porch to take his place among them.

The crowd milled through the front gate and divided, half marching around the house one way and the other half going the other way. For fifteen or twenty minutes they marched around the house, the men shooting off their guns, the women banging their pans and ringing their cowbells, all of them shouting and laughing. The folks stood on the porch and waved and shouted as the lines went by.

Then suddenly the crowd converged on the porch. The women dragged Irma, who was laughing by now and enjoying the excitement, from John's side, and dumped her unceremoniously into a big washtub. She pulled her legs under her hastily as they lifted the tub, swinging it high between them, and carried her around the house.

At the same time the men had laid hands on John. John protested mildly and pretended to wrestle with the men, and it was Hod who seized him strongly and threw him from the porch. Then, setting him astride a rail, they took up their march again.

In a few minutes it was over, and the two were brought back to the porch, disheveled, panting, and laughing. John crippled across the porch, mocking his ride on the rail, and the men called crude jokes at him. Hod looked on proudly. If it was boisterous and vulgar, it still was hearty and neighborly.

When the crowd quieted, Hattie asked them all in the house and served them great cups of black coffee and the four-layer chocolate cake as far as it would go. There was a great deal of laughter and shouting at the young couple, and much merry singing.

Hod went out on the porch to cool off. He sat on the steps, and pulled his knees up under his chin. He sighed gustily. It was a proper thing to be shivareed so successfully. Irma and John had got off to a fine start now. He turned his face against the rough stuff of his jeans and rubbed his cheek against it. Then he straightened briskly. Fiddle! Everything started him moonin' these days! This was no way for him to be actin'!

He was startled when a pair of hands, smelling freshly of perfumed soap, slipped over his eyes. He covered them with his own broad palms. Lily Mae! His heart jumped into his throat and then tunneled to his feet. Lily Mae! He pulled the hands down and turned to face her. "I didn't know you were here," he said softly, his breath coming quickly between his words.

"Did you think I'd fergot?"

She was so close, bending over him. And she smelled so sweet. Even as his senses dipped and swirled, he identified the odor. Honeysuckle! He swallowed. "The way you been actin' I didn't know what to think!"

"C'mon," she whispered, taking his hands and pulling him off the step. "C'mon, let's go out in the yard where nobody kin hear."

"Where nobody can see?" he asked hopefully.

"That's as may be," she giggled, and led the way around the house behind the yellow rosebush.

Eagerly Hod caught her and gathered her close. His arms folded round her softness and the empty ache was filled. He held her tightly against him, feeling her warmth steal over him.

"Hod, yer hurtin'!"

"I aim to! Don't ever treat me like that again!"

She raised his face in her two hands. "Silly," she laughed, "silly! Didn't you know I was yer girl!"

"I'll not let you forget it again," he promised, and he let his arms rest wearily about her waist. Something was at peace in him again.

CHAPTER EIGHT

THE HEAT DRAGGED ON, and the corn and the tobacco burned in the fields. The sun brought the day up by four thirty these mornings, dragging it gray-faced and heavy-eyed over the hills, sponging out as it went any stray clouds left over from the night. Then in hot solitude the great yellow disk whitened the sky with glare, and reduced the earth to a flaccid state of inertia.

The tension built up and up as the brassy sky fought to collect clouds and bank them against the rain. Each day the bank was thicker, heavier, in the west, and when the sun could not shred it into fragments, it sullenly hid behind the dark curtain. Each afternoon there was a far rumbling of thunder down the river valley, and when night had blown cool over the land, the edges of the ridge stood out starkly against the summer lightning. At last one evening the swollen, black belly of the banked clouds sagged and burst, and the rains came squalling out of the sunset.

For two days then it rained — a slanting, cold rain which soaked into the earth and packed it down, muddying the fields and streams. It traced a chill finger in the air and sent the thermometer shivering down into the forties. With stoves down for the summer, the raw, damp cold sent folks huddling around the kitchen ranges. Grampa built up a little fire in the fireplace mornings and evenings and hovered over it. His ankle was still sore and stiff, and he had been housebound now for over six weeks.

"Plague take sich weather," he fumed, "never seed sich a summer. First the sun nigh cooks you. Till you feel as parched an' dried out as shoe leather! Then it comes on to storm an' mighty nigh frosts! Even my bones is shakin' with ague!"

His old, thin blood was miserable with the cold, and the second night of the rain he was sneezing and Gramma was urging him to bed. "Dow, you'll take yer death! Git in the bed an' leave me kiver you up, an' make you a cup of tea! Ain't no use flyin' in the face o' nature thisaway! Hit don't change the weather none to act contrary!"

"Who's actin' contrary! I jist don't want none o' that there bed, an' I ain't aimin' to have none! I been layin' on it most o' these last six weeks, an' I'm plumb tard of it."

Gramma said no more, knowing it was useless, and she watched him come down with a heavy cold helplessly. She wasn't overly alarmed. A summer cold didn't amount to nothin', mostly. She dosed him and physicked him and listened to him fret. Even when the cold went down into his chest and he began to wheeze and shake with paroxysms of coughing, she wasn't too uneasy. She'd seed Dow cough the night through, many's the time. A cold allus had went to his chest.

He had been sick about a week when Tom came home from

84

doing the work one night, his face sober and quiet. "Pa's right sick," he said at the supper table.

"So?" said Hattie, pouring milk into the glasses. "His cold's bad?"

"Hit's settled in his lungs, I'm afeared. He's got a right smart fever tonight. Won't have the doctor, though. Says it don't amount to nothin'. But I thought I'd better go back down tonight an' do fer him. Ma's all tuckered out."

"I'll go with you," Hattie said at once. "Hod, ifen we don't git back 'fore mornin', you see that things git done."

"Yessum."

They returned the next morning, tired from the sleepless night. "Gault an' Becky's stayin' the day," Tom reported to Hod before going to bed, "an' Lem's goin' tonight."

"Is he bad off?" Hod asked. Seemed funny to think of Grampa really sick. As long as Hod could remember he had been a giant of a man, strong, burly, able to outwork nearly any two men on the ridge. It didn't seem real for folks to be watchin' up with him. He'd always been the one to sit up with everybody else.

"Well, he's purty sick." Tom bent to unlace his shoes. "An' he's agittin' old. Pa must be nigh onto eighty. Things goes hard when yer that old."

"Did you get the doctor yet?"

"No. But me'n Gault has decided ifen he ain't no better by night we'll one of us go after him first thing in the mornin'. He's past tellin' a body what to do now."

Hattie and Tom slept until the middle of the day. Hattie fixed dinner then, and kept the fire going to put up some beans that had been picked the night before. "They'll spile if they're left e'er 'nother day," she said. Tom and Hod worked in the tobacco, the rains having packed the soil to where it needed loosening. They worked side by side, their hoes mulching the caked dirt, saying little. Both of them were thinking of Grampa. Both of them were counting memories, a generation apart, but remarkably alike for all that. A great, spendid figure of a man had towered over their days, sweetening them and giving them the imperishable quality of himself.

A man wasn't ever by himself, then, Hod thought. He was himself, and his father, and his grandfather. Suddenly he had a clear vision of Hod Pierce stretching back in time, part of him Pa, part of him Grampa, part of him Jeems, and on back. All his days of living were before him, and he saw with certain clarity how he had been molded and made. Something of each of them and something of all of them had been poured into him. A man was a reservoir into which his people poured the stream of their living, and then it went on out of him, and through him, down on into time not yet lived.

Late that afternoon they were all sitting on the porch, waiting for the house to cool a bit before eating supper. Hattie had slipped her swollen feet out of her shoes and was fanning herself with her apron. Tom was whittling down the end of a new ax handle, curling long shavings on the grass at his feet. Hod was propped against the post, leaning occasionally to pick up a tendril of shaving and wind it around his finger. They were too weary and too hot to talk.

Tom looked up from his whittling suddenly. He leaned an ear toward the road. "Somebody comin' up the hill," he said.

They all listened and turned to look down the road. Hod stood up. "Whoever it is, he's comin' in a hurry."

Tom stood too. "He shore ain't keerin' none 'bout his wagon!"

They still could see nothing, but they kept watching the road. The heavy tunnel of trees ended at the old church, and within a few minutes they saw the wagon coming. The horses were running and the wagon was lurching from side to side on the road.

"Pa, that's Lem's team," Hod said, and started running toward the gate. Tom was right behind him, and Hattie began to struggle with her shoes.

"Somethin's shore wrong," Tom said. "Somethin's bad wrong!"

Hod and Tom were waiting by the side of the road when Lem pulled the horses up. He was standing tall in the wagon, his knees buckling to the sudden stop. Trouble was written all across his face.

"Hit's Pa," Lem said, "he's takened worse. I'm goin' fer the doctor!"

"I've been afeared o' that," Tom said. "Who's there? Gault?"

Lem nodded. Hattie was already turning to go into the house and get her things. She stopped and said, "Lem, you better let Hod go after the doctor an' you go back with Tom an' me."

"No," Lem said, "no. I'd ruther go myself. You all go on. I'll git back quick as I kin. Lord he'p us if the doctor ain't there." Even as he spoke he jerked the team into the road again.

Hod ran to hitch old Buck to the spring wagon. It would be too slow walking down the trail. By the time he drove around to the front of the house, Hattie and Tom were waiting for him. They climbed in and Hod whipped the horse into a fast trot.

"Keerful, son," Tom warned. "We'll not git there no quicker ifen you run a wheel agin a rock."

When the road dipped down the hill, they had to go carefully, and Hod was impatient of the time it took to ease the wagon down the steep, rocky slope. Then they had to wheel around the schoolhouse in the mouth of the holler and go halfway down the holler again. Hod whipped old Buck to a run the last half mile.

A group of men stood in the front yard, hushed and reverent. They stood aside to let Tom and Hattie and Hod pass through. No one spoke. Why, it's like he was already dead, Hod thought.

Gramma met them at the door and threw her arms around Hattie. "My pore Dow," she cried. "Oh, my pore Dow, Hattie!"

"Hush, now, Ma," Hattie said, patting the grief-racked shoulders and smoothing the hair back from the wet, swollen face. "Hush, now. We'll all do all we kin. An' Lem'll be back with the doctor, soon. You come an' lie down, now, an' let me do fer Pa."

Hod watched her lead Gramma to the bed and tenderly lay her down. She brought a pan of water and took a clean rag and bathed Gramma's face gently. Hod know how easy was her touch and comforting. He knew what strength would flow from those thin, brown hands, and how the bastions of hope and faith would be buttressed by them. He knew what calm would pass from them to Gramma.

Gramma grew still under the gentle hands, and Hattie laid the wet cloth over her eyes. "You rest yerself now."

She straightened and lifted the pan of water. "Hod, you kin empty this. I'll go in an' look at Grampa."

"I'll go in with you," he said. "This can wait."

At the door he had a sickening desire to turn back. He didn't want to see Grampa like this. But Hattie had already gone inside and he made himself follow her. Lizzie was sitting at the head of the bed. She looked up when they entered, and when she saw who it was she moved to let them draw nearer. She put a hand on Hattie's arm and said softly: "He's done fer. He's goin' fast."

Hod swallowed and looked at the bed. Only Grampa's white face could be seen. His great head moved restlessly on the pillow and a froth of bubbles blew in and out of his mouth as the slow, gasping breaths came and went. Hod closed his eyes. He couldn't look.

"You two go on out," Hattie said. "I'll stay with him till the doctor comes."

"I'll stay," said Lizzie. "You was up all night."

"Well, then, Hod, you'n me better go out. They ain't nothin' we kin do right now."

They left Lizzie with Grampa and joined the group that was gathering in the next room. Gault and Becky were there. They went in to see Grampa again, and shortly came out. Becky was sobbing, but Gault was dry and tearless. Hod watched, aching for Gault and Lem and Pa, and aching for himself because this was Grampa who lay in the next room. He felt the common blood stream that tied them all together and bound them in a common kinship. He felt it stretching from him to Becky and Gault, to Lem and Lizzie, to Gramma and Grampa. And it went on back to Abigail and Jeems. And it went into the soil of Piney Ridge, and the trees and the rocks and the river. It went into the corn growing green and tender. It went into fuzzy, pale tobacco leaves. It went out all over the ridge, into every morning's sunrise and every evening's dark. It went out and pulled tight and close all the ways of living on Piney Ridge, by all the people on Piney Ridge, and it came back inside Hod Pierce.

Gramma slept, and there was no sound except the whispers. People came and went. Neighbors stopped and sat for a while and murmured softly to one another and to Hattie and Tom and the others. Hit's too bad. He was sich a good man. We'll not know how to git along without him. Hit's untellin' how Annie'll take it when he goes. God knows it's hard to lose yer man. Seems like some o' yer own life goes into the grave with 'im. Pore Annie. Pore Dow.

Hod moved restlessly about the place. He drew fresh water

and drank deeply, but his thirst was not real and the water tasted bitter. When would Lem get here with the doctor? And then he had the hopeless thought, what good would it do, anyhow?

Hattie called him in and set food before him and Tom and the rest of the family. Gramma still slept, worn out with grief and worry. No one ate much, but everyone made a show of swallowing a few bites. No one talked much. It was as if by talking they might shut out the sound they were all listening for. What were they listening for? Hod listened too. What was he listening for? And then he knew. Grampa's labored breathing came through the door like a sobbing undertone of grief. It was a faint sound, dragged out long, dragged in long. It had been there all along, but he had not consciously heard it. Now he knew. They were all listening for it to stop.

He felt a sudden panic that it might stop while he was swallowing this bite of meat, and he wouldn't know. And then he had a deeper fear that he would hear it stop, and he would have to know. He pushed his chair back and went out in the yard. But he was still listening. He felt himself straining to listen. So he went back in the house and sought his chair in the corner out of the way.

Night came on, and Hattie lighted the lamps. Gramma moaned in her sleep, and Hattie and Becky washed up the supper things out in the kitchen. There was a muted waiting — a softened interval of suspense that had no relation to reality. Hod felt the minutes spin out into time, and he drew apart as if he were watching the scene from afar. He himself was a part of the unreality and yet he stood apart and looked on. In a moment now he would find himself at home, sitting on the porch tuning his guitar, or maybe just sitting there, and old Duke, the dog, would be scratching fleas under the floor, making a thumping noise against the boards. In a moment now he would be back, identified with the night and the earth and the stars. He would not be here, waiting on the edge of something intangible and vague and fearful. In a moment now.

And then it stopped. The sobbing, dragging sound through the door stopped. Becky was fanning noiselessly with a folded paper. The paper was caught at the end of its motion, and held, arrested. Her eyes went to the door, as if she could see beyond

89

and, seeing, make the sobbing start again. Hattie lifted her hand toward Hod, but dropped it by her side. Gault was standing by the outside door, and he turned as if to hear better. Tom did nothing. He had been sitting there as still as a stone, except for his right hand which flexed, opening and closing, opening and closing, on his knee. The hand opened, and when the sound stopped, it paused in its flexing a brief second, and then it closed tight and hard. It did not open again.

Hod looked at Tom's fist on his knee. His breath choked in his throat. Open it, Pa! Open it! Open it! He was on his feet and he thought he had shouted the words. And then Lizzie opened the door and her face was wet with tears. "He's gone," she said. No one spoke. Gramma turned in her sleep and moaned once. The sound went inside Hod and shook him, and he stumbled outside into the thick, dark night.

He stopped at the rail fence back of the house and gripped the rough rail tight. He felt its roughness and he closed his hands hard upon it. This is the way death comes. You are breathing, dragging the air into your body and pushing it out again. You are real and warm and living. You can run and swim and laugh and sing. You are brown and lean, and you can swing a hoe in the hot sun. You can feel the tug of the plow in the earth. You can love all the good things of the earth and its seasons. There's all of life ahead of you. And then that sobbing, dragging sound stops, and you are nothing. The world turns and the sun and the moon and the stars are bright, but you are nothing. The corn grows and the fish leap in the river, and the rains fall, wet and silver. Flesh is hurt and bruised and loved. But you are nothing. You, pushed down, unknowing and nothing. You, Hod Pierce, unknowing, forever!

He beat his tight fist on the rail and rejoiced in the hurt. He wanted to feel the hurt deep and lasting. The hurt was real, and he was real if he was hurting. Who is Hod Pierce? A mote of dust on a whirling planet — a breath of air in a cosmic wind — a dust and a breath, lost in forever! The littleness and the awfulness of it pressed him down. This here's Hod Pierce! He pounded it into the rail fence, beating his identity back into himself. This here's Hod Pierce! But the voice inside pushed up and up. Who is Hod Pierce? Who is Hod Pierce?

Grampa was buried on a Monday. He was laid in the Pierce burying ground down in the holler. Abigail and Jeems had buried the first Pierces there, and it was the resting place of all the others who had followed. It was a sweet plot of ground, with honeysuckle and wild roses running rampant over it. And tall trees rimmed it in beneath the hills.

All the Pierces from all over the ridge were there. All were joined together in mourning. The holler was full of Pierces.

Hod stood with his eyes lifted to the hills while the same preacher who had married Irma and John consigned Grampa's body to the earth. Strange. A man of God must join people together, and he must also part them forever. He must begin life, and he must end it. In the beginning . . . Amen.

The preacher's voice was soft: " ' While the sun, or the light, or the moon, or the stars, be not darkened, nor the clouds return after the rain: . . . Or ever the silver cord be loosed, or the golden bowl be broken, or the pitcher be broken at the fountain, or the wheel broken at the cistern. Then shall the dust return to the earth as it was: and the spirit shall return unto God who gave it.' "

The first clods of dirt tapped a knocking on the wooden box. Gramma cried out, a high, thin cry, and Becky and Hattie spoke softly to her. She leaned heavily on them, letting her head fall forward, and they supported her gently.

Hod lifted his eyes beyond the open wound in the earth. On a nearby tree a leaf, dried by the heat and wrinkled brown, swung back and forth in the fan of a light breeze. He watched it and shut his mind and ears to the filling of the grave. Back and forth the leaf swung, gaily, saucily. And then a gust of wind snapped the brittle stem. The leaf, free, floated soft as a downy feather toward the ground. The breeze caught it, turned it somersault, puffed it up again, and then ran away. The brown feather drifted into the open scar and lightly came to rest on a lump of dirt. It wavered and tilted, and then it slid a little to one side. The next moment a shovel was emptied, and the leaf was buried.

CHAPTER NINE

A UGUST CAME IN sticky and steamy. Grampa was gone, but life
went on. The door of the old cabin was swung shut, and Hod
helped the folks move Gramma up on the ridge into Irma's old
room. He felt all her grief added to his own, and tenderly he
packed the belongings which were so shaped by Grampa's ways
and Grampa's living. The old mantel clock. The big wooden
bed. The sagging chairs. The ancient, cracked dishes. Some of
the things Gramma gave away. But she hugged to herself many
more than she could ever use again. Hod knew she had to hold
onto them, to keep for herself those things that were so much a
part of Grampa. She was keeping a little of him. Hattie too was
patient, never warning her there wasn't room for so many things.
She set them around the room, and cluttered up the rest of the
house with them, letting Gramma cluck over them broodingly.

Hod went to the mill the next Saturday as always, and it was
good to sit with the familiar group of men and listen to their
talk. They spoke briefly of Grampa. His great strength and his
goodness. And his ways.

" Couldn't nobody make a cheer like Dow," said one.

" No, sir, they couldn't nobody tech him when it come to
makin' cheers," the rest agreed.

" He'll be missed," another said. " He was a good man." And
there was a silence which was a tribute to the big man who had
gone on.

Then the miller spoke of other things. " I hear they got a
bumper crop o' tomaters over in Indianny this year. Hear they
need ever' hand they kin git aholt of."

" What're they payin'? " someone asked.

" I heared Jim Byron say the two Knight boys come home
from there last Saturday night, an' they tole they was gittin' ten
cents a hamper. He said they claimed they was makin' eight an'
ten dollars a day right along."

The circle of men sagely nodded their heads. " That's a right
smart bit o' money," they agreed.

" Feller could easy make a hunderd dollars clear in a month

over there," the miller said.

"I could shore use a hunderd dollars cash money right now too," said Jim's neighbor; "wisht I could go."

"Me too," said one of the others, "but I git down in my back so easy I couldn't noways hold up to it."

I don't get down in my back easy, thought Hod. I could hold up to it! I'll go! A hundred dollars! Why, that was a fortune! That much money would be the open door for him. His heart sang. This was the way, finally. He knew it was.

"You say the Knight boys came home last Saturday night?" he questioned the neighbor. "Do they come regularly?"

"Come ever' week," Jim said. "Ride down with Cooper, the produce man, in his truck. He's aworkin' over there too. Haulin'."

"What time do they go back?"

"Late Sunday evenin'."

"Reckon they'd have room for one more goin' back?"

"Don't see why not, ifen you don't mind ridin' in the back."

Hod waited for no more. He had to get out to the Knights' place and talk to someone about it. The Knights lived a scant mile from the Gap, on the Pebbly road, and Hod lost no time covering the short distance. Old Man Knight was sitting on the front porch mending a pair of plow reins as Hod walked up. "You Mr. Knight?" he asked.

"Yep," without looking up from his work.

"Johnny and Slim your boys?"

"Yep."

"They pickin' tomatoes over in Indiana this summer?"

"Yep."

"They come home on week ends?"

"Yep."

"Comin' tonight?"

"Fur as I know."

"Goin' back tomorrow?"

"Ifen they come, they will."

"About what time?"

"Five o'clock."

"Does Mr. Cooper pick 'em up here, or do they meet him somewhere?"

"Meet him at the Gap, front o' Weaver's store." The old man

93

looked up, spat tobacco juice expertly to one side of the step on which Hod's foot was propped. "Yer a Pierce, ain't ye? Offen the ridge?"

"I'm Tom Pierce's boy," Hod replied.

"Knowed ye wuz a Pierce the minnit I seed ye. Me an' Tom's coon hunted all over that there ridge, many's the time." The knotted old hands fretted with the leather reins. "You thinkin' 'bout goin' over to Indianny with the boys?"

"Yessir. I'd like to get me a job over there pickin' tomatoes too. I heard Johnny and Slim come home every Saturday night with Mr. Cooper and go back on Sunday. I'd like mighty well to go back with 'em tomorrow night."

"Don't know of e'er good reason why ye shouldn't. Tell ye what ye do. You be at Weaver's by four thirty tomorrer evenin' an' I'll tell Johnny to keep his eye out fer ye. Cooper, he won't mind havin' one more. He don't charge the boys nothin' noway. Says he has to come an' he allus likes company. Might be the boys kin git ye on in the same field where they been pickin'. They been doin' right good this year." He shifted his plug of tobacco from one cheek to the other and shot a thin stream of brown juice into the dust.

Hod mulled over the information, then took his foot off the step and straightened up. "Well," he said, "I'd sure be much obliged to 'em for the ride, Mr. Knight, and any help the boys can give me. You tell 'em I'll be there, ready to go." He shoved his hat back, scratched at his head, and settled the hat firmly in place again. "I better be goin', I reckon."

"You ask yer pa ifen he recollects the night him an' Blackjack Knight treed a jug o' moonshine 'stid of a coon, an' see what he says." The old man's stomach heaved as he laughed in recollection. "I could tell you things yore pa an' me done when we was sprouts that'd make yer hair stand on end, young'un," he went on. "Tom wuz allus a lively 'un. Couldn't nobody ever git him to take a dare. We shore had some high ole times them days." He sighed. "But I reckon it's best to leave the past stay dead an' buried. But you be certain an' tell him ye seen me."

"I'll tell him," Hod promised, and opened the gate. "Much obliged, and tell the boys I'll be ready and waitin' for 'em."

After supper that night he was restless, with his plans mulling through his head. He hung around the front porch for a while, then went out to the barn where Tom was mending a plow. He fidgeted awhile, wanting to talk and not knowing how to begin. Tom looked up finally. "Somethin' itchin' you, boy?" he asked.

Hod's breath sucked in. "Pa, I'm goin' over to Indiana to pick tomatoes. I'm goin' tomorrow with the Knight boys. I heard at the mill today they need hands and they're payin' good. I talked to Old Man Knight and he said I could go back with Johnny and Slim and maybe get on at the same place they work."

Tom put his hammer down. He took a plug of tobacco out of his shirt pocket and carefully pared a chunk off one end with his knife. He put it in his mouth and chewed methodically until it was softened before he spoke. "What does yer ma say?"

"I'm not goin' to tell her. She'd just fuss and take on. It'll be better if you tell her after I've gone."

Tom nodded. "She shore ain't goin' to like it none."

"I know she's not, but I've got to go, Pa. I want a chance to make some money of my own, and maybe go to a trade school in Louisville, or something. I don't rightly know just what I want to do. But I know I've got to get away from here and see for myself."

Tom looked at the boy steadily. A broad band of late sunlight lay between them, filled with sparkling dust motes. The barn smelled of hay, and the warm, steamy odor of animals. Tom spoke finally. "Reckon they ain't no way but fer you to go. This has been a long time breedin' in you. I been watchin' it. I don't want to hold you back none. I cain't say as I hold with it, but I've allus said that ever' man's got a right to decide fer hisself what he's goin' to do. Best thing to do is git it outen yer system, I reckon."

"Can you make out without me?"

"Oh, they's allus ways to make out. Gault an' Lem'll he'p with the tobaccer, an' in a pinch I kin allus git Matt Jasper or Old Man Clark."

"Maybe I could come back to help with the tobacco. Or maybe I'll have enough money to help out with."

"We'll make out. I cain't he'p you none with money, but

95

leastways I kin give you a chancet to make yer own."

Something light rose in Hod. Pa had always been easier than Ma to get along with. All at once he felt a man, a grown man, talking with another man — one who understood, just because he was a man. Hod grinned at his father. "Well, then. You'll tell Ma."

Tom picked up his hammer and hit a strong lick on the plowshare. "I'll tell her."

Hod lingered in the door. "Think I'll go over and see if Lily Mae's at home."

"Better not stay too long," Tom warned. "Tomorrer's goin' to be a big day fer you."

Hod whistled for old Duke and cut across the field back of the barn. The sun slid ponderously down behind the rim of the ridge, and stirred a breeze in its wake. The nightjars started whining, and a bird in the hedge of trees cheeped fretfully. First dark purpled into night as he went, and the breeze blew itself away. It was the dark of the moon, and Hod stepped lightly.

Outside Lily Mae's house he whistled softly. There was a light in the front room and he guessed Lily Mae was there. He whistled again, insistently. The door opened and Lily Mae stood framed in the lamplight.

"It's me," he called. "Can you come out for a while?"

She closed the door behind her and he heard her step on the porch. Then he could hear nothing as she felt her way across the grassy yard. But he could feel her nearness. He could feel it in the prickle of his skin and the familiar quickening of his senses whenever he thought of her or was near her. It poured over him now, and the heady joy of being with her took hold of him. Suddenly she was by his side, and then she was in his arms, pressed against him.

"What you doin' out tonight?" she whispered, when he had lifted his head.

"Tellin' you good-by," he answered, stopping her questions with his mouth.

She let herself go in his arms another moment, her lips soft and moist beneath his. And then she drew away. "Tellin' me good-by?" she asked, running her hand lightly over his hair, drawing one finger down the curve of his jaw.

"Don't," he moved his head restlessly. His hands were still on her waist and he shook her gently. "Don't do that."

She laughed and rested her arms around his shoulders, clasping her hands behind his head. "Where you goin', then?"

"To Indiana. To work in the tomato fields."

"When?" And she let her face rest lightly against his cheek. Her hair tickled his ear.

He laughed and pushed her. "Get away from me," he said, and his voice was rough. "You can't keep me from going that way."

"Who said I was tryin' to keep you from goin'? I jist asked you when you was goin'."

"Tommorow."

"Well, that's tomorrer. This is tonight, ain't it?"

"Yeah, this it tonight. But don't forget I'm goin' tomorrow!" He pulled her close, and their talk stopped for a while.

"When'll you be back?" she asked after a time.

"In about a month," he said. He didn't mention the possibility of going to school. No need to get her riled up about that until the time came. Maybe he would be back in a month, anyhow. And if he wasn't, it would be easier to write her the news than to tell her now and risk spoiling their last time together. First from Hattie, and then from Lily Mae, he had learned that with women there are times when it may be healthier not to be completely honest.

The time slipped by as they whispered together, and then the door opened and Lily Mae's mother called. "Lily Mae? You'd best come on in, now. Hit's agittin' late."

Hod let her go with one last, long kiss. "Don't forget you're my girl," he warned.

"I'll not," she promised, "but don't you stay away too long!"

The Knight boys came down the road at about the same time the truck drove up the next afternoon.

"Howdy, Hod," Johnny Knight said. He was a tall, brown boy, with thin flanks and long, lean legs. His shoulders were broad and swaggering, and his body tapered into the hips, coming down straight and powerful. He had a strong, bold face with good features, a clean-swept jaw line, and a nose that hooked slightly over

97

a long upper lip. His mouth had a quirk at the corner, as if he scoffed lightly at himself and the world. His reddish-brown eyes had a merry light in them, a twinkling gaiety which approved life heartily.

" Howdy, Johnny," Hod replied. " Your pa told you I wanted to go back with you, I reckon."

" First crack outta the barrel, he told us. He takened quite a shine to you. Said he wanted we should he'p you all we could."

" He used to know my pa, guess that's why," Hod said. Slim nodded at Hod and went around on the other side of the truck to join Mr. Cooper. Slim's nickname suited him. He was tall, thin, angular. Where Johnny had an easy, careless attitude of good will toward men, Slim was saturnine, inturned, quiet. He seemed much older than Johnny, although actually he was several years younger. Hod was not drawn to him, while instantly he felt at ease with Johnny. " You think I can get on over there? " he asked Johnny.

" Easy," replied Johnny. " They're beggin' fer hands. The to-maters is fallin' off an' rottin' on the ground account o' they cain't git 'em picked fast enough. We'll git you on with the same man we're apickin' fer, an' you kin stay with us. Rooms is hard to find, an' three in a room'll be cheaper on all of us. We'll git the landlady to put you up a cot in with us."

" I don't want to be any trouble, but I'd sure be obliged to you for helpin' me out," Hod said.

" Hit's no trouble. First time you go over to Indianny it's kinda strangelike an' different from home. But ifen you know somebody that knows the ropes an' kin kinda put you onto things, it goes a heap better. You got any money? "

" No."

" Didn't figger you did. Well, you won't need none 'fore you kin draw yer wages. We'll stand good fer yer board an' room till you git paid, an' Ma allus packs us somethin' to take along an' eat on the way goin' back. There's plenty fer you too."

Hod hadn't thought of all these details. He had started out without a penny to his name, his one goal being to get to Indiana, pick tomatoes, and make one hundred dollars. Rather humbly he realized that he was being befriended generously by two boys whom he knew only casually, and he was beginning to understand how much simpler they were going to make things for him. He felt chagrined that they should have to assume responsibility for him, but he was grateful for their willingness to do so.

"I'll sure do my part," he told Johnny. "I can work as hard and as long as anybody, and I'll see to it that the man you work for doesn't regret hiring me. And I won't be any trouble to your land-lady, either. A cot in your room will be fine for me. I'd rather have it that way myself. I'm not lookin' for it easy over there."

"Hit's not so bad," Johnny said. "After you git used to it, the days go on all right. C'mon now, I think Cooper's 'bout ready to leave out."

They clambered into the back end of the truck and piled the heavy tarpaulins into one end to make a soft heap. Slim got in front wth Cooper, slammed the door, and the truck moved heav-ily onto the road. Hod felt a high, exultant singing in his ears and his pulse was beating like a trip hammer. Already the hundred dollars was in his pocket!

After they went through Campbellsville the way was new to him, and he sat quietly watching the country slide by. Fifty miles from the town he began to notice a distinct change in the lay of the land, the quality of the soil, and the kind and sizes of the farms. They were out of the hills and there was only a gentle, roll-ing swell which stretched off in greater distances than he had ever seen under cultivation. The soil was dark and rich-looking and the pastures were lush and velvety. He saw acres of such pastures, fenced in by neat, cross-board fences, and he saw immense barns and silos and beautiful, picture-book houses.

Johnny spoke. "Ever been up this way before?"

Hod shook his head. "Campbellsville's as far as I've ever been."

"This is good country," Johnny said. "Bluegrass country. All them big farms is rich land. A man makes a mort o' money on one o' them, I reckon."

Hod thought of Pa's stony acres, and the split rail fence around the thin little pasture, and the pitifully patched old barn. His young eyes looked far beyond the voluptuous blue-green grass, back to Piney Ridge. He let his memories linger lovingly on the ridges and the rocks and the thorns. And loyally he thought how the Pierces had come and compelled the ridges and rocks and thorns to make a home. But this was something of what he wanted

99

to see now! This was part of his dream!

It was dark when they reached Louisville and they paused only long enough for him to write a post card to Hattie. Pa would tell her, but he wanted to reach out and lay his own touch upon her. It eased a trembling in him just to write her name. He still belonged somewhere.

To Hod the sprawling city at the falls of the Ohio was only a cacophony of blurred and fantastic sounds, and a mirage of hurrying traffic and neon lights. Then they were across the broad Ohio, leaving the glow of the city behind and spearing the dark of an Indiana highway with the lances of their headlights. Around ten o'clock they reached a little town, and the truck turned off the highway onto a graveled road. It rolled to a stop in front of a shabby frame house.

"Here we are," said Johnny. "Pile out."

Hod grabbed his parcel of clothes, crawled out, and followed Johnny and Slim into the house. "You wait here," ordered Johnny, "an' I'll find Miss Sadie. She'll be out back, more'n likely."

He went off down a narrow, dark hall and Hod stood at the foot of the stairs, shifting uncomfortably from one foot to the other. Mr. Cooper came in and went silently up the stairs. Slim followed him. "Johnny'll git you fixed up," he said as he mounted, "an' I'll see you up in the room."

"Sure," Hod answered. "I'll just wait here." He spoke casually, but he was feeling forlorn and lonely. He looked around as he waited and saw that while everything in the house was worn and shabby, it was also clean. That made him feel better, somehow. It was like finding something Hattie's hand had touched. He told himself: I'll make out. I'll make out fine here.

Johnny came back down the hall and behind him came Miss Sadie. Hod liked her at once. She was a round little lump of a woman, looking friendly and comfortable. She was wiping her hands on her apron. Johnny made a vague motion toward Hod. "That's him," he said.

Miss Sadie laughed a big, easy laugh. "What's your name, son?"

Hod told her.

"Johnny says you're goin' to pick with him an' Slim, an' you want a cot in their room."

100

"Yessum. If it won't trouble you too much."

"It'll be no trouble at all, if it'll do you. Fact is, it'll have to do you. There's not another room in the house, an' I couldn't take you no other way. But if it suits you, it'll suit me."

"That'll be fine, ma'am. I'll make out all right on a cot. I'd rather be with Johnny and Slim anyhow."

"Well, we'll call it settled, then. Johnny an' Slim pays me fifteen dollars a week for their board an' room, an' I reckon I can come out ahead if you'll pay me seven. You can pay me Saturday night after you get paid. If it's handy, you can pay me for this week and next week too. Johnny said you didn't have no money so I won't press you, an' I'll take their word you're all right. It don't pay to let your bills run too long." She turned to Johnny. "Johnny, you get a cot out of that closet under the stairs an' go on up. I'll bring some sheets up in a minute."

She waddled off, and Hod and Johnny rummaged in the dark little cubbyhole until they found the folding canvas cot. They took it upstairs to the room, where Slim had already gone to bed, and set it up under the windows on one side of the room. By the light of the single hanging bulb in the center Hod could see that the room contained a double bed, a big oak dresser, and two straight chairs. Johnny moved some clothes out of one of the dresser drawers and motioned to it. "You kin have this'n fer yer things."

Hod unrolled his parcel and put his clean shirt, the extra pair of blue denim pants he had brought, and two pairs of socks in the drawer. He slipped them out of sight hastily, aware of their meagerness, and somehow ashamed. He would get him some more clothes when he got paid, he thought.

Miss Sadie knocked and came in with an armful of blankets and linens. "If you'll fold these blankets an' put 'em under you, they'll make a right good mattress," she explained. "An' you'll get clean sheets once a week an' two clean towels. The bathroom's at the end of the hall, but there's no hot water except on Saturday. Johnny, you get him up in time for breakfast in the mornin'." She turned back to Hod. "I hope you'll feel at home here, son, an' I hope you do good with your pickin'."

Hod ducked his head. "Much obliged, ma'am. I'll make out fine."

She closed the door, and Hod set to work making up his bed. Johnny went down the hall to the bathroom and Hod undressed and slipped between the cool fresh sheets. They smelled airy, like Ma's, and he pulled the top one close to make the smell a part of him.

Johnny came back, and after asking Hod, " All set? " turned off the light and shoved Slim over to crawl into bed beside him. Out the window Hod could see the Big Dipper tipping its empty cup over the trees. That would be right over the beech grove at home, he thought.

" Johnny," he whispered hesitantly after a moment.

" Yeah? "

" How far is it home? "

" 'Bout two hundred miles."

The room was quiet and Hod let the full weight of two hundred miles press him flat against the curve of the earth and spin him bleakly into solitude. He was homesick, fiercely and terribly homesick, and he felt trapped and bleeding. This was one of those places he had wanted to see. But it was just a room. Less lovely than his own room at home, with two strangers in the bed a dozen feet away. He wanted to start putting his feet down the trail to the holler. He wanted to see Ma turning down the lamps and latching the screens. He wanted to hear Duke thumping at his fleas under the porch. He wanted the curves of his own straw tick fitting easily around him. He wanted to go home!

CHAPTER TEN

THERE WAS NO DIFFICULTY the next day in getting Hod signed on as a picker. Steady pickers were so hard to get that the farmer merely nodded at Hod and told him to go with Johnny and Slim. He helped them load the truck with empty crates, and then they were driven to the twelve-acre patch that had been assigned to them.

Hod learned that a crew of three or four pickers were assigned to a certain patch at the beginning of the season and they picked it over and over until the peak had passed. Four weeks was an average season. In a large field of tomatoes grown for the canneries the vines were not staked. They spread their growth close to the ground and carpeted the field with a mass of creeping vines and fruit. Every six or seven rows, two rows of vines were pulled together so that the truck could be driven down the field. Cooper drove his truck now down the first of these roads and the boys threw the crates out on either side. Later, as they picked and filled them, they would carry the full crates back to the same road where the truck would pick them up. For each crate of tomatoes, which held about a bushel, they would be paid ten cents. The farmer checked in a load of crates from ⅋3 field, and tallied them. The boys kept a tally too. At the end of the week the tallies were checked and the farmer paid off the ⅋3 crew. The crew kept individual tallies and divided the pay between themselves on that basis.

Hod and the others were at the field by seven o'clock, but by the time they had scattered their crates and settled down to picking it was usually eight, or after. They picked steadily, bent over the low vines, until noon. Then they took an hour in which to eat and get the kinks out of their backs before going back to crouch over the vines again until five thirty. Each man picked as steadily as his cramped muscles would allow, for the amount of money coming to him on Saturday night depended entirely upon the number of crates he could fill.

The first few days in the field were days of sheer agony for Hod. Lean and wiry as he was, and accustomed as he was to hard work, the stooped position welded his muscles into armor plate. To straighten was torture; not to straighten was worse. By midafternoon he was usually working in a semiconscious paralysis of mind and body.

The first day he picked fifty bushels. Five dollars! His board and room were going to cost him a dollar a day, so he actually made four dollars. He was satisfied that night as he eased his tired back onto his bed. He knew that within a week he could step up his picking to seventy or eighty bushels. And if he could clear six dollars a day, he could have his hundred dollars by the time the peak had passed.

About the middle of the week he wrote to Hattie, giving her his address. " This leaves me fine and hoping you're the same," he said politely. Then he told her he was doing fine with his picking and he would be home in three or four weeks. Well, he might go home for three or four days, he defended as he wrote it. It was a meager, skimpy little letter but he felt better when he had written it.

He tried to write Lily Mae too. But her image got in the way. You couldn't write to Lily Mae. You could only . . . well, you could only fill yourself from the fountain of her warmth.

He made thirty-six dollars the first week, which Johnny and Slim told him was good. Better than they had done, they said. He paid Miss Sadie fourteen of it, bought some underwear, another shirt, and a pair of blue denims, and hid fifteen dollars in his dresser drawer. "Now," he said. "Now, I've got started."

Gradually his muscles became accustomed to the crouched position and he learned to ease them without losing time to stop and straighten. Doggedly he whipped his aching back down one long row after another, and he was soon keeping pace with Johnny and Slim. He didn't know whether he would ever eat another tomato or not, but, by golly, he was sure pickin' 'em!

The little town was dirty and dingy and had little to offer by way of amusement. The canning factory was the heart and center of it, and it came to life only during the canning season. Then it was a busy, humming beehive during the day, and a tired, snoring mass at night. Johnny took Hod around the square the first Saturday night he was there, but he saw little to interest him. After all he had been used to the Gap and the blue-denimed farmers all his life. This canning factory crowd which milled the streets on Saturday night was only another section of the same thing.

Week nights the boys were too tired to think of fun. But Miss Sadie had an old banjo in the front room; when Johnny learned that Hod could pick it, he bought strings for it, and each evening, before going up to their room, Hod played and sang awhile.

"Sing 'Barbry Allen,'" Johnny would say.

And Hod would plink out the tune to the long, sad ballad. Johnny never tired of it. "'Young man, I think you're dyin','" he went around humming to himself. Hod grew weary of it, but he always sang it.

The second week Hod made forty dollars. He handed Miss Sadie seven and kept three for spending money. That left thirty dollars to bank in the dresser drawer. He counted the forty-five dollars over and over, loving the feel of the bills and exulting in the possession of them. He was feeling fine. He was feeling victorious.

As he was putting the money away, Johnny came in. " Hey," he exclaimed, " how 'bout let's ride as fur as Louisville with Old Man Cooper tonight! I don't feel like goin' down home. Slim, he kin go on if he wants, but I'd ruther see the bright lights myself. Want to? "

Hod's heart leaped crazily. Want to! More than anything he wanted to! But immediately he was sobered by the thought of the money it would take.

" How much'll it cost? " he asked cautiously.

" Five dollars'll do it," Johnny assured him. " C'mon, let's go. Cooper ain't gonna wait all night. He's ready to leave out right now. "

Suddenly Hod decided. All right, it would take five dollars. He had allowed himself three for spending money the next week. He'd add two dollars to it and have one grand time in Louisville! And then he'd scrimp all next week. " Goin' just like we are? " he asked.

" Shore, ain't nobody knows us over there noways."

They were off at once. And almost before they knew it they were crossing the bridge into Louisville. Cooper let them off at the foot of the bridge on Main Street.

" This ain't the main part o' town, though," Johnny said. " Hit's further on down."

They wandered down Main to Fourth Street, and up and down Fourth, Jefferson, and Market. Not knowing, Hod thought this was all of Louisville that mattered. It was enough for him, anyhow. He was confused by the rush of traffic, the blaring street noises, the crowds of people hurrying everywhere. He clung tightly to Johnny to keep from being separated from him. He thought that if he lost Johnny he'd just curl up and die. He'd never know which way to turn.

They found a restaurant on Jefferson and had supper. Hod fearfully noted the prices on the right side of the menu. A dollar for his supper seemed terribly high to him. He wanted steak, but the price was too steep for him, so he followed Johnny's lead and ordered ham and French fries. They weren't too good, the ham

105

being stringy and tough and the French fries soggy with grease. But it was something to be eating at a swell restaurant in the city.

When they had finished their supper, they wandered out on the street again, down Jefferson to the Haymarket. The big market square entranced Hod, and he idled down one aisle and up another eying the fine vegetables and farm produce displayed in the stalls. They spent an hour in the market. Then Johnny grew restless.

" C'mon," he said, " we never come to town to spend the time in a market. C'mon, let's find us a movie or somethin'."

If Johnny knew, he didn't tell Hod that the Haymarket area was said to be one of the most vicious in the city. They hadn't gone far before a man sidled up to them. " You boys just come to town? " he asked, his voice coming at them from the corner of his mouth.

Johnny took charge. " Yeah, but we know where we're goin'."

" Well, that's O.K. Just thought if you was strangers in town I could put you wise to a few things. If you want a couple o' drinks, or something, or if you'd like to sit in on a friendly little game, I can take you right there."

" Beat it," said Johnny curtly. And the man slid away down an alley. " He's in the business," Johnny said. " You don't never want to let one o' them git his hooks into you. Ifen you do, you'll wake up in the mornin' with a knot on yer head, all yer money gone, an' a mighty bad taste in yer mouth." And Hod tucked another bit of knowledge away into a corner of his mind.

They stopped at a little theater near Fourth Street and looked at the billboards. They took their time, eying the pictures judicially. Then they decided to go in. This was Hod's first movie. From the time they stepped into the darkness his eyes were glued to the screen. It was a Western and he watched it tensely, every movement being real and personal to him. He was tied in knots when the villain stole the rancher's money and threatened his daughter. And he felt a tremendous relief when the sheriff took the trail after him. He edged forward to grip the arms of the chair when the gunfire grew rapid and the outcome was uncertain. His breath came shallow and fast as the tension mounted, and he leaned back limply when finally right was vindicated and wrong was justly punished. That was the way things should be.

106

Johnny punched him then, and he pulled himself slowly back to reality. He was loath to leave, but Johnny was already stumbling up the dark aisle. It was difficult, after having projected himself so completely into another world, to come back down to earth. Outside they blinked in the light, and stood for a moment indecisively.

" We got to decide whether we're goin' back tonight or whether we'll stay all night. Ifen we're goin' back, we'd better be gittin' on down to the bus station," Johnny observed.

" Could we stay all night? "

" Shore. I've stayed two, three times. Know right where to git a room. Hit's jist around the corner. You wanna stay? "

" I'd like to. Like to see things in the daylight. "

" Well, let's jist git a room an' then we kin scout around all we want to."

In less than ten minutes they had rented a room in the next block. Hod left all the details to Johnny. When the matter was settled, they went out on the street again and stood uncertainly on the corner.

" Reckon we could go to another show," Johnny said finally, tapping his thumb against his chin. " But I git tired settin' so long . . ."

Hod watched the flow of traffic and grew dizzy trying to count the cars. He didn't know how anyone could ever drive in such a mess. And he watched a neon sign advertising fish dinners. A fisherman pulled in a big fish on a taut line. Just as he landed it, the sign went dark. In a few seconds the fisherman started pulling in the same fish all over again. The movement intrigued Hod, and he wondered how the sign was made. But the perpetual motion wearied him, and he felt the pull and tug of the fish in his arm until it ached. It irritated him and made him restless. He shifted on his feet.

Suddenly Johnny grabbed his arm. " I got it. We'll go out to the park. The amusement park. Boy, it's jist like the Fair out there. Whyn't I think o' that sooner! Now we'll jist have a hour or two 'fore it closes, an' it ain't open on Sunday, neither. I don't know how come me to fergit it. C'mon, we'll have to ride the streetcar, an' the best I recollect it's a coupla squares down the street."

Fontaine Ferry was in a beautiful park in the west end of town.

Here the Ohio curved in the last loop of the great " S " which it traced around Louisville, and here one of the loveliest of the city's parks had been built. To Hod it was like fairyland . . . the luscious, deep green of the carefully kept lawns, the beautifully landscaped drives and walks, the sweep of the river beyond, the park lights shimmering on its rippling surface. He had been accustomed to the wild, uncontrolled beauty of the hills, but he had never before seen cultivated beauty, clipped and swept and controlled. Fleetingly he thought of the difference between a good huntin' dog and a house cat. Well, there's good in both, he thought. Depends on what you want them for.

The amusement park was off by itself, and it was all Johnny had said it would be. For an hour and a half they whooped and hollered on the roller coaster, the Ferris wheel, and the various other rides. Tickets were only ten cents then, and a dollar or two went a long way. Hod thought he had never had so much fun in his life. Johnny was a gay companion, willing to try anything, and Hod let himself go like a ten-year-old boy. He took into himself the brightness and the gay crowd and the laughter, thinking it would always be a part of him . . . a thing to remember over and over again.

Around midnight they stuffed themselves with hot dogs and ice cream and went back to their room. Hod was dog-tired and he undressed swiftly and crawled into bed. Johnny moved restlessly about the room, fiddling with the window shades, the light cord, an ash tray on the dresser, until Hod was in bed.

" Think I'll go out fer a while," he muttered then. " I ain't sleepy. If I don't git back right straight, don't worry."

" O.K.," Hod answered from the pillow, too sleepy to wonder, and Johnny clicked out the light and was gone.

When Hod awoke in the morning, Johnny was snoring on his side of the bed and his breath was faintly sour and acrid. Hattie's strictness had kept Hod pretty much at home, but he knew what morning-after liquor smelled like. Tom kept a bottle in the barn most times, and nipped along on it occasionally. Once or twice in his life Hod had seen him roll into bed pretty full, and he remembered the stale, sour smell of his breath the next day.

He wrinkled his nose now as he caught the odor from Johnny. So that's what he was going out for! Well, best let him sleep then.

He wouldn't wake of his own accord until around noon. That would give Hod a chance to get out and see something on his own.

He dressed quickly and went back to the same restaurant for breakfast. His money was running short, so he had doughnuts and coffee, which didn't fill him up but eased the emptiness in his stomach.

First he wanted to see the river. So he asked a policeman on the corner for directions. He was surprised to learn it was only three short blocks to the river front, and he coasted lazily down the hill, slipping on the cobblestones when he came to the end of the walk. An excursion boat was loading passengers for its first trip up-river. The fare was fifty cents, and the boat went as far as Ten Mile Island upstream. Hod counted his money. He had a dollar bill and a dime. Well, if he ran short he'd borrow from Johnny, or hitch a ride back to Indiana. He had to go on this boat!

The old *Island Queen* tooted its whistle one last time. The dock hands upped the gangplank, and the cumbersome, high-decked stern-wheeler backed laboriously away from the dock. Hod found a place on the deck near the wheel, where he could watch the huge paddles turn slowly, lifting their burdens of water and spilling them in a fall of sun-shattered cataracts. He was held rooted to the deck, feeling the surge of power trembling beneath him. It communicated itself to him, becoming part of him, tracing its quivering finger through his legs and up into his chest and arms. He lifted his head with sudden exaltation of his own oneness with the boat, the water, and the upward push against the current. His breath came deep out of his chest and a wave of sheer joy swept over him.

Downstream the river spread before him, widening to the Indiana shore. In his mind he traced the map. Down there, not too far, the Green slipped into the Ohio. The same Green that flowed heedlessly through the hills of home, and that gentled itself on the breast of the broad, low, flatlands around the ridge. He was sorry the trip didn't take him south, so he could ride buoyantly over the confluent flow of the Green and the Ohio. You couldn't tell one from the other, he thought. But he would know they were all there.

His questing mind then followed the stream on down the map

109

to Cairo, where it joined the Mississippi. So many times he had traced the course in his geography that he could see the twists and turns and looping bends the great river made, until finally it broadened and emptied into the sea. The sense of the mightiness of the water concourse gripped him, and made him strain his eyes to look far and hungrily into the distance. He was going to see it all someday. He felt the distance eating at him with a lonesome, homesick ache and his heart thumped painfully, until a comforting thought came to him. He would never really be far from home. For on whatever land he stood, if water from the eastern ocean touched its shore, a drop of Green River would be lapping, salted and transfused, but remaining yet unchangeably an emerald droplet that had known the hills.

That night, back in his bed at Miss Sadie's, with Johnny and Slim deeply asleep nearby, he went over the evening and morning in Louisville, and he sorted out the things he wanted to keep. The market . . . that was good. The thrill of his first movie . . . that too was good. The clear, sparkling fun of the amusement park . . . oh, yes, that was good. But the best was the river. High above everything else flowed the river . . . into his sleep and his dreams. All the rest but these he rejected.

CHAPTER ELEVEN

Tom turned the horse into the back lot and slapped his sweaty flanks to move him out of the path. He lifted the gate to swing it shut, and the pain which had been a dull ache in his side all day caught him again. He eased to it, and drew in his breath. He and old Buck had been dragging logs up from the lower woods lot, and he had fought a creeping nausea all afternoon. "Hit's the heat," he told himself. "Man gits my age he cain't stand as much as he oncet did. Jist take it easy," he warned himself. But the pain nagged at him constantly.

Now the day was over and there remained only the evening chores. Then he could stretch out on the bed and let the blessed relief of stillness have him. He went to the barn. Even in his pain it never occurred to him to neglect his chores. This is the way of a man on the ridge. He must take care of his animals. They must be brought in out of the weather; the barn must be kept clean and the water must be kept fresh. So Tom forked down the hay, doubling over the long handle and stopping when the pain took him sharply.

He ate little supper, the odor of the food making his stomach rise and fall uneasily.

"You ailin', Tom?" Hattie asked sharply.

"Don't feel none too good," he admitted. "They's a pain in my side been abotherin' me all day. Facts is, hit's been comin' an' goin' two or three days. Seems like it's sorta settled down in my right side, though, today."

"Likely you need a good physic. You go lie down an' I'll fix you one."

Tom eased himself down on the bed, his hand gently massaging his sore side. Hattie allus knowed what to do, he thought, comforted. Hattie was allus good with the sick. There was the tinkle of a spoon against glass, and then she was beside him, holding out the dose she had been mixing. He swallowed it and belched sickeningly.

"By gum, that stuff is shore bitter!" he complained. "Ifen its taste is any sign of its strength, hit orta work. Powerful enough to cure a sick mule, seems like."

"Well, ifen it's that powerful, it orta cure a sick man, then," Hattie retorted. "Git yerself straightened around there, an' let me git yer shoes offen you."

He twisted himself carefully around on the bed, and Hattie slid his shoes and socks off. Even when there was acid in her voice, there was gentleness in her hands.

It was a miserable night. Time and again the physic roused Tom, and each time he must pull himself out of the bed and walk, doubled over with pain, to the outhouse. The pain was sharp now, sharp and heavy, like hot hammers beating in his side.

In bed, between trips, he tossed restlessly and moaned constantly. Hattie built a fire in the kitchen stove and heated water. Then she wrung out hot cloths and laid them against his side. His skin was so hot that when she touched him she drew back involuntarily. It felt thin, and dry and papery, and it burned like a

111

stove lid heated by a slow fire.

When dawn finally came, gray and stealthy and languid, Hattie left Gramma with Tom and hurried down the road to Gault's. Smoke tailed out of their chimney and hung hazily in the still air. They were eating breakfast.

"Tom's sick, Gault," she said, her breath shallow and rapid. "You better go fer the doctor."

Without a word Gault rose from the table and reached for his hat. He had known Hattie a long time now. She was afraid. He could feel her fear, alive and swarming in her, coming over from her to him. If Hattie was afraid, there was need to be afraid, and he had best move in a hurry. "I'll make the best time I kin," he promised.

But it was noon before he was back with the doctor. Meanwhile Tom's suffering had increased until he was jackknifed in the bed, unable to straighten out, and he was delirious with fever. About the middle of the morning the fever went down unaccountably and the pain subsided. Sweating in his relief, Tom dropped off into a deep sleep, after assuring Hattie first: "Hit's better now. Likely the worst has passed." And Hattie went weak with relief herself.

When the doctor came she apologized for having troubled him. "He's a sight better now. He's asleepin'."

The doctor, however, waked Tom and examined him, probing around the sore side, and questioning him. Hattie, at first reassured, took fresh fright when she looked at the doctor's face. "Ain't it passed?" she asked.

The doctor shook his head. "Hattie . . . and Tom may as well hear this too . . . I'm afraid he's got a ruptured appendix. It may be that the attack has just passed, but the sudden easing of the pain and the drop in temperature are very suspicious. So suspicious, in fact, that we'd better get him to the hospital as soon as possible."

If the doctor had hit her suddenly, Hattie's stomach couldn't have sustained a harder blow. But she stiffened herself and laid a hand on Tom's shoulder. "What'll they do to him?" she wanted to know.

"Operate, more than likely."

"I don't hold with goin' under the knife," Gault spoke up

sharply. "Hit's agin nature."

The doctor waited.

"I hold with e'er thing that'll he'p Tom," Hattie said, her voice flat and level. "Ifen the doctor says this is the way it's got to be, then we'd best git busy."

The doctor smiled at her. He had seen these hillwomen face such things before, beating down their fear, stiffening themselves against an unknown danger. Hardly ever did they ask questions. When you told them what must be done they suffered it stoically and patiently. In the hospital they would sit long, long hours in the corridors. Waiting. Waiting. Never bothering nurses or doctors. Just following every move they made with their eyes. Their faces and their bodies would endure all things, but their eyes cried their fear. Tomorrow Hattie would wait in the corridor just that way. If the operation were necessary, she would sit out the long hours, neither asking nor receiving comfort. These hill people had a pride that repelled the comforting word or hand. Inside themselves they found what they needed, or else they did without.

"Make him as comfortable as you can in the back of Gault's wagon," the doctor said, "and when we get to the Gap we'll get a truck to take him on into town. I'll go ahead and make the necessary arrangements at the hospital."

When they got to the hospital, the surgeon examined Tom and confirmed the doctor's diagnosis. He told Hattie they would operate immediately. It was then, while they were preparing Tom for the operation, that she slipped out to a drugstore next door and bought paper and pencil and wrote Hod a short note. That was on Saturday.

On Monday night Miss Sadie handed him the letter as he came in from the field. When he saw it was from Hattie, he was faintly uneasy. Even at that distance he could feel Ma's iron hand. He took it up to his room and opened it. "Dear Hod," she wrote, "Tom's been took real sick and we've got him at the hospital at the county seat. The doctor says he's got to be operated on. You will have to come home and help out."

Hod looked at the words — words which snatched his hundred

113

dollars away from him — and thought numbly: I might have known! I might have known it wasn't meant for me! High and mighty notions are not for Pierces! There's no use trying to be different. There's something stronger than I am pulling at me.

He picked up the letter again, and suddenly the full import of the words struck home. Pa was sick! Hospital! Operation! What was he mooning around for! He had to get moving in a hurry! He yelled for Johnny and feverishly began throwing his clothes together.

"How's the quickest way to get home?" he asked when Johnny came running.

"Git home? Now?" Johnny said, in amazement.

"Now," said Hod. "I've just had a letter from Ma and she says Pa's bad sick and they've got him in the hospital at the county seat. I've got to get there quick!"

Miss Sadie had come panting up the stairs behind Johnny. She sat down on the edge of the bed and fanned herself with her apron while she got her breath.

"Quickest way's to take the next bus to Louisville," she said, gasping out the words. "Johnny, you run down to the store where the bus stops and find out when the next one goes through. Seems to me like there's one due pretty soon. You can change right there in the same station in Louisville," she added to Hod, "and take the bus home. What you reckon's the matter with your pa?"

"Ma didn't say. She said he was goin' to have an operation. Must be something pretty bad for him to need an operation." Hod was trying to roll his clothes into a compact bundle as he talked, but there were a few more of them now, and they made an unwieldy package which kept slipping loose.

"Here, Hod," Miss Sadie said, heaving herself up. "Let me get you a box to put them things in."

While she was gone, Hod counted his money again. Forty-three dollars, and he had eight coming to him for today's picking. He was wondering how he could get that when Johnny came back.

"Next bus comes through at seven thirty. Jist about a hour from now," he reported. "You got plenty o' time."

"Much obliged, Johnny. Say, Johnny, will you tell Carson why I've gone, and ask him to mail me the eight dollars I've got comin' for today's work?"

114

"Shore," answered Johnny, and then: "Well, wait a minnit! They ain't no sense in that. I'll give you the eight now, an' keep yore part Saturday night to pay myself back." And he peeled eight one dollar bills off the roll he carried in his pocket and handed them to Hod.

Hod took them and added them to his own small roll. "Much obliged, Johnny."

"Fergit it. I don't stand to lose nothin' by it."

Miss Sadie bustled back with a box into which she packed his clothes. Then she tied it expertly and tightly. "There," she said, "that'll hold till you get there. And here's five dollars. You're due that much back on your board this week. Better come on down to the kitchen now and eat some supper before you go."

Hod added the five dollars to the rest of his money wordlessly. He looked at Miss Sadie and there was a shine in his eyes, but there was a lump in his throat which blocked the words. She patted his arm. "Come on, now, and eat something."

Fifty-six dollars he had now. It would take three or four to get home on the bus. Say fifty dollars he had left. But Pa might be in the hospital a long time. He wished he had back the money he had spent on the new clothes, and in Louisville. He had been un-thinking for certain.

Miss Sadie and Johnny went to the store with him. They said very little but Hod felt their sympathy like a warm arm laid around his shoulder. As the bus came in sight, Miss Sadie touched his arm gently. "Hod," she said, "I'm sure sorry. I'm sorry two ways. It's bad your pa is sick, but I'm thinkin' too about what you wanted to do with your money. I know how bad you wanted to go to Louisville."

Hod looked at her quietly before he spoke. "You've been aw-fully good to me, Miss Sadie, and I'm much obliged to you. But don't you worry about what I wanted to do with that money. When there's trouble, I reckon things like that just don't seem very important. The money, it'll come in handy right now, and I only wish it was more. I'll make me another chance someday. Maybe I'll be right back up here pickin' tomatoes next summer. I've sure liked stayin' with you, Miss Sadie, and I think maybe I'd have got fat on your cookin' in another week or two."

"It'll take more'n my cookin' to fatten you up, son," she said.

" But there's the bus, now. Try not to worry, and let us hear from you how things go along."

" I will, ma'am. Good-by. Good-by, Johnny. Next time I see you I hope you've learned more of ' Barbry Allen ' than just about the young man dyin'! "

He swung himself up into the bus and was wheeled away in the night.

The trip home, with its change and two-hour wait in Louisville, was tedious. The urge for hurry was riding him hard. His mind wouldn't turn loose of Hattie's short message, and he kept seeing Tom, sick and drawn, in the hospital. What had happened inside of Tom to strike him down so quickly? He saw Tom lying still and lifeless, and the knife drawn fine down the white of his skin. He's real bad, Hattie had said. Maybe by now he was like Grampa. Nothing but the husk of a man. He shuddered away from that thought.

At the hospital, when he told them who he was, they directed him to Tom's room. Hattie was sitting stiffly in a straight chair by the window. Hod's breath sucked in when he saw her. He didn't know what he had expected, but the sight of her still, unbending figure gave him courage. Tom lay strangely quiet in the unfamiliar bed.

In whispers Hattie told him what had happened. " He was took with a pain in his stummick, Tuesday I reckon it was, an' I give him a good, big dose o' physic. But seemed like hit jist make him worse. He was jist doubled up with the hurtin', so I went for Gault. When Gault got there, Tom, he was outen his head with fever. I never seen nobody so hot an' dried out. Gault, he went as fast as he could fer the doctor, but it takened him a spell to git there an' back. Seemed like by then Tom was restin' some better. He'd quieted hisself down some, an' felt a heap cooler to tetch. But the doctor, he acted wearied like. He said it sounded to him like his appendix was busted, an' we'd have to git him in to the hospital as quick as we could. We fixed him up a bed in the back o' the wagon, an' takened him in to the Gap, an' a feller with a truck brung us on into town. They cut into him right straight, an' the doctor was right. Hit had busted wide open, an' now they say

116

they's some sort of infection. I don't rightly know what kind, but he ain't come to hisself sincet we been here."

"What's to be done now?"

"Nothin'. They done the best they could. Nothin's to do now but wait. Hit's in the Lord's hands now."

Hattie's face was still, but her hands smoothed at the blanket on Tom's bed. Like Gramma pickin' at Grampa's coverlet. Hattie was hurt through with Tom's hurt now.

So began the long vigil. Tom's body was strong and it fought valiantly, but the poison had got a mighty hold on it. For days it seemed that no power would keep the infection from having its way. In the little hospital doctors and nurses worked day and night over him, and Hattie left his side only when she was too exhausted to stay awake any longer.

Hod went on home. Someone had to take care of the stock and see to things. Irma came over and did what she could, but she couldn't leave John and her own home for long at a time. Lizzie and Becky and other neighbor women brought food almost daily, and Lizzie took the soiled clothes home with her to wash and iron. Gramma kept the house clean and cooked a little and redded up the kitchen. The menfolks came too, and put in a day in the tobacco or corn. Hod took it all into himself. The kindness. The friendliness. The brotherliness. Piney Ridge folks, he thought, are knit so close together that what is one man's suffering must needs be another's also.

The day finally came when they knew for certain that Tom would live, and it seemed to Hod that the earth turned a little truer on its axis. Not long after, he made the trip to bring Tom and Hattie home. He stopped in the office of the hospital to talk with the doctor and the superintendent. Some arrangement must be made about the tremendous bills he knew had been accumulating. The total staggered him, even though he thought he was prepared for it. A hundred and fifty dollars to the hospital, and the doctor bill was another hundred. That was the surgeon's bill. The doctor from the Gap would probably take his out in eggs and butter.

Hod knew the hospital bill had been pared down almost to the

117

costs. But it had been an expensive illness at best. He had no idea how they were ever going to pay it. The doctor and the surgeon were sitting in the office as he studied it over. All he could say, finally, was, "We'll try to pay you a little along as we go till we get it all paid."

The doctor laid a hand on his shoulder. "When Tom gets on his feet again, you'll make out. Don't fret too much about it."

Hod reached in his pocket and pulled out his small roll of bills. "Here's fifty dollars now, and I reckon we can pay a little more when the tobacco's sold."

The doctor looked a long time at the stern young face. Then, without comment, he took the money from the hands that shook only the least little bit as they offered it. He knew that this was a sacrificial offering.

CHAPTER TWELVE

Tom's recovery was slow. The poison seemed to have inched its way into every part of his system, used it ruthlessly, and left it drained of strength and vitality. For weeks he could do little more than creep around the house, breathless at the slightest effort, and complaining constantly of pain in his legs. Work of any sort was out of the question.

Hod cut the tobacco, working grimly from dark to dark, sweating to get it into the barn. If it cured rapidly enough, he could strip it and get it to the early market. The early market generally paid the best prices, and this year they had to have the best prices. Hattie's jars, on which they leaned so heavily during the winter, were half empty, because Tom's illness had come in the middle of the canning season. That meant they must buy more food from the store than usual. Tom had to have a tonic, a golden elixir of two dollars in solution, every other week. And there was always the debt to the hospital and the surgeon.

That debt walked through the days with Hod. Its harsh reality drove him brutally, dogging him and whipping him with lashing authority. It could be whittled down only a few dollars at a time, and the tremendous total laid claim to so long a stretch of time. There was nothing to do but settle the harness of debt to his back and bend himself to the aching years ahead. It never occurred to him to do anything else. It never occurred to Tom and Hattie that he should do anything else. Tom laid down the troublesome load of responsibility and Hod picked it up. It was that simple.

The economic system on the ridge was elementary. You raised tobacco and you sold it, and you made do with the money you received. What influenced the price and how it was controlled was a mystery. Some years the price was good, and you had a little more; some years the price was bad, and you pulled in your belt and made out the best you could.

But when Hod's tobacco went on the floor at the warehouse that winter, he was stunned by the price it brought. When the entire crop brought less than two hundred dollars, he stood fingering the check numbly. What was happening that good burley could sell so low?

He cashed the check and took the money home to Hattie. She would have to dole out the cash for only the absolute necessities and make it go as far as she could. One thing was certain. Nothing of that slim hoard could be spared to pay on the debt. One more year must be added to the total.

The winter was harshly interminable. Hod worked at every odd job he could get. He cut timber for the sawmill, freezing his hands and face in the bitter winds until the sawmill closed down. Then he split rails for Little Wells's lower pasture fence — split rails until he felt as if he had split his insides loose. He cut and sawed wood and carted it into town to sell. He strung a line of muskrat traps, and ran them in the frozen dawns when his body shook so hard with the cold, and his hands in the icy water turned to such rigid lumps, that he couldn't release the traps. He hunted coons at night, skinned them, and dried their pelts to be sent off along with the muskrats. He did anything and everything to make three, four, or five dollars to add to the dwindling store of cash. Everything but make moonshine, and he grimly considered that. He kept going, somehow, because his lean, gaunt tiredness was all that stood between them and hunger.

But that winter was only a beginning. A whole country was sick and the years of famine were upon the face of the earth. There were long winters of scrabbling like an animal for scraps, pride crawling before the goad of necessity. There were blistering summers of working the tomatoes, running a feverish race of energy against time. The bony spikes of Piney Ridge wore Hod's soul to a keening thinness, and hope was a thing he had forgotten.

Tom laid his hand on Hod's shoulder one day. " Boy, I ain't heared you hollerin' at that ole cliff in a time an' a time! You done fergot yer Hod Pierce? "

Hod lifted the shoulder wearily. " I've not forgotten. But there's not much use remindin' myself."

The summer he was twenty-one Hod came home from working in the tomatoes in Indiana so worn that even to himself he seemed but a shadow. His skin felt dry and drawn, and his bones were painfully sharp. Hattie was alarmed. " Hod," she said, " yer so thin you kin read a newspaper through yer ears! Didn't you have nothin' to eat up there this year? "

" Same as always," he shrugged. " I'm just tired. Don't sleep good, and I don't seem to want anything to eat much."

" Well, you jist rest up a spell, now that yer home agin."

Rest up a spell! How was he ever going to rest again! Each day that dawned prodded him on. Night brought no surcease. There was never any letup. He was racked and strung daily. The tomatoes had paid practically nothing this year, and for all his backbreaking labor he had less than forty dollars to show for the whole season. Tobacco was still to cut, although there was hardly any use cutting it, it would bring so little. Rest up a spell! What was rest?

On Friday Little Wells came by and stayed for dinner. In the summer like this they fared pretty well for food. Hattie's garden could be depended upon to dish up green beans, tomatoes, and corn throughout the season, and the table held plenty for all.

" Well, Hod, how was the tomaters this year? " asked Little Wells.

" Not much good," Hod said, shoving his chair back from the table. " Only paid four cents a bushel, an' a man can't pick enough to do much more than come out even at that price."

They went out to look over the tobacco field. " Looks purty good," said Little Wells. " Growin' tall, an' they's been enough rain, fer a wonder, this year."

120

"Much good'll come of it," said Hod bitterly. "It won't bring hardly enough to pay for loadin' it into town."

"Well, things is bound to git better sometime. I allus say, when they git so bad they cain't git no worse, they've got to take a turn fer the better. An' I'd say they cain't git no worse'n they are this year."

"I sure hope you're right!"

"Anyhow, I'm glad yer home agin. They's some folks comin' over to our place tonight fer a little practice singin', an' I thought mebbe you could come an' he'p out. We got a new songbook, an' they's some mighty good songs in it. We aim to try to learn a few 'fore meetin' tomorrer. Reckon you could come?"

"Don't know of any reason why not."

"We'll be lookin' fer you then. Any time after supper that suits."

"I'll be there."

After supper he shaved and put on a fresh shirt and walked across the pasture. It had been hot during the day, steamy and sticky hot, but, with the sun almost down, the earth was resting and cooling off. A blue haze hung over the beeches when he cut through the woods, and he loosened his shirt collar to let a wispy breeze play around his throat. The ground was springy and easy under his feet, and he wished for time to stop and sink his weary body into its darkness. He felt as if it would go on down and down, and then he could rest.

Across the clearing Little Wells's shabby frame house looked like a sodden slattern. The front porch sagged and the steps were splitting away from it. Paint peeled in scabrous patches from the siding, and there were cardboard squares in several of the windows. Hod supposed the children had broken the panes and Matildy had stuck the cardboard in to make do for the time being. But they gave the house a leering look. Matildy met him at the door and pushed the battered screen open for him.

"Here's Hod," she called to Wells, "and he's brung his gittar! I tole Wells I was hopin' you would. I ain't heared you play all summer. Some o' the others has done come, an' yer girl's asettin' over there on the davenport awaitin' fer you. Looks like you could a went by fer her."

"I didn't know she was comin'," he said, his eyes moving past Matildy into the dim room and to Lily Mae. Lily Mae had been

121

his girl for a long time now. The slow years had yoked them in the familiar pattern, and they and the ridge took the situation for granted.

As he walked across the uncarpeted floor, she made room for him beside her, but said nothing. Ferdy Jones was already there on the other side of the room, and one or two others. Gault and Becky came in soon after Hod, and Becky slipped wordlessly into a chair beside the door. She gets thinner and quieter all the time, thought Hod.

Matildy lighted the lamps and placed them around the room, and Little Wells passed out the songbooks. Lily Mae held Hod's book because he needed both hands for his guitar.

" This looks like a good 'un," said Wells, and he called out the number. When they had all found it, he cleared his throat and hummed a tone.

And they were off, feeling their way through the first line or two. You've got to live your religion every day, the song said. Not just on Sunday, but on Monday, Tuesday, Wednesday, Thursday, Friday, and Saturday. Every day. It's too fast, thought Hod, fingering the strings nimbly, trying at the same time to bring his bass in when Little Wells expected it. Lily Mae's alto beside him was strong and sure. But he never had liked a song that raced itself. To get real harmony you needed time for all the parts to blend into each other.

When they had finished, Little Wells shook his head. " Takes all the wind outen a feller, that 'un does. Let's try another'n. Ferdy, you pick one this time."

Ferdy picked one, a slower one, and they achieved a real melody this time. I'll meet you in the morning, the words promised, with a how do you do! They liked it and tried it again and again. There was a strong part for the bass in this one, and Ferdy kept motioning for Hod to bring it out.

The evening wore on through song after song. New ones, over which they stumbled awkwardly, and the old, familiar ones which brought ease from the harrying burdens of the day. " Rock of Ages." " Amazing Grace! " " Sweet Hour of Prayer." In song, they who were " weary and heavy-laden " brought their loads to " the everlasting arms," which gave them an hour of rest. Long after their voices were tired, they kept on singing, loath to put away these moments of peace, this evening of release.

But finally Gault said they must go. " Have to git up early in the mornin'," he said, " an' ifen I stay up too late at night, I'm druggy the next day." Becky nodded, and followed him out the door.

" I'll walk home with you," Hod told Lily Mae. He leaned his guitar in the corner by the davenport. " If it won't trouble you too much to bring it to meetin' tomorrow night, Wells, I'll just leave my guitar here."

" Shore, shore," Wells chuckled. " You'll likely be needin' both arms on the way home! "

Hod grinned, but made no answer. Lily Mae came through the bedroom door, with Matildy following. " Tell yer ma," Matildy was saying, " that ifen she'll sleep with a dirty sock tied around her neck, hit'll ease that sore throat o' her'n. Many's the time I've did it, an' I've never saw it fail."

" I'll tell her," promised Lily Mae. " You ready, Hod? "

They said their good nights and went out the rickety screen, down the unsteady steps, and across the trodden-down yard to the path that led to the woods. The moon was up, and until they reached the woods, it made a bright road for their feet. But in the woods it could not penetrate the heavy foliage, and all was shadow. Hod's feet knew the path so well that he needed no light to follow it, but Lily Mae stumbled when it pitched downward suddenly.

Hod steadied her with his hand on her arm. She laughed as she recovered her footing. " Reckon you'd ort to of brung yer lantern 'stid o' yer gittar! " she teased.

He let his arm rest lightly about her waist. She slipped her arm around him and they went on down the dim path. " There was a time," he said, " when you asked me to bring my guitar, remember? "

She leaned back against his arm to look up at him. " Hit's been a time an' a time sincet then, though," she said.

Hod brushed a dried blackberry cane from the way. " Mind the thorns," he said automatically, his thoughts going back and back to that night so long ago. So many long weary years ago. So many lifetimes ago. Back to when he was young and gentle and full of dreams. Had he ever dreamed? Had he ever hoped there might be a way? Had he ever been young and tireless?

Forever, it seemed to him, he had been stooped under the cruel load of necessity. He had almost forgotten there had ever been yesterday, and he had entirely given up hope there might be tomorrow! "Yes," he said, and there was a wistfulness in his voice. "Yes, that was a long time ago," and the frailty of his words on the night air sounded his renunciation. They were softly said, and, as softly, the darkness swallowed them and they were gone. And with them went the ghost of his dreams.

Arm in arm they came out of the woods, crossed the pasture, and followed the road to Lily Mae's. Hod felt no inclination to talk and he let Lily Mae's chatter fall unheeded on his ears. At the gate he took her in his arms and kissed her briefly. She pulled his head back down when he would have let her go. "Hod, why don't we git married?" she whispered.

He took her hands away, but he held them gently and swung them back and forth. "How can we?" he asked. "There's Ma and Pa and Gramma already over there dependin' on me. We couldn't set up by ourselves, and you'd not like livin' with Ma."

Lily Mae pulled her hands away. Her voice when it came was sharp. "Ifen you loved me, you'd find a way." She moved toward the house. "I'm agittin' tard o' this waitin', Hod."

He leaned against the gate and felt all his tiredness drain down to his feet. All his tiredness and his hopelessness. All right, he thought. All right. I'll try to find a way. But as he turned away into the night, he knew it was useless. He even knew that he was not too sorry it was useless.

CHAPTER THIRTEEN

The days of the autumn passed. At home things were not much different. Tom was not ill, but he was never very strong. He tired easily so that he could help only with the simplest chores. His shoulders stooped now, and his neck looked stringy and thin. Sometimes, looking at him, Hod thought he looked as old as Grampa.

Hattie too was thinner and more bent. But it was as if she had only stripped herself down for a long race. She worked constantly to make the little they had go as far as it would. She patched and turned and darned their clothes as long as they held together by a shred. She raised her own seed and made her gardens each year, and she found ways to can and preserve everything that grew in them. Nothing was wasted. Nothing was thrown away. Nothing was bought that could be done without. She seemed possessed of a holy zeal to make do, to eke out, to drink the last grim drop of poverty's threatening cup.

On Saturday nights Hod bathed, put on fresh clothes, saddled old Buck if he hadn't been worked too hard that week, and rode over to see Lily Mae. He walked if the horse was too used up. Lily Mae was still his girl. She had never once referred to that dark, summer night. It was a closed chapter for them both.

One Saturday night she met him, excited, flushed, and eager. " I was hopin' you'd git here early tonight," she said. " They's to be a housewarmin' over to Mort King's place. I'd like a heap to go."

Hod warmed to the sparkling glow on her pretty, heart-shaped face. He laid a cool hand against her cheek. "We'll go if you want to," he said. Lord knows, neither one of us has much fun, he thought.

It was a mile down the Gap road to Mort King's new house, and they could hear the sounds of the party before they came in sight of it. On the night wind the singing voices were carried far:

> " ' Skip, skip, skip to m' Lou,
> Skip, skip, skip to m' Lou,
> Skip, skip, skip to m' Lou,
> Skip to m' Lou, my darlin'. ' "

" O Hod, hurry," Lily Mae pleaded. " They're playin' ' Skip to M' Lou,' an' we'll miss out on it! "

He caught her hand and they ran the last hundred yards, joining the circle out of breath but in time to share in the game.

> " ' Lost my girl now what'll I do?
> Lost my girl now what'll I do?
> Lost my girl now what'll I do?
> Skip to m' Lou, my darlin'.

> " ' I'll get anothern, prettier, too,
> I'll get anothern, prettier, too,
> I'll get anothern, prettier, too,
> Skip to m' Lou, my darlin'. ' "

125

An old man was dragging the tune out of an ancient fiddle, and the people chanted the words and beat out the time with their hands. Skip, skip, round the circle, choose a partner. Skip, skip, round the circle, choose a partner. Skip, skip, round the circle, choose a partner. It was such a nonchalant tune; such a gay, uncaring tune. " ' I'll get anothern, prettier, too.' "

> " ' If ya can't get a redbird, a bluebird'll do,
> If ya can't get a redbird, a bluebird'll do,
> If ya can't get a redbird, a bluebird'll do,
> Skip to m' Lou, my darlin'.

> " ' Skip, skip, skip to m' Lou,
> Skip, skip, skip to m' Lou,
> Skip, skip, skip to m' Lou,
> Skip to m' Lou, my darlin'. ' "

The fiddler drained off the last notes from his strings, and the crowd stood getting their breath and fanning their hot, perspiring faces.

" All right, now," bellowed a hoarse voice from the porch, " sets in order! "

There was a scurrying as the squares formed. The fiddle whined up. The caller lifted his voice: " Salute yer lady, an' it's eight hands round! " Then the fiddle broke into the audacious tune, " Little Brown Jug."

" Oho! " someone yelled. " Bird in the cage! " Everyone laughed. The dust in the hard-packed yard shuffled up, under the prancing feet.

> " First top couple to the right

> " Circle four!

> " Bird in the cage, shut the door,

> " Bird flies out, crow flies in
> Crow flies out, bird gits a spin!

> " Swing her in the middle
> An' six hands round! "

When Hod swung Lily Mae, her long, wheat-colored hair flew out behind her, and her skirts whirled until the backs of her knees

126

gleamed white. She was a good dancer, he thought. Always sure of the figure, always ready for the next step. And she loved it! Her head was high and her foot was light, and her laugh rang out from time to time clear and sparkling above the music. He was glad she was having a good time.

"First side couple to the right

"Circle four!"

On around the square the call went until the dance was over. "Draw yer breath, now, while Clem rests his fiddle a minnit," shouted the caller, and the group dispersed to wander around the big yard. Lanterns placed on the porch and on the gateposts made light for the party. "Ain't it purty?" sighed Lily Mae. Hod squeezed her arm but made no reply. It was good to be young, to have dancing feet and a light heart. He was happier than he had been in a long time.

The sets formed and the people danced. The air grew heavy with the dust from the shuffling feet. Before the evening was over, they would all be invited in for supper and to see the inside of the house, but as long as the dancing went on, they were content outside. A barrel of sweet cider stood at one side of the yard, and the folks made frequent trips to dip out cups of the sweetish, sour liquid. Some of the men slipped away from time to time to sip furtively at a moonshine jug which was hidden out back.

During a break Hod found a bench by the fence, and he and Lily Mae gratefully sat down. "You havin' a good time?" he asked her. A lantern on a nearby post threw a feeble light over them, and made quickening shadows on her white dress. Her hair had pulled loose from its ribbons, and she was shaking the yellow mass back before retying it.

"I shore am," she said, "never no better in my life! I jist love to dance anyways! Here, you tie this here ribbon fer me, while I hold my hair back."

He took the strand of ribbon and she turned her back to him, lifting the heavy hair so he could slip the ribbon under it. Clumsily he managed to tie it in a knot and bow. The feel of the skin under his fingers prickled him and he bent, filled with a compulsion to lay his lips against that spot where the hair pulled softly away. He touched it lightly, and thought how clean and cool and sweet

127

it was. There was a faint odor of soap. He let his hands slip down over her arms.

She twisted impatiently. " Not now, Hod," she said, " yer mussin' me." And she pulled away to straighten and pat her hair into place. " Let's go on back," she added. " I promised Ferdy Jones I'd dance this next 'un with him."

Lily Mae pressed her white dress close to her waist, and smoothed its gathers over her thighs. The movement was catlike in its grace. They walked back toward the dancers.

" Come to think of it, I've not seen Corinna here tonight," Hod said.

" She ain't here. She's gittin' too heavy to git around much now. Ferdy come with Little Wells an' Matildy."

Hod surrendered Lily Mae to Ferdy's lanky arms and went to cool off with a dipper of cider. He stretched the drink out until the end of the set and then went looking for Lily Mae. The dancers were milling around, but Lily Mae wasn't among them. Ferdy was gone too, he noticed. Hod frowned. Lily Mae oughtn't to go wandering around like that with a married man. She'd get herself talked about, first thing she knew.

He roamed restlessly about the yard while another set formed and was finished, and another after that. And then he spied Lily Mae coming out of the house, cool, unruffled, and luscious in her thin white dress. He waited for her. " Where've you been? " he asked.

" I been goin' through the house," she answered. " O Hod, it's jist the purtiest thing you ever seen! You'd orta go through an' see. Hit's jist fixed up real nice! "

" Is Ferdy in there too? "

" Ferdy? Why, I don't know. I've not saw him sincet we was dancin' together. I reckon he went off to git him a drink."

Hod didn't know why he felt such relief. He laughed foolishly. He edged Lily Mae toward the gate. " C'mon," he said, " let's go home."

She flashed a quick, bright smile at him. " All right," she said, " let's."

CHAPTER FOURTEEN

They were on their way home from meeting one night when Lily Mae said to Hod: "I'm goin' over an' he'p out Corinna fer a while. I reckon you knowed she was expectin' agin, an' Ferdy says she ain't doin' so good. He's comin' after me tomorrer, an' I'll be gone till after the baby comes an' she's up an' around agin."

Hod frowned. "I don't much like for you to go 'way over there," he said.

"I know," she answered quickly, "an' I wouldn't go, only he says they cain't git nobody, an' he'll pay me five dollars a week an' my keep."

"How long you think you'll be gone all together?"

"Well, hit's three weeks 'fore the baby's due, an' I doubt she'll be up 'fore another week or two after."

"That's a pretty long time. And I can't hardly get over that far to see you very often."

"I know. We'll just have to make out. Will you miss me?"

He bent her head back, and sought her mouth. "What do you think?"

She was gone nearly two months, for Corinna was poorly for weeks after the baby was born and kept her there much longer than had first been intended. Hod didn't know how he would ache for her. She had come to be so much a part of his life that he felt lost without her. He was restless and moody, and he took to staying home nights because there was no joy in a singing or a party without her. In the two months he wasn't able to get away a single time to make the trip over to see her. He was splitting rails for Gault, and by the time the long day's work was over he couldn't find the energy to make the five-mile trip and back.

It was early winter, and the first snow had fallen before she came home. She met him at the mailbox the next day, and he thought she looked tired.

"I am tired," she said, when he questioned her. "It's enough to wear a body plumb out, cookin' an' doin' fer a family as big as

129

that 'un. Corinna, she wasn't stout enough to do nothin' fer six weeks, an' I had the washin' an' ironin' an' all the cookin' to do. She's not learned them girls o' her'n to do e'er thing, neither. They jist set there an' play all the time. 'Course I was gittin' paid fer doin' it, so I reckon I've no call to complain. But I'm plumb wore out jist the same."

"Where'll we go to talk?"

"Matt Jasper's moved an' the house is still empty. We kin go there. You kin build a fire in the fireplace so's we won't freeze to death."

They walked down the road half a mile to the shambling, unpainted old house in which Matt Jasper had housed his brood of epileptic children. Its roof sagged and its sides leaned, and it looked as if you could push it over with one good hard shove. There were a few sticks of wood in the corner of the yard, and Hod gathered an armful while Lily Mae opened the door. She sniffed when they were inside.

"This place smells somethin' awful! I don't reckon Lutie ever cleaned it."

"When would she have time with all those sick kids?" Hod asked, as he knelt and shaved kindling from a pine board with his knife. "Of all the people on the ridge that's had a hard time I've always felt sorriest for Lutie Jasper. I wonder why she ever married Matt."

"Mebbe he was the only one ever asked her."

"Well, I'd have stayed single if I'd been in her shoes!"

The fire blazed up and its warmth began to creep into the bare room. Lily Mae took off her coat and spread it before the hearth. But without it she shivered and held her hands to the fire. " Br-r-r," she said, " this place is as cold as a wedge! "

"Here," said Hod, " come sit by me and I'll hold you and you'll get warm."

She laughed, but snuggled close in his arms.

" I sure missed you," he said, nuzzling her neck and hair. " Don't ever go away and stay that long again."

"It wasn't but two months." She pressed her finger in the dimple in his chin.

" I know, but it seemed more like two years. What's that sweet-smellin' stuff? "

130

"Oh, that's jist some perfume I got awhile back. Don't it smell good?"

"I'd rather just smell your hair the way it always is. Never did like the smell of perfume."

"Well, you'll smell it purty often I reckon, 'cause I aim to use it all I want to."

"Why, sure," he said, puzzled. "I didn't mean you shouldn't use it if you wanted to. I was just sayin' I like you all right without it."

He bent to stir the fire. A shower of sparks hissed up the chimney and the chestnut logs crackled sharply. When he turned back to her she was leaning against the wall, relaxed and still in the glowing heat. Her hair was thrown back and her throat looked unbearably young and vulnerable. He was shaken by a sudden yearning and he snatched at her roughly. "Did you hear me say I'd missed you?"

"I missed you too," she said, but she was strangely unresponsive — passive and dull. "I'm jist tired," she insisted.

"Well," he replied, quoting from Hattie, "you better rest up a spell."

For several weeks they met once or twice a week at the old abandoned house. Sometimes Hod reached the house first and had a fire roaring hot by the time Lily Mae came. Other times she was waiting for him. Occasionally she brought food and they swung an old coffeepot on the crane over the fire and picnicked merrily. Times like this Hod felt close to her — almost married to her. The room closed round them tightly and shut out the cold and the harshness and the dreariness. Times like this he almost wished they *were* married. He felt happy and easy inside.

And then he had to go over to the lumber camp to work for several weeks. A fellow had to make all the money he could. When he returned he found a note from Lily Mae in the mailbox saying that she wanted to see him.

He met her at the empty house again. A deep snow lay on the ground and they both had wet feet. "When I get the fire built up we'd better take off our shoes and dry 'em," Hod said.

Lily Mae bent to unlace hers. Hod set his own shoes beside

her and rid himself of his leather jacket.

Lily Mae played with a loose button on the front of her blouse. "Hod," she said suddenly, "we're goin' to have to git married."

She said it bluntly . . . flatly . . . inevitably. Hod looked at her, startled and questioning.

"Folks are talkin'," she said. "I had a big fight with my brother Saturday, and we've not spoke sincet. He'd been ahearin' things about us meetin' here in this old house. Come right out and point-blank accused me o' carryin' on here with you! Said ever'body on the ridge was asnickerin' behind our backs — asayin' all kinds o' things!"

A deep flush burned up Hod's neck and anger flooded him.

"Who'd he say was talkin'?"

Lily Mae shrugged. "He wouldn't name e'er one person. Jist said he heared it at the mill."

Fleetingly Hod saw the familiar group of men banded around the hopper. Heard them chuckle slyly and slip their tongues over his name. Heard them roll this gossip round and round in their mouths, spitting it out like the constant stream of amber from their jaws. Saw them nudge and poke each other. That Hod, now. He's a good 'un!

His anger flamed. "I'll go down there Saturday and I'll whale the daylights out of every livin' one of 'em," he gritted between his teeth. "They'll not dare say such to me!"

"Hit wouldn't do no good," Lily Mae said, her fingers fumbling the loose button. "You've done ruint my name here on the ridge. You know as good as I do they ain't but one way to put a stop to it. Folks'll never believe e'er thing but what hit's true. But ifen we're married they'll soon hesh up!"

Hod knew this was true. Bitterly he knew it. Once a girl and a boy got married folks let bygones be bygones. But it would be the only way Lily Mae could ever hold her head up again! He felt helpless . . . trapped. He didn't want this! Everything in him protested against it. He worked his knuckles, and his eyes went back to the fire. He watched the flames lick along the logs, sending sparks shooting off onto the hearth. He shrugged. There was nothing to do but make out. He'd have to take Lily Mae home and fit her somehow into the already crowded little house. He reckoned he'd have to take her up in the loft room . . . Gramma couldn't climb those stairs. They'd have no place to be together, no way to be alone, ever. But he couldn't walk out on Hattie and Tom and Gramma. And Hattie would be frashed, and she and Lily Mae would grate on each other.

"Well," he said finally, "when do you want to do it?"

"The sooner the better."

He was silent. Lily Mae slanted her eyes at him. "They ain't no use waitin'," she said.

"I reckon you're right. I'll see if I can get someone to take us into town next week. Will that do?"

Lily Mae nodded and curled against him, comfortable now and relaxed. But the moment had gone flat for Hod. He looked down the years and saw them spinning themselves into nothingness. Already he and Lily Mae were old with the struggle, and when he looked at her again he seemed to see her bright young eyes rheumy and cast over, and her skin withered into wrinkles. He shivered. The hills had closed in and pressed him flat. The tight hills. Forever and enduring. Caught, they said harshly. Now he's caught!

On Monday he walked through the snow to Irma's, thinking to get John to drive him and Lily Mae to the county seat one day that week. Irma was happy to see him. "O Hod," she said, "I'm so glad you come! The weather's been so rough, an' we been housebound so long, yer as welcome as spring! But what in the world you doin' out in sich weather? An' jist look at yer feet! Here, set down by the fire an' take off yer shoes an' dry them feet out!"

"I came over to see John a minute," Hod answered, stretching his wet feet toward the heat. "Is he around?"

"He's jist out choppin' some firewood. He'll be in in a minnit. Is ever'body all right over home?"

"Everybody's fine, I reckon. Pa complains a lot of his back. But that's not new."

Irma shook her head and bent to put Hod's boots by the fire. "I don't believe he'll ever be no account no more. Seems like that there operation takened somethin' outen him."

John came in with an armload of wood and dropped it noisily by the fireplace. "Well, howdy, there, stranger! You ain't been

133

over in quite a spell. Been mad at us or somethin'?"

"Just busy. John, are you aimin' to go in to town any day this week?"

"Hadn't aimed to. Why? You wantin' to go?"

"Yes." He paused before going on. The words came hardly. "Lily Mae and I are goin' to get married, and I thought maybe you'd drive us in to the county seat to get the license."

Irma's hand flew to her mouth. "Oh, no! Hod, no!"

He looked at her in surprise. "You surely knew we'd get married sometime, didn't you? As long as we've been goin' together?"

"No!" she shot back at him sharply. And then, "John, ifen you don't tell him, I will!"

John was nervously fingering his chin. "I'd think about that a long time if I was you, Hod. You'll have to stay married a purty good while."

"Well, I know that! What in the devil's the matter with you two? I've been goin' with Lily Mae off and on for over four years, and nobody's objected before!"

"You ain't talked about marryin' her before!" Irma cried.

Hod looked at his feet and wiggled one toe, up and down . . . up and down. "Well," he said, "I am now."

"Hod," John put in, "I'd make mighty shore about things 'fore I stuck my neck out."

"What do you mean?"

"He means," Irma flared, "he means that ever'body on the ridge knows she's been acarryin' on with Ferdy Jones fer ever so long! That's what he means!"

"Ferdy Jones! Why, you're crazy! He's old enough to be her pa, an' besides, he's married!"

"As if that made any difference to Lily Mae! Him bein' married wouldn't stop her none!"

"How do you know about this?"

"Hit's common talk, Hod. Hit was goin' on even before she went over to take keer o' Corinna. Reckon that's why she went. He's give her presents, an' I reckon might' nigh ever'body's seen 'em one time or another out awalkin' or atalkin' together. Corinna knows, now, too."

Hod was stunned. He remembered the perfume. "I don't understand," he said. "I never dreamed there was anyone else."

"There's allus been somebody else," Irma cried. "You never thought she was true to you, did you? Why, ever' summer you been up in Indianny they's been a different one she's been talkin' to! Jist about ever' man on the ridge by this time! She ain't no idee of bein' true!"

"Why didn't somebody tell me?" he said angrily.

John spoke, kindly. "Hod, I reckon a man's allus the last to hear the truth about somethin' like this. Didn't nobody have the heart to tell you."

"Irma," Hod pleaded, "you're not just tellin' me this because you don't like her, are you? I know you never did like Lily Mae much."

Irma's eyes softened and she reached a gentle hand to his arm. "Hod," she said, "hit's true I never liked her overmuch, but I'm yer sister, an' we growed up together. You he'ped me an' John git married, an' you kin believe me, no matter how much I didn't like her, that wouldn't stand in the way ifen she was the decent girl you thought she was. But ever' word I've said is true, an' John'll back me up, an' half a dozen others knows the same things we do. I'm only wantin' yer happiness, an' how fur could you go toward findin' it with a girl that never knowed the meanin' o' bein' true to nobody."

Hod laughed shortly. "I've sure been a blind fool." He rose and walked to the window, looking bleakly out at the stainless snow. It was ludicrously out of place. He scratched idly on the frosted glass and thought of Lily Mae! Remembered all the times they had laughed and sung and walked the ridge together. Remembered her wheat hair that lay so softly under his hand. Her red, red mouth that lifted so eagerly to his. Remembered, and then let the bitter ugliness shoot through him. Lily Mae! Why, she was his girl! Surely she was his girl!

He swung away from the window. "You think, then, this is Ferdy's doin'?" he asked Irma.

"I know so. Ifen you marry her you'll fall right into the trap they've set fer you. She even made her brags to Corinna that she could allus git you to marry her an' take keer of her."

"We'll see about that!" And he was on his feet, struggling into his coat.

"Where you goin'?"

135

"Does it make any difference?" Slamming the door fiercely he went out into the blowing snow, and Irma and John looked at each other helplessly. Irma began to cry.

"Somebody had to tell him," she sobbed. "He had to know, but I wish it hadn't been me had to hurt him."

John comforted her. "He'll take it better from you than from anybody else. Don't fret, now. His pride's hurt, but his heart ain't broke. Hod's got too much sense to grieve long. An' even if he does, it's better to grieve now than later. She'd a really broke him up sometime ifen he'd married her."

Hod went straight to Lily Mae's home. She was sewing quilt pieces when the wind blew him in, and she screamed at him, "Shut the door!"

"Get your coat on," he said bluntly, "and come outside with me."

"Have you lost yer mind?" she asked, amazed. "Hit ain't fit weather to git out in! Take yer things off an' set here by the fire."

"I said get your coat on and come outside with me! There's something we've got to talk about!"

She looked at him quickly, and a strange, furtive look hooded her face. Without further argument, she put her coat on and went out with him. They walked down the road toward the mailboxes. He stopped when they were out of sight of the house and faced her. "You've got Ferdy's perfume on again, haven't you?"

"What do you mean?"

"What's been goin' on between you and Ferdy Jones?"

She jerked her head up, startled. "Nothin', Hod. Not e'er thing! I swear it!"

"You're lyin'!" and his voice was a growl between his teeth. He took her by the shoulders and shook her until her hair flew wildly around her head.

"Stop it!" she screamed at him, clawing at his hands. "You stop it, Hod Pierce!"

"Quit lyin' to me, then! Tell me what's been goin' on between you and Ferdy Jones!"

"What's been goin' on between me an' Ferdy Jones is my business! An' don't you lay yer hands on me agin!"

"It's my business too, when you try to pull the wool over my

136

eyes! Have you been carryin' on with Ferdy?"

She was stubbornly silent. She bent and scooped up a handful of snow, and stuck her red tongue in it, like a child being deliberately insolent.

Hod gritted his teeth. "If you don't answer me, I swear I'll shake you till every bone in your body comes apart!" He slapped the snow from her hand, and swung her roughly around toward him. "Answer me! And don't you lie to me again!"

She spat the words in his face. "Yes! Now are you satisfied?"

His hands fell limply to his sides. "That's all I wanted to know," he said. He looked at her and let the acid of her lush ripeness eat itself into him. His girl. Ferdy's girl! Anybody's girl! He could have killed her! She gave him back look for look, and even now her eyes were cold — disbelieving. Abruptly he turned and walked away, leaving dragging marks in the snow. As far as Lily Mae could see him down the road, he hunched into the wind, and his boots raised a small snowstorm behind him. He never once looked back.

Shortly after, he heard that she had gone to Louisville to stay with her sister and work. Hattie was the one who told him. "I reckon Lily Mae'll do right good in Louisville. She's a fair hand to work when she's a mind to."

Hod was oiling a stiff harness strap by the kitchen stove. He jerked the strap into an angry knot.

"Didn't you hear me, Hod?"

"Yes."

And he put the grease away, carefully, and went out to the barn where only the animals could see his tight mouth and his burnt-out eyes. He walked like an old man as he went down the path.

CHAPTER FIFTEEN

Hod never knew how he got through the rest of that winter. He only know that all the days ached with him and wept gray tears for weeks at a time. All Piney Ridge was sodden and mired in mud, and he let himself down into his own pit of despair. Spring came, and he went through the motions of planting the tobacco, and another summer soon bore down upon the leafy green. He worked now, not only to make a tobacco crop, but to forget. If he could drive his body through enough merciless hours, he could sleep at night. Otherwise he would lie awake, tormented and haunted, and, above all, empty.

After the tobacco was in the barn in the early fall, he turned to other tasks. He was plowing the field next to the road one day, thinking he would put the corn patch there next spring, when Gault came by.

"Howdy, Hod."

"Howdy, Gault. Whoa, Buck! Whoa there — whoa, I said! How's everything, Gault? Whoa, Buck! Whoa! You dad-blamed, consarned, doggoned idiot, I said whoa!"

"Purty good, I reckon. How's Tom?"

"About the same. He does most of the chores around the place and feeds and takes care of the milkin', but I doubt he'll ever be real stout again."

Gault shook his head. "I allus said I'd never go under the knife. Did the Lord aim fer me to do without some o' my innards, he wouldn't never have give 'em to me in the first place. They takened somethin' outen Tom when they cut into him, an' hit'll never come back."

Hod made no reply. He plucked a stem from a dry vine clambering over the fence and stuck it in his mouth. Tom and Hattie halfway believed the same thing, and he knew they used it to excuse Tom's failure to pick up in strength.

"I hear they're puttin' through a W.P.A. projeck to gravel the section roads," Gault went on. "Thought you might like to know."

Hod wrapped the lines around the plow handle as if he would walk out of the field at once. "Where do you see about gettin' on?" he asked.

"They got a office in the county seat. Wells was in there yesterday an' he said they was a line plumb up to the corner, folks waitin' to sign up. The talk is they're tryin' to put them that needs it worst to work first. I told Becky they wasn't nobody needed it worse'n you, an' I aimed to name it to you first off."

At eight o'clock the next morning Hod was in line. He had walked to the Gap that evening, and from there had hitched a ride to the county seat and had spent the night in the bus station.

The line moved along at a snail's pace, and it was the middle of the afternoon before he was inside the door. Hunger gnawed at him and his head had begun to ache, but he didn't dare leave the line long enough to eat. He might have asked someone to bring him something, but there was only a dime in his pocket and pride forbade his asking a stranger to buy cheese and crackers to bring to him, and he knew of nothing else he could buy for ten cents.

When finally it was his turn to be interviewed, he was swaying on his feet and he sat down suddenly, letting the flood of relief stream through him. The interviewer was a tired man who spent his days behind this desk, asking questions, filling out papers, hiding himself behind the impersonality of red tape. He snapped the questions at Hod. Name. Address. Age. How many in family? Ages. How many employed? Family income last year? What type of work applying for? Qualifications. Education. References. He was impatient with Hod's hesitant replies. How could he know that to the proud hill heart this probing into personal areas was like baring a quivering nerve? Hod felt as if he was begging for alms as the cold, disinterested voice droned on. He was asking for work, not relief! That the man spent his days asking these questions of hundreds of people, and that the replies had no meaning for him except to fill in the proper places on the innumerable forms, Hod never thought. He only knew that he felt a sense of outraged self-esteem and that this man was the instrument which heckled him.

"That's all," the man said finally. "You'll be notified. Next!"

"Does that mean I get the job, mister?"

"It means you'll be notified whether or not your application is approved. If your application is approved, you'll be assigned to a public works project."

"Much obliged," and Hod was out the door, surging with the release of his pent-up emotions. That was that! How in the world a man could hold his head up if he had to go through all that every time he needed a job he didn't know! It made a man feel like poor white trash. Like nothing human. But it was over, and if he was lucky he'd have steady work before long, and a pay envelope regular. He hadn't known he could feel so light and happy! If

139

he could get a regular job, the whole world would be different. They could all have some new clothes and something to eat besides beans and fat back. He could get that plow he saw in the mail order, and, by golly, he'd have him a new guitar! He could pay on the debt regular, and sometime he'd even get it all paid off. A regular job! What a wonderful sound it had!

He saw a familiar figure down the street ahead of him. There was Irma! He lengthened his stride to catch up with her. " Hello there," he hailed her. " Where have you been? "

" Why, Hod," she said, jumping a little, " you skeered me! I should be askin' you where you been! Hit's been so long sincet I seen you! Ever' time I been over home lately you been off the place somewhere."

" It takes a lot of rustlin' these days to keep the wolf from the door," he answered.

" I know it's the truth. What you doin' in town? "

" I just put in for a job on one of those W.P.A. projects. They say they're goin' to gravel all the county roads and build new bridges, and I figured I could swing a pick and shovel as well as the next one. Don't know whether I'll get on or not. He said they'd let me know."

" I shore hope you do, Hod. You've had it hard long enough. An' don't nobody deserve to have one o' them jobs more'n you do. I dunno what Ma an' Pa'd do without you. Hod, do you ever think Pa could do more'n he lets on? Sometimes I think he's jist content not to have to weary no more."

Hod's mouth tightened. " I don't know. I used to look for him to take hold again, but I've quit expectin' it now. And it doesn't help to fret about it. He's the way he is, and there's nothin' to be done about it."

" Well, it ain't right, an' I *do* fret about it. Hit ain't fair to you." Irma shifted her packages and clutched her purse tighter. " Whyn't you come go home with us an' stay the night? They's goin' to be a pie supper at Blain's Chapel tonight an' a spellin' bee, an' we'll all go an' have us a big ole time. C'mon. You ain't been over to see us in a coon's age."

Hod pondered the question a moment. " Believe I will," he decided. " The folks can make out another night, I reckon." Somehow it was fitting that this hopeful day should hold the promise

140

of a happy night.

"Good fer you," said Irma. "The car's parked down in front of the hardware, an' I reckon John's ready to leave out by now."

They set off down the street, and Hod took most of her packages out of her arms. "You been buyin' out the town, looks like," he teased.

"John's goin' to think so too," she laughed. Then she glanced at him cornerwise. "Reckon you've heared Lily Mae's come home."

So. She was back. "No," he answered slowly. "No . . . I've not heard. When did she get back?"

"One day last week." Irma hesitated and then went on. "Oh, she's been tellin' it big about her fine boy friends she had up there. One, she said, had a big Buick car an' takened her out in it ever' night!"

"That," said Hod, "should have pleased her right well."

"You don't act like it troubles you none."

"It doesn't."

Irma smiled at him. The brief exchange of words had told her exactly what she wanted to know. He didn't mean to take things up with Lily Mae where they had left off. He was through.

John's old Model T rested its flat nose against the hitching rail in front of the hardware, and John was waiting comfortably with his feet propped up on the door. He and Hod exchanged greetings. "Hod's goin' home with us," Irma explained, "an' we're all goin' to the pie supper tonight."

"Now that's fine," said John. He moved over and let the two of them in.

Irma's home was still the little two-room tenant house in which she and John had started out. But it was a sweet home, neat as a pin, with bright, clean curtains at the windows and gay, plaited rugs on the floor. Hod loved it because it had such an air-swept, uncluttered look and he thought that Irma must be a fine wife for John. They had lost two babies, both stillborn, but while they had grieved over the tiny, lifeless forms, they had not let it embitter them. It was Irma's way to believe that all things happened for the best, and she had dried her tears after burying her babies and had taken up her life again, glad for John's love, her pretty house, and the fact that in a time of want they had enough and to spare.

141

Folks were already gathering when they reached the chapel that night, and the pies, disguised in gayly decorated boxes, were lined up on a long table at the back of the room.

Soon the chapel was full to crowding and seats were getting scarce. It was almost time for the spelling bee to commence when Lily Mae came in, late, with her mother and Matildy and Little Wells. Hod saw her immediately. She went down the center aisle carrying her box, her eyes searching the room as boldly as ever. She had on a new dress, he saw — a tight-fitting blue silk of some sort. When she saw Hod, she met his eyes full, and then, tilting her chin, she tossed her heavy hair back with the old familiar gesture.

Hod let the spasm of pain which started in his tightly knotted chest run thickly down into his arms and legs. How could he not hurt over this girl who had taken so much of him? Why, every move she made was as known to him as if he had made it himself, so much of him had become a part of her. He saw her clearly. Cheap. Bold. Vulgar. He didn't miss any of that, and well he knew how shameless she was too. But she was part of him and he couldn't tear her out. He turned away, while the pain still ripped through him.

The preacher was talking now, explaining about the spelling bee. And Hod tried to listen though his mind felt numb. John and Little Wells were elected to choose sides. No one was omitted from the choosing, from the oldest down to the youngest, and as they were chosen they lined up along the opposite walls of the building. The preacher, who was to give out the words, took his place behind the table, on which three spelling books were arranged.

Word after word was given out, down both lines, with very few missing on the first round. The next round the words were harder, although they were still fairly simple. A few more persons took their seats. The next round there was a perceptible tightening up and the little fellows began to fall out. They had known from the beginning they wouldn't last long, but it had been fun to try.

The lines were only half as long now. The words flew from one side of the room to the other. " Fascination." " Minimum." " Embargo." " Cynical." One by one the weeding out went on. The excitement grew and the tension mounted, and there were cheers when favorites successfully hurdled a particularly hard word, or moans when they stumbled and failed. Irma went down on " ecstatic." Matildy caught the word on the rebound and took it in her stride. A moment later she was down on " dubious."

There were only four left standing now . . . John, Little Wells, Hod, and a man from Pebbly. Faster and faster the words flew. The preacher was down to the hardest words of all now. The words in a spelling bee had no reality for the people who spelled them. They could spell words of whose meaning they had not the vaguest idea, and which, in a hundred years they would not have used. Words like " heptagonal," " interdependent," " managerial," and " parsimonious." Little Wells went down on that one. Hod picked it up. Wells had used an " e," so he tried it with an " i." " Correct," said the preacher. The man from Pebbly went down on " admonition." John skimmed through it easily. Now only he and Hod stood facing each other. By golly, Hod thought, he's good! I'm goin' to lose me a spellin' bee if I don't look out. He tightened up carefully. But so did John and the match went on. Finally the preacher said: " We've still got to have the pie supper, and it's gettin' late. Suppose I admit I can't spell you men down, and suppose you all call it a draw between you. Will that suit? "

They agreed it would suit and got a big hand from the audience as they took their seats. Hod felt a moment of pride that the two best spellers on the ridge were in the family.

The preacher was talking again. " And now, friends, we're going to auction off the pies. We've got Uncle Billy Barton, from down at the Gap, to do the selling, and you all know that he's the best auctioneer outside of a tobacco warehouse. And the money from this pie supper is going to buy new songbooks for the church. So let's not let a single pie go for less than a dollar. There's some mighty good pies lined up on this table, and any one of them is worth a dollar, to say nothing of getting to eat it with the lovely young lady that made it. Uncle Billy, are you ready?"

" Ready an' rarin' to go," said the sprightly, white-haired little man. " Now, folks, we're goin' to start with this here red, white, an' blue box. This here is the dad-blamedest most patriotic box you ever seen an' it's yer bounden duty to start the biddin' high. Now, what am I offered fer this artistic creation? Twenty-five cents, I hear from the redheaded young man on the back row. Twenty-five . . . twenty-five . . . twenty-five-five-five! Who'll

143

make it thirty? Thirty cents, says the gent in the middle. Thirty cents I'm bid. Who'll make it forty? Thirty . . . thirty . . . thirty . . . Who'll make it forty? Forty cents from the redhead. Who'll make it fifty? "

The bidding went on up, ten cents at a time, until it reached a dollar and a quarter. The redheaded boy then went his blushing way up the aisle to pay for his girl's pie. The hypnotic singsong chant of the auctioneer rapidly disposed of one pie after another. Most of them sold for around a dollar. Occasionally there was a flurry of excitement when a group of fellows ganged up on a boy and ran the pie of his girl up to two or three dollars. It was a point of honor, then, for the boy to stick it out. Manfully he would stay with the bidding until his last cent and all he could borrow was gone. Lord, how young they are, Hod thought. Was I ever that young? His twenty-second birthday had passed in July.

Then Lily Mae's pie went up. Hod knew it by the little bunch of artificial roses she always tied into the knot of ribbon around the box. The hurt, which had eased in the excitement of the spelling bee, clutched him again. Used to be, he always bought that pie. He remembered the first time. He'd had two dollars saved up, and Pa had given him another. He'd been scared to death it wouldn't be enough. That must have been the winter he was eighteen. It had been enough, and he'd always managed to get that pie one way or another. Tonight the boys eyed him expectantly when the artificial roses bloomed in the auctioneer's hand. But Hod sat still.

Lily Mae's profile was carved from stone when he looked at her across the room. Feeling his eyes, she turned to look at him. He held that look steadily, and it was she who looked away first. But the pain flickered through his chest. Lily Mae! Lily Mae! And then it was that Hod learned another truth. There are some things, hurt though they may, that you cannot amputate. Instead you must take them, hurt and all, into yourself, and close them over with the dignity of your manhood. You have done these things. You have known them and felt them. They are part of you now, forever and enduring. You cannot put them away and deny them. The best you can do is let them heal, scarred and roughened, inside of you. In time the jagged edges of the gash would grow together. But the scar was there, for always.

144

The bidding on Lily Mae's pie was listless, and it was knocked down finally to a boy from the Gap. Irrelevantly, Hod thought the roses looked a little faded. Lily Mae had better buy a new bunch pretty soon.

CHAPTER SIXTEEN

DURING THE MONTHS THAT FOLLOWED the mailbox became very important to Hod. Daily he walked down to the crossroads and looked hopefully inside the box. He didn't know when he could logically expect the notice from the office, but each day he would tell himself, today it might come. Each day he would pull the little hinged door down, wishing some magic would make it be there. The box remained empty for so long that finally the edge wore off his eagerness, and while he continued to make his regular trip to the crossroads, the emptiness of the box became a part of the routine.

The circle of time completed the cycle of seasons and brought tobacco-planting time again, and his days were crowded and full. The impregnation of the earth in her period of fertility makes a ceaseless demand upon men who walk behind a plow. The days lengthened until Hod could feel them yawn and stretch; the sky bent a cerulean hood over the world; the soil swelled in gestation and cracked its sides with new life. The winter was past and " the time of the singing of birds " was come.

One day the white envelope was in the mailbox. It looked alien and lonely lying there, and for a moment Hod couldn't remember its significance. Realization dawned slowly, and he reached for it with a shaking hand. Let it be a job, he prayed. Please let it be a job. He opened the letter, searching quickly for the important news. " Your application has been approved . . . you have been assigned to . . . report May 10, to . . ." There it was! In black and white there it was! A job! Regular pay check! Real money! It was all there on the paper. Hod saw it through a mist, and only then did he know how much it had meant to him to have a door opened even to such a stingy release from anxiety. Now, he thought jubilantly, now we'll have it better. Now, we'll be people again. Now, things are going to be different. He felt mighty and strong, and he walked the road home with free, long strides.

Watt Jones was foreman of the project to which Hod was assigned. They were putting in new culverts and bridges on the pike between the Gap and Campbellsville, filling in the wheel-eaten holes and resurfacing the whole pike. Watt looked at Hod's paper when he reported that Monday morning, grunted, and made a notation on his payroll sheet.

"Can you mix cement?" he asked.

"Never have," Hod answered, "but I can try."

"Humph! Well, that's all there is for you to do right now. Go on down the road there until you come to a bunch of men workin' this side the culvert. They orta be mixin' a batch. Tell one of 'em I said they was to let you help."

Hod did as he was told, and when he relayed the foreman's message, one of the men handed him a big shovel. Two men stood on either side of one end of the long frame that held the mixture, and Hod and the third man were at the other end. He noticed how they used their shovels to stir and mix and push the cement, and after a moment he bent over his own shovel and fell into the rhythm of pushing, heaving, and pulling. It was hard work, and before long his muscles felt the drag of the heavy shovel, but he was glad of the ache in his shoulders. It reminded him that he was being paid thirty cents an hour. Thirty cents an hour, eight hours a day, and his notice said he was entitled to fifteen days' work each month. He had added the total a hundred times. There would be thirty-six dollars each month, and thirty-six dollars was more that they had sometimes had in three months. He could afford to ache for that!

For several months he mixed cement, pushed a wheelbarrow, filled cuts, and smoothed gravel. Then one day the foreman called him into the shanty that served him as office. "Hod," he said, "you reckon you could handle the timekeeper's job?"

"If Masters could handle it, I can," Hod said.

"Well, Masters is quittin' this week. Got him another job over at the county seat, and if you want to, you can take a try at it. I been watchin' you. You're dependable and you've got a head on your shoulders. I've seen you more'n once figure out the best way to do a piece of work. You don't loaf on the job and you ain't just tryin' to put in eight hours a day. Timekeepin' will pay you forty cents an hour, and I reckon you can use the extra cash as well as the next one."

So Hod became timekeeper. Each morning he took his lists and made the rounds of the crews scattered up and down the road, checking each man on the list. He wasn't pushed for time, so he frequently helped out the men at work.

He liked to work with his hands — to make things, to handle tools, to put things together. He liked the feel of things in his hands. Something outside came over into him through his hands. A hoe handle made him feel the warm and living earth. The pull of a plow through his hands into his shoulders made him aware of life, pulsing and growing and moving on. If he could touch a thing, and feel its texture — its smoothness or roughness, its thinness or thickness, its grain or pile — he got a knowledge of it that was surer than his mind could give him. And now when he hefted these tools the roadmen used, his hands tested their fineness and sharpness clear up into his mind.

Watt Jones watched him sometimes. That boy would make a good toolman, he thought. So he gave over to Hod the responsibility for the care of tools for the whole outfit. At first this applied only to the commoner tools, the ones the laborers used, checked in and out daily. These Hod worked over, keeping them in fine shape, loving even their coarse edges and heavy bulk. They were things to use — things for a man to put his hand to. They deserved care.

Later, some of the engineers, seeing his way with their instruments, began to let him make minor adjustments and repairs for them. They learned that if a thing had a gadget on it, Hod could set his fingers to probing its inner secrets and make it work. Screws, knobs, hinges, edges, came to life under those searching, patient fingers.

Now he made fifty cents an hour. The summer went by, and the winter, and then another summer. His job on the road project held.

Things were easier at home now too. Hattie, who was always a good manager, did wonders with the cash money. Little by little she replaced their worn clothing, added a few luxuries to their food, and even saw to it that Hod got his new guitar. It sat in the corner most of the time, for Hod was too tired to touch it often, but it was there, a symbol of their progress. The debt had been paid out too. In many ways, life was better.

But as the time went by and Hod took stock, he saw the job for what it was. W.P.A. Temporary. It wasn't doing anything more than stopping the gap. He had not been able to accumulate anything for himself. He had a dollar or two in his blue jeans most of the time, but he could never get ahead. It took all he could pour into Hattie's asking hands to keep them going. Where was the end of it? He saw that he had no identity except that of Joseph, the opener of the storehouse. And a man had to be more than that. However commendable it was for him to do his duty, duty was slim fare as a daily diet.

His resentment flared at times, but not to the point of prodding him to do anything else. And now he was twenty-five.

One day in the late fall, when there was just enough frost in the air to make the beech-log fire feel good, Hod was sitting straddle of a chair by the fireplace when Hattie passed between him and the window. He straightened with a jerk. There was an unmistakable swelling to her silhouette. He flung the chair from him and plunged violently out of the house. No! Not that! Not now! It can't be! Not after all this time! That ought to be all past for them! Why, Ma must be . . . He counted up and with a start he realized that Hattie was only forty-four. He had always thought of her as old. He felt sick, suddenly tired and very discouraged. He flung himself down the road, not knowing where he was going and not caring. He had to get away. I must be blind, he thought. All these years he's been taking it easy around here! And all the sweating I've been doing while he lies around and gets another mouth for me to feed! Another back for me to keep warm! Another ten years on the W.P.A.! I will not. *I will not!* He gets his kids. He can take care of them. I will not. By heaven, I will not, I swear!

He turned off the road through the woods and came to the edge of the hollow. Where the path pitched steeply down the hill, he sat down and leaned wearily against a tree. A hundred drums beat in his head. His lips felt sore and his eyes were dry and hot. Wretchedness flowed its bitter way through his whole body, its gall lapping at the edges of his very soul.

148

Suddenly he twisted away from the tree and stretched his lean frame against the uncomforting breast of the earth. Sobs racked his body, and one clenched fist pounded the rhythm of his pain into the stony ground. The soil soaked up the blood from his cuts, and he never knew that he bled. "God," he cried, beating the prayer into the earth. "God, I've got to get away from here. I've got to get out! I've got to! Let there be a way. Please, please let there be a way!"

CHAPTER SEVENTEEN

Hattie's time came in April. She got up that morning and did the usual tasks, built the fire, made the bread and the coffee. She asked no extra help. But from the way she caught her breath from time to time and bent over to hold to something, Hod knew it was upon her. And Tom was not there for breakfast, so he knew she had sent him to get Becky or Lizzie. This was one of the days Hod was not working and he had expected to mend the pasture fence. "You want me to stay around for a while?" he asked.

She shook her head, and he saw that her mouth was set. "I'll make out," she said. "Tom'll be back in a little. I told him to git Lizzie if he could. She don't never git flustered. You could put some water on to heat in the biggest kittle, an' build up the fire good 'fore you go out."

When he returned from the spring, Hattie was in bed, and from the kitchen he could hear her smothered moans. He set his own teeth and went to the back door to look down the road. He wished they would hurry.

Restlessly he built up the fire again and put the water on in the biggest kettle he could find. Then, noticing the confusion of breakfast dishes, he set to work to redd them up. His hands felt awkward in the unfamiliar task, and he was conscious constantly of Hattie in the bedroom, but he kept his mind firmly on what he was doing. The dishes, then the milk things. Or had anyone milked yet? Yes, the pails were dirty. She must have had Pa milk before he went.

A broken cry from the bedroom brought him running to the door. "Ma? Ma, you all right?"

149

"Go away, Hod. Git on away. I'm all right. See if they're comin'."

He went again to the door. This time he could see the wagon far down the road. Finally they were coming! He called through the door: "They're comin'. They're at the bend in the road now." And he went out to wait at the gate for them.

"You better hurry," he said curtly, when they drove up.

"Is she bad?" asked Lizzie, heaving herself over the wheel to the ground.

"I don't know," answered Hod, "but she's been takin' on a right smart, an' she's been askin' for you."

"She's likely got a good while yit," said Lizzie, but she hurried toward the house. "They ain't none of it easy."

Tom spoke. "I'll drive around an' unhitch," he said.

"I'll do it."

"Well, I kin . . ." Tom's voice trailed off, and he looked at Hod helplessly.

"It's hard on you, isn't it?" Hod's young, thin voice said. "Powerfully hard on you to stand around and listen to what's goin' on in there? Well, you had your part in it. Now get in there and see if you can help!"

There was no effort to veil the contempt in his voice, and Tom was small and helpless before it. Tom stood a moment, as if he would say something, and then he turned and walked toward the house.

Hod jerked the horse around the house. Let him help birth it, he thought. Let him stay there and listen every time she yells. Let him pay a little too!

The day wore on. It seemed to Hod an awfully long time. When he went in that night to look at his new sister he felt no tenderness. He looked at the red, wrinkled little face with no expression on his own. "She looks like a tomato," he said, and walked away.

The birth of the baby broke the straps of the harness Hod had worn for so long. Something that had been warm and gentle in his feeling toward Hattie and Tom hardened and iced in his veins. He had accepted the frustration of his deepest wants most of his

150

life as a matter of course. He had picked up the burden of caring for the family as his duty, not expecting to escape it. He had yearned and dreamed, but he had not particularly resented the fact that his yearnings and his dreams must be put away. But this was different. This ate at him and chafed him, and he was moody and silent through the days. This they had no right to do to him.

On a Sunday in midsummer Hod went to an all-day singing over on the next ridge. He felt listless about the walk over there, but he liked to sing, and maybe he'd feel better if he went.

The singing began about ten o'clock, the leader starting with some of the familiar songs. Everyone sang. The volume of sound that rose to the rafters of the little whitewashed chapel would have amazed a city preacher, accustomed only to the halfhearted efforts of his congregation. This was a noisy, joyous, hearty, lifting up of voices.

On and on the singing went, alternating between the old and the familiar and the new and untried. When one leader grew tired, another took his place. And special numbers by duets, trios, and quartets were occasionally interspersed. The people seemed never to tire. An all-day singing on the ridge was really an all-day singing!

When they stopped for the picnic dinner and Hod followed the crowd outside, he was delighted to see Johnny Knight squatting on his haunches under a big tree.

"Hi, there, Johnny," he called. "Where've you been keepin' yourself all this time? I've not seen you for a coon's age!"

"Oh, I been around," Johnny said nonchalantly. "Been workin' first one place then another. Not doin' much good no place, though. What you been doin'?"

"I've been workin' on the road project for three years now."

"Pretty hard work, ain't it?"

"Not too hard. Don't pay much, though."

They talked of other things and finally the conversation came around to the new conscription act before Congress.

"You think it's goin' through?" Hod asked.

"Shore. Hit'll go through, an' I been thinkin' what's the use o' waitin' fer 'em to come git me. Might as well go on an' enlist an'

151

git it over. I've heared you could name yer pick o' the service ifen you enlisted ahead o' time. I've shore been studyin' on it."

Hod was startled. Why hadn't he thought of this before himself? This was the perfect escape from the ridge. He turned to Johnny suddenly. " I'll go with you. When you want to go? "

Johnny rolled a cigarette and sealed it. " Ifen you mean it, an' I reckon you do, they ain't no use awaitin'. How about tomorrer? "

" The sooner the better," Hod answered.

"Well, meet me at the Gap in the mornin', an' we'll hitch our way to Fort Knox. They'll take us in there."

" I'll be there," Hod promised, and he felt a great lift of his heart. Now he was finally going to be free. The folks could fend for themselves or do without. He was through. No man, he thought, has a right to make himself a way of life that binds another. And Tom, he was convinced, was doing just that. Hod laid down the load this time, and he didn't care whether Tom picked it up.

The next morning he put ten dollars in Hattie's blue bowl on the mantel. Then he shaved, put on fresh clothes, and walked out the door. He didn't even look back as he went down the road. He had said nothing to anyone of what he meant to do. Hattie thought he was going to work, as always on Monday. She could not know, as she watched him down the road, that it would be thirty-three months before she would see him again.

He walked to the Gap, where Johnny met him, and they hitched a ride in to Campbellsville. There they debated the possibility of taking the bus to Louisville and on out to Fort Knox. But with only five dollars in Hod's pocket, and less in Johnny's, they decided against it. So they stationed themselves on the highway at the edge of town and thumbed a ride. They managed, by short hops from town to town, to arrive at Fort Knox by the middle of the afternoon. They were lost in the big camp, but when they stated their business an M.P. directed them to the recruiting office. A young lieutenant sitting behind a desk looked up as they walked in.

" We want to enlist," said Johnny.

" Just a minute," said the lieutenant. He finished what he was doing.

"Now, then. Your names?"

"Johnny Knight."

"John . . . any middle name?"

"Leslie." With a slanted look at Hod.

"John L. Knight. Your name?" to Hod.

Hod had caught on. "Thomas Hodges Pierce."

"Thomas H. Pierce. And what branch of the service do you want to enlist in?"

Johnny spoke up immediately. "Tanks."

"O.K. You'll train right here. And yours?"

Hod would have liked to be with Johnny. He hadn't thought but what they would be together. But he didn't like the idea of tanks, and besides he didn't want to stay this close to home. Guess I'll have to go on my own, he thought. He took a deep breath and plunged. "I'd rather be in the engineers," he said, "but I want to get as far away from Kentucky as possible."

The lieutenant scribbled a moment. "You can take the infantry and be sent to South Carolina, or you can take the engineers and go to California."

"I'll take the engineers and California."

"O.K.," said the lieutenant. "There's a line of men in the next room waiting to go through. Fall in and take your turn."

The line moved fast and, before Hod had time to quiet his heartbeats, it was his turn. He stripped and went through a routine but thorough physical examination. He was nervous about it, for he had some bad teeth and he was afraid he might be turned down because of them. When it was over and he was told to dress again, he asked the officer, "Did I pass?"

"You're O.K.," was the answer. "Get your serial number over there."

He drew his serial number . . . 15042375 . . . and was told to memorize it immediately. "Wait outside," the group was ordered, "and draw your blankets and bedding."

The ceremony of being sworn in the following day was not impressive. The new recruits lined up in the same long room in which they had waited yesterday, raised their right hands, and repeated the oath of allegiance after the officer. Scarcely were the last words said when a busy corporal shouted: "All right. Form

153

outside to draw your uniforms."

Hod felt strange and uncomfortable in his uniform. It fitted him tighter, for one thing, and all the regulations about its proper wear made him uneasy. But at the same time he settled it on his body with a feeling of pride. Another man might have thought of himself as shackled and regimented in the Army. But to Hod it meant freedom, and being Pvt. Thomas H. Pierce was infinitely better than being plain Hod Pierce. Instead of regimenting him, it set him apart.

The three days passed quickly. Johnny was permanently assigned and moved to another part of the camp. But Hod was kept so busy that he had little time to think of it. He wrote Hattie a card during that time — one stabbing sentence: "I have joined the Army." He dug the point of the pen into the period at the end of the sentence. There was satisfaction in waving his banner of freedom.

When they were loading onto the bus to go to Louisville the day they left, Johnny showed up. He didn't have much to say. Just shook Hod's hand and warned him, "Keep yer nose clean."

As the bus pulled into the drive, Hod looked back and watched Johnny walk off. Suddenly he felt friendless and very much alone and there was a knot in his stomach. He liked Johnny Knight. He'd always found him a bighearted guy. That time Tom was sick, for instance. And you couldn't ask for a better guy to have fun with. He remembered the night in Louisville. He wished they could have been in the same outfit. But it was too late to think about that now. A man had to go his own way.

He didn't examine his feeling any further than that. He didn't realize that it was mostly because Johnny was his last link with Piney Ridge that he felt this sudden appreciation of him, and that even while he was fluttering his brave new wings in flight, they were circling once more around home.

CHAPTER EIGHTEEN

THE TRIP TO THE WEST COAST was an enchanted time to Hod. He had seen trains before, but he had never ridden one. And here he was riding for three days and nights in a Pullman. He marveled at the way the beds were pulled down at night and deftly made up by the porter. He stretched out between the crisp sheets and let himself be lulled to sleep by the swaying motion of the train, and felt old and wise and experienced.

He was shy in the diner, studying long over the menu until the waiter helpfully made suggestions. He didn't think the food was anything to brag about. Hattie could beat the cooks they had on the train all to pieces. But it was something just to sit down at that little table, with its snowy white cloth and baffling array of silver, and order whatever you wanted.

The thing that fascinated him most was the broadening country he saw from the car windows. Never had he dreamed of such vastness! Distances, space, the fathomless reaches of the sky shook him, and left him feeling small. He hadn't known or suspected how the land could roll out as far as the eye could see, flat, level, and endless.

When they reached the mountains he was stunned by their magnificence. Piney Ridge was left a puny, paltry little hump against the earth by the side of these sleeping giants. The other fellows poked fun at the way he kept his face glued to the pane of glass by his seat. " He's a regular Kentucky hillbilly," they said. " Never been nowheres before."

But he didn't mind. He admitted quickly he had never been anywhere before. He had to know about them — this new land and these new skies. This was what he had come for.

After two weeks at March Field, Hod was sent to the presidio of Monterey. There he began to learn how to be a soldier. Day after day of close order drill. Inspection. Guard duty. Reveille. Retreat. Gold-bricking. Week-end passes. All the official and unofficial things that make up a GI day he learned. He shook down into the routine, added several hundred new words to his vocabulary, got sucked in on the usual number of old Army games, and gradually the rawness wore off the recruit and a soldier was made. And Hod was a good soldier. Hattie had prepared him well for the discipline of the Army, which expected him to do as he was told, to question no command, and to jump when he heard the word " frog."

On his week ends he wandered through the city, going off alone so that he might seek out the things he wanted to see. He stood on street corners and watched the fast lines of traffic and the crowds of people. He listened to the gabble of voices on the sidewalks and in the stores, and he searched out queer places to eat, trying new foods and not liking most of them. He was like a sponge soaking up every new experience.

Most of all he liked to go to the beach. He would sit hour after hour watching the waves roll up on top of each other. The rhythm of their inward surging held him hynotically and he watched and listened. This was another thing he had come to see — these far waters lapping on the sand. He let a wave roll over his foot and looked at his wet foot strangely. Did these same drops wash up against another land? The ocean was too big for him. There was no comprehending such width and such depth. A man's mind wouldn't stretch that far. He wished he could tell someone about this now. He would say this water is bigger than all the words that tell of it. The waves come creeping up on the sand, like a cat licking cream, soft and smoothlike. He would say the sky comes down to meet it in the west, and the sun is drowned each night in the water. And it paints the water red and purple and gold. He laughed. Anyone on Piney Ridge would answer that he didn't keer for sich!

When he signed his first payroll, Hod found that after all he did care whether Tom picked up the load, and that two thousand miles between him and home did not make it any less home. He sent ten of his twenty-one dollars home every month. The rasping file of his resentment against Tom and Hattie had dulled and he was remembering, nostalgically, only the things he loved most about the ridge. Out from under the chafing yoke, he could have a more selfless understanding of their helplessness to be anything other than what they were. He remembered with shame his indifference to the new baby, and he was careful always to ask about her when he wrote. He sent her small gifts and in other ways tried to atone for his spiritual denial of her.

The months slipped by. Hod dug trenches, built barbed-wire entanglements, learned to purify water, shoveled gravel and sand on roads, and braced heavy bridge girders. He was sent over to

Fort Ord and made his first rating there. After nine months there he moved on up the coast into Washington, and from there he went to Colorado. Wherever he went, he tested the feel of the land and the people.

" This here's a soft country," he wrote home of Washington, " soft with mist like that which wraps around the trees down in the holler. The grass and the trees are a downy green, and the sky blue is like a baby's eyes. There are the prettiest creeks I ever saw. Tumbling and rushing down the hills. But it's a strange-feeling land at that."

Of the mountains in Colorado he wrote briefly: " There are some things just too big to tell about. A man feels like a little ant standing under these mountains. I would be hard put to be content with them towering over me."

The poet mind, which in the little boy had avidly absorbed Tennyson and Keats and Browning, struggled now with these new beauties, to find a way to tell of them. Something in him hurt with beauty, opened wide to it and let it in. And he wanted to let it out again, transformed, made vocal, singing a new song. His letters were full of what he saw, but they hardly scratched the surface of what he felt.

A year and a half went by. There were times when Hod felt as if he had never known any other life than the Army. But there were other times when he looked down at the strange soil his boots strode across and wondered how Hod Pierce happened to be there. Then the Army and Pvt. Thomas H. Pierce, 15042375, were dissolved, and he walked the ridge again, old Duke to heel and his gun cradled in the bend of his arm. Those were homesick moments when he wanted achingly to see the folks, and to ramble through the woods and fields again. Jeems, he thought, must have yearned for Abigail and the cabin in the holler in much the same way.

Along in November he put in for a Christmas furlough. It would be good to be at home for Christmas. Hattie would cook a goose and make a pile of dressing to go with it. They would have a little pine Christmas tree, fragrant and fresh from the woods, star-bright and spangly with ornaments. Irma and John would come over and they would all go to church on Christmas Eve and walk home through the brittle cold. Maybe it would even snow and they could crunch through its crispness, making it squeak under their heels. He would buy Sarah a big doll, and she would be as pretty as a Christmas doll herself! Ah, they would have a wonderful Christmas!

The furlough came through and he wrote saying he would start home on December 20. He was counting the days. Week ends he haunted the stores doing his Christmas shopping. He got a warm, fleecy robe for Hattie, who was up in the night so often . . . and a pair of fuzzy little slippers for Gramma's tiny feet. He held them in the palm of his hand and laughed at their size. " I reckon they'll do," he told the clerk. " She isn't any bigger than a minute."

And he found the big doll for Sarah — a beautiful, lifelike doll with blue eyes and yellow hair. He could see Sarah now, hugging it close. He couldn't wait to watch her eyes when she saw it under the tree!

But his Christmas furlough was not to be. On December 7 the stars changed their courses, and his destiny and that of millions of other men like him was shaped to fit a new world.

The night after war was officially declared, the captain called the men together. It was a solemn moment. " Men," he said, " this is it. We're at war now. Our job is plain. Nothing is important now except winning the war. We're in the Army for the duration."

The duration! Not for one year. Not for three years. For the duration. And no one could know how long the duration would be! The words echoed down the unknown years and rolled on into infinity. No one in the room that night knew where he might be sent before the year was over, or what awful thing might happen to him. The ink in which each man's lease on life was written dimmed and blurred, and the future faded into darkness.

Hod knew his own moment of panic, along with the rest. Then he wrote home: " This war changes everything. I can't come home now, and it's doubtful when I'll get to come. I am mailing you the presents I wrote about. I was going to give them to you myself. But now that can't be. I'll come when I can."

The 19th settled down to the serious business of training for specific jobs. There was a grim purpose now which had not characterized their work before. Hod was counted an old soldier, and in June he was picked to go on a cadre to a camp in Missouri. He felt fine about being chosen to go. It was no mean recognition to be selected as one of the small group of noncommissioned officers to form the skeleton of a new outfit. He had been tool corporal for nearly six months, and he took a pride in keeping the company's tools bright and shining and sharp. It was no accident that on every company problem the men maneuvered to get his tools. "They're always in first-class shape," they said. Going on the cadre was a sort of special reward.

The camp in Missouri was another arid concentration of men who had been drafted to learn the art of war. Hod's job was to teach them what he knew of it. Shortly after reporting in he had been made sergeant, and he was now out in front of a squad, drilling the feet off of them, whipping their curved spines into taut, lean thongs, stripping the fat from their soft sides, pickling, hardening, tightening them against the day when their lives might depend upon their being indurate as steel. Better to be merciless now than sorry later.

But no rookie ever sees past his swollen feet and his aching back, and a top sergeant is always Simon Legree. Hod, having been through the mill himself, knew when they hated him most, but he flogged them hardest then. And when they went into the Tennessee hills on maneuvers that fall they were tough as leather, resilient, stretchy, springy, and unbreakable. He was proud of them during those killing days. Men who had already seen action in Africa shook their heads over the Tennessee maneuvers. "War ain't no worse," they said. But that was the reason for the maneuvers — so that war wouldn't be any worse.

The Tennessee hills were enough like home to make Hod look longingly north over their rolling curves. He would have walked every mile to get there, but there wasn't time for even so much as a week-end pass. He was lucky to get twenty-four hours once, to go into Nashville.

When the 44th went to Wisconsin that October for winter training, Hod went along. There, in weather thirty below zero and in snow up to their knees, those same tough kids did four-, six-, and eight-mile marches with full field packs. The winds jelled the marrow in their bones and congealed the blood in their veins. But

159

they didn't fall out. "They're O.K.," Hod said to the captain. "They'll do." And then, in the middle of the worst cold spell they had had all winter, the 44th were issued tropical clothing, mosquito nets, Atabrine tablets, and were shipped out to Africa!

Hod didn't go with them. The old soldiers were still needed too desperately to make new soldiers. A good top sergeant was often worth more in camp than he was on the beaches. This time he was sent to Texas.

After the misery of his northern winter he couldn't get enough of the sun, and it was paradise to be where it beat down hotly day after day. He scorched himself into brown leather and felt his blood thaw and run free again. But there was little else about Texas that he liked. The brown, wasted reaches of western Texas held no attraction for him. He snorted as he looked out over the vastness one day. Grampa would say this land ain't good enough to raise a fuss on, he thought, chuckling!

It was now that Hod had his biggest chance to become somebody, according to Army standards. And it was now that he learned exactly how much Piney Ridge he was.

After a series of intelligence tests, given soon after he reached the camp, Hod was called into the office.

"Pierce," the captain said, "your I.Q. is in the upper bracket and you've got a good record with the men. We're sending a bunch over to Belvoir next week to O.C.S. You can go along if you like."

Officer Candidate School! The gold bars of a second lieutenant . . . more pay . . . men saluting him . . . responsibility . . . prestige! He wanted it more than anything! And, wanting it, he should have said yes immediately, while he was still Sergeant Pierce standing at ease before his captain. He should never have asked for time to think it over. But some deep-rooted uneasiness took hold of him.

"May I let the captain know later, sir?" And he gave himself time. Time in which to sink back into the timid inertia of Piney Ridge. To sink back into a distrust of change . . . a fear of failure . . . a dark clinging to the slow, familiar things . . . a wrapping of the self in the womb of safety.

He tried to pull himself up to the bars on the shoulders; dreamed of himself at staff meetings . . . in an officer's uniform.

But something else kept saying: That course at Belvoir is tough . . . They really put you through the mill over there . . . It would be tougher for me than most . . . I'm older than the others . . . I wouldn't have a chance in a million to make it . . . I've got a good thing where I am . . . I like my job . . . why should I frash myself?

Thus he argued with himself, and was torn between the dream and the reality. Finally he pulled the blue heights of the dream down to Piney Ridge and leveled it under the thin dust of rationalization. He told the captain he preferred to stay with the outfit. He made it sound as if he thought he could best serve where he was. He could not admit even to himself that the familiar job and the family of enlisted men supplied him with confidence in himself, and shored up his frightened sense of inadequacy. He could not confess that he dared not risk this hard-won security in a new and untried world.

Perhaps a lot of his fear lay in his intuitive knowledge that to him the men in the Army paralleled Piney Ridge. The officers were over across a fence, where the language was foreign, the customs were alien, and the standards were strange. With all his heart he had wanted to climb over that fence. But something that was part of the breath of his life wouldn't turn loose; wouldn't let him frash himself. He put it behind him uneasily . . . tried never to dig it up and look at it. But it lay there, heavy, just the same.

Hod was shifted from squad leader to weapon sergeant. His sentient fingers handled guns with the same genius with which they had handled tools, and not only could he endow them with a personality of their own — he could teach other men to do so too. He turned out gun crew after gun crew who worked together with perfect precision and co-ordination, turning in consistently high scores.

But there was something different about this outfit right from the start. It was in the nightly NCO meetings, the urgency of maneuvers, the nervous energy of the officers, the razor edge of the men themselves. Hod felt it, and let it run through him like quicksilver. This battalion was being groomed for special work. There was no mistaking it. This was it.

They moved over to the Gulf coast for the summer, and the emphasis shifted from road construction and bridge-building to assault landing, removal of underwater obstacles and mines, and the clearing of beaches. They knew then that this was the real stuff. This was invasion engineering; combat engineering. This was the kind of stuff that moved in on the beaches with the infantry. And their minds were full of questions. Where will it be? When does it come off? How soon will we ship out? The rumor factory worked overtime. Men in his outfit asked Hod, " You know anything about it? " And he shook his head, " Not a thing."

But he knew as well as they that they were headed for some long stretch of sand where the far waters lapped lonesomely. Only a man wouldn't have time to stand and watch the waves come creaming up on the beach. He wouldn't want to if he could. He would be too busy trying to keep from getting shot.

CHAPTER NINETEEN

NOTHING HAS CHANGED, he thought, as he started up the ridge from the Gap. It's been a hundred years since I left, but nothing has changed. The rocks are just as sharp, the trees are just as old, and the hills are just as steep. Forever and enduring the hills are the same. The words of the ancient psalm came to his mind: " I will lift up mine eyes unto the hills, from whence cometh my help "! He dug his toes into the acid dust, scuffed it on his shoes, and sniffed the smell of it. Kentucky dust. Kentucky sky. Kentucky hills. Fly away, Kentucky babe . . . fly away . . . but come home to the hills to rest.

He paused in the quiet little woodsy place and laid his hand against cool, white birch bark. He smiled when he saw where he had cut his initials. He remembered the time. Grampa had just given him a new knife. He couldn't wait to try it out! A mockingbird poured a liquid song over him from the treetops, and an old blue jay scolded him from a sumac bush. " Did you miss me? " Hod said softly. " Did you think I wasn't comin' back? "

The last mile of the road seemed eternally long, and when he rounded the bend and could see the low roof of the house, the supper smoke tailing out of the chimney, his heart ballooned into his throat and pumped achingly there. He wanted to reach out his arms and pull it close. He wanted never to let it go.

He hadn't let them know he was coming. Furloughs had started coming through suddenly about midsummer, and when he drew fifteen days the latter part of July, he knew that port of embarkation was just around the corner. By the time he was sure of his furlough, he had known he could beat a letter home.

The front room was empty when he walked in. He dumped his musette bag on the floor and called, " Anybody home? "

Hattie ran from the kitchen. She stared at him, unbelieving, for a long moment. Then she began to cry. " Hit's Hod," she said, and her thin brown arms reached for him hungrily and drew him close. It was perhaps the first time since he was a little boy that she had touched him in affection. But gladness broke down her wall of reserve. She rocked him gently back and forth, her wet face pressed against him. " Hit's Hod," she said, " hit's Hod." Over and over she said it, as if she could not get enough assurance it was really he. " Hit's Hod."

Finally she stepped back and wiped her eyes with the heels of her hands. " Let me git a good look at you," she laughed shakily. " Hit's been so long! Jist let me look at you! " She turned him round and round and pulled and picked at his uniform. " Hit don't seem natural," she said. " Hit jist don't seem right fer you to be wearin' sich clothes! An' yer thin, Hod! Don't you git enough to eat? "

" I get plenty," he answered reassuringly. " They feed us fine. But I walk it off and work it off. Anyway, I've never been fat, and you know it! "

" Well, I jist weary myself plumb to death! Nights I jist cain't sleep, seems like, thinkin' 'bout you, way off somewheres away from home. Nobody to do fer you. Jist seems like it's more'n I kin bear."

Hod pushed away from him the knowledge of how much heavier her nights would be before long. He didn't know how he could tell her. Best leave it lie.

" Where's Pa? " he asked. "And where's Gramma? "

But Hattie darted suddenly to the kitchen. She came back holding a small girl by the hand. " This here's the tomater! " Hattie said proudly.

Sarah was three now. And when she saw Hod, she ducked her head in unbearable shyness and hid her face in her mother's

163

apron. But she peeked out, to blink one wide blue eye at him.

"I don't believe it," Hod said, going down on one knee and holding out his arms. She was a Botticelli angel, head covered with a fluff of silvery duck curls, and chin pressed with the same deep, probing finger as Hattie's and Hod's. She looked warily at Hod, but as he coaxed her she moved inch by inch, one step at a time, toward him. Finally he lifted her in his arms. She was so soft; so almost fluid in her roundness. As he held her, he had a sense of his own loss. If he had married, one like her might be his own. A wave of tenderness for her flooded him and he buried his nose in the feathery down of her hair. I didn't mean you looked like a tomato! I didn't mean it at all!

He followed Hattie into the kitchen where she was rattling pots and pans and poking up a fire. "Law me, Hod," she was saying, "I ain't got e'er thing fitten to eat tonight! I was jist aimin' to have leftovers from dinner. You ortent to come in this way an' surprise a body! I wasn't expectin' nobody but us."

"Don't fret, Ma," he assured her. "Anything you've got'll taste good to me. Just be sure and make me some hot corn bread. I've dreamed about that corn bread of yours. And many's the time I'd have walked five miles for a piece of it. Where'd you say Pa was?"

Hattie laughed. "I plumb fergot you asked! Why, him an' Gault's aworkin' in the tobaccer. They got a new patch over on a piece o' Gault's land. He'll be home directly. An' Gramma's feedin' the chickens."

Tobacco! From everlasting to everlasting tobacco! Now he knew he was at home!

It was good to sit on the porch after supper in the last cool dimness of the day. To pick at his guitar, listen to the gossip of the ridge, and talk quietly. He sat in his old place on the step, with his head against the post, and Tom loomed over him on the porch railing. Gramma squeaked her little rocker, and spat into the dark when her snuff overflowed. Hod thought she had grown even tinier, and her mind wandered these days so that she moved almost constantly in a misty dream of the past. Times, she knew him. Spoke of his boyhood and young manhood. But mostly she thought he was Tom. Or again, appallingly, she thought he was the young Dow. She dimpled then, and hung her head, and chided him for staying away so long. Gramma moved in a dream. But it was a gentle dream which wrapped her from the pain and worry and loss of her life.

Hattie sat near Hod, and her eyes seldom left him. She felt whole and filled full again. She reached out a hand to him time and again, as if her entire being was still saying, " Hit's Hod."

The western sky rested on the tops of the beeches across the road, and fireflies punctured the growing dark like a thousand candles. Katydids sawed on their tuneless fiddles. The cinnamon vine and the yellow rose poured out their sweetness. Down in the holler an old bullfrog garrumphed doggedly, and under the porch Duke thumped at his fleas. Around the world guns were roaring, and tomorrow he would be deaf from their sound. But tonight, in this blessed spot, there was peace. The earth hung suspended, and tonight was all there was of time.

It was Saturday when Hod got home, and he went with the family to church the next morning. The little white church was packed. There always was a good crowd, but on this Sabbath there was a gathering of the clan to welcome Hod. Hattie stood aside while he exchanged howdies with the friends and relatives, quietly refracting the rays of his glory in the prism of her pride.

Inside, even the preacher took note of him. After the opening prayer and song he pointed out that Hod was there, calling him one of the " stanch defenders of our country." Hod was uncomfortable. He hadn't defended anything yet. But it was nice of the preacher to notice him. This was a new preacher since Hod left, and it was doubly nice of him to take note.

" Sergeant Pierce," he was saying, " we'd like to have you lead us in a song. They tell me you used to lead the singing quite a bit before you went in the Army."

Hod, who was holding Sarah, fumbled a moment as he handed her to Hattie. " Well, I never was a real expert, like Little Wells over there. But if you'll put up with me, I'll try." He started up the aisle, the back of his neck pink with embarrassment.

Sarah was struggling to follow him, and when her mother took

165

a firm grip on her and set her down solidly, she set up such a wailing for Hod that the whole church rang with it. Hattie tried desperately to quiet her, but she wouldn't be hushed. " Hod," she kept crying, " Hod," in a bereft and heartbroken little voice. Hattie rose to take her out, but Hod walked back down the aisle, stopped her, and took the little girl in his arms. She rubbed her nose against his chin and sniffed contentedly.

> " ' Faith of our fathers! living still
> In spite of dungeon, fire, and sword,
> O how our hearts beat high with joy
> Whene'er we hear that glorious word:
> Faith of our fathers, holy faith!
> We will be true to thee till death.' "

With Sarah on one arm and the other marking the rhythm, Hod led the congregation in the stalwart old hymn of reaffirmation.

> " ' And through the truth that comes from God
> Mankind shall then be truly free:
> Faith of our fathers, holy faith!
> We will be true to thee till death. Amen.' "

Amen! Hod's heart echoed the solemn ratification. Amen. In this place of his fathers, from which he was going forth, it was good to sing about faith. To touch it in the reality of his people. To weld again his link in the chain that circled the ridge folks.

Irma and John and their six-month-old Johnnie went home with them for the big Sunday dinner that followed church. The table sagged with food. Fried chicken, crisp and brown, piled on platters at either end of the long board. Soft, fluffy mashed potatoes heaped in a tremendous bowl. Rich cream gravy, which made Hod lick his lips. Green beans from the garden and early roasting ears. Great, thick, red slices of tomatoes, and thin, green curls of cucumbers. And for dessert, when they were almost too full to hold another bite, there were spiced peaches and chocolate cake. When he finally pushed back his chair, Hod groaned. " Ma," he said, " the way you cook is a gift from God."

Hattie flushed with pleasure at the compliment. " Well, I orta be able to cook right good," she replied, " after doin' it fer all these years."

While the womenfolks washed up the dishes, Tom took himself to the back room for a nap and Hod and John wandered out onto the porch. They talked of crops awhile, and the weather. John told of a different kind of corn he was going to try next year. " Leastways ifen they don't call me in the Army 'fore then," he said.

" You won't have to go yet, surely."

" No. Not right away, I don't reckon. I ain't any too happy 'bout stayin' out. Sorta feel like I'm lettin' somebody else do my fightin'. But they's Irma an' the baby to think of. An' the farm. 'Pears like they need what we kin raise as bad as e'er thing else. I reckon if they git to needin' me they'll let me know."

" You've no call to feel bad," Hod assured him. " There's still plenty of single fellows that haven't been called. They're the ones to go first."

" You think it's goin' to be a long war, Hod? "

" Well, I think it's goin' to last so bitter long we'll all forget there ever was a time when it wasn't goin' on. I think it's not even good started yet. And I wouldn't care to guess when it might end."

They were silent, pondering the immensity of the octopus that was gripping the world in its tentacles. John shivered. " Think you'll go over across the waters? "

" Bound to." Hod couldn't say he was already on his way.

" Hit'll jist about kill Hattie when you have to go."

" That's what I hate most about goin'. She'll worry herself sick."

John pulled a straw of dry grass and stuck it between his teeth. " Reckon you heared Johnny Knight was killed."

" No! " Hod said, and his chair legs bumped the floor. " No. I hadn't heard. Where? "

" On one o' them little islands out there in the Pacific. Got blowed to bits in a air raid is the way I heared it."

Hod's heels bit into the chair rung. He saw the pieces of Johnny Knight, red and dripping like a butchered beef, hurled violently into the air. No! No! He swung his mind away from it. Johnny, how far is it home? About two hundred miles. It's farther than that, Johnny. It's a heck of a lot farther than that.

The women joined them on the porch, Irma carrying Hod's guitar. " Sing somethin' fer us, Hod," she said, handing him the guitar.

He hesitated. He didn't feel much like singing. Then he reached for the instrument. All right. He'd sing. Requiem for Johnny Knight, blown to bits on an island in the Pacific!

> " ' In Scarlet town where I was born
> There was a fair maid dwellin';
> Made every youth cry well aday,
> Her name was Barbry Allen.

> " ' 'Twas all in the merry month of May,
> When green buds they were swellin';
> Sweet William come from out the west,
> An' courted Barbry Allen.' "

"You goin' to do any courtin' while you're home from out the west?" teased Irma, when the last notes of the song died mournfully away.

"Not a bit," he promised lightly. "I'm savin' my love."

"What fer? A rainy day?"

"For ' the lily maid of Astolat,' " he whispered, only half joking.

The days went by all too fast, and as they slipped carelessly into the past, Hod threaded the present carefully through his fingers and knotted it into himself. He pulled down the hills and packed them into the places that would be empty inside of him. He stored the baby's gay laugh and rippling stream of words into the voiceless regions of his mind, to drink from when the sands were hot and dry. He took the slow, sleepy days and stitched a cushion against the sleeplessness to come. He wrapped Piney Ridge around him and pinned the edges down, tight.

He said good-by.

CHAPTER TWENTY

THE BUS WAS AN HOUR AND FORTY MINUTES LATE at Bowling Green, where Hod made connections going back to camp. And when it nosed its way into the dock, there was still a thirty-minute supper stop to wait out. As the passengers poured off the bus and streamed into the station, Hod watched them hurry past and rest-

168

lessly lighted a cigarette. He wanted to be on his way.

Through the open door of the bus he could see a girl sitting in the first seat. The contagion of haste seemed not to have touched her, for she was fluffing a powder puff against her nose and applying fresh lipstick to her mouth. She slapped a little circle of shiny black straw, not much blacker than her hair, on the back of her head, patted it a couple of times, wriggled her dress into place, and crawled down out of the bus. He watched her walk across the station platform, noticing the free swing of her legs, the slender length of her body, the lift of her head on her throat. He got a whiff of some flowerlike smell as she went by, and he noticed that her eyes were almost as dark as her hair. His tongue probed the rough spot on his tooth. She wasn't a kid. He judged she would be about twenty-seven or -eight. Somewhere near his own age. Then he shrugged her from his mind, and took up again his boredom with the long wait. A paper boy came by and he bought a paper, glanced at the headlines, read the funnies, and folded it to throw away.

"Don't throw it away," said a voice at his elbow. "If you're through with it, let me have it." The girl had come back and was standing just back of him.

"Sure," he said, handing it to her. "You must have eaten in a hurry."

"I didn't eat," she answered. "We're due in Nashville at 8:30, and I'd rather get a good meal there than to grab a sandwich here. Thanks for the paper. They were all out inside." And she got back on the bus, seated herself, and was immersed in the paper before he could think of anything else to say. He liked her voice too. It was pitched low, with a richness that sang. Like the G string on his guitar. He had been surprised when she cut the conversation short. Experience had taught him that when girls opened the way for talk, they were usually opening the way for more. Could be she just wanted the paper, though, he concluded.

The passengers filtered back onto the bus and Hod waited until it was loaded, knowing they were entitled to their former places and he would have to take what was left. When the bus driver nodded for him to get on, he swung up the steps and paused just inside the door to look the situation over. There were two seats, one beside the girl, and one on the long seat across the back. He grinned as he stopped beside the girl. " Is this seat taken? "

She grinned back at him. " Not unless you want it."

" It's taken." He racked his musette bag and hitched up his pants.

The girl had taken off her hat and she handed it to him now. " Put this up for me, please," she said, and by the time he had carefully made a place for it, and seated himself, she was deep in the paper again. Home, James, he thought, and determined to let her alone. Nuts to women who act like the queen of Sheba!

The bus was well on its way, rolling into the sun toward Nashville, when she finished with the paper. She folded it and tucked it neatly down by the arm of the seat. Now she was ready to talk, he supposed. He braced himself. They always said the same old things, and he was weary of the answers. Been in the Army long, soldier? Been home on furlough? Where are you stationed? What branch are you in? What does that shoulder patch mean? It was a game you played to be polite.

But she said nothing for a while. Instead she leaned her head back against the seat and kept her eyes fixed out the window. The bus tires were hissing on the pavement, and the sun was a golden coin dropping into the slit of the hills. She turned to him suddenly. " Did you ever see anything as beautiful as that sunset? Look, it's all red and gold and purple! And look at the way the tops of the hills stand up against it . . . like they've been drawn in with black ink! "

Hod followed her pointing finger. " It sure is pretty," he agreed. " That gold band back of the hills looks like it was sewed to the sky, doesn't it? "

" Oh, yes! " she laughed, delighted. " Yes. With nice, neat seams."

She was quiet for a time, watching. Then: " A sunset's such an extravagant thing, isn't it? Like the day had flung every color in its paintbox into the sky before going to bed at night."

" A sunrise is mighty pretty too."

" Oh, a sunrise is a pale, weak thing compared to a sunset! It's so timid! "

" Well, I've seen many a one that wasn't! The break of day's not always so timid! Especially over the sea. One minute the light

170

is dim, and the next minute the sun has turned it to brass."

"Lovely," she said, and then, suddenly, "What is the most beautiful thing you ever saw in your life?"

"The most beautiful thing I ever saw?" Hod was surprised, but he tried earnestly to think, turning over in his mind all the forms of beauty he had ever stored there. "I don't rightly know. There are so many beautiful things in the world. There are the stars over the holler on a clear night. And mists in the valley early in the morning, rising and curling around the trees like smoke. A rainbow's a mighty pretty thing too. And a crab apple tree in bloom is just about the sweetest sight you could ever hope to see."

"Oh, yes! We had a crap apple tree in our back yard in one of the places we lived once. It has a pinky bloom!"

"That's right. And young beech leaves are soft and pretty when they first come out," Hod went on, "and a dogwood flower would be hard to beat. A field of green corn's mighty sightly too. I don't know as you could say what's the most beautiful. But I believe the hills against the sky, sort of like they are tonight, is just about the best."

"You were born in the hills, weren't you?"

"Yeah. Just a Kentucky hillbilly, and I don't reckon I'll ever get very far away from it."

"Why would you want to?"

"Well, there's better ways of livin' than the folks back in the hills where I come from know about. If you could put good livin' into the hills, I'd have no wish to leave them. But the way it is, it takes the soul out of a man just to scrabble a livin' out of the ground. Hill ground is always poor ground for raisin' crops, and hill people don't usually know enough about makin' it any better. Things sort of jog along. Nobody's got anything, nobody ever expects to have anything. It's that hopelessness that I'm afraid of and want to get away from."

"Is that true of all hill people? Do they all have that feeling of hopelessness?"

"No. No, I don't reckon you could say it's true of all hill people. If you've never had anything, and don't even know there's more to be had, you can't feel hopeless about not havin' it, can you?"

"That's just what I mean! You're afraid of hopelessness because

171

you've been waked up to what it means, isn't that it? "

" Partly. But mostly I think I was born knowin' what it means.
I can't remember when I wasn't strugglin' against it . . . when
I didn't wonder why my family was the way it was . . . why
the Pierces settled on Piney Ridge, and why none of them ever
amounted to anything, or ever wanted an education, or ever
thought of livin' differently. Nobody told me those things to think
about. I was just born different, someway or other. I've been
pulled back and forth between bein' a Pierce on Piney Ridge and
lovin' it, and wantin' something better and not knowin' what it is,
ever since I can remember."

The girl was listening intently, and she was still when he finished talking. After a while she said: " What would something
better be? Do you have any idea? "

" It would be . . ." he struggled for the words, " it would be
makin' something out of myself. When you've not had much all
your life, it sort of gets important to have things. I'd like to have
a good job. And I'd like to have things nice. You know . . . pretty
things, I reckon. Like a nice home . . . nice furniture . . . that
sort of thing. I used to say I was goin' to be somebody! I don't
rightly know how yet, but I still think I'd like my chance at it."

And then he found himself telling her the things he would
have resented her asking. " I wanted more education than I had a
chance to get. And there wasn't any way I could get it. I tried.
Once I thought I had a good start on it. But my father got sick
and I had to go home and take over. And I had to stay on makin'
the livin' after that. And then a thing happened that made me
feel like I had a right to leave. And I joined the Army. All I could
think of was gettin' off the ridge, and I took the Army as the best
way out. I enlisted for three years, and my time would have been
up this summer, but the war came along. Now if I've got any future, it's got to wait awhile. But if I come through the war, I'm still
goin' to try. Somewhere. Somehow. I'll find where I'm supposed
to belong . . . the place where I fit best . . . and the thing I'm
supposed to do."

The girl's finger was drumming on the arm of the seat, and she
smiled at him. " Man looking for his home," she said. " As far back
as the first man who could think, men have been trying to find
their homes in this universe. Some call it security. Some call it

172

peace of mind. Some call it religion. But it's a yearning that's as old as time. 'To be somebody' — that's putting it very well."

Hod was embarrassed suddenly. "Look," he said, "I didn't mean to talk so much. I wasn't tryin' to tell you the story of my life!"

"I'm interested," she protested. "And I want to hear some more. Go on. Tell me about those hills of yours."

"Oh, they're just hills. A little steeper than most. A little rockier than most. They look just like any other hills. The only difference is that I've lived in them all my life. They're down in the southern part of Kentucky."

"And you were born and raised there?"

"Me . . . and my father . . . and my grandfather . . . and his father. That's about as far back as we know."

The girl looked at him, her dark eyes wide and full. "Imagine living all your life where your people have always lived!" She caught her lower lip between her teeth and shook her head a little. "Tell me what your home is like."

"It's a little old house my Grampa built nearly seventy-five years ago. At least he built the first of it. My father built onto it later. It's got four rooms and a loft room." He laughed. "The old cat 'n' clay chimney's still standin'."

"What's a cat 'n' clay chimney?"

"It's sticks and rocks and mud plastered together. Easiest way to build a chimney . . . out of whatever's closest to hand. When the mud dries, it's as stout as concrete almost."

"Doesn't it crumble?"

"In time, I reckon. But it takes a mighty long time."

"What else is your home like?"

"Well, there's a picket fence around the front yard, and a yellow rosebush by the chimney. My grandmother planted it. She got the cutting from Grampa Dow's mother. There's a saying that there's always a yellow rosebush in a Pierce yard. There's dominecker chickens scratching around in the grass in the yard, and there's a couple of cows in the pasture. One has a new calf. And there's old Buck, the horse, and old Duke, my dog. And there's a beech grove across the road, and a spring down under the hill."

The girl caught her lip again and breathed deeply. "It sounds beautiful."

"It is beautiful. It's the most beautiful place in the world. There's times when I want to be there so bad I hurt. But when I'm there too long, it gets to be ugly. Then it hurts me to stay. I get all mixed up."

"Everyone gets all mixed up at times."

"Yes, but I've been mixed up all my life!"

"What about your people?"

"There's my mother — Hattie's her name — and my father, Tom Pierce. And Gramma lives with us since Grampa died. And there's my sister, Irma, who's married and lives about four miles from us. And then there's the baby, Sarah."

"The baby?"

"Yes. She's just three. See," he said earnestly, "Ma and Pa had eight of us, but only Irma and I lived. And we were grown and Irma was married when Sarah came along. That's what made me leave home, like I said awhile ago. I hated the whole business. I felt sorry for myself, I reckon. Seemed like I'd been chained there makin' the livin' for so long, and another mouth to feed was just the last straw." He fumbled with his hands and eased his eyes away. "I'm sort of ashamed of it now."

"The way you felt was pretty natural, don't you think? Most people would have felt that way, I'm certain."

Hod sighed and stretched his long legs out in front of him. "Now, that's enough about me," he said. "It's your turn, now. What about you?"

The girl spread her hands and laughed. "There's not much to tell about me. I teach school in Louisville, and I live in a tiny little apartment there. There's no picket fence, and no yellow rosebush, and no dominecker hens there! Just three little rooms."

"Haven't you got any folks?"

"My father and mother are dead. My aunt lives in El Paso. I have a sister and two brothers, but they're all married and live in the west."

"Were you raised out west?"

"In Texas. My father and my mother were both schoolteachers. My aunt is a teacher too, and when both my parents died, I went to live with her until I finished college."

"How did you happen to come to Kentucky?"

"Maybe I had to find something better for myself too."

"You mean you had to get away from something?"

"No. Not that exactly. But I had to make my own way. I had to find out what would make me myself . . . just like you're looking for yourself."

"Did you find it?"

"Not entirely. Yet."

"Look," Hod was eager. "Look. This is the funniest talkin' I've ever done with a girl. I don't even know your name and I've told you things about myself I've never told anyone before. I feel like I've known you all my life!"

"That's because you don't know me at all, isn't it? You can tell a sympathetic stranger things you wouldn't dream of telling someone you knew well. Just because you don't know the stranger, and he won't be critical of you and judge you."

"Yes, but I do know you . . . now. I know that you know all about me, because I've told you all about me. And I know you feel like I do about the things that are most important to me. I could stand by your side and look at the sunset, and I wouldn't need to say a word. I'd know what you were feeling and thinking. And I know that you know what I mean when I say I have to be somebody . . . have to find myself. Because you've been looking for yourself. How can that happen in an hour?"

"I don't know."

"I don't know, either. Who are you?"

"Mary . . . Mary Hogan."

"Mary Hogan," he repeated the name. "Mary Hogan." He reached over and took her ringless left hand and spread the fingers gently apart. "You didn't say Mrs. Mary Hogan, did you?"

"No," she laughed, freeing her hand. "It's just Mary Hogan."

"Is Mary Hogan promised to someone? Please, I'm not just bein' curious. At least I don't mean to be. It's awfully important."

"No," she answered, "she's not promised to anyone, either."

Hod sighed with relief. "Good," he said. "Where are you goin'?"

"To El Paso. I'm on my vacation, and I usually spend part of it with Miss Willie."

"Miss Willie?"

"My aunt."

"Oh. Hey, you'll be goin' through Dallas, won't you?"

175

"Yes. I have to change there."

Hod did some figuring. "You know this is wonderful. I'm goin' to Texas too. I'm stationed at Camp Swift, just outside Austin. I hadn't planned to go any farther than Nashville by bus. I usually save a little by hitchhikin'. But I can go as far as Dallas with you."

Mary wasn't so sure. "Maybe you'd better not change your plans," she said. "You might be disappointed in the rest of the trip."

"I'll take a chance on that. I wouldn't miss ridin' as far as I can with you for anything in the world! I've dreamed about someone like you! Almost as long as I've dreamed about that something better. Used to call her 'the lily maid of Astolat'!"

"Now, look!"

Hod laughed, quickly and joyously. "Don't quarrel with fate, lady! I think it's wonderful!"

The bus driver, directly in front of them, joined in the conversation then. He had settled down to the run and wanted company. He took over the talk and began telling long stories about the peculiarities of the people who lived in these hills. He was a rambling, loquacious sort of person, talking with a slow, drawling voice which pointed up a story to a fine, dry humor. They laughed partly at him and partly with him, and Hod felt himself slipping deeper into the most relaxed feeling he had known in several months.

The girl bubbled over when she laughed, somewhat like a child, and she laughed readily. There was a gayness about her which transferred itself to him and he caught it eagerly. And her face, when she talked, lighted up with a look of shining intensity. Her eyes took fire then and grew brilliant. She was interested in everything, with an eager, compelling interest, and yet when she was impressed by something she was still, all over still, as if she were taking it into herself. She's different, Hod thought. She's the most different person I ever saw. She's friendly and gay and happy, and yet she thinks about things — 'way down deep inside of her she thinks about everything.

Almost before they knew it, the lights of Nashville were ahead. They would change busses there, and there was a wait of several hours. How best to spend it, thought Hod. How make it memorable.

176

"You know what I think would be fun?" he asked, when he had thought it over.

"What do you think would be fun?"

"When we get to Nashville, let's find some nice place to eat, and let's have the best bang-up chicken dinner in town!" A table was such a quiet place to sit and talk.

"I think that's a wonderful idea! Give me fifteen minutes to freshen up when we get in, and then we'll hunt for the best bang-up chicken dinner in Nashville!"

While she primped, Hod found the men's room, shaved, retied his tie, brushed off, and felt ready to go. There was one thing you could say for a uniform. You were always dressed up — ready to go — as long as you were clean and had a crease in your pants, that is.

They left the bus station and walked up the hill, looking for a place that would serve their chicken dinner. But it was too late, and they finally settled for steaks at a steak house. They found a table over next to the wall, snug in its own lamplight and out of the path of other people. Mary had put on a bright little jacket and had added white gloves to her outfit. She looked quite fine to Hod.

With enormous appetites they ate, enjoying the big, hot steaks; the crisp curls of French fries; the round, red slices of cold tomatoes. And then over coffee they dragged out the full two hours they had allowed themselves, talking and talking, as if they had only these minutes left. When finally the clock on the wall warned them they must go, Hod paid the checks, glad it had been an expensive dinner, and they walked back down the hill to the station.

He queued up to buy his ticket and Mary went to get her bags. The busses were loading by the time he had got his ticket and joined her at the dock. His heart sank when he saw the milling crowd. Three or four sections were running, but if they ever got on one they would have to stand.

"This is goin' to be pretty tough," he said to her.

"Where did all these people come from?" she wondered. It was eleven o'clock at night, and there were young mothers with sleepy, crying babies, struggling to manage the babies and their luggage; there were girls with heavy, tired eyes, worn out from a sleepless week end visiting their soldiers; there were old women with aching lines of fatigue in their faces; and always and every-

177

where there were the soldiers.

"Oh, I shouldn't have come," said Mary. "I'm just taking up room these people need. My trip's not necessary at all. It's purely selfish!"

"Don't say that," Hod begged. "It's *very* necessary to me!"

"I had no idea it would be like this! Will it be this way the rest of the trip?"

"I'm afraid so. From here on we get deeper and deeper into the section of the country where most of the camps are located. People have got to go see their men, and the men have got to go see their people. And that makes a lot of travel."

Just then the loud-speaker behind them blared out: "Two sections for servicemen loading at Docks 7 and 8! Servicemen only! Two sections, now loading at Docks 7 and 8!"

Hod thought quickly. "Mary," he said, "we'll never get on one of these busses. Come with me and I'll get you on the servicemen's bus."

He picked up her bags as he spoke and began shouldering a way for her through the crowd. She grabbed the back of his shirt and hung on, laughing, as he made a wedge of the bags and shoved their way through the jam. He reached the end of one of the lines waiting by the special busses, set the bags down and turned to her. "Give me your ticket," he said.

"My ticket? What for?"

"Don't ask questions! Just give me your ticket. I'll explain later."

Without further argument, she dug down in her purse and brought out the envelope containing her ticket. He took it and placed it with his own. They inched along with the line, and when they reached the driver, Hod handed him both tickets.

"My wife goes to El Paso. I go to Dallas."

"O.K."

Mary's eyes flew wide open, but she said nothing. On the bus they found a seat and settled themselves. Mary nudged him and whispered, "Why did you tell him I was your wife?"

"Because only a serviceman's wife, mother, sister, or some sort of special relative can travel with him on special transportation."

"Couldn't you have told him I was your sister?"

"I preferred the other relationship," and he grinned wickedly.

A journey is a strange suspension of time in space. You have left one place and have not yet arrived at another. In between is a small pendulum of time which is unidentified, unowned, unmoored. In the arc of that swing of the pendulum Hod and Mary talked the night away . . . softly, because the other passengers were sleeping. They found so much to say . . . so much to laugh about. They were the only two people in the world.

When, just before dawn, Mary slept for an hour, Hod turned so that he could watch her face. In the last shining brightness of the moon it was washed with silver. There was a purity in its unguarded stillness which made him long to touch it. Gently he reached one finger to the corner of her mouth, and felt its soft immobility. This is my girl, he thought. Out of all the world, this is my girl! I wish . . . and he flung it bitterly away. A man can't ask a woman to start out on a journey with him when he doesn't know where it ends. Or can he? Can a man find his destination truer with a woman taking one step at a time with him? Mary! Mary! Love me, Mary, and heal me!

" You're wonderful," he whispered, when she awoke.

" At five o'clock in the morning? "

" At any time! "

" That's because we're riding a bus from Nashville to Memphis."

" That's because you're Mary! "

At Memphis they worked out a system. As soon as the bus unloaded, Hod found a porter. " Where does the Dallas bus load? " he asked.

" Dock 6," was the answer. They took their bags to Dock 6 and set them down on the curb.

" Now, I'll stay here with the bags while you go eat your breakfast. Then when you come back, I'll go eat," Hod said.

" We're the first in line this time," Mary observed.

" We'll be the first on that bus," he promised.

A long day and another night went by. There were no more changes until Dallas, and they made a home for themselves of the familiar seat on the bus. They had never lived anywhere else. They slept in snatches and talked interminably. There was so little time . . . only now . . . today, tonight. And beyond that the spread of a sea between them, and the dark night of war. He must know what she thought, what she did, who she was. What kind of little girl were you, Mary? Whom have you loved, and who has hurt you? Do you like squirrel an' dumplin's? Do you like to fish? Do you know the sweetest sound in the world is the G string on my guitar, and do you know your voice is like it? And he must tell her about Hod Pierce. Make her remember Hod Pierce! Make her love Hod Pierce!

All too soon they came to Dallas, in the early morning hours of the third day. The light was strained and thin, and they were lost in it. Their home was gone. Hod drained the cup of the last drop of her presence. There were two hours before her bus left and he drew her to an island around the corner of the station, where they could grab at forgotten words.

" Will you write to me? "

" Of course."

" Mary, don't forget me."

" I won't."

" Even if it's a long time? "

" Even if it's a long time."

" Will you write soon? "

" Just as soon as I get there."

" Mary . . ."

" Hush, now. Be still."

At last he had to take her to the door of the bus. " This is my wife," he told the driver, dedicating himself. " I have to leave her here. I'd appreciate it if you'd look after her the rest of the way."

" I'll do that, soldier," promised the driver, and he placed Mary's small bag and her coat in the seat directly behind him. " You'll ride there better than anywhere else in the bus," he said.

They clung to their last moments as long as they could, but the time came when the driver touched Mary's shoulder apologetically. " You'd better get on now, ma'am."

She turned to Hod and went homing into his arms. She knows, he thought, she knows I have to hold her in my arms, so they can remember. So they won't be empty ever again. He held her hungrily and closed his eyes against the parting. Then he found

180

her mouth and was pulled down and drowned in its sweetness. Suddenly he released her and walked away . . . out of sight . . . without looking back. He didn't want to hear the bus leave. He didn't want to watch her go.

He had sixteen cents left in his pocket. He breakfasted on doughnuts and coffee and then shook the dust of Dallas from his feet. He hitched a ride to Austin, and all the way he remembered Mary . . . Mary.

CHAPTER TWENTY-ONE

BACK IN CAMP, Hod counted the days. If she gets to El Paso tonight and writes tomorrow, then I should hear from her on Friday. He sweated out the days. Suppose she doesn't write. But she said she would. She's not like other girls. She wouldn't promise and then not write.

He was due to go back to the Gulf coast on Monday, and he was desperately afraid he would have to leave before her letter came. Mail call, which had not been overly important to him before, suddenly became the center of his days. Even before Friday he was hanging around, waiting. And on Friday he was panicky. All at once he wished the mail would never come, so he wouldn't have to know she didn't write. He was a fool for thinking it had meant anything to her. There wouldn't be a letter, of course. It was just a pickup on a bus.

But he made himself go over and stand around as nonchalantly as possible. He watched each letter, wondering what it would look like if it did come. Pierce! There it was! Just a little, square envelope, with his name in a free, flowing hand across the front. He was shaking when he took it. He set his teeth and swallowed hard, and the sweat ran down his chin. He slipped the letter into his shirt pocket and walked back to his tent to read it. He wanted to be alone when he opened it. He flung himself on his cot and studied her writing for a time, deliberately postponing the joy of reading what she had written, savoring a little longer the sweetness of suspense.

Then he ripped it open. "Dear Hod: We arrived on time and Miss Willie met me . . . The bus driver took excellent care of me . . . a pleasant trip . . . lots of fun . . . We are going over into old Mexico for two or three days . . ." Three pages of gay, friendly news. She wrote like she talked, giving the details of the rest of her trip in a laughing fashion that made him smile. He read it through again, searching between the lines for something personal and meaningful. But it wasn't there. He could make no more of it than was written.

He didn't know what he had expected, and he felt, suddenly, a little let down. Don't be a fool, he told himself. Did you think she would write she loved you, just like that . . . out of a clear blue sky! His spirits lifted again. At least she had written. That was something. Surely, if he wrote carefully, he could keep her letters coming. That was the main thing right now. He dashed over to the PX for stationery, and although he would have no time to write before night, he was composing his letter as he went.

When Hod's letters began to arrive regularly in El Paso, Miss Willie raised a sandy eyebrow at her niece. "New heart interest, Mary?" she teased. "Army too, I see."

Mary had not told Miss Willie about Hod yet. Now she stood, tapping the letter against her chin, weighing the need to talk about Hod against the need to keep him alone inside her. She felt that her reluctance must have come from her feeling that he was different. She didn't know whether she could do justice to him. And he deserved that.

Suddenly she was telling the whole story, beginning at the beginning, with the delay of her start which had made her have to cancel her train reservation. Her decision when she was free, finally, to attempt the trip by bus. The meeting with Hod. The long hours together. Even the parting at Dallas. She told that too.

Miss Willie was silent when Mary's voice stopped. Her face reflected her conflicting emotions. And then she raised her hand to push her glasses up on her nose, a gesture which was as much a part of Miss Willie as her eyes or her hair or her thin, angular body.

"I know all you're going to say," Mary put in quickly. "I *can't* be in love with this man so suddenly. I've only known him . . . well, I've only been with him once. But remember that *once* was forty-two hours long. And I don't know anything about him except what he told me. And he's a farmer . . . a poor, hillbilly farmer at that . . . uneducated, uncultured. Except that he's *not!* Miss Willie, he's not! He has an educated heart, and a good, quick mind. He may not be cultured in our sophisticated sense of the word. But I can't tell you how weary I am of that anyhow. Hod is naturally a cultured person. He loves beauty and he has a questing spirit. He is gentle and good, honorable and idealistic, and unbelievably sweet. He's warm and big and wholesome. It's been so long since I knew anyone . . . anyone at all like that. Anyone more than half alive! Don't you see? "

Miss Willie sighed. " I see. I see he's very important to you, Mary."

" I'm afraid he is."

There was a silence and then Miss Willie leaned forward and touched Mary's hand. " Mary," she said, " forgive me for saying this . . . but if he continues to be important to you . . . important enough, say, for you to marry him . . . are you going to spend your life defending him so fiercely? "

Mary's breath drew in sharply, and her head jerked as if Miss Willie had slapped her. Her teeth caught her lower lip and her eyes filled. " I needed that, didn't I? How rude I was to him! How unjust! No! No! No, Miss Willie. He needs no defense. Thank you for reminding me! "

It was two weeks before Hod heard again, because the letters had to follow him to the coast. Then there were two on the same day, and in the second one she wrote that she was going home and she wished he could be riding back with her. She didn't think she would enjoy the trip home as much as she had the one coming out! Hope soared high on this meager strand she held out. She had fun with me! She's been thinking about me! He built a high castle with the bricks of his hopes.

The engineers spent another month on the coast and then hurricanes and squalls sent them back to camp. He dreaded any shift in his movements now, because they meant a delay in her letters.

183

Fellows in the outfit had quickly caught on to his concern about the mail, and his nightly absorption in his own letters. They kidded him unmercifully.

"What was it Sergeant Pierce said to you about six months ago, Hough?"

"I remember it like yesterday. He said there wasn't no woman livin' that could interest him enough to make him write a letter ever' night!"

"Yeah? And what would you call what he's doin' right now?"

"Well, it ain't washin' dishes!"

But when they returned to camp, he was in such good luck he could hardly believe it. One of the men in his company went AWOL, to see his girl in Cincinnati, and Hod was detailed to go after him. He could have cut a buck and wing right there! The way to Cincinnati was straight through Louisville, and Mary was in Louisville!

"Brother, I *love* you," he said to the first sergeant, who brought him the news.

"We love you too, dearie," said Jenkins, the sergeant, sweetly. "That's why we pulled strings so you could go. And give our love to Mary," he added wickedly.

He sent her a wire asking her to meet his train, and she was waiting by the steps when he walked through the gate. He saw her first. She's so alive, he thought. She's so terribly alive! She looks like Duke on a fresh coon scent! Even her nose is alive!

And then she was in his arms. She kept nothing back of her gladness to see him. There was no false note of coyness. She seemed to know he had come to her with all of himself, and she didn't betray him with shyness.

They found a corner table in the restaurant in the station where they could eat and talk. He had three hours, and in that time he must tell her all he had to say. He thought he knew what he wanted to say, but the briefness of the time, her disturbing nearness, and the urgency which was pressing him made him say it badly. How does a man find the way to tell a girl she has become his whole life? When he is all but on his way to battle, how does he find the courage to ask her to love him? He stumbled and halted. Mary reached across the table for his hand.

"Are you trying to tell me you love me?"

184

"Yes."

"Then just say it. There isn't need for any more."

"I love you, Mary."

"I love you, Hod."

The shoddy station restaurant became a green pasture, and Mary's words led him beside still waters. He lifted his head and drank deeply.

"I've nothing to bring you but myself, Mary."

"Can a man bring anything more?"

"Oughtn't he to have something to offer? Some money in the bank? A job? Something real?"

"Hod . . . in the hours we were together on our trip you told me all about yourself. You told me about a little boy who wanted to learn everything he could. You told me about a young man who had to step into his father's shoes. You told me about a man, who made of himself a good soldier, and a better man. More than that, in every word you spoke you told me also of a gentle, tender spirit . . . loving beauty, in the hills, in music, in people, in life. You are offering me the only things that count. You've got a mind that is eager, a sense of honor and duty, and gentleness, goodness, sweetness. Those things are real. Nothing else in the world is real, beside them. If you had a million dollars and lacked them, you would have only a barren plain to offer. A man can't fill an empty soul with money and call it riches. And no man whose soul is overflowing is ever really poor."

His eyes misted. "You're wonderful!"

"No. I just love you and I know what you are."

Hod took a deep breath, and Mary laughed gently. "Let yourself down, Hod. Don't look so hard at Tomorrow. We'll handle that together when it comes."

They turned to the food which had grown cold on their plates. It was tasteless straw, but they picked at it.

"I don't even have the money to buy you a ring. A girl should at least have an engagement ring."

"Why?"

"Well, just because . . . well, everybody does, don't they?"

"We're not everybody."

"Don't you want a ring?"

"Yes. A wedding ring, someday."

185

"But I want you to have something now!"

"Give me something of your own then."

He thought for a moment, then he took his engineers' insigne from his lapel and handed it across the table.

She cupped it in her hand and looked at it. "I'll wear this on a chain," she said finally. "It will be my engagement ring, darling."

The thread was spinning short. The war filled stations all over the country with such partings as theirs, and each was fraught with its own grief. But to Hod this leave-taking was unbearable. To leave her so soon! And he couldn't tell her that he wouldn't see her again. That before he could hold her close like this again he would have fought a war. That maybe he would never hold her close like this again. He could only let the bitter-sweetness of her touch flood him with a silent despair, and tear himself apart to leave it.

"I'll write every day," she promised, "and you'll come home the first time you can. The time will pass."

"The very first time I can," he repeated. "The very first time I can!"

Within two months he was at Port of Embarkation. The time there was packed with lectures, instructions, indoctrination. There were changes to make in his allotment, in his insurance, in his whole outlook. The grim preparations for actual conflict were full of implications of life cut short.

With each promotion Hod had increased the amount of money he sent home. When he made sergeant, he felt he could send enough so that the simplest way to handle it would be through an allotment which would regularly and directly be sent to the folks. He had pushed the amount up from ten dollars with which he started to forty dollars a month. Now he must think of saving for himself and Mary.

So he wrote Hattie that he was in love, that he was engaged, and that he was planning to be married just as soon as he returned from overseas, and that he felt he should put aside as much as he could spare for himself. He told her that, with times so much better, maybe they could make out with a little less. So he was cutting the allotment to them to twenty-five dollars per month; he hoped they would understand.

A sergeant's pay, plus the twenty per cent overseas increase, would be ninety-seven dollars per month. He knew he would need very little of it, so he tried then, to make a fifty dollar allotment to Mary. He wanted so much to give all his material wealth into her hands along with himself. He wanted to lay everything that was his before her and say, " I thee endow."

But he ran into the rules against making allotments to persons not related by blood, and had to write her: " I tried, but they say no. So I am making a separate allotment to Ma, and I'm asking her to save it for us."

He felt so good about saving the money. He felt as if already Mary had placed her hand in his and started down the road with him.

·

CHAPTER TWENTY–TWO

Early one Sunday morning in October, the 291st marched aboard a transport and was slipped quietly out to sea. No man aboard was entirely insensitive to the widening distance between him and his native land. In various ways, according to their temperamental differences, they expressed their emotions, ignored them, or controlled them.

Hod stood at the rail and let his eyes hold the dear earth as long as there was the faintest line of it on the horizon. He was leaving so much! Then he went below and sought to re-establish his identity with the familiar things of his own possessions.

Two things served to ease the tension of that first day at sea. The first was a moment of grim laughter furnished by a replacement who had come aboard at the last minute. He had been jerked out of a chair in front of a sewing machine in a quartermaster outfit, being told only that he was going out as a replacement. He uneasily eyed the men as they unpacked their bags and put things away. Finally he timidly approached an officer. " Sir," he said, " this doesn't look much like a quartermaster outfit."

" Quartermaster! " the officer roared. " This is the 291st Combat Engineers! "

" Combat engineers! " echoed the boy, and he keeled over in a dead faint.

Because they themselves were so shaky and tense, the men roared with laughter at this. The poor guy, scared stiff of being with a combat outfit! They were tough and hard. They couldn't tremble. But when a man fainted in fear of their job, the shadow of their own fear was somewhat lifted. Someone else had trembled for them. So they laughed.

The other event was mail call. The last until the voyage ended. And there were four good letters from Mary. She wrote with no foreshadowing of grief. With no portent of loss. She accepted his going as quietly as if he had simply gone around the corner to the grocery store. In the entire two years Hod was away, never once did he receive a letter that placed the burden of her anxiety and fear on him. She carried it alone, as he must carry his. When, later, he saw other men torn and drawn by letters from home, he thought of Mary proudly. He was never afraid to open a letter from her. He knew, always, that they would share home with him in all its small details, and would offer him sanctuary in her out-pouring love.

They set foot on English soil at Liverpool, and thirty-six hours later had once more settled themselves into their routine. This much of home they brought with them. The American Army on foreign soil was never entirely in an alien land. It moved into England, Africa, Europe, and the islands, but it made of every place it touched an American colony.

Along about the middle of December the first of Mary's Christmas packages reached Hod. It was packed thoughtfully, so as to get the most into the small space. And each package inside was gaily wrapped with bright paper and scarlet ribbons. She sent him a little piece of cedar, just for the Christmas smell, she said. And there was a small fruit cake, a fountain pen (he'd lost his old one), a carton of cigarettes, and, wrapped between two pairs of soft woolen socks, a small, black disk. He looked at it for a moment, puzzled. What in the world! And then he knew. She had made a record for him. She had written a letter he could hear instead of read. He waved it at the other guys in the tent. "Hey, look! Mary's sent me a record! She's written me a letter on a phonograph record! "

" Let's see! "

" Well, whaddya know! "

" How you gonna play it? " his bunkmate asked.

" On a phonograph, of course! "

" Yeah, but where you gonna get a phonograph? "

" I'll find one," he swore. " I'll find one! And you guys keep your eyes open too."

And they did. Every man in the company heard of Hod's record, and every one of them kept his eyes open for a phonograph. It came to be a matter of first importance to all of them. And one evening, Jenkins the first sergeant burst into Hod's tent. " Hey! Hey, Pierce! We've found it! Pierce! Where's your record? We've found a phonograph! "

Hod ran to his bag and dug frantically. " Where? " he said, excited, flinging shirts, shorts, and socks heedlessly into the air. " Where'd you find it? "

" Hough found it in a little pub over on the east side. It's an old beat-up victrola, but it'll still play, and they've got some needles too."

The news spread and about ten men went with Hod to the pub. " C'mon," they yelled, " Pierce's gonna play his record! "

Hod knew Mary wouldn't mind. No man's love was entirely private in such a fraternity, and she had become very real to these men who saw her picture daily, who heard excerpts from her letters, and who chaffed Hod over his own nightly letters. They were now entitled to hear her voice.

At the pub Hod was so excited he could hardly set the needle. " Here, let me do it," said Jenkins. But he too was excited, and it took several false starts before the record began to move. At last it took hold, and faintly and dimly the voice came through the wheezy old machine. The men bent closer to hear.

" Hello, darling . . ." And with the first words Hod was lost in memories. He heard her voice saying a hundred things. Did you ever see a more beautiful sunset in your life? The first words she ever said to him were words of beauty, and she had never failed to make it real to him since. Is there anything more a man can offer? The substance of faith. I love you, Hod. The green pasture and the still waters. " I love you, Hod."

The record ended, and he'd lost everything between. "Play it again," he said to Jenkins. And then, "Play it again."

"Who is it?" asked a kid who had come along just because a crowd was gathered.

Jenkins turned on him indignantly. "That's Mary!" he said.

The months turned the pages of the calendar through the long, black winter, and the 291st moved through them bleakly. Their day came on June 20, 1944. Rumor had it that they had escaped Omaha Beach by the flip of a coin. The guys liked to tell that another outfit of corps engineers was ready to go too, and it was a tossup which should go. And the other outfit lost.

On his trip home from Europe a year and a half later, a member of that battalion told Hod about Omaha Beach that day. They had gone in at H hour plus two minutes, and they had been massacred. The battalion was decimated in the carnage of a wave-washed slaughterhouse. The man who told the story to Hod said he was one of ten men out of his company who came through alive. Hod could not say why one should be chosen to go and one to stay. But for the flip of a coin, according to rumor, he might have lain on the riddled ledges of Omaha Beach.

On June 24, Hod's outfit landed on the now quiet beach. The story of its racking pain was everywhere evident in the burned-out trucks, tanks, and jeeps, and in the great litter of ruined materials and supplies which had been discarded. But the torture had moved on and the sands drifted slowly over the scars.

They moved inland fast after landing, and were under fire within twenty-four hours. They were bivouacked in an open field, unloading trucks, settling in for the night. Hod heard a whistling sound and then a dull detonation. A burst of dirt and debris flew up in the air about a hundred yards away. Hod threw himself down, hard. The high whine of another shell could be heard, and then another and another, until they were dropping all around. The noise of the explosions was deafening, and the air was full of flying dirt, pieces of trucks, lumber and metal. Hod dug himself into a little ditch and hunched himself down as low as he could. Fear gripped him and he panted and sweated against it. Nobody could live through this, he thought. We'll all be wiped out! This is the end of the road!

But the barrage lifted as suddenly as it had begun, and Hod stood up and looked around him. It had wrought a terrible carnage. Trucks, tanks, tents were blasted into heaps of burning chaos. But the worst was the wounded who lay where they had been hit. And the dead who were strewn in pieces over the wide field. He shuddered. Artillery fire! He had a new respect for it.

He felt of himself and wiped his face with his shirttail. And he watched other men crawling from their ditches and foxholes. He lost his feeling of shame for having been afraid. They had all been afraid. They crawled out, dirty, torn, and white-faced, some of them with their sickness still staining their shirts. It had been a whole community of fear, and Hod felt close to each one of them. They looked at each other strangely, as if a miracle had happened and they were a part of it. Hod felt his knees trembling and he sat down. "Next time," he said, "next time I'm goin' to dig me a deeper hole."

They swung across France that summer, sleeping lightly in foxholes and slit trenches, alert always for air raids, keeping company day and night with heavy artillery. They grew bleary-eyed, bearded, and dirty. They bathed and washed their clothes only when they hit a river or stream. They forgot what a bed felt like. They celebrated when they could forage eggs or chickens or a bottle of Calvados to add to their monotonous rations. They thinned down, whetted and honed into a tight compact outfit, snarling, cursing, griping, hating, killing, building, and loving.

Gone was all Hod's objectiveness, now. This tight little group of men was the only reality in the world. Mary's letters came as regularly as mail call. He read them avidly, and occasionally he had the feeling she was near. But mostly they were like pages of fiction. She was in the dream of peace and home. But here there wasn't time to dream.

Hod looked around him sometimes at the men and wondered at what was happening to them. There were times when he hated them and felt their coarseness and toughness rub him like a saddle on a sore back. But most times he loved them. Every day he saw an act of heroism. But heroism had become so common that it had ceased to be heroic. These men sacrificed for each other as a matter of course. They cursed at each other, stole cigarettes and writing paper, articles of clothing and bedding, and then crawled out on the skeletons of bridges under the fury of machine-gun fire to drag one another back to safety. Hod won his own bronze star that way. It never occurred to him that he had done a brave thing. He had done what any other man in the outfit would have done for him. Sometimes he thought how war took men and wrapped them round with brotherhood, and, even with the sound of guns in their ears, made them think of one another.

They moved on, always eastward. They bridged the Ruhr that spring, under an incessant and withering stream of fire. It took them three days, and they lost men, but when they had finished, they had built one of the longest single-span bridges ever built by Army engineers. When Hod looked at the casualty list for his own company there was alum in his mouth. Jenkins' name was on the list this time. Every bridge they built took its toll, but the Ruhr was deadly costly.

War's end found them at a little village on the far side of the Danube. War's end! It left a flat taste in their mouths. They were too tired, too beat up, too stretched out. Hod tried to feel elated, but all he wanted to do was to go home and sleep a hundred years on a soft bed. He didn't think he would ever get the tiredness out of his bones!

And there was still a war going on in the Pacific. There was a lot of agitation in most of the outfits about whether they would be sent to the Pacific or not. But the 291st was pretty unconcerned. O.K., they said; O.K. If they need us to help finish it up. But they sure better send us by home first!

And then the outfit began breaking up. The point system started picking them off, sorting them, crating them, and shipping them home. Hod was a high-point man, with his long service, and he wrote Mary in July: "Get your wedding dress ready! I'll be home before Christmas!"

Two years to a day from the Sunday he had steamed out of Boston harbor he stepped off the gangplank in New York. Two long years of such experiences as men can never forget, no matter how deep they may bury them. Hod had not been the sort of man to agonize over the reasons for the war. Finding himself

192

drawn into it, he had gone along, wasting neither time nor tears over something that could not be helped. He had done his share of work, sweated and toiled and been horribly afraid at times. The two years had left their imprint forever. But there had been no worms in his brain — no maggots of hate either for the enemy or for his own Government. A thing had had to be done. And he had done his part. He had come through remarkably sane, remarkably balanced. He was just tired.

The first thing he did upon landing was to drink three pints, one right after the other, of fresh, cold milk, which the ladies of the Red Cross proffered each returning soldier. Hod wondered how even in two years a man could get so thirsty for the sweet, chilled taste of milk. He let it slide down his throat slowly, savoring every drop of it, making it last, not yet realizing he was back where he could have all he wanted.

At Camp Shanks, the first stage of his separation, Hod sent Mary a wire: " Just landed. Will call tonight if possible. See you soon. Love, Hod."

In the phone booth that night he listened while the operator put through his call. Heard the Louisville operator repeat the number, heard the ringing signal, and tried to imagine the small apartment where the telephone was now clamoring out the good news. The palms of his hands were wet, and a drop of sweat under his left arm trickled down his ribs, making him squirm. Soon, now. Soon. Then the receiver clicked.

" Hello. Hod? " There it was . . . the rich, singing voice. He closed his eyes and let the sound of it wash over him, pour into him, fill him and run over! Dear God, how good it was to hear it again! It made everything real. The war, the separation, the land of home. He could say nothing for a long moment, and then he forced his voice past the tightness in his throat.

" Mary . . . Mary, I'm home! "

He reached Louisville on Thursday at two o'clock in the morning. Mary's sleepy voice was startled into full awakening when he called her, and she told him to take a cab; she would dress and be waiting.

Her flying feet reached the door before his finger lifted from the bell. Everything about her was flying . . . her hair, the banners in her eyes, her hands, lifted to his face, and her body fitting itself to his. She flew straight to his weary heart and cradled it in her gentleness; she rocked it to rest with her cool cheek pressed to his; she took the yoke of his bruises upon her warm mouth lifted so eagerly to his. He sighed. Now he could rest.

They were married as soon as it was possible. When they stood before the minister in the little chapel, Hod felt his stomach go shaky, and his knees trembled. He had forgotten how lovely Mary was. In all the months he had kept a sure remembrance of her before him, not forgetting the dark of her hair or the depth of her eyes. But today, in a dress of some soft, white material, she was like a tall, white candle, alight with pure fire. There was a shining look on her face, and her eyes, resting on Hod in tender possession, were still and loving. She was more beautiful than he had thought possible. The faint scent of the small bouquet she carried came to him, and he closed his eyes for a second. I shall never forget this moment, he thought. Not time nor life is going to dull it. For in this hour I am made whole.

They went to Spring Mill in the southern Indiana hills for their honeymoon. The beautiful lodge was set in the midst of the great park like a château Hod had seen on the Aisne. It had the same solid dignity and the builders had captured something of an ancient grace. The drive curved before it in a crescent of white gravel and swooped to a widened stop in front of the entrance. Hod liked it immediately.

They had a wonderful week, sleeping late in the morning, having their breakfast sent up to the room, wandering over the hill trails during the day, visiting the old mill in the rehabilitated village. They had long, dawdling dinners in the evening, and then more often than not they walked out again under a huge harvest moon. They told themselves over and over again that October was undoubtedly the most perfect month of the year for a honeymoon. The countryside was aflame with color, extravagant and riotous and gay. And the air was clear and golden and sparkling.

When they came back to their room at night, they built a small

194

fire in the fireplace and sat before it, watching the flames lick over the logs, setting them to snapping and crackling and to shooting sparks out on the hearth. Mary would sit on a low stool and hold out her hands to the warmth, a soft, yellow robe wrapped close about her. When Hod pulled the big chair up near the fire he made room for her, and she snuggled down beside him. Holding her thus, her hair dark and fragrant on his face and her slender body warm against him, he knew a deep content. This was the way of a man and a woman, then. This oneness of spirit as well as of flesh. This taking in of each other so that never again were they clearly able to distinguish which was which. This merging and blending of self and self. This hidden pearl which a man found only in his wife.

And they talked. Hour after hour they talked. There was so much lost time to make up. And then when they had said it all, they came back ever and again to the miracle of love. To the miracle of being together after the long months of struggling toward each other through the deep fears of the war. To the miracle of holding now, for all time, only love and peace.

They would have liked to stay on at the mill, drawing out the days of their first joy in each other, but the ridge was waiting, and the folks. They left, finally, with a feeling of sadness . . . a putting an end to something they would never have again. Mary looked back as they drove down the curving drive. Nothing will ever be quite like this again, she thought. The first week . . . the first days and nights can never be repeated. And then she turned around and looked resolutely ahead. What lay there, she determined, would be infinitely better!

CHAPTER TWENTY-THREE

THEY BOUGHT AN OLD RATTLETRAP CAR and made the trip to the ridge in it. They wondered if it would get them there, but even the uncertainty was fun. When they came to Campbellsville, Hod began to get excited. "It's only sixteen miles now," he said. "It won't be long."

A few miles out of Campbellsville they left the pavement to follow a graveled road. It had been washed by rain and eaten out by traffic until it resembled a piece of corrugated tin, and it was full of holes which heavy wheels had gouged out. Hod sent the car skimming over it carelessly and casually, and the corduroy ridges made a constant, jarring vibration that shook every bone in Mary's body. Occasionally, when the wheels hit a very deep hole, she was thrown violently upward, and when she came back down, her body was slammed against the cushion with such force that she felt certain the springs would flatten uselessly and permanently.

"Did you ever herd cattle?" she asked finally.

Hod looked at her wonderingly. "No," he said. "Never did. Why?"

"You drive this car like you were an old hand at it!"

Hod laughed. "This road's better for horses and mules at that, isn't it?"

"Next time I think I'll walk," Mary threatened, grabbing at the door as they hit another hole.

"This is the county pike," Hod said. "I helped build this road back before the war. And it was a good road when we built it. Needs to be scraped, though, now."

Just then the road dipped down and to Mary's amazement she saw that a shallow creek wandered across in front of them. Hod shifted gears and nosed the car gently into the water. It was about hub deep. When they had climbed the slight rise on the other side, he didn't bother to change gears. They ground along for a few hundred feet and then dipped down again. There was the creek once more. They forded it and climbed another rise, and then dipped again.

"Don't tell me," said Mary, "let me guess. That's Wandering Creek!"

"That's Wandering Creek!" Hod affirmed.

"It lives up to its name, doesn't it?"

"Why, yes, I reckon it does. Reckon that's how it got its name in the first place. It's a humdinger when it's in flood, too. Spreads out all over these bottoms."

"When it gets up, how do you cross it?"

"You don't."

Mary thought about this for a moment. "When it gets up, then, there's no way to get to town."

"Nope."

"Suppose somebody got sick, or was dying, and you had to get a doctor."

"Well, if you had to have a doctor from Campbellsville, you'd just have to wait. But there's a pretty good doctor over at the Gap, and you can always get through that way by the old road. This creek doesn't stay up long, though. It gets up like a flash, but it goes down in a few hours."

"Why don't they bridge it?"

"It would take a bridge a mile long to make the highway safe. The county hasn't got that much money. A bridge like that would cost a small fortune to build."

The country was pretty here. They had been following the rounded edges of the hills for some time, hills that rose to the left in undulating folds. They were broken up by small ravines and hollows, and back up in each hollow Mary could see houses and barns and small, cleared fields. The houses were little unpainted shacks . . . one or two rooms slanting crazily against the hill, the yards always full of cluttered trash and swarming with children. Some of them were built on the hillsides themselves, and hugged close to the rocky slopes to keep from tumbling down. Some were built down in the hollow, perched up on stilts for safety from high water. Some ventured down near the pike, but these were few. It was as if they guarded their depressing poverty from the knowledge of the world, hiding it in the cracks and crannies of the hills.

To the right the valley stretched fertile and green for several miles to the row of trees which marked the course of the river. The fields were richer here, and the farmhouses were larger and neater, although Mary wondered if all the farmers down here kept their cultivators drawn up by the side of the front porch. They passed no large farms . . . great land holdings such as those in the bluegrass. There were no fine homes. At best there were a few rich acres, and a neat, four-room house. At worst there were the shacks on the hillsides, and a stony corn patch.

"Is this Pierce land around here?" Mary asked.

"No. We've never come this far down in the bottoms. Pierce land lies on the ridge and in the hollers on both sides. Lem, my uncle, is the only one that lives near the pike. His place is right at the foot of the main ridge, where we turn off. When Grampa Dow gave his three boys their choice of land, Lem liked the piece down here on the pike. Gault took the piece on the ridge down the road from the home place. Pa was the youngest, and he took the home place."

They traveled another mile or two, and then Hod said, " That's Lem's place right there," and nodded to the left.

Mary saw a trim white house reminiscent of a Connecticut saltbox, set well back from the road, with a stretch of green yard widening down to the road and with huge barns framing it in the back.

" That place looks right prosperous." Already Mary was developing a comparative sense of values.

" Lem's done right well down here. I reckon he's the best fixed of any of the Pierces now. Reckon he was pretty smart to pick this piece. But it's too close to the pike to suit me." Mary looked at him thoughtfully.

" Here's where we turn up the ridge." Hod was turning off the pike to the left.

Mary looked at the trail he was following. It resembled a road only because there were faint wheel tracks among the rocks and because it cut through the woods in a narrow path. Hod shifted into low, and they inched into the climb. Almost at once they were on a narrow ledge, the hill falling away to the right and rising abruptly to the left. Slowly Hod eased the car up over the gullied tracks and around the sharp bends.

About halfway up, the road became a mere thread lying close to the hillside, and the car brushed the branches of trees and the overhanging bushes as it crept along. The roadbed was solid rock, now, and the tires slipped and bit for traction. To the right Mary could see down into the tops of the trees in the ravines. She shuddered and closed her eyes.

" Would it help any to hold my breath? " she whispered.

" Oh, we're almost up now. That wasn't so bad," and she felt the car ease into a more gradual incline.

" Thank goodness," she breathed. " If it had been any worse I'd have died! " She turned to look back. " Do the folks have to go up and down this hill every time they go anywhere? "

" Just when they go to the pike, or the county seat, or Campbellsville. But that's not everywhere by a long shot. You can go all over the ridge and up and down the hollers without comin' this way at all. Fact is, they don't go in town more than three or four times a year. Do most of their tradin' at the Gap. It's at the other end of the ridge, in a gap in the hills. The road along the ridge is rough, like I said, but the hills ease off down that way more gradually. Pa and Gault and Little Wells and the others that live up here on the ridge have to haul their tobacco and corn to market down this hill, though. Nearest market's at Springfield or Greensburg. But they make out, one way or another."

" Is this Piney Ridge we're on now? "

" This is Piney Ridge. We're in Pierce country now. This ridge, the hollers on either side, and the next two ridges are all what we call Piney Ridge."

The car had nosed up over the brow of the hill and was following a narrow, rutted pattern. It wound a meandering way down the top of the ridge, humping itself aimlessly along. On either side fields stretched to the very rim of the ridge and disappeared in a final cresting wave over the edge. Here and there a wooded section stood out, scarlet and gold against the cloud-locked sky.

They passed a little two-room shack, gray with age, and sagging at the corners. The front porch had fallen in and the screen door hung in tatters from its hinges. The windows had no screens. A decrepit bedstead leaned against an apple tree in the corner of the yard, which was bare of grass, and half a dozen dirty, unkempt children lolled on the splitting mattress.

" Who lives here, Hod? "

" Old Man Clark. This is Gault's tenant house. He lets the old man live there for nothing. None of us have got enough land to need a tenant any more, but the house was there and the Clarks didn't have any other place to go. He's gettin' too old to farm much. He makes out helpin' everybody a little."

" Whose children are those? "

" I don't know. I've been gone a long time, remember. Must be his daughter's, though. Seems to me Ma wrote something about Julie's husband leavin' her."

" Do you suppose they all live crowded up in that little house? "

Hod wrenched the car out of the ruts. " You'll see a lot of that

199

up here on the ridge, Mary. People depend on their folks when trouble comes. And their folks always take them in and help out. Crowding doesn't mean much here. Just a few more plates on the table, and another pallet or two on the floor."

They were coming to a place on the left of the road. The house was built of peeled logs, and looked as if it had two or three rooms. Smoke was curling out the chimney.

"That's a pretty little place," Mary observed.

"That's Gault's place." He smiled and waved as they went by.

"I didn't see anyone," Mary said.

"No, you wouldn't. Becky's startin' supper, but right now she's standin' there behind the window watchin' us go by. Old Man Clark and Mamie were watchin' from somewhere on their place too. Any time you go down this road you can know everybody'll see you. You may not see them, for they'll be behind a door or the window curtain, but they won't miss seein' you."

"You mean they watch for anyone passing?"

"Well, they don't exactly watch. But there's not enough passin' up and down this road but what each one goin' by is a special event. If they know you well, they'll call out as you go by. But today they're all keepin' out of sight because they don't know you. But they wouldn't miss the sight of you for anything in the world. Tomorrow they'll all be talkin' to each other about seein' you go by. They'll know what you look like, what kind of a hat you had on, the color of your dress, and about what you weigh."

Mary straightened up and gave her hat a settling pat. "I don't know that I like that," she protested.

"Oh, you get used to it. That's the way it is here. You can't make a move without everybody on the ridge knowin' it, and you might as well tell all your business straight out. They'll find it out sooner or later."

"But suppose I don't want to tell my business!"

"Then they'll think you're stuck-up and too good for them. They don't mean to be nosy. And they don't interfere. But it's a little, close-knit world here. Every family depends on every other family. In a way it's like one big family, and you can't keep secrets or have much privacy. Comin' from the city, you wouldn't understand that. You're used to havin' people mind their own business and leave you alone. But you don't have neighbors in the city, and you don't depend on each other. Here, everyone is your neighbor. And they stand by you when you need help, and you stand by them."

Mary took a deep breath. She felt suddenly as if she had been picked up and set down in some foreign land. All of this was unreal, alien . . . even incongruous. You read about places like this in books. You saw them from train windows, or from the side of a car speeding across the country. But a road like that one up the hogback of the ridge, and shanties like those down in the hollows, and people like the Clarks . . . they didn't exist in your own world. They were out there somewhere on the fringe. But they were right here in front of her . . . and, furthermore, she had married into them. The hogback and the shanties and the Clarks. This was Hod's land and these were his people. " Thy people shall be my people . . . whither thou goest."

She swallowed . . . hard.

" There it is," Hod said, as they came around the curve. " There it is. That's home! "

Mary saw the low house, weathered to a soft, rainy gray, framed by the picket fence stitched neatly around the tidy yard. She saw the low chimney, with smoke tailing out and skirling lazily upward. She saw it set against a sunset sky and thought, It's like a picture. A pastel in rain-washed gray and blue. Ancient, peaceful, and beautiful.

Hod laid his hand on the horn and kept it there, sending a raucous, glad trumpeting into the air. And onto the porch, railed across the front of the house, swarmed a group of figures who spilled into the yard and onto the pickets of the fence.

Suddenly Mary was frightened. " Hod, I'm scared," she said. She began ineffectually to push her hair under her hat, to straighten her dress and to dab at her face with her handkerchief. " I feel so dirty and mussed. What if they don't like me! "

" They'll like you all right," Hod answered, but he was too excited to comfort her beyond that. This was home, and there were the folks. Mary's words made little impression on him, and what she might be feeling was not conveyed to him at all. In this moment of home-coming he was insulated by his own feelings of

201

joy, becoming for this space of time the boy of the ridge, the returned son, who transcended the husband . . . the lover. He did not consciously remove from his oneness with Mary. He simply returned spiritually to a familiar world, so personally, so intimately, so obviously his own that he went back into himself, where Mary could not yet follow.

They stopped in front of the gate, and the woman hanging to the gate ran out. Hod was out of the car instantly and in her arms, and she was crying over him. A tall, stooped man joined them and laid his arm across Hod's shoulders. Mary sat still in the car and watched, feeling small and alone . . . forgotten. What they said to each other was murmured so low and so brokenly that she could not hear. Don't be an idiot, she warned herself. They haven't seen him for two years either. And he's their son. Can't you be big enough to share him for a few minutes? But the newness of her own possession was still upon her, and she was bereft by this sudden need for generosity.

She studied them as they stood near Hod. Hattie was stooped and thin, and she had run out clumsily in big, heavy shoes. But her cotton print dress was freshly washed, and the bright apron tied around her waist was stiff with starch. Mary watched her face. How finely sculptured it was! Not even age could ruin those high, molded cheekbones, nor the firm, squared chin. The skin was remarkably unwrinkled. It must once have been as creamy as a magnolia petal, Mary thought. Hattie kept tight hold of Hod's hand, and her mouth worked pitifully.

The man, Tom, was taller than Hod, but, like Hattie, he was stooped and thin. When he turned so that Mary could see his face, she was struck by the benign calmness of it. The gentle, patient kindness of it. She thought she had never seen a face on which enduring goodness was stamped so indelibly. Fine lines were etched around the mouth, and deep furrows in the forehead. But there was dignity and nobility written across that countenance, and Mary saw another thing. How much Hod looked like him! Someday his face will look just like that, she thought. Someday. Because he is the same kind of man his father is.

And then Hattie was coming to the car. "Now you're Mary, ain't you?" she said warmly, wiping at her eyes with her apron. "Git out! Git out! I didn't aim to be so unmannerly, but hit's sich

202

a joy to see Hod agin." She searched Mary's face. " Oh, I'd have knowed you anywheres! Hod sent us yer picture, an' he's writ about you a heap. You look jist like I thought you would, only I believe yer purtier. Git out. The menfolks'll bring yer things in. Supper's jist ready, an' I'll bound yer hungry."

They walked up the path, and Mary saw that Hod was surrounded by the group on the porch.

" That there's Irma, an' her man," Hattie explained, " an' their two young'uns. They was all bound to see Hod too."

And then there was Sarah. Mary watched Hod try to make friends with her. At six she was delicately blond, with ash-silver curls. Hod held her in the curve of his arm, squatting to her height. But she kept her finger in her mouth, her eyes on the floor, speechless and timid.

" She ain't talked about nothin' fer a month but Hod," Hattie explained. " Git up in the mornin' awantin' to know if today he was comin'. Go to bed at night askin' if tomorrer was the day. An' look at her now! Cain't you say nothin', Sary? "

" Leave her alone," said Hod. " She'll get used to me."

Mary's heart went out to the little figure. She had seen those agonies of embarrassment in the schoolroom, and she knew the painful tumult that was throbbing through the child. In her own time and in her own way she would break through it. But Mary was glad Hod didn't press her now.

Irma came forward, struggling with her own kind of awkwardness, the timidity of any ridge person meeting a stranger. But there was warmth in her awkwardness . . . a warmth that expressed pride in Hod's choice. Hod had married a city girl. He had done something no other Pierce had ever done. So Irma's greeting, while brief, held that undercurrent of pride, and her eyes were friendly.

For that matter, Mary noticed that except for Hattie no one had much to say. It was only in the quick, fleeting touch of a hand, and in the glad glow of the eyes that she could tell how deeply they were touched . . . by Hod's home-coming . . . by the strangeness of her city presence.

When they went in the house, Hod stopped just inside the door. It was just the same. Forever and enduring the same. Home, embracing and enveloping him. A quietness stole over him. He took

203

in the details. No. It wasn't quite the same. There was new paper on the walls . . . rich red roses climbing up a green lattice, with fat cherubs fluttering from bouquet to bouquet. The seams were not quite true, and Hod could see Ma and Irma struggling to match the pattern. There were new curtains at the windows too. And a new linoleum on the floor. He knew these things had been done in Mary's honor. Hattie and Irma must have worked for weeks to bring the house to this shining state of readiness. But no notice must be taken. That would shame Hattie before Mary.

Mary followed Hod through the house, and where his eyes fondly rested on the familiar things that had surrounded him always, hers took in the bare skeleton of furnishings. Everything was clean, spotlessly clean. But the wide cracks between the scrubbed boards of the floor could not be hidden, nor could the sag toward the middle from each end of the house. The new cushions on the old hickory chairs could not disguise them or make them into comfortable, easy chairs. There was one rocking chair in the house. It had been Gramma's. Mary remembered that Gramma had died while Hod was overseas.

To Mary there was something pathetic in the poverty of the house. Just now she could not see past it. She took in the oil lamps, their chimneys speckless and gleaming. The wash shelf, with the old wooden bucket, and the new white granite basin. The huge kitchen stove with the wood stacked behind it. The long pine table with the fresh oilcloth cover. And from the back door she saw the path that led to the outhouse hidden in a clump of young cedar trees.

She wandered helplessly along behind Hod, trying to sense what he was feeling . . . trying to get over into him long enough to feel a little bit at home. But there was nothing here for her to lay hold of. She had the queer feeling that she had stepped inside a history book and the pages had been rapidly leafed back a hundred years. Time stopped right there on the ridge, she thought. There was no link between her tiny efficiency apartment, with its gleaming porcelain plumbing, its instant hot water, its soft wall-to-wall carpeting and subdued silk-shaded lamps, its vacuum sweeper, electric toaster, and coffee maker . . . there was no link between that and this. There was a yawning gap which she could not leap instantly. She would have to find a hard way . . . she would have to burn oil lamps, draw water from a well, and make trips out back. Try them and experience them, before she could accept them.

But for now Hod was the reality. And she clung desperately to the only familiar thing in this whole, new, strange world — Hod, her husband.

The days flew by. Mild, mellow days which hung ripe in the October air. Hod and Mary went fishing on the river, and he showed her the hole where Little Wells had pitched him in and he had learned to swim. Mary could see the little towheaded boy, years behind the achievements of his cousins, tagging along when he could slip away, finally triumphing, dog-paddling desperately to his own personal victory. Trotting home later, tousling his wet head with his shirttail to dry it so Hattie wouldn't notice. She felt a tender affection for that little boy.

They took long walks through the red-gold beech woods, and Hod told her the habits of birds and squirrels, of coons and foxes and rabbits. He dug back into his boyhood and brought up his store of memories for her, and in doing so he shed the years that had intervened. The tenseness that had first been in him let down, and he laughed and went young and gentle before her eyes.

These days she loved. The country was beautiful. The high pile of trees along the rim of the ridge. The sweeping openings of the valleys. The soft, grayed dawns and the cool, scarlet sunsets, purpling almost instantly into night. The winy haze that sifted over the woods. She filled herself with all this, and called it good. The ridge was truly beautiful.

Sometimes Hod went off with Tom to hunt, and Mary stayed in the kitchen with Hattie. On one of these days, when they had been there nearly two weeks, Hattie was called out front. When she came. back, she was laughing. "That was Little Wells," she said. "He stopped by to tell that him an' a bunch is comin' over tonight after supper to see Hod, an' mebbe to sing a spell. He's allus been one to sing, Wells has. An' him an' Hod has allus loved to sing together. Now that'll pleasure Hod a heap. I'll bound he ain't sung e'er note sincet the last time he was home."

"How many will come?" Mary asked, her mind immediately busy with details.

"He never said. Jist said a bunch of 'em. Like as not they'll be eighteen or twenty, though."

Mentally Mary counted the chairs. Six . . . seven, counting the rocker. And the bench back of the table would seat three or four. There was a stool or two, but counting everything she couldn't see how they could take care of that many people. She gave it up. If Hattie wasn't worried, why need she be?

Hod was pleased. Mary could see his pleasure spreading all over him. "Well, now, that's nice of Wells, isn't it," he said, "to get up a shindig like this for us. Yessir, that's plumb nice of him!" His voice took on the drawl of the ridge talk. Mary smiled. The soft, honeyed speech was one of the nicest things about the ridge.

Hattie bustled them through supper and quickly redded up the house afterward, and while Mary and Hod were dressing, she tied a fresh apron around herself, dampened her hair and brushed it down, and was ready to greet the first comers, who followed on the setting of the sun by no more than a good ten minutes.

"This here's Hod's woman." Mary heard it over and over that evening. Two, four, six, ten, a dozen times. Each time her hand was shaken gravely and a shy, "Pleased to meet you," accompanied the handshake.

They kept coming until the chairs and the bench were full, and then they overflowed onto the bed and the floor. When the edge of the bed was full, those in front scooted back and leaned against the wall, leaving the edge for the late-comers. The wall by the fireplace was soon lined, and a row of feet stuck out into the room like tenpins waiting to be knocked over. Hod brought in a cot and pushed the dresser down the wall to make room for it. He and Little Wells and several other men crowded onto it.

And in between, scrambling over and around and under the chairs and the beds, were the children. Mary counted twenty, and that did not take in the babies that were asleep on the bed in the next room. There were six or eight of them, she knew. She began to understand that no family left its children at home on the ridge. A party for the parents was a party for the children too. It would not have occurred to fathers and mothers to leave their children at home in the first place, and in the second place there was no one to leave them with.

But, even with all the children, there was not the usual noise of

206

a party as Mary knew it. There was only a small hum of talk, and that came mostly from the men's corner. Some of this Mary knew was because of her. She felt as conspicuous as a sore thumb, sitting straight in her chair next to Hattie. She had put on a simple dress, but it was much too fine for this gathering. It would have been better, she decided, to have left on her house dress. She caught the women's corner glances and felt them taking her in. Hod Pierce had married a city girl and they had all come to see. She tried to be pleasant, easy, comfortable. But she had so little in common with these women. Children! She had that in common with them! She taught children. Brightly she mentioned it and talked hurriedly about it for a few flat moments. When there was no response, she let it die a-borning. She looked desperately at Hattie. But Hattie sat, complacent and silent, her hands folded across her stomach. Well. She retired into her own silence. Maybe that was etiquette on the ridge!

" How about a little music? " she heard Hod say, and she sighed with relief.

Little Wells went out on the porch and came in with a stack of paper-backed songbooks. " Jist got these in, Hod. Been awaitin' fer you to come home to try 'em. Hit's the latest Stamps-Baxter book. Orta be some good 'uns in here too."

Two or three of the men unslung guitars and Hod got his from the chimney corner. He laughed as he picked it up. " Been a long time since I chorded a tune on this old thing. The strings are probably rotten."

Briskly Hattie spoke up. " No, they ain't. Tom, he restrung it jist 'fore you all come."

" Ferdy, how 'bout you leadin'? " Wells said.

Mary watched the gangling, overalled man swallow his Adam's apple painfully. " Well, now, I ain't sung in quite a spell."

The others insisted, however, and he took his place in front of them, towering over them. He set the key in a nasal hum, and suddenly his long right arm shot out in front of him. He lifted and swung it, like he was scything hay, and a tumult of sound filled the room. They sang as if they were in an auditorium seating five thousand people, and the room rocked with their voices. The roof fairly lifted.

Mary sat very still. Nothing could have prepared her for this,

207

braced her for it. She looked quickly around, when she had sufficiently recovered, to see if the others had noticed anything amiss. But the placid faces and the folded hands told her this was usual. This was fine singing! Her eyes flicked over to Hod. His bass was growling along happily. His face was red with the effort he was putting into the volume he must attain, but he was attaining it along with the rest, she had to admit. There were no fine attempts at feeling and phrasing. The words and the notes apparently were only the instruments for the voice. The main thing was to lift up your head and shout!

When they had sung half a dozen songs perhaps, changing leaders approximately that often, there was a sudden commotion at the door. Looking up, Mary saw a man and woman coming in, with two children tagging behind them and a third in the woman's arms.

"Why, hit's Matt an' Lutie Jasper," Hattie said, rising. "Come in, come in. Come in an' set, ifen you kin find e'er place."

The man was thin, almost to the point of emaciation, gaunt and shambling. He had a week's growth of beard on his face and tobacco spittle drooled down his chin. His overalls were slick with sweat and dirt, and a foul, sour odor emanated from him. His hair hung down on all sides, lank and greasy-looking. His face had a vacant, staring look, and his skin was pasty and moist like fallen dough.

The woman was almost as thin, the skin taut over her cheekbones. Her dress hitched up in front several inches and left her skinny knees bare and exposed. It was black with grease, and a rent in the skirt had been pinned together. Below the dress her legs were little more than bone and muscle. Her mouth was slack, and a twig toothbrush hung from one corner. Her hair, which had once been fuzzy with a permanent, was now matted and dried like straw.

But the most horrible thing about both of them was the flat, empty look of their eyes. They were as devoid of expression as ovals of glass. Their empty stare made Mary feel as if her look had run into something solid and glanced off. Nothing could penetrate that marbled surface. They were as opaque as if they were turned inward. Mary felt a deep shudder start within her, and her effort to control it raised goose bumps on her flesh. There was something slimy and loathsome about these people.

"This here's Hod's woman," Hattie was saying.

Neither the man nor the woman spoke. They simply stared at her, the woman's eyes roving over her, taking in every detail of her hair, her face, her dress, even her hands and feet. There was no change of expression on her face. Neither interest nor lack of it. The face was blank and the eyelids drooped over the cold, empty eyes. Mary was suddenly reminded of the hooded eyes of a snake. She shivered. I am looking at the substance of evil, she thought. This is the irreconcilable distillation of sin, extracted and poured into the form of humanity. This is the prideless travesty of man. She felt her own dignity assailed, and loathed herself for the horror that filled her. Wildly she looked for Hod. But he was miles away, over there in the corner with the men of his own kind, laughing and joking and picking a nameless tune on his guitar.

He went strange and unknown to her, changing before her eyes into someone new and unfamiliar — as new and unfamiliar as this room, and the people who were packed into it, bulging its sides with their leathered bodies and fetid odors. What was she, Mary Hogan, doing here? How did she reach this place? What did she have to do with these people? And who was Hod Pierce?

A lamp smoked suddenly and a woman's hand reached out to turn down the wick. The dim, sputtering light and the crude smell of oil added the final nightmarish touch of unreality to the scene, and Mary stumbled across the room, through the door, out onto the porch. She clung, nauseated, to the railing and gulped in the good air. I will not go back into that room, she thought. Nothing can make me go back in there!

The door slammed behind her, and at once Hod was beside her. "Mary," he said, and his voice was full of fear, "Mary, what's the matter?"

His arms went round her and pulled her close. She leaned her head against him and shook with deep, shuddering sobs. Oh, blessed relief! This was Hod. This was her husband. Here, holding her. Now, touching her and comforting her.

"What is it, Mary?" he urged. "Are you sick?"

"No," she shook her head against his shirt, her voice muffled and choked by tears. "No. I want to go home, Hod. Please, I want to go home!"

CHAPTER TWENTY–FOUR

GENTLY HOD GOT FROM HER what had caused her panic and her flight. He held her while she let it spin out of her, interrupted from time to time by shuddering gasps. She was cold now, and limp. Spent with the terror of her betrayal by the ridge. She loved it, she assured Hod. It was such beautiful country. But the people. Hod, the people are so unbeautiful!

"Why, that's just poor old Matt Jasper and Lutie," he reasoned with her. "There's not a bit of harm in the world in him. He's simple-minded, sort of, and he has epilepsy, but he's not mean. And Lutie. There's no harm in her either. She's about as feeble-minded as he is, but she's goodhearted when you know her."

Mary wiped her eyes and sniffed. "But you've grown up with them! You're used to them!"

Hod was still, smoothing her hair with a soft hand. He stood cradling her thus for a long time. "Sure," he said then, "sure, I know. I should have known how they would look to you. I didn't know they were coming, or I might have warned you. We can't be unkind to them, Mary. They're ridge folks too. They're neighbors. They're part of things here. Ugly, pathetic, maybe. But they belong here too."

He soothed her, his voice low and gentle, holding her, making her feel close to him again. Until finally he said: "Now, let's go back in. They'll all be wonderin' what's happened. They won't be stayin' much longer. Ma's makin' coffee now, an' gettin' the cake ready. You go on out in the kitchen and help her. And we'll go home tomorrow."

She felt better, now. Weak, craven she might be. But she felt much better. At least Hod had come back to her. And they did go home the next day.

Home was Mary's small apartment. One of those one-big-room-kitchenette-bath affairs. And it was full of Mary's things. There was her piano, her desk, her books, her clothes, and all her personal belongings. It was a gay little apartment, bright with colorful curtains and warm rugs, but it was a tiny, fussy, feminine little place. Hod set his bags down in the middle of the big room and looked helplessly around.

"Where's the rest of it?" he asked, laughing.

"This is all of it," Mary answered, and motioned vaguely with one hand. "We'd better unpack you first."

When they had finished, his things filled every available nook and cranny and overflowed into places never meant for a man's things. Mary found him standing unhappily in front of the wall cabinet in the bathroom looking hopelessly at the bottle-filled shelves. He was trying to find a place for his razor and shaving brush. She swept one shelf clear of bottles. "There, darling. You can have that shelf."

Thus, pigeonholing, they managed to clean out his bags, and stored them away in the basement.

The apartment was so small that they were constantly tangling, bumping into each other, getting in each other's way. Hod was a big man, and he spilled all over the place. He was not a neat man, strowing his belongings carelessly. The apartment more often than not took on a wind-swept, storm-torn look. Mary was careful not to nag, but her orderly teacher's mind could not restrain her from tidying behind him when it got too bad.

They put up with the crowding several days before they admitted the truth. It just wouldn't do. That was all.

Hod let himself down into his chair at breakfast that morning, rubbing his back. "That sofa of yours is about the doggonedest bed I ever tried to sleep on. I get up with a crick in my back every morning."

Mary poured his coffee and defended the couch. "It's always been a good bed for me! It just resents having to sleep two now."

"Well, whatever it is, we'd better get a new bed." He buttered his toast and looked at the lovely breakfast table. It was spread with a fresh white cloth, against which Mary's pink plates, sparkling glasses, and shining silver gleamed brightly. Two pale rosebuds lifted themselves above a slender silver holder in the center of the table. Glasses of fruit juice were nested in cups of ice, and crisped bacon curled around a beautiful omelet with a spot of clear red jelly in its heart.

Mary took her place opposite him and flipped her napkin open.

She was one of those fortunate women who need no make-up except a deepening of the red of her mouth, and she was still young enough to waken fresh, rested, and full of energy. This morning she had tied a yellow ribbon around her hair, and her cheeks were flushed from cooking the breakfast. She was very lovely.

Hod was conscious of the picture . . . the table, the plates, the silver, Mary across the table from him. This all went together, and he felt a full sense of achievement. Somehow this was meant to be. This was just the way it had looked in his dreams.

If, when he buttered his toast and bit into its thin crispness, if then he remembered Hattie's fluffy biscuits, it was only for a second. If, when he helped himself to several slivers of the crisp, broiled bacon and the airy omelet, if he thought then of the old ironstone bowl full of cream gravy, and the rich taste of home-cured side meat sliced into thick, man-sized pieces, it passed immediately. He didn't need to tell himself that he would become accustomed to such breakfasts. He needed no reassurance of any kind. This was what he wanted . . . Mary, and the white table-cloth and the shiny silver.

Mary picked up the conversation again. " We not only need another bed," she said, " we've got to find a larger apartment, Hod. This was fine for me, but it's just too crowded for two. We'll be in each other's hair all the time."

" You know I was thinking the same thing," Hod said, " and wonderin' if you'd mind."

He glanced around. Why, the whole apartment could be set down in Ma's big front room, with space left over in all four corners!

" Oh, no, I don't mind. This just won't do. But it's going to be hard to find a place." Mary's forehead crinkled into a frown. " The town is so full that apartments are awfully hard to find. And high. But," and she rose briskly and set about cleaning off the dishes, " we'll see what we can find. There's nothing like trying, I always say." She brushed the top of Hod's head with her mouth as she went by. " You've got lipstick on your forehead, Mr. Pierce! Tsk! Tsk! "

" That just goes to show," Hod drawled, hitching himself up out of the chair, " what a woman can do to a man. Such a fine, upstandin' young man too. Just gettin' a start in the city! "

212

" You mean I'm a bad influence on you! "

" Why, you're plumb leadin' me to ruin! "

In that mood they washed the dishes, folded the bed back into the sofa, and, armed with the morning paper, which had a scant dozen ads in the " For Rent " column, started out to look at apartments. Hod was full of confidence. With Mary by his side the world was all his. He strode belligerently along, chin up, plunging his long body over the sidewalks as if they had been new-plowed furrows. And Mary reached out her own long legs to keep pace.

They were more fortunate than most couples. One of Mary's teacher friends called her one night and told her there was to be a vacancy in her building. But they'd better come right over and look at it. The landlord would hold it only twenty-four hours.

They hurried over, and immediately they knew it would do. It was an old-fashioned apartment building with large five-room units. The rooms were spacious, with high ceilings and tall, narrow windows. There was a fireplace in the living room, and Mary exclaimed over the fine woodwork and floors. She poked her nose into the big, deep closets and yearned over their ample storage space. The whole apartment was roomy, light, and airy. It was just what they had been looking for. But she trembled when she asked the rent. Eighty-five dollars. Well, that was reasonable enough. It was the ceiling price, the man explained.

Hod tortured his tongue against the rough spot on his tooth. It sounded like quite a lot to him. This business of paying money for a place to live was one thing the Pierces had never worried about. There always had been a Pierce roof over Pierce heads . . . somebody else had paid for that roof generations ago, and it had come down through the years, tight and secure. There it was . . . home. And all you ever paid was the taxes once a year. And they were so small that even Pierces could pay them and hardly miss the money.

But if Mary thought it was reasonable, he supposed it must be. They took the apartment that night, signed the lease, and Hod pulled out his billfold and counted off eighty-five dollars. As he handed the man the money, he thought that he must do this the first of every month. Not just once . . . done and over . . . but every month, come hell or high water, or else he and Mary wouldn't have a roof over their heads. For the first time he felt the responsibility of being married settling down on him. And for the first time he felt a little bit scared.

He looked at the greenbacks as he stuffed the remainder of them back into his wallet. You sold your skill, your time, and your labor to get this kind of money. Well, that's what he had wanted to do. And he was just the man who could do it. He squared his shoulders.

" Now we've got us a place to live," he said as they walked home under the street lamps, " what next? "

" Furniture," Mary answered. " Lots of furniture. That's a big place! "

" Isn't that your furniture over at your place? " he asked, startled.

" Just the piano and desk and odds and ends. A place like that has everything furnished."

" Why hasn't this one? "

" Because it's an unfurnished apartment, silly! "

" Oh."

" Didn't you notice there wasn't any furniture? "

" Sure. But I thought maybe they'd moved it out to clean or something."

Mary laughed and ran her hand through his arm. " We'll not try to furnish it all at once. We'll start with the essentials and work up to it gradually."

The first winter cold had settled over the city, raw and damp and biting. Fog crept in from the river and mixing with the smoke became a dirty blanket of what people in Louisville called " smog." It had an acrid, penetrating odor, sharp and unpleasant in the nose and throat. Soot sifted through it and settled in greasy flakes on the skin. Hod brushed at it impatiently. The street lamps were dull-amber bowls of light, spotting the unfriendly haze spasmodically and inadequately. There was a moon shining somewhere, Hod knew. It had been almost a month since they had spent those first nights at Spring Mill, and walked the tunneled trails where, full, it had shown through in silver shafts of light. Down home . . . down home it was shining. Over the dried fields and the stripped woods. Over the hollers and the tree-locked

214

ridges. Over the road winding ribbonlike down the saddle of Piney. Light enough, likely, to go huntin'. Old Duke would be restless tonight. He would thump the porch floor and wander out to the gate, and maybe rear back on his haunches and bay mournfully. The ground would be crisp with frost, and would ring to your heels . . . but it would give underneath. He stabbed his heel into the pavement. Cement was sure hard to walk on now.

They sat up late that night over their furniture list. The kitchen first. Stove, refrigerator, table and chairs. There were plenty of cabinets, thank goodness. The bedroom next. Bed, springs, mattress. Hod thought of his old straw tick . . . fresh-filled each winter. Nothing lay better. But of course you couldn't use a straw tick in the city. Chest of drawers, dresser, bedside table, lamps, rug, curtains. We'll leave the other bedroom bare for a while. Store things in there. Now the living room. We've got the piano, desk, and bookcases. All right. Sofa, rug, coffee table, one big, comfortable chair, lamps, curtains. That will do for now.

"How much?" Hod asked when the list was complete.

Mary hesitated. "About a thousand dollars."

Hod whistled. They bent over the bankbook. Mary had been saving too, and between them there was nearly two thousand in the bank. She looked at him questioningly. "I can cut a few corners," she suggested.

"No, you don't," Hod said. "We don't start by cuttin' corners. Get what you want. I'll be workin' pretty soon. And that back bedroom's not goin' to stay bare very long, either."

When they had moved, Hod took another two weeks to help Mary clean windows and woodwork, lay rugs, hang curtains, and get settled in, before he started out to look for a job. Mary had taken a two months' leave of absence and the time was running out. She wanted to get the home to running smoothly before she went back to teaching.

At first Hod had protested. "I don't like the idea of my wife workin'," he said. The ridge concept of a woman's place was very strong in him.

But Mary had been firm. "Listen, Hod," she pointed out, reasonably and patiently, "it will just be for a little while. Until we

215

get on our feet and know where we're going. When you've found what you want to do, and have made a good start, then we'll buy a little place and I'll quit teaching and stay home and raise a family. But for a while, another year or two anyhow, it just makes sense for me to earn too."

" You sure you'll be satisfied to quit when the time comes? "

" I'm sure. I want a home and children, but it would be silly for me to quit now and give all my time to keeping this apartment. What I make will help out, and as long as we can't yet afford the home and family, I'll be a lot better satisfied to work."

When she put it that way, Hod had no objection. After all, Mary knew best, he supposed. He would rather she didn't work, but if she would be happier, then that was what really mattered. Mary was good at figuring things out. He swelled a little with pride when he thought of all the ways she was so smart.

The day Mary went back to the schoolroom Hod began looking for his job. As they dressed that morning, she timidly offered to advise him. " How're you going about this? " she wanted to know.

Hod was knotting his tie and he pulled it into place before answering. " Oh, I thought I'd just look around a little. Get the lay of the land . . . I know about what I want to do."

" I'd be glad to call a few people I know, if you think it would do any good."

" We'll see," he said, shrugging into his coat. " You ready? "

" Ready. Got your key? "

He held it up for her to see, and shook his head. Locking a door! He didn't suppose there ever had been a lock on a door down home. But Mary had warned him. " Always keep the door on lock," she said, " and always be sure you've got your key. Even if you just empty the garbage downstairs."

Hod browsed around the city for several days. He had learned since the days he and Johnny Knight came to town all those years ago that there was more to Louisville than Market and Jefferson Streets. He laughed when he remembered that night. Deliberately he went down in that end of town and loafed around. It sure was drab. Thousand wonders two kids like that hadn't got knocked in the head.

216

Hod took his time. He talked with men at several employment places. He had a sense of leisure and of wanting to choose carefully. And at one place he heard first of the plant that interested him immediately. Kentuckiana, Inc. They made furniture, mostly, but they made a little bit of everything that was made out of wood.

Hod asked for details and then went out to look the plant over. It was a huge industrial concern, one of the largest in the state, spread out over acres of ground. A guard stopped him at the gate, and when he said he wanted to visit the plant, he was routed to the main office. He explained once more and was told to wait. A party of visitors were going through in about thirty minutes.

On the tour he walked along silently with the group. He didn't need to ask many questions. He took in the huge machines, the presses, the small precision instruments, the saws and the lathes. And he knew that he would like to work here. Machines . . . instruments . . . tools. He liked the feel of them in his hands. Yes, this was the place.

At the end of the tour he sought out the employment office and filed his application. But he figured it would be buried in such a large place. That night at dinner he asked Mary, " You know anybody out at Kentuckiana? "

Mary thought for a moment. " No. No, I don't. But I know someone who does. One of the teachers has a friend whose husband is in Personnel out there. Why? "

" I'd like to work there. I put in my application today, but I don't think a guy'd have a chance to get on, cold like that. I thought maybe you knew someone out there who could help out a little. But a friend of a friend of a friend of yours is the long way round I reckon."

" Well, I don't know about that," Mary bristled. " She's a pretty good friend. And if her friend's husband is in Personnel, all he'd have to do is O.K. your application."

" I don't want him to do that. What I want is to get an interview, so he'll have something to go on when the application comes up."

Mary leaned her elbow on the table and pocketed her chin in her palm. " You wouldn't care if I said a word to Esther, would you? "

Hod was lighting his cigarette. He blew a cloud of smoke across the table at her. "Nope. I doubt it'll do any good, but it wouldn't hurt to try."

Mary started to ask him why he had picked Kentuckiana. But she bit the question back. Already she was learning to let him alone. He traveled by himself on certain roads.

About a week later Hod was asked to call at the employment office. The card was signed by W. A. Fleming. Mary waved it gleefully in front of his nose. "See! See, what did I tell you! That's Bill Fleming. Nora Fleming's husband. And Nora Fleming is Esther's friend. It *did* do some good after all! "

" Let me see it! " Hod growled, and grabbed at the card. He examined it thoughtfully. "Hmmm. O.K."

He put the card down and walked over to the window and stared out at the courtyard down below. A flight of pigeons whirred past the window and wheeled gently to the ground. Their jeweled wings fanned briefly in the sun and then pleated primly into a pouted, rounded symmetry. Hod stood so still that only his back moved with his breathing. Mary watched him for a moment or two, and then she slipped over to stand beside him. She ran her hand through his arm and nuzzled his shoulder with her nose. "Thinking? " she asked, when he remained silent.

"Yeah." He straightened and patted her hand. "Yeah. I was thinkin' how many years it's been." And then almost absently he pulled in his belt another notch.

CHAPTER TWENTY-FIVE

THE NEW WORK WENT WELL. The first three months Hod was on the job he advanced rapidly. This was partly due to his own initiative and energy, but mostly it was because industry was hitting its stride in postwar production. Men were being hired by the thousands, trained rapidly and briefly, and if they were efficient at all they were pushed ahead.

Another man might have found that work tedious, monotonous, and dull. But to Hod each precisely calculated operation satisfied some tidy, mathematical instinct in him. He liked the feel of metal and wood in his hands, and he liked, when he had finished an operation, to look at the piece and see it in relation to the whole. It wasn't just a panel of wood or a bar of steel; it was a chair, a sofa, a bed, something useful and beautiful.

Part of his liking for his work was due too to the fact that it was new to him. But most of it was because he had imagination with which to enliven it. In the handling of materials, in the precision operations, in the part he played in the whole, he saw an over-all plan, and it had a certain beauty of its own. Like the child who could lose himself in the story of King Arthur's Court, like the boy who felt poetry in hoeing the corn and milking the cows, like the young man who cried out against the unawareness of his people, Hod now saw something of the rhythm and surge of American industrialism, its inevitable forward sweep, its giant strides across the world, taking millions of little people along with it. He was glad to be a part of it. He took a great deal of pride in his job.

He also took a great deal of pride in the contents of his pay envelope. At first it had been fifty, fifty-five, sixty dollars a week. To one to whom ninety dollars a month, overseas pay for a sergeant, had been top pay in his life, this was a magnificent sum. He brought it home and turned it over to Mary each week, with a grand gesture. True, this sense of proportion was only temporary. He stepped up too rapidly, and each time he stepped up he looked back down the ladder, and eventually looked with contempt upon that first fifty dollars. It wasn't until then that he knew how naïve he had been. But it was a thoroughly enjoyable naïveté while it lasted.

He experienced a small return of it the first time he drew a check for a hundred dollars. He looked at the figures, and they were unreal. He remembered hoeing corn for Little Wells . . . ten long hours a day for fifty cents. He remembered the tomato money that first summer with Johnny Knight. He remembered the thirty-two dollars a month on the road project. Those amounts were real. This hundred which Hod Pierce had made in five short days had no tangible value to him. It was fantastic.

But he took tremendous pride in it just the same. Just as he took great pride in the way the apartment shaped up under Mary's capable hands. *Things* became very important to him.

The new, hand-blocked drapes at the windows. The cherry drop-leaf table for the hall. The mahogany beds in the guest room. The exact shade of the rug for the dining room. Even the new automatic toaster and electric mixer and pressure cooker . . . each new piece Mary added was a symbol to Hod. A symbol of success . . . of achievement . . . of being somebody.

And he smoothed off the rough edges from himself too. Clothes had never had any meaning to Hod. He never did have enough of them to give them a second thought beyond whether they were clean or not. Hattie had taken care of them, and up to the time he left the ridge, she had even bought most of them for him. And then the Army uniform had relieved him of all responsibility for nearly six years.

When he and Mary married, he was still in uniform, but shortly afterward they had outfitted him in civilian clothes. He had asked Mary to select these for him. He hadn't particularly liked her selections . . . he thought they were rather drab and colorless. But he had accepted them because he trusted her judgment.

When they went to their first party and he studied the other men in relation to himself, he was glad. Mary had been right, of course. The plainness and darkness of the blue suit, the brilliance of the white shirt, the soft casualness of the hand-knit tie . . . these were right. With only slight variations the other men were dressed the same.

Mary had been a little nervous about that party. It was Hod's introduction to her friends. She told herself she wanted Hod to like her friends. She told herself she hoped he wouldn't find them dull or trivial. But she fussed a lot over Hod as he dressed.

"Not *that* shirt, darling! You wear a *white* shirt tonight."

"Why? I like this blue one."

"Because, darling, men don't wear colored shirts on some occasions! Parties, church, things like that. And your blue suit, dear, not your brown one."

Hod obediently got into the things she laid out. "Tell me about these folks who'll be there," Hod asked, buttoning his shirt.

"Well," Mary slipped one foot carefully down the leg of a fragile stocking, "you've met Esther. She thinks of herself as an intellectual . . . dabbles in art, poetry, music, and stuff. She's a good teacher, though. And Ed travels. Salesman for some hardware firm

220

here in town. And there'll be Joe and Daisy Prentiss. Joe is a salesman too. Daisy has a dress shop of her own, is very beautiful, and very, very sophisticated. Then there'll be Minna and Sid Bowden. Sid is another salesman. And Minna is a sort of frustrated little person. She goes in for civic work and great causes. She's a little picked-chicken sort of person and I don't think she's very happy, but she's dreadfully in earnest about her work. And then there'll be Nora and Bill Fleming. I don't know them. And with us, that's all. They're just people, dear. People like you meet every day in the week."

She preened nervously before the mirror, twisting and turning to see if her seams were straight, to see if any tiny fraction of slip was showing. She turned to the dressing table to dab perfume behind her ears, and leaned forward to redden her mouth. " Oh, I *do* hope you like them, Hod. They're really pretty nice."

Hod caught her waist and swung her around. " That's about the tenth time you've said that! What you really mean is, you hope they like me, isn't it? That's why you're so jittery. You mean you hope I remember to use the right silver at the table, and to keep my elbows off, like I usually don't. And you mean you hope I don't make any slip in my grammar. And you mean you hope I won't get started talking about the ridge, telling jokes about Old Man Clark and his third wife, and so on. That's what you really mean! "

Mary stood still with his big hands warm on her waist and looked helplessly at him. An iron hand in her chest squeezed the blood right out of her heart and sent it, weakening and dribbling, down to her feet. She caught a deep sob as it came up past the lump in her throat. What have I done, she thought. What have I done to you, my darling! In the clear, clean light of his sensitive apperception she went down and down inside herself, and came back up with her own true sense of worth and dignity restored. She lifted her hands, took Hod's face gently between them. Tears blurred her vision. She shook them impatiently away. " No," she said softly, " no, Hod, that's *not* what I really mean. I truly mean I hope you will like them. You are so much finer, so much nobler, so heads and shoulders above them, that I truly, truly hope they may be worth your respect and liking. Truly. Truly! "

Hod pulled her close and wrapped his arms around her. How

221

loyal she was! How terribly, terribly honest and loyal! But he'd be careful. He knew about pride. They had it on the ridge too. He'd sit back and listen mostly tonight, and he'd be careful.

Esther and Ed were giving the party in honor of Mary and Hod. Esther met them at the door. She was a tall, rawboned woman with iron-gray hair, and a high, strident voice. She drew them inside, chattering incessantly, and led them into the living room. Her husband detached himself from a group around the radio and came across the room to greet them. He was a rotund, sleek little man, balding and paunching at forty.

Hod shook hands with him and allowed himself to be led over to the group of men bunched around the radio. "Want you to meet the rest of these boys," Ed said. Hod listened to the names around the circle. Joe Prentiss. Dark, slight, nervous, his long upper lip covered with a small moustache. "Joe's over at Belknap's. My rival. Lucky he doesn't work the same territory."

Sid Bowden. Another round, sleek little man. "Sid's with Brown-Williamson."

"And I guess you already know Bill Fleming. Esther told me you were out at Kentuckiana. Bill's in Personnel out there."

"How are you, sir?" Hod hadn't seen Bill Fleming since the day he had interviewed him for the job. He reached out a firm hand and shook the older man's. The old Army "sir" had slipped out automatically. "I expect I owe my job at Kentuckiana to Mr. Fleming," he added to Ed.

Fleming, who was a big, hearty, heavy man, laughed. "That's what friends are for, Pierce. How're you getting along? They treating you all right out there?"

"Couldn't be better, sir."

Fleming nodded. "I've checked on you once or twice. You're doing all right. This may be a little out of order, and keep it under your hat, but I heard they had their eye on you for section foreman."

Hod flushed, and for the first time he felt awkward. Praise always made him feel that way. "I've done the best I could," he said. Hattie, at home, had always phrased it, "I like to do what I kin."

At dinner Hod sat at Esther's right, with Nora Fleming on the other side. She was a plain, plump little person, almost wrenlike. Immediately she began to talk to him about the country. "I hear you were raised down in Adair County," she said. "That's not far from where Esther and I grew up."

Hod laid his soup spoon down. "Where was that?" he asked.

"In Marion County, near Lebanon."

Esther leaned across. "Nora, you always bring that up!"

"I do, don't I?" Nora said cheerfully. "Well, I was raised in the country, and I like to remember it. And I wish our children were being raised in the country right now. Then I wouldn't worry about them like I do."

"Being raised in the country isn't necessarily the panacea for all ills, dear," Esther remarked.

"Maybe not," and Nora began telling Hod about Bill, Jr., and Anne, who were in high school. "They just go, go, go, all the time!" she said. "They're never at home. I don't even know where they are most of the time. And Bill is always at the office, or off on a business trip. Sometimes I feel like I don't have any family at all!"

Esther's strident voice broke in again. "Are you going to the Ice Follies Monday night, Nora?"

Nora nodded. "I suppose so. We have tickets."

Minna broke in. Minna, Hod thought. Minnow! And that was just what she reminded him of! A darting little sliver of fish. She was quick, thin, and colorless, with a small mouth that puckered when she talked. "Did you get your tickets from my girls, Daisy? You know, the Civic Duty League . . . we got a percentage."

Daisy shrugged her velvet-hugged shoulders. "I really don't know, Minna. I can't keep up with all your causes. We got them at the box office."

Minna looked disappointed. "Oh. Then you didn't. The girls were on the street in booths." She smiled across the table at Hod. "It's true I *do* work for a good many civic causes, Mr. Pierce. But I feel it's my duty. And besides, I think *people* are so important, don't you?"

Mary twinkled a finger at Hod down the table and he winked back to show he was getting along all right.

The dinner went on and the talk frothed around the table.

Finally it settled on Hod's and Mary's apartment.

"Esther tells me you have a beautiful place in that lovely court over by the park. Weren't you fortunate, though, to find something so nice!" Nora said.

Mary launched into an enthusiastic description of the apartment, Esther breaking in occasionally. "It's an enchanting little court," her high, cracked voice cried, "hidden away right in the heart of town. Almost Old World looking. And the apartment is lovely. The only thing," and she laughed brittlely, "the absolutely only thing wrong with it is that awful Van Gogh print Mary insisted on hanging over the fireplace! Darling, no one has Van Gogh any more! Peter Hunt would be better than Van Gogh. But, no! She hangs onto that sweet orchard in bloom as if it were an original!"

Mary's chin came up. "I like that picture! There's something very still and splendid about it. It has repose. None of us can afford originals, so what's wrong with prints? And if you like Van Gogh, what's wrong with him?"

What was a Van Gogh, Hod wondered. And who was Peter Hunt? They must be talking about the picture hanging over the mantel. He liked it too. And Mary was right. There was a feeling of repose in it. And it looked real. He could vouch for that. He should know orchards in bloom!

The talk went on. One of the men asked, "Did you get a pretty good deal on your furniture?"

"I don't know," Hod answered. "I left that up to Mary."

"Where'd you buy?" Ed asked.

"Oh, here . . . and there," Mary said. "I bought wherever I found what I wanted."

"Mary, you fool!" screamed Esther. "Don't you know everything costs you three times as much that way!"

Hod spoke up. "What's wrong with buying where you want to?"

Ed leaned back in his chair and swabbed his mouth with his napkin. "Look, Hod," he began. "I'm a salesman, see? I've got some good connections. I could have got you a good price on everything you bought. The next time you buy anything, let one of us know. That's what friends are for."

Hod smiled down the table at Mary. It's all right, he meant to say to her. We got what we wanted. That was more important than anything else. But he was disturbed a little, nevertheless. He felt as if they had been taken in.

After dinner there was bridge. Hod didn't play and Esther sat out with him. Her agile tongue slipped from one subject to another, dwelling lightly on all, leaving no burden on Hod for reply, and relieving him of the necessity of listening with more than one ear. He sat quietly relaxed in his corner, absorbing the whole scene, letting the people and the room and the hum and flow of talk eddy around him, swishing its edges near him, but not sweeping him away.

The room was expensively beautiful, and temptingly comfortable. From Mary he was learning how rugs, drapes, wall colors, lamps, pictures, and furniture blend to make a pleasing picture, and this one pleased him. Their own apartment was lovely now, but this home said so plainly, I am the result of money as well as good taste. He liked that. But he liked the way it was expressed too. With restraint and with quality rather than with ostentation.

He studied the group around the card tables. The women, even Minna, so well-dressed, so groomed and finished. He felt a swell of pride when his eyes rested on Mary. Daisy was more beautiful in a polished, smooth way. But Mary was prettier in a natural, pleasing way. These were the kind of people she belonged with, though. These gracious, pleasant, cultured people. No wonder she had run away from Lutie and Matt Jasper!

He turned his thoughts to the men, and took in their gloss and finish and easy way of talking and laughing. They were so assured. They had that easy kind of nonchalance which comes from possessing good things — good jobs, good salaries, good living.

Snatches of conversation came across the room. Sid Bowden was talking. Telling Ed about his new car. "You don't have to wait to get a new car if you know how to work it," he was saying. "It's a racket. And you've got to know where to go. It'll cost you a little extra, but what's a coupla hundred in the pocket of the right man. Presto, you've got a new car!"

Ed nodded. He fanned his cards and squinted at them. "Two spades," and he snapped the fan of cards neatly. "I've got to get a new one this year."

"Let me know when you're ready."

"O.K."

Hod thought of the old Chevrolet parked outside. Junk heap! He sucked in his cheeks and let his tongue find the familiar rough spot on the edge of his tooth. Before I'm through I'll drive a bigger car than any of 'em, he thought. Mary'll have the biggest and finest home of 'em all. And she'll wear diamonds and furs with the best of 'em! Nothing's too good for the Pierces. And nothing's going to stop them!

CHAPTER TWENTY–SIX

WITHIN THREE MONTHS the promotion came through, and Hod was made a section foreman. "This is it, Mary," he laughed that night, "this is the first step!"

He was too excited and happy to sit still. He paced back and forth across the r)om, rumpling his hair. Every nerve in his body was electric, and deep, rippling thrills ran clear down to his toes. Golly, he thought, it means so much more than a guy ever thought it could! Even if he has starved for it!

It was beginning to be in his grasp now. He flung himself down on the couch and slipped his feet out of his shoes, stretching back and curling his toes. He felt like that. Like his toes, freed and unloosed. The certainty that he had started on his way up was an unloosening thing. A freeing feeling. A sparkling, winy thing shooting through him, racing in bubbles down to his finger tips. He was on his feet again in a moment, pacing in his socks. He needed to feel something solid under him. "Jeff Martin says . . ." he said.

"Who is Jeff Martin, dear?"

"He's the division superintendent, the big shot. You see, there are about six sections in each division," he told them off on his fingers, "and each section has three foremen, one for each shift. And then there's a division foreman, with about six assistants. But the division superintendent is really brass. He's stuff! And Jeff Martin says I'll be a division foreman in another year. Says he's been watching me. Says if I do all right on this job, he'll see that I get the breaks. It's not being section foreman that means anything. It's where it's leading. And we're going places with it! We're going places, Mary! And nothing's going to stop us! "

But Hod didn't tell Mary about the first foremen's meeting. They were all there — the little shots and the big shots. Reminded Hod of an NCO meeting. Hod sat tight, back in a corner. Like he had in NCO meetings. He remembered the brass had watched him there too, and had picked him for the other side of the fence. He hadn't had the nerve to take it on then. And he knew a moment of writhing shame as he thought of it. Well, he had one leg over the fence again, and he was going all the way this time.

When the big shots left and they broke up into division meetings, the talk came down to local problems. For Hod's special benefit the division foreman, a big, hulking fellow by the name of Conway, outlined the setup. "This is the way it works," he said. "The rest of you guys know all this, but Pierce is new and if he doesn't know what it's all about he'll screw the works for everybody. Now look, Pierce. The division's run on a budget — an expense budget. The company have figured out what they think each division in the plant can operate on. We take that figure and break it down by sections. You section men take it and break it down into shifts. Any questions so far? "

Hod shook his head. It was like analyzing a problem back in the prewar Army.

"Well, then," Conway went on, shifting on his thick, stout legs, "here's where you'll make a good foreman, or not. It's sort of like a war. The men on the machines are out to make as much money as they can. Practically every machine in the plant is on piecework, now. You know that, and you know what the average piecework rate is, and how much it means to a man. How hard he works to get a good one, and how much he likes to draw time on it. Now, I ain't saying we're against the men. If your men don't respect you and work for you, you ain't got a chance. But all the same, you got to make that expense margin. If you don't watch out, first thing you know you'll be running in the hole. And when you go in the hole, the division begins to lose ground, and when a division begins to lose ground, a lotta foremen begin to lose

227

their jobs. That's the way it goes."

Hod was puzzled. The strategy was clear enough, but the tactics were fuddled. "How do you stay within that margin?" he asked. "If you're expected to get out so much work, run so many pieces, you've got to do it, haven't you? And you can't get out work without its costing something!"

"Oh, there's ways," Conway continued. "Get the feel of the job, and try to keep from running behind. Keep it running through smooth and even, so you don't have to use no overtime. Overtime mounts up. The guys like it . . . time and a half, who wouldn't? But too much overtime eats up your margin. And you can always stop a man on a job. If he's running it up into pretty big pay, you can pull him and put him on something else. Pick a machine that don't pay as much. Tell him there's a hurry call for something." Conway laughed suggestively.

The other foremen settled into their chairs and laughed with him, comfortable, deep laughs, rumbling around their cigarettes. Hod tightened his mouth. Yeah. That had been pulled on him too. He had never resented it, believing honestly there must be a sudden run on a certain stock. Hillman always bustled up so importantly. "Gotta hurry this one, Pierce. Hate to take you off the machine right now. But I gotta slip on number 1088's. Need 'em in assembly by four this afternoon."

Hod looked across the room at Hillman, and Hillman winked at him slyly. Hod's tongue probed the rough tooth. He'd quit the job! He wouldn't pull stuff like that on the guys!

But Conway was still talking. "At the end of the year there's a nice fat check waiting for you. A bonus. And the size of it depends on you. If you don't make it, you can close your desk and look for another job."

Yeah. Yeah, he had a leg over the fence all right. And he was the one who wasn't going to let anything stop him. But you couldn't pull that kind of stuff on a guy like, say Demarest, for instance. Demarest had six kids. He needed every cent he could make!

He was a long time getting to sleep that night. The air was close and muggy, and the first spring warmness pressed in. The flicker from the street lamp on the corner made a fretting pattern on the blinds at the window, and streaked bars of light across the bed. The bars became real and solid and took on weight, until at last he threw them off angrily and rose and dressed and went downstairs to the court. He stretched out in the grass, then, and let himself sink into its green softness. Overhead a thin moon cut a silver crescent in the sky. Here the rumble of traffic was dulled to a faint throb, and he could almost imagine he was in the back pasture on the ridge. He listened for the night sounds . . . the lonely, lovely cry of a whippoorwill . . . the sad, sweet mourning of a dove . . . the heart-stopping trill of a wood thrush. His eyes drooped. Maybe, he thought, maybe I won't have to do it that way. Maybe I can manage without it. Maybe. And he slept.

Mary was happy for him, and proud of him. They had a new car now. It was a small car — not the low-slung, powerful convertible Hod really wanted — but it would do for the time being. That would come. In time. The small car was better than the jalopy, anyhow. Sid Bowden helped him get it. And it only cost him a couple of hundred extra.

They went down to the ridge frequently. Hod was like a small boy wanting to show off the car, wanting to give lavish gifts to the folks, wanting to spread around over the ridge and let folks see how well he was doing. He never said so. But there was a swagger in his walk and in his talk that was transparent. Mary smiled over it. She thought he had earned the right to swagger a little.

Each time they started out he piled the back of the car full of things. Clothes for Ma, clothes for Pa, and especially clothes for Sarah. New tools for Pa, a new kerosene stove for Ma, new dolls and dishes and toys for Sarah. He even included Irma and John and their young'uns in his giving. They all protested, but Mary could see they loved it just the same. And their pride in him showed out of their eyes when they spoke of him, or when they welcomed him home. Hod Pierce was really getting to be somebody!

The ridge was becoming familiar to Mary. No longer did the road frighten or shock her. When Hod swung off the pike onto the trail up the ridge, it was just the last lap of the trip to her. The hill was just the familiar old hill up which the new car sped, scorning the rocky ledges and the slipping stones. And the old weathered house no longer seemed bare and poverty-stricken to her. It too was glossed over with familiarity. It had even come to take on a feeling of home. When she closed the door behind her now, the four walls snugged in and held her with possession. She went out from this place and she came back to it, and it never changed. It's enduring sameness was like the rising and the setting of the sun. It stood here, whole and secure. It framed life gently and timelessly. And when they rounded the last curve and came in sight of it, she knew a perfect moment of stilled life within her. Everything was slowed, rested, and blessed.

She came to love the sameness. Frequently when she handled the old ironstone dishes in Hattie's kitchen she had a sentient feeling, as if old, now-dead fingers were quickening, and in her youthful finger tips they were given back their life. To feel again, to wash and scour and dry these same dishes of their own youth. Their life tingled through hers.

They had come to Hattie from Gramma. And they had come to Gramma from Abigail Pierce, Jeems's wife. Mary thought of the scenes these ironstone plates had witnessed. Abigail's tears when Jeems went away to war. She would have bent over the soapy water and let her tears drop unseen into the froth of suds. And her ironstone plates would have been gripped hard in hands that were aching to hold tight to a man they could not hold.

Or, she thought, how the plates would have bounced and clattered when Jeems came home! Oh, Abigail would have tripped so lightly around the table, flinging down the plates to their places! Setting, now, once again, that beloved place at the head of the table.

And then there was Gramma, coming at sixteen to the ridge as Dow Pierce's woman. Inheriting from Abigail the Pierce traditions and the Pierce belongings. And the ironstone plates. Again they would have seen a woman's sorrows and joys. And in her time, Hattie. Hattie too would have gripped them tight, grieving for the little lost babies, grieving for Hod during the long war years, and, Mary's mind probed on, grieving even now for him because he was not following in Pierce ways.

It was then that Mary felt a sense of loss. It was an uneasy, fretful thing, which disturbed her only now and then. Times like this, when she stood with an ironstone plate in her hand. Or when she cut a yellow rose from the bush in the chimney corner. Or sometimes when she walked by the split rail fence down to the pasture. Her feet then felt the pull of the land . . . the ease of it, and the yield of it to the foot. She stood sometimes and leaned on the fence, and smelled the earth, drawing it deep down inside her, feeling the earthy air fill her. Then she had this faintly nostalgic yearning. Out of nowhere it came, like an ache sobbing through her, a feeling in her hand, or in her feet, or a smell in the air. But it said to her: " You are not keeping faith! You and Hod are not keeping faith! "

She began too to know the people. Ridge people have a way of closing out strangers. They hood their eyes and shutter their faces and present an inscrutable countenance to outlanders. Friendship comes first from ridge folks, and when they are ready to open the door. Nothing you can do will force it.

Not that Hod's family weren't friendly. They were. Hattie and Tom, Irma and John, and all the others. There was a gentle courtesy, an inherent graciousness in their manner, but at the same time they withheld themselves. She felt that their conversations were guarded and shielded, deliberately directed and channeled around her, so that she might not come too suddenly and too clearly into a knowledge of their most intimate feelings and thoughts.

A less sensitive person might have forever antagonized these people of Hod's. But Mary, having been in her own time a shy, withdrawn person, having known the meaning of intrusion, did not intrude. She met their courtesy with her own courtesy, their friendliness with her own friendliness. And when, hospitably, they offered their home to the guest she graciously returned the gift. She never pressed against the barrier.

It was late summer, a full nine months after Hod and Mary were married, before the door finally opened to her. And it happened as simply as the sun coming up over the rim of the ridge. Hattie overslept. And she was hurrying and bustling in the kitchen, grumbling: " Hit's been a time an' a time sincet I've did sich a thing! Never even opened my eyes till broad daylight! I'll be behind with my work all day! Mary, run upstairs an' git me a jar o' them plum preserves. They're in the little chest under the window."

Mary scurried for the narrow little stairs with a glad feeling in her heart. Never before had she been permitted to go up those stairs into the back room of their life. The barrier was down, and the guest in the house now became the daughter of the house . . . one to share the depths and the heights of family feeling. One to slip a sly look to across the room and share a family joke with. One to call on to help with the work, and to talk long hours to around the quilting frame. One to tell in soft whispers about Irma's two dead babies, and her long labor with the two living ones. One to laugh with over Hod's frailties, knowing it was loving laughter. One, finally, of the Pierces.

And as the family let down the bars, so too did the rest of the folks on the ridge. Little by little they forgot her city strangeness. It's true, she was quare. Allus wantin' to do the most uncommon things. But more and more she became Hod Pierce's woman, a plumb nice girl when you got to know her. And they began to let her see them as they really were.

She watched Tom and Gault, John and Lem and Little Wells, come together and walk through the tobacco or the corn, feeling it, savoring it, hovering over it. They wore dirt-grimed overalls and they smelled of the barnyard and of sweat. Their hands were horny, and their shoulders had bent from the pull of the plow. But they walked their land, free and unbeholding to any man. There was a dignity in that freedom, and it was reflected in their relationships one with the other. No man hurried them, or harried them. And they, in turn, neither hurried nor harried another. Because they were free, they could leave others to their freedom.

There was the day Little Wells bought a new tractor. The family was at supper. " I doubt that little tractor Wells has got is goin' to do the work," Tom said, pouring his coffee into the saucer and blowing upon it. " Hit looks powerful little to me. My opinion, hit won't pull worth a team o' mules."

" Hit looked so to me too," said Hattie.

Hod also shook his head. " It won't. Those little machines are no good for heavy work like Wells has to do. He'd ought to have got a bigger one."

" Did you tell him that? " Mary asked, surprised.

Tom bent a twinkling eye on her over the rim of the saucer.

232

" Hit would be unseemly to give a man advice he weren't askin'
fer," he said gently.

" But if he needed it . . . to keep him from wasting his
money! "

" He would ask fer it, ifen he felt e'er need. An' hit's his money
to waste or not as he sees fit."

The silence grew and the sounds of the supper table took on
new volume. Mary pondered. " Suppose he didn't have enough
money to buy a big tractor with? "

" That would be fer him to say, daughter. Wells'd know that if
e'er person on this ridge had it, he could borry what he needed
to git what he wanted. Hit'd be fer Wells to think on."

The inviolate right of the individual! To pursue his own way
. . . to make his own choice . . . to make a fool of himself if he
so minded . . . to waste his money if he so wanted . . . to call
on his neighbors if he so needed. But forever and enduring his
right to decide for himself . . . to go his own way . . . to be
himself! The obligation of the neighbor? To stand by if needed
. . . to come to the rescue if asked . . . to make up the lack
caused by foolishness and waste. But never to interfere. This was
a fundamental conception of liberty!

Mary looked down the table at Hod. He had come out of all
this. He had this gentleness, this quietness, this silent awareness
of the inviolability of personality, this tall, upstanding conception
of freedom, born and bred in him. They had made him . . . set
him apart from all other men she had ever known. She hugged
this knowledge of him close. But even as it warmed her it was
shot through with a trickle of fear. Would he keep those qualities
in the city? Would he lose something of himself? And if he did,
would he find anything better?

Don't be silly, she told herself. Hod is Hod, wherever he is. And
don't romanticize the ridge. For all this fine conception there is
still poverty, and ignorance, and superstition. Don't overlook that!
Her mind slewed around the edges of that thought. But it isn't
poverty like the slums, she thought, honest with herself. It isn't
the vicious ignorance of the city. It isn't the deliberate evil of
the tenements.

What about Matt and Lutie Jasper? Even they, she thought,
even they have something here they wouldn't have anywhere else.

They have a place . . . they have neighbors . . . they are treated with kindness. And to the limit of their capacity to enjoy it, they have a fullness of life. That would not be possible to them if they were swarmed into a crowded slum room.

It is ironical, she thought, that as I am drawing closer to the ridge, Hod is pulling away from it. And the thought made her feel alone . . . small, and helpless, between the sky and the earth.

CHAPTER TWENTY-SEVEN

For a few months Hod was happy in the new work. He was full of a surging power, like a man who has climbed a tall hill, and stands, winded but victorious, surveying all he has left behind him. He stood like that, straddled and tall, feeling the keen wind in his face, the sharp, exhilarating thrill of being lifted up, over, and above the flat and level land.

The symbols of his new job were important to him. The little cubbyhole of an office; the paraphernalia on the desk; his signature a hundred times a day on workers' slips; the references to him: " Ask Hod." " Ask Pierce." He liked all this.

He watched his margin carefully and managed to end each month safely. He was pleased when he did that and he tucked away into a back cranny of his mind the bleak possibility of having to cut corners. He wouldn't have to. He had the feel of things now. He had it going.

But there came a month when a sudden rush of work narrowed his margin dangerously, and the necessity became a living possibility again. When the rush carried over into the next month, he doggedly refused to look at the operating sheets and let things take their own course. At the end of the month, when the three shift foremen balanced their sheets, it was obvious that Hod's shift was out of balance. The other two men said nothing. They merely tightened their mouths and stalked out of his office.

He sat for a long time after they left, feet on his desk, a pencil turning idly in his hand. He listened to the hum of machinery out in the plant. Listened to the unspoken accusations of the two foremen. Listened to his own conscience. I'll quit the job! And he threw the pencil on the desk. But even as his feet lowered to the floor, he wavered. There was the money in the bank, rapidly mounting up to the day when they could buy that home they were always talking about. There were the nice things Mary was accustomed to. The little car. The feeling of being somebody. The smooth, easy, glossy way of life. There was the office, the desk, the walk through the plant checking things, his shoulders a little wider than the men's, his head a little taller. He shrugged, and twisted through the door. The men would get it in the neck whether he was here or not!

So Hod's shift never ran anywhere near the low margin mark again. And at Christmas when he got his bonus check, he bought Mary a fur coat. Not mink or sable — it was like the small car . . . a substitute for the thing he really wanted. But into its soft, brown pelt went something Hod had lost. His young, naïve sweetness was gone. The fur coat was the final gesture . . . the last unrelenting demand of honor. He wanted nothing that check could buy for himself.

Once he tried to talk about things to Bill Fleming. " I don't like it, Bill," he said. " It's a dirty trick to pull on the men."

Bill Fleming laughed. He slung an arm across Hod's shoulders and patted his back. " You'll get over that. You've got to look out for yourself, man! If you don't, nobody else is going to do it for you! "

Then Hod became another man. Hard, driving, ruthless. He could be ruthless. He had been when he judged Hattie and Tom so harshly and walked off without so much as a backward glance. Youthfully harsh, then — hurt, and wanting to hurt back. But now there was no desire to hurt. He hadn't that excuse, and he didn't need it. He was looking out for himself. He was getting ahead.

Gone now was the fine beauty of the plant. He no longer thought of it as something big, and grand, and splendid. He saw it now as a great maw, cruel and conscienceless, swallowing people down into its dark depths and belching them up again, crushed and broken. He no longer thought of parts as chairs and sofas and beds. He thought of them as numbers, endless spokes and rounds and surfaces, forever conveyed from here to there, to be pitted against the increasing costs of operation.

With nice, precise calculations he weighed and measured, and cut corners anywhere and everywhere, keeping within the margin. He did it carefully and exactingly, lacing his feelings tightly inside himself. He had only one motive now. To keep getting ahead.

At the end of the year Jeff Martin called him into his office. He sat behind his desk and built his fingers into a temple. " Hod," he began, " you've done mighty well. Your record is absolutely clean this year."

Hod lighted a cigarette and rolled it into the corner of his mouth. He squinted his eye against the smoke and said nothing. Get to the point, he was thinking.

Martin got to the point. " Conway's being transferred to the Detroit plant. How would you like his job? "

Hod tongued his cigarette and spoke around it. " I'd like it," he said shortly. He met Martin's eyes and held them.

" It's yours."

" Thanks."

He unfolded his long legs and pushed his cap back on his head. " Thanks," he said again briefly, and went back to his own cubbyhole.

Martin watched him and his eyes slitted. He collapsed the temple of his fingers. That young man, he mused. That young man. He drummed slowly on his desk. But he let the order stand.

Now Hod was division foreman. And he stood up in front of the men at division meetings. In clear, unminced words he told the new men how to cut corners. He didn't laugh about it as Conway had and there were no innuendos in his speech. He made it deliberately rough. They could take it or leave it. " If any of you have got any idea you can do it any other way, get it out of your minds. Take it or leave it, but this is the way it is."

If their eyes betrayed their contempt, he met it coldly, unwaveringly. This is the way it is. Take it or leave it. And most of them took it. They wanted to get ahead too.

At home he was much the same, except that he was often tired, and he had begun to be troubled with indigestion frequently. There were nights too when he didn't sleep well. " You're working too hard, Hod," Mary accused him. " Let up a little. The plant'll be there in the morning! You're getting a case of city nerves and jitters! "

" Yeah," Hod answered. And he shrugged off her worry.

They seldom went to the ridge any more, either. Mary suggested it occasionally. " Let's go down and spend the week end with the folks, Hod."

" I promised Bill I'd play golf with him Saturday."

" You could call him."

" What do you want to go down there for? "

" Well, we haven't been in quite a while. The folks like to see you. And I thought maybe . . ."

" It's too far to drive down and back in a day. I come back more tired than when I started."

He played golf a lot now . . . with Bill Fleming and Ed and Sid Bowden. And he and Mary frequently went to parties with the crowd on Saturday nights. When he dressed for a party now, there were five or six suits to choose from — suits tailored for him out of fine, rich materials. He no longer needed Mary's guidance. He had developed an impeccable taste, patterned after the men with whom he associated. And when they parked their car in front of Ed's or Sid's or Bill's it was no longer the small new car. Now it was the long, low-slung convertible. This year's bonus check had helped pay for it. And they had taken the balance from their home fund. Mary had protested that. " We don't really need a new car, Hod," she said. " And we have enough saved now for a down payment on a home. We could get a small place out in the edge of town."

" I want the car," Hod answered. " There's time enough for the home."

He knew what he wanted. The car now, and the home later. The home, out in the edge of town, yes. But not a tiny place like Mary had in mind. He had seen those new bricks building up on the long, outreaching roads and lanes, nesting snugly in their broad, sweeping lawns. One of those now. Why not? Division superintendent paid seventy-two hundred. But Martin was division superintendent! Yeah. Still . . . time enough, later.

Mary watched him with mixed feelings. So conflicting were her emotions that she could not find the point at which she was apprehensive. When he sat across the bridge table from her, his steady, smooth game balancing her own rather erratic one; when

237

they dined out and danced together; when he took his place naturally with the other men in a corner of the room; when he handed her into the long, low car, she was extremely proud of him. He had come so much farther in these two years than she had ever thought possible. Even her faith in him, and her love for him, had not envisioned this sure, steady climb on his part. Nor had she foreseen his adaptability . . . to the city, to their friends, to the gracious, easy life of which they were a part.

Well, she asked herself, isn't that what you wanted him to do? What's the matter with you, then? And she couldn't say. It was vague, elusive, a feeling of loss — real only in that it was constant. A troubled feeling that they were missing something. She reassured herself by looking around, telling herself they had everything . . . youth, security, friends, a satisfactory social life, Hod's good job. What was missing? The feeling was too persistent to shake off. And sometimes she looked at Hod and wished he weren't so often tired. Weren't so often engrossed in something he brought home from the office. Weren't so often unhungry and unsleepy.

Not that he wasn't always gentle and good to her. Not that he wasn't still a dear lover. When he had time. When he wasn't too tired. When they weren't going somewhere. There were yet those high moments of the recurring miracle. But they were dimmed by the race of time, the demands of living, the jaded body and spirit used up by the day's work.

She remembered the warm gaiety of the first months. Hod had had a merry, roguish wit which had sparkled for her when they were alone. An earthy, pungent speech, so different, so peculiarly his, that she mixed him and his way of talking all up together. But this too had disappeared. It was as if the inspiration and source of himself had run dry. He could bring forth nothing except clichés. Nothing particularly Hoddish. Apparently his mind was as cubbyholed as his body. Mary mourned for the loss, but didn't despair of it. He's too busy, she told herself. When he's settled down into this job and doesn't feel so burdened, he'll be himself again.

She felt restless. She wanted the settled feeling of home and children. Time was fleeting, and they were both past thirty now. She didn't talk about this to Hod. She was afraid it would trouble him, and in these days she was seeking in every way she knew to spare him additional burdens.

And so the time went by. Went by so tightly and so tensely for so long without surcease that Hod felt an unutterable weariness overtaking him. He thinned down to a flat leanness, and developed a tremor in his right hand. He was never rested. Sleepiness came over him early at night, overtaking him at the table, or even at parties. Overpowering sleepiness, wilting him and making him ill. And yet when he slept, later, it was a sodden, loggy sleep that left him unrested and nauseated with weariness. He felt a compulsion to swallow constantly, and when he tried to eat, he felt sick.

Now he was compelled to look at himself, at his life. His body which had endured the strain for so long now compelled him to think of it. And he could not think of his body without thinking also of the conditions that surrounded it. Not for a long time had he done any objective thinking. He had walked so surely, stepping so firmly from one stone to another, that he had never noticed the stream which he was crossing. Now he had to look down. But so stubbornly dedicated was he to the steppingstones that even as he looked down he denied the necessity. Why, things were going too well. He was on top. Just one more stride and he'd be sitting in Martin's office. All he needed was to take it a little easier. Get a little more sleep. Get out in the open more often. Quit going to so many parties.

The parties bored him anyhow. He sat, now, on the fringe, and looked on with sated eyes. Ed, Sid, Joe, and Bill . . . he saw them in their shiny, bursting skins . . . he knew the line of their talk by memory. Deals, and more deals. So I told him. So I said to him. So I made him an offer. And the complacent laughter that always accompanied the telling. Hod sat in his corner and let his anger and his nausea beat against him. He rarely entered into their conversations any more. And he tried not to listen.

The women were just as bad. Esther, veiling herself in the smoke from her long amber holder, shrieking her eternal cry of culture down the room . . . pseudo art . . . pseudo music . . . pseudo living! Nora, insulated in her country memories, inept

239

with her offspring, escaping her impotence by constant nibbling
at the past. Daisy, lean and lithe, satin-cased and slick, eating
away at Joe, wearing him down with her hatred and nagging. And
finally Minna Bowden. Minna, on her everlasting search for
reality. Running like a rat in a maze after this good cause and that,
shutting her eyes to life and raising them skyward with pious
mouthings.

And what was it any of them wanted? What drove them to this
insane life? What was it they still kept running after? For they
were all in a race — a mad, rat race, chasing their tails, clawing
the barriers, frothing after something else. What would it take to
release them? A little more money in the bank? A little better
job? A little bigger house? A little more powerful car?

What? What? What? He slitted his eyes and let the room whirl
around him until the figures of the people were on a treadmill
before him. Circling like little squirrels running, stepping on each
other's tails, biting and snarling, circling, circling . . . and getting nowhere. The treadmill only went faster. Mary was in the
circle, her black head thrown back and her breath laughing out
of her mouth. And then as the room whirled faster, he joined the
circle, and his long legs hurried to catch up.

In his bone weariness Hod took to walking at night. Maybe, he
thought — maybe if I get tired enough physically, I can sleep.
Sometimes Mary went with him. She was genuinely worried about
him now. And she felt better if she was with him. At first they
walked at random, seeking no special place, thinking no special
thoughts, not noticing the people they jostled or were jostled by.
They rarely talked. But one night Hod spoke suddenly. " Did you
ever notice the faces of people? "

" The faces of people? "

" I mean just people in general. Like these we meet on the
street. Ever look at them good? "

Mary was startled. She thought for a moment. " Not very
often," she finally admitted.

" Take a good look at them," Hod said. " Try it for a block.
Look carefully at the face of every person we meet."

At the end of the block she looked at him. " Well? "

" Did you see anybody who looked happy? "

" I wasn't looking for that."

" Look for it in this block."

Mary shook her head at the end of the next block. " There aren't many, are there? "

" Did you see *one* face that looked happy? "

" I thought maybe that old woman looked happy. Not bubbling over with it . . . but sort of serene and calm."

" Yeah, I counted her too. But nobody else. The faces look tight, screwed up. They look like they're hurting. Even the young ones look stretched out thin. And nobody's got time for anybody else. Everybody's in a hurry, got to get somewhere, fast. Now watch this."

They were walking down Fourth Street, and as he touched her elbow, they stopped to watch a bus load passengers at the curb. The bus was already crowded to standing room, and about thirty people on the sidewalk swarmed around the door as it drew up to a stop.

" Let 'em off," the driver yelled. " Let 'em off, first."

But the packed mob at the curb wouldn't give an inch, and the people coming out had to fight their way through the pack, clothes being pulled, hats knocked awry, bundles dropped. Muttering, they made their way through, only to be caught in the surge of the pack toward the door when the last person cleared it.

" All the way to the back, now," the driver called hopefully, screwing his head around to see if there was room. Outside, the crowd shoved until the starter called: " That's all. Close the doors."

" You'd think that was the last bus tonight," Hod said, and he pointed up the street. Another bus was nosing into the curb there.

" Funny what being jammed and crowded together in a city does to people, isn't it? Seems like they turn themselves wrong side out, and you can only see their worst sides. They've got to get so much for themselves so fast that they haven't got time to think of anybody else. Everybody's out to take care of himself, and the devil take the hindmost."

They walked on up the street and crossed to avoid the starlings that circled the hotel. Since the old post office had been torn down on the square, the homeless starlings roosted there. Each evening at dusk they circled and swarmed, their shrill cries filling

241

the air. Mary and Hod stopped to watch them.

"A starling is such a hideous bird," Mary said. "And it has such a pretty name. A bird with a name like that should be beautiful, with a song like a thrush's. But listen to that hoarse cry of theirs! It's worse than a crow's."

Hod watched silently. Finally he pulled at Mary's arm. There was a bitter taste in everything tonight. "Yeah," he said, "we're like those birds. Those of us who live in a big city. Crowded and quarreling for room and life . . . pecking at one another . . . ruffling our feathers and screaming at each other. We've got no more dignity than the birds. Just a little more modesty."

Mary's mouth fell open. It was the first time she had heard one of Hod's pithy, wry remarks in months and months. She kept still, hoping he would go on. But his ire was spent and he felt the futility of sermonizing. Who am I to talk, he thought. I'm just as unlovely as the rest. And I won't do any more about it than they will.

But he had a sudden vision of a place where time stood still . . . a green and sweet place, where life flowed slowly. Where a man could prop his foot up on a fence rail and spit a puddle of brown tobacco in the dust, and talk about the weather, the crops, the state of the world, with all of time and space to spare. Where people were busy with purpose, but never too busy to stop and be kind and neighborly. Where you were never alone in sorrow, grief, or sadness. Where a man could stop in the middle of a corn row on a bright June morning, if he was of a mind to, and grab his fishing pole. Where, on a moony night, he could whistle up his coon hound and take to the woods. Oh, life is never so sweet as when it is distilled slowly, one drop at a time . . . lived fully, one hour at a time!

Hod was filled with a nostalgic longing for the ridge. But he turned on the pavement and set his heel down hard, denying it.

CHAPTER TWENTY-EIGHT

THE SECOND SUMMER CAME ON. The sun blasted the city day after day and it stewed in its own juice. The streets softened to an oozy, viscous dough, kneaded by traffic until a muggy, smothering wave of steam rose from it, like a solid column, from which there was no escape. The brick buildings absorbed the sun, and gave it off again, blowing a furnace breath into the air. The lowering pall of heat did not cool until late at night. Never completely cooled, really, for morning came too soon.

Hod's office, which had been Conway's, was a box which held the heat like an oven. The big plant sprawled in the sun, taking it in and spreading it through the low, flat-topped buildings. Hod never used to mind the heat, but it wilted him these days. By the end of the day he felt like a starched shirt that a hot shower had spattered.

He was feeling like that late on Friday afternoon just before the five o'clock whistle when Bill Fleming sent for him.

"Sit down, Hod," Bill said when he went in, offering him a cigar. Hod shook his head. He wasn't smoking as much these days.

"What's on your mind?" he asked, tipping the big electric fan so that its current played over him. "I need this more than you do," he laughed.

"Sure," Bill agreed. Bill cut the end of his cigar and rolled it around in his mouth before lighting it. Hod knew Bill would take his time. When he had something he considered important to say, he always played with a cigar that way.

"Hod," when the cigar suited him and was lighted Bill spoke, "how'd you like Martin's job?"

The legs of Hod's chair came down suddenly. "Martin's?"

"That's what I said."

Hod felt a gushing thrill pour through him, like an emptying and draining of all the fluid of his body! Division superintendent! Six sections under him! This was what he'd been waiting for! He grinned at Bill, and Bill's mouth widened in an answering grin.

"Sounds pretty good, huh?"

"Sounds mighty good!" He kicked the chair back and walked over to the window. "Can you swing it?"

"I think so."

Hod drummed his fingers on the windowpane. "What about Martin?"

Bill leaned back in his chair and swiveled around. "Martin?" he said, as if it were a new problem. "Oh. Why, Martin's been slipping pretty badly lately. I guess you'd say Martin's just going to be a casualty."

Hod cracked the knuckles on his right hand. Martin had been pretty good to him. Martin had seen that Conway gave him his first break, and he'd come through with division foreman when Conway was transferred. He hated to see him get it this way. Still. "If I don't take it, who gets it?" he asked.

Bill looked at him a long moment, a bleak look and a final look. He shook his head and when he spoke his voice had a dead, level sound. "Nobody. This job is strictly for you. Take it or leave it, Hod."

Hod knew then. There was nothing wrong with Martin's work. He hadn't played ball with Bill somewhere along the line . . . or he'd got fed up with playing ball, and Bill was putting the skids under him. And Bill was putting a friend of his in Martin's place. Another one of Bill's deals.

"O.K., Bill." What else was there to say?

Mary had learned that the little courtyard was cooler than the apartment in the afternoons when the building next door shaded the tiny grassy plot from the sun. It was far from cool, but it was more bearable than their third-floor rooms. Late each afternoon she moved there with her reading or sewing, taking along a tray of cold drinks, and tried to make herself comfortable. She wished Hod could take his vacation soon, and they could get away from the city. She thought longingly of the mountains, or the sea, or even of the ridge. Any place where they could escape the pavements and the hot buildings.

That Friday afternoon she had been especially fretful. She was trying to decide whether or not to sign her contract for another year. Hod had been urging her to quit teaching. They no longer needed the money, and that had been her principal reason for teaching at first. But she wondered what she would do with herself if she gave it up. As long as they lived in an apartment and had no children, she would find life pretty sterile and empty. If they would only buy a place and get settled!

Hod found her there when he came home. He swept his hat onto the ground and stretched out with a moan, letting his body sink into the cushion of the grass.

" Pretty bad today? " Mary asked.

" Oh, the same old thing! But it's so hot I feel like I've been fried! "

" I know. Something cold to drink before dinner? "

" Yes, ma'am, please! And you can just keep on serving me something cold to drink! I don't care if we never have dinner." He turned over and buried his face in the grass, letting it tickle against his cheek. He bit down on a blade, remembering the pungent taste of crab grass when he was a boy. But this tasted dusty, oily, flat. He spat, wrinkling his mouth.

When Mary nudged him with the toe of her shoe, he sat up to take the drink from her. He sipped, and then drank gustily. " More," and he held out the glass.

" You'll ruin your dinner, Hod! "

" Dinner can wait. What is this? "

" Tea, with pineapple juice and ginger ale."

" Wonderful! "

He leaned back against the chair in which she was sitting, rubbing his head against her knee. " Got some good news."

" A house! "

" No. But we can get the house soon. I'm the new division superintendent."

" Hod! Hod! " Mary's hands flew to his shoulders and shook them delightedly. " How wonderful! Darling, I'm so glad! When did you find out? "

" Today. Just before quitting time. Bill called me in and told me." That was all he'd tell her of that, though.

" O Hod, I know you've been hoping you'd get that job someday. But I thought you'd be lucky if it came five or ten years from now. When Mr. Martin retired. Oh, what about Mr. Martin? "

" He's quitting."

" Quitting? Is he sick? Is he going with another company? "

" I don't know. All I know is that Bill called me in today and said Martin was leaving, and did I want the job."

" Are they firing him, Hod? "

" How should I know? "

" Well, don't you think you *should* know? After all, Mr. Martin's

245

been pretty nice to you."

Hod threw the handful of dirt he had been sifting through his fingers to the ground. He squared around and faced her. His jaw jutted stubbornly and his mouth was tight. "All right, you asked for it! They're firing him."

"Why?"

"I don't know. But I strongly suspect he got tired of playing ball with Bill. I don't know, and I don't want to know the straight of it. But my guess is Bill's got to have a friend in that division job. I'll pat your back and you pat mine. So Martin gets fired, and Pierce gets the job. Pierce is Fleming's friend. I don't know any more than that. I don't need to know any more."

Mary sat there, stupidly trying to take it in. This wasn't Hod talking. She brushed her hair back from her hot forehead.

"Well, say something!" Hod shouted at her.

"You mean —" she said finally — "you mean you'll go along with Bill? You'll let Bill fire Martin, and you'll take his job?"

"Sure I'll do it. It's not much worse than what I've been doing all along. I've been stealing time from the men for two years. Been stealing money from their pay envelopes so I could pad my operating sheets. Oh, not literally," he said when he saw her face. "I haven't really gone into their pockets. But I might as well have. I've kept their wages down and cut 'em out of time. It's the same thing."

"Hod, what's happening to you? Jeff Martin was your friend. You could keep Bill from doing this to him!" Mary's voice was trembling, and it hung broken in the air between them.

Hod was on his feet now, shouting at her. "What's happening to me! Nothing. Nothing at all, except that I'm learning how to get along in the world! I'm learning that you can't be soft. You can't think about other people. You've got to take care of yourself. And when it comes to cutting throats, I'm learning not to let mine get cut, that's all!"

"Even if you cut Jeff Martin's?"

"Even if I cut Jeff Martin's! If it's his or mine, it'll be his! Mary, you live in an ivory tower! If you get ahead, if you ever amount to anything, you can't be careful how you do it. If you have to step all over the other fellow, it's just his tough luck for being in the way! He'd step on you if the cards ran the other way!"

Mary felt sick and dull. This was Hod shouting these terrible things at her. Hod, who was so tender and gentle with her. She hadn't known he could talk like this . . . do things like this! She felt as if he had struck her down and trampled on her. "Then everything I've ever believed in is false," she said. "Everything I've ever tried to teach children to believe in is false."

"You're darned right it's false! You don't get ahead by honesty and integrity. You get ahead by making friends in the right places. And by pulling wires. And by forgetting your conscience. You learn right away that deals are more important than ideals! They're no good to you when you come up against the world. And only a few people like you still believe in them — and you don't practice what you preach!"

Mary's hands cupped her face and she shook all over with the ague of her horror. Let him stop, she prayed. Let him stop talking! But the silence was dead and white, and she dropped her hands limply. "Hod, if you take that job, we're through. You know that, don't you?" There was a trembling down her legs and her chest felt caved in.

Hod's head flung up at her words. "Well, what makes you think your skirts are clean? You cry crocodile tears, you don't soil your lily white hands, but, brother, how you do gobble up all the good things that come your way from somebody else's soiled hands! You wanted solid mahogany furniture, didn't you? You wanted an electric kitchen, didn't you? You wanted a Chinese imported rug, didn't you? And you didn't complain over your new fur coat, did you? Oh, but gee, how shocked you are when I tell you that the way I made the money to pay for 'em was by stepping on people like Jeff Martin! Do you want to examine every dollar I make to be sure it's clean? Well, precious few of them are, I can tell you that!"

Mary's face came clear before him in the haze of his anger. He saw it naked and white and crumpled. A blaze of sunlight through the interstices of the buildings cut across it and marbled the pure white of her skin. He lifted an arm, and then let it fall heavily to his side. He whirled toward the house.

"Where are you going?" Mary cried, running after him.

"Out! Out! I'm going out! I don't know where, and I don't care where! I'm going to see if I can drive far enough to get a breath

247

of clean air! I'm sick of this town. I'm darned near sick of everything!"

"Let me go too!"

Hod stopped and looked at her, and everything inside of him melted and ran down. "Mary," he whispered. "O Mary, forgive me! It wasn't true. It wasn't true!"

She came into his arms and wound her own arms tight around him, hugging him closely as if she couldn't get near enough. Oh, he had been so far away! And then the tears came — wet, freeing tears that drowned his shirt collar and trickled down his neck. He let her cry: "It's such a mess, Mary. It's such a mess."

She smeared her nose on the front of his shirt and lifted a shaky smile. "Let me get a scarf for my hair. I won't be a minute."

Hod drove and drove, not thinking where he was going. He sought the outer edges of town and turned the car loose on uncrowded roads. The wind in his face felt clean, and the dark, sparsely lighted roads were good. Mary sat close, saying nothing. Only her hand on his knee never lifted. From time to time he reached down and took it, held it for a short time, and then laid it back on his knee.

Far into the night they drove, circling and circling, out one road, in another. And then, just as dawn grayed the sky, Mary bent her head against his arm. He thought she had gone to sleep. Looking down, he saw she was crying again. He pulled the car up to the side of the road and drew her gently against him, cradling her and rocking her. She flung her head back then, and sobbed: "Hod. Hod, let's go down home!"

Home! Neither of them thought it strange that she should use that word. Neither of them remembered the other time when she had cried, "I want to go home."

Hod started the car and turned it into the road, and, straight as an arrow released from a taut string, it sped into the rising sun.

Three hours later they were climbing the ridge, and then they were nosing the car up against the picket fence. Sarah poked her nose out the front door, and, seeing who it was, screeched and flew to the back of the house. But Hattie would not admit surprise when she came in, wiping her hands on her apron front.

"I knowed you was comin'," she said. "I was jist cleanin' a chicken. I told 'em all I'd best git ready, fer I knowed in reason you was comin'."

"How could you possibly have known we were coming?" laughed Mary.

"The old dominecker rooster got plumb up in the door this mornin' an' jist crowed fit to kill. Hit's a sure sign. An' I told 'em all right then — I says, 'Hod an' Mary's acomin' an' I'd best git ready!'"

"How long will it take you to fry that chicken, Ma?" Hod asked.

"Not more'n a few minnits! I'll bound yer hungry, an' I aimed to have it ready. But you come a mite quicker'n I was lookin'."

When they had finished eating, Hod folded the remainder of the chicken and a couple of biscuits in an oiled bread wrapper and stuck it in his pocket. Then he started rummaging through the old corner cupboard. "Ma, you know where there's any fishin' line and stuff? I think I'll go down to the river."

"In that there box on the bottom shelf. Right where you allus kept it. I reckon Tom got so used to you puttin' it there he ain't never thought none o' movin' it. Facts is, I don't reckon hit's been used sincet that time when you was home on furlough."

"I found it," Hod grunted. He turned to Mary and kissed her softly on the cheek. He patted her shoulder. "Don't worry if I'm late. I'll be home for supper, though."

When the screen door slammed behind him, Hattie looked at Mary. "Didn't you want to go with him?"

"Not today."

Mary watched him cross the back lot and lift his long legs over the fence into the tobacco patch. He wasn't going away from her, she knew. But he had some thinking to do today, and he had to do it alone.

Hod eyed the length of the tobacco patch speculatively. Looked pretty good. It was waist-high, greening up from the broad, dark base to the curled edges of pale leaves at the top. Spiking the top were the fragile, creamy petals of the blooms, as delicate as oleander. When he looked back, the acre was a small green sea, crested with amethyst foam. There's nothin' as pretty as tobacco in bloom, he thought.

His feet took the path down the holler, following the purling creek. The stones were white in the sun, and tiny, silver minnows darted frantically from shallow to shallow. On past the schoolhouse he went, across Lem's cornfield, coming finally to the river. He cut a reed and wound the line around it, adjusted the cork for depth, baited the hook, and set the pole in the soft, hot soil of the bank. He leaned back and let his shoulders feel the rough bark through his shirt. He sighed. His eyelids drooped from lack of sleep, and he slid down against the thick mat of leaf mold under the tree. He turned over and laid his face in his arms and dozed dreamily.

The ground was warmly spotted with sun streaks through the leaves, and the river ran a rapid, noisy chatter around the rocks in midstream. Here it eddied in toward the bank in a deep pool, but the edges of the pool were restless with the hurry of the shallows in the middle. Hod listened, and the heat and the noisy talk of the river made him want to strip and become a part of the coolness, the wetness, and the noisiness of the stream. He flung his clothes on a blackberry bush and plunged into the pool, going down deep and opening his eyes in the dimness below. There were the white roots of the big sycamore tree sprangled out in the water, and a frightened fish hiding in their network. He went down to the bottom and laid his hand against the cool pebbles. He clutched a handful of them and came up shouting when his head was clear, " Touched bottom! " Wade and Sandy and Little Wells should have been there on the bank to hear him, and to laugh, and make him open out his hand for proof.

When he tired of splashing and swimming, he eased over on his back and floated, letting the water hold him lightly. He looked down his long length and eyed the whiteness of his stomach and legs. Time was when they were brown as a berry by this time in August. He lifted his arm and let the water run in a thin stream down it, back into the river. He remembered another time when he had lain here on the breast of the river and watched a droplet trickle down his arm and join its source again. And he had traced it on down the stream. Past the Beaver Hole . . . he remembered. Past Old Man Smith's place. Past the covered bridge. On down it had gone to the union with the Ohio . . . to the merging with the Mississippi. To the Gulf and the ocean. And what was it he had thought? O free and searching water! He had wanted to be free as the water, hadn't he? He had wanted to travel with it and see all those places out there, hadn't he? Well, he'd been, now. He'd seen them. Free and searching water! Free, but never staying anywhere . . . free, but always moving. Free, but with no purpose. And what had he done? And what had he seen?

He crawled out on the bank, rubbed himself down with his shirt, and dressed slowly. When he had finished, he sat down, drawing his legs up and lacing his arms around them. He let his mind follow on down the path it had ventured into.

Then freedom had to have a purpose, he thought. It's got to be tied to something, and it's got to be going somewhere. Is it freedom if it's tied to something? Is there really any such thing as freedom? What do men mean by being free? What did I mean by wanting to be free? I thought if I could get off the ridge I'd be free. What was it I wanted to be free of?

He squirmed around and looked back up the valley toward the ridge, humped sullenly against the sky. There it stood, forever and enduring. Was that what he had wanted to get away from? The foreverness?

His mind fringed out his thoughts, tracing each to its frayed end, and somewhere along there he remembered the night when he had made Lily Mae mad with his talk of leaving the ridge. It came back to him how he'd said folks on the ridge always did things the same old way, that they never looked farther ahead than the end of their noses, that they were satisfied to make do. He remembered later that night, after Hattie had forbidden his going to the lumber camp, how he had flung his thoughts wildly to the night sky. He wouldn't be caught in the net of that inertia. He would not settle down in a two-room shack on the edge of Pa's land and doom himself to dark risings and dark sleepings, and nothing beyond but the end of a furrow and sweat for his pains. He had twisted under the weight of seven generations of Pierces on the ridge. The dead weight of it, and the wantlessness of it. That's not for me, he'd said. That's not for me.

That was what he had wanted to be free of, then. That dead weight. That inertia. Troubled, his hand sifted the earth through his fingers. He still didn't want that. He twisted the thoughts round and round in his head. Well, what was it he wanted to be free for, then? I wanted to be free to be myself, he remembered. I wanted to find out who Hod Pierce was. What he could do if he had a chance. Where he belonged, and how big a man he could be, the work and the place that would bring out the most in him. That's a man's right, isn't it?

Yeah, he told himself. You thought if you could get off the ridge, you'd be somebody. You thought folks out there had life sweeter. You thought out there lay freedom. Well, you found out, didn't you? He accused himself. You found out that freedom hasn't any meaning at all over there. You thought there'd be green pastures and wide, lovely spaces, and men would live in those spaces graciously and sweetly. Instead, you crawled over the fence right into a little box. A little box two feet this way, measured by the kind of job you had, how much money you made, the contacts you had. Two feet this way, measured by the kind of place you lived in, the kind of furniture you had in it, the number of gadgets you were able to buy for it. Two feet this way, measured by the sort of friends you had, the kind of clothes you wore, the kind of car you drove. Two feet this way, measured by the time you punched in on a clock, the time you wasted at parties, the time you slept, the time you didn't live.

A little box, walled in on all four sides. At first it wasn't so high but what you could crawl over it and get out for a while. And at first you wanted to get out from time to time. And at first you were certain you were going to make it bigger. Bring into it something fine. At first the top was open, and overhead were skies and the stars, fuzzy clouds and new moons. You could look up and see them. But the longer you stayed in the pen, the less often you wanted to get out. The less often the smallness bothered you. The more satisfied you were with it. Until finally you yourself nailed the last board across the top, closing yourself in, shutting out the skies and the stars, the fuzzy clouds and the new moons. They troubled you. They were too bright and big and far away.

You liked the smallness and coziness, and the space outside frightened you. You crouched in your little pen and felt safe and snug and secure. You didn't have to dare anything in that small space. You didn't have to think. You didn't have to reach for anything. You didn't have to do anything different or brave or honest.

252

You just closed the box around you and made yourself little to fit it. And you dried up inside, contented with the pattern of things. You didn't have to *be* somebody to live in that little box. You only had to be like everybody else.

And what did it cost you? You only had to seal yourself into slavery . . . the slavery of making money, of buying and accumulating possessions, of racing breathlessly toward the pie in the sky . . . success. You only had to punch the time clock and bow and say, " Yes, sir." You only had to forfeit every dream of freedom, every last ounce of dignity, every last inch of self-respect. For how could a man walk tall in liberty caged in a pen!

Hod's hand dropped again to his side, fingering the earth beneath it. He crumbled it and sifted it between his fingers. He lifted it and smelled it, sniffing its dank richness. With the feel of the earth in his hands, suddenly he felt the pull of the plow in his arms. The feel of the furrows under his feet. The hot sun on his back. The fuzzy greenness of new tobacco leaves between his fingers. The clean, winy air in his lungs. His head went back and he took a deep, deep breath. It's good, he thought. It's good.

What was it Grampa said once? I've had me a little piece o' land o' my own . . . an' a roof over my head that belonged to me . . . an' I've raised what I put in my stummick an' it set light there on account of it. I've had me a good woman to go along with me, an' kids that's pleasured me. I've had work to lay my hand to . . . work o' my own choosin'. An' folks around to neighbor with. Don't know what more a man could want. Livin' jist about biles down to that, I'd say.

Suddenly the words were shot through with a new illumination. Like blinding light Hod saw it. There's more, Grampa. You didn't say it, but it was there all the time. It was in everything you said, wasn't it? Living like that a man can be a clod, never lifting his head above it. He can be what I wanted to get away from. Dull, and plodding, and oxlike. He can sink down into the land itself, and never rise above it. There's got to be something else running through it like a scarlet thread . . . giving it color . . . giving it meaning. A man's got to have the knowledge that it's good . . . that it's good and true and beautiful. He's got to have the deep and abiding awareness in him of the dignity of his relationship to the earth, or else it loses its dignity and becomes

253

in its own way another kind of slavery. He's got to hold close to him its beauty. He's got to feel that it's the foundation of pride and strength . . . of dignity and manhood.

Grampa had known how good his life was . . . how right and true. And that's what's got to color life and make it live. That's what makes a man free. That's what lifts the weight of the land from his shoulders and makes him walk tall . . . on his own land, where he can walk on it, smell of it, feel of it, plant it and harvest its growth. That's what freed him, because the land he owned was part of himself and in the last analysis he only owned himself.

And then Hod saw he had answered his own most profound questions: Who is Hod Pierce? And why does he live? He saw that a man could search forever outside of himself for the purpose of his life. But until he turned his eyes inward, he would never find the home he was seeking. It wasn't off somewhere in mansions in the sky. It wasn't in the city or in the country on the face of the earth. It was right down inside of a man.

This thought startled him, and he looked backward timidly. Was he going to have to unthink all he had been thinking now? Start from where? He stood up and felt his tallness reaching up, and his leanness filling out. Start from inside the man. Start from deep down inside. There was no other way. If a man could look at himself and the work he had done at the end of a day, and say, it's been good today . . . it's been as right and as fine and as good as I could make it . . . it's taken the best there is in me to do it, and it's made me bigger and better to do it . . . then that man was at home, wherever he was. Even in the little box? Even there?

Even there. You didn't have to nail the lid down on the box. He looked at that thought, wincing. You didn't have to take the foreman's job. The first time you cheated on a guy you nailed down the first board. But you didn't have to do it. He went farther down this path of thought. You didn't even have to crawl into the box in the first place. Your ideas of being somebody were all wrong. You thought getting ahead on a job, making money, and buying things were amounting to something. All your life you were walking toward that box, and it wasn't the box's fault. It was inside of you all the time.

Standing tall, he felt cleansed and renewed. He tightened his belt a little. He could go back to the city. He could make Hod Pierce's life have meaning there. But he could make it have more meaning here. It would be here. Here on the land where his father and his father's father before him had worked out their own lives. He could take on the full weight of seven generations and it would measure him to his tallest height. It would make him the most somebody he could ever be. By the manner of his living, the way of his work, by his own sense of integrity, he would establish his own proprietorship of himself. Free himself, and walk tall. Who is Hod Pierce? A speck of dust, whirling in a cosmic wind. Yes, but a speck of dust with a purpose, whirling in a wind with a pattern. Part of a timeless whole, which without him would be incomplete!

When Mary saw his face that evening, she knew he had found his answer. It had gone young again, smooth and quiet, and peace spread over it like a healing ointment. And she felt it stealing into her, gentling her fears and calming her. A rising tide of gladness choked her throat. Whatever he had decided, it was right. If it made him look like this, it was right.

After supper he turned to her. " Let's walk awhile. There'll be a moon later on."

They went down the road, scuffling the dust, swinging their joined hands like children. The night mist was crawling up the holler, cooling the heat and dampening the dust. The purpling twilight softened the mass of trees on the rim of the ridge, muting their identity. A dog barked sharply, twice, and then was quiet. Across a hill and a holler a sentinel cowbell tongued the knell of the buried sun. The stars blinked out and came closer. Kentucky stars. Just far enough above so that a man must tiptoe to touch them. Around all the world, Hod thought, there's none so beautiful. The stars over a man's home must always be the loveliest.

He held Mary's hand tighter and guided her into the path that led down into the holler. " Where are we going? " she wanted to know.

" You'll see," he answered. " There's a thing I want to show you."

They followed the trail and came to the foot of the hill, and then they crossed the creek, stepping lightly on the stones. They waded the tall grass up to Grampa's unlighted cabin. Hod let down the gate and went through. Mary followed him. She was afraid to speak. She would break the spell.

When they came up to the old log house, Hod laid his hand against it. "This is it," he said. "This is what I wanted to show you."

"It's Grampa Dow's house, isn't it?"

"It's our house."

Mary was still. There was no mistaking Hod's meaning. This was his answer. She thought she must have known it all the time. Known that this was where they would make out their lives together. Known it even that day long ago when he had boarded a bus and racked his bag above her and sat down beside her. Known that this man would take her by the hand and lead her here. Known it, and wanted it. Something in her was fulfilled now.

Oh, it wouldn't all be as simple as that! She would have to change every habit of her life . . . remake herself . . . strip herself of many small vanities and prides. She would hate it sometimes. She would cry from weariness and ache from the hardness of it. She would feel sorry for herself sometimes, moan for her permanents and manicures and trim, tailored suits. She would be frightened and ill sometimes, borne down by the strangeness. But even as she knew all this, she knew another thing. She had it in her to be that much of a woman. By this man's side, she had it. He would call it out of her . . . expect it of her, and make her be that big. She could take on that stature to walk beside him.

She joined her hand with his against the rough old logs. "It will be a beautiful home," she said.

Hod stopped her by the beech tree at the head of the trail when they climbed out of the holler. "Wait," he said. "Listen to this." He cupped his hands around his mouth and shouted long and loud: "Hey! Hey, you! This here's Hod Pierce ablowin' his horn!"

And the echo rolled up in the holler, reverberated against the cliff, and came back to them, clear and strong. Triumphantly it came back, "This here's Hod Pierce ablowin' his horn!"

256

Miss Willie

Janice Holt Giles

———————◆———————

Foreword by Wade Hall

THE UNIVERSITY PRESS OF KENTUCKY

3 in 1 ISBN: 0-7394-3237-0

To
my mother, Lucy M. Holt,
and to the memory of
my father, John A. Holt,
who spent their lives together
in the schoolroom

Acknowledgment

Once again I want, publicly, to acknowledge the help of my husband, Henry E. Giles. I have not written anything, and I doubt if I ever shall, in which he does not have his part. In its deepest meaning, he is a faithful collaborator.

FOREWORD

KENTUCKY authors have written two of the most engrossing and inspiring books about teachers in American literature. Jesse Stuart's *The Thread That Runs So True* (1949) is an autobiographical novel about the trials and triumphs of a male teacher in Eastern Kentucky in the 1920s and 1930s. Janice Holt Giles's *Miss Willie* (1951) is a fact-based story of a female teacher set in the ridge country of South Central Kentucky shortly after World War II. Both Stuart and Giles were describing a profession they greatly admired and a part of the state they knew intimately. Stuart was a native of Greenup County, the setting for most of his fiction and nonfiction, and for many years served as a teacher and a school administrator. Arkansas native Giles was working in Louisville during the war when, on a bus near Bowling Green, she met Henry Giles, a soldier who became her husband. After the war the couple moved to Adair County, which Mrs. Giles made the setting for most of her books. Indeed, two of the characters in *Miss Willie*, Hod and Mary Pierce, are modeled on Janice Holt and Henry Giles. Unlike Stuart, however, Giles was never a classroom teacher, although in *Miss Willie* she pays tribute to her mother, who taught for forty years in the public schools of Arkansas and Oklahoma.

The story is focused on Miss Willie Payne, a second grade teacher in El Paso, Texas, who is bored with her life and her career. As a young woman she had wanted to become a missionary and go to China, but family responsibilities killed that dream. After more than twenty years as a teacher, she feels unfulfilled. "Something's missing," she confides to herself. "I get up in the morning moody and depressed, and I teach all day feeling as if I were getting nowhere and accomplishing nothing." Her life is a monotonous treadmill.

Her niece Mary, whom she reared after her parents died, is also a teacher, but she has recently left her position to marry Hod Pierce, whose home is in a remote community in rural Kentucky called Piney Ridge. Mary writes her aunt joyful letters about her new life. One day Miss Willie receives a letter that awakens her missionary impulses: "Do you remember what the Macedonians wrote to Paul? 'Come over into Macedonia and help us.' Miss Willie, come over to Piney Ridge and help us!" The school she would take over, Mary tells her, is a one-teacher, one-room log building with eight grades and forty students ranging in age from six to sixteen. The school term runs seven months, from July to January. It is a desperately poor community, with people living "only a little above the margin of necessity." Tobacco is their main cash crop, and even that provides but a meager income. Most families have a cow, a few chickens, and a small garden and live in a hovel with a leaky roof and a sagging floor. "They make out, and that's about the best you can say for the way folks live on the ridge," Mary summarizes.

It's a challenge that seems to Miss Willie like an answer to prayer. The forty-five-year-old spinster takes stock of herself: "I am a thin, dried-up old-maid schoolteacher. I am brittle and barren and plain. But they need me!" She has heard the Macedonian call and takes the leap of faith that will transform her life. She will go to what seems like a foreign mission field in the wilds of Kentucky and, like a true missionary, convert the natives to her ways of life. She may not be able to save the world, but she can at least save a little Kentucky corner of it. That will be her mission—and her problem—because eventually she will learn from these backward Kentuckians more about life and love than she teaches.

When Miss Willie arrives at Piney Ridge to take over the Big Springs School, she is overwhelmed by the natural beauty of the landscape. She is also delighted to be moving near her beloved niece, now a woman who has found happiness as a wife and mother-to-be. But Miss Willie soon discovers that there are many serpents in this beautiful new Eden. The people appear to be poorer and more ignorant, backward, and complacent than Mary had described. Nevertheless, with the zeal of generations of Presbyterian true believers in her blood, she accepts the challenge gladly. "Nothing is hopeless," she asserts, and rolls up her sleeves to become carpenter and janitor as well as teacher at Big Springs.

Alas, Miss Willie begins her tenure on the wrong foot when she attempts to establish her authority by holding classes the first day of school and seating her scholars by her rules rather than by local custom. Her autocratic style begins to seem strange and overbearing to the community, but most of the people accept her "quare" ways, even when she goes so far as to begin a community-wide campaign "to wake these people up." Her improvement program is designed to get the people to eat less fried food, become more sanitation conscious, and be more aggressive about reducing ignorance and disease. Furthermore, she announces, something must be done to modernize the open spring that provides drinking water for the school.

Soon she has gained a reputation as a well intentioned busybody with advice for everyone. In the health class she starts for women, she instructs them in how to rid their children of itch and head lice and how to improve their living conditions generally. Indeed, Miss Willie's reform movement has vast implications for the ridge people and their habits and traditions. The women listen respectfully, eat her refreshments approvingly, and go home nodding affirmatively. And nothing happens: "But the children's lunch buckets continued to hold cold biscuits and fat meat, the children continued to come to school with the itch, with colds, and even with whooping cough." Even the reformer herself has caught the seven-year itch and must undergo an embarrassing treatment of sulphur and lard. After one especially difficult day that included encounters with a wild man and a wild animal, she is on the verge of despair: "This is the ridge for you! Start the day with a mad man, and end it with a polecat!"

But Miss Willie is hardly a quitter. She is a tough old bird for whom endurance is a guiding light. For two years she teaches her motley pupils, gradually learning to accept the local customs that cannot be—or need not be—changed. She endures an outbreak of typhoid fever at her school, several violent deaths, including an axe-murder, as well as numerous practical jokes calculated to embarrass and ridicule her.

Except for one boy, Miss Willie is generally respected or at least tolerated by everyone in the school and the community. The exception is thirteen-year-old Rufe Pierce, "the golden boy" to whom she is strangely attracted, despite his active dislike for her. Rufe roams the woods with his dog, digs ginseng, and believes that only he can hear the birds sing. He also takes every opportunity to disobey and humiliate Miss Willie, whom he calls "that mealy-mouthed, pussyfooted, dried-up old maid!" Their relationship reaches a critical point after she becomes romantically involved with his father, a middle-aged widower with four children. The climax occurs when the teacher becomes the student and vice versa. Rufe finally tells Miss Willie frankly why he despises her so much. It is, he says, her superior, patronizing attitude and her refusal to recognize "the mess of living" that exists everywhere, not just in Piney Ridge, Kentucky. Miss Willie has been agonizing for two years about her "calling" to Piney Ridge. Now her epiphany is made possible by the very boy who has been her nemesis. Through the agency of this bad boy with the golden hair, she has learned that this poor and backward community has a thing or two to teach her. In fact, the people she has come to save have saved *her*. Moreover, they have given her a husband, a family, and a new life. The barren spinster from Texas has become a wife with children in her new Kentucky home.

Indeed, Giles portrays Piney Ridge as a community rich in history and tradition. There are citizens slovenly enough to sit at the same table with Erskine Caldwell's poor white trash in rural Georgia, but there are also hardworking, intelligent people whose lives are filled with beauty and joy. There is the handsome, swaggering moonshiner who dies in a shoot-out with the revenuers, but there is also the well mannered, decent Wells Pierce, who woos and wins the teacher from Texas. In fact, he helps her to learn and finally accept the folkways of her new home. It is a way of life in which even the religious services are foreign to her, as she discovers when she attends an all-day meeting at Bear Hollow Chapel and hears the whiny, nasal shaped-note singing for the first time. She learns, however, that this community has been around much longer than she has. She learns that if she is to be a part of it, she must respect its ceremonies and customs—from possum-hunting to moonshining to tent revivals and river baptizings. Even with reservations, she must fit somehow into this male-dominated society, where women wear themselves out with childbearing and child rearing, water toting, food growing and cooking, housecleaning, and husband tending.

Indeed, in *Miss Willie* Mrs. Giles has documented the mid-twentieth century life of an isolated Kentucky community better than a library of government statistics or sociological surveys. She has rendered its hill dialect accurately and sensibly. She has described in lyrical language the landscape in its seasonal variety, and she has set the people in their proper relationship to the natural world. The birth of Mary Pierce's baby elicits this hallelujah to life: "The rhythm of the earth turning around the sun, of corn greening and then ripening, of dayspring and nightfall, and of a woman's time come in the night. It was a rhythm of pain and ecstasy, mingled and blended until there was no knowing the beginning or the end of either. It was a rhythm that was timeless and spaceless—the rhythm of creation."

Miss Willie is ultimately Janice Holt Giles's love song to the land of her husband and his people, a people who, despite their sometimes backward ways, know how to live vital, fulfilled lives. It is a novel of optimism and hope and inspiration, a story that says life will be worthwhile for people who work hard and love each other and the land that sustains them. Mrs. Giles learned the ways of her husband's country like a native. She observed them with the objectivity and freshness of a newcomer. And she recorded them with the sensitivity of a talented writer. *Miss Willie*, the second novel in the author's Piney Ridge trilogy that included *The Enduring Hills* (1950) and *Tara's Healing* (1952), is a reminder of the remarkable ability of Janice Holt Giles to bring a world to life and populate it with believable people we can care about.

WADE HALL

PREFACE
TO THE SECOND EDITION

In 1948, my mother, Lucy McGraw Holt, had to retire from forty years of teaching. This was compulsory retirement. She could easily have taught another ten years and taught well. But in Arkansas all teachers had to retire at 65 and no exceptions could be made.

My mother chose not to do substitute teaching. She decided instead to indulge her love of travel, confined all those summers to brief trips. She had the maximum teacher's retirement pension, a small private income from some rent property, and she was quite independent financially.

In September of that year she came to spend a few months with me before going to spend Christmas with her brother in Florida. We lived in Louisville, Kentucky, where I was secretarial-assistant to the Dean of the Louisville Presbyterian Seminary and where my husband, Henry Giles, worked at International Harvester.

I had written one book, *The Enduring Hills,* at night after my day in the office. It seemed certain of publication although there was no firm contract yet. With my mother visiting and taking over most of the housework for me, I began another book, again writing at night.

Perhaps the fact that my mother was present, that I saw her daily, studied her, thought what a good teacher she had been all those years, gave me the idea of writing a book about a good teacher, much younger than my mother, but experienced and tired of city teaching.

I thought of what a really good teacher could do in one of these foothill Appalachian one-room schools, so I had Miss Willie invited by her niece to "come over into Macedonia" and help out on the ridge about which I had written in *The Enduring Hills.*

I used several of the same characters as those in *The Enduring Hills,* Mary Hogan, Hod Pierce and the Pierce family clan. But this book was much more inventive, based on no facts given me of ridge life. It was all mine and entirely fictionalized. My mother's character formed the basis for the good teacher Miss Willie, but in no other way was she like my mother. And none of the experiences that happened to Miss Willie ever happened to my mother.

The book went easily and smoothly and it was about two-thirds finished when my mother left to spend the rest of the winter in Florida, about mid-December. Shortly afterward I had a telegram saying that *The Enduring Hills* was definitely accepted for publication and that a contract was on the way.

I laid *Miss Willie* aside. We had been planning and hoping to buy a small farm in Adair County, Kentucky, where my husband grew up. The $500 advance which came with the contract, plus most of our savings, was enough to pay cash for the little rocky, woodsy forty-acre farm we wanted (we paid $1100.00 for it!). In May of 1949 we made the move, giving up our jobs and certain income.

Miss Willie was finished that summer "sort of inbetweenst" as one of my neighbors said, for there was much work to be done on that little farm. Henry told me about a strange and oddly sweet experience of his own, that when he was a small boy, that until he was about eleven years old in fact, he believed he could hear things nobody else could hear. He could hear the birds singing. Never in his life had he heard anybody, not his father, his mother, any of his family or neighbors, mention the birds singing. He never mentioned it because he thought he was perhaps an "oddling."

The only change I made in *Miss Willie,* therefore, was to create the new character, Rufus, the little boy who heard the birds singing. He gave me a natural conflict because I made Miss Willie young enough to marry. She married the boy's father, and the boy did not like her. The conflict was beautifully resolved at the end of the book when quite casually one evening Miss Willie mentioned the sweet song of the wood thrush and the boy realized he was not an "oddling" at all.

This is probably the most genuinely creative book I ever wrote and certainly I was happier writing it than with any other book. Not a word had to be rewritten. It was accepted immediately. It was a Doubleday Book Club selection and for many years it was used as supplemental reading in teacher training courses on "The School and the Community."

The book is dedicated to my mother and my father. Not until she read the published book did my mother know that Miss Willie was at least partly herself.

I am glad that Houghton Mifflin is reissuing the book. I hope it has success again and that its emphasis upon good teaching, upon love, upon the open heart, is as timeless as ever.

JANICE HOLT GILES

Spout Springs
Knifley, Kentucky
June 18, 1970

❧

CHAPTER

❧ 1 ❧

THE BOY AND THE DOG FOLLOWED A COW PATH through the woods, the boy's eyes taking in the slick, shiny green of gum and sassafras bushes, the red spray of sumac, the heavy veins of dogwood seedlings. Morning dew hung sparkly and brilliant on every leaf and blade, showering a small rain across the path where the dog brushed against the bushes.

When the path cleared the woods and penciled off through a pasture, the boy and the dog angled on down the ridge. "Ain't no use lookin' fer sang hereabouts," the boy said. "Wait'll we git down in the holler."

The north face of the ridge swelled gently, easily, shouldering itself toward the deep ravine which gashed it midway. Suddenly the easy slope sheered off sharply and plunged downward. Steep and abrupt it fell straight down into the hollow, its sides patched with thick rugs of moss under the trees. The boy dug in his heels and slid from one bed of moss to another, sinking his feet deep in the soft mat, letting its plush brake him against the downhill pull. The dog scampered ahead, waiting in the easy places.

The floor of the hollow was narrow, boxing in a shallow stream which raced rapidly between its walls. White water foamed around the rocks and chattered a noisy song. The boy and the dog drank deeply and then followed the stream up the hollow, branching off into a deeper ravine on the right. Here the floor widened, and was bedded with a heavy leaf mold through which a rank growth of small sprouts and plants pushed themselves.

"Now, this is it," the boy said. "Here's where the sang grows best. I takened notice o' this place last year."

Across a log a bed of ginseng lay dark and green, slender stems spiking proudly upward, pronging at the top to bear the soft, ivy-green leaves. "All of 'em three prongs," the boy exulted. "No! There's one of 'em's a four-prong un. See that there big un next the log, Jupe! Oh, hit's untellin' whenever we've found a four-prong un!"

Jupiter sniffed the log. "You, Jupe!" the boy yelled and the dog fled, tail drooped between his legs.

Gently the boy dug the plants from their beds, and breaking off the tops, he slid the roots into his overalls pockets. "Hit won't take many like these to weigh heavy," he said. "We'll have us three-four ounces 'fore you know it. Bet hit'll bring anyways three-four dollars."

When they had cleaned that bed, he and the dog wandered on, always looking for the dark-veined sang, whose roots, when dried, were good medicine for so many ailments, and which brought sixty cents an ounce when sold to the country store-keeper at the Gap. The boy's pockets filled until they bulged, and the dark hollows grew bright with the noon-riding sun. The dog no longer raced ahead. He lay in the shade waiting, his tongue lolling and his sides heaving. The boy's shirt turned dark with sweat. He squinted up into the sun. "Reckon hit's about time to go home," he said, and he led the dog up the steep flank of the ridge.

They came out of the hollow into a clearing in a grove of beeches. Abruptly the boy stopped. He stood rigid and his hand reached out to hold his dog to heel. The noon sun shafted white columns through the interstices of the trees and turned the boy and the dog into tawny, golden statues.

The boy lifted his head, turned it a little to one side, and listened. An April thrush, up near the sun, was pouring out its song, and the notes fell, fountainlike, down through the trees. Note by liquid note descended, pure and clear and sweet. The song rose rapturously, mounted lyrically, ecstatically, flung sunward in joyous abandon. And the boy's face, lifted to the sun and the song, stilled and quivered under the wash of golden sound.

Suddenly the song broke off. The boy sighed and moved rest-

10

lessly. "Hit's flew away," he said. He waited a moment more and then shook his head. "No, hit's flew away. They ain't no use o' waitin'. C'mon, Jupe."

They moved off, dwarfed by the giant overshadowing of the trees. The boy whistled a few notes and then stopped. "Cain't nobody go like that there old thrush," he told the dog, "even if they could hear him. Hit's a quare thing, but on this whole endurin' ridge ain't nobody but me hears the birds asingin' an' atalkin'. Hit appears they'd leastways be another'n, but they ain't e'er 'nother soul has ever named it."

His bare toe kicked idly at a fallen log lying across the way, and a small, scared rabbit ran for the thicket. The dog yelped sharply and bounded after the rabbit. "Git him, Jupe," yelled the boy, taking after the dog. "Git him!"

His heels flew across the ground and the hole in the seat of his overalls gleamed whitely as the sun spotted the bare skin. The bushes of the thicket shook violently as the skeltering race of dog and boy parted them.

Down in the hollow Mary Pierce stood for a moment in her back door. Hearing the yelping of the dog, she shaded her eyes against the sun to look up the side of the ridge. She caught a brief glimpse of the dog and the boy tearing across an opening in the brush. She chuckled. "Rufe and his dog have jumped another rabbit."

She turned back to the kitchen stove and stirred the big pot of beans simmering there. She lifted a spoonful and tasted. They were done. They ought to be, she thought. She'd soaked them overnight and first thing this morning had put them on to boil in the old iron kettle that had belonged to Hod's grandmother. Hod said white beans ought never to be cooked in anything but an iron kettle, and they ought to simmer slow and long over a low wood fire with a big piece of fat meat gradually melting into soft white sweetness. These beans were just right — tender, the skins peeling delicately, but not mushy. Beans, Hod said again, ought not to lose their individuality when cooked. They should remain whole, every bean apart, unto itself, but communing one

11

with the other in the rich juicy soup with its thick blobs of fat meat.

She glanced at the short ray of sunlight lying across the floor. She must hurry. When it touched that crack by the door, it would be noon and she must call the men to dinner. Quickly and lightly she stepped around the room, placing plates and silver on the table, dishing up corn and tomatoes from her own cans in the cellar, setting the white bowl of beans in the center of the table, heaping the squares of golden bread in a gay basket and covering it over with a red-checked napkin, pouring tall glasses of buttermilk from the blue pitcher, and setting it near at hand.

She stripped her apron from her and stopped for a second in front of the wash shelf as she went toward the door. She glanced quickly at her reflection in the small mirror that hung there and brushed her hair back. Then she wiped a smudge off her nose and went through the door into the back yard.

A dinner bell was mounted on a short pole at the corner of the house, and she gave its rope a swift tug. When Hod was working near the house, a call would bring him; but when he was down in the hollow, in one of the lower fields, he would listen for the bell.

It was a deep-throated bell, with a friendly, urgent tone. And the hills that rose steeply on either side of the hollow walled in the sound so that it went bounding and echoing against the rocks, chased by its own reverberations into the bottleneck which was the upper end of the hollow. Mary tugged the rope once more, and then stood passively in the warm April sun and let the shower of bronze sound drench her where she stood.

She looked down the long meadow of deep grass where the cows moved indolently, lazily switching their tails, and on beyond to the hills that had been split to form this hollow. Wishful Creek began somewhere up in those hills in a bright, bubbling spring, and followed the cleft in the ridge down to the floor of the valley.

This was Wishful Hollow, a narrow, fertile valley, stretching some three or four miles between the ridges. In the two years she had been living here, Mary Pierce had not grown weary of

12

the soft mists that settled over the curves of the creek; or of the long stretch of meadows and fields down the valley; or of the high wall of the hills on either side. Nor had she grown tired of this house to which Hod had brought her, which had been his great-great-grandfather's homestead. The original log cabin was still the main room of the house, and the chimney which Hod's great-great-grandmother had built herself when Jeems was off to the wars still warmed the log room adequately. Hod's grandfather, Dow Pierce, had added two rooms when he lived in the cabin, and Mary and Hod had added two more. The house stood now, low and rambling, weathered by rain and sun, a monument to the hearts of a man and woman who had believed in this land.

To Mary Pierce it stood for clan continuity, for roots probing deep into the land and welding generations of Pierces to it with a passionate love for its ways. It stood for the women of the family — Amelia, Abigail, Annie, Hattie, and now Mary. For their courage and strength, and their loyalty to their men. It stood most of all for her own immortality. Such a family was as ongoing as the surge of the sea, as unending as time, as deathless as truth. And Mary, rooted in that past rich with strength, felt free of mortality in a future that would inherit the past.

Here, now, she was caught in that strong-flowing stream of life. For her own child would soon be born. The sixth generation Pierce on Piney Ridge. She laughed aloud and she felt full of never-ending life. She was glad her child was to be born in this house, and she was glad his feet would tread the land that belonged to him.

Mary was a tall woman, a little past first youth. She was high-bosomed and long-legged, with narrow hips and broad shoulders. There was an easy grace about her which Hod had always compared to that of a young colt. There was the same hint of awkwardness in her movements, overlaid with a swift co-ordination. Her brown hair had the clean, shiny look of a chestnut colt's satin coat, and she had a way of flinging up her head in alarm occasionally when she was startled. Her skin was already tanned by the spring sun, and her eyes crinkled like brown water in the

deep pools of their sockets. Her mouth was wide and full —
sweet and big and compelling — and her chin underlaid it with
a square, firm foundation. Mary had a good face, and a fine
figure. In a quiet way she knew these things. There was no vanity
in her, but there was a proud sense of worth.

Hod and Wells were turning in the back lot now. Hod was tall
and broad-shouldered, fair as a Norseman, with heavy straw-
colored hair rumpled over his head. Even from here she could
see that his face was ruddy from his work in the sun, and his
blue jeans hung lankly on his thin hips. As she watched his slow
plunging walk, she felt the bubbling of excitement that seeing
him at a distance always brought to her throat, and she laughed
as she remembered the ways in which he was tender and good
and sweet. She yearned toward him in love, and she felt her
throat tighten as she watched him moving toward her.

Oh, her friends had said when she married this Kentucky
farmer, what does Mary Hogan see in him! How can she give up
the lovely life she has worked so hard for . . . her beautiful
apartment, her position in the schools, her music, all her friends!
They haven't a thing in common. What can she find in him!

They wouldn't know, of course. And you couldn't tell them.
Their scale of values didn't go far enough. They only knew that
two and two make four. They would never understand that
sometimes it makes six or ten or twenty. No. They wouldn't
know, and you could never tell them of the quick, flashing to-
getherness that made speech unnecessary between them . . . the
startling unity of their minds . . . the intimate knowledge,
shared across a room, across a gathering of people, so perfect that
like darting, sunlit sails their minds had met and gone over the
horizon together. No. That was something one learned for one-
self, and only in company with the other half of that perfect
whole.

You couldn't tell them of the poignant, puissant tenderness in
this man. Of the quality of gentleness and fineness that was almost maternal in its shy and awkward solicitousness. It threw
a veil of safety around one — this knowledge of being so greatly
loved, so deeply cared for.

You couldn't tell them, either, about the naïve idealism that

14

had made it impossible for him to live in the city. He was forever being hurt, forever being crucified by the harshness and bitterness of people massed together. That horrible, anonymous massing that drained people of their personalities, their personal dignity, and even of their humanity. He had valued himself too highly to allow himself to sink into that anonymity.

She drew a deep breath and gave thanks that this man was hers. Thanks for their possession of each other, and for the child that was on its way.

Hod's cousin, Little Wells, who was helping him fence the lower field today, looked short and stocky as he strode along by him. He was a solid, squatty man, swarthy of skin. He was older than Hod by some ten or twelve years, but they had always been good friends. Wells was a merry person, quick to laugh, and with a ready quip on his lips. He had deep-set, twinkling eyes which wrinkled at the corners. Mary had come to like him and to trust him. "Hi, Wells," she called and flung up an arm in greeting.

"Howdy, Mary," he answered. "Got anything a couple o' starving men kin fill up on?"

"Got plenty," she said, laughing. "It's on the table. Wash up, now, and hurry."

"See," Hod said, nudging Wells, "what'd I tell you? Just got me a plumb dominatin' woman. Always orderin' you around! Never any peace!"

Wells dipped his head in the big tub of water sitting on the wash bench by the stoop. He snorted and blew water at Hod. "I'll trade fer her e'er day you say. I could use me a smart woman."

Hod handed him the towel and ducked his own head. Wells flicked him on the back of the neck. "He's agittin' too big fer his britches these days. Must be on account he's goin' to be a papa purty soon. Wait'll he's got seven or eight runnin' around. He won't act so prideful then. He'll be scratchin' an' diggin' too hard tryin' to feed 'em to take much pride in 'em."

"I've never heard you complaining of your four," Mary put in.

"No," Wells said, and his eyes went past Mary down the meadow. His voice softened. "No, I ain't complainin'. They're all I got left of Matildy."

15

He straightened up and threw the towel at Hod. "Well, let's git in there an' git them beans eat. This ain't fencin' that pasture of your'n."

Quickly they put away a sizable meal and left the bowls and platters empty. Mary kept the breadbasket filled, and the milk pitcher overflowed constantly into their glasses. When they had finished, the two men pushed their chairs back and tilted them against the wall. "That shore was good eatin', Mary," Wells said, around the toothpick in the corner of his mouth.

Mary made a mock bow. "I thought maybe Rufe would come in for dinner, I saw him and his dog up on the ridge a while ago, chasing a rabbit from the way they were going."

Wells laughed. "Him an' that dog's allus out wanderin' the woods. I don't know where he's at half the time. I'd ort to git more work outen him. He'll soon turn fourteen, but he's slippery as a eel. Out an' gone 'fore you know it."

Mary turned a little in her chair and eased her legs under the table. "I ought to get up there oftener than I do," she said, "but climbing the ridge is pretty hard for me, and it seems like I have more than I can get done here at home."

"Don't you fret none 'bout it, Mary. Rose does right well fer a sixteen-year-old, an' Abby's gittin' up big enough to he'p a right smart. Manthy's got Veeny over at the Gap, an' we make out jist fine." He poured a little more milk into his glass and drained it with a swallow.

Mary leaned her elbows on the table and cushioned her chin in her palms. "How'd the trustees' meeting come out, Wells?"

"Hit never come out. Whichever way you turn, we're up agin the same old thing. We need a good teacher. Big Springs ain't had a good teacher in too long a time. But we ain't got the money to pay nobody to come here an' teach. Cain't pay 'em but seven months outen the year the way it is. Who's gonna come way back here in the hills an' teach a ridge school fer seven months' pay? Nobody in their right mind, I kin tell you that!"

"It's a pity," Mary said. "These children need a good school the worst in the world. If the Skipper wasn't on the way, I'd be tempted to try it myself."

Wells sighed. "I hate fer my young'uns to grow up like I done,

16

no more learnin' than I got. Seems like a man owes it to his kids to give 'em a better chancet than he got. But I swear back here in these hills might as well be the other side the waters. Looks like the best we kin do is that Owens boy agin. My kids says he don't do much more'n keep books, an' e'er one o' the oldest ones kin outsmart him."

"What does Lem say about it?" Hod asked.

Lem was Hod's uncle who lived down on the pike. He was another of the school trustees.

"Oh, he hates it bad as anybody. But he ain't got no more idee what to do than the rest of us. Lem's been puttin' in his share an' more on the teacher's pay fer a right smart while. Hit ain't fair fer him to do no more. You've give all you kin, an' several others as well. But ifen you cain't raise but so much, that's all they is to it. We'll jist have to make out."

Mary drummed the table with her fingers. "I wish . . ." she said, and stopped. She flicked a crumb to the floor with her thumb. The men waited.

"You wish what?" Hod prompted.

"Oh, nothing." She rubbed at a spot on the tablecloth. "Yes, it was. I was wishing Miss Willie would come out here and teach the school!"

Hod stared at her. "You mean give up her good job teachin' in El Paso and come out here to *this* school?"

"Oh, it was just an idea."

"Who's Miss Willie?" Wells wanted to know.

Mary pushed her chair back from the table and stood up. "She's my aunt. The one I lived with after my father and mother died. She teaches in El Paso. But it wouldn't be fair . . ." she stacked the plates and folded the napkins. "Only I was just remembering. Hod, you know Grandfather was a preacher, and Miss Willie always wanted to be a missionary. Even when she was a little girl she wanted to be a missionary, and she always planned to go to China. Then just when she finished college and was about ready to go before the Board of Missions, Grandfather died, and Miss Willie had to take care of Grandmother. Now that Grandmother's gone, Miss Willie is free, of course, but it's too late for her to be a missionary. She must be in her middle forties by now."

17

"Was you thinkin' she might be interested in comin' here to the ridge?" Wells asked.

"I was just wishing she would, Wells. She's a wonderful teacher. My goodness, what she would do for those children!"

"She's used to gittin' good pay, I reckon."

"Yes. She makes a good salary, as far as teachers' salaries go. But she has a little income of her own besides. She doesn't have to depend on her salary entirely. Grandfather left some land and there's a big oil boom out in West Texas just now, so she gets a pretty good income from her oil leases. You know, Hod," and Mary's voice quivered with excitement, "the more I think about it, the more I think maybe we've got something here. This is just the sort of thing that might appeal to Miss Willie. You know how interested she's been in this country ever since we came down here. . . . Maybe she'd like a change from city teaching. Maybe she would . . ."

"Maybe she'd what?" he asked.

"Maybe she'd like to do a little missionary work on the ridge."

The three were quiet for a moment, thinking it over. "What do you think, Wells?" Hod wanted to know.

"Boy, ifen she'd come," Wells said, "I'd say we'd be beholden forever to her. She'd be doin' us a favor we couldn't never repay!" His voice was warm and thick with feeling. "Why, jist me by myself would welcome her an' uphold her on account o' my own kids. An' they's half a dozen others'd feel the same way!"

"Why don't you write her then, Mary?"

"Just like that? Just write her and ask her to come teach the Big Springs school? Doesn't someone have to act officially?"

"Well, I'm actin' officially," Wells snorted indignantly. "What you reckon I'm a trustee fer? Go ahead an' write her! I'll guarantee the rest'll back her!"

18

CHAPTER

❧ 2 ❧

I<small>T WAS FIFTEEN MINUTES YET</small> before the second grade would be dismissed, and the children were restless in the sticky, unseasonable heat of the April afternoon. That was the worst of this crowded condition. The afternoon group were not at their best, especially as the spring came on and the days grew hot and long. Miss Willie sighed and pushed her glasses up on her nose. It was a thin nose, and her glasses were constantly slipping down. The habit of pushing them back in place was so old as to be automatic, and it had become a part of Miss Willie's personality. Hundreds of second-grade children would remember this mannerism. They would remember too the clear, lustrous blue of her eyes behind the glasses; the slight slender figure that stood so uncompromisingly erect; the heavy coil of fine, soft hair which had never been cut and which lay in a thick figure of eight atop her head; the wide, generous mouth which could smile so approvingly.

Thirty small heads were bent over drawings on the two long tables by the wall. Thirty little bodies wiggled and squirmed. It was a sign of fatigue that Miss Willie had set them to an aimless task for the last thirty minutes of the day. Weakly she had set out fresh paper and allowed Marie and Salvador to get out the colors. She had told them to draw what they pleased . . . anything at all. It was sheer busy work and Miss Willie despised busy work. She was convinced that only a poor teacher ever resorted to it. But this had been a long day . . . and the April heat had been close.

She glanced around the familiar room. At the gray-green walls and the sprigged yellow curtains. At her low rocker near the front of the room and the hooked rug before it. At the border of drawings pinned along one side of the room, and the small chairs and tables before the windows. She felt an objective distaste for the plants growing in pots on the window sills. They seemed suddenly to be silly substitutes for gardens and lawns and widestretching spaces. She had always taken pride in the comfortable,

19

homelike atmosphere of her schoolroom, believing ardently that for small children, venturing so insecurely into the wider world, the schoolroom should offer a measure of the feeling of home. So she had brought her little rocker and her hooked rug and her pots and green plants to school to give it a warmer and a snugger look, to draw in the horizons of the new world to a safer, more enfolding circle. She brought her knitting also, and many times when she sat in her little rocker, knitting, she watched a feeling of contentment, security, safeness, spread over the room, the purring, satisfied contentment of a child who can sprawl happily over his work because his mother sits nearby with her sewing. She believed all this was good. Where, then, had her satisfaction in it gone?

She straightened her thin, bony shoulders and rubbed the place in the small of her back that ached so dully and so persistently. Somehow, somewhere along the twenty years she had been teaching in this room the spring had gone loose in her. Had come unwound. There was a bitter taste in her mouth, as if she had breathed too much chalk dust. She ran her tongue over her dry lips and swallowed. Soon, now, the bell would ring, and these thirty restless small bodies would be released.

Out of the corner of her eye she noticed that Billy Norton was edging over near Donny Brown. She ought to nip that in the bud right now. Donny must have a crayon Billy wanted. If she didn't stop him, there would be trouble. But she didn't move. Maybe the bell would save Donny's crayon.

But it didn't. And in one fleeting second she saw Billy snatch quickly, saw Donny grab futilely, and then there was a wail as Billy made off with the crayon, scuttling crabwise down the room. "He got my color, Miss Willie!" Donny cried, waving his hand wildly at Billy. "He got my purple color. It's my color, and I was making a purple tree. I just laid it down a minute and he grabbed it!"

Miss Willie pushed her glasses up her nose. "Billy, give Donny his purple crayon," she said sternly. "You know you mustn't take another person's things."

Billy was sullen. "It's not his color! The colors don't belong to anybody. You said so yourself. You said they belong to the school

20

and we could all use 'em. I can have any color I want!" His lower lip stuck out ominously.

"Donny was using the purple crayon, and while he was using it, it belonged to him, Billy. Give it back to him immediately." Miss Willie started toward the table. The rest of the children had stopped and were watching warily.

Billy looked at the crayon in his hand and then looked at Miss Willie moving relentlessly toward him. He clutched the crayon tightly for a moment, and then, his defiance melting before the inevitable approach of authority, he flung the offending crayon blindly at Donny and collapsed weeping in his chair. "I wanted to make a purple tree too," he sobbed. "I like purple trees best too, and Donny gets the purple color every time. He always makes purple trees, and you always let him. You like Donny best!" The small voice was accusing.

Something quivered inside Miss Willie and came achingly alive. She reacted always to this inconsolable yearning of all small children. This uncertain need for love and affection. This out-reaching, hungering longing for the security of adult approbation. "I don't like Donny best," she said, reaching for Billy's bent head. "I like all of you best. You and Donny and all the others. All of you. I couldn't get along without any of you. But see what happens when you quarrel? You are unhappy, Donny is unhappy, and all of us are unhappy. It hurts every one of us. Now, hush, and pick up the crayon and give it back to Donny. He didn't know you wanted to draw a purple tree. Perhaps if you had told him he would have been glad to give you the purple color."

Billy sniffed and rubbed the back of his hand across the end of his nose. He caught his breath in a sob and walked across the room to pick up the crayon. At the sight of the envied purple color his grief mounted in him again and his eyes filled and over-flowed. His lips puckered and trembled. But he held out the crayon to Donny. "Here," he said, bluntly.

Donny took the crayon and cut his eyes at Miss Willie. And then he thrust it back at Billy. "You can have it," he said, "I'll make me a pink tree."

The bell rang and Miss Willie let a limp and thankful sigh es-

21

cape her. "May Billy have the purple crayon at drawing time tomorrow, Donny?" she asked.

"Oh, sure," Donny said nonchalantly, sticking his hands in his pockets. "If he wants to make a tree like mine, I'll help him."

"Well, we'll see. Maybe he'd rather make his own kind of tree. Pick up the papers and put the colors away now. You can finish the drawings tomorrow." She guessed weakly that there would be a drawing time the rest of the spring.

The second grade swarmed to the cupboards with their unfinished drawings and put the crayons neatly away in their boxes. And then they hovered briefly around Miss Willie.

"Good-by, Miss Willie."

"Good-by, Marie. Good-by, Sanchez. Good-by, Katherine. Don't forget to bring your kitten tomorrow so we can see her. Good-by, Donny. It was nice of you to give Billy the purple color."

Beaming, Donny ducked his head. "Aw, I didn't want to make another old purple tree, anyhow. He can have it every day if he wants it."

Miss Willie laughed. "Well, it was nice of you anyhow."

She was setting the room to rights when her friend Louise Wright came to the door. "Come on in, Louise," she said. "How was your day?"

Louise taught the third grade. She was a tall, rangy woman with big shoulders and broad hips. Her voice was deep and heavy like a man's. She crossed the room slowly and stood before the windows, playing with the pull on one of the shades. "Just like every other day this year. I'm a little tireder than usual. Guess it's the heat."

Miss Willie opened the top drawer of her desk and dumped an assortment of odds and ends, pencils, erasers, paper clips, and two or three broken crayons, inside. She closed the drawer with an unnecessarily hard shove. "I don't know what's wrong with me, but all at once I am horribly bored with everything . . . El Paso, my home, the children, school, everything. I get up in the morning moody and depressed, and I teach all day feeling as if I were getting nowhere and accomplishing nothing."

Louise shrugged her shoulders. "Oh, all teachers have that feeling occasionally. Along toward the end of the year, mostly. It wears off with vacation, and you come back at the beginning of the year ready to go again."

"Yes, I know. I've had it before . . . but only for brief periods of time. I always had down underneath a conviction that what I was doing was important, and as long as I felt that, I knew my lethargy was only physical and that a rest or a change of scenery for a few months would take care of it. This is different. Ever since Mamma died . . . no, since before then, since Mary left, I've been restless. And the last three or four years I've had to take myself in hand to keep from being indifferent about things."

"Partly your age, don't you think?" Louise suggested.

"Yes, partly," Miss Willie admitted. "I do get tired quicker than I used to. But that's just rationalizing. Something's missing. Something vital has gone."

Louise laughed her strong, deep laugh. "You need somebody to take care of, Willie. These children here don't really need you, and you know it. Any good teacher can do what you're doing here. You can't get over having to be a missionary. That's all that's wrong with you. Me, I'm very glad not to be concerned about anyone but myself. It suits me just fine not to be needed."

Miss Willie pinned her hat to the bun coiled on top of her head. She smiled at her friend in the mirror. Then she let her arms fall limply and stood looking out the window. The days ahead of her. The long days stretching ahead. A woman alone is so terribly alone, she thought. However she might fill these days of hers she could never quite get them full. Always there was a last thin edge of emptiness. She shrugged. "Come go home with me for dinner."

Louise shook her head. "Term paper to do on that course I'm taking. I'll drive you home, though, if you like."

"No," Miss Willie answered, gathering her purse and a couple of books off the desk. "No. I like to walk. I'll go on."

She walked down the street slowly, a slender little figure bordering on thinness. Usually she walked with short, rapid steps . . . purposeful steps that knew exactly where they were going. But today she moved slowly. The street was lined with

23

thick-walled adobe houses. Miss Willie liked the adobe houses. They sat so solidly against the ground, so thick and squatty, looking as if they had grown up out of the ground itself. There was no meeting place between them and the earth. They seemed all of a part with it.

The sky was a brilliant blue bowl cupped over the earth, and its brilliance hit hard against the white and cream houses. Miss Willie squinted in its glare. The heat bit down between her shoulders, and she felt a trickle of perspiration run tantalizingly down her back. A heavy haze hung over the mountains across the river in old Mexico and turned them purple with distance. If this heat keeps on, Miss Willie thought, everything will soon be sun-baked and dry and Constancia will be wanting to go home to her people.

Constancia was her maid of all work, and each year when the summer season came on she became enamored of the greenness of her father's irrigated farm down in the valley. Miss Willie had long since resigned herself to doing without help during the summer months. She might have replaced Constancia, but in her own way the woman was faithful and when the heat had passed she turned up on the doorstep like a good dog come home again.

Her slow steps brought Miss Willie to a small adobe house set back from the street in a walled garden. The house was a smooth, creamy white, with a bright-blue door. Miss Willie smiled every time she saw her blue door. There was a saying that long ago among the Spanish-speaking people a blue door signified the presence of a marriageable daughter in the house. It amused Miss Willie to paint her door blue in spite of the legend . . . or perhaps because of it! For certainly she had been a marriageable daughter for a good many years! Inside, the house was always cool and dim, and it was with relief that she pushed open the blue door and stepped within.

There was a little entrance hall, and to the left and one step down was the living room. Its walls were whitewashed and almost empty of ornaments. Miss Willie liked their virginal cleanness. There is something about a clean, white wall, she said. Something which gives a feeling of depth and space. It takes you out of yourself into a third dimension . . . a dimension of quiet-

24

ness and calmness. A flat surface is peaceful, drawn out, refined. She always came into this room with a feeling of gratitude for its pool of quiet. With its white walls, its few pieces of fine furniture, and its absence of clutter, it was sanctuary to her.

Constancia appeared in the doorway, her head bound with a red bandanna and her hands floury. "A letter," she said, nodding toward the table under the window. "It come today."

"Yes, thank you, Constancia," Miss Willie answered, taking it up. "Oh, it's from Mary! How nice! You remember Mary, Constancia?"

"Sí," Constancia beamed. "She the nice lady come three, four years ago."

"That's the one."

"Sí. The phone all the time ring when she here. The soldier all the time call up. *¡Hijo!* We do not have such an excitement in this house before!"

No, Miss Willie thought. We do not have such an excitement in this house before. Not in this house. She smiled as she remembered that time. Mary, arriving tired and worn-out from the long bus trip, but radiant with some strange inner glow. Mary, with a romantic, exciting story of a soldier she had met on the trip. Mary, warm and happy, answering the phone which seemed always to be ringing. Long distance from Camp Swift, night after night. The romance had brought fresh life to the house, and to Miss Willie. She had captured something of its radiance for herself during the brief time it had been housed beneath this roof. Such an excitement in this house!

"She marry the soldier, no?" Constancia was saying.

"She marry the soldier, sí. And now she lives on a farm in Kentucky and she doesn't teach school any more. Are you making cookies today, Constancia?"

"Sí. I make the seedcakes. They be done soon."

"Well, don't hurry supper. It's too hot. Let's wait until the sun is down and have it in the patio. I want to bathe and lie down awhile before eating."

Constancia nodded. "You read your letter. I finish the seedcakes."

Like a child wanting to save the best for the last, Miss Willie

25

laid aside her niece's letter until she had bathed. Then, in a cool, thin wrapper, she stretched out in her big long chair and gave herself up to reading what Mary had written. It was a thick letter. "Miss Willie, love," it began.

CHAPTER

❧ 3 ❧

Miss Willie smiled. "Miss Willie, love," the letter said. "This leaves me fine and hoping you're the same. My book of ridge etiquette tells me all proper letters begin with that formula. I should never want to be improper or impolite in a letter to you.

"Truly, I *am* well, and I have never been so happy in my life. I am overwhelmed and overflowing with happiness. No one ever told me that I'd literally walk on clouds during this whole nine months! I needn't tell you that we can hardly wait till fall to welcome the young man.

"Our spring planting is going on apace. Hod has been fencing a new field which he intends to put in corn this year. The tobacco beds are exquisitely beautiful just now. The plants are a pale, delicate green like mint ice cream. Oh, you really should see a tobacco bed when the plants are only a few inches high! They look as if they had been dipped in moonlight!

"And now, Miss Willie, I come to the point of this letter. Do you remember what the Macedonians wrote to Paul? 'Come over into Macedonia, and help us.'

"Miss Willie, come over to Piney Ridge and help us! There is a little school here . . . the only one for miles around. There are about forty children enrolled, and they range in age from six to sixteen, and from the first grade through the eighth. The school term is only seven months long. It can't begin until July because the children are needed in the fields in the spring and early summer, and it closes in January because the weather gets so bad that the roads can't be traveled later than that.

"The children attend very irregularly, and I suppose it's very rare that any one child gets as much as a full five months' schooling. Almost any excuse is good enough for them to stay at home,

26

or for their parents to keep them out.

"I don't know what the physical facilities are, for I haven't been inside the building. Hod tells me there are desks, of a sort, and that when he went to school, there was at least one blackboard and a map. Heat is provided by a huge wood stove, which sits in the middle of the room.

"The water comes from a big spring situated about a hundred yards up the side of a hill, from which the school gets its name . . . Big Springs School. You cannot imagine anything more primitive. And yet it *is* a school, after a fashion!

"The problem, of course, is to find teachers. The pay is meager, a little better than a hundred dollars a month, and when you think that the term is only seven months long, and when you think further of the physical limitations of the school itself, you can understand easily enough why no one wants to teach at Big Springs. In all conscience we here on the ridge cannot blame them.

"This year the trustees are up against the same old problem. Of course there are ramifications which they do not see. They believe if they had money enough to pay a good teacher, somehow, miraculously, they would have a good school. Actually they are pretty blind about the physical conditions of the school. Here on Piney Ridge what was good enough for 'Grampa' is good enough for the kids. That, generally, is the opinion of the trustees, with the possible exception of Hod's cousin, Wells Pierce. I believe he truly has a greater sense of responsibility. But at least a start would be made if we could just get a good teacher. And I cannot get it out of my mind, Miss Willie, that you are that teacher!

"First, of course, you are an excellent teacher. You would do wonders for the school. Second, the salary would not have to be a major consideration for you, although that shouldn't excuse the school from paying the most it can. But at least you would not have to depend entirely upon the tiny salary. And last, but by no means least, it would be good to have you near me. There are so very many Pierces here on the ridge! Sometimes I get mighty hungry for my own kith and kin!

"When I think of what I am asking you to do, the enormity of

27

it stuns me. You have a good position, well-paid, with the honor and prestige due you as a reward. You have a lovely little home and your life is well ordered, comfortable, and full of beautiful things. In one sense of the word you have earned the right to spend the rest of your days as easily and comfortably as possible. And here I am asking you to give it up!

"I won't minimize the hardships you would know here. You would live sixteen miles from the nearest town. There is not a musical instrument on the ridge except my piano and the various guitars and banjos scattered here and there. There are no books and there is no library. There are a few cars up and down the ridge, but by and large the principal means of travel is still a wagon and a team of mules. It's the only thing that will get through these roads. There is no electricity. We all burn kerosene lamps here. There is no plumbing, except the 'necessary' out back. Every drop of water must be drawn from a well, or dipped from a spring. There are no furnaces or central heating. In the winter you will shiver and shake until the wood stove is hot enough to warm the room. There is literally nothing here . . . except the people and the country!

"I shan't plead with you, because you must decide for yourself. I must say just one thing more. We *need* you! This is April, and the school term starts in July. Could you face it, do you think?"

Miss Willie let the letter drop into her lap. She leaned her head against the back of the chair and closed her eyes. This niece was very dear to her and almost the only family she had left. When her sister, Mary's mother, and her husband had died within a few short months of each other, Mary had been a young girl, yet in high school. She was the youngest of four children, the others already married and established in homes of their own. Miss Willie had watched her thin, tearless face at the second funeral, and had known that the girl was suffering an anguish that only the tightest hold on herself could control.

What is to become of the child, she had thought. It would be more natural for her to go with the sister than with one of the sisters-in-law. But there was a span of twelve years between the

28

two, and Miss Willie knew that to Mary the older sister, who had been married and gone from home almost as long as she could remember, would seem like a stranger. It was in her face during those days, the fear and the dread of this arranging of her life.

Miss Willie had seen her shrinking helplessness before the situation, and had watched the frightened, lost, small-animal look grow to terror in her eyes. She could not bear it! So, suddenly, warmly, generously, she had said, "Mary, would you like to come home with me?"

Mary had flung her a startled look, and her eyes had widened darkly. She drew in her breath sharply, and bit down upon her lower lip. "For a visit, Miss Willie?" she had asked, "or to stay?"

"To stay."

Mary had curled her long legs under her and leaned her head against the back of the chair. Miss Willie remembered how dark her hair had looked against the pale blue of the chair, and how white and lustrous the skin had been drawn over the high-modeled cheekbones. She remembered, too, how nervously the child's hands had worked in her lap. She had lifted one hand and gnawed worriedly at a knuckle. "Will they let me?" she asked.

"I think they will." She had not hurried the girl. "It will be strange, dear, and it may not be easy at first. There's Grandmother to remember, and she's an invalid. But at least we shall be all women in the house together, with a more or less common point of view."

Mary had brought her eyes back from distance and fixed them upon Miss Willie. They were dry and strained, with dark circles lying shadowy underneath. Miss Willie went on. "This is a cruel thing to happen, Mary. To lose father and mother almost at once, and to be thrown helplessly into a new life. But we have no control over such things, and the only thing we can do is to pick ourselves up and go on as best we can. Your brothers, and Beth, have their own families and their own homes, and any one of them will make a place for you with them."

Mary's mouth had quivered. And Miss Willie had hastened on. "But they have small children, and their lives are busy and full . . ."

Mary had interrupted. Passionately she had cried: "I don't

29

want to live with any of them! I don't want to be taken in and given a home! I don't want to be a burden to anyone. I want . . ." and she had bent her head in her hands.

Miss Willie's voice had been soft and warm, then. "You want to be loved and wanted, as you have been, so tenderly and so deeply, all your life. Of course, dear. That's why I think you would be happier with Grandmother and me. We can't take your father's and your mother's place. Bitter as it is, you have to accept their going. But we *can* love you in our own way, and you *can* know that you are loved and wanted, and, even more, that you are needed. For we *do* need a young person in our house." Miss Willie had smiled wryly then. She herself was only twenty-eight, but she felt as old as time. "We're in a rut, Grandmother and I, and we're drying up. We need your youth and vitality and your fresh interests. This isn't entirely an unselfish offer, Mary."

So Mary had come to live a few brief years here in the little adobe house. She had come, and, at whatever costs to herself, had made the adjustments necessary to that house, dominated and controlled by a sick old woman. Miss Willie had ached over the quiet, poised little figure, and had loved her and protected her as much as possible from the autocratic old invalid.

She had seen to it that there were gay new clothes, gracious meals together, just the two of them, and shared hours before the corner fireplace listening to her vast collection of records, or reading, each in her own place on either side of the flickering fire. Little by little Mary had let down, and Miss Willie had watched her stretch and grow in the security of love and home again.

Near the end of the first year Miss Willie's mother had died, and then out of the blossom of Miss Willie's love for the girl had come the full fruit. She lifted the letter and looked again at the free, flowing handwriting.

The next two years with Mary had been so perfect, so beautiful, so completely happy for them both. The tight-closed bud that had been Mary the first year had opened out full and generous. The quiet, withdrawn child had bloomed quickly into a beautiful, gay, winsome girl. Miss Willie remembered — oh, so well she remembered! — those years. When the house was overflowing

30

with Mary's belongings left carelessly helter-skelter; when the record cabinet became stacked with Glenn Miller and Benny Goodman records; when the refrigerator was never full enough to satisfy the hunger of the raiding gangs of boys and girls that gathered so often; when the ring of the phone had brought Mary flying swiftly and eagerly to answer it; when Mary had become at last so rightly and so safely a normal, happy girl. Those two years had been a flawless gem to Miss Willie, to be taken out and polished and looked at again and again.

And then Mary had gone away to college . . . four long years at the university. There had been her letters, frequent and long and full of her activities. There had been her times at home, summers and during holidays. And when Mary had majored in education, Miss Willie had hoped she would teach here in the city and their life together might go on for a time. Selfishly she had hoped it, for Mary filled her heart and her days with an overflowing interest.

But that was not to be. For almost upon the heels of her graduation Mary had gone to Kentucky. They had talked of it one night. Mary had sat there, on the edge of the bed, her arm braced behind her and one foot swinging idly as she talked. "I want to be on my own, Miss Willie," she had said. "I could teach here, of course, but I should always be Miss Willie Payne's niece. I would always be following in your footsteps . . . nothing but your shadow. I want to see what I can do on my own!"

Miss Willie had felt her heart plunge in a sickening downward motion. She had wanted to plead with the girl. But what of me, Mary? she had wanted to ask. What about me? She wanted to tie the girl to her and hold her and keep her close. What of me, now? The years have been so dear . . . so short . . . so sweet. How can I go on alone, after filling myself so full of you? How can you expect me to cut myself loose from you?

But she had said nothing of that. She had cried the tears she had to shed, alone, and had said to Mary: "Of course, Mary. You must do what you think best." She had freed the girl of her own close-drawn love and let her go, unfettered, to make her own destiny. She, who had never been free, knew its glory so well.

31

So Mary had gone to Louisville, and the years had passed. There were still her letters, and always her vacation months spent with Miss Willie. Miss Willie had expected her to marry soon, but somehow the time had gone, and although there were always a few men in her life, Mary hadn't married early. She seemed, instead, to be testing, and searching, and questioning life.

And then had come the war, and the summer Mary had come home full of the soldier she had met on the bus; and at war's end had come the marriage to the soldier, and the end of Mary's teaching and the beginning of her life on Piney Ridge. Now, here was her letter.

A fine thread of excitement ran through Miss Willie . . . a fine silver thread which began deep inside her and fled in narrow, tingling chills out to her finger tips. Well . . . she thought. Well! This is April, and the school term starts in July! How wonderful!

Abruptly she rose from her chair and walked with her quick, rapid steps over to the long mirror that hung over her dressing table. She looked at herself a long time, stripping herself down to find the last small ounce of her strength. Objectively she looked at the small, slender body reflected there. At the soft, fine, mouse-colored hair piled on top of her head. At the calm, blue eyes, and thin, narrow nose. Automatically she pushed her glasses back in place, and let her hand drop slowly to her side. I am forty-five, she thought. I am a thin, dried-up, old-maid schoolteacher. I am brittle and barren and plain. But they need me!

The fine silver thread spread to her legs and her toes. They need me! She looked around at her lovely room . . . at the wide, soft bed, and the pale walls . . . at the exquisite porcelain of her Chinese lamps . . . at the wall of books, and the glint of her mahogany radio. And in one all-rejecting moment she denied them. They need me!

She hurried to the kitchen. "Constancia," she called, "Constancia! I am going to Kentucky to live!"

CHAPTER
❧ 4 ❧

THE REST OF THE SCHOOL TERM sped by so rapidly that almost before she was aware of it her last days in El Paso were upon Miss Willie. She went about the city attending to the last details of leaving, with no regrets and with a fine excitement mounting within her.

She debated selling her house, but decided against it, renting it instead, furnished, except for the few personal things she felt she wanted about her wherever she was. These, and her books, she packed carefully and shipped ahead of her to Piney Ridge.

She was amazed at how easy the parting came. After all these years she had supposed it would wrench her to break the ties. But she was already projecting herself into the future, onto the ridge which she knew so well from Mary's letters. She looked ahead with gladness, feeling wanted again, feeling needed. The days took on a new shine, and she felt welling up in her a vigor and strength that had lessened these last years.

She had followed Mary's instructions and made application to the county school board, and had in due time received their approval. Now it was the middle of June and time for her to be going. She went by train to Louisville, and then by bus to Columbia, the county seat, where Hod and Mary did all their business.

Hod met her at the bus station. Miss Willie had met him only once before, when he and Mary had visited her in El Paso one summer, but she remembered his lean longness, his sun-browned face, his straw-covered head on which he never wore a hat. When she saw him through the bus window she thought, He'll always look like that. If he lives to be a hundred he'll just add a few wrinkles, and maybe a few pounds, but out of his eyes he'll always look the same. As if hills and hollows and cornfields and tobacco patches were mirrored in them, at home in them. Like any man who knows where he belongs and is contented there.

"Where's Mary?" she asked him.

"She decided not to come." He laughed. "You'd ought to re-member that Mary doesn't like to say hello or good-by to people in public! Said she'd rather see you the first time at home. Any-way, she gets tired pretty easy these days, and ridin' over the kind of roads we've got back here in the hills is not too easy on her."

"Ah, I was forgetting," Miss Willie said. "But she's well?"

"Fit as a fiddle." And Hod loaded her bags in the back of a rickety old car. "Got to go to the bank a minute, Miss Willie, if you don't mind. I meant to get that done before the bus got in, but I was runnin' a little late."

"That's all right, Hod."

Up on the square, Miss Willie looked around at the quaint old town. Columbia was built, as are so many old Kentucky towns, around the courthouse, which housed a huge clock in its tower. In most towns built in a square, the streets enter at the corners. But here, Miss Willie smiled to notice, they entered directly in the middle of each of the four sides of the square. These sealed corners snugged the square around the courthouse, like a hen's wings covering her brood.

On the courthouse steps loafed a crowd of men, talking and spitting, and around the four sides of the square people walked, unhurried, stopping to talk with passing friends, or looking in the store windows. The town had a sleepy, lazy look in the sun-drenched afternoon; a quiet, villagey look which the slow glossing of time had given it. Miss Willie felt that life would keep step with the slow movements of time here. That it would not rush at one, and strike one down. Instead, it would hold back its keen edges and, paced by the heavy hands of the courthouse clock, lead one graciously through the years.

She sighed and let the tiredness of the trip have its way with her body. It was good to be nearing the end of her journey. She wanted to see Mary. She hoped Hod would hurry. And then she smiled at the incongruity of her thought. Hadn't it just occurred to her that hurry was a word that would have little meaning here?

Hod was back then. He crawled into the car and stepped on the starter. He nodded at the bank. "That's the bank Jesse James robbed one time," he said.

Miss Willie peered at the building. "Bank of Columbia," it said across the windows. "Why, I didn't know Jesse James ever got over into Kentucky!"

"He did, though. Must have been pretty exciting too. Old Mr. Martin was killed during the robbery. The bank keeps a picture of the old fellow hanging in the front to this day."

So, Miss Willie thought. Life wouldn't strike out at one here! How ridiculous! Life strikes out wherever it pleases, and a sun-drenched, lazy little town couldn't hide one from its suddenness.

Miss Willie was prepared for the narrow, winding, dirt road out to the ridge, but even so its deeply gouged ruts and the bouncing of the car from one side to the other made her clutch her hat and hope fervently that her partial plate would stay put. Hod grinned at her and yelled, "Hold tight, Miss Willie!" She grinned back and held tight. She was glad Mary hadn't come.

Much of what she saw along the way was already familiar to her through Mary's letters. The beautiful, rolling countryside, with its green, swelling hills, wide-stretching valleys, and little, rushing creeks. It was so green, so lush, so softly lovely, after the wide, dry reaches of Texas.

She was prepared too for the evidences of poverty she saw when the road took them deep into the hills. "This is a poor country," Mary had said. "People scratch the barest sort of living out of the thin soil, and exist only a little above the margin of necessity. They depend on one crop, tobacco, for cash. Most of them have a cow, a little flock of chickens, and a garden patch. They live in two- or three-room houses, with a leaky roof over their heads, and a sagging floor under their feet. They make out, one way or another, from one year to the next, mostly on what the women put up from their gardens, and the milk and butter and eggs they sell. They make out, and that's about the best you can say for the way folks live on the ridge. Beauty, graciousness, even comfort, are things ridge folks have no conception of."

When she saw with her own eyes what Mary had written, she knew there had been no exaggeration. She saw too that it was

35

what economists had been writing about Southern farmers for years. But to most people it remained forever academic, textbook material. She drew in her breath deeply. Well, she was going to open the textbook, now, and make it come alive. She was going to *do* something about the things she had only heretofore read about! This was what she had come for. She was needed here.

Piney Ridge was a part of a chain of hills called the Tennessee Hills. This chain laid itself ponderously across southern Kentucky, and northern and eastern Tennessee. After it entered Tennessee, it humped itself higher to become part of the Cumberland range. But here in Kentucky the hills were long, saw-toothed, and sharp, bending and folding over themselves with countless steep ravines and hollows between them. A little to the north, between this range of sharp, edgy hills and the narrow band of peculiarly conical hills known as the Knobs, lay a fertile and fruitful plateau called the Pennyroyal Plains. Actually the Tennessee Hills were geologically in that section. But there was little either of fertility or fruitfulness atop their shallow, spiny furrows.

Miss Willie knew that one of Hod's remote ancestors had settled this country on a Revolutionary War grant, and she knew also that up and down the straggling ridge backs lived innumerable Pierces, descendants of that old soldier. If she wondered why they, and Hod, continued to live, precariously and poorly, on these ledgy slopes, she said nothing. A man's reasons for calling one place home are innumerable, and they are usually voiceless, coming as they do from the heart and not the head.

The sun was banding the hills with streaks of gold, and purple shadows were creeping across the sky, when they turned off the road up the hollow, leaving the ridge humped solidly to their left. Miss Willie knew that up on that ridge was where Hod had been born and reared, but he and Mary had chosen his grandfather's old home down here in the hollow.

The car crept cautiously down a narrow trail which opened up in a heavily wooded section. Although it was little more than a path, the floor of the trail was smooth . . . smoother than the road, and it wound in and out under the tall, dark trees. The last of the sunlight was gone here, and the shadows hung ghost-like around the trees.

"What a beautiful place!" said Miss Willie. "This is like a forest straight out of Hans Christian Andersen! Gnomes and dwarfs and elves should dwell here!"

"Maybe they do," Hod chuckled. "Mary loves this piece of woods too. She comes here a lot."

"I don't wonder. Does it belong to you?"

Hod nodded. "All my land is down in the hollow and on the other ridge."

They threaded their way through the woods for about half a mile, and then the road slanted down an easy slope into the open. The next ridge had edged over into this one, folding itself gently against it, and almost at once they were in the cup of the hollow.

"You can see our house down there now," Hod said, pointing straight ahead. "This is the head of the hollow, and that's Wishful Creek there."

Miss Willie looked down the hollow and saw the weathered gray house held there in the curve of the creek, as if in a loving embrace, the hills rising steeply on either side. The supper smoke was curling gently upward, and the trees around the house bent softly toward it. Wishful Hollow! No wonder Mary loved it! Here in this beautiful valley, bounded by the hills, she must have found a whole new world. Living here must be like living in the hollow of God's hand, borne ever aloft in beauty and in loveliness. The gray-green picture blurred, and Miss Willie dabbed impatiently at her eyes. She wasn't going to meet Mary with tears in her eyes!

"We come up to the back of the house this way," Hod said. "It fronts down the hollow. There's Mary now!" And he sounded the horn.

Miss Willie felt a knot in her throat, as she strained to see Mary. Ah, there she was, waving from the back gate. She hasn't changed, thought Miss Willie. She hasn't changed at all! And then she checked herself. Why did I think she would have changed? And how did I think she would have changed? What a snob I am after all! I know better than anyone else what she has gained by marrying this man and coming to this place to live! Better than most I know how little she had before, because that's all I ever had. How convention betrays one! Of course she

37

hasn't changed, except for the better!

When the car stopped, Miss Willie was out the door in a flash, and into Mary's arms. "Mary, Mary," she cried, straining the dear figure to her.

"Now, Miss Willie," Mary laughed — "now, Miss Willie, you're not going to cry, are you?"

"Oh, let me cry if I want to! Let me! Be still and let me look at you! Oh, you're beautiful, beautiful! Isn't she beautiful, Hod?"

"Well, I wouldn't go so far as to say that. But she's a right nice-looking woman to be as long-legged as she is."

"Oh, shut up and go get my bags! Mary, I'm here! Now it's real! I'm here! The last three days have had a dreamlike quality as if I were still back home and only my thoughts were projected into the journey. But this makes it real. To be here with you!"

"Miss Willie, Miss Willie! I've had a thousand doubts since I wrote that letter! I shouldn't have asked you to leave all you had to come here to the ridge."

Miss Willie drew away from her and looked at her. "Why, Mary! What did I have? What did I have, Mary? What did I leave? Surely you know how little it was!"

Mary's mouth trembled. "That makes it all right, then. That's all I wanted to know. You'll not be sorry if you feel like that."

"No. I'll not be sorry. No matter what happens now, I'll never be sorry, Mary. I'm glad I'm here."

Hod interrupted them. "You all go on in the house and I'll bring these things in."

"Come on, Miss Willie," Mary said, "I want to show you my house."

They moved around the corner of the house, by the old stone chimney. Mary laid her hand on it as they passed. "Hod's great-grandmother Abigail built this chimney herself, with stones from the creek bed there. I've written you about it. And the yellow rose here she planted. The family say that Amelia Pierce brought a cutting of this rose from her home in Virginia when she came to Kentucky. Abigail brought this one, cut from that plant, and now there's always a yellow rose in every Pierce yard. Those old apple trees were set out by Great-grampa Jeems. See how gnarled and ancient they are?"

"And these logs were cut and shaped by him, weren't they?" Miss Willie touched a corner of the log house.

"Yes. He felled and squared these logs and raised a one-room cabin. This part of the house is over a hundred years old."

Across the front of the house was a wide, screened porch. When they stepped through the door, Miss Willie saw that it was comfortable, with chairs and tables grouped at one end.

"Hod makes those," Mary said. "You know he has a workshop out in the old woodshed where his grandfather made chairs."

"Yes, you told me," Miss Willie answered.

And then they were inside the big log room. A lamp was lighted, and in its flickering light the logs were burnished copper. Miss Willie stood and let the feel of the room creep over her. The floors were wide and darkly gleaming, with ovals of braided rugs scattered across them. Mary's piano filled one corner of the room, and the huge fireplace took up the opposite wall. An old pine dresser stood against another, and a deep couch covered with a quilted pattern sat beneath the windows. Big easy chairs were grouped before the hearth, and a low, polished table stood between them. The roof lifted high overhead and the great, smoked beams stretched from wall to wall. It was a lovely, gracious room, and Miss Willie let its charm flow over her.

"And here is your room," Mary said, opening a door. Here was the same ancient charm . . . a high wooden bed, softly shining in the lamplight . . . a tall mirror over a marble-topped chest of drawers . . . a deep pine blanket chest at the foot of the bed . . . a low rocker with a quilted cushion, and the same gay, braided rugs on the floor.

Miss Willie turned to Mary. "You have a lovely home, my dear. Another person might have ruined it, but you've kept it beautiful."

"So much of this was already here, Miss Willie. I've just tried to restore it. This bed belonged to Abigail . . . this little rocker too. This blanket chest was Gramma's . . . Grampa Dow made it for her. There aren't many things in the house that have been 'fotched on.' I've only had to put them together again."

"Even so, you've done a lovely thing here. You've given Hod the heritage of his forefathers. It might so easily have been lost."

39

"Someday it will be the Skipper's, Miss Willie. Besides what it means to Hod and me, I want our son to know his past, how rooted it is in this place. And I want him to grow up loving it. You know what my life was like . . . always moving . . . never putting down roots. Not once in my life until I married Hod had I slept under a roof I could call my own. Not once had I walked on land that belonged to me. O Miss Willie, I've learned that the most fundamental pride in the world is the pride you have in owning a little piece of land! You've got to live on your own land, walk on it, work in its dirt, to know the final pride of being free. And I want my son to know that, always. I want him never to know what it is to be rootless and insecure. I want him always to know where he belongs."

Terribly moved, Miss Willie felt her throat knot. "You're a big woman, Mary Pierce. And Hod and the Skipper are mighty fortunate men!"

Mary laughed. "Here we stand talking! And you're hungry and tired! I'm forgetting the very first rule of Piney Ridge hospitality! There's fresh water in the pitcher there, and when you've freshened up a bit, supper will be ready."

After supper they sat on the wide screened porch and talked of the thousand and one things two women can find to talk about when they haven't been together for a long time. Talked of Texas and Miss Willie's friends; of this acquaintance Mary would remember and that one; of Miss Willie's trip and her anxiety over the ribbony, black-topped road down from Louisville; of Mary's first days here on the ridge; how she and Hod worked so hard remodeling the house. And inevitably again to the long history of his family here on Piney Ridge. "Tell her, Hod," Mary said.

And Hod tilted his chair against the wall, drooped his eyes, and lifted his voice in Grampa's endless tale. "Old Tom Pierce, he come here from Virginny, back in the olden days. He was a soljer in the Revolution, an' they paid him off with some land in Kentucky. He brung his woman an' their young'uns, an' house plunder through the Gap in a wagon, an' settled this land an' raised his kids. His name was Tom Pierce. An' he fit the Injuns an' plowed his land an' lived an' died right here on this ridge.

Give it the name o' Piney Ridge . . ."

His voice droned on and Miss Willie smiled. All Hod's love for his old Grampa Dow sang richly through his voice. But more than that, all his love for this land and these people was in it. In every word, every tone, every slow, drawling inflection. She had expected to love this man for Mary's sake, but in that moment she began to love him for himself.

The June night rested softly on the hills, and the stars arched the sky from ridge to ridge with a spangled bridge. Under the trees a white mist curled slowly from the creek, and fireflies pricked the shifting veils with dimmed and softened lanterns. An owl hooted up on the hillside, and in some dark, quiet pool a frog grumbled deep in his throat. A late thrush sent a fluting trill across the meadow, and on the very rim of the ridge, high and far away, a thin, silver moon cut a crescent out of the sky.

Miss Willie felt an ineffable peace within her. This is going to be all right, she thought. This is going to be fine!

CHAPTER

❧ 5 ❧

Miss Willie was awake early the next morning. She knew it was early although the sun was streaming in her window. The air had the texture and the feel and the smell of something new and unused. Like a freshly minted coin, bright and shining. There was a crisp vigor in it and an energy waiting to be put to work . . . a lightness and a strong excitement. It lifted and bore one aloft. Only in the very early morning was this so. Later the air would take on the burdens of the day. It would be heavy and tired.

Early as she knew it was, Miss Willie heard the sounds of breakfast stirring out in the kitchen. The smell of coffee came drifting into her room and she sniffed eagerly. Coffee, she thought, smells brown . . . like it looks. Rich and heavy and brown. Suddenly she was hungry . . . ravenously hungry, and she threw the blanket back and rose and dressed quickly.

When she went into the kitchen, Mary looked up from the

41

dough board where she was cutting biscuits. "You were supposed to rest this morning," she scolded.

"Too excited," Miss Willie confessed. "I'm like a child on a visit . . . eager to be up and around. Are you making hot bread this morning, Mary?"

Mary laughed. "I make hot bread *every* morning, lady! My husband comes from a long line of biscuit-for-breakfast people!"

She whirled quickly toward the stove. Taking the lid from a deep skillet, she frowned anxiously over the chicken which was frying, turning first one piece then another, setting the lid back in place finally and shoving the skillet toward the back of the stove. "Chicken's almost done," she said. "Miss Willie, you want to run down to the creek and get the fruit juice and cream? Down by the tall sycamore you'll find a little springhouse built over the creek, and the cream is in a blue crock and the orange juice is in a fruit jar."

When Miss Willie returned, Mary was piling fried chicken on a deep platter. She set it in the warming oven when it was full. "Now you can set the table if you like. The dishes are in that corner cupboard."

"Where's Hod?" Miss Willie asked.

"He's milking and feeding. He'll be in pretty soon, though. He ought to be through by now." As she talked, she opened the oven door and glanced in. "Biscuits are nearly done." She went to the back door and looked out. "He's turning the cows out." And then she was back at the stove again.

"Mary, is this corner cupboard cherry?"

"Yes. Grampa Dow made that. And this dough table here. All these things were Hod's grandmother's."

Miss Willie clucked softly to herself. "Your house is full of museum pieces, isn't it?"

"And right here's where they'll stay." Mary was stirring gravy at the stove.

Hod came in with the foaming buckets of milk. "You're up bright and early, Miss Willie. Hardly an hour past sunup! Sleep good?"

"I slept fine, Hod. I thought I was going to be so stiff I couldn't move from all that bumping yesterday, but, strangely

42

enough, I'm not! And I feel as though I had enough energy for a dozen people."

"Breakfast is ready," Mary called, pouring coffee into the big, ironstone cups.

Miss Willie looked at the table. Mary's love of beauty was evident in the bright blue cloth, and the pot of flowers in the center of the table, but Hod's needs were evident in the hot biscuits piled in the basket, the platter of fried chicken, the deep bowl of cream gravy, and the jars of jam and jelly clustered about the butter dish. Miss Willie thought of her own breakfasts in the little adobe house. Fruit juice, toast, and coffee, and she frequently only nibbled at the toast. On Sundays she sometimes broiled a bit of bacon and added a spot of jelly. Year in and year out her breakfasts had been the same. Drawing a good breath, she opened a biscuit as she saw Hod doing, and floated it in the thick white gravy. Then she took a piece of chicken and bit into it. Heavenly! At this hour of the morning too.

"Well, what you two goin' to do today?" Hod asked.

"I thought we'd walk down to the schoolhouse this afternoon. Unless Miss Willie needs to rest. I imagine she's anxious to see it and to begin to get her bearings."

"Oh, no. I'm not tired at all," Miss Willie said. "I'd like that. When does school start?"

"July twelfth."

"I'd better see the schoolhouse, then. And we had also better begin to think of where I'm going to live."

"Why, you're going to live right here," Hod said.

"Oh, no, I'm not."

"But, Miss Willie, that's what we've planned all along. That's your room that we've got ready for you," Mary protested.

"Well, you'll just have to unplan then. I have no intention of staying here with you and Hod. If this were a visit, I should love to stay here. But I have come to Piney Ridge to stay awhile, and I want a place of my own while I'm here."

Hod pushed his chair back from the table. "Miss Willie, this ain't El Paso. There's water to draw, and fires to build, and lamps to keep cleaned and filled, and wood to chop. A woman can't live by herself in this country. It'd be too hard on her."

43

"Oh, I didn't mean a house of my own. I know that isn't possible. I meant a room somewhere."

"Is this idea of yours for our sake or for your own?" Mary wanted to know.

"Both. You and Hod don't need anyone else around just now. And I like to be alone at times. We are too much alike for you not to understand that, Mary."

Mary looked across the room at Hod and smiled. Hod pulled at his nose. "O.K., Miss Willie. Mary said that's what you'd say. But we'd have liked to have you."

"I know you would. But it will be best the other way. Now, do we do the dishes, Mary?"

That afternoon Mary and Miss Willie set off down the hollow for the schoolhouse. "Should you be walking, Mary?" Miss Willie asked.

"Oh, yes. I puff and pant a little when I climb the ridge, and I don't do some of the heavier work as I used to. But otherwise I follow my own inclinations. It's only about a mile to the schoolhouse, and it's a pretty walk."

They were following an old road which tunneled a shady path under the close-hanging trees. And the creek rolled and tumbled along beside them. There was a scent of clover and dry, sunbaked soil, intermingled with the damp smell of leaves close-packed under the trees. It was a soft blending of odors overlaid with the lazy heat of the afternoon. When they walked near the stream, Miss Willie could see the minnows darting here and there in their abrupt, swift way. Their movements were broken into flashing forays from dark to light pools, behind rocks, over ripples, and under roots tangling the water.

"This is going to look pretty bad to you," Mary warned. "Nothing I wrote can give you any idea of what it's really like!"

"I'm not expecting much," Miss Willie said. "I shouldn't have been interested in coming if it had been a good school. I was in a fine school where I was, remember?"

The road came out in a widening meadow which was lush and deep in grass. Out of the opposite woods came a man and a

44

woman, with three small children straggling behind. The woman was carrying a fourth child too small to walk.

"Oh, heavens!" Mary exclaimed, "there's Matt Jasper and his brood. Of all people for you to meet the very first day you're here!"

As they came nearer, Miss Willie thought of the characters in *Tobacco Road* or *Grapes of Wrath*. She had the amazed feeling that she was watching them come to life. They don't live outside of books, she thought.

The man was slight and bony, his overalls hanging sacklike over his thin frame. His scant beard was a week old, and his shirt collar buttoned loosely around his gaunt, stringy neck. His mouth worked constantly around a cud of tobacco, and spit drooled from the corners onto his chin. His battered old felt hat was pushed down around his ears, and his long, shaggy hair curled up all around the edges. He had a flat, vacant look on his face.

The woman was filthy, emaciated, and stupid-looking. Her mouth was packed with snuff, and she spat sloppily at her feet when they stopped. The child in her arms was covered with sores, mewling and crying fretfully as it turned its head restlessly from side to side. Its skin had a blue tinge, and its legs hung thin and spidery from its swollen stomach. Miss Willie felt her own stomach heave uneasily. She swallowed hard.

The children drew up behind their parents. The oldest one, a boy, had a large head — too large for the rest of his body — covered with a thatch of coarse red hair. His face had a sly, foxlike look. He stood scratching his chest, running a grimy finger inside his shirt front.

The other two were girls, less repellent than the boy but obviously stupid and simple. They were skinny little things, with sharp, whetted features. All of them were unwashed and uncombed and clothed in filthy rags.

Mary had stopped. "Why, hello, Matt . . . Lutie, how are you? Have you all been to the store?"

"Howdy, Miss Mary," the man spoke, after shooting a thin stream of tobacco juice to one side of the road. "No, we wouldn't have nothin' to go to the store fer. We're goin' sang diggin' up the holler, if it's all right with Hod. Hod, he said they was some up on that fur hillside. Told me oncet I could allus have what I found on his land. But I reckoned to ast him, jist the same."

"I'm sure he won't mind," Mary said. Turning to Miss Willie, she went on. "This is my aunt, Miss Willie Payne. She's come to teach the Big Springs School this year."

"How do you do?" said Miss Willie, although her voice was thick with effort.

"Howdy," said the man. The woman didn't speak. She simply stared. And the children drew up in a tight huddle behind the man and woman. Miss Willie felt all their eyes fixed on her. All the eyes, blank, expressionless, unmoving, simply lying on her, heavy and solid. Their look was thick with substance, and she shivered with a chilling omniscience of evil. She moved closer to Mary and touched her arm.

"We'd best be gittin' on," the man finally said, and they shuffled on up the road.

"Dear Lord, Mary," Miss Willie sighed, when they had passed on. "Are there many like that here on the ridge? They made me feel positively unclean!" She groped for her handkerchief and wiped her face and hands.

Mary shook her head. "I know. I know. The first time I saw them I was so nauseated I almost disgraced Hod. I had to get away from them where I could be sick. No. There aren't many like Matt and Lutie, thank goodness. Matt is simple-minded and epileptic."

"And the woman! What about her? She was as repulsive to me as the man!"

"Lutie? Lutie is normal, as far as anyone knows. She has just been dragged down by hard work and forever bearing children. I don't know how many she's had, but these are all that are living. Most of them die either when they're born or soon after. That one she's carrying is about two, and she lost one last year. Oh, something ought to be done about things like that! I tell Hod, and I tell him. And he says what can you do? And I don't know what you can do! Matt ought to be institutionalized! But someone would have to go through the legal process of having him committed, and no one is willing. Not even Hod. He says Matt isn't crazy, and that he would die if he were put away somewhere. He says Matt lives in fear of that happening. He has a brother who was sent to Danville, and he has a horror of it. He hides away in the hills when he feels the convulsions coming on. Hides back in a cave somewhere and stays for two or three days at a time, to keep people from knowing. But to keep on bringing children into the world of parents like that! If we were a more civilized people, it wouldn't be allowed! They could never have married!"

"Why did she marry him, do you suppose? If she's normal, surely she wouldn't have married him!"

"Miss Willie, do you know how old Lutie Jasper is?"

"She looked about forty to me."

"She's twenty-five! And she married Matt when she was four-teen! How much sense has a fourteen-year-old girl got? Besides, Matt didn't start having these seizures until he was grown. They had been married several years when he had the first one. Hod says he can remember when Matt Jasper wasn't a bad-looking boy. He was sixteen when they married."

"How can children that age get a marriage license? Aren't there any state laws here?"

"Oh, yes. But fourteen is the minimum age, with parents' con-sent. And the kids forge their parents' signatures, and that's all there is to it."

"Don't the parents ever do anything about it?"

"No. Not on the ridge. No one wants to get mixed up with the law. Once it's done, it's done. Oh, I'm sorry we had to run into them today. I wish you could have seen some of the good things about the ridge, first. And I wish you could have met some of the good folks. Because there's more good than bad here, even with the bad as awful as it is."

"It'll balance in the long run, Mary. I'll see the good too. These folks leave a bad taste, but after all they're people, and we shouldn't draw away from them."

They had come to the wide mouth of the hollow, and in a flat open space at the foot of the ridge the schoolhouse hugged the hill. Back of it the trees climbed the steep slope in serried ranks, and formed a solid green backdrop against which the great square logs were painted in bleached gray. Those logs had soaked up

47

a hundred years of sun and wind and rain, and from them had been drawn the strong yellow of the pines and the poplars and the fine white cleanness of the oaks. Little by little they had been washed and dried and sunned into the present ancient silver and were beyond further saturation.

A lofty elm, majestic, kingly, and august, allowed its lower branches to sweep delicately over the shingled roof, and in its intense shade the curled boards had put on a covering of moss — rich, vivid velvet, green against the gray.

The schoolyard had been tramped down by generations of running feet, and the bare ground looked white and beaten under the trees which still enclosed the space. These were nearly all giant elms — ancient trees — with a few tall maples and half a dozen beeches.

"There," said Mary, pointing. "There it is, and you may rue the day you ever saw it!"

They had stopped at the edge of the grove, and Miss Willie had been still, taking all this into her. Nothing could be too bad, she thought, that was so quietly beautiful. I should have lived a hundred years ago, her thoughts went on. I should have been a little girl going to school here. I should have heard the wind and the rain crying through these trees. I should have had a young love to carve twined hearts on that great elm. Is there something in all of us, she mused, that keeps one longing heartbeat in the past? Is that the only way we can bear the present? Do we all of us belong in another age with some part of ourselves?

Mary was walking through the grove and around the building. "Here," she said, "is the family tree." And she pointed to a gray-beard beech. "See, there are Grampa Dow's initials on that side. And here, a little lower down are Lem's and Gault's and Mr. Tom's. And here, still young and clean, are Hod's. Someday the Skipper will cut his just below his father's." She stood looking at the tree, and then she turned. "Miss Willie, is there always something selfish, something inevitably personal, in our desire for goodness? It's because of the Skipper that I want a better school, isn't it? If it weren't for him, would I have bothered?"

"If it weren't for him," Miss Willie answered, "you would have bothered so much you wouldn't have sent for me! You would have done it yourself. Of course the pattern of goodness is centered in some personal want, Mary. It has always been so. All conceptions of goodness have had their beginnings in the minds of people . . . people who found their happiness in thinking good, or doing good, or being good, or wanting good. Goodness can't be abstracted from the personal. But it isn't any the less good for being personal! Let's go in. I want to see the worst of this at once."

Inside, the building was long and dim, its windows high and on one side. The desks were very old and battered, and many of them were broken. They were all of the same height, and Miss Willie saw that the short legs of the younger children would swing painfully from them.

In the front of the room was a pine table, which was evidently the teacher's desk. On the wall back of it was one small blackboard, cracked and gray with age. In the center of the room was a round, drum stove, rusty and sagging, the door missing from the front.

"Isn't it horrible?" said Mary.

Miss Willie didn't answer. She was wandering around the room, trying the seats and running her hand over the desks, looking at the inevitable carved initials marking their tops. "Here is Hod's place," she said, "he must have sat here once."

Mary hurried over to stand by Miss Willie, looking down at the carved name. "Well, at least I don't see Mr. Tom's or Grampa Dow's. The desks must be newer than their time!"

Miss Willie laughed. "Isn't it unbelievable? When I think of the equipment we have in the cities! A quarter of it would seem like riches here!" She shook her head, and repeated, "It's unbelievable!"

They went outside again. "And where is the spring?" Miss Willie asked.

"Here," Mary said, "on the hillside."

A wooden washtub had been embedded in the slope of the hill, and a tiny stream of water ran constantly into it over the pebbly soil. It came from farther up the hill and it had channeled a narrow furrow in the shaly earth. It ran clear and sparkling over the moss and rocks, and dripped in an invariable and

49

regular stream. It ran off down the hill in a ditch which had been dug for that purpose. Even so the ground was wet and muddy around the tub.

Miss Willie looked up the hillside at the narrow stream of water. "This is dangerous, Mary."

"Of course it's dangerous! The spring is a hundred feet up the hill. It may be pure . . . it probably is. But it runs in an unguarded stream over the ground, and people or animals passing can wade right through it, to say nothing of any other sort of pollution. But this is one of the blind spots I mentioned. We have not been able to get anything done about it. But it *must* be changed! I only hope we don't have to have an epidemic of some sort to get it changed!"

"Changing it is part of my job?"

Mary laughed. "Your conscience wouldn't let you leave it unchanged, would it?"

"No. I'm afraid not." Miss Willie squared her shoulders. "Well. It's pretty bad. Worse than I imagined. But nothing is hopeless. We'll just have to see."

Mary moved toward the road. "We'd better start. I thought we'd go by the ridge road and stop at the folks' for a while."

Miss Willie followed, turning once or twice to look back at the ancient trees and the weathered old log building. As a schoolhouse it was pretty terrible. As a beautiful old structure it had the grace that time lends all old things, and the charm of faded and blended colors. She liked it. She thought she was going to be very happy in it. And there was real challenge in this place.

They followed the road back down the hollow until they came to a path which crossed the creek on a foot log. Here they stopped for Mary to rest. The shade was very heavy, and the air was cooled by the creek. They sat on the foot log and swung their feet over the swift running water. Miss Willie bent over to watch. "Makes me dizzy," she said, straightening.

"Oh, there's Rufe," Mary said suddenly, and she waved across the creek. A boy, about twelve, maybe fourteen, and a dog were standing there under a tall tree. The boy waved, and then he and the dog disappeared. "That's Wells Pierce's boy," Mary explained. "I wrote you about Wells. You'll have Rufe in school."

50

Miss Willie was watching the woods where the boy had disappeared. "Why did he run away?" she asked.

"Oh, that's just Rufe," Mary said. "He and his dog roam the woods all summer. He digs ginseng, I suppose, and the dog jumps rabbits. You're likely to see them 'most any time you're out."

"Wells is one of the school trustees, isn't he?"

"Yes. He's Hod's cousin. We're very fond of him. His wife's dead. He lives on up the ridge past the folks'. He's kept his home going somehow, though with four children to look after I don't know how he's done it. Well, three. His sister took the youngest when Matildy died. Fortunately the oldest is a girl, Rose, and although she's just sixteen, she does a pretty good job of taking care of things."

"Four children?"

"Yes. Rose, and Rufe — Rufe's about thirteen, I guess — and Abby. Let's see, Abby must be nearly eleven. And Veeny, the baby. I imagine she's six or seven now. But Manthy has had her since she was less than a year old."

"Was his wife nice?"

"I never knew her. She died before Hod and I were married. While he was overseas. But Hod says she was a fine woman. Short and dark and sort of plump, and a happy, easygoing sort of person. From what I've heard she and Wells must have been very happy. Hod says they always seemed to have such a good time together."

"How did she die?"

"Of pneumonia. Took a cold and didn't take care of herself. And before they realized she was seriously ill, she was gone."

Miss Willie was quiet. Everything she had heard about Wells Pierce was good. He had had more to do with her coming to the ridge than the other trustees, because he was a man interested in a better school for his children. He was also a man who had somehow held his home together after the death of his wife. And he was a man of whom Mary and Hod were very fond. Yes, she looked forward to meeting him.

"We'd better go on," Mary said, and they crossed the log and pushed on up the steep and rocky path.

They came out at the silver birch just below Gault Pierce's place. Becky was sitting on the front porch. "Hi, Becky," Mary called. "Can we have a drink of water? We've been down to the schoolhouse and have just climbed that hill from the hollow. I'm as thirsty as old Buck when he's been plowing all day."

"Why, shore," Becky answered, rising from the slat-backed chair drawn to the edge of the porch. "Jist git you a cheer, an' I'll go git the bucket. I jist went to the spring not more'n fifteen minnits ago, so I know the water's still cold."

Mary and Miss Willie sat on the edge of the porch, Mary leaning back against a post. Becky returned with the bucket of water and offered them the gourd dipper which hung from a rafter. The water was as cold as ice, and there was a faintly sweet taste to it from the gourd.

"This is my aunt, Miss Willie," said Mary. "And Becky is Hod's Uncle Gault's wife."

"Pleased to make yer acquaintance," murmured Becky, offering a limp hand. She was a small woman, even smaller than Miss Willie, and frail-looking. Her black dress hung on her in folds, hardly touching her body anywhere. Over it was tied a crisp white apron, its ruffles fluted into frilly stiffness. Her head was no larger than a child's, and the hair was skinned back from her face so tight that her eyebrows seemed to be drawn up at the ends. Her face was wrinkled and brown, and her mouth was bunched with a dip of snuff. She spat over the edge of the porch when it overflowed.

"You've come to teach the school, ain't you?" she asked.

"Yes," said Miss Willie. "We've been down looking over the building. There's lots needs to be done."

"They is that, fer a fact. Hit's a sight the way things gits run down when they ain't used. In jist five months that schoolhouse kin git so spider-webby an' dusty hit takes three, four days to red it up. I'll be glad to he'p ifen yer a mind to git at it soon."

Miss Willie looked at Mary. It hadn't occurred to her that she would be expected to clean up the building before school began. She made a wry face. Of course there would be no janitor here. If it was to be bright and shining for the opening of school, she would have to do it, with the help of anyone who offered.

52

Mary spoke up hastily. "That's good of you, Becky. But I think we'll get some of the men to do most of the work this year."

Becky sniffed and squirted a thin, brown stream expertly into the grass. "Never seen a man yit could red up a place like it ort to be! Takes a woman to scrub an' clean. Best count on me'n Hattie he'pin' out."

"We'll let you know," said Miss Willie pacifically. "I want someone to help me make some curtains for the windows, and I'd like to have two or three bright braided rugs. Do you know where I could get them?"

"Braided rugs? Well, upon my word an' honor! What you want with them in the schoolhouse?"

"I think they will brighten up the room. I want some pretty yellow curtains too."

Becky shook her head. "Kids go to school to larn, don't they? Cain't see why you need rugs an' curtains."

"They learn a lot more than what's in books, Becky," put in Mary. "Anyhow, you just leave this up to Miss Willie. Do you know who's got some braided rugs or where we could get some made?"

Becky folded her hands in her lap. "I've sorta caught up on my work lately, an' ifen you think they're good enough, I could whip you up a couple I reckon."

"I was hoping you would say that," laughed Mary. "Becky makes the prettiest and the best rugs on the ridge. Everybody will tell you that!"

Becky's face glowed with pleasure, but she disclaimed such credit immediately. "They's a heap kin make 'em purtier'n mine," she said. "Mine is jist hit-er-miss. I don't never foller no pattern like some does."

"That's what makes them so pretty! Well, there, Miss Willie! There are your rugs practically made!"

"An' I'll he'p with them curtains if yer set on 'em," Becky offered.

"I do thank you, Becky," said Miss Willie. "You'll see what a difference they make."

"Doubtless they will. Hit's a unknown sight what a splash o' color will do. Air you all goin' to the singin' Sunday, Mary?"

"What singing?"

"Over at Bear Holler. Brent an' Dude Johnson's goin' to hold a all-day singin' . . . dinner on the ground. I allowed you'd be goin' on account of Hod lovin' to sing so good."

"I didn't know anything about it, and if Hod knows, he hasn't mentioned it. Are the rest of the family going?"

"Hattie an' Tom is. Me'n Gault is goin' with 'em. Hattie's already abakin'. Said if you all went, they wasn't no use o' yer havin' to bake. She'd jist bake up enough fer all."

Mary rose and shook the skirt of her dress and hitched her stockings up. "Hod'll want to go I'm sure. And I'd love for Miss Willie to go to an all-day singing. I imagine we'll be there. If we go, we'll see you over there and we'll all have dinner together."

"Oh, hit's a spread. Ever'body jist puts their stuff together."

"All right," said Mary. "Come on, Miss Willie. The sun's almost down. We're not going to have time to go on to the folks' now. I'm going to have a hungry husband in about half an hour. We better go back to the hollow."

On up the ridge Matt Jasper stumbled down the road, Lutie, sagging under the weight of the child in her arms, following him. The children were strung out in a long and straggling row behind. Matt was muttering under his breath. "Old Hod don't like me no more. Old Hod's gittin' mean to me. Don't like me. His woman don't like me, neither. Looked funny outen her eyes too. Don't nobody like me no more. Ever'body looks funny at me outen their eyes."

He swung around suddenly, facing Lutie. She stopped abruptly, and her hooded eyes narrowed. "*You* look funny outen yer eyes too," he accused. "You don't like me no more neither!"

Lutie shifted the toothbrush in her mouth. "Le's git on home, Matt. Hit's gittin' late. Don't git none o' yer idees."

"Idees come an' idees go," he mumbled and started on, lurching from one side of the road to the other. His breath was foul with whisky. "You better not look funny at me," he warned. "You better not go tellin' the law to git me." He stopped again, his frail body shaking. His voice rose and he screeched at her, a trembling

54

finger pointing. "You better not! I'm atellin' you! I ain't goin' to no 'sylum. I'll kill anybody turns me in. I'll kill 'em dead! You better be keerful an' not git no idees yerself!"

Lutie changed the child from her right arm to the left. "C'mon, Matt," she said. "Ain't nobody got no idees but you. This kid's powerful heavy, an' I'm tard. Le's git on home."

CHAPTER

✹ 6 ✹

SUNDAY MORNING THE SUN CAME UP over the ridge into a cloudless sky. Miss Willie was aware of a tingling anticipation. This was the day of the all-day singing. She had been so afraid it would rain and spoil everything. But the blue dome rounding over the hills promised a blessing on the summer day.

All day yesterday she and Mary had been busy preparing for the dinner — dressing chickens, boiling potatoes for salad, baking beans, and a double quantity of Mary's snowy, light loaves of bread. Miss Willie had churned again, although they had churned only the day before. Mary wanted to take extra butter along. They had visited the cellar, prying about in the dimness among the jars for pickles and spiced peaches and corn catsup.

"Surely you needn't take so much, Mary," Miss Willie protested.

"There'll be those who can't bring enough, Miss Willie," Mary had answered. "The Jaspers, if they come, and Old Man Clark's family."

And as she dressed now, Miss Willie could hear Mary out in the kitchen and could smell the heady odor of frying chicken. The singing would start at ten o'clock, Hod had said, and you wanted to be there for the beginning.

Miss Willie was terribly excited. Her thin face was flushed and her eyes sparkled. She hummed a gay tune as she pulled on a crisply ironed wash dress. She laughed as she recognized "Turkey in the Straw." They had had some music last night, Mary at the piano and Hod with his guitar, and Hod had tried to teach her the words to that song. It fitted her mood today. It was a sort

55

of prancing tune, and prancing a little herself, she went out to help Mary.

After breakfast they packed four huge baskets with food and gave them to Hod to store in the back of the car. Miss Willie was thoughtful as she watched him carry them out the door. In those baskets was nothing that had not been grown here on this farm. Nothing except flour and salt and sugar. Hod had only a meager thirty acres all told, and yet from it he produced all the food the household needed; raised his nine tenths of an acre of tobacco and fifteen acres of corn. There was no want here, and yet she remembered the gray, rubbling shacks that hugged the hollows down by the pike, the leaning walls of Old Man Clark's house, the tenant place on Gault's farm, and the shambling, prideless beggary of Matt Jasper. It was true, then, wasn't it, that men were not created equal, even if they were offered equal opportunities. Matt Jasper had once had a farm as large as Hod's . . . and Old Man Clark had once owned one twice as large. He had sold off small chunks of it until there was none left to sell; then he had thrown himself on the mercy of the neighborhood and had accepted the charity of Gault's tenant house.

Must society always carry on its back the old man of the sea? Were there inevitably those too inert to labor, too shiftless to toil? And were they therefore a responsibility of all those who did? Was it better to take along enough lunch to feed them too, or was there hope of their ever being able to feed themselves? And was it loving your neighbor more to feed him or to instruct him? She wondered.

In that moment she felt a reinforcement of her conviction that she was here with a sense of mission. There was something she had to do here on Piney Ridge. She, Willie Payne. She was too good a Presbyterian to doubt that she had been led to this place, even as she chuckled at the conceit that lay back of her conviction. "The Lord's been running Piney Ridge a mighty long time without you, Willie," she cautioned. And then she giggled. "Maybe that's why He sent for you!"

Bear Hollow Chapel was set in a grove of trees at the head of the second hollow over from Wishful Creek. When they drove up, a crowd had already gathered. The grove was thick with vehicles

56

of every sort — wagons, buggies, carts, and ancient and broken-down automobiles. Hod's car, which was at least ten years old, was the best-looking of the lot. Mules and horses were hitched to the fence and to the wagon and cart wheels. People were milling around, talking in groups which were constantly being broken as those on the fringe moved on.

Miss Willie looked eagerly at the restless throng. She saw that the oldest women were dressed in their shapeless dark cottons, tied about with spotless aprons, Sunday sunbonnets knotted firmly under their chins. The dark dress, the starched apron, the slatted bonnet were apparently their uniform.

Women of Hattie's age ventured timidly into a discreet gaiety with their colored cottons. They were restrained to pale blues, pinks, yellows, and greens, with infinitely varied patterns of tiny flowers. It was as if at forty and fifty one might delicately own to the last fading moment of youth and indulge it cautiously in the pastels of the rainbow. Not yet must these shy women of middle age put on the black and brown of age. The aprons too were left off, a further mark of the still present energy to work. The white apron represented the time of sitting in the corner. Only Becky had put on voluntarily the garb of her elders. Miss Willie wondered about that. Neither did this middle group wear bonnets. On their heads were perched the flowering straws of Montgomery Ward and Sears, Roebuck.

It was among the girls that color rioted boldly. In cheap rayon and jersey dresses they flaunted their young loveliness, letting the brazen stripes and gaudy floral arrangements of the manufacturers wrap themselves lovingly around their slender curves. Their permanented heads, frizzy with curls, daringly took the sun and the wind, and their tanned young legs were innocent of stockings. They gathered in groups, chattering shrilly and laughing loudly, conscious of the boys gathered in similar groups on the other side of the yard. In a single, lucid moment Miss Willie knew the aching excitement they were feeling, and her mouth trembled into a smile when one girl's laugh rang high above the others. It was so important to be noticed!

The men, Miss Willie noted, were not so sharply delineated as the women. Most of them were in faded but clean overalls and

57

denim shirts. A few, like Hod, had on fresh white shirts and slacks, but none had on coats or ties.

The boys, like the girls, bloomed colorfully. Their shirts were gay checked and plaid sports shirts, and a few had even braved the heat in loud blue, green, or brown coats.

A battered old Ford drove up and two men got out, reaching into the back of the car for their guitars. "That's the Johnson brothers," Mary whispered. "They're to lead the singing today."

They greeted people with loud howdies, circling around the crowd. Then there was a general movement toward the doors, and a breaking up of the smaller groups. Hod came back from taking the baskets to the picnic grove and helped Mary from the car. "About time to start," he said. "We might as well go inside."

At the door they stopped a moment, and Miss Willie saw that the men were all seating themselves on one side of the room, the women on the other. She looked questioningly at Mary, whose eyes were twinkling. "That's the way it's done down here," she said, putting her hand under Miss Willie's elbow and urging her gently toward the women's side. She spoke over her shoulder at Hod. "See you at noon."

He nodded. "Try to save me some of your things," he said.

Mary smiled and motioned him away. He joined the men across the wide aisle, and Mary and Miss Willie seated themselves beside Hattie and Becky.

Miss Willie looked around. The chapel was small, but it was light and airy and pleasantly clean. The walls were pine, painted white, cut by long, narrow windows which let in broad beams of sunlight. At the front of the room a platform was built up about a foot higher than the floor. A lectern made of stained pine boards sat near the front of the platform. The benches upon which they sat were sawed, ten-inch white pine planks, and one rail had been nailed to uprights at intervals to form a back. For an all-day singing this was going to be powerfully hard, thought Miss Willie.

There was some milling and stirring on the platform, and almost immediately the Johnson men, who were tall, lanky, and rawboned, were passing out songbooks. Miss Willie took one and passed the stack on down the row. She looked at it curiously. It was a pink, paper-backed book with *Gospel Tide* written across the front in tall letters. Inside the cover, the title page carried the legend "Stamps-Baxter Music and Printing Co., Inc. Price, 35 cents a copy. Shaped notes." She opened the book to the first song. Shaped notes. She had heard her father talk of the old hymnbooks when he was a boy. They had shaped notes. But this was the first time she had ever seen one. The notes were really shaped, then. Some were full diamonds, some half diamonds. Some were full squares, others were triangles. Some were full circles, others were half circles. But what did they mean? She nudged Mary and pointed to the notes.

Mary whispered behind her hand. "Each shape represents a tone. Do, re, mi, fa, sol, la, ti, do."

Miss Willie scanned the hymn. She shook her head. "I never would get it straight. Why aren't the notes of the scale just as simple to learn?"

"Because they're fixed tones. This way, 'do' is always the key-note of the song. In whatever key the song is written . . . here, I'll show you. Here's one written in B-flat. B is 'do' in that song."

Miss Willie puzzled over it a moment, then she giggled. "That doesn't make it any simpler."

The tallest and lankest of the Johnson brothers stepped to the front of the platform, announced the song, made a little pep talk, and lifted his arm for the down beat. The guitar-playing brother threw his head back and swallowed his Adam's apple and plucked a rich chord from the instrument. A thrill of anticipation ran over Miss Willie. Now she would hear some real old country singing!

The volume of sound was terrific! Everybody knew the song and there wasn't a silent soul in the house. The full impact of a hundred voices raised in unison, each to its loudest pitch, struck Miss Willie without warning. Involuntarily she shrank from it, and in spite of herself her hands lifted toward her ears. She glanced sidewise at Mary, and felt Mary's tremble of laughter, then she set herself to endure it. Singing? Well, that was one name for it!

The leader's brassy baritone brayed out over the heads of the people. Apparently he must be heard over the other ninety-nine! But they must make the effort to drown him out! Loudly, stridently, nasally, the voices filled the house, the women's with a high, whiny whang; the men's with a bellowing, grating harshness. The rhythm was broken into short, choppy phrases, and there was never the slightest degree of feeling for the words, nor the slightest shading of tones. There was perfect time, perfect harmony, on a dull, flat, monotonous plane.

To Miss Willie's ear, trained to Bach, Handel, Haydn, and Mozart in church, this was a travesty of all sacred music. She had listened too long to exquisite and singing blending of tones, to high, exulting sweeps of emotion, to perfect poetry of feeling, to accept this as music. These people knew shaped notes, it was true. Most could read them and carry a tune. They had a sense of rhythm. But they could neither sing nor make real music. She felt flattened by the force of the noise, and by the end of the first song she knew that the day would be torture for her. Four verses of that high nasal whanging told her that. When the brassy, harsh voices came to the end of the song and held the last flat note dully, Miss Willie shuddered. She would have Hod teach her this do, re, mi business, and they would see about some singing in the schoolroom! At least her pupils were going to know the difference between good singing and bad singing!

Only once after that was Miss Willie really stirred, and her Calvinistic soul denounced that as a sort of sacrilegious stirring. The Johnson brothers announced they were going to do a special number. "Hit's real easy-like. You've heared it over the radio, likely. Hit's called the 'Golden Boogie.'"

Dude Johnson tuned the guitar, twanging the strings noisily; then he bent low over the instrument and, cuddling it close, picked a chord from its bosom — a chord so infinitely soft that it floated into the air and brushed the ear like a butterfly wing resting on a honeysuckle bloom. Then he straightened and sent his fingers solemnly walking up the neck of the guitar in a slow boogie rhythm that was purposefully solid and sweet. He grinned at the crowd.

Brent was twitching his hips and shuffling his feet. He bent over and clapped his hands together. Straightening, he flung his arms wide, and the guitar-playing brother broke his walking fingers into a run:

60

"When the bells are ringin' all the folks start flockin',
When the bells are ringin' all the folks start rockin',
Flockin' and arockin', rockin' and aflockin',
To the golden, gospel bells.

"When the bells are ringin' sinners all start shoutin',
When the bells are ringin' Satan, he starts routin',
Shoutin' and aroutin', routin' and ashoutin',
To the golden, gospel bells."

"C'mon, ever'body!" the man shouted, "you know the tune by now, c'mon an' join in!"

Laughing, the crowd picked up the solid beat and began chanting the words, their bodies swaying. Somewhere in the back hands began to clap softly. The sound spread and swelled and was like the beat of a drum, sharp and regular. Miss Willie was horrified! Boogie! "Golden Boogie"! The idea! But the rhythm was so contagious, the beat so solid, the glory so infectious, that she found herself swinging along with the crowd, her foot tapping in time, her hands clapping along with the rest. It reminded her of the old-time Negro camp meetings. All it needed was old fat Angeline cutting a buck and wing!

And then it was noon and time for the picnic dinner.

The picnic ground was a grassy plot to one side of the yard. The trees formed an arch over it so that it was heavy with shade. In this shade and on the grass the women had spread white cloths in a long streamer, and then the food from all the baskets had been set out upon them. The folks gathered around, children greedily eying everything, plotting, while they waited for the blessing, what pieces of chicken and what big chunks of cake they were going to get. The older people lined up on both sides and stood quietly. Brent Johnson lifted his hand. "I'm goin' to ask Gault Pierce to say grace."

Gault's deep voice rumbled forth unhesitatingly. Miss Willie knew that the ease with which he prayed came from long experience. So had her father prayed at the table. No doubt Gault's voice was lifted in thanks to his Maker at every meal in his house, and so comfortable was he in conversation with Him that the presence of others did not dismay him.

61

At the end of the brief prayer Brent Johnson took charge again. "Now ever'body eat hearty. They's aplenty fer all. Pitch in an' fill yerselves up, an' then we'll call intermission until two o'clock to let it settle. Don't nobody stand back an' be bashful. Ever'body he'p theirselves."

No one needed urging. Mary took two of the paper plates she had brought and filled them, giving them to Hod and Miss Willie. She laughed as she handed his to Hod. "All of that's mine," she said. "Isn't it flattering, Miss Willie, to have your husband like your cooking so well he won't eat anyone else's?"

"You like it," Hod grunted, gnawing on a chicken leg.

"There's Wells," Mary said, and, standing, she waved across the crowd. "Come on over, Wells."

Miss Willie watched him as he made his way around the end of the table, laughing and joking with the men as he passed. Like the other men, he had on faded, patched overalls. Patched, more than likely, by his own hands, Miss Willie thought, as she noticed the long, uneven stitches. His shirt was a blue denim, open at the throat and laid back from his strong, short neck. The shirt had been smoothed by an iron not too hot, for it was still wrinkled, but it was clean and the man himself looked soaped and scrubbed. His powerful, broad shoulders stretched the stuff of his shirt tight at the seams, and where his sleeves were rolled back, his arms emerged thick, heavy, and muscular. They were matted with a mesh of sun-bleached hair, wiry and golden against his brown skin.

As he came up to them he shoved his hat back on his head and ran his hand over his face. "Howdy, folks," he greeted them. "Ain't seen you all in some time. Didn't know whether you'd git over here today or not. This yer aunt, Mary?"

Miss Willie winced at his grammar.

"Yes, this is Miss Willie, Wells. Wells is Hod's cousin, Miss Willie, and he's a very important man to you. He's one of the school trustees, so you'd better do a little bowing and scraping."

Wells laughed and held out his hand. "I don't reckon she's goin' to be able to do much bowin' an' scrapin' with that plate full o' stuff in her hands. Howdy, ma'am. I'm powerful glad yer here. I been aimin' to git over to make you welcome, but I been right busy lately. We're bankin' a lot on you this year down at the school."

Miss Willie set her plate down and took his hand. It was a square, brown hand, with a horny palm which felt rough and hard to her own. She liked the firm clasp of it. It seemed friendly and solid, somehow. She liked, too, his brown, sunny face, open and merry and genial. Don't be an arrogant fool, she chided herself. Of course he talks like the rest of the ridge folks. How else would you expect him to talk! Here is a good man, her thoughts went on. Good like Hod is good. Honorable, gentle, and kindly. She noticed his eyes, warm, brown eyes set far apart, frank and sweet. Yes, here was a good man.

"Don't look for too much, Mr. Pierce," she said, wanting honestly that he should know she admitted of human frailty. "I'm afraid Mary has led you to think too highly of me. This will be a new experience for me, and I am very likely to make many mistakes."

"Why, shore," he said cordially, "ain't nobody but makes mistakes. More'n likely you'll make yore share. But the main thing is yer a good teacher, an' a good teacher is a good teacher wherever you put her. What I had in mind to say, though, was to tell you to call on me fer e'er thing you need. I ain't so wearied about you makin' mistakes as I am you'll git so disgusted with us you won't stay. If e'er thing comes up to weary you, jist holler, an' I'll come arunnin'. Mary an' me, we cooked up this scheme, an' we feel honor bound to stand back of you. Bein's you was good enough to come when we ast you. My kids, some of 'em, will be in yer school, an' I'd like to say right now I don't want none of 'em givin' you no trouble. If they do, jist light into 'em an' frail the dickens outen 'em. They's some you cain't. Folks is tetchy. But I'm aimin' fer mine to respect the teacher. An' I ain't goin' to stand fer no foolishment from 'em."

"I hope that won't be necessary," said Miss Willie, who had never frailed the dickens out of one of her pupils in her life.

"Did the children come with you, Wells?" asked Mary.

"No. They went over to Manthy's yesterday. She was aimin' to take 'em to the county seat to git their school clothes, an' she allowed she'd keep 'em the night. Hod, gimme some o' that food 'fore you eat it all up!"

"Nobody's holding you back," Hod said, making way for him by his side. "You heard what Brent said. Plenty for all."

"They'll be aplenty gone 'fore long, too," Wells laughed. He filled a plate and moved over to squat by Hod.

Miss Willie looked at the short, solid figure squatting there, and she felt a great tenderness for him and a deep respect. Four — well, three — motherless children to care for, and he could keep a placid poise that turned a laughing face to the world. Whatever his own sense of loss, and whatever his deepest confusion, he had not allowed them to shadow his life.

She felt again her own restlessness, and she wondered if there were times when he felt completely alone and unanchored. He was not an insensitive man, she knew, so his hurt must have bitten deep. But he had laid it over with the necessities of fatherhood, and had not allowed its acid to etch into the core of his being. Or perhaps the sweetness of his memories was enough for him. After all, wasn't most of life remembering?

The women had begun to gather up the scraps of food, repacking baskets and piling the refuse in heaps. Mary moved over to help. "I must get my things," she said. "I'm going to pack all this stuff in one big basket and make Wells take it home with him. The children will enjoy it."

Becky came up just then, and Miss Willie stayed to talk with her. "Have you started my rugs yet, Becky?" she asked.

"Oh, I got one about done," Becky said, smoothing her apron. "Hit don't take me no time to whip up a braided rug. How big you want 'em?"

Miss Willie thought for a moment. "About four by six, I guess. If I put one in the front of the room and one by the stove, that ought to do."

Becky nodded. "That's jist about what I figgered. I'll have 'em done fer you 'fore school starts. How're you likin' the singin'?"

"I'm liking it a lot," Miss Willie answered.

"This ain't a really good singin'," Becky said, apologetically. "Them Johnson boys cain't lead near so good as Ferdy Jones over on the ridge, or Wells or Hod, neither. I jist wisht they'd let Wells an' Hod git up there . . . they'd show 'em up in no

64

time."

"Why, I didn't know Hod could lead singing!"

"Yes," Becky said, and her mouth was prim with pride. "Yes, he's follered leadin' singin' sincet he was jist a boy. Hit comes natural with him. All the Pierces is good at it."

"And Wells too?"

"Wells is actual better'n Hod. But then he's older — he'd ort to be. Ifen you kin git Wells an' Hod an' Ferdy Jones, an' Matt Jasper fer the tenor, I've heared folks say they ain't no better singin' anywheres in the world."

"Matt Jasper!"

Becky nodded vigorously. "He's got about the truest tenor in these parts. Used to sing a heap. But you cain't hardly git him to no more. Hit's worth listenin' to when you kin."

The therapy of music! Where had it failed with Matt Jasper? Or had it been drowned in the faithlessness of life for him? What fears had he known that kept him from standing before his friends in pride, winsomely lifting the sweetness of his voice before the altar of their approval? Hod had said Matt Jasper had once been a good-looking man . . . and now Becky said he had the truest tenor in these parts. How much the iron of degradation must have seared his soul! Like a leper he was scarred by his disease, and like a leper he must walk before the world crying: "Unclean! Unclean!"

Miss Willie turned her thoughts from him with an effort. "Becky," she said, "I must find a place to live. Do you know of a family on the ridge who has room for me?"

"Why, ain't you goin' to live with Hod an' Mary?" Becky asked.

"No. I may be here several years, and it wouldn't be right to stay with them that long. Besides, I'm more comfortable in my own place."

Becky was silent for a time. She fingered the frill of her apron and eyed Miss Willie askance. She cleared her throat several times, and finally, ducking her head, she said: "You kin stay with me, ifen yer a mind to. I'd like it a heap myself."

"Why, Becky, how wonderful! I was thinking it might take me several weeks to find a place, and here you make room for me the very first thing! I'd like it a heap myself, Becky. When can I come?"

"E'er time you say. Ain't no reason I know of you cain't come on over tomorrer."

"No, not tomorrow," Miss Willie said. "I have to get Hod to take me to town first, and pick up my boxes and trunks and things. But when we've done that, I'll move right in. How good you are to let me stay with you!"

Becky's eyes were fixed on her feet. "Hit ain't good," she blurted out. "I liked you the first time I laid eyes on you. I was awishin' you'd be clost enough I could see you ever' day. Hit's me I'm a thinkin' of. They's other places you'd maybe ruther stay, an' maybe like better. But I've sich a likin' fer yer company, I made bold to offer you to stay with me. Hit'll be sich a mort o' pleasure fer me."

Miss Willie was touched. "It'll be company for me too, Becky. And I thank you for wanting me. Now I'd better help Mary before she gets everything done."

There wasn't much difference, after all, Miss Willie thought, between Billy Norton, who grabbed at crayons, and Becky, who grabbed at friendship. The same essential loneliness moved them both. That loneliness which pervaded all mankind, which was inherent at the partition of birth and was never assuaged until death sent the spirit back into the darkness of time from which it had come.

Again Miss Willie had the feeling of being led. There was something she and Becky could give each other.

CHAPTER

❧ 7 ❧

Miss Willie, you can't stay with Becky." Mary was vehement in her protest. "Becky has only two rooms. It's physically impossible!"

"But, Mary, why should she offer to let me have a room! I just don't understand." Things had taken a bewildering turn. Miss Willie had been so pleased to have this arrangement with Becky. She had spoken of it to Mary confidently, happy to have it

66

settled, and feeling certain that, since Gault was Hod's uncle, he and Mary would approve. Mary had been dismayed.

"Becky didn't tell you she had a spare room, did she?" she wanted to know.

"No," Miss Willie admitted, "not actually. Not in so many words. But surely she would know I meant . . . why, she wouldn't possibly think of having me in her own room!"

Mary laughed. "In hers and Gault's, you mean. That's just what she did mean, though. It wouldn't occur to Becky that there was anything improper in your sleeping in the extra bed in her front room. That's her sitting room, parlor, and bedroom. Here on the ridge, when people come to spend the night, they occupy whatever beds are available. It doesn't matter if there are two or even three in one room. Neither does it matter if men occupy one bed and women and children the others. Darkness is their privacy."

Miss Willie was aghast, and she pushed her glasses up on her nose in agitation. "What in the world shall I do? I might spend *one* night like that, but I can't spend months in such a situation. My goodness, Mary, it's positively uncivilized! Oh, I should have let you and Hod make some arrangement for me! I had no business to go barging ahead like that!"

They were sitting on the screened porch where Mary had brought her churning, and Miss Willie was sorting over Hod's socks in the big darning basket. She pushed the needle unhappily through a huge hole. "What are we going to do about Becky?"

Mary lifted the churn lid to peer inside. "It's nowhere near come," and she replaced the lid and started the dasher going again. It made a comfortable slushing noise, cavernous and full. "One of us will just have to tell her it's impossible. Because you simply can't do it. I'm afraid her feelings may be hurt too. She's such a queer little person. I don't even pretend to understand her. She's so withdrawn and remote . . . always wears those black dresses. Goes around so quietly."

"Wonder why."

"I don't know. Nobody knows a lot about Becky, to tell the truth. Hod's mother says Gault brought her home one day and said they were married. None of them had ever seen her or heard of her before. She came from over near Elkhorn somewhere in

67

those hills. And the only folks she seems to have is a sister over there she goes back to see occasionally. I've always felt there's a mystery somewhere about Becky. But if there is, it belongs to her. And she's a good, dear soul in her own way."

Miss Willie was silent. The morning was soft and still. Down the hollow an amethyst haze hung over the wrinkling hills. The sun was lazy getting up over the ridge, and the grass and bushes were still sparkling with the heavy dew. Hod's dog, old Duke, came around the corner of the house and dropped his fat, ancient body heavily to the ground.

They were quiet for a time, Mary shoving the churn dasher up and down, Miss Willie pushing her needle back and forth. Then she let the darning drop in her lap. "We're not going to hurt Becky's feelings, Mary," she said. "I'll move up there and something will happen. I can manage for several nights and then we'll see. But whatever else I do, I am not going to disappoint Becky. Her face positively beamed when I was talking to her. It would be like punishing a child to take her pleasure away from her."

"Miss Willie, really you can't do it. Hod will be able to tell her so that she'll understand."

Miss Willie shook her head. "Oh, I'm sure she could be made to understand. But all the understanding in the world wouldn't keep her from being disappointed. By now she has it all planned and she's probably been cleaning and polishing that room until it shines. No. I got myself into this and I'll get myself out of it. How, I don't know. I think I'll leave that to the Lord. He should have been watching me a little closer anyhow!"

Mary got up and moved toward the door. "I've got to get some water to make that butter come," she said. "That's a pretty large order for the Lord, Miss Willie. You don't know what you're getting into!"

Hod added his word to Mary's that night. "I aimed to speak to Ma, Miss Willie," he said. "They've got an extra room now that Irma and I are both married and Gramma's gone. You would be comfortable there, and you'd have a place for your books and things. Becky meant well, but she'll understand. I can tell her you have to have a place to read and study. I don't believe she'd be the least bit hurt."

Miss Willie shook her head. "No," she said. "I spoke impulsively to Becky, but the more I think of it, the more I believe there is a reason for my going there. I don't see it clearly just yet, and I don't know how I'll manage, but it will work out. Things usually do, if you give them time."

Mary was near tears. "Miss Willie, you have no idea . . . you just don't know . . ."

Miss Willie laughed. "Then I'll find out. Now don't fret over it any more. I'm going to pack tonight, and Hod can drive me up there tomorrow. I want to get settled before school starts."

When she went to her room, Hod puffed on his pipe and scratched at old Duke's ears. The dog thumped his tail gently against the floor. "Kinda hardheaded, isn't she?"

Mary gathered up her sewing and crammed it into the basket. "No," she said slowly, "not really. She just has a strong sense of duty."

"Becky's part of her duty now?"

"Yes. I talked too much today."

It was left that way, and the next afternoon when he came in from the fields, Hod drove Miss Willie and her luggage and her boxes of books up the ridge. "Well, it's just a whoop and a holler down to our place, Miss Willie," he assured her; "you can run down to see Mary any time you like, and she can come up to visit you. But I hope you get something better worked out before long."

Becky was on the porch, and she rose to greet them. "Come in," she called heartily, "come in. Hod, I'll fetch ye a cheer."

"Not for me," Hod said, "I've got to get on back. I just came to bring your new boarder. I'll unload these things and then I've got to get along home."

"I was lookin' fer you," Becky said to Miss Willie. "I allowed you'd be along this evenin'. I've got the place redded up an' supper's a waitin'."

69

"That's nice, Becky," Miss Willie answered. "Where shall Hod put my things?"

Hod had set two large bags on the porch and he was dragging out the cartons of books. "Is all them your'n?" Becky wanted to know. "Law, I knowed in reason you'd have a suitcase, but I never thought on you havin' sich a passel o' stuff as that! We'll make room fer 'em, though. Jist set 'em here on the porch, Hod. Miss Willie kin figger out where she wants to put 'em inside."

Miss Willie thought of her trunk, which was still at Mary's, and the packing boxes of small articles she had brought from home — an Italian print she especially loved; a quaint old wine flask which she used to hold flowers; a cloisonné box; a piece of tapestry; an India shawl that she had liked; and a jade figurine. Small things which she had thought would help make a room into a home. Well, they could stay where they were until she could see her way more clearly. This was enough for now.

When Hod left, Becky led the way inside. It was a sparsely furnished room that Miss Willie saw, the two beds standing in opposite corners. A few chairs and a dresser and an old tin trunk were the extent of its furnishings. Becky's braided rugs were scattered about, and the stone of the huge fireplace had been freshly whitewashed. An old clock ticked peacefully on the mantel, and above it hung a framed sampler, its faded red stitches praying, "God bless our home."

"This here bed's your'n," Becky said, pointing to the farthest one from the fireplace. "Gault, he allus likes to sleep clost to the fire. I cleaned out the bottom drawer of the bureau fer you, but I don't reckon hit'll be enough fer all them things you got. Mebbe we kin clean out that there trunk tomorrer. I keep my rags fer my rugs in it, but I kin put them somewheres else."

"Don't worry about it, Becky," Miss Willie said, "I'll keep my things in my bags until we decide about something. I'll just bring them in and slide them under my bed. And the boxes are full of books. They can stay in the boxes for a while. We'll just shove them back on the porch for tonight."

"Well. Hit don't look like rain, an' they ain't e'er thing to bother 'em. Ifen you don't need 'em, we'll jist leave 'em be till mornin'. Now, supper's a waitin'. I'll go call Gault, an' then we'll

70

eat. The wash place is right by the door here in the kitchen," she called back, "reckon you'll be wantin' to wash up."

Miss Willie followed her to the kitchen and dabbled her fingers in the cool water Becky poured for her. "Ain't you goin' to wash yer face?" she asked when Miss Willie reached for the towel.

Obediently Miss Willie bent her face over the basin. Dear Lord, she thought, just help me get through these next few days . . . and let something turn up mighty quick!

When Gault came in, he and Miss Willie sat down to the table. He was a tall man and thin, but there was no stoop in his broad shoulders. His frame was big without being massive, and was as flat as a strap. He had a shock of iron-gray hair, which he had dampened and combed at the wash bench before coming in, but Miss Willie knew by its look that it was coarse and unruly and that usually it sprang up like bleached straw over his head. His face was thin, deeply tanned, and seamed with lines. There was a kindly look in his eyes, and his full underlip kept his mouth from being severe. Here was a man of conviction, she thought, poised in his assurance of himself, and quiet in his unquestioning faith.

Gault bent his head and quietly blessed the Lord for his care of them and asked him to use them in his service. Miss Willie liked his voice and the way he spoke. There was no unctuous holiness in his prayer; it was a friendly, manly thank-you, and a recognition of his obligation in return. When they lifted their heads, Gault turned to her. "Now, jist fall to an' he'p yerself, Miss Willie. I reckon Becky's got plenty, an' if she ain't, we'll git it."

The table was burdened with food — fried chicken, green beans, creamed corn, pickles, stewed tomatoes, half a dozen jars of jelly and preserves, fruit pies stacked twelve inches high, and a tall four-layer cake. There were two kinds of bread, corn bread and biscuits, and Becky diffidently offered boughten bread in addition. "Knowin' you was used to it, I thought to git some from the huckster yesterday," she explained.

"Now, don't buy special things for me," Miss Willie said. And then, noticing that Becky was standing to one side of the table, she asked, "Aren't you going to eat now?"

71

"I'll wait on you all," Becky said.

"We can wait on ourselves," Miss Willie protested, "come on and sit down with us."

Becky looked at Gault out of the corner of her eye. Gault was taking out generous helpings of food on his plate. Without pausing, he said quietly: "Hit's a woman's place to wait on her menfolks. Becky'll eat when we git done."

Miss Willie choked and coughed.

"Git Miss Willie a glass o' water, Becky," Gault directed. "She's got somethin' down her Sunday throat."

When the meal was finished, Gault went outside to finish up the chores. The evening light was fading and the kitchen was dim and pleasant. Miss Willie sat on at the table. Becky fussed around the stove and took up the remainder of the food. "Now you go on inside," she said, "an' set down. I'll jist eat a bite an' red up in here."

"No," answered Miss Willie. "I'll sit here with you. It's nicer. And then I'll help you wash the dishes."

"Oh, I didn't aim to set down. I mostly eat comin' an' goin'. I jist nibble on somethin' while I'm doin' up the work."

"Well, you're not going to nibble on something tonight! You sit right down at this table. I'm going to wait on you!"

Becky's mouth dropped, and then she laughed. "Law, Miss Willie, you've got the quarest idees. Why, they ain't nobody waited on me sincet I was a young'un."

"It's time they started, then. Now sit down. What do you want to drink?"

Becky sat down and filled her plate. "I reckon I'll take buttermilk." She sighed. "Ain't this nice? To be asettin' here with someone to talk to? I knowed in reason you was goin' to be a pleasure to me, but you ain't called to wait on me. I don't know as Gault'd like it."

"What Gault doesn't know won't hurt him," snapped Miss Willie. "A woman's place to wait on her menfolks, my eye!"

"Don't you go gittin' Gault's back up, Miss Willie," Becky warned. "He's easygoin' mostly, but he's got some strong idees about wimmin."

"I've got some strong ideas about men too. But I'll not anger

72

him if I can help it."

When Becky had finished, she took the two water buckets from the wash shelf. "I've got to git up the night water," she said, "down at the spring. You jist git you a cheer an' rest yerself."

"I'll go with you."

"Now, they ain't no call in you doin' that. Hit's jist a steep old pull back up that hill from the spring. Hit'll jist git you all winded."

"No, I want to go. I can carry one bucket."

Becky gave in and handed Miss Willie a bucket. They crossed the yard and followed a winding path through the back pasture to the edge of the hill. They came then to a barbed-wire fence, and Becky set her bucket down and rolled expertly under the fence. "Keerful," she warned Miss Willie. "Don't git yer dress caught an' rip it. I been after Gault hit's untellin' the times to make me a gate in this here fence, but jist looks like it goes in one ear an' out the other'n. I don't rightly mind packin' water from the spring. Hit's good water, an' cold, an' not too fur to be unhandy. But I shore git almighty tard o' rollin' under that there bob-war fence!"

Miss Willie scrambled under the wire and looked back at the fence. "How long have you been carrying water from the spring, Becky?"

Becky's face showed her surprise. "How long? Why, ever sincet me an' Gault was married. Twenty-five year, I reckon."

Miss Willie started to speak, but she thought better of it. She was too new yet on the ridge to speak her mind plainly.

When they were back at the house Miss Willie was winded and her arm was aching from the long climb with a heavy water bucket. They lighted a lamp and washed the dishes in its soft yellow glow. There was a contentment in the familiar task, and the big room enfolded them gently. Miss Willie hummed as she put the plates and bowls in the corner cupboard, and she smiled when she caught Becky's eye. "You're going to be a pleasure to me too, Becky," she said warmly. And Becky ducked her head and scrubbed a knife vigorously.

When Gault came in, they went in the other room, and Becky lighted another lamp. "I kin see to read by this 'un," Gault said,

73

"no need wastin' coal oil."

"I jist thought mebbe Miss Willie'd like more light," Becky answered.

Gault looked at Miss Willie across the room inquiringly. She shook her head. "No. You needn't light another lamp for me, Becky."

Becky turned the lamp down and blew the small flame out. The room was dimmed and muted around them. Gault took a large book from the mantel and went back to his chair. He opened the book and thumbed through it, and then, finding his place, cleared his throat. "We allus foller readin' the Scriptures 'fore goin' to bed," he explained.

"I'd like to listen," Miss Willie assured him.

He put on a pair of glasses and settled them on his nose. Involuntarily Miss Willie pushed her own in place more firmly.

"I'm a readin' from The Book of Isaiah, the sixth, seventh, and eighth chapters. We read straight through the Bible ever' year. Three chapters on weekdays, an' five on Sundays." He cleared his throat again and began. " 'In the year that king Uzziah died I saw also the Lord sitting upon a throne, high and lifted up, and his train filled the temple.' "

The vision of Isaiah! Gault's voice was unusually beautiful . . . deep, slow, and rich. He never stumbled over the words, and he gave them a cadence properly belonging to their poetry. " 'I heard the voice of the Lord, saying, Whom shall I send, and who will go for us? Then said I, Here am I; send me.' "

That's for me, Miss Willie thought. She remembered hearing the words when she was a child. A visiting missionary was preaching in her father's pulpit. He had talked of his field in China, speaking with passion of the people and their needs . . . pleading for help for them. "Here am I; send me." Miss Willie had sat tensely in the front row, echoing the words in her heart. That had been her moment of dedication. "Here am I; send me" . . . and she had consecrated her life from that time to the high purpose of ministering to the Chinese. That she had been thwarted she felt was the Lord's will. He had other work for her to do. And now, after all those years, she felt again a moment of dedication. This might not be China, but the needs of these people were just as great.

When Gault finished the reading, she leaned forward in her chair. "That was beautiful, Gault. Thank you for reading that portion of Isaiah tonight. It has always been one of my favorite passages."

"The Scriptures is all good readin'," he reminded her, putting his glasses away. "You kin turn out the light now, Becky."

Becky looked at Miss Willie. "Is they e'er thing you want outen them bags, Miss Willie?"

Miss Willie was startled. "Are you going to bed now?" she asked.

Gault was already slipping off his shoes. "They ain't no reason to stay up, fur as I kin tell. The beasts an' the fowls is a sleepin', an' man had best be gittin' his rest too."

Miss Willie drew a deep breath. "Just let me get a few things, Becky," she said. "It won't take me a minute."

She took a nightgown from her bag, and looked wildly at her toothbrush. Better let my teeth go tonight, she thought. It would be just like that old coot to turn the light out on me while I was brushing them. Becky waited patiently.

"All right, Becky."

"Ain't you goin' to take yer hair down?"

"Oh, yes, I forgot." She looked over at Gault's corner, but he was winding the clock. She slipped the pins out and let the long loops fall over her shoulders.

"Ain't it purty," Becky said, reaching out her hand and touching it. "I jist knowed it would be soft an' fine like that. Jist like a little girl's. I was hopin' you'd take it down where I could see."

Gault was fidgeting and Miss Willie hastily braided it. "I'll not brush it tonight," she said. "Now you can turn the light out, Becky."

"Let me git me a chaw o' terbaccer," Becky said to Gault. She glanced apologetically at Miss Willie. "I allus have to have a leetle piece to go to bed on."

O Lord, Miss Willie thought. Just get me out of this in a hurry! Just get me out of here!

75

In the darkness Miss Willie took off her outer clothes and slipped the nightgown over her head. Under its cover she timidly removed her underwear. Her hands shook, and she hurried to crawl into bed. She had trouble finding the sheets, and then she realized that there was only one sheet and it was on the bottom. A light quilt was the covering.

What *is* this mattress made of, she thought, as it rustled and gave beneath her. It must be hay, or straw, she decided. Over in the other corner she could hear Gault and Becky settling themselves. This is indecent, she thought. Positively indecent! Even in China perfect strangers don't sleep in the same room! Or do they? If Louise Wright could see me now! And suddenly she giggled. Indecent or not, it certainly would make a wonderful story to tell.

I'll never go to sleep, her mind wandered on. It's far too early. She turned on her side. Her bed was drawn up under the window and the night sky leaned intimately down. The thin crescent moon of last week had swelled to adolescence, and it hung naïvely over the far-flung stars. The air was clean-smelling and fresh. She listened to the night sounds, thinking how little they disturbed the tranquil peace. From a pasture down the ridge came the muffled tones of a bell, swinging in staccato rhythm. Near at hand there was the sweet, sleepy twittering of birds and the drowsy monotone of cicadas. Miss Willie tucked one hand under her cheek like a tired little girl, and slept.

CHAPTER
❦ 8 ❦

SEVERAL DAYS PASSED in the slow cadence of summer. The mornings were light and unburdened. Dawn came quickly up here on top the ridge, the sun heaving itself powerfully up over the eastern rim of trees. Miss Willie stood on the porch watching its round, disklike edges cut through the thin pink sky, waited for the pale pastel streaks to deepen and darken, and felt the sweeping climax of the morning as the full red ball lifted itself clear of the hills, majestically diminishing the heavens. The pale greens and pinks and smoky grays were washed out by its radiance, and only the blue of space sustained its brilliant gold. Far down in the valleys the mists smoked hazily, curling under the increasing light toward the tops of the hills. Each morning was a new delight to Miss Willie. And each morning she claimed this time as her own, while Becky and Gault were busy with chores.

Later, the air became somnolent and sluggish, and they moved lazily about the tasks of the day. Gault came in for dinner and slept through the heat, rising in late afternoon to go back to the fields. Becky moved like a shadow about the house.

The evenings were another miracle of quiet, blued by dusk and the darkening sky. Then the hills seemed ancient and tired, resting tranquilly in a hushed stillness, waiting for the transmuting of night. In that brief time between twilight and dark, before the sounds of night began, Miss Willie felt caught up in the transcendent moment, lifted above and beyond time and space. She had a feeling of absolute stillness within herself . . . an absence of all unrest and conflict. Always one thought came to her at this time: "Be still, and know that I am God."

That moment broke with the stirring of the leaves in a lifting air, for with the breeze came the first notes of the evening nocturne — the call of a mourning dove; the high, descending lyrics of the whippoorwill; the low, insistent drone of the insects; and the deep bass drum of the frogs.

Later, there was the ordeal of going to bed in the same room with Gault and Becky. But Miss Willie had lessened it by staying outside long past their bedtime, thus gaining for herself a measure of privacy. And, she said to herself honestly, one gets used to anything.

It was the first of July when she said to Becky one morning that she was going to walk down into the hollow back of the house. She had wandered down the road in both directions, and across the fields to each side of the house, but down the steep hill past the spring lay an unexplored land.

"They ain't nothin' down there but rubble an' weeds," objected Becky. "You'll jist git yerself het up fer nothin'."

"Well, I want to see," Miss Willie answered. "I like to know what's all around me."

77

She borrowed one of Becky's bonnets and crawled through the fence of the back lot and made her way down the steep slope. She was disappointed in what she found, for, as Becky had said, there was nothing to be seen but gravelly ledges and waist-high growths of weeds.

Turning back, she climbed the hill, arriving at the top breathless and hot. She went through the barnyard again, and under the shade of a big walnut tree stood fanning herself with the bonnet. That's funny, she thought. I haven't seen that little log house there before. And then she noticed that the woodshed stood between it and the house. She walked over to it, curious as to its purpose. It was small, not more than twelve feet square, but it was complete with roof and chimney. Its high windows were empty and open, and the door sagged on rusty hinges. Except for a few places the chinking was still good, and along one wall an ancient and untidy rosebush climbed sturdily.

She peered in through the gaping door and saw that it was filled with odds and ends of junk — old broken furniture, pieces of rusted farm equipment, harnesses, stacks of feed, and so forth. Gault must use this for a storeroom, she thought. She was turning to go when the idea struck her: Why couldn't this little cabin be made into a home for her! She could still take her meals with Becky. And maybe Gault would let her use wood from his woodpile this winter. She could learn to build a fire. It would be worth cold mornings to have her own place! If Gault just had some other place he could put all that stuff!

Excitedly she squeezed past the sagging door and picked her way over the piles of feed and other things. The floor was still good. A board or two missing and several places that needed repairing. But it would do. She looked at the walls and quickly decided that wallboard would be the quickest and best way to take care of them. Painted white, she thought. Leave those beams too, but ceil the inside of the roof. The fireplace was filled with heaps of rubbish, but it looked all right. Paint the stones white, ruffle that old mantel with unbleached muslin, tie muslin curtains at the windows. Two of Becky's rugs on the floor. The idea was fast taking hold of her.

Gingerly she poked and prodded at the furniture. There was

78

an old wooden bed leaning against one wall. She pinched her lip between her fingers and studied it. Wash it down with soap and water and give it a coat of shellac, new springs and mattress. There was a table in the corner. She ran her finger over it, then hastily picked up a feed sack and cleaned the dust off the top surface. "Why, it's cherry," she said. It's a beautiful drop-leaf cherry table! Her excitement mounted. There was a rocker too, with the springs sagging and the cushion frayed. A spoke or two was gone in the back, but it would sit there by the fire on long winter evenings and gently rock the hours away. Oh, this was perfect! This was the answer. This would make a lovely home.

Everyone on the ridge helped get Miss Willie's house ready for her. The womenfolks came with scrub brushes and strong lye soap and soft, clean rags. They scoured and mopped and cleaned until the little cabin was spotless. Then Wells Pierce came, and Hod, with saws and hammers and nails, and soon the floor was whole, new windows were in place, the roof mended, and the clean white wallboards nailed over the old logs.

Miss Willie worked on the furniture with paint remover out under the big walnut tree, and was filled with joy when the soft patina of old cherry emerged, not only on the table, but also on the old bed. She exclaimed over its rich depth, and ran her hands lovingly down the sweetly curving posts. "Oh, it's beautiful!" she cried. "See how lovely it is!"

The table was mended and rubbed down with wax, and it took on a rich, glossy sheen. Wells put new spokes in the back of the rocker and Gault tied the sagging springs in place. Miss Willie then took a square of pieced quilt work and tacked it over the cushion.

There were trips to town for muslin and curtain rods and paint, and finally Hod brought the big packing box up from the hollow.

The day came when it was finished. Miss Willie stood in the door and drank it in, spreading out full and wide with contentment. The windows were softly draped with the muslin, and a frill of it banded the dark old mantel. Over the mantel hung the

79

India shawl, its fringe drooping gracefully around the Seth Thomas clock Becky had found for her in the loft room. On either side of the whitewashed stones stretched the bookshelves Hod had put up, and the blue and red and green bindings of her books blended in the dark tones of an old masterpiece.

In one corner stood the bed, the new mattress bulking high and comfortably under the woven coverlid Mary had brought. The cherry table was against another wall, the Italian print hanging over it, and the exquisite gray-green figurine reflected in its shining surface. From Hod's mother had come the chest of drawers in which even now Miss Willie's clothes were neatly put away, and Becky had massed a huge armful of her beautiful peonies in a tall, creamy pitcher on its marble top.

And finally there was the floor — Miss Willie loved the floor. She had painted it a dull, berry red, varnished it, and waxed it, and it now was a glistening pool of color, against which two of Becky's rag rugs lay softly.

Miss Willie drooped with tiredness. It had been hard work. Terribly hard work. But when she slipped between the sheets of her own bed that night, she was happy. I am in my own home, she thought. Tonight I shall listen to the heartbeat of the ridge in my own home.

CHAPTER

❧ 9 ❧

School started the second Monday in July, and Miss Willie left for the hollow bright and early. As she picked her way down the path, she felt a bright glow of anticipation — a keen tingling of joy at the task that lay ahead of her.

It was a beautiful morning, sharply clean and shining. Beads of dew hung in great, glistening drops on the bushes along the way, and the cobwebs that barred the path were frames of intricate lacework, hung with colors borrowed from the rainbow where the sun touched them gently. She went around them to keep from breaking them. They were too perfect and too fragile to touch.

80

Down in the hollow the shade was deep and sweet with clover smell, and Wishful Creek ran swiftly and noisily over its white stones. The fog was low here, and her hair clung damply to her forehead. This walk would be too long when winter came, she knew. She would have to have a horse to ride, and she would have to go down the ridge and around the road. But as long as she could she would walk the mile and a half, both morning and evening.

When she came within sight of the schoolhouse, she looked at it with pride. It had become hers now. This was her place, and here was her work. In the past week she had placed her stamp upon it, and in the next years it would hold her influence and her personality. The school ground had been freshly raked and cleaned. Hod and Wells had done that, and they had also brought from town, at her command, several dozen tin cups for use at the spring. She intended that each child should have his own cup, at least.

Inside, the room had been swept and scrubbed. Hattie and Becky and Mary and other women from the ridge had worked with her two days cleaning and scouring. Becky had helped her make the yellow curtains that hung at the windows, and there were two bright splashes of color on the floor — one in the center of the room by the stove, and one by her desk. She had decided two were enough. Hod had built her a row of shelves under one of the windows, and she had stacked dozens of books there. She had selected those books carefully, hoping they might open doors of adventure to eager minds. She wouldn't press that now, but the books would be there and the day would come when young hands would reach for them.

On her desk she placed a bowl of Becky's marigolds, letting their fringed green leaves frame the brilliant yellow. She looked around her, taking in the room. Everything was ready. Hod and Wells had cut off the legs of several of the benches in front, so that the smallest children could sit more comfortably. On a table at the back of the room she had placed stacks of paper and boxes of crayons. The one square of blackboard had been freshly painted and there was a new box of chalk. A roll of maps had been hung. Beside her desk were the cartons of textbooks, de-

81

livered last week from town. At least the state furnished free textbooks to these almost forgotten children!

There were voices outside, and she glanced at her watch. Seven thirty. Half an hour yet before time to ring the big dinner bell there on the corner of her desk. She smiled when she looked at it. How many years had that bell, vigorously rung, called these Piney Ridge children to their books? The handle was smooth and shiny, and there was a small crack in the rim of the bell. She had lifted it one day last week and let the clapper fall gently against the cup. The tone had been richly mellow and vibrant, in spite of the crack. It would ring out strongly in this hill-rimmed hollow, and send its deep-voiced summons to every nook and ledge.

Miss Willie went over the outline of her program for the day. Names and classification first. Then the distribution of books and assignments to the older pupils. While they were studying, she would work with the smallest ones. Then they could go outside with an older girl while she heard the first of the classes. She wondered how she could have eight grades in one room. How she could pack that much into each day. But others had done it, after a fashion, and she must do it too.

There would be a handful of small children, just starting to school. These would require time and patience. There would be another handful just beginning to read and write; a few more who could read a little better and write a little more legibly and who would be struggling with elementary number work. And then there would be at least three full grades with geography, history, reading, arithmetic, spelling, language, to say nothing of writing, music, and any science and art she could wedge in. She felt the same sense of frustration she had felt when she first looked at the hodgepodge of textbooks. How can you be expected to do it! Well, she would have to find some way to overlap things, to give less emphasis to some subjects — and here her mind chortled, What things are less important than others? — and perhaps she could work out some system whereby the older and obviously good students could help her. At least she didn't have to do everything today. Today she must make a start, and that was all.

At eight o'clock she stepped to the door and rang the bell. She had been conscious of the confusion of many voices as she studied her program, but as she looked out over the schoolyard, she felt suddenly afraid, and her heart sank dismally. There were so many of them! Forty, Wells had said. There seemed to be twice that many!

They lined up in front of the steps, the girls in one line and the boys in the other, the smallest in front and the tallest in back, making twin stairsteps ascending from her feet to the level of her eyes, slanting back into the yard. She had been on the point of turning back into the building, expecting them to come trooping in after her. But this was an orderly and expectant double file of freshly combed, cleanly washed children. But what did they expect? Heavens, she thought. What I am supposed to do now? Why hadn't she asked Mary or Hod or even Becky or Gault more about the procedure? Hod had warned her to do things the way they had always been done, until she had the confidence of the people.

But no one had told her these youngsters would line up the first thing in the morning and stand stiffly straight with their eyes glued on her, waiting for something, she knew not what. Maybe I'm supposed to make a speech, she thought wildly. But she dismissed that immediately. They might have clustered around the doorway if that were true, but they would hardly have lined up in this precise and orderly fashion. Maybe they sing before going inside was her next guess. But that didn't seem plausible either.

And then a middle-sized boy waved his hand. "Kin I beat the time?" he asked, when she nodded at him. Of course, she sighed. They lined up and marched in. "Yes," she answered and stood aside. The boy went to the big tree at the corner of the building and picked up a piece of iron leaning against it. He pounded a warning note on a broken wagon spring which hung from the lower limb. The lines straightened as if by magic, and then the boy slowly beat out a rhythmic one, two, three, four, to which the lines moved forward, up the steps, and through the door, keeping time to the clanging iron.

Inside, the boys seated themselves automatically on the left side of the building and the girls took the seats to the right. Miss

Willie's mouth quirked at the corner. "Male and female created he them." Even to the six-year-olds!

Once seated, the boys and girls looked around the room curiously. There was some whispering and snickering and pointing to the curtains and rugs and flowers, but she ignored it and went directly to the business at hand. "The seats in front," she said, "have been shortened for the little folks. Will those of you who are older and larger move to the rear and make room for them?"

There was a general scuffling and shifting, and some hesitation on the part of the least ones to leave older sisters and brothers. But Miss Willie waited, her attitude plainly saying she expected no difficulty. One small redheaded girl whimpered as her sister led her up front, and hid her face and clung to her sister's hand when she tried to leave her. Miss Willie reached out and patted the red curls. "She's skeered," the older sister explained.

"She'll be all right," Miss Willie promised. "You go on back to your seat."

The little redhead hitched herself around on the seat and watched her sister go back to the rear of the room, and the tears flowed steadily down her cheeks. Miss Willie kept her hand on the bright curls, occasionally patting them, but otherwise she made no attempt to comfort the child. So far and no farther, she knew, could one go into the unknown with another. This child was having her first experience in venturing beyond the walls of home, and she must do her venturing for herself. As she turned loose from the old and familiar, she must have something warm and real in the new, but it could only be a touch, a quiet hand and a steady voice. Tomorrow that hand and voice would be a part of her, and her enlarged horizons would take in the new personality and add it to the family.

When all the little folks were up front Miss Willie collected them and took them to the table at the back of the room. "Here are colors and paper," she told them. "I want you to make something for me. Think of something you saw on the way to school this morning — something lovely, like a flower or a bird. Draw it for me and paint it some beautiful color, like red or blue or purple or orange."

When she turned back to her desk, Miss Willie pondered the

situation. It would be best to have them seated by grades. Then she could move from one class to another easily. She pushed her glasses up. Yes. That would be best. She faced the group, smiling. "Today," she said, "today we shall start by getting acquainted and by enrolling. All of you know each other well. You have known each other all your lives. And I suspect you also know that I am Miss Willie Payne, Mary Pierce's aunt. But I shall have to learn who you are. Suppose I ask all who are in the eighth grade to stand in the back of the room for a moment."

Perhaps a dozen moved from their seats. "Now give me your names, please. One at a time."

A tall, thin girl with bleached blond hair was first. She kept her eyes on the floor.

"Your name," Miss Willie prompted.

"Pearly Simpson," the girl giggled and slewed an oblique glance across the room at the boys' section.

"Your parents' names?"

"Jodie an' Quilla."

"And how old are you?"

"Sixteen."

Sixteen, and in the eighth grade. Was that usual here, or was the girl just slow?

A couple of boys were next. Bill Johnston. Joe Sanderson. And then a plump, round, berry-brown girl gave her name as Rose Pierce. Ah, Wells's Rose, who kept house for her father and mothered the younger children. Miss Willie looked at her sharply. She was short and stocky, like her father, and she had her father's merry brown eyes. They crinkled now under Miss Willie's look, and her small, red, full-lipped mouth widened in a smile. "We're might' nigh kin to you," she laughed, "seein' we're Pierces too."

The girl was pretty in a wholesome, healthy way. She looked like a plump little brown wren, Miss Willie decided, and she laughed too as she answered, "Yes, that's true." Rose was sixteen also.

Miss Willie had the eighth grade sit down in the rear of the room, and then she took the seventh grade. Here was Sarah Pierce, Hod's little sister. The baby born so late in his mother's

85

life, whose coming he had so bitterly resented. Miss Willie had heard from Mary the story of this baby sister whom Hod had called "the tomato" once, but whom he now adored as if she were his own child. She was a shy, beautiful girl, and Miss Willie smiled at her gently.

Then came the sixth grade — a huge, milling group of children. There were Hickses, Squireses, another Simpson, two of Old Man Clark's boys, and Ewell and Sewell and Bewell Jones, Ferdy's triplets. There was also Sylvie Clark, a slender, silvery-haired child with an elfin face pointed with tiny, perfect features. Miss Willie felt a quiver of joy when she looked on this beauty. How could the child be a Clark, she wondered. She thought of a lily with its roots mired in mud.

A thin, overalled boy was next.

"Name?"

"Rufe Pierce."

Miss Willie looked up sharply. He was lean and brown, as were all the boys, with a shock of yellow, tousled hair. His face was honed down and hollowed, and over the cheeks the fine bones looked as if they had been rounded by firm thumbs. His jaw line was sharp and lean, and the chin squared off under the mouth decisively. There was a deep cleft in the chin, as if a probing finger had left its mark, and Miss Willie remembered that Hod had the same sunken spot in his chin.

The boy's eyes met hers boldly. Eyes that were so clear a blue that they blazed with light. At Miss Willie's quiet look they dropped, and the lashes lay tenderly and girlishly long on his cheeks. With that moment of dropping his lids, Miss Willie drew her breath quickly. His whole face changed. When the blue blaze of his eyes was quenched, the face softened and the straw-colored curls and the tawny lashes and the sun-drenched, tight-drawn skin were merged in a golden suffusion. Somewhere in Italy she had seen a head like that. A boy's head painted in those same warm sun tones, the flesh overlaid with deep gold so that it ran into the edges of the hair, the lashes dusty with gold laid gently against the chiseled bones of the cheek. The effect had been that of warmth and richness. The feel of the earth and the sun and winds and rain. Yes, now she remembered. It was in that

86

little church in Taranto. She had stood there in the dim light, on a gray day, while the weary rain fell outside and blotted out the sun, and she had felt the warmth of the sun steal through her chilled body from that golden head. She remembered thinking that the artist must have loved that child very much to have painted him so warmly. Putting all of the sun into his hair and eyes and skin . . . making of him a young golden god. This golden boy now . . . this Rufe Pierce!

Suddenly she was conscious of the passing of time. "Your father's name?" she asked.

"Ever'body on the ridge knows Wells Pierce is my pa," he said.

"But I'm new on the ridge," she smiled at him. "I wouldn't know."

The lashes dropped again and he said nothing. Miss Willie felt rebuked. She had known, of course. The question had been automatic.

On and on the enrolling went. How many children there were! In the fifth grade there was another of Wells's children. Abby, little, thin, and blue-eyed, looking not even remotely related to Rose and Rufe. But finally it was done. The textbooks were distributed then, and Miss Willie went through the weary business of making assignments.

"We don't never go to school the first day," volunteered one of the older boys.

"What do you do?" Miss Willie asked.

"Well, the teacher jist gits us all enrolled; then he ginerally goes to git the books. We don't actual start till the next day."

"Well, we already have the books. I think we might as well go ahead with school today." Miss Willie was pleasant as she dismissed the question.

She turned then with relief to the youngest children. They were like old friends to her. These little ones she understood. Quietly she moved among them, learning that this one was Jimmy Clark, that one Jewel Simpson, this one Clarissa Jones, and here was Hod's sister's little boy, Johnnie Walton. He held up a stork-legged bird with brilliant plumage for her to see. She nodded seriously. "That must have been a beautiful bird you saw this morning, Johnnie."

He ducked his head and grinned, showing four wide spaces where he had lost his teeth. "I think hit was a blue jay," he said. "He was flyin' so fast I couldn't make out fer shore, but that's what I think he was."

"Blue jays don't have all them colors," snorted another boy.

"This un did," stoutly insisted Johnnie.

"Of course," said Miss Willie. "Let's get your books now, and then you may go out to play."

When she turned around, Rufe, who was far to the middle of the room, raised his hand. "Are we goin' to set in these seats all the time?" he wanted to know.

"Not necessarily," Miss Willie answered. "As soon as we get things straightened out, you may be assigned permanent seats. But I think it will be best if each grade sits together."

"We ain't never done it that-a-way before," he insisted. "I've allus set next the window there. Hit's been my seat ever sincet I started to school."

"We'll see," Miss Willie promised.

The boy bent his head. Cranky old maid, he whispered under his breath. Cranky, ugly, old maid teacher. Allus have set by the winder. A feller kin look out an' see the woods, an' watch the wind apassin' through the leaves, an' see old Jupe settin' out there under the tree waitin'. An' hear that leetle ole mockerbird that's got a nest clost by. I cain't noways stand to stay all penned in here in the middle, he muttered. Hit ain't right. Only way I kin stand to go to school is to set by the winder. He laid his head in his arms and wished he hadn't come today.

It was ten o'clock, then, and Miss Willie dismissed the entire group for the midmorning recess. She handed some of the older girls the stacks of cups and asked them to see that they were distributed at the spring. "Make sure each person has a cup," she said. "Here are black crayons. Mark each one's name on a cup for him."

The girls giggled, took the cups, and went outside. Miss Willie went to the door and watched the yelling, milling crowd of children for a moment, and then she turned back. She would start with the reading classes, she decided.

She was busy the entire thirty minutes and was hardly conscious of the noise outside. After this she must get out too, but today there was too much to do. Before she realized it, the time had sped by and she must ring the bell for "books" again. She stepped to the door. It was only then that she noticed how unnaturally quiet it was. She looked around the schoolyard and saw the girls huddled in small groups, watching the door, giggling and whispering among themselves. Not a boy was in sight except the very smallest ones. Well, perhaps they played somewhere on farther down the hollow by themselves. She rang the bell and the girls came slowly toward her. They didn't line up this time, but passed her in the doorway, eying her solemnly, and moving slowly to their seats.

She waited for a moment and then went to her desk. I shall not ask them where the boys have gone, she decided. She felt the tension in the air and knew that something serious had happened. Her heart beat fast and a frightened feeling settled in her stomach. I shall not be disconcerted, she said to herself. Whatever has happened, I shall not be humiliated before these girls. Her mind was whirling with her thoughts, and a deep feeling of dismay spread over her. But she stood calmly behind her desk, and deliberately pushed her glasses into place.

"We shall have the third- and fourth-grade reading classes now," she said quietly. "And while I am hearing these classes, the sixth, seventh, and eighth grades will work the problems assigned this morning."

The room was so still that not a breath was heard. Pearly Simpson and Rose Pierce looked at each other, and then bent over their books. As if that were a signal, the other girls opened their books, and Miss Willie took a deep breath. At least the girls were not going to rebel!

Somehow the day moved on. Through the morning, the noon hour, and the early afternoon. Through arithmetic, geography, and history. And still there were no boys. Miss Willie began to suspect that they were not going to come back, and there was a heavy weight in her chest. On my first day, she thought. It will be all over the ridge! What did I do that was wrong? And how do you handle an open revolt? What sort of big stick were these boys waving over her, and what did they want? What were they trying to do? She had heard tales of how new teachers in country schools were deliberately tried to see if they could handle the school. Was this what lay back of it?

Just before four o'clock, as she was getting ready to dismiss the group, the boys filed in through the door, one at a time, Rufe Pierce leading them. When she looked up and saw them, Miss Willie's anger flared. The little tramps, she said to herself. The little ruffians! And that beautiful, brazen, golden boy! He must be the ringleader!

The boys had stopped just inside the door. Rufe looked at her boldly. "We don't never go to school on the first day," he said. "An' we want our old seats back."

Miss Willie's head went up, and her anger spread so rapidly and so thickly over her body that she trembled with the effort to control it. She had to try twice before she could speak. "You are not going to sit anywhere," she said, and her voice sounded harsh even in her own ears. "You are not even coming back to school until you bring me written excuses for your absence today. You left school without permission, and you can't come back without permission. Do you understand that?"

She whirled quickly and spoke to the entire group, rapidly and sharply, the words dropping like pellets from her mouth. "Listen to me, all of you. I may be a new teacher on the ridge, and I am a woman. But I will *not* have rebellion in this school. I don't want to be a dictator. But if we have to have authority in this school, I want every one of you to understand that *I* am that authority. If I *have* to issue orders, I certainly shall! And please understand another thing. I am not easily frightened. You *cannot* force me to do anything, either by threats or by action. Now you boys get out of here, and either bring written excuses for your absences tomorrow, or don't come back!"

Her knees were weak and shaking, but her voice remained calm and icy. Each word had been spoken precisely and without tremor. But she was thinking, Now I've done it. Now I shall probably have all the parents on the ridge on my neck, and shall have to leave here in disgrace, and Hod and Mary will be shamed before their relatives and friends. But she could not check the angry flow of words. She was madder than she had ever remem-

90

bered being in her life, and she was determined that these boys should *not* get by with this sort of threat.

"School is dismissed," she said curtly, and she began stacking the papers on her desk. I shall have to see Lem Pierce at once, she thought. He was the chairman of the trustees. And Wells, and Hod. Hod wasn't a trustee, but she wanted him there. I shall have to tell them what has happened and what I have done. If they don't stand behind me, then I shall have to leave. And Jodie Simpson. He was a trustee. But no teacher can be bullied and retain the respect of her pupils, she told herself. This had to be faced, and I've done the best I could.

She felt a certain peace then, and turned to the smallest children with a smile. They had not understood her words, but the tone of her voice had left them wide-eyed. She made her voice warm and friendly to them as she said good-by, and she spoke gently to the girls gathering around her. Rufe swaggered out the door, the rest of the boys following him. Once outside they went whooping off up the hollow and over the hill. She wondered if there would be any boys in school this term! She wondered if there would be any school!

CHAPTER

❧ 10 ❧

THAT NIGHT SHE SAT IN HER SMALL CABIN with Lem and Hod and Gault and Wells and Jodie Simpson around her. All Pierces but Jodie, and he had married a Pierce.

"I'm goin' to tan that Rufe's hide till he cain't sit down fer a week," Wells said when she had finished her story. "He's jist been ahonin' fer trouble. He's gittin' too big fer his britches. I'm goin' to take him down a peg or two. Don't you weary yourself none, Miss Willie. He'll not lead off no gang o' boys agin soon!"

"No," Miss Willie said, "that's not the answer. Whipping the boys isn't going to help. I called you here just to tell you what has happened. I felt the boys took the law into their own hands, and I didn't think they should be allowed to get by with it. They have to learn to respect authority and to live under discipline.

91

Maybe I shouldn't have told them to bring written excuses, but I did, and I shall stand by it. They don't come back to school without them."

Lem and Hod had not yet spoken. Lem was stroking his long chin. "They ain't no doubt but what you done right, Miss Willie. Ifen you'd let 'em git by with it you might jist as well of packed yer things an' went. They wouldn't of never give you no peace. They's been more'n one teacher hounded outen Big Springs. But I dunno whether they'll ever bring them there excuses you want or not. That's what's wearyin' me."

Hod spoke then. "I think the trustees had better take united action on the whole matter. Then there won't be any doubt but that they're back of Miss Willie. Lem, you're the chairman. You call a meetin' at the schoolhouse for tomorrow night. The boys didn't count on this gettin' as big as it has, and they're goin' to be plumb scared of what they've started if we ring the parents in on it. But they've acted like little hoodlums down there long enough. They might as well learn right now Miss Willie don't stand alone."

Gault nodded his head in agreement. "Hod's right."

But Wells rocked back on his chair legs and twisted a forelock of hair. "I dunno," he said. "Believe I'd wait a day or two. See how many o' them excuses comes in tomorrer. Might be better to let the thing simmer down."

Miss Willie thought about it. "I believe Wells is right. Let's see what happens tomorrow before you take any action."

Hod and Lem and Gault shook their heads. She knew from the look on their faces that they doubted the outcome. "Well, I reckon a few days one way or the other ain't goin' to hurt," Gault said, "an' if she kin bring 'em to taw by herself, hit might be best."

When they left, Wells lingered. "Miss Willie, I shore hate this. Special since my Rufe was the cause of it. I wisht you'd let me git in after *him* anyways."

"No," Miss Willie answered. "I'm afraid you'll just make him hate me. Wells, he's a beautiful boy."

"Beauty is as beauty does, Miss Willie. He's a quare young'un. Never give me no special trouble, though. But he's allus roamed

92

the woods . . . him an' his dog. I ain't never understood the boy, but he's mostly been quiet-like an', like I said, not give to makin' trouble."

Miss Willie laid her hand on his arm. "Well, let's not worry too much about it. Maybe it will all blow over."

Wells put his hat on. "Hit will that. You'll see, Miss Willie. Jist don't give it e'er 'nother thought. Hit'll be all right."

He said good night and left her to her troubled thoughts. Her first day had ended disastrously. But the worst disaster was not the rebellion of the boys. The worst was that she had lost her grip in her anger and had reverted to pure schoolteacher type. She had let her sense of outraged pride make her become the autocrat . . . the disciplinarian . . . the typical unbending, unyielding, ununderstanding old-maid schoolteacher. Oh, she had spoken bravely of not wanting to be a dictator. But hadn't she been? Didn't she really want obedience . . . immediate, unquestioning obedience? Hadn't she cracked down, not only with her own authority, but with the authority of the trustees too? And even now wasn't she comforted by the knowledge that the trustees thought she had done right? Hadn't she fled to them, wanting them to pick up her lowered flags and fly them for her?

She twisted and turned in her bed, flaying herself with her own self-contempt, and driving herself into first one corner then the other. There had been so little excuse for what she had done! Just the excuse, she thought wryly, of what else could she have done! If she had controlled herself and had asked the boys to sit down and talk the matter over? If she had tried reasonably to get to the root of the matter? No. She knew better than that. The boys were trying to force her hand, and the only answer they would understand or respect was force.

If that's true — and she knew it was — then I wasn't so far wrong. Whatever I did that made them behave so, once it was done I have surely done the only thing I could do as a consequence! She felt better. Not good, yet. But better. She had no idea what she was going to do next. No plan would come. But she laid it away until tomorrow, making her mind quit seeking a lighted way, stilling her tired body and letting it sink deep into the mattress. A last chuckling thought raced through her mind

93

before she drowsed off to sleep. Well, *veni, vidi,* but evidently not *vici!*

The next morning she was frankly nervous. Gault and Becky watched her as she tried to eat breakfast. Finally she pushed her plate aside. "I'm scared," she confessed.

Gault poured half his cup of coffee into a saucer and blew on it. "Got good reason to be," he said, sipping noisily. "Boys down at Big Springs is allus a handful fer e'er teacher we ever git. Allus has been that-a-way. Ever sincet I kin recollect. We was a handful, an' Hod's gang, they was, an' I reckon boys ginerally ever'- wheres is a trial to their teachers. Hit'll blow over, though. Don't know as I'd let it weary me too much. Jist go along with 'em. Don't believe I'd insist too hard on 'em asettin' diffrunt, though. Hit sort of goes agin the grain. Jist let 'em set where they're used to settin'. Let 'em come up to the front fer their classes like allus."

"Is that the way it's done? I intended to go to them for the classes."

"Hit does 'em good to git up an' stretch a little, an' move around."

"Gault," said Miss Willie, "tell me just exactly how the day should go? I think I need some help!"

The old man buttered a biscuit and took a big bite before he answered. "Well," he said, "I'll tell you how we allus done it, an' I reckon they ain't changed none sincet then. We marched in an' then we stood up an' sung 'America' or 'The Star-Spangled Banner,' or 'My Old Kentucky Home,' or somethin' ever'body knowed. Then we had the Lord's Prayer. Then we started off with readin'."

"How do you mean, started off with reading?"

"One class at a time come up front an' set on the benches in front o' the teacher's desk an' read to her. Mostly ever'body read one paragraph. That was all. Then we had spellin'. She jist give out the words, first to one then another. After recess we had arithmetic. That takened a longer spell. Then after dinner we had language an' history. An' then geography. They've got hygiene too now. But we never had none o' that."

94

Miss Willie took a deep breath. "And what about the first and second grades?"

"Oh, mostly the teacher jist called them up to her desk one at a time an' had 'em read to her. She jist kinder worked with them when she could. She never tried to have no class with 'em."

"And what did they do all the rest of the time?"

"I don't rightly know. Jist set there, I reckon. Drawed a little, mebbe. Sometimes when the weather was nice, she'd let 'em go outside a spell."

Miss Willie rose. She had a dazed look on her face. "I'll try," she said.

Miss Willie was early again that day and she deliberately stayed in the building until time to ring the bell. She thought she could hear boys' voices, but she made herself stay at her desk. When she stepped to the door, the bell in her hand, she glanced quickly around the yard, and then she sighed with relief. Apparently the boys had come back. The yard was full of them, and a vigorous game of baseball was going on. At the sound of the bell they came trooping toward the door, shoving and pushing and yelling, and lined up on their side of the steps. Once the lines formed, there was quiet. She stood still and watched them. Her eyes went down the line and took in each face, meeting the glance of each boy.

Rufe Pierce stepped out of line. "You want these here notes we got now, or after we git inside?"

"I'll take them now, please," she answered, meeting his challenge. Rufe moved forward and laid a folded bit of paper in her palm. His eyes met hers with a straight, deep look, a look that blazed at her, and she felt a long shuddering down her back. The look was full of hate.

One at a time the other boys brought their notes to her. Every boy in the line had his note. Every boy stepped out and laid it in her hand. Some were bold, as Rufe had been. Others were awkward and would not meet her eyes.

"Thank you," she said, and stepped back to the door. "Will someone beat the time, please."

"Hit's our time today," one of the girls said.

"All right. One of you older girls go ahead."

95

Inside, they filed to the places they had occupied the day before. Miss Willie laid the little stack of notes on her desk and turned to face the group. There was something queer about every boy being back in school today, with his note from his parents. But she wasn't going to ask any questions now. Whatever lay behind it, this wasn't the time to go looking a gift horse in the mouth! "Now," Miss Willie said, "we can just forget that whole episode. You may take your old seats if you like."

There was a moment of quiet, and Miss Willie looked at Rufe. There was an amazed look on his face. Miss Willie chuckled. We'll see who has won this first round, she said to herself.

She waited until the confusion of the shifting around had died away. "Now," she said, "we shall stand and sing 'America.'"

When the last note of the song had echoed through the room, she bowed her head and began the Lord's Prayer. One by one the clear young voices joined in. They stumbled when she automatically said "debts" instead of "trespasses," but recovered and went on to the end.

When they were seated again, she pushed her glasses up on her nose and cleared her throat. "We shall now have reading. Fourth grade, come forward, please."

Compromise? Her mind accused her. Of course. She lifted her chin and picked up a fourth reader. "Ewell Jones, will you read the first paragraph?"

CHAPTER

❧ 11 ❧

How's SCHOOL GOING, Miss Willie?" Mary asked. It was a Sunday morning about two weeks after school had started. Miss Willie had slipped down to Mary's for a long talk. The burden of the air hung heavy over them and they sat quietly on the long screened porch, Miss Willie fanning herself occasionally with the bonnet she had borrowed from Becky. Hod was stretched out in a big chair, his feet propped up on the table nearby. Miss Willie laid the bonnet down and pleated its big back ruffles between her restless fingers.

"I don't know, Mary," she said slowly, "I just don't know. I got off to a bad start. There isn't any doubt about that. I ought to have found out how things were done here on the ridge. But it just didn't occur to me that even the children wouldn't be budged from the way things have always been done!"

"Now, Miss Willie, you're taking that entirely too seriously. It's all settled. The boys brought their excuses and came back, and you haven't had any more trouble, have you?"

"I still think there's something fishy about that. It isn't reasonable to suppose every last one of those boys went to their parents of their own accord and asked them to write an excuse for them. And the notes all sounded suspiciously alike. I asked Gault about it, but he wouldn't say a word. Said just to let well enough alone."

"That's just what I'd do too, if I was you," Hod said. He puffed a lazy smoke ring toward the ceiling. Miss Willie fanned industriously.

"I think somebody went to those parents," she said after a moment, looking at Hod intently; "somebody went to see every one of them after you all left my cabin that night and told them what had happened, and furthermore told them what to say in those notes. It couldn't have been you, could it?"

"It could have. But it wasn't."

"Then you admit somebody did."

"I don't admit nothin'. I just said it could have been me, but it wasn't."

"Well, I don't think Lem would have done it, and I know Gault didn't. Wells . . . of course! Rufe was the ringleader and he felt responsible. And he told me not to worry. Why, of course! That's just what happened! Now, look here, Hod . . ."

"*You* look here, Miss Willie. You're just guessin' at something. Forget it. Leave it lie. When you've stirred up one hornet's nest, it's just plain sense not to stir up any more. If Wells took the sting out of this one for you — and I'm not sayin' he did or he didn't — you better just be glad it don't sting no more, and forget it!"

Miss Willie looked at Mary, and caught the merest suggestion of a wink. Her angry retort died aborning. She pleated the ruffle and then fanned, and then went back to pleating the ruffle. "Well, that doesn't sting any more," she said finally, "but there are little

97

things. You know all those tin cups I bought so that each child could have his own cup? They just disappeared last week. Every single one of them! Saturday I sent by Gault to get some more, and Monday they all disappeared. No one knows a thing about it, of course. When I ask, there's just a blank wall of silence. I don't know what to make of it, and I don't know what to do."

Hod spoke. "Who you think's doin' it?"

Miss Willie hesitated. "Hod, I'm afraid Rufe's at the bottom of this too."

Hod nodded. "That's what I think too. You'd better let Wells get in behind that young man."

Miss Willie shook her head. "No. I'll have to work it out myself. But I don't know what to do about the cups."

Hod shifted his feet and leaned forward. "Miss Willie, I went to that school when I was a kid, and I know how kids think down there. They're lined up against the teacher. They'll dare you every way they can, and as long as they can get by with it, they'll keep on daring. They're used to a teacher that lights into them with a hickory stick, and that's all they'll pay any attention to. Every time they get by with something they're gigglin' and snickerin' behind your back. They're bestin' the teacher, see? I tell you, there's only one thing they respect. Either you'll have to make up your mind to tan that little scamp yourself, or let Wells do it. He'll not give you any peace until you do."

Miss Willie pleated the ruffle of her bonnet. "I don't believe that," she said, finally.

"You'll see," Hod said flatly.

Mary eased herself in her chair. "I'm sorry, Miss Willie," she said gently. "I'm so sorry. I hate to see you troubled like this, and I didn't know how it would be or I would never have got you into it."

Miss Willie straightened her thin shoulders. "Now, Mary, don't you go feeling sorry about things. I'll lick this thing yet. I'll get it straightened out. You'll see. And don't you think for one minute I'm sorry to be here. This is just one small problem, and it'll take more than this to make me sorry I came. I've about decided to keep the cups locked in my cupboard and give them out myself at recess and noon, and stand there like a policeman while they're being used, and then gather them up and lock them up again when they've finished with them. I can't let Rufe get the best of me, and that's the only thing I can think of."

Hod laughed. "It'll be a lot of trouble, but I reckon it'll work. I still say the easiest way would be just to whale the tar out of that young man. That's something he'd understand and respect."

Miss Willie laughed too, but she still shook her head. "I'll try my way first."

A comfortable silence settled over them, and the noon sun rode hot overhead. A bottlefly buzzed lazily at the screen door, and Hod's dog snapped angrily at it.

"When you aimin' to have the school openin' party?" It was Hod who spoke.

"The opening party?" Miss Willie's voice lifted the question in amazement.

"Sure," he said lazily, "always open school with a big shindig."

Miss Willie collapsed against the back of her chair and she fanned feebly. "Oh, dear," she sighed.

"Miss Willie, you don't have to," Mary interrupted. "It's too much for you, just getting started and running into this trouble with the boys. Don't try it."

"Have they 'allus' done it, Hod?" Miss Willie wanted to know.

"Allus," he replied solemnly.

Miss Willie knocked her thumb against her chin. "That settles it," she said gloomily, "whatever has allus been done, I must do or die trying! What sort of party do they have?"

"Oh, usually a pie supper or spellin' bee. Or a box supper. Ridge folks always want to eat at their shindigs, but they don't mind bringin' their own food. Just announce at school when you're havin' the party, an' they'll all come."

Miss Willie looked at Mary and raised her eyebrows. Mary laughed. "We'll have a party, then," Miss Willie said. "When would be the best time?"

"About a week from Friday night," Hod put in. "That'd give 'em time to get ready for it."

"I thought you said it wouldn't be any trouble!"

"I did. And it won't. But folks'll have to have time to spread the word around and bake up their pies and such."

"It's so hot for a pie supper," Miss Willie objected.

"It's not ever too hot for a pie supper," Hod insisted.

"Why couldn't we have an ice-cream supper?"

"Take a powerful lot of ice cream. And folks would have to get ice from town. Now that'd be real trouble."

Miss Willie thought for a moment. "I could get several freezers already made. Would the men and boys be willing to pay for it . . . I mean, buy it like the pies?"

"Why, I reckon they would. They always buy the pies or boxes. Don't see there'd be much difference."

"They could draw for partners and buy the cream for them. And why couldn't we have a little program? Have some singing and let the young folks play games and have a speech or two," Miss Willie was getting enthusiastic. "I know — we could get Lem to make a speech, as chairman of the trustees . . ."

"And Miss Willie," Mary said, "as the new teacher of the school."

"No, no. That wouldn't be necessary."

"Oh, you'd have to say a few words anyhow," Hod said. "The teacher allus does."

"Here we go again," Miss Willie laughed. "Well, just a few. Just a welcome. Oh Mary, this may be fun! I'll get to meet all the parents! Mary, do you think we could find enough small tables and chairs so that people could sit around and be comfortable while they eat their ice cream? Maybe outside where it's cooler. Lanterns in the trees? Wouldn't that be pretty? Oh, we'll make this a really nice party!"

"We'll take the car one day, Miss Willie," Mary promised, "and scour the ridge for tables and chairs. And we'll get flowers to decorate. All the women will help."

Miss Willie went in the house to get pencil and paper to make a list. "I always forget something," she said as she went through the door.

Mary looked at Hod, and the corner of her mouth drew down. "You be sure and take your guitar that night," she warned, "and tell Wells to bring his!"

Hod let another smoke ring curl upward. "I'll remember," he promised.

Plans for the party went forward. Miss Willie announced the date at school and the news spread rapidly. A sparkling expectancy rose over the ridge. An ice-cream party! Well, I never!

"They ain't never been no ice-cream party fer the school openin' that I know of," Becky said.

"There's going to be one now," Miss Willie insisted. "And I want all your spoons and that little table, and all the flowers you can spare."

"Shore," Becky said, "we'll jist strip the yard. They ain't goin' to last long noways. With the heat an' all."

Mary brought the car, and for two or three days before the party she and Miss Willie drove over the ridge collecting tables, chairs, and spoons, marking them meticulously to avoid mixing them.

On Friday, Hod went to town and brought back with him the freezers of cream and a dozen rolls of white crepe paper. Miss Willie had dismissed school at noon, and she and Mary and Becky had been working all afternoon. The schoolhouse was gay with flowers. Late roses, gladioli, zinnias, and marigolds sprayed their brilliance around the walls, and over all honeysuckle drooped its sweet fragrance. The desks were moved back against the wall, and tables were set up in the yard. When Hod brought the crepe paper, the women set to work and soon had the tables covered with white squares, scalloped and crimped. Miss Willie gathered up the tin drinking cups and covered them with the white paper and set one full of flowers on each table.

"Doesn't it look pretty?" she asked.

"Hit shore does," Becky agreed. "How you aimin' to git enough light out here to see by?"

"Oh, we've got lanterns to hang in the trees," Mary said. "We borrowed all the lanterns on the ridge. How'd we happen to miss yours?"

Becky giggled. "More'n likely 'cause we don't have e'ern!"

Mary put her arm around Miss Willie. "You run on home now. You're all worn out. Lie down and rest a minute before you dress, and we'll come by for you early tonight."

When they had lighted the lanterns that night, the school yard looked unbelievably lovely. The dim, flickering lights swayed in the trees, casting long shadows over the white-covered tables with their bright spots of color. Miss Willie felt the familiarity of the place slipping away from her. This was not the school ground where the boys romped and ran and yelled, and the girls grouped themselves under the trees. This was a shadowed terrace, cool and softly lighted, where gracious people could walk and talk and sit quietly sipping their frosted drinks, and where muted music would presently flow gently over all.

Miss Willie pushed her glasses up and smoothed her dress. She had worn a thin white dress, belting it with a soft gold sash. Her fine brown hair was piled in an orderly mass on top of her head, but she had pushed a pearl-studded comb into the back of it, and had pinned one perfect yellow rose at the throat of her dress. She felt very splendid indeed! Her mouth crinkled. And for what reason should she want to be very splendid tonight? Her mind poked a ridiculing finger at her finery. She tossed her head impatiently. Must I examine every motive, she asked herself. Must there be a reason? Well, then, I should like to make as good an impression as possible on the parents of my children! Oh? Isn't it wonderful, then, that Wells Pierce is a parent? Oh, be quiet!

By dusky dark the crowd was gathering. Hod and Mary stood near Miss Willie, at the entrance of the room, greeting each newcomer and introducing him to her. Quietly and shyly they greeted her. Some of them she had already met at the all-day singing. Others she was meeting for the first time. They were all resplendent in their Sunday best, and awkward in their movements. "Pleased to meet you," they said. Or, "Glad to make yer acquaintance." Or, "Hit's a pleasure, ma'am." They shook hands gravely and then moved stiffly to the seats, which had been moved to line the walls. A respectful silence was observed.

Miss Willie looked at them sitting stiffly and grimly around the room. Oh, dear, she thought, why can't they move around and talk and laugh a little!

"It's time to start," Hod whispered, "ever'body's here that's comin'."

They moved forward to the chairs that had been set apart in

one end of the room. Lem joined them. It had been planned for him to make a short talk and introduce Miss Willie. Loosely and easily he stood before them.

"Folks," he said, "I ain't goin' to make no speech, although Miss Willie here has done ast me to. But you ain't wantin' to hear me. I'll jist say that we're proud you come, an' we want you all to have a good time. I'll jist say too that we got the best teacher this year we could of got. You all know who she is . . . Mary's aunt, Miss Willie Payne. She's been ateachin' school fer a good long time, an' she knows how's the best way to teach our young-'uns. Me an' the rest o' the trustees has got full confidence in her. We have done told her we'll do all in our power to uphold her, an' I'm repeatin' it here where you kin all hear it. We aim to do our part, accordin' to our lights. On account of we know she'll allus do her'n. As fur as we're concerned, whatever Miss Willie says in this here school goes. An' I want her to have her say-so right now."

The audience applauded when Lem walked over and brought Miss Willie to the center of the room. She felt confused for a moment. What could you say after an introduction like that? She had planned a little speech of welcome, but Lem had already done that. Funny. They had been coming to this schoolhouse for years. And yet she was their hostess tonight. She let her glance sweep around the room. There was Becky, primly proud and expectant. The teacher lived at her house. She had a right of ownership tonight. There was Gault, tall, lean, and ragged-headed. There was Hattie, Hod's mother, her starched apron fluting stiffly around her waist, her finely chiseled face profiled against the wall. There was Tom, Hod's father, lean like Gault but more stooped, honest face cleanly scrubbed. There were the Joneses, Ferdy with the gulping Adam's apple and Corinna with the newest baby asleep already in her lap. They were Ewell and Bewell and Sewell's parents. There was Old Man Clark and Mamie, and their brood cluttering around them. There were the Simpsons and the Taylors and the Jordans from over Bear Hollow way. There was even Matt Jasper, drooling spittle down his chin. But he was alone. She must talk to him tonight, and see why the children weren't in school.

103

Her eyes stopped finally on Wells Pierce, standing in the far corner of the room, his solid frame leaning easily against the wall. His clean blue shirt was open at the throat, and she saw how strongly his neck rose from his shoulders, and how wide and solid his shoulders were, straining under the shirt. He smiled at her when her eyes passed on over him. By his side stood Rufe, tawny and golden in the half-light, and near by sat Rose.

Oh, she had no welcome for these people! Rather, they should welcome her. She spread her hands slightly apart, appealingly. Well, say that, then. Say you want them to take you into their hearts and make you one with them. Say you have been lonely for too many years, and you want to be at home with them. Say what you hope and dream for this school. Say what you hope and dream for yourself and for them, here together. Say you want to walk the dark hills with them . . . let the streams of their lives flow through you, thread through you, quicken you. Say you want to walk under the moon and stars of Piney Ridge and bring them down to you . . . to fill yourself with them . . . you, who are empty. Say you want to fill the emptiness. Say it! She found Wells's eyes again.

She flung her hands wide and let them drop. Oh, no. Not yet. She stammered through a little speech, gaining poise as she went along. She hoped they could be friends. She wanted very much to have their help. If they ever wanted to suggest ways in which she could be more helpful, they were to tell her frankly. She would welcome such suggestions. She went on to talk of the school. Of the boys and girls who were her pupils. Of some of her hopes for them. She mentioned her own joy at being here, spoke gently of Mary and Hod, and ended with the reiterated hope that they might all be friends. She felt confused and foolish. She, who was usually so sure of herself!

When she had finished, she told them they had planned a few games, and she tried desperately to direct them in a silly guessing game, "Who am I?" Brightly she went among them, trying to enliven them, to draw them out. Their faces were wooden, and only a few were brave enough to speak out. Abandoning that, she went on to the next thing she had planned. Another mixer. But they wouldn't mix. How could you draw people into games who refused to be drawn? She tried two or three games, and her despair grew. Only Hod and Mary and Wells were responding. The party was dying of dullness. Did they always sit like sullen bumps on a log, she wondered.

"Let's sing awhile," she said brightly. She moved before them, her white dress glinting in the soft light. "Do you all know 'Flow Gently, Sweet Afton'? Let's start with that," and she led out bravely into the beautiful words. Mary's voice followed stoutly, and Hod's. Wells didn't know the words, but she saw that he was trying to follow her, and his deep voice lent power, even with its humming. No one else made any attempt to sing. Falteringly she came to the end of the first stanza, and the song died of its own weakness. Wildly she looked toward Mary and Hod. Hod was lifting his guitar from the corner. And then from the side of her eye she saw that Wells was coming forward with his guitar. Oh, yes! Let them take over! Let them stir some response from these lumps of clay! Let them resurrect this deadness, if they could!

Wells stepped easily to the front. "Miss Willie here has ast me an' Hod to he'p out with the singin'," he said, thrumming ragged chords from the guitar as he spoke. "C'mon, Hod, git yer chair over here. An' let's sing!"

The two guitars lifted their singing chords high, and the two men stormed into a gay, fast tune:
"'She'll be comin' round the mountain, When she comes.
She'll be comin' round the mountain, When she comes.
She'll be comin' round the mountain,
She'll be comin' round the mountain,
She'll be comin' round the mountain, When she comes.'"

The rollicking stanzas went on: "She'll be drivin' six white horses, When she comes"; "Oh, we'll all go to meet her, When she comes"; "We will kill the old red rooster, . . . When she comes." And soon every hand was clapping, every foot was patting, and every voice was shouting the loud, lusty song. "And we'll all have chicken and dumplin' When she comes."

Miss Willie looked at Mary and lifted her hands helplessly. Ridge people knew what they liked! And you couldn't fool them with "Flow Gently, Sweet Afton."

The two men swung the crowd into "O Susanna! Oh, don't you

105

cry for me!" and from that into "Buffalo Gal." They kept them shouting and clapping and stamping their feet with the fast-running rhythms. And then Hod stood up and shouted at Ferdy Jones, "Ferdy, come up here"; and to the crowd: "Form sets for a singin' game! Ferdy, you call 'em!"

Wells threw his guitar to the floor and grabbed Miss Willie around the middle, swinging her into the center of the floor. Ferdy threw back his head and yelled, "Balance all!" and Hod pranced his fingers up the neck of his guitar and rocked his shoulders.

"First young lady all around town," Ferdy bawled, and Wells seized Miss Willie and swung her twice around. Her glasses slipped down her nose and she pushed at them with her free hand. Wells let her go and the next man on her right grabbed her and started swinging. She hung on and let her feet fly on the corners. Her breath was coming fast, and the perspiration was tickling her back.

"Swing on a corner with a step and a swing!" and the next man in line grabbed her. Her glasses were on the end of her nose now, and she felt them bounce as she hit the floor between swings. They hung on her chin a moment, and hung there balanced carelessly by the earpieces. She clutched them as Wells came around again, and slid them off to safety as she promenaded home. The knot of her hair had slipped crazily to one side and she was raining hairpins. Oh, let it go! The music was getting inside her, and she was finding her second wind.

"Swing and do-si-do. Promenade all. Take your partner and we'll all run away. Second young lady all around town. Swing on a corner with a step and a swing." Wells was swinging her now, prancing with a shuffling step down the line. She bent her knees and let her legs go loose. "Oh, swing on the corner and we'll all go home." When they passed Hod, she saw his hands furiously plucking the strings, his head thrown back and his mouth shouting the words. Ferdy Jones was bellowing over the music. "Swing on the corner . . . and balance to your places!"

"Git yer breath, now," Ferdy called. "Next 'un'll be 'Shoo Fly.'"

Miss Willie stood where Wells had released her, her breath heaving violently out of her chest.

106

"Hey, Miss Willie," Wells laughed between his own gasping breaths, "you kin shore swing a lively leg. Now wasn't that grand?"

Miss Willie nodded, unable to talk. A lively leg! Miss Willie Payne! Suddenly she was laughing . . . great gusts of laughter shaking her, and the tears were running down her cheeks. A lively leg!

Wells joined in with his great roar. "Now, wasn't that somethin'? Miss Willie, how you like this here clambake?"

"Wells," she said, still gasping, "I like this here clambake!"

But she wouldn't dance any more. She wanted, rather, to stand and look on. They were having so much fun now. This was what they wanted then. And she remembered the white-covered tables outside, with the glow of lanterns on them. Gracious people walking and talking while muted music flowed around them. No. Lusty people, shouting and stamping, while lusty music flowed through them and within them. Ridge people singing their own hill songs, dancing their own hill dances . . . ridge people, dark with the soil, dark with the hills. Born and bred in the deep darkness of the hills. Hills as old as time. People rooted in them, timeless as the hills. She felt a new sense of timelessness herself . . . one with the earth and the earth's people.

She noticed Rose dancing with a tall, dark boy. He hadn't been there at first. His hair was black like a crow's wing, and his face was sun-reddened mahogany. He had bold black eyes and flashing white teeth. There was the look of a pirate about him. A predatory, swaggering look. He was too daring, too handsome, and he held Rose too tightly when he swung her.

"Becky," Miss Willie asked, "who is that boy dancing with Rose?"

Becky turned to look. "Him? Why, that's Tay Clark. Old Man Clark's boy by his first woman."

"I haven't seen him around before."

"No. He don't live here on Piney no more. He up an' left out when his pa married Mamie. Some says he's stillin' over on Wanderin' Creek."

"Stillin'?"

"Moonshinin'. Makin' likker."

Miss Willie's eyes widened. "Why, do they still make liquor here in these hills? I thought since prohibition had been repealed there wouldn't be any need for making moonshine any more."

"Some likes hit best. An' anyways, Adair County's dry. Allus has been. An' hit's a fur piece over to Marion County to git a drink. They's allus some makes it nearabouts."

When the music ended, Miss Willie watched Rose slip out the door with Tay Clark. She saw his arm hold itself around her plump waist and wondered if Wells would like that. Surely not, if the boy was a lawbreaker. She turned around to find him. But Mary was at her side. "Miss Willie, we'd better serve the ice cream now. If you want them to choose partners, you'd better get started."

"No," Miss Willie answered, "just get Hod to tell them the ice cream will be served outside. We'll let them do as they please about eating. And, Mary, tell Hod not to say anything about paying for it. This party's on me."

In the darkness under the trees Tay Clark and Rose stood. No light filtered in this closed place, and trees sheltered deeply on all sides. Tay pulled the girl into his arms. He bent his head and let his mouth down upon her lifted one. "Rose, Rose," he said softly, pushing her head back and laughing a little, then bending to drink deeply of her mouth again.

"We cain't stay long, Tay," she warned, "somebody'll miss us."

"Not fer a minnit yit," he begged. "I don't git to see you hardly ever. Days is so long over there by myself. An' I git to thinkin' of you. Someday I'm goin' to run off with you!"

"Not yit," she said, letting her lips run lightly over his chin.

"Don't do that!" and he pulled sharply away.

She laughed and, stretching on her toes, locked her arms around his neck. He pulled her close. "Yer pa'd take his shotgun to me ifen he could see us like this," he growled.

"He ain't goin' to see us," she said.

"What's he got agin me?" Tay grumbled. "Ifen you'd let me, I'd tell him to his face we was aimin' to git married soon as we kin. Hit ain't no sin to want to git married."

"He ain't got nothin' agin you personal, I reckon. But he don't like what he's heared about you. Says you been a wild 'un all yer life. An' he wouldn't noways put up with that there stillin'."

"Cain't a man change hisself?"

"I doubt he'd think so."

They heard the sound of the people moving outside the building. "I got to go back now, Tay. They're comin' out to eat the ice cream. You go on around the schoolhouse, an' I'll go back the way we come."

"Wait," he held her a moment longer. "You goin' to school?"

"Yes."

"I'll come up the holler when I kin. Listen fer a owl. I'll hoot three times, an' then three more times. I'll be in the pine woods."

She listened intently. "I'll git away when I kin. Ifen I don't come soon, don't wait. Hit'll be because somethin's holdin' me. Now git around that buildin', quick!"

People were milling around the door as he dropped a last light kiss on her lips, and she slipped easily under his arm into the darkness.

The ice cream disappeared like magic. Miss Willie and Becky dipped it up as fast as they could, but there was always another dish held out for more. There was an easy flow of talk and laughter now, and a high, good-natured give-and-take of fun. Miss Willie, so tired she couldn't stand, sat behind the freezers, full of contentment. Hod and Wells had saved the party, but that was not important now. What was important was that folks were having a good time.

Then Hod came to her. "Miss Willie, I'd like to end this party with a song from Matt Jasper. He can really sing, an' I think folks would like it."

"Of course, Hod."

Hod brought Matt into the lantern light, where he stood before the crowd, gaunt, dirty, and fumbling, his head hanging and his eyes darting. He had made some attempt at cleaning himself up, for his hair had been cut and his face was clean-shaven. Miss Willie saw with surprise that his lean, thin face wasn't bad-

109

looking. She had thought him hideous when she and Mary met him and Lutie down in the hollow that morning. Now she saw that the bones of his face were chiseled into sharp, fine contours, and that his weak, mobile mouth was pathetically young.

He wet his lips nervously a time or two. Then he cleared his throat and lifted his head. He fixed his eyes at some point beyond the heads of the people and opened his mouth. A sweet, clear voice rose soaring above them all. Clear and sweet and soft, it floated over them. He was singing an old spiritual: "And I, If I Be Lifted Up, Will Draw All Men Unto Me." "If I be lifted up" . . . Miss Willie's eyes stung. The truest tenor in these parts! Matt Jasper used to be a fine-looking man! The voice lifted and fell, like a sweet-blown bugle in the night, full, clean, and fine. "If I be lifted up"! For this transcendent moment Matt Jasper was lifted up. Lifted out of the dull, prideless clod that walked the hills by day, lifted and changed somehow into something clean and noble. For a moment, this shining present, he was a man.

The voice rose to the last high, unbearably sweet note and held it suspended, as fragile as a star, letting it linger and fade, gently and softly, until it whispered into nothingness in the trees. A sob rose in Miss Willie's throat. It was too much that this man whom you couldn't bear to look upon, whose touch you would shrink from, who was foul and diseased and unclean — it was too much that from out of *that* should come that pure, sweet voice. This ridge . . . these people! She would never understand them!

When that last high note had been lost in time, the people wiped their eyes and cried for more, more! But Matt shook his head and shambled out into the darkness. The pure look that had lighted his face while he was singing was washed away, and the old sly, furtive expression crept back as he slunk off. Miss Willie watched him, and her throat was knotted in an aching lump.

And then the party was over. The first folks to leave came by as she stood there, ice-cream dipper hanging limply in her hand. "Hit was a real good party, Miss Willie." "Hit was a heap o' fun." She heard that repeated dozens of times. "Hit was a good party. Hit was a plumb nice party."

At the last Hod and Mary and Wells were left with her. While the men took the tables and chairs inside, Mary and Miss Willie stacked the little paper plates and crumpled the white table covers. They made one huge trash heap and burned it, and piled the littered spoons in a basket for the next day's returning. Miss Willie's feet ached, and she felt hot and weary all over.

"We'll take you home," Mary said, when they had finished.

"I'll take her home," Wells said. "I've got the spring wagon. Hit'll save you all the trip up the ridge an' back."

"Yes, Mary," Miss Willie agreed, "you go on. You must be as tired and worn out as I am. Wells has to go right by my place anyhow."

Wells helped her into the wagon and she settled herself on the quilt which was folded on the seat. He crawled up beside her and clucked to the team.

When they came out from under the trees, the moon was riding high and a froth of stars was following in its wake. The night was full of sound, and the wraiths of mist were curling in the low places, shot through with moonlight. There was a ghostly stillness which the singing insects could not disturb. A stillness that is full of sound, but that belongs only in the country.

As the wagon jolted down the road, Wells's shoulder moved against her own, and Miss Willie felt a hand of peace laid across her weariness. This man was so good, so solid, so earthy. He was part of the ridge, absorbed into the soil, bound to it, tied and yet free. He gave off an earth feeling, a closeness to land and trees and streams and animals. He had not lost his essential bondage to the earth which gave him his full, free manhood. He was not wasted or emptied. His shoulder here, so broad and strong, rubbing through the thin stuff of her dress, was built for swinging an ax, or pushing a plow, or handling a team. Or, she was honest, for cushioning a woman's head. She drew a deep breath. And he turned to her, speaking for the first time.

"You're jist plumb wore out, ain't you? Jist frazzled down. This here party was jist too much fer you."

"I am tired," she confessed, "yes. But it's a good tiredness. Do you think they had a good time, Wells?"

"Why, shore!" He was astonished. "Didn't you see 'em prancin' around alaughin' an' asingin'? Why, they shore did have a good

111

time!"

"That was because of you and Hod. The party was dying on its feet until you all stepped in. Wells, when am I goin to learn?"

"Miss Willie, hit'll take the rest o' yer life to learn the ways of the ridge. You have to be borned here to know 'em all, an' to fit ever' time. Ifen you stay here the rest o' yer life, you'll git easy-like with 'em, but they's things that'll allus puzzle you. But it don't matter, Miss Willie. Jist keep this in mind. They don't ex-pect you to be like 'em in most things. They think yer quare, but that ain't goin' to keep 'em from likin' you, an' bein' proud yer their teacher. Hit won't keep 'em from buckin' you when what you want don't suit, neither. But I reckon they'd be a mite let down if you wasn't some quare. Hit gives 'em somethin' to talk about. As fur as tonight goes, they'd of had a good time if Hod an' me hadn't of stepped in. They'd a set around an' takened it all in, an' et the ice cream quiet-like, an' they'd a went home an' talked about how purty the schoolhouse looked, an' how purty Miss Willie looked in her white dress, an' how good the ice cream was. Hit was smart of you to give 'em somethin' diffrunt. They liked it. Ifen you'd jist had another pie supper an' spellin' bee like they allus have, they'd a enjoyed it, too, but hit wouldn't of been in keepin' with what they was expectin' from you. Me an' Hod jist thought we'd as well mix in a little of the old with the new to satisfy ever'body. But don't go thinkin' that was all of it. Hit was you, in yer purty little white dress, an' yer nice speech, an' the flowers, an' ice cream 'stead of pie, an' tables an' chairs, an' lanterns in the trees. Why, they'll brag about this school openin' party fer years!"

Hot tears pricked Miss Willie's eyes. "Thank you, Wells," she said. "Thank you. For everything."

But when she was drifting off to sleep she could remember only one thing he had said. "Hit was you in yer purty little white dress." He had noticed the dress then!

CHAPTER

❦ 12 ❦

Aᴜɢᴜsᴛ sᴛᴏʟᴇ ᴏᴠᴇʀ Pɪɴᴇʏ Rɪᴅɢᴇ with its long sun-filled days, and its cool, sighing nights. Miss Willie walked the mile and a half to Big Springs, watching the changing fields. The corn was browning and the ears hung heavy on the stalks. Broom sedge along the way was losing its silky look and turning light and yellow. Goldenrod was heading up and sumac was beginning to redden.

The tobacco was bleaching in the sun, standing tall, crowned with the pale, amethyst, oleanderlike blooms. They looked so waxen and so creamy that she stopped by a field one day and gathered an armful for the schoolroom. The children laughed when they saw them on her desk in a tall urn. "Terbaccer blooms," they snickered. "Teacher's got a bouquet of terbaccer blooms!"

"Beauty is where you find it," Miss Willie insisted stanchly, "and if you're looking for it, you can find it anywhere, even in tobacco blooms!"

The nights were starlit and still. The cowbells in the pasture carried far over the hills, and the incessant drone of katydids and nightjars hummed out of the shadows and dark places. And always from the creeks and ponds came the bass growl of the frogs. To Miss Willie the night sounds formed the perfect accompaniment for drowsy contentment. Night after night when she lay on her old cherry bed under the window watching the moon and the stars circle the skies, these sounds lulled her to sleep. And she slept so deeply and awakened so refreshed! If the days took their toll of her strength, the nights filled and replenished her, giving her in the cool dawns a sense of power and grace. The spring of life was rewinding. She felt full of health and an inner sap which flowed through her joyously. She was well, she was busy, she was happy.

And she felt she was beginning to accomplish some things. Her little scheme about the drinking cups had worked. She felt

113

a little guilty about that. It was another compromise. But at least the cups hadn't disappeared again, and however she had won the victory, it was still a victory. Things had quieted down at the school.

And she was beginning to get somewhere with her plan to make Gault have a well dug for Becky. She giggled as she thought of it. She hadn't even told Becky she was working on that. She had just started helping Becky bring up the night water. A time or two she had noticed Gault watching them. Once or twice she had dragged behind with her bucket so that Gault, coming to the house, had overtaken her. "Becky's back gets so tired," she had explained, "carrying water all that long way up the hill." Gault had not offered to carry the bucket, but she'd have him doing that next. Let him see how heavy that bucket was once, let him roll under that barbed-wire fence and carry two full buckets of water up that hill, and he'd start thinking about a well!

She jogged along in Hod's old car, keeping it in the ruts of the road, letting it nose along slowly. She had borrowed it to go calling. She wanted to know the parents of all her children, and she wanted to see for herself the homes they came from. Right now she was headed toward Wells's place. Not that a call there was necessary. She saw Wells frequently, but she admitted to more than a little curiosity about his home. Out of what had Rose and Rufe and Abby come? How did they make out, now, with Rose keeping the house? Mary said they did very well. But she wanted . . . what did she want? She just wanted to see Wells's home. She was compelled, somehow, to see where he lived, and how. Compelled to . . . to what? To be where he was? To stand familiarly where he slept and ate and worked? To look at the four walls that enclosed him daily?

The house stood off the main ridge road, on a high point in a long sweep of fields. A grove of trees surrounded it and shaded it from view until you were right up on it. Miss Willie drove the car up to the fence and got out. It was a big house, larger than most on the ridge, two stories in front with a T added in back. But it had a neglected look. The grass and weeds had overgrown the yard, and the fence sagged badly. The house had once been painted, but now the paint was scaling off, leaving dead and

114

patchy places, like scabs on old sores. There were cardboards in the missing windowpanes across the front, and when she stepped up on the porch, a loose board gave treacherously under her. She felt a shock of sympathy and pity. A man alone had so little time for beauty.

When she called, Rose came to the door and pushed the sagging screen outward to let her in. "Why, hit's Miss Willie," she said. "Come in. Come in, ifen you kin git in. I wasn't expectin' nobody today an' the house ain't cleaned up or nothin'. Git you a chair, Miss Willie."

Miss Willie looked around the room. Rose was right. The floor was littered with odds and ends. In one corner was a bed, not yet made, and across from it stood an old bureau, its top cluttered with bottles, boxes, Rose's purse, an old hat of Wells's, and as much other stuff as could be gotten on it. The faded blue wallpaper had come loose in the corner over the bed and hung sagging and bellying in the draft that swept through the open door.

Hanging on the wall were several brightly colored calendars, and hooked up near the ceiling, by cords passed under their arms, were three dolls. Miss Willie remembered that here on the ridge little girls did not play with their best dolls. Only the old, ragged ones were to play with. The best ones were hung on the walls.

Over the fireplace was an enlarged and tinted photograph of a woman, hung at that precarious angle which was considered correct on the ridge. It was a gaudy, cheap piece of work, framed in a wide and ornate circle of gilt, and the glass bulged drunkenly over it. But neither the gaudy colors, nor the cheap ornate frame, nor the bulging glass could detract from the winsomeness of the brown-haired, brown-eyed woman laughing down from the wall. Her eyes crinkled at the corners and her mouth spread widely across her face. That's Matildy, thought Miss Willie. That's Wells's Matildy, who used to sit here before this fire and laugh with him, and hold her children close, and laugh with them. These four walls closed safe around them and their laughter, and held them tight. She looked around as if the walls had moved closer in. And then these four walls didn't hold them tight any longer. Wells, trying to hold the bits together. And the bits flying farther and farther apart. How empty Matildy's going had left

115

these four walls! A slow ache spread over Miss Willie, squeezing her and smothering her. How empty Matildy's going had left Wells!

She rose abruptly. "I'd like a drink, Rose," she said.

"Yessum," and Rose led the way into the kitchen. Rufe sat near the door, cleaning his gun. He looked up when they entered, but ducked his head when Miss Willie spoke and went on drawing the oiled rag through the gun barrel.

The flies swarmed through the unscreened windows and settled in a heavy cloud over the uncovered table. The dishes and the remainder of the breakfast food still sat there, greasy and sodden-looking. Miss Willie felt a tremor of nausea.

Rose took a bucket from the wash shelf and emptied its contents out the door. "I'll jist draw up a fresh pump," she said, shooing a chicken from the stoop as she went out.

Suddenly Miss Willie turned. "Rufe," she said, "why don't you keep the yard trimmed, and the fences mended? And why don't you fix the screens, and the windows? Your father has so much to do. He can't do everything. But you're a big, strong boy, and you could be such a help to him if you would. Instead of hunting and fishing all the time, why don't you try to be more thoughtful of your father?"

A closed, sullen look crept over the boy's face. "I he'p him," he said. "All I kin, an' all he wants." He snapped the bolt of the gun in place and stood it in the corner. Miss Willie spread her hands helplessly. And Rose sloshed water across the floor lifting the bucket to the shelf.

Miss Willie turned to her. "Rose, I'll help you do these dishes while I'm here."

"Miss Willie, they ain't no need o' that. I'll git to 'em sooner or later. They ain't no hurry."

"Oh, let's do them now. Two of us will make fast work of it."

"Yessum," and Rose put a kettle of water on to heat while Miss Willie set to work stacking the dishes.

"Do you always have flies this bad, Rose?"

"Yessum. The screens is bad, an' Pop don't git around to fixin' 'em, looks like. An' they jist swarm outside the door, what with the chickens flockin' around, an' ever'thing."

116

"Can't you pen the chickens up somewhere? They oughtn't to run loose in the yard. And, Rose, if you wouldn't throw water close to the house there wouldn't be so many flies. Or garbage and refuse. Take it away from the house, and empty all the water somewhere else. Those things draw flies, and you'll find there won't be so many if you take care."

Rufe snorted and went out the door, slamming it behind him. Miss Willie flushed, and heat poured up into her face and neck. "I don't mean to interfere, Rose," she went on, though, "but you'll have a home of your own someday, and you'll want it nice and clean, and if you don't learn now, it will be hard for you later on."

"Yessum."

Miss Willie had a hopeless feeling. Rose was so compliant, so soft-spoken, so agreeable. But she doubted if a word she had said meant a thing to her. O Wells, Wells! How truly empty had Matildy's going left this house!

When Miss Willie returned the car that night, she was tired and white-faced. She handed Hod the keys and sank into a chair, her knees trembling and her back aching. "Mary," she said, "I wouldn't believe what I have seen today, if I hadn't seen it with my own eyes!" She rested her elbows on the arms of the chair and put her hands over her face. "I have been in ten homes today, if you could call them homes. They are where people live, at any rate. Where the parents of those school children live! In not one have I seen the least comprehension of the necessity of sanitation, cleanliness, or even comfort! I can't quite believe even yet what I have seen!"

Mary laid her knitting aside. "I know, Miss Willie. I've tried to tell you."

Miss Willie shook her head. "You could never tell anyone what the actual circumstances are. They beggar telling. You have to see this sort of thing for yourself. Mary," and she sat up straight, "I stood on the porch at Mamie Clark's and watched her separate her milk. The flies were so thick they drowned in the milk as it poured from the separator, and Mamie reached in with her hand — her hand, mind you — and dipped them out, and went right on

117

separating!"

"And at the Joneses'," Miss Willie went on, "the baby was sick — 'summer complaint,' Corinna called it — and do you know what she was giving it? Soot water! Water, with soot from the chimney stirred in it! Said it was the best thing she knew for stopping summer complaint. And the poor little thing lay there, crying and fretting! She gave it a cold rind of bacon to gnaw on to hush it!"

Miss Willie's hand fretted nervously in her lap. "And at the Simpsons', Quilla is down with her stomach ulcers. 'Stummick trouble,' she called it. I asked her how long she'd had stomach trouble, and she said she didn't rightly know. All her life, nearly! She lay there and told me in the calmest sort of way how she had spit up blood this time. I asked her if she'd seen the doctor, and she laughed and said it wouldn't do any good. She'd been once, a long time ago, and he'd told her to stop eating soda bread and chunk meat and soup beans, but she said she didn't like the stuff he told her she could eat, so she'd just gone ahead eating like always!"

Miss Willie sat forward in her chair and pointed her finger. "Mary, half the people on this ridge have ulcerated stomachs! You can't think of a family but one or two have stomach trouble. And they go right on eating hot soda bread three times a day, fried chunk meat, boiled beans — greasy and soupy — and raw onions! They raise wonderful gardens and they don't like garden stuff! They get plenty of good, rich milk, but they separate their milk and sell the cream to the creamery, and drink coffee or skimmed milk! Fried meat! Fried apples! Fried potatoes! They only know one way to cook anything, and that's to fry it! Oh, I always thought people in the country had the best, the most wholesome food in the world! But not here, they don't! They literally eat themselves to death on their greasy, fried foods!"

In her agitation she got up and took to pacing around the room. She stopped in front of Mary and shook her finger again. "And do you know that in five of those ten homes — five of them, mind you, exactly half — there wasn't even a toilet! No outhouse of any sort! They use the barn! A whole family, eight or ten people, and they use the barn! And in three of those homes they carry water from a spring. There wasn't any well! I asked why they didn't

118

have a well. It costs money to dig a well. 'Then,' I said, 'why don't you have a cistern? All it would take is a little energy to dig a hole, just a small amount of money to line it with cement and to trough the eaves of the house.' Drink rain water! They looked at me as though I'd lost my mind! They wouldn't think of such! I said they could keep it pure with chloride of lime, and they would know positively it was clean. Well, they knowed the spring water was clean. Why, it was so cold it hurt your teeth, and so clear you could see yourself in it! No matter, of course, that cows drink from it too! No matter that lizards and snakes and bugs crawl all around it, and maybe in it! No, the spring water was clean and pure! Oh, it's terrible! Terrible!" And Miss Willie sank back into her chair and shivered.

Mary moved restlessly. "Well, these are our people, Miss Willie, and that's the way they are."

"That's what's so hopeless about the whole thing," Miss Willie cried, "you've expressed it exactly! That's the way they are, and there's no changing them this side of heaven! That's the way they've 'allus' been! That's the way they're satisfied to be! How on earth can you help people who don't even know they need helping?" In a fury of frustration she flung her hands wide. "Never in my life have I been so angry, and never have I felt so completely helpless! It makes me furious that here in this country of ours, the wealthiest in the whole world, there are people living as these people on the ridge are living! But that's not the worst of it! The worst is their lethargy. Their not wanting anything better or different! They have no conception of what it is to live freely, and graciously, and healthily and cleanly! They make out, just like — " she paused — "I started to say just like their fathers had before them. But I believe these people have sunk farther into apathy. They don't have the initiative their fathers had. Their fathers and their grandfathers turned their minds to work and made them serve them. The women spun and wove and stitched and sewed. The men sawed and hewed and experimented. They had to. There was no alternative. But these people have lost all the things their fathers knew and have learned nothing new. They sell their healthy, wholesome living for the cheap things they can buy. They'd rather have sardines and bologna and bottled pop

119

from the huckster than their own good milk and eggs and garden stuff."

Her glasses slipped down her nose, and in her agitation she shoved furiously at them. The nosepiece snapped with a sharp, brittle sound. She snatched the broken glasses off and glared at them. "Now," she said in exasperation, "now, that's just the last straw! That's just the end of all I can stand today! I'm going home, Mary. I'm no fit company for anyone in the mood I'm in!"

She strode across the room, turning at the door to brandish the broken glasses at Mary. "But you wait and see! You wait! There's a way to wake these people up, and I'll find it! I'll think of something! And then I'll do it!"

And she stumped doggedly out of the door.

CHAPTER
❧ 13 ❧

Aᴜɢᴜsᴛ ɪɴ ᴛʜᴇ Pɪɴᴇʏ Rɪᴅɢᴇ country was also the time of revivals and great preachings. Big white tents mushroomed in the hollows and on the ridges, each ministering to a particular neighborhood. It mattered not what denomination sponsored the revival; the folks came, tanned and leathered by the summer sun, to hear the power of the Word. To shout and pray together, and to fall, abashed, confessing their sins at the mourners' bench.

Piney Ridge had its meeting too. Out of the flatlands beyond the hills came a traveling preacher with a tent. He set it up in Matt Jasper's field, about halfway down the ridge, at the corner where the roads crossed, and where the mailboxes were set. Gasoline lanterns gave a brilliant white light which filled the tent and spread out over the field, throwing long shadows across the clover and the bushes that edged the field.

The people came and filled the tent, and sat in the clover and crushed it so that its sweet, spicy smell mixed with the odor of sweat and tired, soured bodies. Night after night the people came, believing, with perhaps the last sure belief left in this sophisticated land of ours, in their sinfulness and in their need for redemption. Sin was real here on the ridge. There was none among

120

these people who had not sinned. Who had not gossiped, or cursed, or drunk from the flowing jug, or dealt a hand from a deck of playing cards, or been tempted in the ways of the flesh. Sin rode hard upon their shoulders, and nightly they came and writhed under the lash of the preacher's words.

The sin that he laid upon them the hardest was that of the tobacco crop. It was a crop inspired by the devil! "Them that uses it," he shouted, "is doomed! Them that raises it is damned forever . . . forever and endurin' damned!"

But how else were they to feed the house full of young'uns that overran the doors and porches? How else clothe them against the winter's cold? Tobacco was hard money in their overalls pockets. There was no other crop to bring them cash. They fought and groveled and promised. But always they made another tobacco crop.

Miss Willie went one night with Mary and Hod and sat bewildered and confused on the back row. She felt as if she were witnessing a scene lifted straight from Dante's *Inferno*. These moaning, sobbing people were not her neighbors. They were actors upon a ghostly stage, with the dirty sides of the tent providing a slovenly backdrop, and the sputtering, spitting lanterns hissing a monotonous orchestral accompaniment. It was lurid, tawdry, and gross.

This was the crying out of a tortured people, of a burdened and sin-laden people, begging for deliverance. She saw neither dignity nor truth there. Only frenzy, and emotional fury, and chaos. She went no more, for it had saddened her inexplicably. She left it, impersonally, to itself.

But it didn't stay impersonal, for one night Mary told her sadly that Irma had professed during the revival. Irma was Hod's sister. Little Johnnie's mother.

"Well," Miss Willie said, "each of us must decide his religious beliefs for himself."

"If it were just for herself, we wouldn't be worried," Mary answered. "But this religion Irma has taken up believes in faith healing. They don't believe in having the doctor when you're sick. And Irma is the mother of a family. Suppose little Johnnie or the baby gets sick? Or she or John? This will affect all of them,

121

don't you see? We are terribly disturbed, Miss Willie. Hod just can't understand how Irma could have been so influenced by this faith."

Miss Willie rubbed her hand against the glossy arm of her chair. "It's just the ridge again, Mary. Just the lack of knowledge, experience, wider horizons. What else can you expect? Instead of arousing themselves to do something *now* about the drudgery and the sorrow and the sufferings of life in all its harsh reality here on the ridge, they go along apathetically, and find their release in some bright and shining state of life in heaven. Irma is the product of her environment, that's all."

"So was Hod."

"But Hod, my dear, is one in a thousand. And, say what you will, he got off the ridge long enough to look at it in perspective. He got away from it long enough to find himself. Had he never left the ridge, he might now be sunk in this same lethargy."

Mary found no answer to that. She turned restlessly to the piano, and her fingers sought comfort in a Chopin nocturne.

The big baptizing followed the revival. There were always twenty or thirty people who had been converted to be baptized. Some of them had been converted every summer, year after year, but during the long winter months they always fell from grace and had to be converted and baptized again the next summer. The time between revivals was too dragged out, and the Word was forgotten and the spirit became weak. So the people backslid and had to come under the Power again, and be dipped once more in the blood of the Lamb.

"Miss Willie," Becky asked that Sunday afternoon, "you goin' to the baptizin' with us?"

"I don't think so," Miss Willie said, shuddering away from another spectacle of rampant holiness.

Becky went on. "You better come go along. Hit's allus a sight to see."

"Do they preach and go on like they did at the revival?"

"Oh, no. The big preachin's over, an' the convertin's done. This is the bringin' in of the sheaves."

So Miss Willie decided to go. At least this was broad daylight, and the scene would lack the infernolike quality the glaring lanterns and the dark night outside had given to the meeting.

She dressed and went out to the back lot, crawled into the big wagon, and took her place in the hickory-bottomed chair Gault placed for her back of the wagon seat. They jolted down the road toward the pike and the Green River bottoms. The baptizing was to be held down below the bridge, where the water was shallow but where there were also pools deep enough for the immersions.

Miss Willie felt taut and she halfway wished she hadn't come. But, she argued with herself, I should know the *whole* life of the ridge. If this is part of it, I should know it. She couldn't say why the meeting had filled her with such revulsion. Perhaps it was because it had been so stark . . . so raw and so animal-like. She felt as if the people had stripped themselves before her, and she felt sore and ashamed when she thought of it. As if she had witnessed the most private and indecent baring of humanity's soul.

"Becky," she said, "did you know Irma professed the other night?"

"Yes," Becky answered tightly.

Gault slapped the reins against the backs of the horses. "Come up," he grunted.

"Don't you all go to these meetings?" Miss Willie went on. "I don't believe you went a single night."

"We don't hold with no sich," Gault said. "When hit's a reg'lar meetin', we go like the rest."

Miss Willie felt a sudden relief pour over her at Gault's words.

"What will Hattie and Tom think of Irma's being converted?" she asked.

"I'm thinkin' they'll not like it," Gault answered briefly. "We have allus been decent, God-fearin' people, abidin' by the Scriptures."

"The Scriptures says they shall speak with tongues," Becky murmured.

"Becky," Gault turned on her fiercely, "you ain't called on to interpret the Scriptures! I am the head of this house, an' I am beholden to speak what the Scriptures says as best I kin. Hit ain't fitten fer a woman to seek wisdom beyond what the head of the house has got. I have told you that before. Yore rebellious tongue frashes me, times."

123

Becky shriveled into herself and Miss Willie subsided. The head of the house had spoken!

When they came down off the ridge onto the graveled pike, they joined a procession of others going to the river. There were wagons and buggies and a few cars which pulled around the slower moving vehicles, raising immense clouds of dust which fogged down upon the road in an opaque veil. Miss Willie kept her handkerchief over her nose and fanned helplessly at the thick cloud which settled inevitably over her clean dress and made her hands and face feel gritty.

When they came to the bridge, they followed the others off the pike down into a beautiful green, parklike area under the trees. Many were already there, teams unhitched and tied to the backs of the wagons. And the crowd wandered up and down the riverbank, waiting.

The women who were to be baptized were gathered together under one tall tree. Young and old, big and little, they were dressed in white. Some of them had on long, flowing robes, evidently made from bed sheets, while others had on simple white dresses. Other women were going among them, kneeling and stooping and moving from one to the other.

"What are they doing?" Miss Willie wanted to know.

"They're aputtin' little rocks in their hems, to keep their dresses from floatin' on the water," Becky said.

"Oh."

The men to be baptized were gathered under another tree. Their clothing looked no different from every day. Except that their shirts seemed gay and colorful compared to the angel white of the women's robes. A man detached himself from the group, and, taking a long staff, waded solemnly out into the river.

At this point the stream was clear and emerald green. The white pebbles on its floor gleamed like crystal through the sparkling water, and the current eddied slowly around the man's trousers as he walked carefully into the water. He prodded with the staff before him, setting it down and then taking a step forward. He waded straight into the river until the water was waist deep, and then he turned toward a pool that was shaded by the overhanging branches of a willow tree. Here the water deepened

124

gradually. When he had reached a place where he stood chest deep, he stopped and, turning to the crowd on the bank, called to the preacher, "This here's about right."

The preacher, in a long, black, shapeless garment, waded in next. When he reached the man, he turned and raised his hand. Two men stepped to the side of the first of the women and supported her into the water. Slowly they made their way through the emerald current, stepping carefully over the stones and easing the woman's way. When she reached the preacher, he turned her toward the crowd, and at his raised hand a song was lifted into the air:

"'Shall we gather at the river? . . .
Yes, we'll gather at the river,
The beautiful, the beautiful river.'"

The rocks sewed into the hem of her garment weighted the woman's robe so that it hung wet and heavy on her. She was as white as her robe. The preacher's voice could not be heard above the song, but his mouth moved. Then he placed his hand over the woman's face and bent her back into the water until she was lost to sight. When he raised her up, she flung her arms over her head and started shouting, and the crowd on the bank shouted with her and started crying and weaving back and forth and singing.

"'Yes, we'll gather at the river, . . .
That flows from the throne of God!'"

This was the first of many. The two men brought the woman back to the edge of the stream, and she fell to the ground, moaning and crying. They took the next woman into the water, and she was trembling so that her robe quivered around her. Miss Willie saw that this was Irma, Hod's sister. Little Johnnie's mother. Little Johnnie, who drew blue jays with red and green and purple feathers, but who didn't know for sure whether hit was a blue jay because he was flyin' so fast!

Irma was quiet in the water, spent and subdued, and when she rose from the wet burial of her living flesh, she didn't shout and cry. Instead, her face was uplifted and transfigured. There was a radiance on it that glowed and shone. There was a look of muted joy and an illumination of some inner light shining through. She came to the shore and moved quickly through the shouting women, as if they stood in her way. Miss Willie watched her go into the bushes to change her clothes. She shivered in the heat, and her own perspiration-damp clothes felt cold and clammy.

After the women came the men, and the afternoon waned before the baptizing was over. The river was muddied from the dragging feet, and the preacher dipped the gay shirts methodically now. The song had died away and the last man was immersed in a sudden stillness, so that the words of the preacher came across the water strong and clear: "In the name of the Father, the Son, and the Holy Ghost."

A finger of sunlight stole through the shadows and laid itself directly on the head of the man waiting quietly by the preacher's side. The scene was sharply etched before Miss Willie's eyes and there was a clean, fine dignity in the strong look of the man, and in the firm, loud words of the preacher.

"That's Irma's man," Becky whispered. "That's John Walton. Irma must of talked him into it too."

The man was bent backward and the water closed over him with scarcely a ripple. And then he was making his way, dripping and sodden, to the shore.

The people scattered to their wagons and buggies. There was a hurrying and a scurrying and a calling back and forth. Teams were hastily hitched up, and wagons turned onto the pike with a scattering sound of gravel thrown from under quick wheels. There was no friendly dallying for talk. It was getting late and the nightwork was still to be done. And the baptizing was over.

CHAPTER
❧ 14 ❧

AND THEN IT WAS SEPTEMBER and a feeling of fall was in the air. The days were still summery and lazy, but they were growing shorter. Now when school was out at four o'clock, the path through the hollow was darkened by the long shoulders of the ridge. The hillsides were taking on the look of an artist's palette, with the solid green background broken here and there by brilliant splashes of color. Some of the trees were hasty with their giving to autumn, abandoning themselves freely and easily, strutting early in their gorgeous colors. But the great oaks and the tall elms hesitated. A few leaves had mottled and veined into a dull reddish-yellow, but mostly they still clung stubbornly to their pristine, virginal green. It was as if they offered, grudgingly, one leaf at a time to the season, counting miserly their remaining hoard. As if they knew the splendid gold and scarlet garments so gaudily worn by the other trees were but a brief prelude to the inevitable and withering nudeness of the winter. In their wisdom they postponed the time when their black ribs would be stripped and exposed, frozen and shrunken. Winter was a long, long time.

Miss Willie picked her way down the ridge path one morning, thinking she must absorb all this color and beauty, for the time was so short now that she could walk. All too soon she would have to ride around the road. These few days in September were all that were left. She must breathe deep and let her eyes drink the full cup of the hills and the hollow and the creek. She must spread out and take in all the green and the gold and the red, a savings against the gray days ahead.

A noise in the bushes off to her right startled her. It was a rattling and scratching, as if some big animal was thrashing around, loosing pebbles and shuffling the dried leaves. She stopped. But quickly she decided it must be one of Hod's cows wandering off up the hillside, and she started on. She had taken a few steps when she felt fear crawling up her back, raising the hackles on her neck. A cold wind blew down her spine, freezing and paralyzing her. Her stomach was gripped by an iron hand, squeezed and knotted, and her legs felt limp and heavy. When her fear reached the border of panic, she whirled, her mind instinctively telling her to face the unknown danger.

And then she saw him. Matt Jasper was clawing through the bushes, a little back of her and to the right. He was staggering and reeling drunkenly, pulling himself along by the bushes. He fell to his knees and frantically crawled along on all fours, careless of the undergrowth which tore at his face. He pulled himself heavily to his feet and staggered a few steps toward her, and then fell and rolled to her feet. She screamed then. One high, rending scream which rose spiraling over the hill.

127

But Matt was clawing at her feet. "Don't let him git me. Don't let him git me. Please, Miss Willie, he's acomin' after me. He's acomin' up the trail down there. Hide me, Miss Willie. Hide me. Don't let him git me." He was plucking at her shoes, his face drawn and taut, his eyes fixed and staring. Foam had gathered in the corners of his mouth, and his teeth worked over his under-lip, gnawing it raggedly.

Miss Willie made herself stop shuddering, and she swallowed the tightness in her throat. "Who's coming, Matt? Who is it that's going to get you? This is just Miss Willie. There's no one else here."

"He's acomin' up the trail. I seen him down there in the holler. He's acomin' to git me. He's agoin' to take me to Danville to the 'sylum. I ain't agoin'! I ain't agoin'! Ain't nobody agoin' to put me in no 'sylum! I'll kill 'em! I'll kill 'em!" His voice rose shrilly, and then his body stiffened and his back arched high. He began to jerk and his head twisted on his neck. His mouth drew into a grimace, and the muscles of his face twitched and jerked in a chorea of tiny movements. His hands beat against the ground, and his feet pulled and twisted.

A spasm of nausea gripped Miss Willie, but she felt the weak-ness of relief surge through her. This was just an epileptic seizure and he was harmless now, at least. But what should she do? Run back to the house and tell Gault? Run down in the hollow and get Hod? Nerveless she stood there, and while she waited inde-cisively, she heard footsteps on the path. Fearfully she turned to meet this new threat. The path was full of evil this morning. All the beauty had fled.

The steps neared the big rock, and then a lusty voice broke into song: "Git along home, Cindy, git along home! Oh, git along home, Cindy, I'm goin' to leave you now!" So great was her re-lease from tension when Wells rounded the rock and came into view that Miss Willie sagged against a tree and let herself slide ignominiously to the ground. She dropped her face into her hands and let the tears flow, catching her breath in great, gasping sobs.

Wells took in the whole scene at a glance. Matt Jasper's inert form on the ground. Miss Willie's collapse. But he ran first to Miss Willie, dropping to his knees beside her and pulling at her

128

hands. "Miss Willie! Miss Willie! He never hurt you, did he?"

Miss Willie let her forehead sag forward and rest against that big, broad shoulder. Oh, it was so solid and safe! And his voice was so warm and comforting. The urgency of it filled her with security and safety. She shook her head and rubbed her nose against his shirt. "No," she sobbed, a hiccup catching her between words, "no, he didn't hurt me. He just scared me half to death!"

"Why, hit's jist old Matt Jasper, Miss Willie. He's harmless. He's sort of natural-like, but he wouldn't hurt a flea. Them fits of his'n is skeery, but they ain't dangerous. He allus comes outen 'em as mild as a baby. But he's not harmful. I thought fer a minnit mebbe he'd grabbed at you, or fell over you, or somethin'. You shore had me skeered!"

Miss Willie drew away and pulled herself up. She pushed at her glasses and straightened her hair and blew her nose. "I don't usually go to pieces like this," she apologized, "but he frightened me so!"

"Tell me what happened," Wells said, brushing the twigs and leaves off her dress.

"I was walking along, feeling awfully gay and happy, sort of dreaming, I guess. Thinking how pretty the hills looked and thinking it wouldn't be long until winter, when I heard a noise off to one side of the path. It startled me, but I thought it was just one of Hod's cows, and I started on. Then I just felt as if something terrible was right behind me. Something awful and repulsive. When I turned around, there he was, coming through the bushes, clawing and reeling and falling, and frothing at the mouth. And then he fell right at my feet. He kept saying: 'Don't let him git me. Don't let him git me.' And when I asked him who was trying to get him, he said it was a man from Danville coming to take him to the asylum. And he said he wouldn't go. He'd kill him first." Miss Willie's hands were picking at her handkerchief as she talked, and Wells reached out and stilled them between his own large palms. She wrenched at them and then let them lie quiet. "He said he saw the man down in the hollow."

"I reckon he seen me. I been down to Hod's to take his saw back. They wasn't nobody else in the holler as I know of. Hit

129

must of been me he seen." Wells wrinkled his forehead. "Wonder what's come over him to think ever'body's fixin' to send him to Danville. Jessie said he threatened him one day down at the store. Ain't nobody aimin' to send him off to the 'sylum. He's bright enough when he don't have them fits."

Miss Willie drew a long, shuddering breath. "Wells, I'm not so sure he's not dangerous. If he's got this fixation about being sent to Danville, and if he didn't recognize you and thought you had come after him . . . I think something ought to be done."

"Aw, shucks, Miss Willie. Ever'body here knows Matt Jasper. Knows he has fits an' is sort of quare. But he's harmless. He'll git over this spell o' thinkin' somebody's goin' to take him to Danville. But I'm real sorry he skeered you. Look, he's acomin' to, now." And Wells turned to the lank form lying in the path. He bent over it.

"Matt," he called. "Hey, Matt. C'mon, git up. You had a spell here an' might' nigh skeered Miss Willie to death. C'mon now. Git yerself up from there." He shook the limp shoulders and slapped the limber neck, rubbing his hands up and down Matt Jasper's back and over his face. "C'mon, now, boy."

Matt slowly sat up and rubbed at his mouth. He looked blearily at Wells and past him to Miss Willie. He shook his head and felt of the back of it. "Doggone," he said, twisting and craning his neck, "that'n shore was a good 'un."

Wells helped him to his feet. "You better git on home, now. Tell Lutie to give you somethin' to eat. You ain't got no business walkin' the ridge 'fore breakfast!"

Matt grinned sheepishly and ducked his head at Miss Willie. "I'm shore sorry I skeered you, ma'am. I cain't never tell when one o' these spells is comin' on, but I hate fer you to of seen it." He slapped his old hat against the leg of his overalls and pulled it down over his ragged hair. "Thank ye agin, Wells," he mumbled and started off up the path.

Miss Willie sighed as she watched him lurch up the trail, and shook her head. "He's not like the same person, is he?"

"Matt Jasper was as fine a boy as ever lived on this ridge," Wells said, "until he started havin' them fits. But his pa had fits, an' I reckon hit was jist in the blood. Old Man Clark's woman,

Mamie, is Matt's sister, an' she has 'em too. Now, you come on. I'll walk the rest of the way with you."

"Oh, no. You needn't do that, Wells. I'm all right now."

Wells grinned at her. "Well, you don't look it. Don't give me no bad time, now. C'mon, I'm goin' with you."

The mention of Old Man Clark reminded Miss Willie that she had meant to ask Wells about Rose and Tay Clark. But she found it hard to bring up. They walked in silence down the trail, Wells occasionally whistling little bits of the song he was singing as he came around the rock. Finally Miss Willie summoned her courage and blurted out, "Wells, does Rose go with Old Man Clark's son, Tay Clark?"

"Not that I know of. And she better hadn't," he answered grimly. "Why?"

"Oh, nothing. I just noticed her dancing with him at the party the other night, and wondered."

"Oh, them kids allus dance with ever'body. Hit don't mean a thing. I reckon he's tried to talk to Rose, but I told her not to have nothin' to do with him. He's allus been sort of wild. I'd hate fer Rose to git mixed up with him."

"Yes." Miss Willie found that she couldn't tell him she had seen Rose slip out into the darkness with Tay. Maybe it didn't mean anything, anyhow. Maybe Rose flirted a little with all the boys. And Tay had just been the handiest one that night. She couldn't run telling tales. There was just this uncomfortable feeling that there was something between those two. The boy's eyes had possessed the girl, and his arm had crooked too knowingly around her waist. But she had no right to trouble Wells, especially if the trouble was only in her own mind.

He left her at the schoolyard. "I'm agoin' to bring you a horse," he promised. "You cain't walk this fur much longer. Hit'll set in to rain 'fore long, an' after that winter'll be here. I got a good little mare you kin use this winter. Gentle as a baby, an' she rides easy. I'll bring her over next week."

"Can I buy her?"

Wells hushed her. "Nope. You cain't buy her. Come spring, I'll be needin' her. Jist count it part o' yer pay. I'm a trustee, remember?"

131

Miss Willie laughed. "You're awfully good to the teacher, Wells."

"Well, she's sort of easy to be good to. Ifen e'er person ever asts, you kin tell 'em I like the teacher a heap. Been studyin' about goin' back to school, jist so's I kin be around her more."

Miss Willie felt her face go hot, and she became very busy with her belt. "I've got some studying to do right now! Thank you for bringing me to school, though. And I'll take good care of . . . what's her name? The horse's, I mean?"

Wells's chuckle rippled between them. "That's who I thought you meant. Her name's Pet. The horse's, I mean."

Miss Willie giggled. "That's a nice name." She hesitated, then offered him her hand. "Well, good-by now."

She walked stiffly toward the schoolhouse, not looking back. Don't be a fool, Willie Payne, she scolded herself. At your age! Blushing like a schoolgirl! There's nothing so ridiculous as an old maid simpering around a man! Her head came up at that, and she sniffed. She had *not* been simpering, and why not blush? Goodness knows there had been precious few opportunities for her to blush when she was a girl, and none at all for the past sterile twenty-five years! Why not blush! It was good to have a man speak admiringly, even if it was only in fun! Come to think of it she had a lot of blushing to catch up on, and after all there was no one except herself to jeer at an old maid's vanity!

As she rounded the corner of the schoolhouse, a sidewise glance of her eye caught the shadow of a fleeting, shifting movement behind the tall elm. There was just time to see the vanishing outline of an overalled figure, topped by a tawny head. She frowned. Now what was Rufe doing at school so early?

In the two months since school had started Miss Willie had settled herself into its routine. She had organized and shaped a schedule, bending it as best she could around eight grades, and while she felt frustrated at many points, on the whole she thought she had made as much headway as could be expected. Hod and Gault had constantly emphasized, "Go slow." And she had contented herself with a few things in which she could take genuine

132

satisfaction. The bookshelves were being used now. Not to any great extent, true, but each day someone wandered over to the shelves and took down a book to explore, even tentatively, its hidden treasure. The first- and second-graders now had low tables and benches behind her desk, and she managed to give them greater freedom of movement than at first. By using the older girls to supervise them, they had more frequent playtimes outside. Rose had proved especially good with them. And from her own income Miss Willie had furnished extra books and colors and learning toys. From these smallest ones she reaped her greatest happiness.

In addition to the bookshelves for the older ones, she had set up a long table along the wall, which she called a science table. It was rapidly becoming loaded with specimens of rocks, birds' nests, various pressed and mounted flowers, ferns, leaves, and anything at all that took the eye of a boy or girl on the way to school. She had been amazed at the enthusiasm with which they had received the idea, and at the knowledge of their own land that they displayed. She had encouraged every interest, and several group projects had developed. The sixth grade, for instance, had worked two weeks on a project that began with a hornet's nest one of the boys had brought. The nest had been carefully cut apart and its cellular structure examined. The bookshelves had been resorted to for information, and the interest of the whole school was caught and fanned by the intensive research. Finally a notebook on the hornet was assembled, painstakingly illustrated by drawings and mounted specimens.

She could take pride in these things. They were good. But there were still the major questions of the short school term, the irregular attendance of many of the children, the open spring, and the primitive outhouses. And she could not close her eyes to the fact that she had made little or no headway there. But she reminded herself that there must be first the acorn and then the oak. Except for Rufe, who remained stubbornly aloof, she was winning the confidence and friendship of the school. And she hoped by the end of the term to be able to show the parents so much improvement that they would trust her judgment about the more important things to be done. At the end of the term she meant to make a report to the chairman and the trustees. And she meant to include in it some strong recommendations. But for the present she was satisfied.

The September day heightened to noon, and waned toward four o'clock. It was Friday, and, in accordance with the custom of the school, the last quarter of the day was given over to a program. This program consisted of stories, songs, recitations, and it was varied sometimes with a spelling match or with games in the yard. Today the little folks were excited because they were to do a dramatization of the story of Little Black Sambo.

Irma's little Johnnie, who was Sambo, was near apoplexy with his pent-up feeling of importance. His small earnest face was beet red, and his tongue licked nervously in and out of the empty space where his front teeth were gone. Miss Willie watched him fondly. He was such a sturdy little fellow. So independent and resourceful, and so alert. His mind was eager and quick, with a farseeing, visionary quality that made the distance between the real and the fanciful very short for him. His imagination soared lightly over whatever he did, touching his thoughts and his dreams with enchantment. Little Black Sambo was very real to him today.

The children were grouped to take their parts, and after much whispering and shuffling around and some giggling, they waited for the story to begin. Miss Willie turned to her book and read the opening lines.

Suddenly Johnnie cried: "Wait! Wait, Miss Willie! I have to get the tiger!" And he ran out the door before Miss Willie could stop him. She was puzzled, because redheaded little Sarie Simpson was supposed to be the tiger. Sarie stood now, her head drooping and her thumb in her mouth. "I was the tiger," she quavered.

"You're still the tiger," Miss Willie comforted. "When Johnnie comes back, we'll go on with the story."

And then Johnnie struggled through the door with his arms full of a strange, striped animal. And with him came an awful, penetrating odor! As he came down the aisle, the odor spread, growing stronger and more powerful with each step. Johnnie's face was screwed up in a knot, and his nose wrinkled away from the stench he was carrying. It dawned on the boys and girls and

134

Miss Willie simultaneously what the animal was, and as Miss Willie rose to her feet, there was an uproar from the pupils and the schoolroom emptied in a mad rush for the door. Johnnie and the skunk were shoved aside, and in the confusion Johnnie loosed his hold upon the animal and it fled to the farthest corner, still pouring out its dreadful, protective stink.

Miss Willie could hardly breathe, but she found Johnnie and led him outside. He was sick from his close proximity to the animal, and he reeked of the oily smell. Irma would have to scrub him with her strongest soap, Miss Willie thought, and his clothes would surely have to be burned! For that matter, every person in the school would have to be scoured and scrubbed, including herself! The children stood huddled in the schoolyard now, waiting for some word from her. They were fanning themselves, and pulling at their repulsive garments.

When Johnnie got through being sick, Miss Willie took him to the water tub and bathed his face. He was a wretched little chap! When finally he could talk between his sobs and his retching, he said mournfully: "He never smelt like that when Rufe give him to me! He never smelt atall, Miss Willie! An' he was so purty. Rufe said he'd make a awful good tiger on account of his stripe down his back. The pitchers in the book had stripes on the tiger, an' I was goin' to s'prise you!" He buried his face in Miss Willie's skirt.

She patted his head gently. "Never mind, dear. Never mind. It's all right." And then she disengaged his clutching fingers and walked over to the group of older pupils. She felt her anger rising within her until it boiled up and burned her face like fire.

"Where is Rufe?" she asked the group.

No one knew, and then Miss Willie remembered that she had not seen him since the afternoon recess. No. He wouldn't stay and risk contaminating himself! He would just turn it loose upon the whole school while he got safely away! What a dirty trick, just to take one more lick at her!

"Did anyone else have any part in this?" she asked.

"No, ma'am!" The answers were vehement, and accompanied with emphatic shakings of heads. She had no doubt they were truthful. No one, knowing what was to happen, would have

135

stayed around to see it. The penalty for that would have been too great. The smell saturating these boys and girls was proof enough that Rufe had perpetrated his trick alone.

"You may go home, then," she told them. "And I'm terribly sorry for all the trouble this is going to cause your folks. A harmless joke is fun for everyone, but a joke that causes trouble is no longer a joke. It's just plain meanness!"

"That Rufe Pierce," one of the girls scolded. "He'd ort to be whipped! Stinkin' up all our clothes like this! My mamma's shore not goin' to like it."

"This is my best dress," another one chimed in, "an' I'll bound the smell won't never come out!"

"Your mothers will know what to do with them, if anything *can* be done with them," Miss Willie said. "Now run along home."

When they had scattered, Miss Willie set out determinedly for Wells's house. The awful stink that went with her was settling into her skin and hair, and she wondered if she would ever be clean of it again. But this had to be settled with Mr. Rufe immediately!

At Wells's she stopped outside the gate and called. Wells came to the door and seeing her started down the path. "Come in," he shouted, "Come on in."

"I can't," Miss Willie answered, "I smell too bad. And don't come any closer. You'll get it all over you."

Wells stopped and looked queerly at her. Being downwind of her, he had just got a whiff of the odor she was carrying. He sniffed and wrinkled his nose. Then he laughed. "I declare, Miss Willie! Don't you know a polecat when you see one? I thought ever'body knowed what a skunk looked like!" He pinched his nose between his fingers. "Whew! You must of got hold of a powerful one!"

Miss Willie's lips firmed and she shot him a malevolent look. "I know very well what a skunk looks like, Wells Pierce. I haven't been playing with any polecat! It was forced on me very much against my will! On me and the whole schoolroom, as a matter of fact. Where is Rufe?"

Wells sobered quickly. "You ain't sayin' Rufe turned a skunk loose in the schoolhouse, are you, Miss Willie?"

136

"I'm saying just that," she snapped, "only it was worse. He played a mean, scurvy trick on little Johnnie . . ." She went on to tell the whole story.

When she had finished, Wells's face was flinty and set. "Miss Willie, I don't keer what you say, I'm goin' to take keer o' that young gentleman my way this time! This here business o' bein' a troublemaker has got to stop. They ain't but one way to handle a young'un that's gittin' outta hand. A good, stout strop laid acrost his backside'll make him think twicet afore he does any more meanness! An' I'm jist the one kin lay it on. I've had all this foolishment I'm goin' to put up with!"

"No," Miss Willie answered, "this is still between Rufe and me. Is he here?"

"No, he ain't here yit. He don't hardly git home from school till a little later. I reckon he's hidin' out somewheres, waitin' till time to come in."

"Oh. I wanted to talk to him myself." She thought for a moment. "I'll be by early in the morning. I'm going to take him to the schoolhouse and see that he scrubs that building from one end to the other. If you don't mind, that is."

"Mind! I'll go along an' see that he does it!"

"No, you'll not! Wells, I don't know why Rufe doesn't like me. Right from the start he has been set against me. It's hard for me to believe he could hold a grudge from that first day of school, and I don't understand what's wrong. He does well enough in his schoolwork, but he never says one word more than he has to. There's a reason for it, and something is building up inside him. And I hate to add fuel to the fire. But he can't keep on doing things like this."

"I don't know what's wrong, either, Miss Willie. Hit's been a sight o' trouble to me. An' I shore hate it a heap fer him to weary you like this. I'll do e'er thing you say."

"If I could just get at the root of it. If I could just once get close to him. But he won't let me. It's as if he held me in contempt. He will have nothing to do with me!"

They stood there, a short stretch of grass between them, Miss Willie's polecat smell eddying around them, one young, tawny-headed boy filling the moment with hurt. That he was by nature

137

a mean boy Miss Willie did not for one second believe. She had spent too many years with children to believe that. Something was troubling the boy. Something connected with herself. Something as yet nebulous and vague. And until it opened up of itself, she must simply go on with him, taking one thing at a time. If only the parents and the trustees didn't grow tired of this conflict between them!

When she reached home, Becky clucked sympathetically over her and helped her heat gallons of water with which to scrub her hair, her skin, and her clothes. They filled the tubs in the woodshed and Miss Willie laboriously rid herself of the horrible stench. When she finally stretched herself wearily on her bed, she thought cynically: This is the ridge for you! Start the day with a mad man, and end it with a polecat!

A silent boy accompanied Miss Willie to the schoolhouse the next morning. He was ready when she went by for him, armed with scrubbing brushes, soap, and buckets. He spoke pleasantly enough when she greeted him, and there was no trace of sulkiness on his face. There was no expression at all. It was as if he had deliberately wiped it clean of his thoughts and hooded his eyes before her.

He took up the load and walked with her, keeping his steps down to match hers, whistling occasionally, but otherwise making no sound. Miss Willie matched his silence with her own.

At the schoolhouse he filled the buckets and set to work. The smell was still strong and heavy. Miss Willie took the curtains down and washed them, and then she took the bright rugs outside, and laying them on the grass scrubbed them thoroughly with one of the stiff brushes. She left them there to dry and air. Then she joined Rufe inside and worked with grim determination by his side, scrubbing down the walls and scouring the desks and the floor. From time to time he emptied the buckets and refilled them with fresh water. But this was the only interruption to the steady swishing of the brushes.

When they finished, shortly after noon, Miss Willie's arms hung limp and nerveless, and her back ached with a throbbing pain.

But most of the smell was gone and the room was fresh and clean again. She laid the still-damp rugs back on the floor and gathered the curtains from the bushes where they had been drying, to take home with her to press.

With every muscle in her body begging for rest, she trudged back up the ridge with Rufe, the silence between them still deep. If he had felt any shame or remorse over his trick, he didn't show it. He had needed no direction in the work, and he had worked quickly and well. Miss Willie had no way of knowing what he thought about it.

At her gate she took the buckets from him and turned in. And then he broke the silence. "You needn't to of went," he said. "I'd a done it jist as good without you there."

She flung her head up and looked at him. His eyes were blazing at her and his face was red. How *was* it he always put her on the defensive? Her own eyes took fire and she threw her words at him angrily. "I didn't go to make sure you would do the work well! I went to help! But you must admit your behavior has not been such as to make me have any confidence in you!"

He appeared to be measuring her before he spoke. "That works both ways," he murmured.

Why, she wanted to cry out, why don't you have confidence in me? What have I done? Why don't you believe in me? I have done nothing to you! I have not wanted to hurt you! I only want to help! But she would not plead with this fourteen-year-old boy who stood half a head taller than she, making her feel small, defeated, frustrated. Helplessly she saw that the rift had only widened. "Well," she said, her voice betraying her weariness and hopelessness, "we got the work done, anyhow."

Rufe bent his head cavalierly. "Hit's been a pleasure, Miss Willie," and he turned on his heel and walked away, leaving her battling her tired tears.

And something inside her bled as her tears flowed. O Rufe, Rufe! She wanted to call to him, to run after him, and to hold his bright head close. She wanted to tell him how much she loved him. How dear he was to her. She looked hopelessly after him, watching his thin, awkward body stride down the road. And she thought how tonight he would take his dog and his gun and walk the ridge and the hollow, restlessly knocking at some closed door which only his own heart sought with understanding.

How little we know of one another, she thought. How little we can commune with each other! We spend our lives together, coming and going and working and living together, and we never really get to know each other. What is deepest inside is hidden, and there is no way of crossing over. Of becoming even for one second that other person. Of feeling with his feelings, of thinking with his thoughts, of aching with his hurts. So complexly egoistic are we that we can never get outside ourselves. There is a veil around each one of us, which no other hand can draw aside. But some of us desperately need to rend that veil!

CHAPTER

❦ 15 ❦

As IF TROUBLE NEVER CAME SINGLY, the next Monday afternoon Miss Willie came home to show Becky an itchy breaking out between her fingers and around her wrists. "I believe I've got a touch of poison ivy, Becky," she said. "Look here." And she spread her fingers and pointed to the whitish rash. "It's just about set me crazy today, itching. I couldn't let it alone, and I've kept scratching and clawing at it all day."

Becky pulled her to the door and looked closely at her hands. Then she laughed. "That ain't no poison ivy, Miss Willie. That's the pure old seven-year itch!"

"Itch!"

"Yes, ma'am! An', gentlemen, I mean to tell you hit's plumb troublesome to git rid of. You got a old pair o' gloves you don't mind spoilin'?"

"Why, yes. I can find a pair."

"Well, I'll make up a batch of sulphur an' lard, an' you'll have to spread it over yer hands ever' night, an' sleep with them gloves on. Worst is e'er thing you got has got to be washed an' scrubbed. E'er thing you've tetched is polluted, an' you'll jist take it agin as fast as you git rid of it. Hit shore is a plumb sight to git rid of."

Miss Willie collapsed on the side of the bed. The itch had been

140

something they talked about in whispers behind their hands when she was a child. Nice people didn't get it. It was a badge of poverty and dirt and shame. The kids from the other end of town were always having the itch, and you avoided them and kept even your skirts from contamination. Miss Willie spread her hands and looked at the white blisters, and disgust crept over her face. Things were piling up too fast! After the polecat, the itch! Now that was too much!

"How do you suppose I got it?" she asked.

"From some of them kids, of course! They's allus itch in a school. Cain't hardly ever git shet of it. An' I been aimin' to tell you to watch yer head, too!"

"My head!"

"Fer head lice. Might' nigh ever' year they's a regular go-round of them, an' they kin spread awful quick-like ifen jist one young'un has 'em."

Miss Willie's hand flew to her hair. Her scalp crinkled as if tiny legs were creeping over it already, thousands of tiny legs invading and infesting her skin, nesting and settling around the hair roots. The very thought sent shivers of horror over her.

Becky went to the kitchen and began to hunt around for the sack of dry sulphur. "Ifen you ever find one when yer a combin' yer hair," she called, "jist let me know, an' I'll go over yer head with coal oil an' a fine-toothed comb. They ain't nothin' better that I know of. Hit usual kills 'em right now. Sometimes hit takes two or three goin' overs, but that ain't common. Mebbe, though, you've heared of somethin' better yerself."

"No," Miss Willie said weakly, "no. I've not heard of anything better."

For a week she slept each night with the sulphur and lard mixture smeared on her hands. It smelled to high heaven, but Becky told her it would get rid of the itch. So she endured it. But not patiently. "I'm going to clean up that school," she vowed to Becky. "I'm going to get the itch and lice and everything else those children have got out of there! I'm going to see every blessed woman who's got a child in that school, and I'm going to have them meet here at my house next Saturday afternoon. There's no sense in that sort of thing. Just a little cleanliness and patience will prevent such things! You just wait and see!"

She stormed through the week, her anger at her own infection sustaining her. Each night when she anointed her hands with the stinking mixture she boiled up again. "There's no sense in it," she muttered. "There's just no excuse for it! Just plain shiftlessness. Anybody can be clean, no matter how poor they are!"

So she rode the little mare all over the ridge after school those evenings. But she was canny with her invitations. "Better not say yer havin' a health meetin'," Becky cautioned. "Folks hereabouts don't take to meddlin' with such like. Jist say yer havin' a party." So Miss Willie said nothing about the itch. She merely invited the mothers to her cabin for a little party. "So we can all get to know each other," she urged.

One and all they accepted. "Hit's right nice of you to give us a party, Miss Willie," they said, and they all promised to come.

"Saturday afternoon at two o'clock," she said.

"Yes, ma'am. We'll be there."

All, that is, but Irma, Hod's sister. It was late in the afternoon when Miss Willie hitched the little horse to Irma's front fence. She had saved this call to the last because she looked forward to it so much. It had promised her a special reward since she had become so fond of Johnnie.

She looked around her curiously as she knotted the reins about a spike paling. Mary had told her how Irma and her husband, John Walton, had started out eight or ten years ago in the tenant house on his father's place, and how they had added a room every two or three years as they added children, until they had changed the tiny tenant house into a sizable home. It was a low, rambling place hugging close to the ground, and its gleaming white paint shone cleanly in the late evening sun. The mat of grass in the yard was neatly clipped, and the last of the summer flowers bloomed gaily around the porch's edge.

Irma herself came to the door. She was a beautiful woman in her late twenties, with red-gold hair crinkling back from her brown face. Her figure was softly rounded, neither thickened with the bearing of her children nor stooped from the burden of farm work. Her face broke into a smile and she spoke warmly. "Come in. Come in," she said. "I'm that pleased you've come.

142

Johnnie's spoke of you a heap."

Inside, the house was bright, airy, and fresh-smelling. Irma was a good housekeeper. Everything was scrubbed and neat, and the curtains and braided rugs were spotless. Like all the other homes on the ridge, it was sparsely furnished, but there was no feeling of emptiness. Rather, there was the feeling of space and uncluttered living.

They talked for a time of school, of Johnnie's progress, of Miss Willie's fondness for him, and Irma spoke proudly of his affection for "teacher." And then Irma wanted to know how Miss Willie was liking the ridge. "I've heared you've got a peart little cabin o' yer own," she said, "all fixed up over there at Becky's. Mary was tellin' me how you fixed it up."

"I like it," Miss Willie answered, "and I'm beginning to feel very much at home there. I brought a few of my own things with me, and it's nice to have them around me."

"Yes," Irma agreed, "hit's allus nice to have a body's own things. Makes you feel more settled. I'd like a heap to see it."

"I'd like for you to come," Miss Willie said. "As a matter of fact, I am having a little party for the school mothers Saturday afternoon. Couldn't you come, then?"

Irma's face shuttered immediately. She shook her head. "We don't hold with worldly things like that no more," she said. "I reckon you know me an' John has been converted, an' we don't go seekin' frolickin' like we useter."

Then Miss Willie explained. "This is not really a party, Irma. What I actually want to do is to get the women interested in organizing a sort of health club. Right now there is an epidemic of the itch in school, and the only way it can be checked is for everyone to co-operate. And there are other things the mothers should know about the general health of their children. This isn't a worldly frolic at all."

But Irma continued to shake her head. "We don't hold with no doctorin', neither."

"You don't believe in doctors and medicine?"

"No, ma'am. The Bible says to have faith in the Lord. Hit tells of the healin' of them that believed. Ifen you believe, you don't hold with no doctorin'."

143

"But what if some of the children get sick? Or you or John?"

"Hit would be the Lord's will. An' ifen hit was the Lord's will, we would be healed."

"But, Irma," Miss Willie protested, "the Lord intended for people to use the knowledge of science and medicine in healing disease! He meant for doctors to help people!"

Irma's face was blank. "The Scriptures says the Lord heals them that has the faith. Hit don't say nothin' about doctorin'. The Lord don't need no doctors to he'p him in his healin', Miss Willie. All he says is to believe on him. *He'll* do the healin'. Ifen hit's his will."

"But don't you think the Lord uses people to do his work in the world?"

Irma's head jerked quickly in denial. "No, ma'am," she said flatly. "The Lord, he don't need nothin' nor nobody to he'p him out. The Lord is powerful enough to move mountains. Hit's jist the conceit o' men to think the Lord needs e'er one of 'em." Her voice softened. "Don't the Scriptures tell of him ahealin' the lame an' the halt, the sick an' the bruised, an' settin' free them that was captive? Ifen you believe, Miss Willie, he sets you free. They ain't no bonds no more."

Miss Willie was silent. The sun had bedded down behind the hills and the last of the day was being drained from the sky. Across in the east the reflection was pink and pearly, and in the fading light Irma's face was strong and quiet. Her eyes looked past Miss Willie across a far-flung space, and they held an ageless peace in their brown depths. Miss Willie felt as if Irma had gone away and left her standing there, emptied, spent, and alone. Irma's spirit had winged its way to heavenly heights.

Miss Willie mounted the little mare and turned her toward home. She rode slowly down the road, her thoughts churning. She tried to sort them out and fix upon something solid. They were fringed by dismay, and a foregathering of anxiety and uneasiness. Like ragged edges, they surrounded something she could not get at. Their frayed threads kept her from the center. On the surface was her concern for the physical welfare of the little family. Inevitably Irma's faith would affect not only herself but her children as well.

144

But Miss Willie's uneasiness went deeper than that. Irma's confidence and strong faith had thrown her back upon herself. It had made her uncomfortable and defensive of her own faith. There! That was it! The core of her feeling was an uncertainty, a troubled sense of guilt. The fountain-spring of her own faith was challenged. She turned her thoughts this way and that, remembering Irma's words. He don't need nothin' nor nobody. Oughtn't a good Calvinist to agree that God needed nothing and no one to do his work? Wasn't one of the foundations of her own faith that cornerstone of God's all-powerful reign over his world? Yes, of course. But there was a difference in interpretation.

Unconsciously Miss Willie tipped her chin upward. A cultured, educated mind sustained a faith that was just as real as this hill woman's. It did not require that one be naïve and literal like Irma to have an honest and absolute faith. But here her mind doubled back around another thought. How absolute was her faith? How complete was the faith of anyone she knew? "Except ye become as a little child." Could one have an intellectual faith? Doesn't faith require that one give himself completely into the hand of God, simply and unquestioningly?

The little mare clopped a measured rhythm down the dusty road. And Miss Willie's thoughts threaded out to their fine ends. But could one do that in this day and age? I believe in the Lord God, she stated defiantly. And then, honestly she added, I believe also in Miss Willie. Wasn't that the amendment to all life nowadays? Thy will be done. But unless thy will is my will, my will be done. Wasn't that, too, the modern version of the Lord's Prayer?

Inexorably she forced herself to consider further. How many times she had heard her father say, "We are in God's hands." And as a child how comforting that had been to her! She fled swiftly back to her childhood, and remembered how her days had been surrounded with the secure, confident knowledge that all was well with her and her world. Nothing could go very far awry if you were in God's hands. She had had a child's conception of that broad palm holding up the world, and she had felt certain Texas was in the center of it, safely distant from the rounded edges where one might fall off. China was off there near the edge. And Africa. And India. When she had dedicated herself to missionary

145

service that day so long ago, she had felt not only the necessity to serve; she had also felt, she now acknowledged, a certain chilling thrill of fear. The same kind of thrill one had when one stepped across the line on a dare. It would be going so close to the edge of safety.

That child's conception, however, had given her life a security and a sure sense of fast foundations. It had stood firmly between her and fear, and had hedged her around with certainty. As Irma's faith was doing for her now. But somewhere along the line of maturing wisdom such childlike faith had been tempered with caution, and with what she was pleased to call common sense. Being in the hands of God had ceased to be the final security. That implicit trust was tinctured with the reality of everyday living, and somehow it got glossed over until it no longer had the same meaning. It bogged down in the necessity of becoming a responsible citizen of the world. And although this generation gave lip service to the phrase, wasn't it usually true that a man must be backed into a corner and brought to his knees before he could genuinely and humbly put himself into the hands of God? Until then wasn't he usually confident and sufficient unto himself? And was his faith not something faint and thin, seeping through Bach fugues and chorales along gilded organ pipes, strained piously through the muted prism of stained glass windows, hushed sanctimoniously by the thick, plushy depth of red carpets? Nebulous. Unreal. Distant. Having little to do with man himself, being reserved, like bonds in the bank, for a rainy day?

Miss Willie's soul was horrified at herself!

When the little mare halted in front of the back lot, Miss Willie eased herself down from the funny, awkward sidesaddle Wells had brought her, and led the horse through the gate. When Wells first brought her the horse and saddle, she had wondered where on earth he had found the thing. Not since her childhood had she seen a sidesaddle. She had laughed and poked fun at him.

"You wait an' see," he said. "You cain't be dressin' to ride astraddle ever'day. An' yer goin' to be aridin' this thing ever' day, don't fergit. This here sidesaddle'll take you, however yer dressed, an' hit'll rock along easy as one o' Becky's rockin' chairs."

And Wells's wisdom had been greater than her own. She

146

crawled up on Pet in whatever dress she might be wearing, and she now crooked her knee around the horn as easily and familiarly as if she had never ridden any other way.

At supper that night she told Becky about Irma. Gault was not at home, having gone to the county seat for court that day. He would be gone overnight, so Becky and Miss Willie were two women comfortably alone. Becky listened quietly as Miss Willie talked. "It worries me, Becky," Miss Willie finished her story.

Becky leaned her elbows on the table and braced her chin in her palms. Her eyes took on the same faraway look that Irma's had held. "I was raised in the faith, Miss Willie," she said. "Hit don't sound unnatural to me. I never knowed nothin' else till I married Gault, an' he forbid me to have e'er thing to do with 'em. Hit's a comfortin' way o' believin', an' I don't reckon they's a thing kin take its place to them that believes thataway. Hit's like leanin' on the everlastin' arms, knowin' they're goin' to uphold you. Hit's agivin' over to man the keer of the little things in this world, an' aleavin' to God the keer of all the big."

She stirred and moved the lamp to one side. "The way I see it, Miss Willie, is that ever'body is bound to believe accordin' to their lights. An' whatever is the most comfortin' an' satisfyin' to a body is the true faith fer him. I don't reckon nobody is enlightened to the whole truth. That would be puttin' too much on one pore, sinful human. But at the last I don't reckon the Lord's goin' to argy too much about the diffrunce in the way people has believed. Ifen I was him, I'd keer a heap more about how they follered what they believed. I don't hold with preachin' one thing an' doin' another. If they's one thing I cain't abide, it's a hypocrite. Ifen Irma holds with the faith, an' holds hard an' strong, then I'd say it ain't nobody's business but her'n!"

Becky rose and began stacking the dishes. Miss Willie scraped her own plate thoughtfully. Becky could speak very strongly when she chose. Evidently she had been a dutiful wife when Gault had commanded her to have nothing more to do with those of her own faith, but it was equally evident that the fire of that faith still burned steadily. Gault had not dampened it with his

147

Baptist theology or with his stern prohibition. Gault was the head of the house, and in all outward ways Becky obeyed him. But Gault could not control Becky's spiritual house, and Miss Willie was surprised at its wide rooms and high-spired roof.

As the dishes went through the strong, sudsy water under Becky's hands, and came to her own from the hot, clean rinsing kettle, Miss Willie remembered something Saint-Exupéry had written in *Wind, Sand and Stars* — something about whatever was right and good and fine for a man being *his* truth. She wiped a glass until it glistened in the yellow light. Odd to hear almost that same thought from the lips of this ridge woman. There was a fine vein of wisdom in Becky. It flashed to the surface only occasionally . . . as on the first night she was here, and again tonight. Wisdom threaded through with humor, and far back beyond the present, with sadness. Wisdom that took people for what they were, and let them alone to be themselves — hating only, as she had said tonight, the false in them. That was pretty fundamental when you got right down to it. That was the essence of love.

"You're a mighty good woman, Becky," Miss Willie said at last.

Becky lifted her hands from the soapy water, letting them drip on the floor. Her mouth quivered. "Don't say that," her voice rasped sharply. "Don't never say that, Miss Willie. I have been the blackest sinner of them all. Hit lives with me night an' day. The Lord ain't never forgive me fer what I done. Don't never say I'm a good woman." Careless of her wet hands, she hid her face in them, and her thin, humped shoulders shook.

"Why, Becky!" Miss Willie dropped her dish towel and hurried to throw her arm around the bent, scrawny back. "You've no right to say that. Why, your own faith tells you that the Lord forgives every sin. No matter what you've done, he doesn't hold it against you. Besides, you can't make me believe you're such a sinner as all that!"

Becky let her hands drop and braced them on the table. "You've got no idee," she said. "I've prayed fer a sign, but hit's never been give to me. He has turned his face from me. I've got no right to talk about e'er other soul bein' a hypocrite! Ifen the folks on this ridge knowed the truth about me, they wouldn't be seen aspeakin' to me! An' if you knowed, you wouldn't stay e'er other night on this place!"

"Now, I don't know about the folks on the ridge, Becky," Miss Willie answered, "but as for me, there's nothing you could have done that would make me leave you, or that would change my feeling for you."

But Becky only shook her head. "You don't know," she said in a low voice. "You don't know." She dropped into a chair and wrapped her hands in her apron and rocked back and forth, misery creasing her face.

"Then suppose you tell me," Miss Willie said, pulling a chair up close.

Becky's voice when she began to speak was harsh and grating. "Oncet," she said, "oncet I was a purty young thing, gay-like and happy. You wouldn't believe it, I reckon."

"I would believe it," Miss Willie said.

"I lived on yon side the Gap with my pap an' stepma, an' I loved ever' bit o' livin'. Hit was purty where we lived — down in a holler between the hills, an' the woods come up in back o' the cabin right up to the door. In the spring the dogwood was lacy-like an' the redbuds was like little fires aburnin' the limbs. You could allus hear birds asingin', an' they was a little creek went runnin' free an' easy down the holler. Hit was a purty place, an' I was happy there. I growed up never knowin' nothin' but the hills an' the holler, never feelin' nothin' but love fer ever' livin' thing."

She paused and rocked her chair back on its legs. "They was a boy lived up on the ridge. Him an' me used to meet down by the creek when we got through in the fields. An' knowin' better, but lovin' him so good, I done wrong with him. Hit didn't seem a sin, he was so fair an' sweet. Hit jist seemed natural an' right. An' then his folks moved away — clean over to Casey County. I never faulted him none, an' I never knowed till he was gone I was in trouble. He aimed to write, an' he allus said he'd come git me soon as they was settled. An' I waited an' waited, but he never wrote. An' he never come. An' I knowed I had to do somethin'. I knowed my pap would turn me out when he caught on, an' the time was gittin' clost when he'd notice. So I jist left out one day. Hit was a bright mornin'. The sun was ashinin' down, warm an' soft-like.

149

But I turned my back on ever'thing I loved an' went away."

"O Becky, Becky!"

"I walked into the county seat, an' I got me a job cookin' fer a woman. An' I stayed until I had me enough money to git to Louisville. I didn't know what I was goin' to do there, but I knowed hit was a big enough place that I could hide away in it. I was awalkin' up an' down the streets, not knowin' where to turn, an' not havin' much money, when a woman stopped me an' started talkin' to me. She takened me home with her, an' I stayed with her until my baby was borned." Becky's voice was even, dry, toneless now. Her hands were restless under the apron, but the voice went on. "Hit was a little girl, an' sweet an' purty to look on. But the woman, she takened it away. I never seen it but oncet. She said it would be better if I never learned to love it. But I loved it from the start. She said she knowed some people would take it an' raise it like their own. Said they'd do fer it better'n I could. So I let her give it away. She wouldn't never tell me their names."

Miss Willie felt a twisting ache knot her stomach. She wanted to reach out and take one of the restless hands, but Becky was looking beyond her . . . back into the past. So this was why Becky wore black. This was the grief and the loss she still mourned. This was the sin she was still trying to atone.

Becky's shoulders bowed over her hands, and she rocked back and forth. "When I was well agin, the woman she said I owed her fer takin' me in an' takin' keer of me, an' I was bound to stay an' work fer her. I didn't keer, fer I didn't keer fer nothin'. Hit was like I was dead, an' jist my body awalkin' around. I stayed an' worked fer her a year, an' then we reckoned our accounts was even. She never rightly wanted me to leave. Said I was a good worker, but I was homesick, so I left out an' come home. Never told e'er soul what all had happened. Jist told my pa I'd been amakin' my own way in Louisville. He never ast no questions. So I jist come home an' takened up where I left off. Only somewheres I got a little girl I give away. An' the Lord ain't forgive me, fer he ain't never let me have no more."

Becky let her chair come to rest at last, and she stilled her hands. Her face took on a granite hardness, and it grayed around

150

the edges of her mouth. The lamp flickered as a small wind went searchingly across the room, and a curtain lifted and folded and dropped limply back against the wall. A white moth fluttered into the pool of light around the lamp, quivered ecstatically in the warmth of the chimney, and then plunged headlong into its fire, falling singed and blackened to the floor.

These things were embossed on Miss Willie's mind, standing forth in relief, graven and carved like the individual features of a statue. There were harsh edges to the room and the woman and the scene. Miss Willie's face was wet, and she had to speak past the tightness in her throat. "Becky," she said, "Becky, look at me."

Becky brought her eyes back from their gray memories and let them fix upon the present.

Miss Willie spoke softly, her voice steady and firm now. "Becky, listen to me. You're a good woman, Becky. You're a fine woman. One of the best I ever knew!"

The sharpness of Becky's face changed. It became diffused and softened, its seams folding gently together again. The dingy black dress burdened the bent shoulders limply. The lamplight washed over her quietly. Not until then did Becky's own tears flow. As if from some released spring within her they filled her eyes and streamed unheeded down her face. "You kin still say that?" she asked, "after me atellin' you? You kin still say that?"

"I can still say that, and I can mean it even more after what you've told me. You're not only a good woman, Becky; you're a brave one. Not one woman in a hundred could have rebuilt her life as you have done, and made a good wife and a good neighbor. That's what counts, Becky. Does Gault know this?"

"Oh, yes. I wouldn't of married him without."

"What did he say?"

"He said hit was over an' done with, an' best forgot. He ain't never named it agin sincet I told it to him."

"And Gault was right. And if Gault saw the goodness in you, don't you suppose the Lord sees it, too?"

"But he's left me barren an' without child! I've prayed an' prayed fer forgiveness, an' I thought hit would be a sign ifen he'd only give me a young'un agin. But he never did, an' now hit's too late."

"Becky, there could be a dozen reasons why you're childless! It's not because the Lord hasn't forgiven you."

"He don't trust me with a young'un is all I kin make of it. He give me one, an' I give it away. An' I reckon he never would trust me with no more."

"No, Becky, that's not the answer."

Becky stood and went back to the dishpan. She laughed quaveringly. "This here water's as cold as a wedge! But I feel better, atellin' you. I've not liked knowin' I was hidin' e'er thing from you."

"I'm glad you told me too, Becky. It makes me feel closer to you."

Becky's eyes were shining as she built up the fire to heat more water. "Hit takes a load offen me. Knowin' you know, an' don't fault me none. Hit makes me feel a heap better."

They had turned back to the dishes when they heard the sound of a car chugging down the road. They stopped their work to listen. Becky walked to the front door. "That's Hod's car," she said.

Miss Willie's heart jumped into her throat. "Hod's car!"

"Yes. Mary's time has come. He's agoin' after Hattie."

Miss Willie could feel her heartbeats pulsing in her wrists. For an exalted moment she knew the pulse of the universe was beating there too — the rhythm of tides and moons rising and waning, and winds blowing strongly, and rain drumming steadily. The rhythm of the earth turning around the sun, of corn greening and then ripening, of dayspring and nightfall, and of a woman's time come in the night. It was a rhythm of pain and ecstasy, mingled and blended until there was no knowing the beginning or the end of either. It was a rhythm that was timeless and spaceless — the rhythm of creation. Mary's time had come!

CHAPTER

❧ 16 ❧

Mary's baby was a boy. A lusty, strong-lunged child who barreled a fine, rounded chest up under his blankets and loudly voiced his opinion of this new world he was in.

"Mercy," Miss Willie said, coming into Mary's room the next morning, "has he got a pain?"

"Naw," Hod said, grinning. "He's just tryin' to make up his mind whether he wants to stay here with us or not. Mary bought everything she could think of for this baby, but she forgot one thing. She didn't get him a muffler! And if he keeps that up, he's goin' to need one!"

Mary looked tired, but amazingly recovered and beautiful. There was a shadow under her eyes of remembered pain, but already it was fading. "Isn't he wonderful?" she asked, stretching to see over the edge of his crib. "Did you ever see such a marvelous baby?"

"Well, if you'll both get back and let me see him, perhaps I can judge a little better," Miss Willie said, dryly. She elbowed Hod and squeezed past him.

Hod bowed deeply out of her way. "Make way for a lady!"

"Make way for a great-aunt," she snapped at him, and bent over the crib.

The baby had hushed, and was lying placidly blinking his deep blue eyes. He stared at Miss Willie unseeingly, with an ageless profundity, as if he had retreated into an ancient wisdom, some boundless space of eternal knowledge. His head was covered with a downy, yellow fuzz, which grew longer on the sides and curled back up over the tips of his tiny, perfectly shaped ears. Miss Willie touched it experimentally and sighed at its silky softness. His nose was a round little button fastened between his cheeks, which bulged fatly on either side. Miss Willie ran her finger down the side of his cheekbone, which ended in a chin that jutted strongly under his puckered mouth. The family mark was fissured deep in the flesh of this newest Pierce man. He had a dimple sunk sweetly in his chin, like Hod, and like Wells.

"I'm glad he's got the dimple," Miss Willie said.

"He'll cuss it, come the day he starts shavin'," Hod answered casually.

"Just the same, I'm glad he's got it. He wouldn't be a Pierce without it. What are you going to name him?"

Mary laughed. "Ask his daddy!"

Hod stuck his tongue in his cheek and leaned his shoulder into the doorframe, scrubbing it roughly up and down. He examined his thumbnail minutely. "Well, I tell you," he said finally, "he's got a right smart name. We couldn't hardly leave anybody out, so we just sort of tacked 'em all onto him."

Miss Willie raised her eyebrows. "How many generations did you feel it necessary to include?"

Hod scratched his jaw, his hand rasping over his beard. "Just four. Miss Willie, meet young Jeems Dowell Thomas Hodges Pierce!"

Miss Willie and Mary exploded, and Hod joined in their laughter sheepishly. "But I reckon we'll call him Jeems."

"Why didn't you save one of the names for the next boy?" Miss Willie asked.

"Might not be boys," Hod drawled.

Mary yawned and stretched. She ran her hands down her sides luxuriously. "Golly," she sighed, "I feel like I could sleep a week!"

Hod strolled over to the baby's crib and looked down at him. "Ain't he a doodlebug, though? Look at that head, and look at those hands! Looks like a heavyweight already. Gentlemen, he's shore goin' to handle a plow right handy one of these days!"

Mary's eyes rested on Hod affectionately. "You're glad he's a boy, Hod?"

"Yes," he said simply. "A man likes his first to be a son."

Hod's heart spoke through his voice and implied the things his words left unsaid. That a man felt a need of the drawing out of himself into a man-child to come after him. That to become a whole man there must be this extension of himself, this division, and this passing on of his bones and flesh into the male succession. That this sonship was the continuing stream of life, threading simultaneously through their masculine veins, carrying for-

154

ward forever the power of generation.

Further, Hod's voice was saying that one day this boy of his would walk the fields and the woods alongside him, shouldering a fishing pole or a gun, and he would talk with him of many things. They would walk the dark hills, the ridges and the hollows, under suns and moons and stars, and he would show him the growing things all around him and teach him how they grew. He would teach him to fish and shoot and hunt and swim, and they would explore together the mysteries of life. And one day he would curl his own great hand around the boy's small one, and curve it lovingly about the handle of a plow. "This is my beloved son," Hod's voice was saying. "My beloved son."

Miss Willie's eyes pricked and a feeling of tenderness welled up and poured over inside her. A man with his first-born son was a beautiful thing to see. She cleared her throat. "I'd better be going. Mary needs to rest, and I've got cookies to bake this afternoon for my party tomorrow. Becky's all in a dither over the party. And she doesn't think I can cook at all. She'll dog my steps from the cabinet to the stove, breathing down my neck and cautioning me every move I make." She rose and moved toward the door. "This is going to be a right smart crusade, Mary. I wish you could be there."

"Keep your flags flying, Miss Willie," Mary warned.

"I intend to! Big Springs School is going to be itch- and louse-free, come next Saturday, so help me! Ugh-h-h!" And she wiggled her hands distastefully in front of her. "That was the nastiest stuff Becky made me use! But it got rid of it! I'll come again, Mary."

"Miss Willie," Hod complained, "haven't you learned yet the proper way to take your leave on the ridge?"

"I forgot! You all better come go along!"

"Cain't," Hod drawled, "you better stay."

"Cain't, got to be goin'."

Hod's mouth quirked at the corner. "Get a little more drawl in it next time, Miss Willie, and bring it out through your nose a little stronger. We'll make a ridge runner out of you, yet."

Miss Willie giggled. "Maybe," she said. "Maybe," and she waved as she went out the door.

The party went nicely the next day. About twenty women from all over the ridge and the neighboring hollows came. There was Quilla Simpson and Corinna Jones, Mamie Clark and Lutie Jasper, all from right down the road on Piney Ridge itself. And there were the Harpers and the Taylors, and the Simmses from Coon Ridge. There were several Miss Willie didn't know at all, but word had been sent by the children. She was dismayed at first because they all brought their youngest children, and Mamie Clark brought all of hers. Becky sniffed when she saw them coming up the road. "Mamie's heared you was goin' to have somethin' to eat, an' she's figgerin' on fillin' up all them kids o' her'n, so's she won't have to cook tonight."

Miss Willie was doing rapid calculation. "Becky," she said distractedly, "I don't believe I made enough cookies."

"Oh, don't weary yerself," Becky said. "I knowed they'd all bring their young'uns. I made a batch yestiddy mornin' whilst you was down at Mary's. They's aplenty."

Miss Willie relaxed. "I don't know what I'd do without you, Becky."

The children were sent to play in the yard, and the women settled down to talk. The group was stiff at first, and Miss Willie caught them stealing sly looks around the cabin at her furniture, the pictures, the books, and the curtains and rugs. She knew they were fixing them in their minds to discuss them later. No doubt they would think all of them "quare." But since Wells's talk with her, she knew they expected her to be queer about some things, and would be disappointed if she weren't. They expected her to dress, act, and talk differently. And if they also expected her to know by some remote instinct the areas in which they assumed she would be like themselves, she must stumble across them alone and unaided. If she ran into the barriers their own long years of walking the earth as free people erected, she must pick herself up and go on, unhurt. The untrammeled hills had given these people a way of life which had its own pockets of pride and its own guarded sense of worth. An outsider must discover those for himself, or must go defeated. So inherent were these things that it was not so much a matter of the hill people being unwilling to explain and share them, as it was an inability to understand why

156

they would need explanation, and an unquestioning expectation that they would be shared. "Why, hit's allus been that way," they would say in amazement. And if you argued it wasn't that way outside the hills, they looked puzzled and remarked, "That goes plumb foolish!"

Under Miss Willie's friendly guidance the first awkward moments passed, and soon the group were talking freely of their homes, their families, the local gossip, the size of their cream checks, and the price for a pound of chunk meat. Miss Willie let this go on until someone mentioned casually an illness among her children. Then she craftily led the conversation around to the prevalence of itch in the school. There was a nodding of heads and a telling of favorite remedies and the scandalous agreement of what a nuisance it was to get rid of. When Miss Willie suggested that they all combine to make a unified fight against it immediately, they agreed without a murmur. "Hit shore would be a good thing," they said. "About the time you git yer own young'uns cured up, one asettin' alongside of 'em gits it, an' hit's all to do over agin."

When she mentioned making minute and concerted searches of heads, also, they received the suggestion favorably. She had supposed there would be some who would haughtily denounce the whole proposal. But evidently these were ancient complaints, to be taken in one's stride and without fuss and bother. It was also evident that they were common enemies, shared alike and without distinction by every family sooner or later. There was no other end of town here on the ridge. No one could conveniently draw aside her skirts here.

When Miss Willie poured hot tea for them in her thin china cups, they accepted it gingerly, handling the cups carefully and examining them cautiously. They sipped at the tea, patently meaning to do the right thing, but obviously not enjoying the unfamiliar drink.

"Hit'd go a sight better ifen they was a slug of moonshine in it," Mamie Clark opined.

"You hesh, Mamie," Becky scolded. "This here's fine Chiny tea Miss Willie's got, an' you'll not see its like ever agin!"

"Well, I ain't aimin' to fault her none," Mamie went on. "I jist

157

was sayin' hit'd go a heap better."

"We heared you the first time," said Becky, bitterly.

Lutie Jasper, whose mouth looked slack without its hump of snuff, twisted around in her chair to look at Mamie. "Is Tay astillin' over there on Wanderin' Creek yit?"

Mamie nodded and crunched a cooky between the yellow stumps of her front teeth. "He's adoin' right good over there," she said. "Runs off a batch ever' week. But he come over yestiddy. He's a talkin' to some girl hereabouts, I reckon. They was a big mess o' lipstick on his shirt collar. The old man was jokin' him about it, but he never let on who it was. He come up from the holler, though."

"Why, hit's Rose Pierce," Lutie said. "Me an' Matt's seen 'em time an' agin on the side of that hill down by the schoolhouse when we was sang diggin'."

Miss Willie was startled. "How could that be?" she asked Lutie. "Rose is in school every day. She hasn't missed a day since school started!"

Lutie shrugged her scrawny shoulders and drained her cup of the last drop of the tea. "Hit ain't none o' my put-in," she said, "but I seen what I seen, an' they's no mistakin' hit was Rose an' Tay."

The women eyed each other slyly, but there was no further comment. Tongues would lick over this later, and Miss Willie was troubled and puzzled. Rose was such a willing helper with the younger children, always ready to supervise their more frequent play times outside, always at school, rain or shine. How could she be meeting Tay, then? She shook her head and turned back to the talk idling around her.

Lutie was still talking. She hiccuped noisily. "That least 'un o' your'n is shore fleshenin' up, Mamie," she said. "He's jist afillin' out all over."

Mamie yawned. "Well, I don't know whether he is or ain't. Hit might jist be bloat. We had one oncet jist bloated up on us an' died. You cain't never tell."

Miss Willie's mouth went dry and she hastily swallowed a gulp of tea. Just as if she were talking of a hog, she thought. It was this callousness that made some of these people seem on the level

158

of beasts to Miss Willie. If they had any finer perceptions and emotions, they were seldom evident. They worked, ate, slept, and raised young'uns, sunk in apathetic and dull acceptance of a sluggish and brutal existence. If they saw beyond those horizons, it was not apparent. Something like shame crept over Miss Willie every time she was around such people. Shame that anything human could be so porcine and brutish.

The party began to break up early because everyone had evening chores to do, and most of them had some distance to walk. They gathered around Miss Willie and said their good-by's. "Hit shore was a nice party," they said, over and over. "Hit was plumb thoughty of you to have it."

And thus Miss Willie's health class was organized. She pranced around the room after they had left, exulting mightily. "I told you so, Becky," she said. "I told you so!"

Becky, picking up napkins, emptying cups, straightening chairs, said nothing.

Miss Willie flung her arms up and reached on tiptoe to touch one of the old blackened beams across the ceiling. "It's a start," she said, her voice deepening with her pleasure. "That's all I wanted. Just a start with them. Just for them to trust me. Now, we can move along."

"Miss Willie, honey, don't count on it," and Becky poured the last drop of tea from the pot and drank it down. "They'll come, an' they'll drink yer tea, an' they'll listen. But they ain't likely to *do!*"

"All right, then, they'll listen! But they're going to listen every time I open my mouth! I'm not going to stop preaching against itch and lice and flies and skimmed milk and fried apples as long as I've got any voice left! If that's all they'll do, listen, then I'll see they have something to listen to!"

Becky's eyes twinkled. "I'll bound you will, at that!"

Miss Willie went to the door and looked off down the ridge where the trees bent and broke over the rim, disappearing down the hillside. A lavender haze smoked up from the hollow. There was a sea look to it, of far distances, as it filled up and lapped at

159

the edges of the ridge. As if it stretched out to the horizon and beyond. Back of it the sun sliced thinly into the sky, striking through the haze with a light that was like golden sherry, a light that was so delicate and fragile that it looked as if it could be shattered with the finger of a touch.

Miss Willie's breath caught in her throat. There is so much beauty on this ridge, she thought. Every hour of the day, and every season of the year brings its own gift of loveliness. And it stretches one's body until the skin is taut and tense, and until it spills over and runs like liquid through all the senses. So much unbearable beauty. In the hills. And the people? A sadness ran through her filling her with exquisite pain. There *must* be beauty in the people too.

She turned back to help Becky, and her mind ran on to what Lutie had said of Rose and Tay Clark. "Why do you suppose," she said musingly, worrying her lower lip with her thumb, "why do you suppose it's Wells's children who worry me so much? Rufe, and now Rose. What must I do about Rose and Tay Clark?"

"Nothin'." Becky's voice was uncompromising.

"But Wells doesn't want Rose to go with Tay," Miss Willie protested.

"Miss Willie," Becky said, crumpling a napkin in her hand, "they ain't nothin' Wells nor nobody else kin do. Rose is sixteen year old. Ifen she's a mind to be seein' Tay Clark on the sly, an' ifen he's takened her fancy, she'll do it, come hell or high water! Wells jist as well to make up his mind to it, an' hit's none o' yore put-in. You'd best leave it alone."

"If she's slipping off from school to meet him, it's some of my put-in! Wells is going to a lot of trouble to keep her in school another year, and I'm not going to stand by and see her pull the wool over his eyes!"

Becky shrugged. "They's nothin' you kin do."

"I can tell Wells. I can do that!"

"Shore. You kin tell him. An' he kin bawl her out. An' all it'll do is make her an' Tay take keer a little better. Hit'd be a heap better if Wells'd jist come out in the open an' let him court her fair. Tay ain't sich a awful bad boy."

"How can you say that when he's running a still and everybody

160

knows it! It's a wonder to me someone doesn't turn him in!"

Becky whirled suddenly. "They's a thing you got to know, Miss Willie. We don't go turnin' in our own to the law on this ridge! Ifen the whole countryside knowed Tay was stillin', they wouldn't nobody do a sneakin' thing like that! Wells wouldn't hisself! An' you better not go gittin' no notions of yer own like that."

"My goodness, Becky, I'm not intending to turn him in!"

"You'd have to leave the ridge if you did! Jist mind yer own business, Miss Willie."

Miss Willie stiffened, and her temper huffed immediately. But at almost the same moment that questioning, reasonable part of her mind began to function. *Was* she examining these people with critical eyes, weighing them in scales balanced by other standards and other values? Was she assuming that those other standards and values were absolute? Were there, then, relative areas of right and wrong? On the ridge, evidently there were. Tay Clark was stilling, breaking the law. But on the ridge the law cut across a man's freedom. Freedom to do what he would with the corn he raised or bought. Freedom to earn his living in a familiar pattern. It was the law that was wrong to these people, and they took their own way of keeping it. If a man wanted to make moonshine, he hid a still back in a hollow, and all the ridge threw a protecting guard across his path. It was a man's right to make likker if he wanted to. It was the law's duty to find it out if it could. No one sat in judgment on the man who made moonshine. No one sat in judgment on the revenue officer who did his duty. Each was doing right as he saw it. But the ridge folks were on the side of the moonshiner. Inevitably their flag was raised on the side of freedom as they saw it.

Becky turned to Miss Willie as she stood brooding by the fireplace. She laid a timid hand on her arm. "Don't be ill with me, Miss Willie. Hit's jist that yer so right down ignorant about some things."

Miss Willie patted the roughened hand and smiled wryly. "I know, Becky. I know. And I'm beginning to think I'll always be right down ignorant about some things. The way people on this ridge think is something I don't think I'll ever understand." She shook her head. "But thank you for trying to help. I don't know

161

what I'd do without you."

She kicked absently at the little rocker by the fireside and set it moving to and fro. And then, as if coming to some decision and putting it behind her, she turned and vigorously attacked the remaining disorder. "Come on, let's get through with this. Wells and I are going down to see young Jeems Dowell Thomas Hodges Pierce tonight!"

CHAPTER

❧ 17 ❧

COON RIDGE LAY ABOUT HALFWAY between the Piney Ridge convolutions and the pass in the hills called the Gap. It was deeply ribbed with lapping folds and it speared the mother ridge sharply at its joining. Back in one of its deepest wrinkles, Wandering Creek slipped from the hillside in a pure freshet, icy cold from the spring that gave it birth, and crystal clear. It twisted and turned down the hill, gullying a course between rocks and boulders, and, after it reached the hollow, scratching a channel in the loamy soil. In one place it doubled back upon itself in a deep, rounding curve, pressing upon the hill a peninsula almost entirely surrounded by the stream.

It was here in this hugging curve that Tay Clark had hidden his still. And it was an almost perfect place for it. The trees were thick on both sides of the creek, and beneath them the underbrush filled in with a heavy growth which hid the flat arm of land completely. In the circle of trees there was a clearing, sandy, shaded, and protected. The still was in the clearing.

Back of it, jammed hard against the hill, was a shack, which he had thrown up out of rough, weather-beaten lumber. There were no doors or windows, but a burlap sack hung across an opening in front. Sheer rock rose behind it. Inside the shack Tay had a cot and an old chest of drawers. And he kept his sugar, cornmeal, bottles, and other supplies stacked in one corner out of the weather. This was the only home Tay Clark had.

Tay took a pride in his likker. He often said you couldn't beat good, clean Kentucky corn and Kentucky limestone water to make moonshine. The way he made it, he'd stack it up agin bourbon any day in the week. And they was plenty that liked it a heap better. Men that had a strong taste for their likker. And these Kentucky hill men would not have been able to translate the Celtic phrase "usquebaugh," or even the Latin parallel, "aqua vitae." They would not have known what the first old monks meant when they spoke of their fermented juices as "aqua de vite." But, gentlemen, they would have agreed that in any language Kentucky moonshine was truly the water of life!

On a crackly, frosty dawn early in October, two men stood by the fire in the furnace, hunched close to its warmth in the new chill of the day. The air was so light and so thin that the first cautious rays of the sun splintered it and shattered it into fragments which smoked and rose in curling wisps over the winding stream. A silver rime plated the ground and sheathed the trees and bushes. It was cold for the first week in October.

Tay stood with his hands in his pockets, shivering and yawning. "You takened yer time gittin' here this mornin', Matt," he grumbled. "Hit's broad daylight already. They's aplenty to do today."

Matt Jasper worked his chunk of tobacco around his mouth from one cheek to the other, and spat a hissing stream of juice into the fire. A week's stubble of beard blackened his jaws, and his chin dripped where his mouth had overflowed. "I cain't allus git away so early," he complained. "Lutie don't like to stir so soon these cold mornin's. An' a man's got to have his breakfast 'fore he kin git out to do e'er thing. I git here quick as I kin."

Tay yawned again and stretched, rumpling his black hair sleepily. He stood tall and loose in his joints, easy on his feet. There was a careless grace about every movement he made, and when he reached his arms up over his head, the gray work shirt tightened across his shoulders. He was flat and narrow-hipped, and his leanness boned up beneath the stretch of his blue denim pants. Tay Clark was a handsome lad.

"Criminy, it's cold!" he shivered. "Git a pot o' creek water an' put it on," he told Matt, "an' the coffee's in the shack. I'm goin'

163

to wash up."

He strode to the creek and doused his head under, yelling with the cold. But he splashed his face and neck and wetted down his hair before he went sprinting back to the fire. "Come winter, I'd like to hole up like a bear," he grumbled, wiping his face on his shirt tail.

Matt had put the sooty granite coffeepot on to boil, and stood turning his hands before the fire. "What you aimin' to do today, Tay?" he asked.

"Mash down a batch, an' I reckon you kin bottle yesterday's run. I'm aimin' to git away from here about ten o'clock."

Matt snickered. "You goin' hootin' agin?"

Tay looked at him darkly. "What you know about me hootin'?"

"Oh, I know." Matt threw a handful of coffee into the pot and stirred it down. "Me an' Lutie's seen you over at the schoolhouse. We was sang diggin' over there, an' we heared a old hoot owl, a whooin' soft-like. I knowed hit wasn't natural, so we sneaked around an' peeked. We seen Rose Pierce come to that there grove. The kids was all aplayin' an' amakin' a noise, but I reckon she was listenin' fer them owl signs."

"E'er other person seen us that you know of?"

"Not that I know of."

"Well, keep yer trap shet. Wells, he don't like me, an' Rose don't want him knowin' she's atalkin' to me."

"You aimin' to marry Rose?"

"That's fer me to say. Hit ain't none o' yore put-in. You jist keep yer trap shet, like I say. An' don't go sang diggin' round the schoolhouse no more. How about that coffee?"

"Hit'll do. Mought be a little on the weak side, but hit'll do." He poured a tin cup full and handed it to Tay. "Tay, kin I have me jist a little bottle today? I'll not tetch it till I git through workin'."

Tay gulped a mouthful of the scalding coffee. "I reckon," he said. "But if you git drunk 'fore yer through, you'll not work e'er nother day fer me. Hit costs cash money to make this here stuff, an' I ain't aimin' to have a batch ruint."

"I'll be keerful," promised Matt, and he settled himself against a log to drink his coffee.

That afternoon a blustery, cold wind blew up, and the rain squalled fretfully against the schoolhouse roof. Although it had stopped by the time the afternoon recess was due, Miss Willie decided that it was too cold and raw for the children to be out a full half hour, so she sent them out for a brief ten-minute run. "It's dark and gray," she explained, "and it's turning colder. We'll dismiss an hour earlier today instead of taking recess."

They were hardly settled in their seats again when Rose's hand waved apologetically. Her face was demure, and she slid her question upward toward Miss Willie from downcast eyes. When Miss Willie raised her eyebrows in surprise, Rose reddened, but she nodded her head vigorously. Miss Willie shrugged her permission, and the girl slipped quietly outside.

Just as she reached the door, an owl hooted softly. It was hardly more than the echo of a sound, but in the quietness of the schoolroom it sounded low and insistent, with a quality of urgency. Something about it penetrated Miss Willie's consciousness, and her head came up sharply. What made her look at Rufe she didn't know, but when her glance fell on the boy, there was a listening look on his face, a foxlike, animal look of interpreting some message. His head was turned toward the door, bent just a little, and he threw a sly, cornerwise look at her, and then jerked his head back, his eyes blazing.

Suddenly Miss Willie moved quickly and quietly to the door. She opened it slightly, and through the crack she could plainly see Rose running toward the grove. She closed the door and stood leaning against it for a moment. So. The owl was Rose's signal to come to the grove. And it was so common a sound in the woods that only listening ears could hear it. And it was timed for a recess period, of course, or one of the play times of the younger children, when Rose would be outside. The noise of the playground would mute it except for Rose, who must always be waiting to hear it. And it was only an accident that it had come today during a quiet time. And it was only an accident that she had somehow caught it herself. They were very clever, Rose and Tay. And Rufe, knowing too, had never given it away. Not until today. How stupid she had been not to realize that their scheme would be so simple!

Outside, Rose ran swiftly to the grove. Tay stepped from behind a tree and caught her hard in his arms, lifting her and swinging her off the ground. He closed his mouth eagerly over hers and held it for a long time. He ran his hands over the girl's shoulders, slipping them down to her waist, then he bent to her mouth again. "Glory!" he muttered when he raised his head again.

Rose pulled loose and held him off. "I cain't stay," she said quickly, "they ain't no recess today on account o' the rain an' cold, an' I had to make like I had to go outside to git away when you called. But I'll have to git right back. She'll suspicion somethin' if I don't."

"Hit's allus like this," Tay growled, pulling her close again. "Sneakin' over here two, three times a week, hidin' around, waitin' to see you ten or fifteen minnits at a time! They ain't none of this to my likin'."

"Well, it ain't to mine, neither. But I don't know of e'er thing we kin do!"

"We kin git married!"

"Not till school's out."

"What diffrunce does it make?"

"Hit makes a heap. Pa wanted me to go through the eighth grade. He fixed it so's I could go this year, an' I ain't aimin' to quit till I'm through. Hit ain't so long."

"Have it yer own way," Tay laughed.

"Have it Pa's way, you mean," Rose said. She turned in his arms restlessly, but she tarried a moment longer. "Tay, what you reckon it'll be like? Bein' married, I mean. Hit's goin' to be powerful quare."

Tay bent her fingers back and then crushed the small brown hand in his own. "Hit's goin' to be powerful good to me! Us bein' married. One thing, cain't nobody fault us none, oncet we're married an' I'm workin' regular."

"You goin' to quit stillin' like you promised?"

"I'm aimin' to quit. I done told you that, an' I aim to keep my word. I wouldn't foller stillin' now, except I don't know no other way to git the money fer us to git a start."

"I ain't so shore," Rose laughed, hugging him hard. "Yer kinder venturesome. An' I've wondered some ifen you jist don't

166

like to go agin the law."

"You've no call to say that," the boy protested. "I been sort of wild in my time, but I promised I'd quit all that when we was married, an' I'm aimin' to keep my word. You ain't got e'er reason to doubt me."

"I'll not doubt you, never," Rose whispered, "but I don't reckon it'd make much diffrunce noways. A girl hadn't ort to love a boy so good, ifen she wants peace o' mind."

Tay stopped her words with his mouth. "You shet up," he said when he lifted his head. "How much peace o' mind you reckon I got? I spend all my time athinkin' about you," he said, shaking her gently and rubbing her face with his rough cheek. "Nights over there on that lonesome crick I dream about you, an' think of how it'll be when we kin be together. When I sit by the fire, I kin see yer face in it, an' seems like the crick water is a mumblin' yer name whilst it is runnin' over the stones. I don't do nothin' but think of you!"

"An' make moonshine," Rose teased.

"An' make moonshine," he agreed, laughing.

"I got to go now."

"Wait."

"No. Leave me go."

"Git along, then. I'll be back a Thursday."

"I'll be listenin'," she promised and slid out of his arms. By the time she reached the edge of the grove, he had faded noiselessly into the depths of the thick-grown trees and was lost to sight.

When she sidled back into her seat, Miss Willie raised her eyes and looked at her long and steadily. "I want to see you for a moment when school is out, Rose," she said.

She knows, Rose thought. She's caught on! But her heart was strangely light. It didn't really matter. They'd find another place and another way to meet. Tay could think of somethin'. Tay wouldn't never let 'em be parted. Ifen she jist don't tell Pa, she thought. That's all that wearies me. She darted a look at Rufe and he drooped one eye cautiously. Yes, she shore knows. "Yessum," she answered Miss Willie, meekly.

When the others had left and there were only the two of them sitting in the schoolroom, Miss Willie asked Rose to come to her

167

desk. "Rose," she said, speaking slowly and carefully, "I think you've been meeting Tay Clark in the grove ever since school started. I don't like to say this, but I must. What happens on the school ground is partly my business, and you can't go on meeting him here. Your father thinks you are in school when you're here, and in good faith he is making a real sacrifice so that you can have this last year of school. He doesn't like Tay, and he doesn't want you to go with him. That much of the affair is between you and him. But when you use the school ground for a meeting place, it becomes my affair too. And it can't go on."

Rose's eyes were on the floor while Miss Willie was talking. When she ceased, the girl lifted her head and looked straight at Miss Willie. "I'll not meet him here no more," she said softly.

Miss Willie picked up a ruler and laid it with a pile of pencils under her hand. "I wish you and your father could get this straightened out. But, as I said, that's between you and him. I only wanted to say you couldn't go on meeting Tay here."

"Pa jist don't know Tay," Rose said unexpectedly, her voice warm and full. "All he's got agin him is that he's Old Man Clark's boy, an' he's been kinder wild-like. An' the stillin'. Pa don't hold with stillin'. I don't neither, but Tay ain't goin' to foller it allus."

Miss Willie tapped the ruler gently against the desk. Oddly enough, now that they were talking, she felt a sudden sympathy for the girl. Tay was a handsome lad — there was no denying that. And most of the boys on the ridge went through a more or less wild time. No doubt Wells himself had sown a few wild oats before settling down. Maybe, if Wells would let them see each other openly, the affair would wear itself out. Or maybe the boy could be influenced. One thing was sure — a hidden flame always smoldered dangerously. Maybe she should talk to Wells after all. He was touchy about this subject, but she had got to know him pretty well. And maybe a woman's hand was needed in the matter.

But she said nothing to Rose except: "Well, that's all. If you and Tay meet here any more, I'll have to tell your father."

"Yessum," Rose said, turning toward the door. "I've done said we won't meet here no more. I'll keep my word."

She ain't goin' to tell Pa, Rose was thinking. That's the main

168

thing. We kin find another place. We don't need her old grove. But she ain't goin' to tell Pa, leastways. We've jist got to be more keerful. Tay'll have to think of somethin'.

A short distance from the schoolhouse Rufe was waiting for her. When she came up to him, he spoke. "She caught on?"

Rose nodded. "She wanted me to promise I wouldn't meet him in the grove no more."

"You promise?"

The girl's laugh rang out. "Shore I done so. Hit don't make no diffrunce. I was skeered plumb to death, though. I thought shorely she'd say she was goin' to tell Pa. Hit would of been natural to her. But she said ifen we seen each other at the school-house e'er 'nother time she'd tell him. I told her quick-like we wouldn't do that no more. I reckon she knowed, though, I wasn't givin' my word not to talk to him no more. She acted kinder sad-like."

"I figgered she'd caught on," Rufe said. "He give that owl agin jist as you was leavin', an' it come all over the room plain as day. She give me a look an' then went scootin' to the door. I figgered you hadn't got time to git clean to the grove yit, an' she seen you. She never said nothin', though. Jist closed the door an' stood there alookin' at the floor."

"She never takened on much. Jist what I said. I'm jist glad she ain't aimin' to tell Pa. Course he'll have to know soon or late, but we ain't aimin' to git married till school's out, an' that's some time, yit. Reckon what Pa'll do when I'm gone? Git Aunt Manthy to take Abby too, an' you an' him batch?"

"Oh, we'll git along I reckon."

Rose giggled. "Pa'll mebbe give you a new ma one o' these days."

"He'd better not!"

"He's been alookin' right sweet at Miss Willie, an' atakin' her around right smart. How'd you like her fer a ma?"

Rufe spat and snarled, twisting his mouth to one side. "Her! That mealymouthed, pussyfooted, dried-up little old maid! Ifen I was a man an' couldn't git better'n her, I'd do without!"

Rose was thoughtful. "I don't know, Rufe. She's got real nice ways, an' they's times, when she gits all het up about somethin',

169

when her face reddens up an' her eyes sparkles an' she's almost purty. An' you kin say what you like, she loves kids as good as anybody I ever seen. She'd do fer the least uns like they was her own. But I don't reckon she'd have Pa."

"He ain't good enough fer her, huh?"

"He ain't her kind is all. Reckon she's used to perfessors an' sich. Pa's good, but he ain't real educated. An' hit's bound to be quare fer her here on the ridge. I kinder like her, though."

"Well, I don't! Hit was a sorry day when she come here, nosin' around, tellin' ever'body do this an' do that! The sooner she leaves out, the better I'll like it! I ain't got no use fer her at all!"

"You're jist jealous," Rose teased. "You're afraid Pa *will* like her!"

"I ain't!" Rufe denied fiercely. "I jist don't like her, that's all!"

"All right, then, you ain't," Rose said. They were nearing the pasture fence just around the bend from home. "You go on an' git the cows up, an' let's git the work done up. I got a heap to do tonight."

Rufe whistled off key and ducked between the wires of the fence, his yellow head scraping the wire. "You're goin' to pull them curls o' your'n out by the roots one o' these days," Rose warned. "But I'd ruther see you do that than tear a hole in yer britches."

Rufe wrinkled his nose at her and streaked across the field. Rose watched him a moment and then hurried on to the house.

That night Miss Willie sent Gault over to get Wells.

"You aimin' to tell him?" Becky asked.

"No," Miss Willie said. "I told Rose I'd have to tell him if she met Tay at the schoolhouse any more. I suppose that's a sort of promise not to tell this time. I just want to talk to him . . . see if I can't get him to let them go together openly. He's driving them to meet secretly the way it is. Maybe if he'd let them alone, the whole affair would wear itself out."

Becky shrugged. "I've my doubts."

"Well, I feel like I've got to talk to Wells about it, anyhow."

She felt very unsure of herself, timid about interfering with his family affairs. But she kept remembering the wild, handsome grace of Tay, and the still look on Rose's face when she spoke of him. Admit, she told herself, that Wells knows more about this boy than I do. Admit he knows Rose better than I do. Admit that Rose is too young to make a wise choice — too young to be making any choice at all. But here on the ridge the sap rose early in slender green trees, and who was to say that slender green trees couldn't root themselves firmly and bend and sway before the wind without breaking? Who was to know whether the cup of this girl's love was for this man or that? And who was to say whether its measure should be full and running over before it was tipped to the lips of any man, or drained before it had filled? Who but Rose could know how full it was? Who but Rose could hear the high, wild notes of love that bugled in her ears, could feel the beat of her heart send the blood surging wave after wave through her body, could see with sure eyes down the long, twisted trail of tomorrow? Shouldn't she have a fair chance to listen to her heart? Or to deny it, if she must?

You fool! Miss Willie admonished herself. What do you know about love? Love between a man and woman, that is. Dream a fine dream about bugle notes in the air, blood coursing thickly through the veins, visions of tomorrow! What do you know about it? Dream it . . . and call it by its right name! She rubbed her thin hands together and shrank them against her chest. I know enough, her heart whispered, to know what I've missed! Dream or not, I know when I'm empty! She flung her hands wide. Is it Rose or Miss Willie that's dreaming? Is it Rose or Miss Willie that hears that wild bugling? Is it Tay's voice that calls, or Wells's? She stood before her mirror and watched the slow blood creep up into her face. Fool, she accused. Thou fool!

When Wells sat before her fire later, a cup of coffee cooling on the table at his elbow, she felt fluttery and nervous. He sat in her rocker, his stocky body filling it and his broad shoulders spanning the back. How like him, she thought, to sit there, still, solid, motionless, rocklike in his strength! His face was clean-shaven, smooth and faintly pink beneath its deep tan. There was a fresh smell of soap about him — soap mixed with the clean smell of his clothes, wind- and sun-dried after their washing. He lighted his

171

pipe and leaned his head against the tall back of the rocker, and the smoke curled lazily between them, veiling his face. The smell of his pipe blended with the other smells, and they became whole, the essence of maleness. And his presence overflowed the chair and filled the room, and washed over into Miss Willie until she was faint with its compelling insistence. She reached out a hand to steady herself and jingled the spoon on her saucer in her tremor.

"This shore is nice," Wells said, kicking a foot against the floor and setting the rocker in motion. "This here's purty an' homey. Them curtains o' your'n, the rugs, an' all. You shore did make you a purty little home outen this old log cabin. Hit takes a woman ever' time to figger things out."

"I like it," Miss Willie said. The coffee was hot, and as she sipped it, she steadied. It felt warm and heavy in her stomach. A log snapped in the fire, cracking sharply in the silence and sending a shower of sparks out onto the hearth. Wells leaned forward to juggle the log with the poker.

"I like chestnut wood," he said. "Hit burns mighty purty, but hit makes a heap o' noise doin' it. Sounds like them little firecrackers agoin' off."

"Yes."

When he had fixed the log to suit him, Miss Willie put her cup and saucer down. "I suppose you're wondering why I sent for you," she said.

Wells looked at her quizzically and grinned. "I ain't so curious," he said. "Whatever hit was, I'm powerful beholden to it fer givin' me a chancet to come an' see you."

Miss Willie felt her face heat. "It's about Rose," she blurted out.

Wells sighed and set his own cup and saucer on the table. "Well, I knowed in reason you had somethin' on yer mind, an' I reckoned it'd be about one o' them young'uns o' mine. I was afeared it was Rufe agin."

Miss Willie shook her head.

"What's Rose been up to?" he asked after a time, when Miss Willie said nothing further.

She had been searching for the right words, hoping to find some tactful way of barging into his personal affairs, and wishing

172

she had never started the whole thing. She shook her head again. "It's not that. It's just . . . Wells, do you think it's best for you to forbid her seeing Tay? Don't you think maybe if you'd let them go together openly, they would eventually tire of each other? Are you sure you aren't driving them together this way?"

The urgency in her voice turned his face sober. She looked at him anxiously to see if he resented her questions. But his face only reflected a seriousness and earnestness that paid tribute to her and her opinions. She breathed easier.

He cupped his hands about his updrawn knee. "No," he said slowly, "no; I ain't a bit shore but what I'm doin' jist what you say. I ain't so blind but what I know they're a meetin' sly-like. That's jist what I knowed they'd do."

"Well, then, why don't you let them go together?"

"Hit's like this, Miss Willie. Here on the ridge we do things different, I reckon. But ifen a girl's folks don't make no fuss about her talkin' to a boy, hit's jist the same as givin' 'em leave to stand up before the preacher. An' I cain't in conscience give my consent to her marryin' Tay Clark. That's jist what it would be if I give 'em leave to talk. I look fer 'em to up an' git married one o' these days. But leastways, if they do, hit'll not be on my conscience that I give her over to sich as him. Folks cain't fault me none about that."

Miss Willie studied. "Would you rather have the good opinion of the people on the ridge, then, than to lose their respect trying to help your daughter?" Her voice was dry.

"Hit ain't jist thataway, Miss Willie," he explained patiently. "Hit's all mixed up, an' I ain't shore I kin explain it so's you kin understand, you bein' new to the ridge. You see, Miss Willie, Tay an' Rose knows where they stand. Rose, she wouldn't understand if I tried to tell her she could talk to Tay but couldn't marry him. Hit would jist tangle her up like. She wouldn't make no sense o' me givin' her leave to talk to him, an' not givin' her leave to marry him. But this way hit's all open an' clear. Her an' Tay, an' folks all over, knows I don't give my leave. Ever'body knows they're meetin', an' likely they'll up an' git married. But I've took my stand, an' I'm bound to stay by it. Folks expect it, an' Rose an' Tay expects it. Hit would go agin the grain all round if I

173

didn't, now. A man's called on to take his stand on some things, an' he cain't noways go agin the grain an' call hisself a man. I couldn't never sleep nights ifen I was to out an' out give my leave to Rose marryin' sich as Tay Clark."

"But suppose she marries him anyhow?" Miss Willie's voice raised sharply. "You just said that more than likely she will! What happens then? You'll just lose your daughter, that's what!"

Wells's look was puzzled. "Why, no, Miss Willie. Ifen they git married, hit's done an' over . . . water over the dam. Likely they'll jist move in with me, an' Rose'll jist go on akeepin' house fer us like allus. Hit'll jist be Tay amovin' in with us."

"You mean you'll object until they're actually married and then it won't make any difference?"

"I reckon that's about the size of it. A man's called on to take his stand. But if his young'uns don't bide by it, hit's outta his hands. Ifen Rose an' Tay gits married, he'll be in the family then, an' nothin' to do about it. You don't turn on yer family."

Miss Willie closed her eyes, and her hand made a futile brushing gesture across her face as if to brush a cobweb away. And that's exactly what she felt she was trying to understand. The cobweb of ridge ways. The fine distinction that only ridge people could possibly fathom! It was beyond her!

She stood and picked up the empty cups. "Well, then," she said, "I've just butted in where I had no business again. Forgive me."

Wells looked up at her and smiled wistfully. "That ain't a word I like, Miss Willie. They's no call fer one human bein' to forgive e'er 'nother one. I don't rightly know that they's e'er one of us good enough fer that. Hit's like a body was settin' hisself up over the other. Hit ain't a thing e'er one of us ort to feel, seein' as we're all liable to the same mistakes. An' besides, Miss Willie, I'm catchin' on to you. You was jist doin' what you thought was yer bounden duty. I kin jist see you mullin' it over in yer mind, adecidin' you was called on to have a talk with me. Ifen you don't take keer, Miss Willie, folks is goin' to be sayin' you an' me is talkin' instead o' the young'uns!"

Miss Willie let her breath out sharply. "Don't be silly!"

"Hit ain't so silly, Miss Willie. Me, I kind of take to the notion!"

174

Miss Willie's eyes brimmed and cooled suddenly with tears. "Well, now," she said brightly, "let's talk about something else. Tell me, is it all right for the school to have a Christmas tree and a program, or is that something that isn't done on the ridge?"

The rest of the evening passed swiftly, but when Wells finally left, Miss Willie lay long awake remembering his bulk in her little old rocker, his laugh ringing around the rafters, his pipe smoke wreathing his brown face. The deep tones of his voice lingered in her ears: "Hit ain't so silly, Miss Willie. Me, I kind of take to the notion!"

She snuggled under her blankets and watched the last of the fire settle itself down for the night. It glowed softly and with a red sheen, and her own happiness and contentment glowed within her. I kind of take to the notion too, Wells! She took a deep breath. But, not too fast, she warned herself. Not too fast.

CHAPTER
❧ 18 ❧

NOVEMBER CAME IN ROARING on the high-winded tail of a sleet storm. The last leaf was driven before the gale, and the bones of the trees rattled in their nakedness. The ridge was stripped, and it reared its scrawny spine against the slashing knives patiently and with stony endurance.

"Hit's goin' to be a hard winter," people told Miss Willie as she stepped the little mare carefully down the icy road. "Winter of 1918 set in jist like this. Had twenty-two snows that winter, an' oncet we never seen the ground fer two months on end."

By Thanksgiving the prophecy was well on the way to coming to pass. Twice the earth had been blanketed with snow, and the earliest hard freeze ever known in the country had locked the little creeks and their tributaries into stillness. The surface of the earth shivered and tensed and hardened itself into plated armor. The little mare's feet rang when she stepped now, as if she were walking on sheet metal, and they struck sparks that hissed in the frozen air.

The houses were haunched against the ground, huddled and

low, their shoulders humped up against the wind and the pelting snow. Smoke from the hearths rose slowly, loath to leave the fire, and it hung in wreaths around the sooty stones of the chimneys, hugging the warmth one last time before ascending into the icy air.

Miss Willie had Thanksgiving dinner with Mary and Hod. Afterward they sat, stuffed and sleepy, before the fire. The sleet hissed softly against the windowpanes, and outside the black-boned trees iced themselves with glassy plate. Miss Willie was knitting an afghan for the baby, but her fingers plied the needles automatically. She lifted her eyes from time to time to glance smilingly at Hod, who sat in his big armchair, his son cradled in the curve of his arm and his pipe dangling from one corner of his mouth. Mary wandered over to the piano and let her fingers drift into soft, improvised chords, which resolved themselves finally into the sweet minor notes of a song.

"What is that?" Miss Willie asked after a time.

"It's an old English melody. The words are a Christmas song: 'What Child is this, who, laid to rest, on Mary's lap is sleeping?' " She continued playing, sometimes singing the words, sometimes humming. "I don't remember all of it," she said. "It's been a long time since I thought of this song. My primaries used to sing it during the Christmas season."

"It's beautiful." Miss Willie counted stitches and turned. "And that reminds me. Could you spare some time to help me with the Christmas program at school?"

Mary's hands dropped from the piano. "I guess so. If Hod's mother can stay with the baby. What kind of program are you going to have?"

"Wells says it's customary to have a tree the last Friday night before the holidays. And I thought it would be nice to have a sort of pageant. Maybe have someone read the Christmas story from Luke, and dramatize it with some simple scene, and use the Christmas songs as much as possible. That's where I want you to help, Mary. Children's voices are so beautiful when they're properly trained, and I'd like the people to hear some real singing for a change!"

Mary laughed. "No 'do, re, mi,' is that it?"

"That's it. That song you were just singing would be nice, wouldn't it?"

"Beautiful. High, soft, and minor. And it isn't too difficult. I think we could manage something pretty good."

"Wells is going to get a big cedar tree, and we thought we'd put it up in the corner of the room at the back, and after the program we'd give all the children bags of candy and nuts, and an orange maybe. What do you think of that? I've got so I'm scared to make a move without asking Wells or Becky or someone if it'll go 'agin the grain' here on the ridge. But Wells told me the Christmas tree and program would be all right."

Hod laughed. "I reckon you've had to learn the hard way, all right."

"I certainly have," Miss Willie sniffed.

"The whole thing sounds lovely, Miss Willie," Mary said.

"I thought maybe we could dramatize the manger scene, and let the shepherds come, and the Wise Men bringing gifts. We could use a big doll for the child. I'd like for Johnnie to be Joseph." Miss Willie pinched her lower lip as she thought. "I wish we had some way of lighting it. It would be so much more effective with spots on the scene."

"I wonder," Mary said — "I wonder if you can still get those little boxes of magnesium powder we used to use for tableaux when I was a little girl. Where did we use to get them, anyhow?"

Miss Willie clapped her hands. "Why, Mary, that's the very thing! We got them from a school supply house! There surely is still some demand for that sort of thing. I'll start trying to locate some at once!"

Mary laughed. "I never could keep from jumping when the powder first flared up. I knew it was harmless, but as many of Mamma's tableaux as I was in, I always had to steel myself against jumping when that first bright light flared up. And I remember how it smoked."

"Yes, but it does make an effective scene. That was a real inspiration, Mary. We'll have some sort of curtains, and Hod and Wells can stand in the wings and light the powder at the right time. Red on one side, and green on the other, I think."

Hod shifted the baby. "Hey, look! He's tryin' to sit up!"

177

Mary looked at Miss Willie. "He can't wait until the baby sits alone, and tries to walk and talk! He'll have him following a plow by the time he's a year old!"

"Well, it seems like he's takin' a long time bein' a baby," Hod complained. "I wanna know what he's thinkin' about when he rolls his eyes around and puckers his mouth at me! He gets such a doggoned faraway look on his face, I'd like to know where he's gone!"

"Pooh," Miss Willie said loftily, "more than likely he's trying to make up his mind what sort of person he's drawn for a father. The way you go on with him sometimes I'll bet he thinks he's out of luck!"

"That's all right, son," Hod confided to the baby. "Don't you pay any attention to 'em. That's just woman talk, an' you'll be hearin' it all your life. Just let it go in one ear and out the other. That's the way I do. You and me, we're menfolks, and one of these days we'll have some good old man talk."

Mary chuckled. "Well, you better let me have a little woman talk with him right now, and give him something to eat!" She rose and went across the room to lean over the man and baby, and lifted the child high in her arms. "You may be menfolks, little fellow," she said, shaking him gently, "but all your life the womenfolks are going to be mighty important to you. How would you get your milk right now, huh? And who would teach you when you start to school, huh? And who's going to marry you someday, and raise your young'uns for you, huh? Don't you let your daddy belittle the womenfolks to you!"

Hod's laugh echoed round the room. "I haven't got a chance," he said to Miss Willie. He stood and pushed his chair back with his heel and strode to the fireplace. He poked a log into place and put another one on top. Then, turning, he leaned his elbow on the mantel and looked fondly at the two of them as Mary bent over the baby. Funny, he thought, how the sight of your wife holding your son made you feel so much of a man! It poured through you and washed out everything but the cleanness of pure manhood, made you taller and straighter. It made you grow clear up to the stars, somehow. Made you ache and at the same time healed the aching; stripped you down, and at the same time

178

wrapped you around with the mantle of fatherhood. Drained you and emptied you, and at the same time filled you full. This business of living. Of being a man and a woman, and of having a son! There's nothing like it in the world, he thought. Nothing to compare with it!

The afternoon light was waning when Miss Willie dropped her knitting in the bag by her side. "It's growing late," she said, "and I'd better be going. Hod, will you saddle Pet for me?"

"Just take the night, Miss Willie," Hod suggested.

"No, I'd better go home. Becky and Gault might worry. Besides, Wells is coming over for supper with us."

"Ah, *there's* the reason," Hod gibed, and Miss Willie's face turned rosy. "She must brave sleet and storm, for Lord Randall is comin' courtin' tonight!"

"Hush up!" Miss Willie said. "I don't want that kind of talk to get spread over the ridge. And the best way to start it is to tease about it."

Hod bowed with exaggerated politeness. "Just as you say, Miss Willie. Just as you say, but," he continued softly, "I'll bet a plugged nickel it's done started in yore heart!"

"Hod," Mary warned, and he left the room chuckling.

Miss Willie looked slantwise at Mary and fumbled with her hat. "Wells has been a big help to me," she said, "and of course he comes pretty often. After all, he's one of the trustees, and then too I've had quite a problem with Rufe and Rose."

"Why, of course, Miss Willie," Mary said quietly. "Hod's just teasing."

Miss Willie went to the window to watch for Hod and the little mare. She stood there fingering the shade pull and doodling on the moist windowpane. Mary pinged one note over and over on the piano. Miss Willie squared her shoulders suddenly. "I like him, though," she admitted, her voice loud in the quiet room. "I don't mind everybody knowing I like him . . . a lot."

"We all like Wells," Mary said. "He's a grand person. Next to Hod, I think he's the finest man I ever knew."

Miss Willie's mouth trembled into a smile. "Well, not being married to Hod, I can't say that I put him first."

Mary crossed the room to lay her arm around her aunt's thin

179

shoulders. "Be careful, Miss Willie. Be careful, and make sure. There's an awful lot to be considered."

Miss Willie nodded and reached to kiss Mary's cheek. "That's what troubles me. Oh, pshaw!" and she shook herself vigorously. "Christmas is coming, and we're going to have a lovely pageant, and everything is fine! I am simply going to enjoy myself these next few weeks, and refuse to be troubled about a thing. I'll pick up my troubles after the first of the year. Right now I want to sing and be happy and gay!"

"Is that the way he makes you feel?"

Miss Willie giggled like a child. "That's exactly the way he makes me feel! Young and light and carefree! He makes me feel important and needed. And he makes me feel beautiful and womanly and feminine. And it's a good feeling, Mary. Especially when you're a dried-up, musty old maid!"

"Miss Willie," Mary said softly, "I'll put my plugged nickel right alongside Hod's!"

Wrinkling her nose, Miss Willie picked up her knitting bag. "There's Hod." She opened the door and the wind blew her next words across the room. "You wouldn't lose your nickel, Mary."

Excitement rippled over the ridge as children went home from school and told the news. Miss Willie was goin' to have a Christmas program . . . they was goin' to be a play thing, somethin' she called a pageant . . . an' a Christmas tree with candy an' stuff fer ever'body! "An', Ma, I got to have a costume. I'm goin' to be a shepherd, an' I've got to have a costume. Miss Willie said she'd ride over here an' tell you what to fix."

Miss Willie rode from one end of the ridge to the other, helping mothers devise simple costumes. Burlap sacking for the shepherds, and sheets draped with bits of bright colors for the Wise Men. Hod and Wells made the beards out of lambs' wool, and the boys made the shepherds' crooks from rugged, knotty hickory limbs.

All the ingenuity of women long accustomed to making do with what they had came to the front. And at school the children were busy practicing. Those who did not have part in the pageant

180

were in the choir, and, sensing their desire to be costumed also, Miss Willie suggested that sheets or table covers could be draped over them for choir robes.

Mary came for several days to help with the songs, but once the children learned them, Miss Willie could manage alone. "Softly," she cautioned them over and over again. "Softly."

She had asked Rufe to read the story.

"No, ma'am," he said.

"But Rufe you have such a nice voice, and you read so well," she pleaded.

"No, ma'am," he said. There was no sullenness in his voice. Just an immovable stubbornness.

She was hurt and disappointed, but her pride would not allow her to press the matter further. She had envisioned Rufe in the part, his golden head shining tall in the lamplight, his full young voice reading the beautiful lines. He would have been perfect. But she hid her disappointment and gave the part to one of the Jones triplets, Sewell. She coached him carefully, and he quickly learned the detail of the dramatization: when to wait for the pantomime, when to pick up the story again, when to pause for a song, and when to resume. But his reading was flat and uninspired, and she sighed over his meticulous monotone. Rufe would have made the lines come alive. He would have made the pageant live and move. But . . . no matter. Corinna and Ferdy would bask in sunny pride over Sewell's reading, and doubtless no one else on the ridge would find anything amiss with it.

Now it was less than a week until the program, and the boys and girls were working feverishly on the decorations for the room and the tree. The green and red paper chains grew by yards and were draped in gaudy festoons from the ceiling. Strings of popcorn and cranberries were ready for the tree, and as the week wore on, the children brought armfuls of cedar and pine boughs to place in the windows and around the room. At night Becky and Miss Willie, and sometimes Gault and Wells, sacked candy and nuts for the tree.

The day of the program there was no attempt to have school. Wells brought the tree and the oldest boys put it up. In happy confusion it was decorated. The manger was set up on a platform

181

and strewn with hay, and the curtains, made from sheets, were strung on tight wires across the platform. Wells and Hod came to help and set the pans to hold the tableau lights. One last rehearsal of the pageant was held, and Miss Willie explained the tableau. "Don't be afraid," she told the children. "It will flare up and make a bright light, but that's just what we want. That will be the tableau. Don't move. Just stay in your places and hold your poses, and when the lights die down, Wells and Hod will pull the curtains. Don't move until then."

Everything was ready. The tree in the corner was tall and green, giving off a spicy, pungent smell of cedar. Its boughs were hung with the popcorn and cranberries, and the red and green paper chains. Tinsel stars sparkled here and there, and the bags of candy and nuts, and the bright round oranges weighted down even the tips of the branches. It was a beautiful Christmas tree.

The people gathered early. By deep dark the school ground was crowded with teams and wagons. It was a warm, friendly crowd, laughing and calling out to one another as they saw the tree and the gay room. It was a congregation of neighbors coming to see their children perform, and to share the ancient tradition of a festive tree. Small shepherds and Wise Men bustled importantly up and down the aisles until Miss Willie herded them behind the curtains, and finally sent them filing to the back of the room to await their cues.

At a signal, Sewell started the reading, and Hod and Wells slowly parted the curtains. Miss Willie settled back with a sigh. Johnnie and Sarie were in their places by the manger, and the large doll rested comfortably in the straw. The choir took up the story with the song of the shepherds, and the first shepherd came forward somewhat sheepishly, hitching at his burlap tunic, but carefully and slowly as he had been taught. The star over the manger swung tipsily and revolved endlessly on its length of wire, but it shone brightly just the same.

Then the choir sang the song of the Wise Men, and the first of the Wise Men, splendid in purple and gold, strode haughtily down the aisle, kneeling properly before the manger to present his gift.

The scene moved flawlessly on. Sewell never faltered in his

182

reading. The choir of young voices came in at exactly the right moments, their voices blending softly and sweetly in the old songs. The young actors moved through the pageant with familiar ease and practice. Miss Willie let her hands relax in her lap. There remained now only the tableau. All the actors were on the stage, the choir was softly chanting "Silent Night," and Miss Willie nodded to Hod, who was peeking through a fold of the curtain. There was the flare of matches from either side backstage, and then the full glory of the red and green lights burned up. As they reached their most brilliant light, there were two sudden, sharp explosions of sound, filling the room and reverberating from the ceiling.

There was a stunned silence, and then, "Hit's a *explosion!*" someone cried, and instantly the audience was on its feet screaming and milling senselessly. There was a panic-stricken rush for the door, and a rush toward the stage by terrified parents to rescue their children. Frightened, the children broke and ran, crying and stumbling about in their costumes. Smoke from the sulphur and magnesium mixtures was filling the room with a heavy pall. "Fire!" someone shouted. "Fire! Clear the room. Hit's a fire!"

Miss Willie had been paralyzed at first. She could only think that somehow the powder had been defective and had actually blown up! The crowd jostled her and shoved her aside, and she was pushed gradually against the wall. A complete sense of disaster overcame her, and she thought futilely that she ought to get up on one of these benches and shout and make herself heard and bring some sort of order out of the confusion.

Then she noticed that Hod and Wells were jerking at the curtains, and then Wells stood before the group. He cupped his hands over his mouth and bellowed at the crowd. "Set down, you fools! They ain't no fire, an' that wasn't no explosion! Set down, I'm a tellin' you!"

When the stentorian voice roared out above them the people turned. "Set down," he bellowed again. "Set down!"

The rush toward the door stopped. A few sat down on the back seats and others followed their example, sliding hesitantly onto the benches.

"I'll be back in a minnit," Wells yelled, and he started lunging

183

through the crowd toward the door. "Ever'body jist set down an' wait fer me."

He disappeared through the door. There was an uncertain milling around of people, and the burr of sharp talk rose around the room. Hod appeared from behind the curtains with the pans in which the tableau mixture had been burned. He held them up for the crowd to see. "You can see for yourselves," he said, "there wasn't any explosion. There wasn't any fire. This is just a harmless mixture of magnesium and sulphur. When it's lighted, it flares up brightly and burns for a few seconds, and then it dies down again. There's no way it could possibly explode!"

There was a disturbance in the back of the room, and Wells pushed his way through the crowd, dragging Rufe by one arm and marching Tay Clark ahead of him. Tay walked carelessly and nonchalantly, his hands in his pockets, a malicious grin on his face. At the front of the room Wells halted them.

"Here's yer explosion," he said. "Long as you fellers been huntin' these ridges an' hollers, I'm ashamed you don't know a shotgun when you hear it! This smart-alec young'un of mine, an' Tay Clark here, thought it'd be fun to play a dirty trick on ever'- body. Skeer the daylights outen 'em, an' start 'em trompin' one another down to git outta here. An' that's jist what they done! I knowed as soon as I heared it, it was a gun." Bitterly he went on. "I ain't claimin' no excuses fer my boy. But I aim to see he don't fergit this. As fer Tay, mebbe he'd better say fer hisself."

Tay shrugged his shoulders. "Aw, we never meant no harm. Hit was jist a trick." His grin widened. "You all shore did look funny stampedin' around in here. You ort to of seen yerselves!"

"An' you ort to be ashamed o' yerself! Playin' a fool trick like that, growed man that you are! Somebody might of got hurt!"

Tay laughed and ran his hand over his black hair. "Well, I tell you," he said, "I reckon I been samplin' my own goods a little too much. Hit jist seemed like a good idee all at oncet. Don't hold it agin Rufe too hard. Hit was mostly my idee."

"I'll hold it agin him," Wells promised. "I'll hold it agin his backside when I git him home! An' right now that's where he's a goin'."

Miss Willie had not taken her eyes off Rufe during the entire

184

scene. When his father turned him loose, he had straightened himself and stood tall before the crowd, looking over their heads into space. By not so much as one troubled look had he given any notice that he heard anything Wells said. The winter was bleaching his summer tan, but the golden wash over his face and hair was still there. There was a still look of endurance on the face now. A withdrawn look, as if he had pulled himself in tight. It would be better, Miss Willie thought, if he were insolent, like Tay. If he would flaunt his contempt, openly.

For she was certain that once again Rufe had found a way to show his enmity for her. She felt her breath tighten in her throat. Why did this boy hate her so? What had she done, or what had she failed to do? She felt as if a fog had closed in around her, blanking out familiar landmarks. There was nothing she could hold to . . . nothing she could see, except the misty currents of dislike that eddied between her and this tawny-headed boy.

"Now git on home," Wells was saying. "You cain't stay fer the tree, nor fer nothin' else. Git yerself home. But wait up. I'll tend to you when I git there."

Miss Willie stood up. "No, Wells," she found herself saying, "no, don't make him go home. Let him stay for the tree." She started toward the front of the room

Rufe looked at her then. Directly. Steadily. "I wouldn't keer to stay," he said.

Miss Willie stopped where she stood. Her teeth caught her underlip and it quivered slightly. She felt as if he had struck her. But the years of her pride rose within her, and she made her voice steady as she answered him. "Just as you like, Rufe," she said.

And he walked past her without again looking at her.

When the door closed behind him, there was a rumbling of talk through the room. Some of the men looked at each other and laughed sheepishly. The women were complaining in undertones, and there was an occasional shrill whisper against such goings on. "Ifen he was mine, I'd take a strop to him, an' I reckon that's jist what Wells'll do too."

There was a virtuous gathering of their own children to their sides, and Miss Willie felt as if Rufe had been outlawed. Bleakly,

185

she heard Wells telling Tay he had better get going too, and in her alienated misery she watched him swagger down the aisle. At the door he waved to Rose, holding the door open so that a gust of wind made the lamps flicker.

"Shet the door," somebody yelled, and he laughed and banged the door behind him. Miss Willie wondered if the reason he had thought of this trick lay in her own refusal to let him and Rose meet on the school ground. Wearily she shrugged the thought away. No matter now. She had done what she must.

When Tay had left, the tension eased and people started laughing and joking together, jeering at each other. "Gault, I seen you jump two foot when that there gun went off," Tom said, poking Gault in the ribs.

Gault laughed. "Hit shore skeered me outen ten years' growth," he admitted.

"I never jumped," Tom bragged.

"No, you was too busy makin' fer the door," Hattie accused dryly.

There was a shout of laughter, and then Hod was calling for quiet. "Let's have the tree, now," he shouted. "Ever'body turn around and face the tree, an' Miss Willie'll give out the presents!"

Miss Willie made her way to the foot of the tree, and Hod crawled up on a ladder to hand down the sacks and oranges. Remembering her joy in planning this night, Miss Willie was shaken by its dreary ending. A chill of shivering fled through her, and she steadied herself against the ladder. And then the bright, expectant faces of the children focused before her, and she thought, Why, the evening hasn't been spoiled for them! She looked around the room, and in the soft lamplight the faces of the people were friendly and warm. It hasn't been spoiled for them, either, she thought. Just for me. Me . . . and Wells. And maybe Rufe.

She drew herself up and handed the first two sacks of candy and nuts and the first two oranges to Sarie Simpson and Johnnie. They beamed at her, and Sarie ducked her red head shyly. Johnnie's round face broke into a toothless grin.

"What do you say, Johnnie?" Irma prompted.

"Thank you, ma'am," Johnnie said importantly.

"You're quite welcome, Johnnie," and Miss Willie tousled his hair fondly.

The next sack she handed to Lutie Jasper. "Fer me?" Lutie questioned. "I thought it was jist fer the kids."

"For everyone," Miss Willie answered. "Christmas gift for everyone!"

"Christmas gift! Christmas gift!" the voices shouted around the room. High up on the ladder Hod started singing "Jingle Bells," and soon everyone had joined in.

When the tree had been divested of the last sack and the last orange, people began to leave. "Hit was a nice program, Miss Willie," they said. And: "Don't you feel bad about yer lights. Hit come right at the last, an' never spoilt a thing."

It was Ferdy Jones who mentioned the choir. "The kids sung real good, Miss Willie. Hit's a pity, though, they never sung out good an' loud. Reckon they was too skeered."

Miss Willie was too tired to reply. It didn't matter anyhow.

But, tired as she was, she tossed sleeplessly on her bed later. I could fight a grown man, she thought. I would know how to go to him and have it out in the open. But Rufe's stony and implacable barrier of enmity thwarted her in the way a tangled skein of yarn baffles one. If only you could find one loose end! It would take patience to ravel the knots, but they could be managed and eventually they would come smooth, if only you could find the starting place! She had tried. Goodness knows, she had tried. She had tried to interest him in reading, but he wouldn't even take the books home. She had tried to interest him in the science table, suggesting he collect things on his wanderings through the woods. She had said: "Rufe, you know the woods so well. Why don't you look for things when you're out with Jupe, and bring them for us to see? Indian spikes, unusual flowers, insects or small animals. You could add a lot to the table." He had only looked off through the window and shaken his head.

Restlessly she turned and wrinkled the smooth sheets, until finally in exasperation she rose and straightened the bed. Crawling back beneath the blankets, she rationalized. School's nearly over now. Maybe it will work itself out this summer. Maybe by the time the next term starts I'll find the answer. Maybe the Lord

187

will pass a miracle, she jeered at herself! Well, go to sleep now, she commanded her tired mind. You're not called on to settle everything tonight.

CHAPTER

✹ 19 ✹

Scʜᴏᴏʟ ᴄʟᴏsᴇᴅ ᴛʜᴇ ᴍɪᴅᴅʟᴇ ᴏғ Jᴀɴᴜᴀʀʏ, earlier than expected. The weather was so bad after Christmas that attendance dropped to a mere fraction of the enrollment. Only those children living near the schoolhouse could brave the deep snows and the bitter cold. The trustees decided to close two weeks early.

Miss Willie worked hard over a written report she wanted to make to the trustees. She dwelt at length upon the things that had been accomplished, pointing them out with pride. And then she concluded by summing up the things that were still wrong, and with her own frank suggestions as to how to right them. She wrote in her bold, schoolteacherish hand: "The school term is much too short, but as yet I see no way to deal with that problem. The children must come such long distances, over such bad roads, that at present it is physically impossible for them to attend when the harsh weather of winter sets in. We need improved roads, so that a car can travel the year round. Perhaps the trustees could lead in a fight to get the county to do some work on the roads."

Then she went on to point out: "I must protest against the open spring from which the drinking water comes. In its present condition it is dangerous. An epidemic of almost any kind could easily start, since the water from the spring flows for some distance in an open channel. It may be fouled by cattle and other animals, and even by people. I strongly urge you to cement the spring in an enclosed box, and to pipe the water to the schoolhouse. The cost of this would be small in comparison to the satisfaction in the security offered the children.

"The open toilets are another thing that should be corrected. New buildings are needed, and modern chemical disposal units should be installed. In their present condition they constitute a health hazard of the gravest sort, to say nothing of being ex-

188

tremely offensive to the eye. Education," she went on to say, "is not simply a matter of learning from books. Children learn from their total environment. Ugly buildings, offensive sanitation units, careless health habits are teaching them things just as surely as the textbooks in arithmetic and geography. They are teaching them that, although their hygiene books stress sanitation, no one takes it seriously. They are teaching them that, although 'teacher' talks about beauty and encourages them to develop an appreciation of it, the unbeautiful things within a stone's throw of them are ignored.

"We have accomplished much this school term. We can take pride in many things we have done. But I appeal to you as the trustees, and more important, as fathers, to consider seriously these things I have called to your attention, and to act upon them before the beginning of the next term."

There, she thought, when she had finished, now that's said. They can't sit back smugly and pat themselves on the back and say: "Miss Willie shore done a good job this year. Best school we've ever had." That report's got something in it that ought to make them stir their stumps!

But she was glad she didn't have to report some other things in which she had fallen short. The health class had had to be abandoned when the weather began to break, and she had to admit to herself it was just as well. As Becky had prophesied, the women had come and had drunk her tea and eaten her cookies, and listened. For she had been as good as her word and she had preached and preached. Diet, sanitation, health, cleanliness — she hadn't left anything untouched. And the women listened docilely, nodded their heads in agreement, and said, "Yes, ma'am," to everything she asked them to do. But the children's lunch buckets continued to hold cold biscuits and fat meat, the children continued to come to school with the itch, with colds, and even with whooping cough.

And she winced every time she remembered that neither had she got very far with Becky's well! When she thought of that, even yet, it made her face go hot with chagrin. Gault had neatly circumscribed her on that! As long as she lived she would never forget the morning he had gathered up his tools and some slabs

189

of old lumber. "Well," he had announced to her and Becky, "reckon I'll make that thar gate Becky's been awantin'. Hit was bad enough long as hit was jist her arollin' under that bob-war fence, but ifen they's goin' to be two of you arollin' I won't never see no peace."

And he had had the audacious nerve to cut a gate in the barbed-wire fence across the path to the spring, so that she and Becky could carry water without rolling under the fence! She could have sworn there was a ghastly twinkle in his eyes when he did it too!

She copied the report and mailed it to Lem as the chairman of the trustees. And then for several weeks she waited for him to reply. She expected him to call a meeting of the trustees to hear the report read, and she thought he might ask her to be present to discuss the details of her suggestions.

But the time went by and nothing happened. At first she was not restless. The weather was bad, and she thought Lem was waiting for a break in the cold. She spent the days quietly, either reading and studying by her own fireside or up at Becky's, helping her. The long winter months which forced the ridge folks inside gave Becky her best opportunity for plaiting and sewing her rag rugs, and for stitching the infinitesimal pieces of quilt tops together. Hour after long hour passed with Becky on one side of the fire and Miss Willie on the other.

"Yer right handy with a needle," she told Miss Willie one day. "Yore stitches is littler than mine. Seems like I cain't see so good no more."

"You ought to have your eyes examined," Miss Willie said, bending over to select another color from the basket. "You probably need glasses."

"Doubtless I do," Becky agreed. "I told Gault if he'd give me the next calf, they was two things I'd like to do with the money. Git me a pair o' glasses, an' git me a wrist watch. I've allus wanted one o' them little wrist watches."

Miss Willie was silent. She knew better than to suggest that maybe Gault would give her the next calf, or even that maybe he would get her the glasses and wrist watch. Gault would do exactly what he pleased about it, as befitted the head of the house. And

190

Becky would not want him to do differently. She knew that too now. Becky had been as proud as punch of the new gate in the barbed-wire fence! So Miss Willie kept quiet.

After a time she asked, "What is this pattern we're working on now?"

"This here's the Double Weddin' Ring," Becky said. "Wait till we git it all together, an' you'll see. The rings all lap over an' makes the purtiest pattern! Hit's one of my favorites. Some folks makes it all one color, but I like to mix 'em up. Hit's brighter thataway."

"I like it better mixed up too."

Becky rose and went into the kitchen, returning with the granite coffeepot, which she set in the ashes at the front of the fire. "Reckon a mite o' coffee'd go purty good, wouldn't it?"

"It would," Miss Willie said, without looking up. Then, "Becky," she asked, after the coffee had been poured, "why do you suppose Lem hasn't said anything about my report? It's been nearly a month since I sent it to him, and I haven't heard a word from him. Has he said anything to Gault about it?"

Becky eyed her quizzically, and then shook her head. "Not that I've heared of."

"Well, I think it's very queer he doesn't do something about it."

Becky poured her coffee into the saucer and blew on it meditatively. Then she sipped carefully. "Miss Willie, he ain't goin' to do nothin' about that report o' your'n. Hit'd surprise me if he's read it.. Likely he jist looked at it an' laid it away, aimin' to git around to it one day. An' if he's read it, I doubt he'd do one thing about it. Things jist moves slow here. You'd ort to of learnt that by now. You'll jist have to take yer satisfaction from knowin' you've done what was right, an' hope you started a idee in somebody's head. Mebbe five, ten years from now somethin' will come of it."

Miss Willie laid her sewing down. She shoved her chair back and, getting up, started pacing back and forth in front of the fire. "Isn't there anything else I can do about it?"

"Well, you kin write you out enough reports to go clean around the trustees, an' that's about all. But if ever'one of 'em has it, leastways they'll know what you had to say. I reckon Hod an'

191

Wells would be fur e'er thing you said, but they ain't the whole shootin' match. Send Old Man Simpson one, an' Gault. Gault, he'll go along with you as fur as he kin, but he kin be powerful mule-headed when he wants to be. But don't look fer too much from it. Like I said, about the best you kin do is git a idee started, an' hope it ketches on."

Miss Willie pushed her glasses up furiously. "Oh, this ridge!" she muttered grimly. "I'd like to take the heads of these stubborn people and knock them together. Maybe I could knock some sense into them. I never saw people so set in their ways! They won't listen to anybody! If it's 'allus' been done one way, it's 'allus' got to be done that way! That spring's got to be cemented. There'll be an epidemic of dysentery or typhoid one of these days, just as sure as anything. It's just got to be fixed!" And in her agitation Miss Willie pounded one fist into the other. "It's just got to be fixed!"

She stopped and pinched her lower lip, thinking. "I know," she said so suddenly that Becky jumped. "I know what I'll do. I'll just have it fixed with my own money. That's one of their excuses. They never have the money. If it's fixed and doesn't cost them anything, they can't object."

Becky raised her eyebrows and stuck her tongue in her cheek. "I wouldn't do that if I was you, Miss Willie."

"And why not, for goodness' sake?"

"Hit's allus best to let folks do fer theirselves. You jist keep on atalkin'. Jist keep on apoundin' it in. But don't take the bit 'twixt yer teeth an' run off with it. Let 'em work around to it their own way when the time's ripe."

Miss Willie sat down and picked up her sewing again. She sighed heavily. "I suppose you're right. You usually are. But it needs doing so badly, and they may take four or five years! If they could just see what a menace it is!"

"Time passes, Miss Willie. Hit comes an' hit goes. You're all frashed about this now, but jist remember that there spring's been givin' drinkin' water fer the Big Springs School fer more years that you been livin'. I don't know as any great harm has come from it yit."

"That attitude is just what I mean! All of you say the same

192

thing! How do you know how many cases of typhoid fever could be traced to that spring? Didn't you tell me that Gault and Tom and Lem all had typhoid when they were little? And hasn't nearly every other family on the ridge had a case of typhoid at one time or another? How do you know where they got it? How do you know?" Miss Willie's glasses slipped down her nose again.

Becky laughed. "You needn't preach at me, Miss Willie! I'd like to see you git that spring boxed in, bad as you would. I'm jist tryin' to tell you not to kick over the milk bucket 'fore you git through milkin'."

Restlessly, Miss Willie got to her feet again and walked to the window. She pushed the curtains aside and peered out.

"Is it fairin' up?" Becky asked.

"I think so. The wind's dying down too, I believe."

"Hit'll be clear, come night."

"Becky," Miss Willie called suddenly, "Becky, here comes Wells!"

"Reckon where he's goin' this time o' day? Is he afoot?"

"No, he's riding Pet." She went to the door and flung it open. A biting wind blew through the room, scattering the fire and making Becky jump.

"Land sakes, Miss Willie, wait'll he gits here 'fore you open the door!"

"He's here. Hello, there," she called. "Come on in!"

Wells came in, stamping his feet noisily and slapping his gloves free of his hands. "Howdy," he called, and the room shook with his voice. "Howdy, there, Becky!"

"Git yerself inside," Becky answered dryly, "an' shet the door! Freeze a body plumb to death!"

"Nice warm welcome a feller gits when he comes to this house!" Wells laughed.

"Hit'd be a sight warmer if Miss Willie didn't blow the fire all over the hearth lettin' you in!"

"Quit grumbling, Becky," Miss Willie said. "Wells, how about a cup of coffee?"

"Jist the thing," Wells answered, letting his chunky frame down on the floor by the fireplace, propping his back against the warm stones and stretching his legs out in front of him. "Jist the thing."

193

Miss Willie handed him the coffee and sat near him on the small stool. "You haven't been over in quite a while. What brings you today?"

Wells set his cup down on the floor beside him and took his pipe out of his pocket. He took his time about filling it, tamping the tobacco down carefully and flinging the shreds in the palm of his hand into the fire. He peeled a splinter from a log on the pile near him and lighted it from the fire, carried it to the bowl of his pipe, and drew slowly until the pipe was going. He puffed a time or two. "Why, I thought you all might like to know Rose an' Tay got married yesterday," he said finally.

Miss Willie looked at him in amazement. He had said it so casually. "Married?" she repeated, as if not comprehending.

"Yep. I been lookin' fer it, like I told you last winter. An' I take it kindly Rose went on an' ended up the school term before she done it. Hit wouldn't of surprised me none if she hadn't of, but I reckon she figgered she'd ort to do that much like I wanted, at least."

"Reckon they went in to the county seat," Becky put in.

Wells nodded. "They come in about suppertime last night. Said they'd jist got spliced. Hit's all legal. I seen the papers."

"Well, Rose could of done worse," Becky said, never missing a stitch. "Leastways she's married now, an' you'll not have no more wearyin' to do over her."

"I'm relieved hit's done," Wells agreed. The two, understanding each other perfectly, spoke comfortably together. "Long as they was jist atalkin' I never knowed. I couldn't rightly give her over to Tay Clark, an' I was allus afeared he was jist foolin' her. Hit would of gone hard if he'd a done wrong by her."

Becky nodded. "Hit's best. Likely he'll settle down now an' make her a good man."

"That's what I'm hopin'. If he'll give over stillin', I kin use him on the place. They's plenty o' work fer two growed men. Rufe is too spare yit to do a man's work. Tay kin be a big he'p if he will."

"Are they going to live with you?" Miss Willie asked.

"Fer the time bein'," Wells answered. "He's got a little money saved up, an' they allowed they'd like to build 'em a place o' their

194

own soon. But they's no hurry about it. They's room an' aplenty fer 'em there."

He drank the last of his coffee, knocked out his pipe on the hearthstone, and pulled himself up. "I got to be gittin' on. Jist thought I'd stop by an' pass the news along. You all come an' see 'em now."

"We'll come," Becky promised. "Tell Rose we'll git around."

Wells started to the door and then he stopped suddenly. "By golly, I was about to fergit! Miss Willie, how'd you like to go possum-huntin' tonight? Me an' Hod's goin', an' Mary said if you'd go, she would. They kin git Hattie to come take the night an' stay with the boy. Hit looks like it'll be a good night. Wind's clearin' up the clouds, an' hit'll be cold an' moony."

"You tell Mary I'd love to go!" Miss Willie said. "I'll just jump at the chance to go! I've been indoors too long lately. A little more and I'd be house-crazy!"

"You'll freeze yer front teeth out, goin' out sich a night," Becky grumbled. "An' at yore age!"

"What's wrong with her age?" Wells wanted to know. "She kin outwalk an' outlast e'er person on this ridge, I'll bound ye. An' we won't let her freeze. Gits too cold we kin allus build up a fire."

"Sure!" and Miss Willie's chin went up. At her age! Becky talked like she had one foot in the grave! She'd possum hunt right along with the best of them. Becky would just see!

When the door closed behind Wells, Miss Willie stood at the window watching him mount the little mare and ride off down the ridge. "He didn't seem at all upset about Rose, did he?" she said finally.

"Nothin' to be upset about," Becky said. "Hit's like he said. Hit's a relief to him that it's over an' done with. You never acted very surprised yerself!"

"Oh, he told me about it some time ago. Remember that night I asked Gault to tell him to come over? You remember I wanted him to let them go together openly. He explained it to me that night. And he said then that he expected them to marry sooner or later. So I wasn't surprised. But I was a little surprised at him. He acted almost like he was pleased about it."

"Why, shore. He don't like Tay so good. But cain't nobody he'p

195

bein' pleased when young'uns gits married. Hit's sich a happy time fer 'em. Hit would be a pore makeshift of a human that'd begrudge 'em their rightful happiness. They ain't no lovelier sight in the world than two young'uns like that that's jist got spliced. Hit's jist like they owned the moon an' the stars an' the sun fer a time. Course, later on when the babies starts comin' an' the goin' gits hard, hit ain't so easy, an' they got to settle down. But a new wedded pair is the apple o' the Lord's eye."

"I must try to think of something to give Rose," Miss Willie said.

"I'm aimin' to give her this here Double Weddin' Ring quilt. I had it in mind all the time," and Becky looked sweetly and intimately across the room at Miss Willie. "Hit'll be right nice, won't it?"

It was good dark when Wells came by for Miss Willie and they set off down the road toward the hollow. It was a cold night, tingly with frost. The stars glittered with a frozen pallor, scarcely blinking in their remoteness. Underfoot, the ground was as hard as iron, and their footsteps rang bell-like against it. Miss Willie saw her breath puffing warmly from her mouth, a thin veil of vapor before her. She felt snug in her heavy wraps, small and isolated from the cold and the night, and Wells's bulk was very heavy and solid beside her.

They talked very little, both feeling the night and the starry skies and the insulation of the dark. Miss Willie tried to remember when she had known this snug, wrapped-in-the-dark feeling before. Long ago, she knew it was. Back, back down the years. When she was a child. Yes. Yes, now she remembered. She had gone with her father, alone, to evening service. He had carried a lantern against the night, and, bundled warmly, she had followed in his huge footsteps, feeling safe and secluded and secure against the dark and the cold. She remembered the exalted feeling of being alone with him, just the two of them at the center of warmth and light. Darkness held at bay out on the fringe of the lantern glow.

Instead of a lantern, Wells carried a flashlight, but the feeling was just the same. Only the two of them, at the heart and core of space, the night held off, and the two of them safe and warm. She dropped behind and tried to stretch her short legs to Wells's long strides, placing her feet carefully in his big footsteps. This was the way it was that night with her father. A little girl, safely following a big man, who held all darkness away from her; who stood between her and the night, and all things unknown and fearful.

Miss Willie stopped abruptly. All things unknown and fearful! A big man who stood between! Broad shoulders, sturdy body, strong arms and legs. Between her and the night. Between her and . . . insecurity? Loneliness? Lovelessness? For heaven's sake, she cried at herself. *Must* you go psychological about everything? Must you go back to beginnings and analyze every feeling? This is a possum hunt. This is Wells Pierce. And this is Piney Ridge. Come down to earth, Willie Payne!

"What you doin', Miss Willie?" Wells called back, and she realized that he was a hundred yards ahead of her. She giggled. If she didn't watch out, the big man wasn't going to be standing between her and the night very long!

"I'm coming," she called. "I got to thinking."

"Well, upon my word an' honor! You better wait an' do yer thinkin' in front o' yer fire some night. You got to keep movin' out in the cold like this!"

"I'm coming," she repeated, and caught up with him.

The walk to Hod's place didn't take long, and soon he and Mary were with them. "Where'd you reckon to go, Wells?" Hod asked.

"Head o' the holler, I thought," Wells answered. "Hit used to be a good place."

"Good as any," Hod said, and turned his dogs loose.

With an excited barking, the dogs struck up the hollow, and the four of them followed. The night, the cold, the dark, and the hunt were exhilarating to both Mary and Miss Willie, and their mood struck sparks from each other so that they were giggling and laughing like a pair of schoolgirls. They stumbled along and lagged and bumped into things in the darkness. Until finally Hod turned and said sternly: "Now you girls got to keep up. We don't

197

want to miss a possum because you all are lost somewhere behind. And we can't wait for you, once the dogs strike a trail. It's every man for himself then, and you'll have to keep up, and you'll have to be quiet."

Rebuked, they were subdued and they bent themselves to keeping up. Up and up the hollow they went and the ground got rougher and rougher. As the hollow pinched in, the trail was lost, and they broke through underbrush, vines, dried canes, and rank, matted growth at every step. The men set a fast pace, crossing the creek and climbing the straight, steep sides of the far ridge when the dogs ran out of the hollow. No one offered to help either Mary or Miss Willie. And they had to work desperately to stay up.

The hillside was so steep that they climbed, literally, a ladder of rocks and ledges. Miss Willie scrambled and fell and grabbed at whatever handhold she could find, her chest heaving and her heavy coat smothering her and weighing her down. She wished now she had worn only a windbreaker, like Wells. Branches and brambles clawed at her face, and her short legs ached as she pulled them up the steep climb. She stumbled over stones and logs, and she slipped and slid on the slippery leaves underfoot. She was determined to keep up, though. When she looked at Mary, she saw that she was having just as hard a time, puffing and panting just as much, slipping and sliding just as often. She hoped the men would wait up when they got to the top of the ridge!

The hill was interminable, and she lay flat getting her breath when Wells finally gave her a hand over the last ledge. Well, she was up. At whatever cost! And then the dogs tore down that awful hill again and off across the creek to the far side. Suddenly they gave tongue and the night was full of their sharp, excited yelps. Yip-yip-yip, came from the bottom of the hollow, and yip-yip-yip it went on up the other hillside!

"Trail!" yelled Hod, and plunged over the rim of the ridge.

"Trail!" yelled Wells, and followed on Hod's heels.

"Trail!" sung out Mary, and she disappeared in the night.

Miss Willie crawled over to a tree and pulled herself up. She knew she couldn't get down that hill again, across the creek, and

198

up another hill. It was physically impossible to do it. The human body, hers at least, was built to stand just so much, and it had stood it! It would never take her through what lay ahead!

But they had gone off and left her! She couldn't stay here in the dark and the cold alone! She had to follow! Well, she thought, recklessly, you can die only once, and she might as well do it trying. So, "Trail!" she echoed feebly, and then she simply sat down on her backside and let nature take its course!

She passed Mary and Wells and Hod somewhere along the way as she went slipping and slithering down, and she remembered the horrified look on Mary's face in the faint glow of Wells's flashlight as she flew by.

"Hit's Miss Willie!" Wells shouted.

"She'll be killed!" Mary screamed.

She tried to call out that she was all right, but just then she brought up against a tree with such a solid thump that all the breath was knocked out of her. She lay motionless, wondering if all her bones were broken, while she struggled for breath. When she could move, she felt of herself gingerly. She seemed to be all in one piece. By golly, she was down that dratted hill, and she was still alive!

And then the others were crowding around her, talking all at once, and Mary was crying.

"Oh, for goodness' sake," Miss Willie said sharply. "I'm all right. I just wasn't going to try to walk down that hill!"

Wells took in a big lungful of air and let it out explosively. He looked at Hod, and suddenly the two men started laughing. They laughed and they laughed, bent over double, tears streaming from their eyes, slapping each other on the back, until they were weak and gasping, and leaning against each other.

"I don't see anything funny about it," Miss Willie said testily, and she indignantly replaced the glasses which she had been holding clutched tightly in one hand. Mary had sunk weakly to the ground and laid her head against her knees. Her shoulders were shaking too.

Miss Willie eased herself up, limped a step or two, brushed off the leaves and twigs, and: "Come on. Let's go possum-hunting," she said.

"You'll do, Miss Willie," Wells said, his voice still shaky with laughter. "You'll shore do!"

"Listen!" Hod's voice was sharp.

The short yips of the dogs had changed now to a deep, long bay — a mellow, bell tone — which echoed through the hollow and came back off the hills. "They've treed!"

And once again the chase was on. Across the creek and up the hill. And then there was the possum, high in a tree, sullen in the beams of light from the flashlight.

"We'll have to shake him out," said Wells, and he started skinning up the tree. Now that she could stand still and get her breath, Miss Willie was crawling with excitement. She watched Wells inch up on the possum and shake the limb until its hold was loose and it fell sprawling to the ground. At once the dogs were upon it.

"Hold it, Duke," Hod called, and the dog stiffened with the neck of the possum between his teeth. "It's a nice, big, fat one," Hod yelled, and expertly he slipped it into the big burlap sack he had brought along. "Good dog," he said, patting the dog's head. "Good dog."

But already the dogs were restless, and when Wells was on the ground again, Hod turned them loose. "One up an' two to go," Wells said. "We allus git three."

In her ignorance Miss Willie had thought this was all. They'd caught a possum, hadn't they? Two to go! She stiffened her spine. O Becky, Becky, how right you were! At my age I should be home by the fire knitting!

But she set her teeth and she stayed with it, and along toward midnight sometime she saw the third possum sacked. The dogs were weary, Hod and Wells were weary, and Miss Willie and Mary were practically crawling when they turned homeward. And there was all that long way to walk yet!

Hod and Mary were in front, and Hod had his arm around Mary, helping her. A cold, lonely moon had risen over the gaunt trees and hung frozen in the sky. Miss Willie stumbled. Wells held her and gently drew her hand through his arm. Arm in arm they walked, then, and the heat from his warm, stocky body crept up Miss Willie's arm and through her veins, coursing vitally

200

through the living streams of her body. It warmed her clear to her toes.

"How'd you like the possum hunt?" Wells asked finally.

Miss Willie leaned her forehead tiredly against his shoulder. "I liked it. But, Wells, I got awfully tired!"

Wells chuckled low in his throat. "So did I, Miss Willie. Just between you an' me, so did I. We better leave this possum-huntin' to the young'uns, I reckon. Yore little rockin' chair an' the fireside's a heap more in keepin' with us!"

Miss Willie lifted her face and saw a star blink twice. She laughed softly. And then a scud of clouds thinned over the moon and left a shredding trail of mist behind.

CHAPTER

❧ 20 ❧

It came on to snow the last of February. There was no sun that morning. Only a pale thinning of the gray overcast in the east. The sky came down flat to the edges of the ridge, thick and smoky and opaque. Trees and houses were anonymous in the murkiness, losing their sharpness and their solid lines. The level stretches of pastures and fields reflected the smokiness of the day and took on the dull look of a gray, calm sea, changeless, monotonous, endless. The cattle herded together in the low places, still and wise, hunched against an unborn wind. Head to rump they stood, as if building a barrier. There was a waiting feeling in the air.

Just before noon the first flakes fell. Big, wet, woolly patches of white which covered the ground within thirty minutes. Then a wind blew out of the north, moaning low around the eaves, whistling shrilly down the chimneys, squeezing and shaking old timbers, and whining like a fine wire around the corners. Before it, the harassed snow whirled giddily, driven in a crazy, mad swirl to seek a resting place.

Half a day the wind blew, and then as if some giant had been amusing himself puffing his stormy breath at the ridge and had tired of his fun and gone away, a great calm fell, so quietly and silently that the absence of motion and sound was like a great

201

noise itself. But the snow continued to fall.

Early in the storm, when the first wind came screeching across the rim of the ridge, Gault had gone down to Miss Willie's cabin. "Hit's comin' on to storm," he told her, "an' from the looks of it, hit's goin' to be a good 'un. You better bring some things an' come on up to the house."

Miss Willie peered out the window. "I've got plenty of wood, Gault," she said. "I'll be all right here."

Gault shook his head. "Hit might be you couldn't git to the house to eat, Miss Willie. You better do like I say."

So Miss Willie packed a bag with a change of clothes, several books, her knitting, and went back to the house with him.

The slow hours passed. Outside the storm wind blew and the snow pelted against the windows. The room, with its blazing fire on the hearth, was shut in, imprisoned by the gray blanket outside. Becky hunched over her quilt pieces and Miss Willie knitted and read. Gault slept most of the day away, rising when the room darkened to see about the animals at the barn. He wrapped himself in a heavy coat, tied a scarf over his ears, and pulled his old cap down securely over it.

"Gault, how can you find the barn in this drift?" Miss Willie asked.

"I'll foller the fence to the barn lot," he answered, pulling on his gloves, "an' it's jist a piece from there. I'll make it all right. Leastways, I got to try. The animals has got to be fed."

When he opened the back door, the snow swirled high through the room, the door swinging crazily on its hinges until he could catch it. It took all his strength to pull it closed behind him.

"Gentlemen! This here's a real blizzard," Becky shouted to Miss Willie from the kitchen. She was sweeping up the loose blown snow and she stopped to peer anxiously out the window. Miss Willie joined her.

"You think he'll make it?" she wanted to know.

"Oh, shore," Becky said, putting the broom back in the corner. "He'll foller the fence like he said."

Becky built up the fire in the cook stove and set about making bread for supper. Miss Willie set the table and put out the butter, preserves, and milk.

202

"How long do you think it'll keep this up?" she asked.

"Hit'll die down durin' the night, likely," Becky answered, her hands working the biscuit dough.

"It looked pretty deep out there already."

Becky nodded. "Oh, hit's liable to be a good two foot 'fore it gits through."

Gault came in just as the biscuits were browned. He shook his head as he stamped the snow from his boots and shed his big coat. "Hit's shore a storm," he said, unwrapping the scarf from his head. "That there wind like to blew me clean offen the ridge! All I could do to hold onto the fence. But ever'thing's fine at the barn. Cows is in, an' the horse. I got 'em down a right smart bit o' hay. They'll do all right now."

Miss Willie felt an elemental satisfaction in all this. The storm keening against the small house. The four walls snugged in around the fire. A man keeping his responsibility for his animals. A woman making a hot meal in the lamplight. This was meeting nature head on, asking no quarter, bedding down to endure. This was man close to nature, with nothing to hold it at bay. No steam-heated rooms, no storm-sashed windows, no deep-comforted warmth. No tempering of the wind. Just man and woman, with the storm howling at their heels, tiny and alone, but neither helpless nor afraid. This country made tough, fibrous men and women, she thought. And she felt a heady sense of being spectator to a living drama.

Then the wind died down, and the snow came straight down, heavy, thick, and full of substance. All night it fell, and the next day. Late in the evening of the second day a timid sun blinked down at the shimmering earth, and then ducked behind its gray curtain again. It snowed for another hour or so, but that night a full moon cleared the sky and rode a high promise for fair weather toward the dawn.

On the morning of the third day the world glistened under a heavy fall of snow. It lay unbroken, save for Gault's trail to the barn, widening and softening the ridge top, stretching out beautifully pure from one horizon to the other. The crystalline surface glittered in the sunlight, sparkling like a jeweled blanket. The trees bore heavy crowns of white, and the fence rows marched

203

like ghosts across the fields.

Miss Willie looked down the road. No track had yet marred its smooth whiteness, which glinted like cake icing in the sun. Down the ridge a wisp of smoke curled up over the trees. Old Man Clark's folks were making breakfast then. Up the ridge another wisp of smoke curled. Hattie and Tom were up too. Miss Willie wondered if Hod and Mary were all right, and then she looked far down the road, knowing she could not see, but looking for smoke from Wells's house.

"I can see smoke from the Clarks', Becky," she called out to the kitchen, "and from Hattie's place too. I guess everyone's all right. But I wish I knew how Hod and Mary made out."

"Don't weary yerself, Miss Willie," Becky called back. "Hod's a old hand here on the ridge. He kin read the weather as good as Gault. He made ready fer this. We'll shore be housebound fer two, three days, though."

After breakfast Miss Willie bundled up and took a shovel to help Gault clear a path to her cabin. She felt invigorated and childishly happy to be outside again after the long time indoors. She took deep breaths of the cold, clean air and swung her shovel energetically, throwing snow in tall mounds on either side of the path. In a short time she was puffing and blowing like a porpoise. Her shovel moved slower and slower until Gault laughed and said, "Better rest yerself a mite, Miss Willie."

She leaned on the shovel and pushed her glasses up on her nose. "I guess I'm out of condition," she admitted.

"This here's hard work," Gault said, going on with his shoveling. The path was two feet wide, and Gault's side was clean and sharp. His shovel bit into the solid white wall precisely and took out a huge square with each lift. Miss Willie eyed her side. It was chewed and hacked, with here a deep cave in the wall and there a fat bulge. She giggled. "As a snow shoveler I'd never qualify as an expert."

"Yer doin' fine," Gault assured her. "Hit don't matter none how you git it out. Gittin' it out's the main thing."

The sound of bells — gay, jingling bells — came from down the road. Gault slanted his head to listen and Miss Willie turned toward the road. And then they saw a team plodding heavily

204

through the thick piled snow on the road.

"Who in the world . . ." Miss Willie wondered.

"Well, I'll be dad-blamed!" Gault laughed. "Ifen that there Wells ain't put runners on his old buggy! Well, I swear! Hit takes Wells ever' time to think o' things!"

Down the road came the team, bells jingling from their harness with each step, and cutting through the drift behind them was Wells in the old buggy. It was slow going, heavy going, but they made progress. He waved to them and pulled up in front of the house.

"Howdy," he called, "Miss Willie, c'mon an' take a ride with me!"

"Where you goin' in that there rig?" Gault yelled.

"Nowhere special. I figgered Miss Willie'd like to see if Mary an' the baby was all right."

"When didja make them there runners?"

"Oh, I smoothed 'em out durin' the storm. Couldn't do nothin' else. You wanta go, Miss Willie?"

"Why, shore," Miss Willie laughed. "Gault, you tell Becky where I am."

Wells gave her a hand and she crawled into the buggy. He tucked the blanket around her and she felt a rich warmness at her feet.

"Did you bring a stove along too?" she asked.

Wells grinned. "I jist het up a big rock. Figgered it'd keep you warm till we got there. Hit's purty cold."

He pulled the team into the road again, and they set off down the ridge. Miss Willie settled herself under the blanket comfortably. "Wells, this is fun! How did you happen to think of it?"

"Nothin' much else to think of, an' like I said, I knowed you'd be frettin' to git down to Mary's soon as the storm was over. An' then, I allus did like to git out after a snow with a sled. Don't git many deep snows like this'n, an' I thought it'd be right nice. Hit'll be a heap better when it's melted some an' hardened over. Runners'll go smoother then."

"This is nice the way it is. And the bells sound so merry and gay!"

"I figgered you'd like them too." Wells stuck his tongue in his

205

cheek. "I'm atryin' ever' way I kin to please you."

Miss Willie felt her neck heating and the flush rising to her face. But she looked at him bravely. "Have you been taking lessons in pleasing ladies from Tay lately?"

Wells's great laugh shook the buggy. "I'll have you know, Miss Willie, I don't need e'er nother man to give me no lessons in how to please a lady!"

"I wouldn't think so, either," Miss Willie agreed softly. "You do right well on your own."

"Thank you, ma'am," and he bent over in a mock bow.

"How silly we are!" Miss Willie giggled. "Tell me. How are Rose and Tay?"

"Snug as two bugs in a rug! Jist as happy as if they had good sense! Rose, she has a fit ever' time she opens a present, an' the folks is shore doin' right by 'em too. Never seen so many nice things. Becky, she sent over a quilt, an' Hod an' Mary, they sent 'em a set o' chairs Hod made. An' Hattie give 'em a box o' canned stuff. They're gittin' set up right off."

"That reminds me. I want to give them something, but I don't quite know what. I wondered if Rose would like one of the pictures I have packed away. I have several very good ones. Do you think she would like something like that?"

Wells nodded. "I know in reason she would. She'd think a heap of it, comin' from you."

"Well, as we go home, I'll get it and you can take it to her."

The runners hissed through the snow and the old buggy ran smoothly. It was hard to believe that this was the road so eaten and rutted that usually you had to hold on to keep from being bounced out.

"Wells," Miss Willie said after a while, "do you think Tay will quit making moonshine now that he and Rose are married?"

"Hit's hard to tell, Miss Willie. I'm hopin' he will. I'm a givin' him ever' chancet to work on the place, an' I'll split even with him on the crops if he'll work right. I'm afeared stillin's in his blood, though. Hit's a easy way to make big money, an', besides, Tay's allus been a wild one, adrinkin' an' aplayin' cards, an' arunnin' with a crowd over at the Gap. Come clost to trouble a time or two. But seems like he's powerful in love. Only thing is, when the

206

new wears off he's liable to go back to his old ways. Cain't tell yit, though, an' it ain't fair to say."

Miss Willie sighed and leaned back against the seat. "I do hope he settles down now and makes Rose a good husband. Rose is a good girl. I do so want her to be happy."

"You an' me both, Miss Willie. Rose *is* a good girl — a heap like her ma — an' I'd not like to see her wearyin' over him."

Miss Willie was quiet a moment. Then: "Wells, tell me about Matildy. I noticed her picture one day when I was over there."

Wells pulled a rein through his hand and straightened it before answering. "Ifen you takened note of her picture, Miss Willie, you seen how she was. Ifen you could of knowed her in the flesh, you would of said the same."

"How did she look, Wells? Was she tall or short? Fair or dark? Plump or slender? If it's none of my business, tell me. But I've wanted to know."

"I don't mind tellin' you. She was short. Little bit of a thing, allus plump as a partridge, an' mostly you'd say fat, I reckon, along towards the last. She had brown hair, curled up sweet-like at the ends . . . big, brown eyes, sort of crinkly-like at the corners. Allus alaughin'. Nothin' never frashed Matildy fer long. She'd git fretted over the young'uns, times, but soon's they was straightened out, she was alaughin' an' ajokin' agin. Some thought she done too much of it. But I allus liked her fer it. I'm turned the same way, an' hit makes fer easy livin'. We was first cousins, I reckon you know. Some thought we ortent to of got married, but I never held with that. An' Matildy, she never did, either. We growed up here on the ridge together, an' never had no thought from the time we was little but what we'd git married someday. Hit worked out fine too."

Miss Willie's hands were gripped tight under the blanket. "I wish I could have known her, Wells. I know she must have been a wonderful person. And I know you must miss her an awful lot."

Wells's eyes were on the road ahead of the horses. "Hit was hard at first. Hit was like havin' part o' yerself gone. Seemed to me like I never would git used to her not bein' there. An' it was bad fer the kids. Rose, she stepped in an' done the best she could, but Matildy had allus done ever'thing an' Rose hadn't

207

never carried the full load. But she done good. Rufe, he takened it awful hard. He thought a heap of his ma. The night she went, he takened his gun an' the dog an' went off in the woods, an' never come home till after the funeral. An' he's never named her agin to this day."

Tears pricked Miss Willie's eyes. "That's mostly what's wrong with him, then."

"I allowed so too. But he's got no call to keep on bein' so wearisome. Boy or man, he's got to learn to take trouble as it comes. You cain't side-step trouble. Hit comes to all. I made allowances fer him fer a while, but I been wearied about him. He'd ort to of pulled hisself outen it by now. But don't seem like nobody kin git next to him. Ifen he keeps up thisaway, he'll end up in some real trouble time he's growed!"

"I wish he'd be friends with me. I don't know why he doesn't like me, but it seems as if he hates me sometimes."

Wells laughed. "He's jealous, fer one thing."

"Jealous!"

"Well, I don't reckon he's figgered it out. But he feels it jist the same."

"How could he be jealous of me?"

"He ain't. He's jealous of me. He knows I think a heap of you."

"O Wells!"

Wells called to the horses, and when they had stopped, he squared around on the seat. "Listen, Miss Willie. I've told you how it was with Matildy an' me. I wouldn't try to tell you it'll ever be jist like that agin fer me, with nobody else. They's jist one time when yer young an' lighthearted an' yer girl is young an' sweet alongside of you. But they's another time when yer settled an' knowledgeable, an' the fire, mebbe it don't blaze so high, but it burns mighty steady-like. Hit ain't that bright, new blaze, but it's a warm burnin' jist the same. An' they's ways mebbe it's a heap more satisfyin'. I wouldn't never ast no woman to take Matildy's place. I wouldn't want no woman to. But, Miss Willie, I'd like to ast you to take yer own place alongside of me. Yer own rightful, proud place."

"Wells, what are you saying?"

"I'm a-astin' you to marry me, Miss Willie."

A thin, high note bugled through the air and sang sweetly in Miss Willie's ears. It pierced her with its exulting song and lifted her heart, filling and stretching it until she thought she must burst. Her throat was tight with the feeling of it and the fullness of it. And the singing made her dizzy and she closed her eyes, swaying gently to still music.

Wells's arms went hard around her, and before her eyes flew open, his lips had laid themselves against her own, warm against the coldness of her mouth, warm and soft, but firmly insistent. Not for twenty-five years had a man's mouth been pressed against her own! And never before in love. Only the light kisses of youth had come her way. Lightly given and lightly received. Never before this hungry warmth, this seeking firmness, this taking from her the source of her strength! She felt as if this man pulled from her the last drop of her coursing blood, and left her drained and sapped.

When she could no longer stand it, she pulled her head back from him and pushed her hands against his chest. Even her hands trembled at the touch of that solid chest. "Don't, Wells," she murmured, hiding her face against his shoulder.

Wells gathered her hands in his own and bent over her again, "Miss Willie," he said softly, "Miss Willie, don't say no."

She let him have her mouth again, savoring the wine of his maleness, the faint odor of shaving soap on his face, blended with the smell of tobacco on his breath. She let herself drink up the feeling of his strong, hard mouth, the feeling of his thick shoulders under her hands, the feeling of his heart beating against her own. She gave herself over completely for one long moment to the transcendent joy of being joined with him. She let her hands slide around to cup his face, feeling it clean-shaven, but with the roughness of his beard just underneath. The eternal symbol of the full-grown man! She wondered fleetingly at it, and at the thrill that went through her fingers. And then she pushed him away again. "Not any more, Wells," she protested. "No more. I'll have to think. You'll have to let me think."

Wells laughed triumphantly and he gathered up the reins. "All right, Miss Willie. Think all you like. But don't fergit what you jist felt! That was a growed man tellin' you he loved you!"

Miss Willie pressed her hands against her hot face. Where had the cold gone! A moment before she had felt the quivers of chill down her spine, and her face had been frozen. Her mouth had been numb. Now there were needles of fire pricking her lips, and her cheeks were burning!

"How long you want to think, Miss Willie?"

"Oh, I don't know, Wells. I don't know." And she repeated that trite expression, "This is so sudden!"

Wells pulled his pipe out of his pocket. He handed the reins to Miss Willie. "Here, you drive while I git my pipe to goin'."

When he had it lighted, he took the reins again. "You mean to say you never expected nothin' like this?"

"I don't know. I really don't know what I thought or felt or anything, Wells. Should I have? I thought you were awfully nice to me, and I have liked you so much. Oh, I haven't let myself think about it! I'm forty-five years old, Wells! I'm past the time when a woman thinks of love and marriage!"

"I'm forty-five years old too, Miss Willie. An' I shore ain't past the time when I think of love an' marriage! An' I'd say it was high time you was givin' it some thought. What you got to think about, anyhow? Didn't you feel like you loved me a minnit ago?"

Miss Willie wouldn't meet his look, but when he persisted, "Didn't you?" she answered bravely. "Yes, I felt it. But there's more to it than that!"

"What more?"

"Oh, a lot!" How could she tell him? The ridge, and everything. How did she know she wanted to live here the rest of her life? And Wells himself — overalled most of his days, happy to follow a plow, butchering every rule of grammar, crude, uncouth in many ways. Kind? Yes. Good. Heartwarmingly good. But there was so much difference in them. How could she tell him that? She couldn't. She could only repeat, "There's a lot more to it than feeling."

Wells pulled on his pipe and sent a cloud of smoke over their heads. "Well, I reckon yer right at that. I've give it some thought, though. I ain't to say well off, but they's aplenty, the way we live here on the ridge. You've seen the house. Hit ain't nothin' extry, but it could be made right nice. An' they's allus a good livin' off

210

the place. I'd ort to tell you they's close to two thousand dollars in the bank at the county seat. A woman *had* ort to think o' them things."

"But I wasn't thinking of them, Wells," Miss Willie said. He didn't know, then, of her own income. But it didn't matter. "I wouldn't worry about material things. Oh, it's all mixed up. Just let me think about it for a while."

Wells shifted his pipe to the other side of his mouth and slapped the reins on the fat backs of the team. Miss Willie was trembling, and the cold seeped through her, sending a ripple of chills down her back. She shivered. Wells reached over to pull the blanket closer around her. "Yer gittin' cold, ain't you?" he asked.

She nodded, biting her lips. Suddenly she wanted to cry. She wanted nothing so much as to burrow her head against Wells's shoulder and weep and weep. She wanted to cry away all the problems and have him hold her close and tell her everything was all right. She wanted him to make her feel safe again, like a child. You can't cry things away, she told herself sternly. You have to face them.

"What about Rufe?" she asked, after a while, and in spite of herself her voice quavered.

"Well, what about him?"

"He wouldn't like for us to be married."

"He'd jist have to git used to it. He'd be all right in time."

Miss Willie shook her head. "And what about Rose and Tay?"

"Oh, me an' Tay'd build them a little place. They's room aplenty. They want their own place, anyways."

They rode silently for a time. Then Wells slanted his eyes at her and grinned. "Ain't you goin' to ast me what about Abby? An' Veeny?"

Miss Willie smiled at him. "I wouldn't worry about Abby. And your sister has Veeny. Abby and I would get along fine."

"You an' the others'd git along fine too. Rose, she'd like it straight off, I'll bound. An' Rufe wouldn't be no worse off than he is now. In my opinion, he'd be a heap better off, oncet he got used to the idee. If you got to make up yer mind on account o' my kids, don't go decidin' what they like 'fore you know. Fur as I kin see, the main thing is if yer goin' to let them make *you* unhappy."

They were coming up in front of Hod's place, and Miss Willie fidgeted with her scarf and her gloves. She pushed her glasses up and patted her hair, loosening the scarf tied over it and retying it. Wells chuckled. "You reckon Hod an' Mary kin see that there kiss smack in the middle of yer mouth?"

"They can see a whole lot more than you think they can, Wells Pierce!" Miss Willie bristled. "And don't you say one word about this until we decide something. You hear!"

"I hear. Cross my heart, I'll not say e'er word. When you reckon we'll decide?"

"Oh, let me alone, Wells! You know what I mean. And don't you go taking anything for granted, either!"

Wells grinned. "I'll not. Say, that there's John Walton's team hitched in the back there. What you reckon he's doin' over here? Must be somethin's happened to Irma or one o' the kids to git him out in this here snow!"

He pulled the team up by the gate and got down and tied them. Wading back to the buggy, he said: "You better let me carry you to the porch. Hit's deeper along here where it's drifted."

"I've got on galoshes," Miss Willie protested. "I can walk. Just help me down."

Wells lifted her to the ground, where she sank in the soft snow to her knees. "I thought you had on galoshes," he heckled.

"I have!"

"Powerful lot o' good they're doin' you, buried down there! Here," and he bent in front of her. "I ain't carried nobody piggyback sincet the kids was little. Yore size is jist about right."

Before she knew what he was doing, his arms swept under her knees and she was lifted to his broad back. "Here we go," he shouted. "Hey, Hod! Open the door!"

Stumbling, half falling, through the deep, soft snow, he plunged toward the porch. Mary opened the door, surveyed them with a startled glance, and then started laughing. "Hod, come here," she called back into the house. "Look who's coming!"

Hod appeared in the door. "Hey, Wells," he yelled, "what you got there? A bag of beans?"

"Nope. Jist Miss Willie!"

212

Miss Willie was giggling. She waved at Hod and Mary and called out: "Miss Willie Payne, on her personal and private puddle jumper! Gangway, you two! I can't stop him!"

Laughing, they tumbled through the door, and Wells eased Miss Willie onto the couch. He was puffing and snorting. "By golly," he said, "you weigh a heap more'n I thought you did. You ain't as much of a lightweight as I'd guess!"

"Nobody asked you to carry me," Miss Willie huffed.

"Well, it was a sight better'n wadin'. Howdy, John."

John Walton was standing in front of the fireplace. He had laughed with them when they tumbled through the door, but almost immediately a strained look had come over his face. "Howdy, Wells," he answered.

"What brung you out in all this snow?"

"I come over to git Hod," John said, his troubled eyes seeking Hod and Mary on the other side of the room. "Johnnie's sick. He's bad sick, an' I cain't git Irma to let me git the doctor. I thought mebbe Hod could talk her into it."

"Fer the land's sake! Why don't she want you to git the doctor?" Wells's voice was brittle with astonishment.

Hod was lighting a cigarette, and he threw the match into the fireplace viciously. "It's that fool religion she's taken up with! Don't you remember she was baptized last summer?"

"Hush, Hod," Mary's voice was soft, and she put out a hand to still him.

"Well, what am I supposed to do — stand by and say nothing while the kid dies? From what John tells he's got pneumonia, or nearabouts, anyhow."

"Oh, no!" Miss Willie said, her hand coming up to cover her mouth. She leaned hard against the back of the couch.

Wells rubbed his jaw. "I'd plumb fergot that," he said. "Wasn't you baptized too?"

John nodded. "Irma wanted it. An' I didn't keer one way or another. But I ain't got the faith like her. I cain't jist set there an' look at the pore little feller an' pray like she kin. I want to git a doctor, quick. But she won't hear to it. Says a doctor won't do him no good. Says the Lord'll cure him, ifen it's his will."

Hod was on his feet again. "Well, I'm goin' to help the Lord's

213

will out a little! Come on, John. We'll go get the doctor. You're the kid's pa, and you've got as much right as Irma to have a say about this."

"Don't you think you'd better talk to Irma first, Hod?" Mary asked.

"No. It wouldn't do any good to talk to her. We'll get the doctor. Wells, you take Mary and Miss Willie over to Irma's, and Mary, you tell Irma we've gone to the Gap and we're bringing the doctor back with us. Tell her any way you like, but tell her that the doctor is coming, and he'll look at little Johnnie when we get there with him!"

"John, is this what you want Hod to do?" Mary asked, going over and laying her hand on John's arm.

John studied the toe of his boot, and then he raised his head and looked at Mary. "I reckon it is, Mary. I hate to go agin Irma, but I cain't stand it no longer. Ifen he died, it'd be on my conscience the rest of my days."

"Well, let's get goin'," Hod said, bundling into his heavy coat. John reached for his coat, and the two men went out the door.

Mary turned to Miss Willie and Wells. "I can't take the baby out in this cold," she said. "I didn't think of that."

Quickly Miss Willie spoke. "I'll stay with the baby. You go with Wells."

Within a few minutes Mary was ready, and Miss Willie stood at the window and watched her and Wells drive off down the road. All the gladness had gone from the day. There was this cold fact staring them in the face. Johnnie was ill, desperately ill, and there was a chasm between his father and mother. This day, whatever its outcome, would leave scars on both of them. Scars that might never be healed. Irma's faith stood on one side of the chasm, and John's fears stood on the other side. Between them was a deep and dark divide.

And then Miss Willie thought of Johnnie, remembering him that first day of school showing her the bird he had drawn and telling her in his slow, exact voice that he thought it was a blue jay. Remembering him the day Rufe had given him the skunk to use for the tiger in the play, remembering how his round little face had screwed up as he carried the smelling animal into the

214

schoolroom. Remembering what a stanch little Joseph he had made in the Christmas pageant. And remembering, Miss Willie found her prayers joining with Irma's: "Let him be all right, Lord. Let Johnnie be all right!"

The hours went by and night came. Miss Willie found wood piled on the back porch and she brought in plenty for the night. She fixed herself something to eat, fed the baby, and put him to bed. And then she sat alone before the fire. There was no sound, either in the house or outside. A log burned through occasionally, and fell with a chunking sound into the ashes, sending sparks flying up the chimney. She kept the fire going and kept a lonely vigil with her thoughts. They would not leave the bedside of Johnnie. Finally she lay down on the couch, pulling the bright afghan Mary kept folded there over her, and along toward morning she slept.

She was awakened a few hours later when Mary and Hod and Wells returned. Sitting upright, and startled, she searched their grave faces for news. Wells shook his head at her. "He's mighty sick," he said.

Mary sank into a chair and covered her face with her hands. "It's horrible," she whispered, "it's horrible!"

"Did you get the doctor?" Miss Willie asked Hod.

He nodded. "We got him. He's still there. Said he'd stay till the worst was over."

"Who's there with Irma now?"

"Ma. We stopped an' got her as we came back with the doctor."

"How did Irma take it — the doctor, I mean."

"Quiet. She just stood to one side and let us in, and then she never went near Johnnie's room again all night. She was on her knees in the next room, and you could hear her prayin' sometimes. I don't know what's come over her. Irma used to be such a common-sense girl." He flung his coat over a chair and dropped to the couch. He leaned his head back and closed his eyes.

Mary rose and went toward the kitchen. "I'll fix some breakfast. Was the baby good?"

"He was fine. There's not been a sound out of him all night.
215

Mary, I want to go over there. Do you think it would hurt anything?"

Mary stopped at the kitchen door. "I don't see any reason why you shouldn't go if you want to," she said. "There's nothing you can do, of course. Hod's mother is helping the doctor. But if you want to go, go ahead."

Miss Willie turned to Wells. "I know you're worn-out, but will you take me before you go home?"

"Why, shore," Wells said, "there'll be little enough rest e'er one of us'll git till they's a change one way or another. I ain't aimin' to go home."

"Eat some breakfast first," Mary called from the kitchen.

After they had eaten breakfast, Wells drove the long miles through the snow again. John let them in. He shook his head when they asked if there was any change.

"Where's Irma?" Miss Willie asked.

"In there," and he motioned with his head toward the back room.

Irma was sitting quietly in a chair, looking out the window across the wide, white fields. She looked up when Miss Willie entered the room, and a brief smile flitted across her face. "Hit's good of you to come," she said.

Miss Willie choked. "O Irma. I've been thinking of you all night. And of Johnnie. And I've been praying that he will be all right."

"He's all right, Miss Willie. Johnnie's all right. He's in the Lord's hands."

"Yes," Miss Willie murmured.

There was a look of absolute peace on Irma's face. A calm look of certainty and assurance. Miss Willie's eyes went blind with tears, and she stumbled from the room. What if he dies, she thought. She is so sure. So certain. What will happen to her if he dies!

Wells lay down on the couch and slept, telling Miss Willie to call him if he were needed. The morning wore itself out. Hod came back, and at noon Miss Willie set food on the table. She roused Wells and they all tried to eat.

Late in the afternoon, just as the sun laid its last brilliant band of gold across the ridge, Johnnie died. He had not been conscious all day, and as the fever rose he had weakened, struggling with decreasing strength against the virulent infection that had him in its grip.

It was John who went back to tell Irma. The others sat stunned, and sunk in the depression of fatigue and grief, by the fire.

As the doctor was leaving, Irma and John came into the room. Irma stood tall and straight, and although John was beside her, she seemed to stand alone. Her face was as quiet and as calm as it had been in the back room.

"I'd like to thank you all fer what you've done," she said. "Fer comin' an' helpin' the ways you thought best. John done what he had to, I reckon. I don't fault him none fer that. An' you," she turned to the doctor, "hit was good of you to come out in the cold an' the weather, although I wouldn't of troubled you. Hit was unneedful." She turned back to the others. "But now I'd like you to go."

Hod kicked at a log on the fire. "All yer prayin' for the Lord to save him didn't do no good, did it?"

Miss Willie saw Irma's lips moving, but when she turned to Hod her voice was level and quiet. "Hod, I never prayed fer the Lord to save Johnnie. I prayed fer the Lord's will to be done, an' I prayed fer him to give me strength to abide by it."

She turned quickly to the others and flung her hands out in a motion of appeal. "I want you to go, now. All of you. An' leave me with my own!"

And then she turned and went into the room where Johnnie lay, closing the door gently behind her.

CHAPTER

❧ 21 ❧

THE REST OF THE WINTER CREPT BY, softly, whitely, slipping the days through the week like a kitten making sly tracks in the snow. Little Johnnie was buried and the snow covered him over, leav-

217

ing no new-mounded scar to stand raw and hurt against the earth. But there were hearts that bore deep, bleeding scars.

There was Hod, whose hurt was as bitter as gall in his mouth. He could not and he would not understand Irma's attitude. Not that he continued to quarrel with her about it. But he brooded over it and had no patience with it. There had always been a warm friendliness between him and his sister. Now there was a rift in the warmth.

There was Mary who yearned over Irma and the emptiness she must now be feeling, and who looked at her own healthy, round-cheeked boy shudderingly, remembering how swiftly Johnnie's life had been snuffed out. And she clutched small Jeems tightly and fearfully.

There were Hattie and Tom, who had buried eight of their own eleven. Hattie, more than most, would know what it had cost Irma to lay little Johnnie in the winter ground. She had laid so many of her own there.

And then there was Irma herself. Whatever peace her new-found faith brought her, it could not keep her from listening for Johnnie's quick, running footsteps through the house, for his high, sweet voice calling through the rooms, for his rumpled curls so soft under her palm, and for his chubby, skinned knees so often needing washing. Faith might comfort, thought Miss Willie, but it couldn't rub out all the memories, and it couldn't fill up all the emptiness.

And there was John, who must put away now the dream of his son growing tall alongside of him. Who must forget the things he had planned to teach him, and the hours he had hoped to spend with him. Who must tide over the loneliness of the future years, which had loomed so full and so content with a man-child to stand beside him. There was John, who must also remember that he had gone against the wife of his young years in trying to save his boy, and who must go through the days knowing he had doubted, and would always doubt, her faith. Knowing there was this road he could not walk with her, although he had tried. Knowing there would always be this wall between them, and that again and again it would build itself up and divide them.

And then there was Miss Willie, who had her own special grief

218

and bewilderment. That first day of school Johnnie had walked into her heart and part of it had belonged to him ever since. It was almost more than she could bear to think of his bright, blue look, lifted so quickly and so lovingly to her voice, forever gone, closed off, shut out. To remember his grubby little fist closed tightly around a crayon, his tongue between the gaps in his teeth, trying so stubbornly to make his birds and his trees and his houses fit the proportions of the paper. To remember his voice, serious and sweet, in the Christmas story, and its breathy catch when his mother had reminded him, "What do you say, Johnnie?" when Miss Willie had handed him his orange and candy. "Thank you," and it had been like a song. The gift had been so overwhelming!

But besides her grief over the child and her sense of personal loss, Miss Willie was troubled by a growing feeling of strangeness. She felt bewildered and confused. Little by little she had lost her first feeling of strangeness on the ridge. She had not, it is true, presumed even to herself that she understood these people and their ways. And she admitted honestly that she had done very little of what she had set out to do. But she had lately felt as if she had settled into a place of her own among them. Mary and Hod, Becky and Gault, and, most of all, Wells had sustained and strengthened her. She felt safe and secure in their friendly affection.

But as the days blew cold and icy, she felt alien again, as if they had withdrawn from her. Hod was so moody and silent, and Mary was so wrapped up in the baby. Not that they weren't kind to her. They were. But she realized too suddenly that she was not at the core of their lives at all. They were complete without her. She was only on the fringe of the circle. They loved her, but it was not the glowing flame of the love that bound them together. And that was right, she scolded herself. That was as it should be! But even its rightness didn't make it any the less cheerless.

And Becky too had grown remote. As if she herself had lost another child. The winter bound them in the house together, but the warmth of the days before Johnnie's death had gone, to be replaced by a chilled and shrunken companionship. Becky shriveled into a thin, warped little shadow, hands eternally busy, but

219

silent and broody on her side of the fireplace. Miss Willie knew that because Becky had grown up in the same faith, she had banded herself with Irma against the outspoken censure of Hod, the silent criticism of Hattie and Tom, and her own lack of sympathy for the belief. She knew that Becky had slipped a portion of the guilt that they all were placing on Irma's shoulders to her own. And because Miss Willie was on the other side, with those who did not understand and keep the beautiful comfort of the faith, Becky had, forsooth, to draw away from her.

And the cold and the snow and the ice kept Wells from coming. Not entirely. Occasionally he rode by for an hour or so beside the fire. But he did not try to recapture the mood of that day. Only once did he refer to what had passed between them. "You been thinkin'?" he asked her.

She had shaken her head mutely, and he had let her alone. That day she had been been particularly restless, poking the fire, wandering around the room, pulling at the window curtains. This Kentucky winter was so different from the ones she had known in Texas. The days were so brief and so dark. The sun so seldom shone, and there was a damp rawness in the air which chilled her to the bone. She longed for the sun again. These gray, dreary days on the ridge beat her down into herself until she felt caged and imprisoned, and the low-ceilinged rooms stifled her.

Wells sat stolidly by the hearth popping corn, and in a sudden, angry despair she had resented his bigness and his calmness. Marry this solid, hulking man? This broad, heavy-shouldered creature who walked with a lumbering stride and whose hands were calloused and hard and rough? This ignorant, insensitive person who butchered the most common rules of grammar every time he opened his mouth? Marry him, and spend the rest of her life feeling the house shake every time he walked awkwardly across the floor! Having his horny hands touch her! Listening to his illiterate language day in and day out! Marry him? She had been crazy to think of it for one small second!

"If the winter would just pass," she said wearily, leaning her head against the frosty windowpane. "The days are so short and we are so closed in! The sun doesn't shine for weeks and weeks, and the mornings are dark and the evenings are dark! We *live* in darkness, like moles crawling around!"

"Hit is wearisome," Wells had answered. "Along about this time of year, hit gits awful tiresome. Seems like time has jist stood still. But hit'll pass. Hit allus does. Spring'll come before you know it."

"Oh, go away," Miss Willie had muttered, fretfully. "Go on home!"

She couldn't stand his everlasting "hits" and "alluses" another minute! "Leave me alone, Wells," she cried, "go on home, and don't come back for a long time. Just leave me alone."

He had wrapped his big, ugly Mackinaw around him and gone. And perversely she had wanted him back at once! He needn't have taken her so literally! What was the matter with her anyway? Why had she taken her restlessness out on him! He was good and kind and didn't deserve to be the victim of her nervous tongue. She was turning into a regular shrew! But he was gone, now. Maybe, she thought, he understands a woman pretty well. Matildy must have lashed out at him sometimes too. Maybe he knew that during times like this a woman couldn't abide a man's big and comfortable ways. Maybe he guessed they only frashed her more. There, she slapped her hands together in exasperation! She was getting to where she talked like the ridge too!

Somehow the time passed and March went by. When Miss Willie turned the big calendar on Becky's kitchen wall to April, she felt her heart lift. It was cold yet, and the buds on the trees were hard, frozen little knots. But the promise of spring was at hand. Just another week or two and the hard, frozen little knots would unfold and leaf out greenly. Just a little while and the whole ridge would be soft and lazy with the sun. Flowers would bloom. Birds would sing. And up and down the ridge people would come out into the open again. Men would work the fields and women would sit in their yards, and there would be laughter and lightness once more. Miss Willie felt a singing in her veins and she wanted to shout for gladness. The winter was almost over.

Becky stood in the kitchen door and sniffed the air. "Hit ain't fur off," she said, turning, and she smiled with her old, friendly smile at Miss Willie. "Spring's nigh. I kin smell it on south wind. We'll be havin' poke sallet agin you turn that calendar leaf oncet more."

Like a forgiven child, Miss Willie felt a high moment of exaltation. She seized Becky's hands and danced her around the room. "Spring is here! Spring is here!" she chanted, and Becky lifted her skirts and cut a fancy step or two.

Gault's footsteps on the porch sent her flying to the stove. "Don't you be tellin'," she warned Miss Willie.

"I'll not," promised Miss Willie, but the song danced on through her body and made her feet light the rest of the day. Spring was here and Becky was her friend again.

Three weeks later the ridge was a bright, clean world, fresh and shining and newborn green. The maples were almost fully leafed out, and the hickory and beech were slowly unfolding their own tender leaves. Redbud was blushing on the hillsides and dogwood was opening shy, white buds. Pastures were greening and tobacco plants were pushing at the white canvas covers over their beds. Plows were being tried in garden patches, and women washed and starched their bonnets against the heat of the coming sun.

Miss Willie threw a light jacket around her shoulders after dinner one day. "I'm going to see if I can find some violets in that woodsy place down the road," she told Becky.

Becky laid a clean cloth over the food on the table. "Hit was allus a good place," she said, "likely you'll find you a nice bunch."

Miss Willie followed the road down past the old, abandoned church. She held her head high and breathed in deeply the spiced, tangy air. The sun fell warm and bright on her head and shoulders, and the earth was springy beneath her feet. The sun, she exulted. The sun! No wonder ancient men worshiped the sun. It's the center and the hope and the promise of life! Just let the sun shine, Lord, she pleaded, and I can do all things!

Miss Willie stretched widely and laughed. She felt strong and invincible. This was going to be a good school year, she promised herself. She would set herself to all the old problems, and she would somehow, someway, make things move! She would even resolve that old hurt of Rufe!

She gathered her violets in the quiet, wooded place. A double handful, enough for Becky too. And then she crawled through the fence and wandered idly up the road, just looking and soaking up the sun and being glad spring was here. A wagon jounced slowly around the bend back of her and she stepped aside to let it pass. It drew up beside her.

"Where you goin', Miss Willie?" It was Wells, with Rufe on the narrow seat beside him.

She held up the violets. "Been flower-pickin'. Where you goin'?"

"Got to go down to the holler an' git a load o' cook wood. Winter's run us kinder short. Come go along."

"I won't be in the way?" she asked eagerly. The afternoon stretched long ahead, and it would be fun to rumble along with Wells in his old wagon.

"Why, shore not!" he said, and reached down his hand to give her a lift over the wagon wheel. "Rufe, you git in the back." But as Miss Willie clambered up, Rufe disappeared over the tailboard.

Out of the corner of his eye Wells saw him and turned to call: "Rufe! Rufe, you git back here. Rufe, you hear me?"

But Rufe was already in the edge of the woods. Miss Willie sank to the wagon seat and looked at Wells. "He's run away because of me, hasn't he?"

Wells was watching the woods. He set his jaw. "I'm shore goin' to have to lay onto that boy. They ain't no call fer him to act like that. I cain't make him out. Seems like they's jist a streak o' meanness comes out in him e'er time he gits clost to you. Don't mind, Miss Willie. Don't pay him no mind."

Miss Willie laid her violets sadly on the floor of the wagon. "I do mind," she said. "I do mind a lot. But there doesn't seem to be anything I can do about it. Unless I give up and leave the ridge." She laughed, and the laugh broke midway.

"Now, Miss Willie," Wells said quickly, "don't you go talkin' like that. Hit'll all work out some day. Jist don't go givin' up

223

thataway."

Miss Willie shook her head ruefully, and then determinedly she straightened her shoulders. No use letting the boy spoil the afternoon. "Let me drive, Wells," she said. "Let me see if I can."

Wells handed over the lines. "Shore you kin! Jist keep a easy hand on the lines. Don't tighten up. Steady, but easy, an' the team'll never know the difference."

Miss Willie settled her glasses firmly and stiffened her elbows to her sides. Steady but easy! And the team nodded their heads on down the road, the wagon swaying and bumping along behind them.

Down in the hollow Wells took the reins again and pulled the mules off the road onto a dim track in the woods. "Got some hickory already cut over here a piece," he explained.

When they came to the pile of wood, Miss Willie crawled down and helped load it into the wagon. It felt good to be reaching and bending and lifting and swinging. She missed the wagon occasionally, but Wells laughed and didn't seem to mind. They worked easily and slowly together in a companionable silence. Wells *was* a good companion. He didn't talk too much, and you didn't need to make conversation with him. The silences that fell between them weren't awkward. They were natural and easy, and if they stretched out for an hour at a time, they still filled the space between them. It ought to be that way with a man and a woman, Miss Willie thought, heaving a heavy stick. The silences should be as full as the talk.

Wells straightened up suddenly and stood listening. Miss Willie held the stick in her hand to listen too. They heard the murmur of voices coming down the track. And in a moment Matt Jasper slid between the trees, followed closely by a big, heavy-set man whom Miss Willie didn't know. Miss Willie looked at Wells, but he was watching the two men, a frown puzzling his forehead. They stood quietly, the trees hanging a heavy screen over them, and the men went on down the track, never glancing in their direction. When they had gone, Wells still looked after them.

"Who was that with Matt?" Miss Willie wanted to know.

Wells shook his head. "Don't know. Never seen him before. Looked like a city feller to me." He shrugged his shoulders and went back to his loading.

When they had finished, he eased down on the ground against a tree. "Let's rest a mite 'fore we start back," he said, and he rolled a cigarette and cupped a match to it.

Miss Willie perched on a down log nearby. Wells puffed a few smoke rings. "Miss Willie, I'm might' nigh shore Tay's astillin' agin."

"Oh, no, Wells!"

He nodded his head. "Ever' sign's apointin' that way. He's takened to goin' off ever' few days, an' he's slacked up on work around the place. Oh, he done right well fer a spell. I had hopes he wouldn't turn to it no more. But the winter got him twitchy, an' he commenced aramblin' off 'fore the thaw set in. He makes out like he's workin' over at the sawmill. But I've my doubts about that. Worst is, Rose is expectin'."

Miss Willie studied her feet, and noticed absently that she had scuffed the toe of one of her shoes. Funny, she thought, how you'll notice a thing like that at a time when you're hunting for something to say. What *was* there to say? Wells had known, if Rose hadn't, that you couldn't change a boy like Tay Clark. You couldn't take a boy who had never learned to yield to any control but his own wild will and expect marriage to control him. There wasn't even any justice in expecting it.

A pity for Rose stole over Miss Willie. A girl was always so certain her love would be enough. So certain that no matter what a man was before, marriage would give him the last ultimate contentment. Would fill him and satisfy him forever. For her, it sufficed. She built her life around her heart and could not believe so wondrous a thing as their deep and secret knowledge would not also fill him to overflowing. And her love was a trap, stretching her body to bring forth new life as often as the man, roaming free, returned to her side. Poor Rose.

Miss Willie lifted her head. "I'm sorry, Wells." There was nothing else to say.

Wells threw his cigarette away and pulled himself up. "Time we was goin', I reckon," he said, and he helped Miss Willie over the wheel. He pulled the team back into the track and Miss Willie felt his shoulder slump heavily against hers. He shouldn't have to be so fretted over his children, she thought. He needs Matildy. He needs you! But she slid her mind away from that thought, and pushed it from her. The mules settled into the climb up the ridge and Wells slapped the reins against them. "Come up, Beck," he called. "Come up, Sal."

The wagon swayed and Miss Willie slipped her arm through his. "Don't worry too much, Wells," she said. "After all, they're married, and it's their life to live. You can't face life for your children. There always comes a time when they must do it for themselves."

Wells smiled at her. "Thanks fer he'pin' me load the wood, Miss Willie."

"Thanks for letting me," she answered. She picked up her violets from the floor of the wagon. They had drooped a little. But, she thought, they'd freshen up when she put them in water.

CHAPTER
❦ 22 ❦

MAY BROUGHT WARMER DAYS and tobacco-setting time. Miss Willie was learning that the seasons on Piney Ridge were counted around tobacco. Along about March she and Becky had gone with Gault over into the far woods and had there watched him stake off his plant bed. "Why don't you put your tobacco bed closer to the house, Gault?" she had asked.

"You want to grow yer seedlin's in new ground," he had answered. He lined off a long, narrow, oblong piece of ground, framed it with sapling logs, and then piled brush on it and slowly burned the brush to ashes. These he mulched with the soil; then he sowed the seed. Becky sowed her tomato, pepper, and cabbage seed around the edges. Last of all he stretched the fine, sheer tobacco canvas across the frame and tacked it securely.

"Now what?" Miss Willie wanted to know.

"Now hit grows. Come May, we pull them seedlin's an' set 'em out."

Now it was May, and the fields had been plowed, harrowed, and fertilized. Miss Willie put on her wide straw hat and went out to help. Gault had gathered a tubful of the young, pale-green plants, and he told Miss Willie to fill her basket and walk ahead down the rows, dropping a plant every eighteen inches. Gault came along behind her with a sharpened stick and bored the holes, pouring a small amount of water in each one. Becky came last, crawling on her hands and knees, sticking the plants in the holes, and firming the ground around them.

Miss Willie and Becky changed jobs occasionally, and after one row of setting the plants, Miss Willie's knees were raw, her fingers sore, and her back kinked into a tight knot. "There must be an easier way of setting tobacco," she said.

"They is," Becky answered. "Down in the bottoms on them big farms they got a contraption drops the plants, waters 'em, an' firms the dirt around 'em. But hit costs a sight o' money. Ain't nobody on the ridge kin spend fer sich as that."

Miss Willie laid the flat of her hand against her aching back and crawled on to the next plant. She was remembering that someone had written a book about tobacco-growing, and had called it green hell! He was right! The whole long process was tedious, torturous work. After this stuff was planted, it would have to be plowed and hoed. Then when it had grown enough, it would have to be topped, and, after that, suckered. Finally it must be cut and speared onto sticks and hung in the tobacco barn to dry. When it had cured sufficiently, the dried leaves would have to be stripped from the stalks and bound into hands, and finally, along about the middle of December, it must be hauled to market and sold. It took a whole year to make a tobacco crop. But since the Government had taken over control of growth, it brought a fair price.

"I kin remember," Becky said, "when yer terbaccer never brought enough on the market to pay yer haul bill. Ten cents a pound fer prime burley! Now, hit allus brings a right good price. Forty or fifty cents a pound."

"How much will you make off this acre?" Miss Willie asked.

"Last year Gault takened in might' nigh a thousand dollars offen it. But that's the best hit's ever done. Hit was mighty good terbaccer, an' you cain't expect to hit ever' year like that. But we'd ort anyways to git seven, eight hundred dollars."

227

And that was the cash for the year. A thousand dollars. But Miss Willie wondered if Gault and Becky used even half of that!

She fell into bed that night certain her back was broken. But she was out the next day, stiff and sore, determined to finish the job! It took them a week, for the ground was hard and dry. "If it would jist come a season," Becky moaned.

"What's a season?" Miss Willie asked.

"A good, hard rain. Hit'd soften up the ground an' we wouldn't have to water the plants none. We could jist fly."

But the rain held off. Wells came by one day and helped, but he had two acres of his own to set and couldn't spare them much time. "I'd like to borry yer help," he joked with Gault.

Gault eyed Miss Willie dubiously. "Don't know as she'd last out," he said finally.

Miss Willie crippled over to a stump and rested against it. "Wells, does being a farmer's wife mean she has to do things like this all the time?"

"Miss Willie," Wells said, "e'er time you want to take me up on that there proposition I made you, you kin rest easy hit won't include no field work!"

Miss Willie inclined in a mock curtsy. "That takes a load off my mind, I assure you."

"Offen yer back, you mean, don't you?" And Wells raised his brows and squinted at her provokingly.

Miss Willie went back to her tobacco-setting. "Don't think I won't remind you of that, if I ever need to!"

"Ifen you ever need to, you'll not have to remind me," his answer shot back.

"What in tarnation them two atalkin' about?" Gault fretted to Becky, offering his cut plug.

Becky cut herself a chew and put it in her mouth. When she spat, she said, "They're courtin'."

Gault humphed and gouged his tobacco stick a little deeper. "Quare courtin'," he said.

Almost before she knew it another school term was starting. This year Miss Willie was on familiar ground. The faces before her were known to her now, and the habits of each child were an old story. She looked around her the first day, missing the old eighth grade. Pearly and Bill and Rose. Ah, Rose. Last year a schoolgirl. This year a bride and an expectant mother. Time didn't stand still for young folks. But then time hadn't stood still for her, either. She had come a long way since this time last year.

Rufe moved up to the seventh grade now, his beautiful golden head a little browner than last year, a little less boyish. Sylvie Clark, tanned by the summer, but still elfin and nymphlike with her silvery curls, moved up with him. There was no need this year to separate the classes. There was no discussion of seats. There was just the familiar routine, known to them all.

There were five new faces in the first reader and Miss Willie looked at them lovingly. I shall always love the little ones best, she thought. Standing before them, with their expectant look fixed upon her, she wondered why. Because they are so young, so fresh, so trusting and lovable. Children grow out of that lovableness very soon, she thought. Or is it, her mind pursued the thought, because they are so malleable! You've been a teacher long enough to like the malleable ones!

Aware suddenly that the group was watching her patiently and waiting for her to speak, she shrugged the thought away. "The short seats down front are for the little ones," she said, "let them come forward, please." And the pattern was smooth and the year was begun.

Swiftly it moved through July and August and into the first cool fall days of September. Miss Willie walked to school with a joyous energy running through her. The sumac had turned scarlet, and the first maple leaves were yellowing in the brittle sunlight. Goldenrod was tawny in the fence rows, and ironweed had a shaggy, purple crown. Corn was in the shock and great, golden pumpkins were piled around its edges. Late apples glinted red on limbs fast becoming bare, and the katydids sawed at their incessant question slower and slower. It was a time of sharp, cold mornings, warm, winy noons, and hazy, purple evenings, There was a feeling of gathering in, of making ready, of harvesting, and of snugging down before the cold.

And it was in this beautiful golden time that the thing Miss

229

Willie had feared from the first came about.

It was Wells's own Abby who came down first with typhoid fever. She was not at school one day. Other children might stay at home on the slightest pretext, but Wells's children were always there. Rain or shine, cold or hot, unless they were really ill, Wells saw that they came to school.

"Is Abby ill, Rufe?" Miss Willie asked.

"Yessum."

So when school was out that afternoon, Miss Willie went by to see her. She found Abby listless and feverish, although she was dressed and languidly up and about.

"Have you had the doctor?" Miss Willie asked Rose.

Rose shook her head. "Not yit. Pa said if she wasn't no better tomorrer, he'd take her in to see him."

"Where is your father?"

"Out shockin' corn."

"I'm going out there to see him, then."

Rufe was helping Wells. When they saw Miss Willie coming across the field, they stopped and Wells flung an arm up in greeting. "Hi, Miss Willie!"

"Wells," she said without preliminary, "I don't think you'd better wait until tomorrow to have the doctor with Abby. Children take too many things with a slight fever and that listless, languid look. She may be coming down with something serious. If I were you, I'd have the doctor this evening."

Wells looked surprised. "Why, I never thought but she was jist a little puny. Mebbe she eat somethin' didn't agree with her. She ain't complained to amount to nothin'."

"Maybe not, but that doesn't mean she might not be seriously ill. I'd feel a whole lot better about her if you'd have the doctor immediately."

Not even to Wells was she going to say what she feared. What she had feared ever since she saw that open spring at the schoolhouse, and even now she prayed that Wells might be right. That Abby was just upset from something she'd eaten, or maybe she was coming down with a cold. But she felt a scared, cold queasiness in the pit of her stomach, and she had to know one way or the other as soon as possible.

230

Rufe skipped a stone across the field and watched the two sullenly. Wells scrubbed his hands down the side of his overalls. "Well, reckon if you feel thataway about it, I'll git ready an' go fer the doctor. I aimed to take her tomorrer ifen she wasn't no better."

Miss Willie picked up a dried corn leaf and rustled it between her fingers. "She should be in bed, Wells. I know it's hard on Rose to take care of her just now, but until we know what's wrong it would be safer to keep her quiet."

Rufe sniffed. "Aw, she's just eat too many apples. Ain't nothin' wrong with her."

Miss Willie gave him a bleak look. "That's for the doctor to say, Rufe."

"Yeah," Wells agreed. "Hit's best we find out."

And he and Miss Willie started back across the field. Rufe picked up an ear of corn and slammed it against the ground. There she was agin! Buttin' in! Tellin' folks what to do! Wrappin' Pa around her little finger! Reckon Pa'd ort to know what was best fer his own kid! But e'er time that old maid come around poppin' off, looked like Pa was jist ready to do whatever she said. He kicked at the pile of corn lying ready to shock. Hit'd be the gladdest day of his life ifen she'd jist up an' leave this here ridge! Wasn't nobody had e'er peace o' mind sincet she'd come!

When the doctor had finished examining Abby that night, he told them: "It may be malaria, but I strongly suspect typhoid. Can't tell until I hear from the laboratory on these blood tests. Where do you get your water?"

"Deep bored well," Wells answered.

"Let me see it."

And Wells took the doctor out to the well. When they came back he shook his head. "Should be all right. No drainage or seepage from the outhouses and barns."

Miss Willie took her courage in her hand. "Doctor, I think possibly it's the spring at the school. It's an open spring, and I've been afraid of something like this ever since I came here to teach."

The doctor pounced on her words. "Open spring! My Lord, I thought they'd all been condemned! How many children in that school?"

Miss Willie quivered. "Forty," she managed to say.

The doctor stared at her. "Haven't you got any better sense than to expose forty children to that sort of thing? What are you a teacher for?"

Wells stood up suddenly. "Now, here," he said, "don't go blamin' her! She's been tryin' ever sincet she come to git the trustees to do somethin' about that there spring! She's preached about it night an' day. Hit ain't her fault!"

The doctor turned on his heel. "All she had to do was report it to the county health board," and his voice was dry. "Open spring! I didn't know there was one left in the county!"

"Then you don't know much about this county!" Miss Willie snapped, smarting from his barbed tongue.

The doctor merely looked at her. "You'll have to close the school. I'll report the spring and tests of the water will be made. In the meantime, be sure to report any other cases of illness. Every child in that school will be suspect for several weeks. I'll let you know about these blood tests. Keep her in bed," he cautioned Rose, "and I'll probably be back day after tomorrow."

Miss Willie's heart had stopped when he said she should have reported the spring to the county authorities. The one simple, sure procedure she should have taken had never occurred to her! Bitterly she watched the doctor put his thermometer back in its case, stick it in his vest pocket, and then bend to close his bag. Of course she should have reported it to the county! Not only was it the simplest way of getting the spring either condemned or improved, but it was the authoritative, the organized way of doing it! Why hadn't she thought of it? *Why!*

She'd been too busy trying to do something about it herself, that's why! Miss Willie Payne, who saw what needed to be done, and did something about it! She reviled herself, and felt sick at the thought of all the children who might now have to pay for her thoughtlessness. She turned abruptly toward the window to hide the tears that burned her eyes. She felt old and worn and bruised. Again she had floundered and done the wrong thing. Was there

232

no end to the things she had done wrong here on the ridge? Was there no way of learning? She was a teacher, but she couldn't teach herself!

When the doctor had left, Wells looked helplessly across the room at Miss Willie. "I reckon you was right," he ventured finally.

Miss Willie looked at him. Like all men in the presence of illness, he looked big and awkward and helpless. His face had that worn, blank look of confusion and frustrated strength. She went toward him, touched and moved by his awkwardness. She laid her hand on his shoulder. "We'll just have to do the best we can, now, Wells. I'll dismiss school tomorrow, and then I'll come help Rose."

He reached up and enclosed her small hand in his own two big paws and he laid his forehead against it. "Yer good," he said, "yer good not to condemn me. Hit was as much my fault as e'er other one. I'd ort to of made 'em listen to you. Hit's like the hand o' the Lord strikin' back at me, Abby bein' the one to take down thisaway."

"Don't, Wells," Miss Willie said, rubbing the black, wiry hair with her free hand. "The Lord doesn't strike back at people. It's more my fault than anyone's, if we are to start condemning. But that does no good now. We'll just do the best we can. They have new ways of treating typhoid these days. It's not as serious as it used to be. Let's not get discouraged about Abby yet."

Wells freed Miss Willie and stood up. "I jist pray they ain't no more takes it. I'll feel the burden of 'em all till we know."

And so will I, Miss Willie thought. And so will I.

It was typhoid, and within the week three other children came down with it. One of the Jones triplets, Ewell; a Simpson child; and Sylvie Clark. Sylvie, the elfin, the moonlight nymph! Something clutched at Miss Willie when she thought of that pure, crystalline beauty lying fouled in the squalor of the Clark home. To her Sylvie had been like a lily, stemming slenderly and splendidly up out of the mud of her roots. But now she was brought down among them.

With school closed, Miss Willie shuttled back and forth to the

233

homes of the sick ones. She threw herself into a frenzied doing of the actual chores of the home . . . cooking, washing dishes, mopping floors. And when there was nothing else for her to do, she sat quietly by a sick child, reading to him or talking to him, feeding him and tending him. She found a sort of surcease of guilt in driving herself thus. She left her own cabin early in the morning, and she rarely returned to it before dark.

Becky and Mary both remonstrated. "You'll make yourself sick, Miss Willie," they scolded.

"No, I'll not," she answered. "I'll not be sick. But I *have* to do what I can. Surely you can see that!"

And they let her alone then.

The Jones boy and the Simpson child were never very ill, and shortly they were well on the way to recovery. Abby too responded surprisingly well to treatment. She had looked frail and thin, but there was a core of strength in her slight body which reacted well. But Sylvie was dangerously ill from the start. She didn't react to any of the injections or to any other treatment given her, and she lay day after day, her small, slender body burning itself up. The doctor looked grave when he spoke to Miss Willie about her. "There are too many things wrong," he said. "She's undernourished, and her heart's bad."

As soon as the others were out of danger, Miss Willie devoted herself to Sylvie. As long as she lived, she would never forget her first visit there. When she stepped inside, the foul, fetid air struck against her like something solid, closing her in and smothering her. Even this early in the fall, the heating stove was up and a hot fire was going. Every window was shut tight, and the doors were closed.

There were three beds in the room, huddled into corners. They were ancient, decrepit iron bedsteads, leaning crazily in all directions, and Miss Willie wondered what held them up. The mattresses were very thin and lumpy. She saw that there were no sheets and that the ragged, torn quilts were crusted with dirt and grime. Sylvie lay upon the bed nearest the door, her hair uncombed and matted about her face, her eyes listless and heavy, and her cheeks flushed with fever. Her single garment was a princess slip, made of flour sacking, grav with unwashed age, and

234

crumpled from the child's tossing.

The floors were littered with dirty clothes, scraps of food, parts of the cream separator, bucket lids, and other odds and ends the smallest children had been playing with. It was hardly possible to take one step without wading through things, or without kicking them out of the way.

Miss Willie picked her way through the litter toward Sylvie's bed, and out of the corner of her eye she caught a movement along the wall. She stopped. A line of bugs was streaming up and down the window facing. An infinite variety of bugs, some of them large, some of them small. Roaches, silver fish, ants, and the flat bodied chinch bugs. In fascinated horror she watched them, and then she saw another stream of them over by the door. And another by the kitchen door. They were everywhere, infesting the whole place, a steady river of bugs going and coming up the walls. Her stomach squeezed, but she made herself lift a garment off the only chair in the room to sit down. From under it dozens of bugs scuttled off in every direction. What shall I do, she thought frantically. What can I possibly do?

She shivered as though the bugs were already crawling on her own flesh, and then, to her utter horror, she watched Sylvie, on the sour and soiled bed, brush languidly at two that were inching up her arm! Miss Willie froze stiff, and the skin on her own arms prickled into quivering bumps. At the same time, however, something in her snapped into action. There was just one thing to do. She must get Sylvie clean and comfortable if she had to kill every bug in the house with her own hands. She turned to Mamie with quick determination. "I'm going home," she said, "but I'll be back in a few minutes."

She made two trips, carrying clean sheets, two of her own blankets, nightgowns, soap and cleanser, and half a gallon of fly spray. She told Mamie to put buckets of water on to heat. She wrapped a towel around her head, tied one of Becky's clean aprons around her waist and set to work with murderous intent. She moved Sylvie into the next room, and then she swept and mopped and scrubbed. She took down the beds and scoured them, and she made Mamie put them up in the other rooms. "No one should sleep in this room with Sylvie," she said.

235

"But, Miss Willie, hit's the only room with a stove. We'll freeze come a cold night, off in that plunder room!" Mamie said.

"You'll just have to pile covers on, then," Miss Willie said, shortly. "Sylvie has to have peace and quiet, and keep the other children out of here!"

Mamie was frightened enough to obey, and she even fell to work helping Miss Willie. They put Sylvie's bed back up and Miss Willie spread it with clean, fresh-smelling sheets and the soft woolen blankets from her own blanket chest. They had a sweet, piney odor. Then she brought Sylvie in, bathed her, and slipped a white, lavender-scented nightgown over her head.

Sylvie slid her hands down over the smooth material in a caressing movement, and then she fingered the narrow blue satin ribbon at the neck. "Hit's so purty," she said softly, "hit's so purty, and soft." Then she laid her fair hair back on the pillow and rubbed her cheek against the pillow slip. "Ever'thing smells so good," and she sighed and drifted off to sleep.

Miss Willie fought a daily battle thus for Sylvie's comfort and care. The bugs crept in from the other rooms and she harried Mamie into giving them a semblance of cleaning. Mamie grumbled, but she did what she was told as best she could. Her idea of cleaning never reached Miss Willie's conception of it, but she got rid of most of the litter and surface dirt, and Miss Willie herself kept the whole house sprayed.

She also made Mamie keep out half a gallon of whole milk each day for Sylvie, and keep the freshest eggs for her. "We cain't git along without the cream checks," Mamie said, "an' the egg money. Hit's what I use to buy meat an' beans with."

"Drink the milk and eat the eggs yourself," Miss Willie snapped, "and quit buying that greasy fat meat and so many beans. You'll be a lot healthier!"

"Don't none of us like milk an' eggs," Mamie sulked.

Miss Willie faced her. "You can do as you like about the rest of the family," she said, "but Sylvie has got to have good, whole milk, and plenty of it, and lots of eggs. Do you want to kill the child?"

"No, ma'am."

"Then do as I say!"

So Mamie strained out half a gallon of fresh milk each day for Sylvie, kept half a dozen eggs for her, and Miss Willie made her good, rich eggnogs, custards, and milk toast. She had Becky make soups and broths, and every hour or so during the day she poured nourishing food down Sylvie. Valiantly she fought against all the odds, a shrew and a termagant when the way was balked, pitting her own energy and strength against the slothfulness and slovenliness of Mamie, against the fever, against the malnutrition which had sapped Sylvie's body of recuperative power, against even the murmuring and protesting heart in the child's shallow chest. She fought grimly and she would not give up.

And she won. The day came when the doctor stood by Sylvie's bed and smiled across it at Miss Willie. "She's going to make it," he said, "she's all right, now. But she owes her life to you."

Miss Willie's knees gave way under her and she pulled a chair up under them. She'd won. She felt her hands quivering strangely, and she wanted to lay her head down on the bed and cry and cry. She was so tired! But she'd won! Ah, no. Sylvie didn't owe her anything. She had owed Sylvie her life. Sylvie and those other children. Thank God the debt hadn't been any greater than four out of the forty! And thank God the toll exacted hadn't been extreme for any one of them! They were all recovering. None of them had died. She had been let off lightly, after all.

CHAPTER

❧ 23 ❧

A SUDDEN COLD SPELL CAME on a late October morning. A Saturday it was. There was a whippy wind scudding across the face of the earth, sending leaves skittering through the air, piling them in heaps in the furrows and ruts, and mounding them against the sides of low banks. It tore at them and heckled them and battered them into the ground. It was a wild kind of day, with clouds swelling at each other and racing wildly around the sky. It was a lowering day, full of frowns and growls.

At the still, Tay worked swiftly bottling his likker that morning, hurrying so that he might finish and make his deliveries early. He cursed the wind as he worked, tugging his old hat tighter on his head, eying the storm clouds to decide whether or not he must take his work inside the shack. But he kept on at the bench outside.

Matt Jasper corked the bottles and set them in rows against the wall of the shack. Occasionally he clinked a bottle against another, and the full gurgling tinkle made Tay raise his head. "Don't break e'er one of them," he warned. "I've got ever' drop of this sold, an' I ain't aimin' to lose a penny on this run."

"I'm bein' keerful as I kin," Matt said. There was a changeless futility about him which made it impossible for him to work effectively. He moved frantically, his hands flying like those of a scarecrow flapping in a cornfield, but he seldom found the right-sized cork for a bottle the first time. He made a dozen impotent motions to complete one operation, so that Tay constantly grumbled at him under his breath. "Dodderin' fool," he growled at him, "they ain't nothin' you kin do right!"

Matt's mouth worked tremblingly. "I'm atryin' to keep up, Tay."

"Git me some more bottles there in the shack," Tay ordered.

Matt shambled through the opening in the front of the shack, and Tay straightened his tired back as he waited. The fumes of the likker hung heavy over the bench, and his eyes stung. He closed them and rubbed them with the back of one hand. In that single moment Tay's fate closed in on him, for when he opened his eyes, it was to see a man with a gun advancing over the clearing. He whirled to leap quickly for the shack, but the man's voice stopped him: "You're covered, Clark. Stop where you are."

From the corner of his eye Tay saw that another man was advancing from the left. He turned his head slightly and saw another one coming from the right, and as he looked, two more broke cover in front of him. He eased his feet on the ground and hitched his pants higher on his hips.

His mind gnawed on the hinges of this trap like a frantic animal gnawing his own foot off to find release. It surged and clawed and ran desperately down corridors of escape. His own gun was under his shirt. But they'd take it, likely. He saw no way out. Five men coming at him with guns made a barrier he could not climb.

238

In that moment of surrender his thoughts went to Rose, and his heart wept and its tears were bitter salt. Rose, Rose! Her name was like a dirge in his ears, and the remembered warmth of her mouth died cold on his own tightened lips. But he slitted his eyes and shuttered his face, blanking it of all expression, and when he turned to face the first man, his features might have been chiseled from stone. "Hit takened aplenty of you," he commented grimly.

"Never mind how many of us it takes," the man said. "The point is we've got you." He called to another man. "There's another one in the shack. Get him."

A man stepped from the circle and pulled aside the burlap curtain. He dropped the curtain behind him, but emerged shortly. "Ain't nobody in there," he said.

"I saw him go in there myself not two minutes ago. He must be in there."

"Well, see for yourself. There ain't nobody in there now."

Tay laughed a short snort through his nose. "He's got away. You wouldn't be thinkin' they was jist one way in an' outen that shack, would you?"

The man motioned for two more men to enter the shack. "Search it," he said. "Get whatever you need to take with you, Clark. We'll be going to town."

Tay reached for his coat hanging on the lower limb of a tree and shrugged into it. "How'd you find this place?" he asked.

"Oh, it wasn't hard," answered the man, motioning Tay toward the creek. "There's always folks that'll talk."

Tay looked at him straight and hard. "They ain't nobody on this here ridge that'd knowingly talk to the law. Ifen e'er body on this ridge told, hit wasn't intentional. You got it outen somebody unknowin'."

"Somebody like your partner there?"

Tay's lips firmed. He might have known! Stupid, dull-witted old Matt! He'd been a fool to let him hang around here! That's what he got for feeling sorry for him and letting him make a little extra money! He'd been a fool!

"Move on, Clark," the man said. The two men came out of the shack. They joined the procession heading toward the creek.

"There's a hole in the back wall of the shack," they reported,

239

"Got an old chest rolled in front of it to hide it. It comes out behind that big rock there on the side of the hill. The other one probably ducked the minute he heard us."

"We'll get him," said the leader. "We know who he is. We can pick him up any time."

"He ain't got nothin' to do with this," Tay said. "He jist works fer me oncet in a while. Jist he'ps out some. He don't know nothin' about this business. An' besides he's natural an' simple. He wouldn't even know what you was gittin' him fer."

"We'll take care of that," the man answered. "There's a car down the hollow. Keep moving. Casey, you and Martin break up that still! Don't leave a whole piece. Bust the bottles and see that there's no likker left either. Bring one bottle along for evidence. And don't go samplin' it!"

Tay laughed. "Hit's right good stuff, boys. Good corn meal an' pure spring water. You couldn't ask fer no better moonshine! Hit's might' nigh as good as bourbon!"

He felt a sudden exaltation. They weren't going to search him. A great contempt for them flowed over him. Muddlers! Fools! Didn't they know about a shoulder holster? But he had his gun. He'd have a chance now.

They splashed through the creek and headed down the hollow. Tay looked back once as he heard the ring of an ax on the metal drum. The man had started wrecking the still. "That was a plumb good still," he murmured. "Hit's a shame to bust it up."

When Matt Jasper had heard the voices outside the shack, he had known instantly what was happening. Tay had told him that no one else knew the exact location of the still. There was always the possibility that someone out hunting, sang digging, or herb-gathering would stumble over it. But that was not too serious. They would be ridge people, with the ridge loyalty to their own. Nearly everyone knew that he had located a still on Wandering Creek, and most could guess that it would be somewhere back in the convolutions of Coon Ridge. "Hit's jist better," Tay had said, "fer as few to know as kin. Ifen they don't know, they ain't likely to give it away."

Tay had further warned him that raids came quietly and swiftly. There would be no warning of the presence of officers. They would be lucky if there was the rattle of a loose stone, or the spatter of creek water as a foot slipped, to give them time to move. And then Tay had showed him the hole in the wall of the shack and had added: "Ifen the law ever comes, an' yer caught in here, likely you kin git away. Make a try fer it, leastways. An' you kin be shore I'll do the same. In this business hit's ever' man fer hisself. Ifen we're ever caught, strike out on yer own. Don't think none of what'll happen to me. Fer one thing's shore, I'll not be thinkin' none of you, neither. Git out with a whole hide, if you kin."

So when Matt heard the strange voices outside, he dropped quickly to his knees before the old chest, and pulled it gently away from the hole. There was no indecision in his movement. Tay had told him to get away if he could. He eased his thin body through the hole, coming out behind the big rock pressed against the hill. From here he could peer around and see that all the men were preoccupied with Tay. He noted their guns and their encircling movement. Only a second did he pause, and then he began to climb up the steep wall, screened first by the rock, and then by the thick growth of bushes. He crawled along flat against the ground, inching his way gently, hoisting himself gradually by pulling from one bush to another. Silently and smoothly he ascended the hill, and, for all his crawling along, he moved rapidly up the steep slope.

He did not stop until he reached the rounded cap of the hill, far above the clearing and the still. Here on this gentler level, out of sight and hearing of the men below, he allowed himself to stop and ease his breath. This far Matt Jasper's mind had functioned normally, reacting to fear in the same way as any other man's would have done, needled and frightened, and pushed by the necessity of reaching safety, but at the same time keeping its balance and sanity, not yielding to panic.

When he stopped to breathe on the easy slant of the hilltop, however, this changed. The sound of a single shot reached him, immediately followed by a fusillade of shots and a chorus of yells. It was then that panic overtook him, and his timid mind began to chase itself, circling madly round and round. That man . . . that man, down there. He'd had on a blue coat. That 'un that come around all time fer a while, he had on a blue coat too. The guards at Danville wore blue coats, he'd heared. Danville. The asylum. Blue coats. Guards. One thought caught the tail of the other and they surged and pressed in on him, until he lifted his hands and pounded them on his head to make them quit. Blue coat . . . blue coat . . . blue coat! Round and round they went. Men and blue coats and bars over windows and Danville, and more men and blue coats, and Danville again. And him inside the bars. They wasn't lookin' fer Tay. They was lookin' fer him!

His breath came harshly, tearing out of his chest, ripping at his throat, and he tore his shirt collar open and gasped the air in great, rasping sobs. The pupils of his eyes dilated and fixed themselves unseeingly on space. His nostrils flared and whitened, and the drooling spittle frothed at the corners of his mouth. His hands clenched and the fingers worked convulsively. The muscles of his face twitched in an uncontrollable dance of tiny movements.

At the height of the spasm, when rigidity usually came, his rabbity mind caught hold of another thought. "Somebody turned me in. Somebody told 'em I was crazy! Somebody . . . somebody . . ."

And then a cunning idea occurred to him. "I know who done it," he whispered slyly. "She's been lookin' funny at me fer a long time. She done it. She turned me in to the law. She told 'em I was crazy!"

His eyes drooped and softened and shuttered over the dilated pupils, and the drooling mouth relaxed and curved gently at the corners, sweetly, like a child's. Every tense muscle in the body of the man, which a moment before had been screaming in spasmodic seizure, eased into looseness. His shoulders sagged down and rounded and his arms hung limp by his sides. His head lolled to one side and a vacuous grin stretched his mouth. He studied a bird hopping on the ground in front of him, giggling nervously. He hiccuped, and swallowed noisily. The purposes of his mind were forming, now.

As they steadied, his fingers fumbled at the buttons of his shirt, and when the last final necessity of thought was reached,

242

he jerked upright and snapped his body tense again. "I'll fix her," he said. "I'll fix her good. I'll fix her so's she cain't never turn me in agin. That's what I'll do."

And he set off at a dog trot over the hill. Thus did Matt Jasper's tormented mind flee its last moorings and slip unrestrained into madness.

CHAPTER

❧ 24 ❧

LATE THAT SATURDAY MORNING Miss Willie and Becky walked to the mailboxes, and Becky took along a basket of quilt scraps for Lutie Jasper. "The pore thing is allus needin' new covers," she said.

The wind whipped at them and they felt a winter bite in its teeth as they bent into it. Miss Willie was glad she had worn her knitted cap and gloves. Her finger tips were cold as it was, and she dug them deep in her pockets. "Such a day!" she yelled at Becky, the words torn from her mouth and sent flying swiftly with the wind. "I never saw such a wind!"

Becky's scrawny shoulders were hunched against the cold. "Hit is a flyaway day, ain't it? Wouldn't wonder if it ain't acomin' on to snow."

When they came up to the Jasper house, a small smoke was tailing out the chimney of the lean-to. "Reckon Lutie's startin' dinner," Becky said.

They called from the front gate, and when there was no answer, they let themselves in and went up on the porch. "They couldn't possibly hear us in this wind," Miss Willie said.

The door was closed, but Becky pushed it open, calling at the same time: "Lutie? You home, Lutie?"

It was then that they saw Lutie lying in the middle of the floor in the dreadful pool of her own blood, her head bashed in and horribly mutilated, even her body cut and slashed almost beyond recognition. Life had long since drained out of such gaping wounds, and she lay hacked and distorted, like a butchered animal.

Miss Willie stood frozen and paralyzed just inside the door,

243

unable to move or to take her eyes from the body, and as horror seeped through her, her own blood slowly congealed in her veins. Her heart pumped painfully hard, and in the region of her stomach an iron fist closed tightly, sending a sudden, stabbing thrust of pain down her legs. She swayed and clutched at Becky, and whimpered like a child having a bad dream.

Becky stood, shaking, her free hand holding her quivering mouth. "Lord God above," she whispered. "A fiend from hell must of been here! Who could have done sich a thing!"

Her quilt scraps dropped to the floor at her feet, scattering an incongruously bright patchwork of color across the gray floor. One small square floated delicately into a scarlet pool, and Miss Willie felt a queer compulsion to pick it up. It will be wet, she thought. I must get it, *now*. It will be ruined. She knew her mind was working slowly, refusing to face this horror. It felt as thick and hardened as the fingers on her hands, as numb and jelled.

But it hit upon one thought. "Matt," she said, and to her surprise her voice moaned out of her throat like a sobbing wind. "It was Matt! I told Wells. Oh, I told him that man was dangerous! Why didn't he listen to me? Why didn't I make him listen!"

"Sh-h-h," Becky whispered, and Miss Willie's eyes followed Becky's look.

As if in answer to his name, Matt Jasper slid through the kitchen door. Like a spectral shadow, he inched through it, sidewise, and then he crabbed along the wall, making no noise as he slipped into the room. Even in that mad moment which Miss Willie was sure would be her last, she had time to wonder briefly where Matt Jasper had found the costume he had on, and why he had it on. For over his grimy, filthy overalls he had put on a gorgeously regal, purple-satin princess slip. It hung from his thin shoulders in loose folds, and its heavy lace gathered about his knees. It was spattered and bloodstained, but as he leaned loosely against the wall he touched it lovingly, smoothing its shiny richness over his hips with a caressing hand. He crooned over it and whimpered a small song in his throat, nodding his head on its limp neck, patting the purple folds and preening himself carefully. His eyes were shuttered and his mouth drooped childishly. The corners curved softly into a smile, and little crying, whimpering songs whispered across the room. In the other hand he still held the ax. It hung lazily, swinging gently as he swayed back and forth against the wall.

He began to hum, and then in a quavering voice he started singing. " 'And I, if I be lifted up . . .' " The voice was small and thready at first, but then it strengthened, and the pure sweetness of it rang out and filled the room. " 'If I be lifted up . . . will draw all men unto me!' "

Miss Willie leaned against the wall, and sobs shook her and the tears poured down her face. Dear Lord! Dear Lord! It's too late! It's too late for Matt Jasper to be lifted up! It's too late!

" 'And I, if I be lifted up . . .' " the song went on. Suddenly Becky moved toward the man. Miss Willie put out her hand, but Becky brushed it aside. "Matt," she said, her voice loud and strong. "Matt, you better give me that ax. You cain't sing so good holdin' onto it thataway. You better give it to me."

Matt drew back and clutched the ax. The song stopped and he eyed Becky slyly. His face widened into a grinning mask, and then a terrified look crept over it. "Hit was the wind an' storm," he whispered, his eyes going past Becky to the door, and filling with terror. "Hit was a powerful wind an' storm. Hit come. Hit come all at oncet, an' hit takened me up on high. I was lifted up! Hit takened me up, an' hit blowed an' blowed! The lightnin' an' the thunder squalled. The lightnin' an' thunder kept asquallin'. The lightnin' went streakedy, strikedy, an' the thunder went baw, baw, yanny, yanny. That's what it kept sayin'. An' I was lifted up! Clean up above the world. Up over the trees an' the fields an' the houses. Clean up above the world! Baw, baw, yanny, yanny. Baw, baw, yanny, yanny! The lightnin' went streakedy, strikedy, an' the thunder went baw, baw, yanny, yanny!

"An' I had my ax in my hand, an' hit was powerful heavy. But I didn't dast let go, fer had I done so, hit would of split the world in two! The wind an' the rain an' the storm kept awhirlin' an' aturnin', an' my arm got heavy an' tired. But I helt on. An' the lightnin' an' thunder kept asquallin'. Baw, baw, yanny, yanny. An' I had to let go! I had to! I couldn't noways hold onto the ax no longer. Hit was too heavy. An' it hit pore Lutie! See! See, where it hit pore Lutie an' busted her head wide open! The Lord

245

told me not to let go. But I couldn't noways hold onto it no longer. Hit was too heavy. Too heavy. An' hit went baw, baw, yanny, yanny, an' I couldn't noways he'p it." The eyes drooped and the head dropped and Matt Jasper sagged against the wall.

Becky reached him then. "Here, Matt. I'll hold the ax for you. I'll not drop it. I'll hold onto it, tight."

Before his eyes closed, Matt looked once more at her. "You shore you kin hold onto it? You shore? Hit wouldn't noways do to drop it no more. Hit would certain split the world in two this time."

Becky's hand closed around the ax handle and she slid it out of his unfolding hand. "I'll not drop it, Matt. I'll promise I'll hold onto it tight."

He sighed briefly and slid into a grotesque huddle on the floor. Becky turned. Her face was ashen, but her voice was steady. "Let's git them young'uns, now."

Miss Willie hunched over. "I can't, Becky. I think I'm going to be sick."

Becky took her by the shoulder and shook her hard. "No, you ain't! You ain't goin' to be sick! They ain't time fer you to be sick! I don't know whether he's asleep or dead, but we got to git them kids an' git out. You kin be sick when we git away from here!"

Miss Willie's teeth chattered, but she clenched them and took a deep breath. "All right," and she found that she could make her legs support her, and that she could swallow her nausea.

The children were huddled on a bed in the next room, the covers drawn around them. They were frightened, but, except for a sobbing whimpering from one of the smallest ones, they were quiet. The oldest girl held the baby hugged against her, and when Becky took it, Miss Willie saw that it was asleep. There was a strange unreality in the fact that even a baby could have slept through all that had happened here! And Miss Willie fought off a hysterical desire to laugh. Sleep! She would never sleep again!

Becky hurried the children into wraps and hustled them out the other door. She didn't want them to see Lutie in the next room. Miss Willie followed with the baby.

"Hit don't seem right," Becky said, when they were down the

246

road, "hit don't seem right to leave her thataway. But I've heared you shouldn't ort to tetch a body that's been kilt. Hit's the law, I reckon. But it don't noways seem decent."

Miss Willie shuddered. "No. You mustn't touch anything."

Becky took the baby, and it stirred in its wrappings and mewled plaintively. She patted it tenderly and bent over it. "Pore little thing," she murmured, "pore little motherless thing." She wrapped its shawl tighter against the wind, and as the two women and three children moved slowly down the road, there was a shining look on her face.

CHAPTER

❧ 25 ❧

THE NEWS THAT MATT JASPER HAD RUN AMUCK and killed Lutie traveled swiftly over the ridge, and Wells had gone immediately to do his part in whatever must be done. He told Rose not to look for him back before morning. Likely he'd be kept all night.

Heavy and awkward, within four weeks of being brought to bed, Rose moved through the afternoon, wishing for Tay and watching the road. She was restless and fretful, without knowing why. Why don't Tay come home, she wondered. Ever sincet he'd takened to goin' off two, three days a week, she'd been uneasy about him. Not that she mistrusted him. He was makin' right good money sawin' them ties over at the sawmill. But she wisht he'd come on home now. Hit give a body the creeps, knowin' Lutie was alyin' over there. Ifen Tay was here, she wouldn't noways feel so quare.

She'd start supper early. If she kept busy, the time'd pass quicker. She picked over a basket of late beans and put them on to cook. Then she went out and hacked up a little cook wood. She stirred about, doing first one small chore then another, and the sun slipped lower behind the ridge, the air chilling behind it.

When she heard a horse out front she ran, flinging the door wide, eager to feel Tay's arms about her, and to hear his comforting voice. But it was Wells, heavy and tired and sober-faced. She turned back to the house and he followed her. "I thought you was

Tay," she said, listlessly.

Wells laid his hands on her shoulders. "Honey, you got to be a brave girl."

Rose slipped out from under his hands, and she faced him, her face suddenly white. "Somethin's happened to Tay! Somethin's bad happened to him! I know. Tell me!"

The white stillness of her face frightened Wells. "Rose, set down, honey. Jist set down an' try to be calm."

"Tell me! Jist tell me an' be done with it!"

And then he had told her, as kindly as possible. But no kindness could gloss over the brutal fact. Tay was dead, riddled by bullets from the officers' guns. "He'd been astillin' agin," Wells told her. "I don't reckon you knowed that. But I suspicioned it away last spring. An' the law, they tracked him down. Way they tell it is, they takened him without no trouble. He was bottlin' up a run. He acted like he was peaceable enough, an' they could see he never had no gun ashowin'. They was five of 'em, an' they never figgered he'd give 'em no trouble. Said they was takin' him to the car when he whirled, quick-like, drawed a gun outen his shirt, an' started firin'. He never fired but one shot before they got him."

"Where is he?" The words were short, sharp, explosive.

"They takened him to the county seat. To the mortuary over there."

Rose ripped her apron off and caught up her old brown coat from behind the door. "Let's go," she said.

"Rose," Wells begged. "Honey, let me go. I'll bring him home to you. They ain't no call fer you to see him over there."

Rose turned on him swiftly. "You think I'll let e'er other hands tetch him to do fer him but mine? He's mine! You hear? Cold or warm, he's mine! I'll fetch him home, an' I'll do what's to be done fer him. Let's go, I said."

Dully, Wells followed her outside and went to the barn to hitch the mules to the wagon. He thought to pile a load of sweet straw in the wagon bed, to soften the ride home for the lifeless body. He had not overly liked the boy. But that was not important now. The boy was dead, and his girl was stricken and grieving. His own grief rose instantly to walk beside her.

248

So Tay Clark was brought home, and that Saturday night three bodies lay corpses on the ridge. For Matt Jasper was dead too, when they found him huddled against the wall, wrapped splendidly about by his royal purple princess slip.

Gault and Hod and Tom went to sit up with the Jaspers. Wells and Rose kept lonely vigil over Tay.

The tragedy stunned the ridge. Nothing like it had ever happened there before. There was always death on the ridge. Every family knew its stalking footsteps at the door. Men had been mangled in the sawmills, or shot when out hunting, or drowned while swimming in the river. The various forms death took were not new on the ridge. But this violent purging of life dazed them and stupefied them. People walked on tiptoe and talked in whispers as if the ghost of Matt Jasper might still be lingering near. No one had dreamed he could ever really do harm. He was just Matt Jasper, who had fits, and who had wandered like a lean, lank shadow among them, drooling his tobacco spittle and upon occasion lifting his sweet voice to the hills. There had been kindliness in their attitude, and indifference. There had been tolerance and pity, and a kind of shaming ridicule. But now they clustered together and remembered his disintegration. His fear of being taken to Danville. His conviction someone was coming after him. His haunted, terror-stricken days, when he ran away and lived in the woods, avoiding everyone. Two by two they put things together.

They even tried to understand the purple petticoat. "Matt give it to Lutie one Christmas," they said, "a long time ago. She wouldn't never wear it. Said he'd ort to of spent the money on somethin' to eat, instead o' wastin' it on foolishment!"

It was known, too, that Matt had been helping Tay over at the still. And it was also known, now, that Matt's careless tongue had prattled all his knowledge of the still, proudly, to an officer away last spring. They'd taken their time, folks said. Had made sure of their man, and then had moved in relentlessly. "The wages of sin is death"! Sagely the men and women of the ridge nodded their heads. You could mock the Lord jist so long in yer wrongdoin'. But hit would ketch up with you, jist the same. "The wages of sin is death"!

Over at Becky's house Lutie Jasper's baby thrived, sleeping and eating and fattening under Becky's loving care, neither knowing nor caring whence it had come or where it was going. Becky moved its cradle and the few poor clothes Lutie had provided it to her home after the funerals. So far as the ridge knew, there was no one to take the baby except Mamie Clark, and she had her hands full with her own young'uns and the rest of Lutie's. No one disputed Becky's right to the baby. No one else wanted it. They reckoned if she wanted the pore little thing, she could have it. After all, she was the one that found it and takened it first.

Only Miss Willie argued with her about it. "Becky," she said one morning when Becky was bathing the baby, her face alight with love and her hands gentle on the tiny form. "Becky, have you thought how much grief there may be ahead for you in this child? Remember that her father was an epileptic who went insane, and that her mother was little better. How do you know this baby won't grow up and have fits like her father?"

"I don't," answered Becky, wrapping a towel about the baby. "I don't know but what she'll have fits, or mebbe go crazy like Matt. But," she said, holding the baby close, "is that e'er reason why she ortent to have a home, an' have a ma, an' have somebody to love her an' keer for her? What are you goin' to do with little 'uns like this? Throw 'em in the crick?"

She lifted the baby to her shoulder, patting its round little backside softly. "No, Miss Willie. This here's my baby. The Lord sent her to me. I ain't athinkin' he made pore old Matt go crazy an' kill Lutie so's I could have me a baby. I ain't a thinkin' that atall. But he aimed fer me to find this little 'un. He led me, plain as day, so's I'd find her, an' he aimed fer me to have her an' to raise her up. He'll take keer of the fits an' the craziness. But they ain't nothin' goin' to stop me from lovin' her an' makin' her my own."

Becky laughed. "You know what I'm goin' to name her, Miss Willie? I'm goin' to call her Hannah, after my own little 'un. An' Gault says we'll git papers on her, so's she'll be a Pierce right an' true! Hannah Pierce! Ain't that a purty name?"

CHAPTER

❦ 26 ❦

M ISS WILLIE CAME DOWN SICK about a week after the funerals. Belatedly the hard work she had done during the time the children had typhoid, and the shock she had suffered at finding Lutie and seeing Matt, told on her, and she lay abed, listless, feverish, and spiritless.

Becky sent for Mary, and in a panic Mary made Hod go for the doctor. He could find nothing seriously wrong. "She's just worn out," he told Mary. "All this has been too much for her. Let her rest. Feed her and try to interest her in something else."

So Mary had packed her up and moved her home with her. "I want you where I can look after you," she had told the protesting Miss Willie. "I can't be running up here every day. Not with young Jeems just at the age to get into everything. And besides Becky has her hands full with her own baby. You come on and don't say another word."

The days at Mary's were slow-moving and peaceful. Miss Willie slept long, restful hours; ate, at first sparingly then more heartily; and sat before the fire while Mary played for her, knitting, sewing, playing with the baby. Young Jeems took up many of the hours. He was beginning to walk now, and his eager pattering feet took him exploring in every nook and cranny of the house. He was a fat, healthy, boisterous youngster, and he bestowed his favors upon Miss Willie as impartially as upon his mother.

Miss Willie loved him, but she felt only languidly interested in him. Everything seemed too much effort to her. She was too worn and too bruised. Nothing was worth doing any more. And suddenly Texas seemed very dear to her. She began to think with longing of its wide, flat spaces, of its far horizons, and of its deep, deep skies. If she could just go home again! If she could just get away from the ridge! Maybe then she would purge some of this horror from her mind, and some of this languor from her body.

The sense of failure rode hard upon her shoulders. She brooded over it, and she found a whipping boy for her own sense of guilt in the ridge. It wasn't for her, after all. It was a monstrously inhuman place. Ugly, uncouth, bestial. It was a place where she could no longer dwell. She must put it behind her. Such thoughts kept running through her mind. And she lived in a deeply despondent and depressed mood most of the days.

On one of the worst days Wells came to see her. Jeems was playing piggie with his bare, pink toes on Miss Willie's lap when Wells came in. He promptly transferred his affection to Wells, and when he sat down across the hearth, Jeems crawled down from Miss Willie's lap and padded across to clutch at Wells's knee. Wells took him up. "We'll be havin' a fine lad like this at our house soon, I reckon. Rose's time is due."

Miss Willie's hands fretted together. Wells brought it all back with him. The ridge and the trouble. The ugliness and the failure. She noticed that his face was seamed with tiredness and his eyes were dull and apathetic. Why did he have to come? Why did she have to think about any of it again? Why couldn't the ridge stay up there where it belonged and let her alone? Why did she ever come to this awful place, anyhow?

She paced across to the piano and ripped her finger down the keys. "How is Rose?" she asked grudgingly, finally.

"She's takened it awful hard," he said. "I reckon she's about as well as could be expected, but I look fer her to have a hard time birthin' the baby. Seems like she don't keer about it none at all. Don't never name it, or act like hit's even comin'."

Miss Willie's hands flew to her face. "I don't blame her!" she cried. "I don't blame her! I wouldn't want it either! Why bring another child onto this awful ridge! Oh, I don't blame her!"

Wells rose quickly and crossed the room to lay a broad arm about her shoulder. "Why, Miss Willie," he said, softly reproachful, "you don't mean that. You're jist upset!"

Miss Willie shook his arm off. "I do mean it! I do! What has Rose's child, or any other for that matter, got to look forward to in this horrible place? What has *she* got to look forward to? I do mean it! And I'd feel just like she does, in her place."

Wells patted her arm awkwardly. "Now, Miss Willie," he soothed, "now, Miss Willie. I tell you! Let's you an' me go fer a little walk. Hit's not too cold out today. Git yer coat an' let's jist

252

walk up the holler a ways. Hit'd do you good."

Miss Willie snubbed her tears and mopped at her eyes with her small handkerchief. "Here, take mine," Wells said, offering her his own huge square of white, "hit's man-size an'll do some good."

Miss Willie took it, but it smelled strongly of harsh soap and she shuddered away from it. "No, I'll get something," she said, thrusting it back into his hand, and she went into her room, leaving him looking at the unused handkerchief.

I don't want to go walking, she thought listlessly. The very idea of walking with Wells made her tired. She wished he would go away. She didn't want anything but to be let alone. To be let alone and to forget everything that was ugly and tragic and ignorant and dirty. Everything that was foul and diseased and coarse and uncouth. Oh, everything that was the ridge. The fields, the hills, the streams, the school, the children, and most of all, the people! The heavy, plodding, animal people! Forget it! Forget it! But she got her coat and went with him. She hadn't the heart not to. He tried so hard to please her and to help her. It would be so rude not to go.

They walked up toward the head of the hollow into the clean wind which swept down off the hills. Wells walked awkwardly, lumberingly, by her side, silent, as if he knew she would rather not talk. Miss Willie ducked her head against the wind and braced into it. It cut through her coat and she shivered. She had been a fool to come! She was going to freeze, and it would do no good.

When they came to the edge of the woods, the trees screened them from the wind and it was warmer. They walked into the woods a way, and Wells found a down tree. "Would you want to set down a spell?" he asked.

"We might as well," Miss Willie said wearily.

They still found nothing to say, and Wells picked up a pronged stick and dug absently in the dirt with it. A dog nosed around the end of the log and sniffed at his feet. "Why, there's Rufe's old Jupe dog," he said. He turned to look around. "Rufe must be somewheres clost by. Diggin' sang, likely."

Miss Willie eyed the dog disinterestedly, and after a moment it wheeled and made off in the woods again.

253

Miss Willie pulled at a loose piece of bark on the log. Suddenly it came free and she flung it down. Rising abruptly, she stood in front of Wells, ramming her hands deep in her pockets. "Wells," she said, "I'm going back to Texas."

When he lifted his head, startled, she went on swiftly: "Oh, not right now. I'll finish out the school term. If I'm able," she added ironically. A rasping file of irritation fretted out to the ends of her fingers, and she made them into fists in the pockets. "There's no use my staying on. You must see that! There's nothing here for me to do! There's nothing here for anyone to do! The people won't listen to me. They don't want to learn anything. And I've not got half a chance with the children if their parents won't help me. It's no use struggling any longer."

Wells prodded with his stick. "Surely you can see," Miss Willie went on, "you can see how it is. Nothing will ever be different on this ridge. Folks will always go right on doing things the same old way. They don't want to do any different. They're your folks, Wells, but they're not mine, and I've got to say it. They live so poorly, and they're content that way. Most of them are dirty, uncouth, don't-care people. They live and they die without even the common decencies of life. Patched-up old houses, patched-up old barns, patched-up old fields! Flies, dirt, disease! Water from springs and old wells! Never a balanced meal in the whole of their lives! And you can't get them to do any different! You could bear all of it, if they'd just try! But you can't even get them to eat wholesome food if they had it! They wouldn't like! And here on this horrible ridge, if folks don't like, that's all the excuse they need not to do a thing!"

Miss Willie's hands trembled, and the quiver ran on down into her knees. Her voice was shaking too. "I'm going home! That's all. I shouldn't have come. But I had to learn the hard way that there are some kinds of people you can't help at all! I thought all people could be helped. I came to help! But not ridge folks! You can't help ridge folks! They won't let you! So I'm going home. Back where I belong. Back where if a man is crazy something is done about it, and he isn't left free to kill his wife! Back where people have the doctor with a sick child! Back where there is decency and cleanliness and comfort in living. Back where you can hear beautiful music, and not this everlasting whang-whang of hillbilly quartets and guitars! Back where there is some graciousness to life . . . some culture . . . some . . . some . . ."

Suddenly Rufe was with them, coming around the end of the log, his hand on the dog's head. He stepped over his father's feet and came straight up to Miss Willie, his head flung back and his eyes blazing, his face set and hard. He came so near that involuntarily Miss Willie stepped back. And then he stopped and his chin jutted forward. "Back where they's some easy livin', ain't that what you mean, Miss Willie?" he said, and his young voice was brittle and thin with contempt. "Back where you won't have nothin' hard, like we do on the ridge. Back where you flip a thing on the wall an' yer lights come on. Back where you turn a faucet an' the water runs out. Where yer bed is soft an' springy an' they's rugs under yer feet. Where you turn a little gadget an' yer fire's lit. No coal oil lamps, no drawin' water, no bare floors, an' no choppin' kindlin' ever' night. Back where things is easy an' soft, an' they's nothin' to turn yer stummick, like Lutie Jasper alayin' in her own blood!"

A sudden wind blew down off the hills, cold and chill. It caught Miss Willie's shoulders and ran down her spine and set her to shaking and shivering. She hunched against it and set her teeth to keep them from chattering. Her mouth was trembling and she covered it with a hand.

Wells jumped at the boy, laying rough hands on his shoulders "Rufe!" he thundered, "yer fergittin' yerself!"

The boy broke loose and hit out at the man with his free hand. "No, I ain't!" he said, "I ain't fergittin' myself! Hit's her that's fergot herself!"

"Let him alone, Wells," Miss Willie said between her teeth. "Let him say what he's got to say."

The wind ruffled the boy's hair as he squared away before Miss Willie again. "Don't they never have no murders back in Texas?" he asked. "Don't they? Don't they never have pore people that's dirty an' ignorant an' hungry? I reckon ever'thing's clean an' sweet an' pure-like back in Texas! I reckon they ain't no dirt nor craziness nor moonshinin', like they is here on the ridge! Nor no flies nor no dishwater throwed out the back door nor no window-

255

panes out!" He pointed his finger at her to emphasize his words. "You know they is. You know good an' well they is! They's meanness an' dirtiness an' poreness an' craziness ever'wheres! You've jist shet yer eyes to it all yer life! You've lived nice an' easy an' never looked at the nastiness! Hit was there, though, all the time. Only thing is, up here on the ridge you cain't shet yer eyes. You got to look at it. Hit's there, an' hit's right in front of you. You cain't turn away. Hit's too clost to you. Hit's yer own folks, likely! But you don't like the sight of it, do you? You want things clean, an' easy, an' nice! You don't want none o' the mess of livin', do you?"

The words fell like hard little pellets on Miss Willie's ears. She closed her eyes, but the brittle young voice kept on and on. Make him stop, she prayed, make him stop!

"You come up here on the ridge like you was God hisself, tellin' ever'body do this an' do that! Handin' out what you knowed so high an' mighty! Like nobody but you ever knowed e'er thing in the world! Nosin' around into ever'body's kitchen, squawkin' over dishwater an' flies an' sich! Turnin' up yer nose at folks 'cause they wasn't as clean as you! Thinkin' you was better than folks! What did you think ridge folks was? Pigs? Ridge folks is folks jist like ever'body else. They got feelin's. They got rights. They got a right to live their own way! An' as fer you thinkin' you could he'p 'em! How could you he'p 'em? What have you got to he'p 'em with? They need he'p, same as all folks does. Ain't nobody kin git along 'thout he'p, times. But they ain't no way you kin he'p 'em none. You was right about that! They git along together here, an' they he'p one another. That's their way of doin', an' they don't need none of yore puttin' in, neither!"

The boy was sobbing now, his anger running out into tears, and he hiccuped between words. His shoulders shook, and even in this moment of despair Miss Willie felt a deep tenderness for him, and wanted to lay her arms about him and comfort him. His hurt was so deep.

"I reckon Pa'll whup me when he gits me home fer talkin' like this," he went on, and the words came wildly, "but even my pa, even my own pa you think yer better than! You won't marry him 'cause he don't talk right, an' he wears overalls, an' he plays

256

a gittar! But he's a heap sight better'n you are! I kin tell you that right now. He's good, an' he never hurt nobody in his life, an' he don't think he's better'n other folks. But you wouldn't think none of that! He's ridge folks, an' ridge folks is jist mud under yore feet! Well, all I got to say is, Go on back to Texas! Go on back! Go back where you belong, an' leave us alone!"

He flung himself around and ran toward the woods. Miss Willie saw him swiping his eyes on his coat sleeve as he ran. The dog was close on his heels. "My son! My son!" her heart cried, and the salt of her tears was bitter on her mouth.

Wells stood beside her, too stunned to speak or to move. Miss Willie touched him gently. "Go with him, Wells," she said softly, "go with him. And don't scold him."

Wells hesitated.

"I'll be all right," she promised. "Go with Rufe, and stay with him tonight. Stay close to him, so he'll know you're there."

When they had gone, Miss Willie started walking again. She took little note of where she was going, following the creek aimlessly. She did not feel the wind or notice the cold. Hands deep in her pockets, head bent, she plowed up the hollow. The sun struck warm against her face, and without thinking she turned toward it. There was no peace for her until this thing was settled within her. The boy's words had been like a sword piercing her heart. They had knifed deep and drawn blood. But they had forced her to her knees. Humbly now she sought the truth. With relentless honesty she compelled her mind to look upon herself and to face reality. She must search herself, discover her motives, find her utmost integrity and courage. She must learn, now, what manner of person was Miss Willie Payne.

You want an easy way of living, the young voice had accused. You want things soft and nice. You don't want it hard. That's not fair, Rufe. And it's not entirely true. I haven't had it too easy this year. And I haven't missed the easy ways of life outside too much. I've built my own fires and done my own washing, and carried water from the spring. And I haven't minded too much. It's only human to want life to be as gentle as possible. I'd like the comforts, but that's not what I've missed the most, nor minded doing without.

But you don't want none of the mess of living, he had said. And she winced from that. No. No, I didn't want it, she admitted. The ugliness, the dirt, the disease, the ignorance . . . the mess! I drew my skirts aside from that, she confessed. I didn't want to touch it. I didn't want any part of it. I didn't want to look on it. Back in Texas? You were right, Rufe. It's there too. But it was over on the other side of the tracks from me, and I never went over there! I didn't have to look at it. "But here on the ridge," the young voice had said relentlessly, "here on the ridge you've got to look at it. It's too close to you! It's your own folks, likely." Your own folks! But she had told Wells, "They're not mine!" She had denied them!

"Come up here like you were God himself, telling folks to do this and to do that!" But she hadn't meant to! She had only wanted to help! Surely it was right, when you had superior knowledge and experience — ah, there it was! Superior! Omnipotent! Like God himself. The only knowing one! Hadn't she, even in her most gracious moments of sharing her knowledge, felt superior? Hadn't she always in her heart felt herself better than these people? Hadn't she always patronized them?

Remembering her first days on the ridge and her missionary zeal, she took her thoughts down another trail. Were all zealots, then — all those who, convinced of their own rightfulness and eager to convert — were they all guilty of the same patronizing? Could you honestly set out to help people without believing yourself better than they? Didn't you first have to believe in yourself and in the righteousness of your convictions? And believing thus, didn't you then set out to convert people to your way of thinking? Your way of doing things? Your way of life? Didn't you set out to convince them that *you* knew better than *they* what was good for them? You, from your heights would reach down and help them up from the lower levels!

She had come to the ridge thinking: These poor people! They need help so badly. They need me, Miss Willie Payne, so badly. She had been horrified and shocked at conditions, and she had gone about preaching and lecturing. She had known the right

258

way to do all things, and she had never hesitated to say so. She had pitied these people and patronized them. And what people of pride ever wanted pity or patronage!

But she had tried so earnestly to help them! She *had* tried. The wrong way, maybe. But she had tried everything! Everything? Now her heart told her. Everything . . . but love! She remembered crying out to Mary: "Where can you start? Where can you start?" You start with the people . . . and you start with love for the people! "The gift without the giver is bare"! And she had never given herself! Her time, her energy, her knowledge. But not herself! She winced from that thought, but she faced it in all its bitter gall. She had never loved them! Not even when she had fought so hard for Sylvie Clark? She pleaded for that time. Not even then? Relentlessly her mind closed down the hope. Not even then. She had fought so bitterly because she had been at fault. She had failed, and she would not let her failure be absolute. She had had to be certain that Miss Willie Payne did not pay the ultimate price for her failure.

Love was the way. And lovelessness had been her greatest sin. Out of a dim, long memory Miss Willie remembered a text of her father's. "Take my yoke . . . and I will make it easy." The words came back to her now, and repeated themselves over and over. "Take my yoke." "Take my yoke." That most perfect One had lived "together" with the people. What did He mean by His yoke? "Take my yoke . . . and I will make it easy." Could He have meant — was it possible His yoke had been living and working with people who never understood Him? Common, ordinary, ignorant people, who wouldn't listen and who wouldn't change? People who didn't want anything better than they had? People who were dirty, diseased, and foul sometimes, and who were clean and noble and fine other times? People who loved and hated, fought and made peace, witnessed against their neighbors and then stood by them? Could He have meant living with them and loving them just as they were, unchanged and unchanging?

Like the eastern sun flooding the sky with light, Miss Willie understood in a flashing, transfiguring moment what it meant. It meant to live *together* . . . under the yoke, together! Not one standing above, reaching down to pull the others up! Not one saying, "I must help these people"! It meant, instead, the banding and linking of people, one to another, in love and pity and yearning. It meant saying, "My people"; not, "These people." It meant getting under the yoke alongside of people, one with them, pulling the load with them. Not standing aside telling them how to pull! It meant grieving with them, and sorrowing with them, and laboring with them, and laughing with them, and, most of all, it meant loving with them. "Take my yoke"! He had been yoked with the people. He had meant, then, live with them where they are. Love them as they are. Take the yoke, and lift it. All lift together!

This was so precious a thought that Miss Willie clung to it tightly, treading softly, lest it vanish before she had made it completely hers. It was so fragile. So perfect. So true. "Take my yoke." Take the yoke of the ridge. Get down where the people lived. Live there with them. Don't reach down. Get down yourself. Then lift up! Ah, there was the pearl at the heart of the thing! But could she do it?

As if meeting a challenge, her step quickened. She could try. She could try, and the way was clear! Over there at Wells's house there was a man, lonely and heartsick, who needed a wife. There was a girl, beset with trouble, who needed a friend. There was a boy, rebellious and frustrated, who needed a mother. Wife, friend, mother. It mattered not what you named it. All of them needed love. Not Miss Willie Payne. They could get along without her. But they would die for lack of love. And she would die for lack of love. She needed them! Husband, friend, son. Desperately she needed them!

She saw with surprise that it was dusky dark, and when she lifted her eyes, the first stars were stabbing the cobalt sky. She turned and quickly started home. She would be late and Mary would be worried. She felt as if wings had been added to her feet, so lightly and so swiftly did they go. This warm glow won't last always, she warned herself, chuckling. You know yourself too well for that. You'll be taking on a mighty big job, and there'll be hard days in store. You'll get frashed with Wells, you know you will! Times he gets to sitting there in front of the fire like a bump on a log, you'll feel like bashing him over the head with something just to make him stir! And Rose is lazy and shiftless, and there'll be the new baby soon. At your age that baby will set you screaming sometimes. And there's Rufe. You're starting out with him set against you! You're walking right into a hornet's nest with him! It would be a lot easier to go on back to Texas and finish out your life quietly and peacefully — you know it would!

She grinned in the dark wryly. Ideals are fine . . . fine and fancy. Take my yoke! But it was going to drag mighty heavy sometimes, just the same. Go back to Texas and dry up like a piece of withered moss! Go back to Texas! Not in a hundred years!

CHAPTER
❧ 27 ❧

THEY WERE MARRIED ALMOST IMMEDIATELY, in Mary's big living room, standing before the fireplace. Wells was still bewildered by Miss Willie's sudden decision. He told Hod over and over again that day: "I jist cain't believe it! Hit don't jist seem true!" But his face wrinkled into beaming smiles as the people began to come, and he pumped the men's hands and seated the ladies joyfully.

Miss Willie had said at first: "Just a quiet wedding, Wells. Just home folks."

Wells had laughed until his shoulders shook. "That'll be ever'-body on the ridge, then, won't it, Hod? They ain't nobody but home folks lives around here."

And Miss Willie, knowing it was so, and further knowing how disappointed Wells would be, gave in. So the folks from all about, the hills and the hollows, came to see them married. Becky and Gault and small Hannah. Hattie and Tom and Sarah. Irma and John and little Sue. The Simpsons, the Clarks, the Sandersons, the Joneses. From all over they came. Rose was there, dispirited, big, untidy. Rufe was not.

This would have troubled Miss Willie once. But the time was past for that. She had thought she must win the boy to her before she even considered marrying his father. Now, all thought of winning him to her was gone. She was only concerned with giving him something he had long been needing. A home, and a mother,

261

and love. Whether he knew it or not, that's what he had been seeking . . . in those long hours in the woods, in those bitter quarrels with her, in the deep hurt of his anger. He might never be won to her. She had to take that chance. But, however Rufe felt toward her, he could not help taking in some of the good that would come out of a clean home, good meals, loving-kindness, and the happiness she hoped would prevail.

The folks crowded into Mary's living room and sat or stood during the simple ceremony. Miss Willie, in a soft green wool dress, greeted them all and then went to stand beside Wells and give herself over to his keeping. She felt a solemn sense of dedication then. A new kind of dedication, and when she heard Wells's deep voice in the first response she felt a thrill of pride. This man, with his big human heart, with his work-roughened hands, with his friendly, kindly smile, loved her. And she loved him. That was all the dedication any woman needed. To love!

And then it was her own time to answer and she found her voice coming out strong and true. She felt no fear trembling through her. No sense of strangeness. Instead, there was only an infinite peacefulness, as if she had been waiting all her life for this moment.

After the ceremony there was much merrymaking. It was a noon wedding, and Mary and Miss Willie and Hattie and Becky had worked long and hard over the food. It was no delicate wedding breakfast that they served. It was ham and chicken and beans and salads and pies and cakes! It was a big meal for a lot of people! And it was Wells's hearty voice that yelled, "Come an' git it!"

The table was long, and they crowded around it, and there was music and laughter and singing and the inevitable friendly, teasing jokes. Wells was in his element, at the center of his friends and kinfolks, dispensing hospitality, proud of Miss Willie, and proud of his place beside her. She had dreaded this part of the day, but she found that after all it had a folksy, homey feeling that drew her into its heart. She wasn't just Miss Willie now. She was Pierce kinfolks!

When it was over, and the last good-by said, she and Wells crawled into his old wagon, he clucked at the mules, and they

262

went away from Mary's home to Miss Willie's new one. Both she and Wells thought a wedding trip would be silly. There was too much to be done at home. And besides they couldn't leave Rose at such a time.

Miracles didn't start happening when Miss Willie married Wells Pierce. That winter was just as hard as she had thought it would be. At times it was even harder. But at the bedrock of Miss Willie's nature was a fund of good common sense, and while she felt she had a new and sweeter understanding of her role here on the ridge, she didn't let it make her abandon habits she felt were of intrinsic worth. She was prepared to make adjustments in this new relationship she was entering, but she did not once make the mistake of believing she must make them all. If she had a new humility along with her new understanding, she did not allow it to become Uriah Heepish. Instead, she made it a proud humility which expected the family to do their own part along with her. She knew herself too well to suppose that she could give over the habits of a lifetime of cleanliness, orderliness, neatness, and she did not feel it incumbent upon her to do so. She felt that love could include those things, and should.

So she set about making the old house clean and comfortable. It was a big job. Wells painted the outside, with Rufe's sullen help, and they tidied up the yards and mended the fences. Inside, Miss Willie scrubbed and scoured. She and Wells ripped off all the old wallpaper, and between them they made a fair job of putting on new. Wells leveled the sagging floors and Miss Willie painted them and waxed them, and then she strowed dozens of Becky's braided rugs around the rooms. New panes were put in the windows, and they were washed to a state of gleaming spotlessness. Then fresh curtains were hung in every room.

Miss Willie sold her Texas home and had her furniture shipped to the ridge. When it came, she distributed it around the roomy old house, and when she finished, she found she had a lovely, gracious home. It was a farm home, geared to the comfort and convenience of a farm life, but that did not detract from its beauty or its graciousness.

263

Wells and the children had not used but three rooms of the ten that rambled sprawling everywhere. But Miss Willie took them over and made them all habitable. She gave Rose a room for herself and the baby, and she delighted Abby's little-girl soul with a small room done in candy-pink-and-white sweetness. She also told Rufe to choose a room for himself. He was startled at the thought of a room of his own, and at first paid no attention to the suggestion. Miss Willie let it ride a few days and then, firmly, she said to him: "Rufe, you are going to have a room of your own, whether you select it or not. It would be better if you choose the one you want, and fix it up to suit yourself."

"You mean I kin fix it up any way I like?"

"Of course."

Then he became enthusiastic about it, and Wells took him to town to choose his own curtains, rugs, and furniture. He used remarkably good sense in arranging his room too. He wanted one of the narrow bunk beds, and an Indian rug on the floor. He built shelves all around the walls, and put his collection of rocks, shells, and arrowheads on them. He made a rack for his gun, and he even brought in one day a huge, dry hornet's nest. "Reckon you wouldn't let me have this in my room, would you?" he asked Miss Willie.

"Has it any hornets in it?"

"Naw. Cain't you tell it's dry?"

Miss Willie had laughed. "I don't know much about things like that, Rufe. But if it's safe, why, of course you can have it in your room."

Miss Willie didn't consciously assume any policy in working with Rufe. She was much too busy. She simply included him in all the plans that were made, in all the work that was done, in all the fun that was had. He was aloof and sullen sometimes, but she paid no attention to those moods, going right on, instead, including him. She made no issue of discipline with him. She implied that he would want to do whatever she asked of him. He didn't always, of course. But at least there was no open rebellion.

At first he was suspicious of her. Resentful. She had expected that and she ignored it. But when he saw that she didn't tattle to Wells, that she wasn't constantly heckling him, he relaxed a little. Grudgingly, and then more willingly, he let down in the home. Miss Willie had put all her faith into the belief that what Rufe needed was the order, the discipline, the security of love, and she was right. In spite of himself he reacted to it. He wouldn't have admitted it, but he liked the clean, shining house, the regular, well-cooked meals, the feeling of something to be done each day, the bustling energy Miss Willie brought to the whole family. He didn't mean to, but he soaked it up and it softened him.

Miss Willie never made any deliberate approaches to him. He was the son of the house — the dear son, she never failed to let him know — and as such he had his own rights and privileges. She never stepped over the door into his room, and if he stayed in it a great deal, she never asked him why. Neither did she question him about his wanderings in the woods. Nor were they curtailed, except as he was needed about the place.

One day he brought home three squirrels, killed and neatly dressed. "I thought mebbe these'd be good fer breakfast," he said, offering them.

Miss Willie didn't like small, killed things. But she suspected this was the first of Rufe's sharing with her. "They sure will," she said, taking them and salting them down until morning.

He frequently brought home small game after that. Thus he brought what had belonged to him in solitude into the home which was slowly enfolding him.

At Christmas Miss Willie asked him to find a tree for them. "Aw, what you want a tree fer?" he had asked sulkily. "We ain't never had none before."

"We're going to have one this year," she had replied firmly. "Will you get it for us, or shall I have your father get it?"

"I'll get it," and he had put on his cap and coat and gone out. He may have gone unwillingly, but she noticed it was a beautiful, full, green tree, perfectly rounded. And he had set it up, straight and level. He hadn't taken any part in decorating it, but he got up Christmas morning and came down for the opening of the presents. And when he saw the new gun for him, his eyes had glowed.

And he loved Rose's baby. The baby had come just ten days

after Wells and Miss Willie were married. A beautiful girl child, looking so much like Tay that Rose had wept bitterly upon seeing it. But when the child was actually form and flesh, and she could hold it in her arms, Rose had lost her careless unconcern for it, and had cuddled and held it tenderly. She called the baby Taysie.

Rufe would spend long hours with her, caring for her so that Rose might be free to help Miss Willie. And when Miss Willie passed through the room and saw the young face, washed so clean by his love for the baby, so tender and so raptly attentive, she knew that Rufe, even without his knowledge, was safe among them.

Yes, it was a hard winter, and a long one. There were times when Miss Willie went to bed so tired that every bone in her body ached, every muscle was sore, every nerve quivering. Times when the baby was so tiny and colicky and got them all up in the night when she wanted to cry in frustration. Times when Wells's mood didn't match her own, and she wondered if two people so completely different in temperament could ever make a good marriage. Times when Rufe's sullenness hacked away at her and she wanted to take him by the shoulders and shake him hard. Times when Rose's shiftlessness made her want to take the broom and sweep everything that belonged to the girl outside. Sometimes she flared up and the whole family skittered before her temper. But nearly always she controlled it, or got outside and walked or worked it off.

Little by little they settled into a family, with a routine of chores and work to be done in common. Cows to be milked, meals to be cooked, dishes to be washed, the baby to be bathed and tended, the house to be kept clean, stock to be cared for, the tobacco bed to be burned, fences to mend, a new barn to build. They had a community of interests and each had his part in them. It can never be true that people who live together don't have anything in common, Miss Willie thought. They have *everything* in common!

Neither did miracles begin to happen in Miss Willie's relationships with the people of the ridge. Mamie Clark went right on straining her milk with the flies swarming around her. Quilla Simpson nursed her ulcers in contempt of the doctors, and Corinna Jones kept on adding a new baby to her household each year. But Miss Willie found that when she quit trying so hard, when she quit preaching and lecturing, when she quit being so critical, she could find much that was good in each of them. Mamie, for all her slovenliness and do-lessness, was a loyal and good neighbor. She came when the baby was born, and she took over the chores and the hardest work. Not until Rose was up and about again did she stop coming every day. There was something worthy and good in each of them, and Miss Willie began to feel an encircling bond stretched around her. No one had to bear his burdens alone here on the ridge. There was a grieving, suffering, helping hand extended in time of sorrow. A glad, rejoicing, sharing hand in time of joy. She began to know intimately what it meant to live "together."

Miss Willie found she could let her neighbors alone, but there were some things about which she remained adamant. The school and the improvements were one. When she and Wells were married, she had not gone back to the schoolroom. On the ridge a wife and mother had no time to work out, even if a husband were willing, and few were. A woman's place was in the home. As a matter of fact, life revolved around her and a home was helpless without her. But Miss Willie went, as sternly and defiantly as ever, before the trustees and demanded new outhouses and better roads and a school bus. There was this difference. She was no longer Miss Willie, the teacher. She was Miss Willie, Wells Pierce's woman, with children of her own in the school. She said *our* children, now. She was one of them, and could lift up with them.

Partly because of the typhoid scare, but mostly because they would listen to one of their own, a few things were done, and Miss Willie had faith that in time the rest would be done. It made a big difference, being Wells Pierce's woman!

So the winter passed and another spring came around and Miss Willie sat in the back yard under the apple tree, sweet with blossom. The day was washed with warmth, and the sun laid a golden bar across the baby's head. She lay stretched across Miss Willie's lap, reaching for the shadowy leaves swinging overhead. Miss Willie hitched her chair a little farther in the shade. The baby grabbed her finger and held it tight. Miss Willie laughed at her and shifted her to her shoulder. Wells would soon be coming in from the field, and it was time to be starting supper. But she lingered yet a while in the April evening.

Rose came to the door and called, "You want I should lay the the supper fire?"

Miss Willie called back, "If you will, please, Rose."

Rufe and his dog came around the corner of the house and dropped onto the grass nearby.

"Come take the baby, Rufe," Miss Willie said. "I must cook supper."

He settled the baby on his arm and she turned toward the house. From the nearby beech grove came suddenly the high, sweet, soaring song of an early thrush. Like a golden stream, its liquid purity drenched the apple-blossomed air, the fragrance and the sound blending to a breathlessly perfect whole, becoming inseparable in an unbearably fragile and sweet moment. Miss Willie stopped, and her hand went to her throat which ached with bird song. "Listen, Rufe," she said softly. "Listen! The first thrush!"

The boy's head had been tilted toward the bird. At her words his face turned slowly toward Miss Willie. There was an unbelieving look on it, and then it was swept by such joy and gladness that it blazed with glory! "Miss Willie!" he said, and the tawny, golden head of Taranto stood before her again. "Miss Willie! Kin you hear the birds sing too?"